THE MORTAL FATES

THE
CROWN
OF OATHS
AND
CURSES

THE MORTAL FATES

THE CROWN OF OATHS AND CURSES

J BREE

To Orion,

named for his sister in the stars, and sent to our family by all of those who have left us too early.

Your sisters have had many dedications already,

this one is just for you.

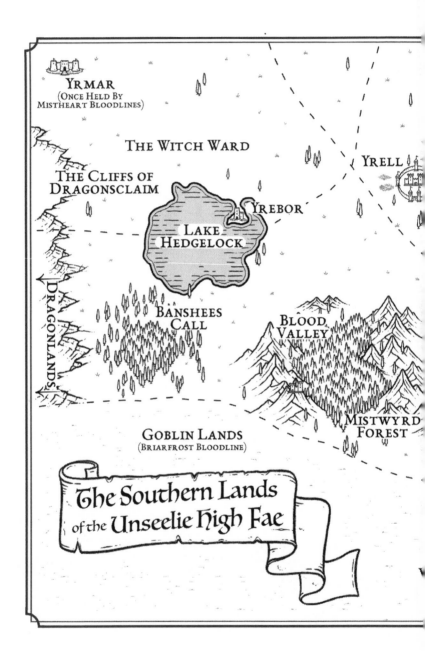

YRMAR
(ONCE HELD BY
MISTHEART BLOODLINES)

THE WITCH WARD

YRELL

THE CLIFFS OF
DRAGONSCLAIM

YREBOR

LAKE
HEDGELOCK

DRAGONLANDS

BANSHEES
CALL

BLOOD
VALLEY

MISTWYRD
FOREST

GOBLIN LANDS
(BRIARFROST BLOODLINE)

The Southern Lands
of the Unseelie High Fae

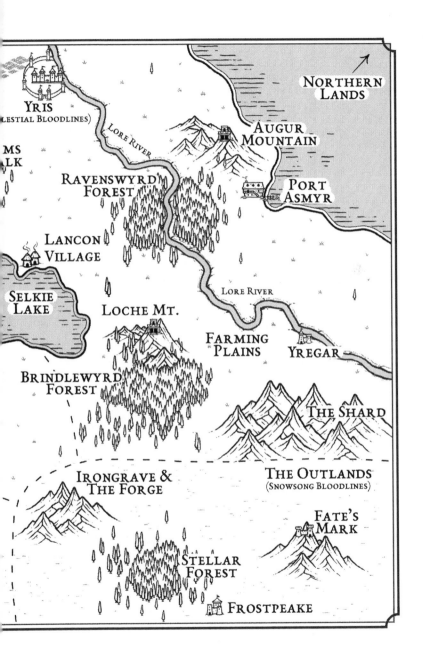

NORTHERN LANDS

YRIS
(CELESTIAL BLOODLINES)

MS
LK

AUGUR MOUNTAIN

LORE RIVER

PORT ASMYR

RAVENSWYRD FOREST

LANCON VILLAGE

SELKIE LAKE

LORE RIVER

LOCHE MT.

FARMING PLAINS

YREGAR

BRINDLEWYRD FOREST

THE SHARD

IRONGRAVE & THE FORGE

THE OUTLANDS
(SNOWSONG BLOODLINES)

FATE'S MARK

STELLAR FOREST

FROSTPEAKE

PART ONE

ROOKE

The Fates have blessed you with a mate.
His name is Prince Soren Celestial, heir to the throne of
the Southern Lands, and your union will unite a shattered
kingdom.
The bloodshed that has ravaged the Southern Lands shall end,
the lands shall be restored, and the old ways shall be honored
once more.
The Fates will guide you to him when your heart is ready.

As waves lap the sides of *the Shepherd*, I ignore all the eyes trained on me and enjoy the last moments of my journey home to the Southern Lands. It is the last peace I may know.

Returning to a kingdom ravaged by the evils of my own kind is not a path I'd ever have chosen for myself, but the Fates have made their demands of me. Surviving the war in the Northern Lands taught me the catastrophic but unavoidable lesson of what befalls a kingdom when a fate is broken, and while my heart is anything but ready, I know it's time to return home as surely as I know the songs of the forest in my heart. No matter how far I traveled, the sorrow of the trees never left me, and I long to see them once more.

It took months to unravel myself from the life I had built, time to be discharged from the Sol Army and to train healers to take over my work for the Seelie Court, to convince my friends and family that the Fates could no longer be ignored and that I must do as they'd bidden. But as the peak of summer crept closer, I made the last of my preparations and found myself passage on a ship. By some act of the Fates, it was the same vessel that carried my brother and I north two hundred years ago—a sign if I ever saw one—and I began my journey back to the kingdom that was once my home.

The Shepherd constantly travels the waters between the two closest high-fae kingdoms, mostly carrying cargo but with room for travelers as well. Old but well maintained, with a small crew of fiercely trained sailors, she's provided a concern-free voyage home. I paid for and received a cabin all to myself, an easy achievement with very few fellow passengers on board.

No one wants to journey to the Southern Lands anymore.

I'm dressed in simple clothing, nothing fancy or restrictive. It distinctively marks me as a witch. The silver pins that hold my cloak around my shoulders and the bands of fabric around my torso are nothing more than fastenings, no ornate nature to them at all, but as the sun glints off them, they make what I am clear, even though I have no telltale markings on my face.

I've always been steady traveling the ocean, having natural sea legs despite my ancestors only ever existing in the Ravenswyrd Forest until my brother and I left. I suppose my father might have found himself on a voyage during his ventures before he met and married my mother. Maybe I'd come by these legs of mine honestly, but my family all died long before I could ask them.

The sun, which started off scorching hot when we left the Northern Lands, has been slowly losing its luster the closer we get to the Southern Lands. While it's still summer here, the season is far milder in the south, and after two hundred years of heat soaking into my bones, I'll have to reacclimate to the cooler, darker lands of the Unseelie Court. I clutch my cloak tighter around myself.

As we approach the port, the water beneath the ship changes from flat and calm into a churning and vicious sort of ice sludge, echoing the ice that seems to encase my heart. My scars from the Fate Wars are far more extensive in my mind than on my body. With every lurch of *the Shepherd* against the waves, I greet my homeland with nothing more than a deep sense of dread and despair. The land itself seems to warn me.

You are not welcome here, Rookesbane Eveningstar.

The Ravenswyrd Coven is gone.

The captain of *the Shepherd* comes down from the upper deck and glares at the gaggle of crew and passengers until they go back to their work and their own business. Cloaks are thrown over shoulders and caps set on heads, the sun no longer warming everyone the way it did days ago in the north, and the crew works hard under the captain's watchful eye.

He comes to stand next to me, resting his gnarled hands on the aged wood of the side of the ship as he looks out over the water. He's a part-blood, more Unseelie high fae than anything else, and his face doesn't give me any true indication of his age. With his close-shorn hair and pale but sun-damaged skin, he could be a hundred years old, or a thousand.

I never was good at guessing at anyone's age.

He doesn't look at me as he speaks. "Are you sure that you wish to return? A lot has changed since you left, little witch. There's nowhere left for you to go that the high fae won't find you…or Kharl's armies. He won't tolerate a witch without loyalty to his cause living on her own."

I shrug, shooting him a small smile at the term of endearment that he's held on to all these years. Perhaps it's something he calls every female witch he takes across the seas, a small kindness to those fleeing from the horrors of the war in the south. Either way, I'm grateful for his certainty that I don't intend to join the witch commander Kharl Balzog and his witch armies. To know that a few here in the Southern Lands still have some common sense is promising, but I'm not holding my breath about the majority of the population.

I cross my arms and thread my hands into my sleeves to fight the chill in the air. After two hundred years away, I'm unaccustomed to the cold. The air is more than a little brisk, and no matter how strong my Unseelie blood is, it's going to take time to acclimate.

Until I do, I'll long for the sun-soaked days of the Northern Lands.

"I return here for my fate. I can't wait any longer, not without angering the Fates themselves. I'd never do such a thing."

The captain's eyebrows furrow, but he nods, scratching at the shadow of a beard on his chin. The high fae I've known haven't ever grown facial hair like that, and I'd guess that he has some human blood. Or perhaps witch blood—maybe that's why he's always had a soft spot for me. His eyes aren't silver, and without that clear marker or witnessing an act of magic, it's impossible to tell. I won't pry by reaching out with my own magic to check. Some secrets are better left alone.

There isn't a person between the two lands who isn't aware of the war that just ended. The Fate Wars began after the king of the Northern Lands broke his fate, chose a different path, and ruptured the very fabric of the world, spilling forth monsters that threatened to wipe out the entire northern kingdom. The Sol King's people were being wiped out, city by city, entire bloodlines of high fae and lower fae alike, and there weren't enough magic-wielders within their ranks to counter the Ureen, creatures impossible to defeat without magic. Thousands of them ravaged the lands. In his desperation, the Sol King sent out decrees to all of the kingdoms under the rule of the high fae.

Join me to win the war and you'll have a place in my kingdom, with prosperity and glory for all.

Two hundred years ago, my brother Pemba and I fled the Southern Lands to join that war. We'd learned to be soldiers and made a new life for ourselves there, met friends and lovers and people we now called family. Even in our darkest days, I was content with the choices I'd made to bring us there. I'd run from my destiny and thought it was possible to turn my back on it forever but, instead, in the midst of the most horrifying battles the Northern Lands had ever seen, I learned an important lesson.

There is no escaping fate.

The king of the Northern Lands himself couldn't do it, and hundreds of thousands of people had died because he'd tried. That's a heavy burden to carry, and I have more than enough regrets in my life. I don't need any more.

The captain makes an unhappy noise under his breath. "You should at least wear something else. There are more than enough females your size on the boat. We can find something that will conceal you more. How far do you have to travel for your fate? Let me send some guards with you."

I have never forgotten the kindness this man showed two humble witches with no money and no clue how bad the War of the Witches had gotten when we first sailed north. When I approached him to return home, I did so with a large bag of gold. He tried to refuse it, his pride strong, but times have been very hard.

Not many people want to leave the Northern Lands now that it's safe there, and there aren't many people left to leave the Southern Lands. Importing and exporting has slowed down significantly as well, the relations between the Seelie Court and the Unseelie Court more fraught than ever before, thanks to the Unseelie persecuting witches and the Seelie welcoming them to live in the north. Not Kharl, of course—the Sol King wouldn't offer sanctuary to such a male—but the witches who were forced to flee their forests and their homes, hunted by the high fae and their ruthless laws.

I've never been reckless with my life, having always been one to overthink the consequences of my actions, but there's a hollowness within my chest where my heart once beat that no longer cares what will become of me due to my fate. My only regret is leaving my brother behind in the Northern Lands, but Pemba had no choice but to stay. I suppose it's better that he's not here for the next part of my journey. His overprotective nature would struggle hard with what I'm about to do, and I've already had to talk my way around a million questions about my fate during our two centuries in the Seelie Court.

While I was able to convince all those I left behind that the Fates are guiding my journey, I'm not so certain about how much damage I'll endure along the way.

"Don't worry so much, Captain. I know the path ahead of me, and I have no doubt that the Fates will see me through safely. I'm not the naïve little witch who left the forest anymore."

The corners of his mouth turn down, and he nods slowly. "There's no doubting the Fates when they call on us, but I'm not sure you understand what you're walking into. Things were bad when you left, but not as bad as they are now. When we drop anchor at port, it will be treason for me to even speak to you—treason for you to be on this ship. Your life will be forfeit the moment your foot hits the dirt. If we can conceal you a bit, it would be easier on us all. A larger cloak with a hood, to start, and perhaps we can find you a dress."

That changes things.

I have no doubt that the Fates will get me where I need to be unharmed, but even the idea of risking the captain and his crew merely because I'm not ashamed of being a witch is unconscionable.

"I'll wear a cloak and hood until I'm away from the port and you're no longer at risk. No need for a dress—these robes are all I know, and I'll be sure to cover them carefully in the village."

The scowl on his face deepens. "I wasn't saying it for me. I have more than enough gold in my possession to get out of an accusation of treason. The regent's guards are easy enough to convince of such things, but there's no amount of gold in the world that can make them forget what you are. They don't care whether or not you side with the witches here. All they care about is eliminating your kind."

Eliminating.

I suppose that's a kinder expression than *mass genocide* to describe murdering people for nothing more than the species to which they were born, but I understand the motives of the high fae, if not their unyielding resolution.

My own family was massacred by the same witches. Anyone who didn't join Kharl's ranks was considered a traitor to all. My family, the Ravenswyrd Coven, was always neutral, but neutrality in a time of war is seen by both sides as nothing more than an act of aggression.

We were damned either way.

The captain leads me down to the cabins under the deck, barking out orders until one of his crew appears with an armful of fabric. The thick, hooded cloak lined with fur is big enough to be pulled over my head to obscure my black tresses and the silver hue of my eyes.

I should count myself lucky that I don't have any obvious witch markings to hide—apart from my eyes, the only signs of my magic are small marks on the insides of my elbows, and my sleeves take care of those. But it's a fact that pierces my heart even through my numb state, because my mother died before she could give me the markings of the Ravenswyrd Coven. I could have been marked by another witch; Pemba offered a hundred times over the years. My best friend, Hanede, the last Brindlewyrd witch and the only male in the history of the covens to hold and wield a relic, offered to mark me as well, but my grief wouldn't let anyone bestow such an honor in my mother's stead.

The shipmate fumbles as she hands me the cloak and then ducks her head and apologizes profusely. I can smell her fear of me, or perhaps of the consequences of aiding one of my kind, but she does as her captain orders nonetheless. With the green hue of her skin, there's no mistaking that she's a part-blood goblin, but there's a distinct void inside of her where magic could be.

Half-human, as well.

The world would not have been kind to this young female.

I place my hand over hers and thank her quietly, then turn her hand over and slip a piece of gold into it. Her eyes widen in shock, and her fingers clasp it desperately.

The captain pays his staff well, but money is tight no matter where you come from, and there's every chance this piece of gold is the first she's ever held.

"Thank you for giving me your cloak. I hope this covers replacing it in the ports."

She nods profusely. "This will more than cover it. You do not need to give me this. The captain already said he would pay for it. Here, take it back!"

Her hand shakes, and I can see how hard it is for her to open her fingers and offer me back the money.

With a smile I close her fingers back around the coin. "Where I'm going, I have no need for gold anymore. I would rather you have it for showing me such kindness, even at the risk of being accused of treason."

She startles as though I've reminded her of the peril, but

a determined look falls over her features as she nods. "The captain told me where you've come from and what you've done. Fighting that war…we all know the Ureen would've come to the Southern Lands once they wiped out everyone and everything in the north. All the stories say they're mindless monsters who want nothing but to consume. I would never have been able to run off to a war as a young girl like you did. I don't believe you're evil just because you're a witch."

It's treason, I'm sure, to say such a thing, but I simply smile at her and pull the cloak tighter around my body before climbing back up the steps to the deck as I hear the captain yell, "Land, ahoy!"

I step back into the sunlight, and my breath is taken from me as I see, for the first time in two hundred years, the Southern Lands of the Unseelie high fae. The place I ran from so desperately.

The one I have no choice but to return to, the Fates calling me home as surely as the forest sings in my heart.

As the ship docks at Port Asmyr, the captain is still deeply unhappy with the situation. He disembarks first and speaks to the high fae soldiers charged with checking the cargo and taxing the ships. Nothing can happen until those males are paid, and so the rest of us wait.

When the soldiers finally allow us off the ship, the captain stays with me for as long as he can. I make my way toward the nearby village of Asmyr, which clings to the coastline, and when the high fae soldiers stop the captain to pay customs and taxes on his load, he's careful not to look in my direction. Every inch of his body points away from me as he does everything he can to avoid tipping them off to the fact that I'm not a simple traveler like the rest of them.

I'm careful to position myself at the edge of the crowd, not wanting any of the other travelers to be accused of aiding me if I'm discovered, and I keep my head down as I go into the village.

The travelers slowly break off from each other as they find their own paths, some stopping at the tavern while others find the family and friends waiting for them.

There's no celebration or joyous welcome to be seen.

Even here at the edge of the water, where there should always be provisions thanks to the bountiful ocean, I can see that the villagers are far too thin. There's a desperate look to them as they shuffle along the cobblestone roads, their hair lank and their skin sallow, ill health showing even through the myriad skin tones.

Not the regent's guards, of course, all of them high fae and impossibly clean in these filthy streets. They all wear cloaks of a deep, navy blue trimmed with silver, broadswords buckled at their belts, their pale skin and white-blond hair standing out like beacons in the crowd. They're made even more distinct by their height, each at least a foot taller than the rest of us, their shoulder span wider than even the goblin part-bloods. Physically, there's no denying their superiority but, if the rumors are to be believed, they lack the basic morals I've come to hold as nonnegotiable in my own life.

I won't bow to any of them without cause.

They all look as though they've never missed a meal in their lives, and yet everyone around them in this small port village is starving. There is much talk in the Northern Lands of the regent and how he rules in his nephew's stead. After the untimely murder of his brother, Solas Celestial had taken the mantle of the regent and demanded respect as though he felt no mournful weight of such an undertaking, something that had certainly raised suspicions across the other kingdoms. News of his capricious nature and wanton ways reached the Northern Lands centuries ago, as did the choices he's made to the detriment of the lower fae and part-bloods. Faced with the catastrophic results of his actions here in the port, I find him detestable.

I've gotten used to the hypocrisy of social ranks, which are clear even in the Northern Lands where the kingdom is more bountiful, but that doesn't mean they don't set my teeth on edge. I suppose that the deckhand is one of the lucky ones, having a job that provides all her meals. She didn't look as rail thin as the rest of these folks.

The captain wasn't exaggerating when he said a lot has changed.

My original plan was to purchase a horse to ride to the Ravenswyrd Forest and trust the Fates to lead my mate to me there, but I can't do that without the regent's guards seeing my face, so I'm forced to walk. A little farther down the road and through the village, it becomes clear to me that there are no horses to buy anyway.

There's no food either.

If I could make my way into the tavern without anyone spotting the silver hue of my eyes, I'd be able to find a tankard of mead and maybe some bread, but there are no markets or food stalls anywhere, none of the provisions and typical signs of life that were here when my brother and I left the Southern Lands, so I have no choice but to make my way out of the small village on foot.

It's not so bad.

I haven't lost my ability to walk for days on end. My time serving in the war strengthened such things. My only complaints are the aches on one side of my stomach and on my back, where my scars are, but I can ignore them well enough. I was seen by one of the best healers—aside from myself, of course—in the

Northern Lands, but wounds caused by the Ureen never heal without leaving a mark. My scars will ache in the cold until my last breath.

The Fates don't care about such things, and now I've returned to the Southern Lands where there's no shortage of chill.

I walk for the rest of the day, watching the sun climb above me and then descend slowly in the sky. The farther I walk, the more desolate the land becomes. It's summer here, but there are no signs of life in the ground around me.

There should be wildflowers everywhere and livestock grazing in large expanses of pasture. This deep into the season, there should be signs of farmers readying for a plentiful harvest, and yet there's nothing.

Devastation stretches as far as the eye can see.

When I stop for the evening along the well-worn path, I still have at least a full day's walk ahead to reach the Augur Mountains and the Ravenswyrd Forest beyond them. I find a small cluster of dead trees and make camp between them, my stomach clenching at the sight of their stark branches. These trees should be covered in foliage and greenery, and yet there's nothing here. No sounds of birds singing in the dusk, no insects calling out their tunes of hard work, no sprites or imps playing in the barren fields. If I wasn't absolutely sure of the season I left behind in the Northern Lands, I would assume it was winter, though a rare snowless day.

I dig my hands into the dirt beneath me, my own pool of magic reaching deep into the ground to find a sign of what's gone wrong, but all that comes back is a void, same as I'd felt in that human part-blood who lacked something so intrinsic to me.

There's no magic left.

Deep in the recesses of the earth, magic should flow freely, the natural springs of the essence of life that have been here longer than the Unseelie. Sorrow blooms in my chest, an old wound opening up once again.

No one is taking care of the land.

The high fae gave up such practices long before I was born, but when Pemba and I left, there were still witches taking care of the solstices and equinoxes. There had to be for the land to continue to provide for the fae folk. Whether the practitioners fled after we did or gave up the traditions, without magic and sacrifice, the land is on the brink of true destruction.

One it won't be able to come back from.

None of the witches care about the lands anymore, proving that their war has never been about taking back power from the high fae to protect those who are more vulnerable. When Pemba told me that rumor, I refused to believe it, but what I'm seeing confirms those suspicions. Kharl's war has never been about redistributing power. He doesn't care about the lands or the traditions of our people.

My brother and I learned a lot about the War of the Witches in the Northern Lands, and Pemba became obsessed with finding out who killed our family and coven.

It was the same name on every lip. Kharl Balzog of the Renfyre Coven.

In his witchling days, he traveled long and far to cultivate a deep-seated hatred of the high fae, the Unseelie Court and the Southern Lands bearing the brunt of his animosity. In the whispers passed on to Pemba and me from other refugee witches, his reasons were never clear, but he started an uprising with nothing but his magic, his charismatic personality, his ability to convince covens that the Fates are on his side, and a wanton disrespect for life and the land.

His name is carved into my soul right next to the mate the Fates picked out for me, two facets of the same fate to end the war and save the fae folk from senseless death and violence.

A path laid out before me that is so terrifying, I ran from it the moment the Seer dismissed me from her temple.

Many other witches fled the war before we did, hundreds from all the different covens in the forests, but not many made it out after us. Pemba obsessively questioned them about what happened, trying to glean the truth of Kharl's plans and how he'd convinced so many covens to follow him. Each and every witch Pemba questioned looked at him as though he was stupid, and it was only when they heard the Ravenswyrd name that they understood our naïvety.

The forest protected us from the horror of the truth.

For hundreds of years, unrest simmered until it boiled over and turned into all-out war, and yet we'd known none of it. I often questioned myself about whether our parents could have known. There's no way to tell; they never let it slip to us. Not once did we catch any of the elders murmuring amongst themselves about evil acts, the curses and the distortion of our ways poisoning the witches so deeply that their blood turned black and rotted in their veins even as their hearts still beat in their chests. Part of me believes they couldn't possibly have known how bad things were, because Pemba and I couldn't have missed whispers of that.

If they had known, maybe they would've survived. Maybe our coven wouldn't have been so trusting of outsiders, and we would've questioned whether the forest could keep us safe from our own kind. Maybe the Favored Children would have made it through the night.

Instead, we were betrayed.

I unpack the small bedroll from my backpack, feeling the cooler summer night air of the Southern Lands over my exposed skin. It feels like months ago that I packed my bag, careful to bring only the most basic essentials. I left so much behind in the Northern Lands, every luxury I fought to earn for myself, as well as everyone I love.

I left my brother behind.

Memories are the only thing that can break through the hard shell I've encased myself in. One thought, and tears fill my eyes. I blink them away with a soft curse. I can't afford weakness right now, but the tears keep coming.

I take off my cloak and bundle it to cushion my head, then lie down and look up at the stars still bright overhead. By habit, my hand drifts to the pocket of my dress, seeking out the small ribbon I usually keep there as a talisman but finding nothing. When I first arrived in the Northern Lands and found myself homesick for the forest and the old ways, Pemba tried to cheer me by continuing our coven traditions, asking soldiers in our training ranks until he'd gathered a small collection of supplies. I spent my meager free time in the Sol Army desperately holding on to the traditions of the Ravenswyrd, and the ribbon became a testament to that, a long, thin scrap of silk that I embroidered. It wasn't valuable to anyone but me, a record of my story told in the images woven in the threads.

The morning I left Sol City, I tied the ribbon to the Ravenswyrd scepter, my family's most precious relic, and tucked them both away inside my magic for safe keeping. It was the first time I'd been without the ribbon in decades, and I'm bereft without the feel of the silk against my fingers.

The scepter itself is an ancient object of great power, and though I once feared it, I learned to wield it with confidence. It's far too valuable to carry visibly in the Southern Lands, and I made my peace with traveling without the ancient wood warming my hands long before I stepped foot on the ship.

I force my mind to empty so I can fall asleep, one of the greatest tricks my time as a soldier taught me. We all learned to sleep at a moment's notice under any conditions, to shut our brains off just enough to get the rest we needed while still being aware enough to sense the enemy creeping up on us.

It's come in handy more times than I can count, and it takes only a breath or two before I fall into a dreamless sleep. I get a few short hours of rest before I feel the presence of others in my proximity.

I keep my eyes shut tight, my heart beating slowly in my chest as I control my reactions. I don't need to be scared.

I will trust in the Fates to see me through this without harm.

The sounds of branches crunching and leaves rustling underfoot break through the silence of the night. Whoever these people are, they're doing themselves a disservice. With all the noise they're making, I could've drawn a blade and killed them with my eyes shut.

Through my hearing alone, I can tell that three are approaching. One is heavyset and breathing with difficulty, one has a limp, and the third has already drawn a weapon and is inching towards me on feet that are less clumsy than his companions' but still far too loud to do any good.

"What do we have here, boys? Wearing robes like that, it's a witch! I thought there were none left out here. You're a long way from your comrades, girlie."

I open my eyes and sit up on the bedroll, then stare down the speaker until a flicker of nervousness enters his eyes. He's a part-blood with elf and goblin heritage that has given his body unique proportions. His huge hands look even stronger at the ends of his smaller arms, and his head looks petite where it sits over a set of massive shoulders. Looking at him, I'm grateful I won't be relying on my own physical strength to get me out of trouble.

The longer I hold his gaze, unwavering and without a drop of fear in me, the more obvious his discomfort becomes, a twitch in his jaw quickening until a snarl rips out of his chest. His lip curls as he fights the fear that's slowly filling his aura, clearly thinking himself to be a brave, alpha sort of male and enraged that I don't view him the same.

"Dragon's fire! A witch all the way out here without one of the Savage Prince's soldiers finding her first—the Fates have blessed us today, boys! One of you get a gag in her mouth before she can use magic against us."

The larger male snaps back with a smirk, "Their kind don't have any magic left. They give it all to the High Witch for his stores. I'm not putting my hands on one of *those* beasts, thank you."

High Witch.

There's no such thing, it's just some stupid title that Kharl gave himself in an attempt to seem more important than he actually is. None of Kharl's long and twisted deceptions have done anything to bring me to his cause; they've only convinced me of his deranged state.

Before I returned here, I visited the Seer again, in her new temple in the Northern Lands. She filled me in on some vital details.

I keep my mouth shut and move very slowly, pulling myself onto my knees and then getting to my feet, holding my hands out so they won't assume I'm trying to hurt them. I'd rather not waste magic on any of these men tonight, not when there are far greater dangers in my future.

"If you're going to take me prisoner, can I at least pack up my bedroll? I'd rather not lose it."

A nervous chuckle works its way through them, and then the sword is pressed beneath my chin, the steel cold in the darkness.

"You don't need a bedroll where you're going, witch. There'll be a lot of gold slipping into our hands for one like you, and I know exactly where to sell you for the highest sum. We just have to get you there without bumping into a high-fae battalion, so get moving."

I stare him down, my gaze boring into his until he gulps audibly, the sword pressing into my skin. Even when a trickle of warm blood rolls down my neck. I have no fear to give him.

I know my fate.

TWO⊙

SOREN

*The Fates have blessed you with a mate. You will find her
at Port Asmyr the morning after the summer solstice, nine
hundred and eighty-eight years from today. The Fates demand
your patience, a virtue of importance for a king to hold, and
your steadfast obedience.*
*You cannot defeat your enemies without your mate at your
side.*
With your union, you shall end the war and take your throne.

The clash of steel rings in the air and I brace myself for impact, ensuring I don't fall from my horse as I swing my sword. An ear-splitting screech cuts through the noise and ends abruptly when my blade cleaves the witch's head from his body. It thumps to the ground.

The snow never stops falling in the Outlands and the mountain ranges that form the gateway to the southernmost point of my kingdom, and even with the summer solstice edging closer, there's a fine powder coming down around us. The Shard looms behind us, the ice that covers its peaks formed into jagged sheets of looming death. The witches lured us in here in a last-ditch attempt at victory.

In the slush of churned-up snow, the entire battlefield

descends into chaos. Blood and magic and the brute force of steel swung by vastly trained high fae soldiers blends as my forces push back the deranged witches. We're outnumbered three to one, but with our iron shields and armor, we have the advantage.

All the magic in the world won't help if their offensive can't land on us, and we've always been stronger, faster, and better equipped at hand-to-hand combat. The only strength they have against us is their numbers, and as I plough through the crowd sword first, killing every last witch I can reach without leaving my saddle, the odds become far closer to one to one.

I hear my cousin Tauron yelling my name, cursing my inability to hold the line and stay within his reach for protection, but I turn Nightspark and sweep back through without waiting for my soldiers to catch up. I let go of my title and every constraint holding me back and become nothing but my sword, killing for my people and for our future.

The bodies pile up, magic spilling out of them in a black acid that rots flesh until the entire battlefield reeks with the stench of dead witches. If we don't take the time to burn them, the land will be poisoned and nothing will ever grow here again. Their blood is a foulness that permeates everything, the stink of it filling my nostrils and coating my throat until I'm not sure I'll ever be rid of it. Bile churns in the depths of my gut even as I ignore it in favor of killing more of our enemy.

One pass turns into two, three, four, and I slash through the witches with my soldiers trailing behind me, picking off any survivors of my rampage. The weight of my sword in my hand is a comfort to me, and even when I'm coated in blood and dirt and blackened in witch bile, I don't stop until every last witch is dead.

Thankfully, though we've taken injuries, the iron armor worked and we haven't lost any men.

I'm keenly aware of our numbers and how finite they are. I've always been a strategic leader, weighing every move that my armies make to mitigate the loss of lives, but as the war wages on and the curse the witches laid upon the high fae continues to kill entire generations of our people, my ability and willingness to fight has become vital to our survival.

The witches' numbers never seem to wane.

"What exactly is the point of naming me your Royal Guard if you're just going to throw yourself headfirst into every stinking witch-blood battle without so much as a thought in my direction? You're a stubborn brute, Soren, and when you end up losing a Fates-cursed limb, I won't feel an inch of sorrow for you," Tauron snaps, pulling up his horse alongside me with a snarl on his face that would terrify a lesser man.

Roan, my best friend and the only one of my inner circle I'm not related to, directs the soldiers behind us to move the bodies of the witches.

I'd love nothing more than to leave them here to rot.

It's not an option for us though. We learned that lesson the hard way early on in the war. We're already struggling to grow crops and feed livestock throughout the kingdom, and to lose any more land to the poison of our enemies is not an option. The Shard has never been a location for farming, but I won't risk any further losses to the witches, regardless.

Tyton, Tauron's brother and the last of my inner circle riding with me today, is already seeing to the injuries of our soldiers. His natural affinity for magic means he can do rudimentary healing, enough to get the wounded home. The maids who pass as healers back at Yregar have barely any more experience than he does, but we've made it work well enough.

"—we're absolutely ruined if you get yourself killed, Soren. At some point you're going to have to—"

"I was never in danger. We need to get moving—we have

a long journey ahead, and if we're ambushed on the way, we won't make it."

I don't have to say what *it* is. They all know, and Tauron's mouth shuts with a click. I'm not using it as a trump card, and yet there's no quicker way to get everyone moving quickly.

Within minutes the corpses are burning, the flames crackling as they flare green and blue from the magic in the witches' blood. The stench intensifies until half the soldiers are pulling their cloaks over their faces to stifle it as best they can.

Roan nudges his horse closer to mine and murmurs, "The wind is blowing north. The witches will know of this loss before nightfall."

I glance at the bright orange burst of dusk as the sun quickly disappears, taking the last of its warmth with it and leaving us with the cool breeze from the snow-capped mountains ahead. I give him a curt nod, and Roan calls out commands to move with haste, the risk of an ambush great. We can't afford a delay.

Not today.

We ride through the short night and all through the next day, the air heating up the farther north we travel. We don't stop for anything until we arrive at Yregar Castle the following evening, just as those same orange streaks across the sky harken the arrival of the summer solstice. My soldiers are well versed in what to expect from me and what I demand from them, trained to serve without question, and so there's not a single complaint about the hard journey home.

I need to leave again quickly, but I also need to bring Roan back to his wife.

My cousin, Princess Airlie Celestial Snowsong, is the strongest and most capable female I've ever met. A danger to the snakes within the Unseelie Court in her own right, she's no wilting rose who needs to be coddled by her husband or the males in her family at all, but there are extenuating circumstances.

She's pregnant.

After losing their first son to the curse the witches cast on all full-blooded high fae, for reasons she's been unable to explain to me, Airlie decided to try again. Centuries have passed since the last high fae baby was born to the Unseelie Court and yet, my beautiful, intelligent, stubborn cousin insisted on it.

I'm both horrified at what may come to pass for her and desperate to break the curse before it takes another babe from her arms. This one is due at the autumn equinox, but with the swell of her belly growing daily and the way she already clutches at the furniture around her with random bouts of pain, I fear she'll go into the birthing rooms early.

When we arrive at the stables at the base of the castle, we find her waiting for us, her belly round and her cheeks flushed, her hands on her hips as she watches us dismount and hand off our horses to the waiting stable hands.

Without preamble, she scrunches her nose at us. "You all smell like rotting witches. I'll be damned if any of you are invited to dine with me tonight like *that*. Fix it."

As he removes his helmet and hands it to one of the squires, Roan's eyes twinkle at his wife. The blood of our enemies still drips from his gloves as he unbuckles his iron breastplate and lets it fall from his body. It's been too badly damaged to use again, so he's not worried about babying it.

Where Airlie looks every inch the Unseelie high fae princess she is, all pale skin, blue eyes, and white-blonde hair that falls to her waist, Roan's lineage shows in his own coloring. Brown skin, golden eyes, and tightly curled dark hair that he keeps cut close to his scalp. They're a striking couple, and one the Unseelie Court always has a lot to say about.

I couldn't care less that Roan's mother was a princess of the Seelie Court, beyond the fact that, ever since she married his father—a fated union—she was loyal to me and to her son.

I've long since suspected my own mate is a Seelie princess, and if she's half as loyal, capable, and beautiful as the Outlands princess was, then the Fates will have blessed me beyond measure.

Impatience itches down my spine, the last few hours of waiting possibly the worst so far, but I fix a blank look on my face to hide it from my family. Years of longing for my croí have helped me develop a cold and impassive mask, hiding the maelstrom of frustration the Fates have cursed me to bear. Even a single word from her has been denied to me because of her captivity, and the deaths I will deliver to those who took her from me loom, the wait finally drawing to a close.

"Beloved, that's the exact welcome I have been dreaming of all these nights away from you. You never fail to sweet-talk me, though I don't deserve such a reception from a princess like yourself."

Her eyes narrow at his irreverent reply, but a frenetic sort of joy oozes from them both, a relief at being reunited despite the death that surrounds us. "You're not going to talk your way out of this, Roan Snowsong. If you don't climb into a tub of boiling water and start scrubbing right this instant, you'll be sleeping in the kitchens with the rats!"

He clutches his chest, and Tauron drawls, "There had better not be any rats down there. I haven't eaten anything decent in weeks. I'll have someone's head."

Tyton shudders before he cackles, nudging his brother with his elbow as though Tauron's told some great joke.

Airlie rolls her eyes at them only to focus on me, her brows whipping up alarmingly. "Well? Any news, or are we just going to continue on in this hellish wasteland forever?"

I'm hyperaware of the bodies around us, the soldiers working diligently to untack and rub down the horses while the stable hands get them all fed and settled in their stalls for a well-deserved rest. In the distance, the gardeners are moving about the yard, trying to keep up the appearance that the castle is unaffected by the war and the toll on the lands.

It's a game I play with my uncle, the regent, his whispers of my savage nature and unworthiness for the throne rising every time the Unseelie Court arrives at Yregar only to find it operating as it always has. The façade is rapidly failing, the land too far gone now, but that's always been the regent's plan. He stays safely in Yris, untouched and suspiciously well-fed, while he lets the kingdom die to keep the power he holds.

My uncle's apathy for the war combined with the sigil carved into his shoulder that matches marks I've found on our enemies' corpses has confirmed to me that he's complicit with Kharl's madness. The High Witch incited the war by killing my parents as they slept, aided by my uncle's treason to gain access to the impenetrable castle at Yris. He then sent war bands of witches through the kingdom to kill any high fae, lower fae and part-bloods under the rule of the Unseelie throne. He's responsible for the curse on the Unseelie high fae and the reason entire generations of high-fae babies have died.

As I answer Airlie, I unbuckle my own armor and hand it off to one of the squires waiting to assist me. "We took out one of the smaller war bands. It was a win for us today."

Only Airlie's closest family and friends could tell that my words are a blow. Her face doesn't change save for her lips tightening just a little as one hand slips down to rest over her swollen belly. Every time we return with news of killing witches but nothing about the curse itself, I see another little piece of her crushed, the weight of her first son's passing to Elysium still heavy on her heart.

It's cruel of me, but I can't tell her that there's no need for her devastation. Never have I let slip the details of the time and day of the arrival of my fate, but she's here, finally within my reach, and with our union will come the end of this war and of the curse that has taken so much from us all. Her voice is still clear in my mind, shyly speaking the name she gave me because I hadn't told her my own. Every syllable and turn of phrase she used during those weeks that our mind had connected through our shared fate before she was ripped away from me echoes in my memory. The Seer told me, time and again, that the Fates were teaching me patience, and no matter how hard I tried to find a way around it, they forced me to wait nearly one thousand years.

During that time, my kingdom fell further into ruin while I was forced to watch, unable to save my people from Kharl or my uncle's indifference. Here at Yregar, I've protected a tiny fraction of the population—a handful of villagers and refugees, my family, and those most loyal to my claim to the throne—but the rest have suffered and starved at the whims of the Fates.

No more. The wait is finally over.

We ride out tomorrow to find my mate.

Dirt and ash, as far as the eye can see.

After a long bath and a terrible night's rest, Tauron, Tyton, and Roan are accompanying me—along with a small and carefully chosen group of my most trusted and capable soldiers—to meet my fate. With weapons dripping from our bodies and cloaks in the royal colors draping our backs, we leave absolutely nothing to chance. Without the use of the fae door, the journey is difficult, but I'd make it a thousand times over.

We're three days' ride from Yregar Castle, and it's here, at the cusp of Port Asmyr and closing in on the easternmost coast of the Southern Lands and the outer edge of my kingdom, that the toll taken by the War of the Witches is at its most stark.

Everything is dead.

It's been decades since the war became destructive on such a widespread level, long enough that it's no longer a jarring experience to see the lands like this, and yet I can't help but feel despair as I take it all in. There's a great shame inside me that it's come to this. Shame that I've failed my people and my land at such a catastrophic level. Knowing that I'll meet my mate today only makes that feeling fester inside of me.

She's going to see the failure I've been to my kingdom and the fae folk within, all the ways in which my hands have been tied, that every advancement I might have made has been thwarted by my enemies and my own blood alike. I'll be forced to bring her home to a pack of devils in disguise and teach her how to tell an ally from a foe even when they all look and act the same.

I'm going to bring her into a battlefield all its own, and one I would never choose for her. That feels like the biggest failure of all—a fate given to me because I had to wait so long for my Fates-blessed mate, and for what?

Patience.

One word, spoken by the Seer a thousand years ago, that has wielded disastrous results. When I'd traveled to see her, just months after my own parents were murdered, she'd given me a fate that almost ended my world, with no sign of remorse or sorrow for compromising the entire kingdom. Supposedly, the Fates had decided that I needed to learn patience, and the best way to teach me that was to make me wait almost a thousand years for my mate.

The person without whom I cannot become king.

Part of me wonders if this has all been a plot against me, an attempt to keep me trapped in this war with no way of ending it. Though he's not the king, the regent holds power over the resources I can use, and at every opportunity we've had to wipe out the witches once and for all, he's moved forces around under the guise of protecting royal family members.

Entire bloodlines have been wiped out thanks to his moves.

During all these long years of waiting, I've fought against my fate. I've hated every second of forced submission, but it only got worse when, for a brief fraction of time, I was able to hear my mate in my mind. A few short months of her honeyed tones drifting through my head like salve over raw wounds, only for her to be silenced once more. Two full centuries have passed since I last heard her, but no matter how brief our acquaintance, no matter how guarded we both were as we learned what we could of each other, I would recognize her in a crowd even without any of my senses. I can feel the tug of the Fates in me now, guiding me to her, every fiber of my body alight with her call to me.

Patience.

A thousand years have passed, and finally, the day has come. The hour is quickly approaching, and everything I've waited for is within my grasp.

I've been very careful about keeping the details of my fate a secret, never letting slip a single thing. Especially not the exact moment we are to meet, in case someone tried to dispose of my mate before I could make it to her.

As the years have passed, treachery has grown deep within the Unseelie Court.

The longer my uncle stays regent, the further away my crown becomes. Every day he's eroding my claim to the throne through his gossip and court games.

I've been planning this day for a long time.

Every moment has been thought out and considered, obsessed over and moved around until I was sure that everything would run smoothly. I planned how I'd explain my movements to the Unseelie Court, the ways that I would slip away from the regent's guards so that I could surround myself with only the people I trust most. The only high fae I trust to bring my Fates-blessed mate back to Yregar Castle and to safety before the regent finds out she exists. I've been so very careful to ensure her safety throughout the kingdom, no matter how bleak the path home will be.

Whatever happened to her that stopped her from communicating with me, I want her to know that she can trust me. That I'll ensure nothing terrible ever happens to her again, and that when I learn who kidnapped her and kept her from me, I'll pursue them to the ends of the earth and enact vengeance. If they still hold her now, their death will be instant and blood-soaked. Whatever it takes to rescue her and bring her home with me.

My hands tighten on Nightspark's reins. My horse is as black as the night sky of the winter equinox, and his temper is just as unpredictable. My jaw tightens until I think my teeth might break as we ride through the Augur Mountain range.

We're close to the mountain where the last of the Seers once resided. Not long after my final visit to her, she fled the Southern Lands for fear of the witches. Kharl led the charge against the voices of the Fates themselves, and the other three Seers who once lived in the kingdom were murdered, one by one, in unprecedented acts of terror.

The witches once offered sigils of protection and worship to the Seers, females chosen from their own ranks to become vessels of the Fates. Now they hunt them to extinction.

The mountain looks more bleak and desolate than ever before, and the very sight of it rankles me.

It shouldn't be like this.

The idea of escorting my Fates-blessed mate to Yregar Castle through such bleak lands galls me, and I decide to take her home through the fae door. There's one here in the Augur

Mountains, a mysterious empty structure created by the First Fae when they first came to the Southern Lands, and though its magic is waning, it's still an invaluable tool. I didn't risk using it today—too many potential eyes on my movements—but once my mate is safely by my side, we'll travel home that way.

As we crest the final ridge of the mountains and the ocean comes into sight, I pull up Nightspark and pause for a moment. We're running ahead of schedule. I have time to take a breath and keep myself under control. It will do me no good to arrive at the Fates-designated meeting place and scare my mate.

"You're taking this a lot better than I thought you would," Tauron murmurs as he halts his horse alongside me and looks across the water with narrowed eyes.

His mount stamps its hoof as if unhappy at how hard we've ridden, but Nightspark stays calm beneath me. None of my cousins are as in tune with their beasts as I am, and it shows on rides like this.

"I'm envisioning exactly how I'm going to murder whoever has her, and that alone is keeping me calm." I speak in the old language, one that, of this group, only my cousins, Roan, and I speak, because some admissions are best kept to the closest of friends.

Tauron nods and strokes a hand down his horse's neck, calming it under his firm touch.

Tyton is mumbling behind us unhappily, this path always wreaking havoc on his inner peace. Roan answers him in soothing tones. We got too close to the trees of Ravenswyrd Forest again.

The old forest began speaking to Tyton years ago, crying out in a way that only he can hear, but the pleas have been getting louder. Every time we're forced to ride past it, the perimeter of safety for him bows out a little further, until I'm sure my cousin is going to lose his mind the moment we cross the Lore River.

Soon there won't be an inch of the Southern Lands where he'll be safe from whatever madness lies within the forest.

It begs us to heed its warning, but no matter how hard we've turned the request over in our minds, we have no answer.

Return the Favored Children to us.

No one knows who the Favored Children are, no one knows what happened to them, and I have more important things to think about at the moment.

Nothing in the world can distract me from my Fates-blessed mate. There are only a few months until the winter solstice, the perfect time for a wedding and an ascension to the throne, and as soon as I have control over the entire Unseelie Court I can stop playing paltry games in the War of the Witches and move our remaining resources to where they need to be. I can send the high fae princes and princesses back to their own lands to return to farming and replenishing the stores of food within the kingdom.

I can stop the stupid balls the regent keeps throwing, frivolous parties that waste resources, until the witches are gone and the lands have been healed. It's not going to be the easiest life for my mate to marry into, but I'm determined to give her everything she could ever want while doing what needs to be done. While unions blessed by the Fates don't necessarily guarantee a happy marriage, I know many who have found love through their fates, and I'm determined to know the same peace and fulfillment that my parents shared. My croí is already buried deep in my heart, and I'll prove myself to her, whatever it takes.

I'll save my kingdom, I'll heal my mate's trauma from being kidnapped, and I'll be the king my people need.

Tauron glances at his brother, ever watchful, but when he sees that Roan has a handle on the situation, he turns back to me. "If she's being held captive and you kill her captors in front of her, you're only going to traumatize her more. Maybe getting her out of the port and back to Yregar should be your priority. We can always hunt them down later."

Unacceptable.

I shoot him a look and speak once again in the old language. "Or I can hand her off to Roan, who's very good at soothing traumatized females. Once he has her out of sight and earshot, I can brutally rend them limb from limb and then stake out their bodies publicly so that everybody sees the consequences of touching my bride-to-be."

Tauron purses his lips and nods, looking as though he is thinking a lot about this, and then a grin slowly stretches over his lips. "I suppose that's a good plan. Roan will be *thrilled* to know that his years of marriage to Airlie will come in handy to you."

The sun bursts over the horizon, lighting up the ocean as dawn finally breaks, and I feel a swell of triumph in my chest. Finally, the patience that was forced upon me and dragged out of my stubborn soul has come to an end.

My Fates-blessed mate is just moments away, and with a quick glance over my shoulder at Tauron and Roan, I nudge Nightspark on, directing him down the side of the mountain. We move carefully, slow and considered, thanks to the loose rocks beneath the horses' hooves, but I'd factored this into my timing as well.

Every last second of this morning had been planned, and I'll ensure that it goes off without delay. I will find the female chosen for me by the Fates to rule at my side. A high fae princess for whom I will accept nothing but the best.

My little croí, whom I have longed for, the soft, melodic tones of her voice in my mind so deeply missed but never forgotten. I reach out one last time to reassure her that I'm coming, that I won't take no for an answer this time with the Fates backing me, but when I encounter the barrier in her mind one more time, I don't feel the despair that usually takes hold. The hours are counting down, and whether I can reach her now or not, nothing will ever part us like this again.

I only wish that my reputation as the Savage Prince wasn't so prevalent throughout the lands.

If she's been traumatized by her captors, then I'm sure the idea of a scarred brute for a husband will be hard for her to accept. Another failing that grates at me.

I direct Nightspark past the fae door that stands farther up the mountain, and the moment the loose rock of the decline becomes the solid ground of the deadened plains once more, we break into a full gallop.

I'm not waiting for my fate any longer.

Port Asmyr is the only seaport within the kingdom. The small village is still heavily populated, the rations the regent delivers enough of an incentive to keep the workers here and the ships catered to. It's manned by the regent's guards, and the markets are a trading hub for both the ships that arrive less frequently now and the meager produce of the fae folk who live in nearby villages. Despite a scarcity of goods, the markets still seem unusually well attended. Though slavery is outlawed throughout the high fae courts, I've long suspected the regent's guards are turning a blind eye to the sale of flesh here.

I've watched this place ever since the Seer told me it would be my meeting point for my fate, and when we arrive, I make my way to the inn and find Jaceon, a part-blood scout I stationed here decades ago. He took over the flagging business from a family I took in at Yregar after the regent's guards terrorized them into leaving.

I find him greeting travelers at the door, a grim look on his face as he ushers them into the slowly deteriorating building. I doubt he's charging them much for the stay, if anything at all. The folk who frequent Asmyr are mostly rake thin, dirty, and reeking of desperation, and the scout is well-known for offering what little aid he can to those in dire need. It turns my stomach to see how haggard the fae folk here are, how bleak and lifeless the children look as they clutch at their parents' legs.

Jaceon bows his head the moment he spots our approach. When people on the street see the royal colors, they scurry away like frightened mice.

I slide off Nightspark and hand the reins to Roan, then approach Jaceon, the scout well trained and not one to waste time as he jumps past pleasantries and straight into a report.

"There've been more guards here in the past few weeks. A ship from the Northern Lands docked yesterday and left again this morning. The guards showed a lot of interest in it."

The corners of my mouth tighten. "What cargo did the ship bring in? The Sol King doesn't trade with the Southern Lands anymore."

My mate was on that ship.

The Fates tug and pull at me, their demand playing across my skin happily as they direct me, but I can't just run off into the crowd without knowing what I could be facing. Ignorance and arrogance could get my mate harmed, and I'll never allow that to happen.

Jaceon's brow furrows, and he meets my eye with a grim look. "People. A handful got off the boat. Most appeared to be part-bloods and lower fae, and the travelers stayed the night here before they left on the boat this morning."

He looks around once more before he says, "Five of the regent's males boarded the ship to travel to the Northern Lands. They wore plain clothing and cloaks, but I can spot a guard better than most."

My eyebrows creep upwards, and I glance over my shoulder at the crowd milling behind us. They give our horses a wide berth, setting a perimeter without direction from us. I know they don't give the same treatment to the regent's guards, having seen them posted in the area for centuries and clearly distinguishable by the off-tone blue of the colors they wear.

Jaceon is perceptive, it's why I chose to station him here in the first place. "The folk here know it's never a good thing to see a high fae prince riding through the backwoods areas of the kingdom. Bad luck always follows."

I nod and hand over a purse full of silver, because no one here could break a single gold coin let alone a bag of them. As I climb back into Nightspark's saddle, my uncle's possible motives churn through my mind, none more likely than another. I let myself consider them for only a moment before pushing the regent out of my mind, my mate the priority today and my uncle's schemes something to worry about later.

How she escaped notice is a concern. Maybe she was concealed by magic.

I curse under my breath for not arriving yesterday and seeing the ship for myself. It was a careful decision, made to stop my uncle from sending guards to follow me. We left at the last possible minute so no one could beat us here, but in doing so, I might have missed a vital clue to my mate's disappearance.

"I think there's a disease going around," Roan mutters to me as we ride onto the main road through the port village, looking down his nose at the guards as we pass them.

As they bow, every last one of them stares at me defiantly, emboldened by my uncle's reign and his not-so-subtle surety that the throne will stay in his power. Rumors of what will happen if I don't marry soon have grown more rampant, the tasks my uncle assigns me have grown more dangerous, and the gossip mongers among the Unseelie Court have become far too bold.

I look around at the lower fae and part-bloods, but I don't see whatever it is that Roan does.

When I meet his eyes, he merely shrugs. "The guards out here are supposed to feed them. There are supposed to be rations for all. If they aren't doing so, it's treason against the regent, as it was his decree. If they are, then there's definitely a disease running through the population. Most look ill."

The idea of my Fates-blessed mate catching something and ailing when we have no true healer sets fire to my blood.

Whoever brought her here is going to die.

Surely she must have guessed who I am by now; my thinly veiled efforts to conceal my identity from her during those few brief months that we communicated can't have held up, and she must know exactly who she is fated to be with.

I'm sure of it.

I worry sometimes that it was my fault she was kidnapped in the first place. There's every chance that my uncle sent his guards or paid mercenaries to keep her from me and buy himself time to steal the throne from underneath me. Bloodlines be damned—if he's responsible for her disappearance, I'll kill him too.

Those words have never passed my lips, not even to my cousins and closest confidants. What a sad state of affairs, to be forced to slaughter your own blood, but I doubt similar hesitations have crossed the regent's mind. To loathe your brother so much—to loathe the very air your nephew breathes—simply because you were born second and felt you were owed more.

When we reach the center of the village and the decrepit market there, I dismount from Nightspark once more and hand his reins to one of my soldiers, instructing half of the group to stay put and watch the horses and the other half to follow me through the booths.

We didn't bring an extra horse for my mate.

Most high fae princesses travel in carriages, and it's a very real possibility that my mate doesn't know how to ride a horse or will be wearing clothing that will make it difficult for her. My uncle and his spies would've known exactly what I was doing if I traveled out of Yregar with a carriage for her though, so I left it behind. Nightspark is more than capable of carrying the added weight of another high fae, and with my mate in front of me, even at a slower pace, we'll make it to Yregar by nightfall thanks to the fae door.

The idea of learning her name—the real one and not just some pet name of affection—shoots a possessive streak of fire deep into my gut.

I packed extra provisions and planned where we could stop with a female to keep her safe if, for some reason, we're unable to travel by the fae door. Every scenario has been considered, the paths home assessed and listed in order of preference, and as the Fates pull harder on me, I'm glad for my obsession as my mind becomes possessed by the drive to find her.

Roan follows me, his gaze on the marketplace around us before he sweeps off his cloak in one fluid motion so his sword is more accessible. The villagers around us avert their eyes, as if merely looking at him will cause that sword to swing in their direction, but his own eyes stay sharp.

Tyton seems to have shaken the demons from his mind. He follows Roan's lead and shrugs his own cloak off, the summer sun finally warming the chill of last night away and rendering the extra layer unnecessary. His eyes have cleared, now that we've made it to the valley and put enough land between us and the mourning trees of the Ravenswyrd.

Tauron tucks himself closely to my side, a wall of protection I'm sure I don't need.

When I shoot him a look, he shrugs. "You're distracted. No

47

matter how hard you deny it, you cannot convince me that your mind is not elsewhere right now. Even with those keenly honed senses of yours, someone could get the better of you."

I know exactly who he's referring to. Even in the old language, he won't say it out loud for fear of who might hear it and understand. If my uncle was the one to take her, he could have laid a trap here to finally be done with me.

If she also knows this is the time and place that we are destined to meet, they could have gotten that information out of her. Without knowing her lineage or her upbringing, there's no way to tell how experienced she is with court life and the games we play to survive.

I give Tauron a curt nod and continue into the markets, a Fate-fueled energy that feels like magic filling my veins. She's here, I can feel it. I can hear the Fates speaking to me, urging me to find her and be with her. I curl my hands into fists to control myself, my entire body filling with tension.

The simple stalls around us sell mostly food and weapons, though several merchants stop negotiating when they see us coming. Without a doubt in my mind, those are the ones who sell flesh. I don't need to focus on them to memorize their faces, a simple glance is all it takes. I'll remember them until I'm able to hold them accountable.

It'll be one of the first things I do once I take the throne— send soldiers back here to wipe this market clean. The idea of the flesh trade having something to do with keeping my mate from me is enough to warrant the decimation of the place.

There's a commotion toward the edge of the market, gasps and jeering breaking through the noise, and I feel the tug in my chest.

I ignore Tauron's muttered curses and take off in that direction, oblivious to everything but that invisible thread pulling me forward. My friends surround me to ensure that my uncle can't finally let his executioner's sword swing for my neck.

My senses tunnel down until I'm plowing through the crowd regardless of who's in my way.

The mutters and gasps turn into screams of terror, anyone who sees the savage determination on my face blanching and scurrying back in fear, and the crowd parts before me.

Three mercenaries stand there, swords buckled at their sides and disheveled leather clothing that has seen better days covering them like low-grade armor. They look fed and well-kept in a way no one else around us does, so they're either outsiders, or taking bribes from someone more fortunate than themselves. They stare at me like I'm their worst nightmare come true—an apt observation on their part—but my eyes focus between them, and I forget the vengeance that burns within me.

Flanked by the mercenaries is a female about a foot shorter than I am, with her back to me. A black braid secured with a leather strap hangs down one side.

At the commotion of the crowd, she turns to face me, and a few wisps of those inky locks tumble over her sun-kissed cheeks. There's no hunger in the rosiness of her complexion or the curves of her body beneath the dark folds of fabric that cover her. Her face is unmarked and vibrant with good health, her natural beauty shining through as she stands before me. A smattering of freckles stands out over her nose and under her sooty lashes as she blinks, but my gaze is pulled down to the gag stuffed in her mouth. The tight fabric digs into her cheeks, and a bruise blooms at her throat.

The further down I look, the deeper into my rage I fall.

Her hands are bound in front of her with iron, the thick bands clamped directly on the tender skin, and blood drips down her slender fingers and falls to the cracked cobblestones at her feet. The copper tang of her blood breaks through the assault of scents in the market and fills my lungs with the call of my mate.

The Fates scream within me, demanding I kill the males touching her and all those who look on, gouge out their eyes for daring to look upon what is mine and for me alone.

My Unseelie nature kicks in, and my hand drops to the pommel of my sword, the sapphire there warm to the touch as the power of my ancestors lingers. Bloodlust blinds me for a moment before my senses finally return and, with them, the true horror of what stands before me.

Staring back at me, with contempt in her undeniably silver eyes, is my Fates-blessed mate.

A witch.

Every inch of me rejects my reaction to her. My lip curls, a snarl bubbling out of the fiery pits of my gut, only for the wall in my mind that has separated us for two hundred excruciatingly long years to disappear and the voice I've dreamed of to finally echo inside my head once more.

The blood in my veins turns to ice.

Hello, Donn.

THREE

ROOKE

I know when my Fates-blessed mate arrives in the village.

Like a bolt of lightning running through my blood, a tingling starts in the scar at my waist and works its way through my limbs until I feel as though my skin is going to slide right off my bones. There's a tugging feeling at the center of my chest, as though my fate is pulling me to him, and my stomach clenches around the fluttering feeling there. The physical reaction is out of my control—I know exactly which male is hunting me through the crowd, and I'd rather cut off a limb than feel this way about *him*. The sensation is uncomfortable, to say the least, and it's only the presence of the three mercenaries that stops me from shaking out my limbs to ease the feeling.

I'm beyond the point of running.

I did that as a young girl when I first learned my fate, but now, after centuries in the Northern Lands fighting against the Ureen in the Fate Wars, I've come to accept that certain things cannot be changed. Not without a catastrophic loss of lives and land, a burden I could never carry.

The mercenaries pull me behind them, a swagger in their gait as they parade their prize through the crowd that gathers as though by accident. There's a murmuring from the villagers as they stop and stare, their eyes looking unnaturally large in their faces due to how thin they all are. The high fae guards we pass are all in perfect health, clean and vigorous as they accept silver coins from my captors and wave us past without really looking in my direction. The stark difference in their physical condition sets my teeth on edge, my contempt at the call of my fate simmering even hotter.

The iron shackles around my wrists itch, though they do little more than irritate my skin because my magic is strong enough to keep the metal from burning me. The real pain flooding my body radiates from my scar, the mottled skin on my stomach and my back from my time in the Fate Wars. I was struck by a Ureen, one of the mindless creatures that descended from the tear in the sky over the Northern Lands, and now I have a close relationship with the Fates themselves. I sense their whims and desires in ways I never could have imagined before.

It's a useful but constant reminder of the numbness that has filled me since the war ended, still holding my mind apart from my body as I catalog the sensations without truly feeling them or caring about the damage being done to me. Even when the mercenary tugs at the iron chains and the shackles break my skin, my blood dripping freely from the wounds, I do little more than murmur a prayer to the Fates in the old language for the land to accept the blood as an offering so it isn't wasted.

At first, the shock and whispers that move like waves through the crowd are centered on me. I suspect this is the welcome any witch gets in the Southern Lands, thanks to Kharl and the evils of the war. I don't blame these people for their reactions, not even those who call out for my death. The endless attacks on the lower fae and part-bloods and the devastation to the land that has destroyed the food supply here can be blamed directly on the witches, and I can't find any emotion within myself for the villagers but pity.

I also don't cower or drop my gaze from any of them.

I am a Ravenswyrd witch, the last Mother of the coven.

We've always held neutrality in this land, caretakers and healers to all without question, and I'm not ashamed of the blood that runs through my veins. No whispers or war can change that.

The murmurs and whispers change. The mercenaries lose their confidence in one fell swoop and come to an abrupt halt, the chains clattering on the ground, and I step in close behind them. The murmurs grow louder and louder, until I hear his name so clearly through the crowd it seems to be whispered directly into my ear. The tugging in my chest almost pulls me off my feet.

He's here.

The Savage Prince.

A ripple courses through the crowd, and then it parts as the villagers scramble away from four high fae princes, each more beautiful than the last. Two centuries of living amongst the Seelie high fae in the Northern Lands has dulled the impact of high-fae beauty on me, but I hold myself rigid to hide my breathlessness at the sight of them.

Each of them is tall and powerfully built, not the type of high fae to sit around and make decrees rather than join a fight themselves. I'm not surprised; I wasn't expecting a pampered group. Three are typical of the Unseelie, with pale skin, long blond hair, and icy blue eyes. The fourth has Seelie blood in him, brown skin, dark hair, and golden eyes, with a face as breathtaking as the rest.

There's no doubt which one is the Savage Prince.

If the Fates singing to me the moment my gaze touches him isn't enough, the scar is a dead giveaway, the angry slash marring an otherwise perfect face. Whispers of his temperament and legacy reached even the Northern Lands, though I did my best to avoid them.

I tried to forget his name.

I spent years shoving it out of my mind and losing myself in a war that was not my own, fighting for good people in a land as far from here as my brother and I could get.

The white slash that cuts through his beauty doesn't detract from it at all, but only adds to the heartbreaking tension in my chest as my gaze traces over him. I couldn't look away even if the Fates themselves commanded me to, though admittedly, I don't try hard.

He's armed to the teeth and wears well-worn leather boots in the traditional high-fae style I hate and a Celestial-blue cloak lined with fur. His clothing is slate gray and trimmed in Celestial blue, the royal crest standing out proudly on his chest. Every inch of his solid body screams high-fae prince, but the arrogance with which he holds himself is different from that of the guards we passed on our way into the market.

I know a soldier when I see one, and this male stands like he's prepared to take a blow. Which is good, because he's clearly just taken the biggest hit of his life.

The look of disgust on all four of their faces has a smirk tugging at my lips, muted some by the gag shoved roughly between my teeth. I suppose the Fates did not warn him that his mate is a witch.

I see rejection in his eyes, and my own frustrations at our cursed fate has me sending him two words through our fate connection, a simple and irrefutable connection between mates that I'd closed down the day I learned his name and ran away from the horrors in store for me.

Hello, Donn.

I close myself off before he has the chance to answer me or find a way into my mind but the tactic is effective all the same. He physically recoils, the hand on his sword tightening as I imagine he fights the urge to kill me and be done with the chaotic mess we're trapped in together. The action startles the mercenaries out of their silent stupor, and the world sharpens around me once more as I remember that other people exist. The Savage Prince and I are the spectacle of Port Asmyr and its pathetically paltry marketplace.

"Your Highness, we were bringing the witch to the guards here! She's a prisoner, and we haven't spoken to her. We meant no act of treason." The mercenary fumbles over his words, but as he holds up the other end of the chains, I turn to look at him and raise an eyebrow.

I'm well aware that they were not bringing me to the guards.

The Savage Prince continues to stare me down with a look of pure loathing, but with a quick glance in his direction, one of the other Unseelie princes steps forward to speak. I'd guess he's the Savage Prince's second-in-command and has realized that his superior has been struck dumb at the sight of me.

"Where did you find her?"

The mercenary holds out the chain again, rattling it in the prince's direction for him to take as though the iron is a venomous python rearing its head. "Half a day's ride. She was camping by herself. You can tell by the clothes she's wearing that she's come off the last ship from the Seelie lands. Returned from the war there, I'm sure."

The prince takes the chains with a gloved hand, crystals around the cuff sparkling in the sunlight, and I make note of them. He doesn't have enough magic within him to protect himself from the iron. I don't smell any magic on him at all, but one amongst their group certainly has it. I can guess which one, but without getting closer to the group I can't be sure.

Magic is a fickle thing, needing a capable and highly trained user to be effective, and gauging high-fae magic is like trying to catch sunlight in a glass—fantastical and impossible.

"What did she have with her?" the prince asks, his voice still icy cold.

The mercenary with a limp grabs my backpack and hands it

over to the prince with a small bow of his head.

When the third mercenary does not reach into his pocket, I turn and face him with a look. He sneers back at me, sweat breaking out over his forehead at my silent accusation.

"Get your eyes off me, filthy witch," he snaps, and then he shoves me.

I have far too much training to be pushed over so easily, my stance widening as I absorb the hit and stare him down.

As he lifts his hand again, the prince grabs his wrist. "What else do you have of hers?"

His lip curls at me and he mutters under his breath, "Nothing. She's a lying bitch. You can never trust a witch."

The prince with Seelie blood steps forward and grabs the mercenary's other arm, then starts patting him down. When the telltale sound of coins clinking together rings from his pocket, the male begins to struggle in earnest. The prince reaches in and pulls out a small satchel.

He opens it up and peers inside, clicking his tongue. "You said she came from the Northern Lands. This is Seelie gold. Trying to keep it for yourself?"

The mercenary's lip curls, and he spits at the ground. "A male has to eat! The high fae are more than happy to take everything from the lands and leave the rest of us to starve. That will feed my family for the next year."

I might have had some sympathy for this male, but I'm well aware he doesn't have a family. During the entire journey here, he lamented loudly that they were running on a tight schedule and so he couldn't stop to have his own fun with me on the way. He joked constantly about the things he could do to me, even offering to make a spectacle of it for his friends, and the way they laughed and joked along with him made it clear it wouldn't have been the first time.

I'm of the opinion that he should starve so he can't do the

same again to another less capable female.

The Seelie prince steps back and hands the satchel to the Savage Prince, who takes it without looking at it, still silent as he stares at me. I can feel the rage and disbelief rolling off him, but it takes another moment before he jolts out of the stupor the reality of his fate struck him into.

His gaze traces the crowd for a moment, but he says, low voice dripping with cruelty, "Find another horse. It's not riding with me."

He then turns to the prince with an armful of mercenary and snaps, loud enough for the entire crowded marketplace to hear him, "Kill them. Anyone transporting a witch without direct orders is committing treason."

A low gasp sounds around us, but the princes don't hesitate, loyal to their savage leader. The mercenaries begin to protest, exclaiming and cursing under their breath at him, but the high fae are too fast for them as they draw their swords and cut each man's throat without another word.

I watch it all even as their blood spatters my cheeks and stains the front of my cloak. The coldness that filled my body long ago hasn't thawed, leaving the entire show of butchery like nothing more than a typical carnival play.

The fourth high-fae prince, who hadn't said a word so far, turns to the Savage Prince and murmurs, "There are no horses to purchase here. No one outside of the castle has access to them anymore due to the regent's decrees. If you won't ride with her, then she'll have to go with one of us or walk, but at that pace it'll take an extra three days to return to Yregar."

The Savage Prince turns back to the Seelie prince, watching as he wipes the blood of the mercenaries from his blades and slides them back into their sheaths.

"Then it walks. I'm not touching it, and neither are any of you."

The journey by foot through the Southern Lands is vastly different from the one my brother and I took when we left. Chained and gagged the way I am, there's nothing for me to do other than take in the landscape of the kingdom. A small crack pierces the ice around my heart, and tears blind me. The gag chokes me, a lump growing in my throat until I struggle to breathe at all.

Everything we pass is dead or dying, no signs of life in the charred remains of the fields. Witches are supposed to be the caretakers of the earth, protecting nature and the seasons by pouring our magic into the land and letting it replenish us in return. But it's clear that none of the rituals that keep the lands flourishing have been undertaken for a long time.

I don't know if this is a strategy of Kharl's to win the war, but it's heartbreaking to see. The witches of the Southern Lands have always been caretakers of the land, nurturing it and holding rites to honor all that it has blessed us with, and to know that my kind have wrought this destruction is devastating. The stories I was told by other witches who fled to the Northern Lands had sounded impossible, embellished, and yet the truth of their testimonies resonates in the barren remains of my once-thriving homeland.

One of the high-fae princes bolts my shackles to the back of his saddle so I'm forced to walk as fast as his horse.

I do so without a word.

I can't speak around the gag in my mouth, but there are still ways of communicating with them if I wanted to. I could open my mind to speak directly to the Savage Prince again, but I've put the wall back up between us, and it stands as strong as it did when I first created it at the Seer's temple two hundred years ago. The disgust emanating from my mate still permeates the air around us, and no doubt he'd react poorly if I spoke to him that way again.

Back then, giving up the comfort of his presence was a great loss to me. Grieving as I already was for my family, it felt especially cruel to lose him too. Time didn't heal the wound; with every snippet of news that came to the Seelie Court from the Southern Lands, the pain only intensified and burrowed deeper within me. No matter the tactics I tried, my memories of his voice and honeyed promises never faded.

The Fates are cruel and fickle, but I've had a long time to come to terms with that.

The high fae ride in silence, though I sense it's more of a cautious thing. I'm sure none of them know what to say, and it makes me curious what the Savage Prince knew of his fate.

Did he assume he was meeting the perfect female, some high-fae beauty, only to find his greatest enemy staring back at him? I should have sympathy for the male, but, staring at him, I find that I'm as cold and empty as ever. I feel as hollow now as I did standing on *the Shepherd* returning home to a place that had left me with nothing but heartache and sorrow.

Never did I think I would return. I never imagined I could leave my brother behind in the Northern Lands to come back and face my fate, though I'm glad Pemba isn't here to see how they're treating me.

I can hear his voice in my head right now.

Kill them, Rooke. Kill them and be done with it. Return to the Northern Lands, to me, to our friends and family, to everyone who loves you.

He never wanted me to leave the Northern Lands in the first place.

Without telling them the future the Seer had laid out before me, it was hard to explain to everyone that the Fates were calling to me– that I'd seen too much death and destruction for the sake of an unfulfilled fate and I couldn't let that happen again. We barely survived the Fate Wars, and I don't need to look around now to know that the Unseelie Court is far less equipped for such a war than the Seelie Court was.

The entire Sol Army was almost wiped out before we defeated the Ureen, and I doubt these Unseelie princes have as much support behind them.

The second-in-command speaks again, this time in the old language. "We have to stop for the night, Soren. We can't keep walking until she dies, even if that seems preferable right now." The sun has long since set, and we've continued marching in the moonlight.

Prince Soren Celestial, heir to the throne of the Southern Lands.

The name was imprinted on my heart at the tender age of eighteen, soaked with poison and wrapped in terror. He became my own personal ghoul, a demon who lived in my mind to torment me.

He doesn't look so frightening now.

"The iron isn't burning her wrists. Are we sure that she's a full-blooded witch? If she has magic, it should be roasting her by now."

Interesting.

They clearly don't understand the laws of magic, if that's what they believe.

The fourth prince shakes his head. "I could smell the magic on her from across the marketplace. She's got it. I don't know if witches can cast to keep iron from burning them, but she's definitely a full-blood."

So he *is* the one with the magic. His gaze never touches me, as if I might bewitch him in some fashion with one glance, but the Savage Prince does not share such concerns, throwing repulsed looks in my direction at every opportunity.

"The iron stays on. The gag stays in. We'll take her back to Yregar, put her in the dungeon, and then figure out what the in Fates good *fuck* we're going to do."

The Seelie prince groans and rubs his eyes. "I think we know what we're going to do, Soren, because the Fates haven't given you many options. Actually, they've given you only one."

The Savage Prince cuts him a look that could flay a male alive, but he doesn't say a word.

We continue walking, the irritation of the princes palpable, though the other soldiers with us follow obediently. When the Savage Prince finally stops the group and barks out orders to make camp, I prepare myself for a very uncomfortable night.

I've slept in worse situations.

"Tie it to that tree. We'll take turns standing guard, and we'll leave again at dawn. I'll take first watch."

The other high fae princes share looks between themselves, and then the Seelie-blooded prince begins to sort out the horses. The prince who dragged me behind his horse comes to bind me to the tree the Savage Prince pointed out, snapping the chains to get me moving faster.

He's extra careful as he triple checks the restraints, and then he stares at me before turning on his heel and walking away to make camp with the others, contempt rolling off him. It's only when they have a small fire burning and food being shared between them that conversation breaks out about something that isn't me.

"We're too close to the forest. I can hear it," the one with magic says, and the Seelie-blooded prince groans under his breath.

"There's nothing we can do about that tonight, Tyton. If you need to drink to get some sleep, I have extra packed."

Tyton shakes his head. "It won't block them out. We've

tried it before. It wants the Favored Children back."

My head snaps up, catching their attention, and the Savage Prince sneers in my direction. "Take your eyes off us before you find yourself without them."

The soldiers all seem to stop breathing, even the ones trying to get some rest, but I stare him down for a moment before I lean back against the tree. I rest my head against the trunk and shut my eyes so none of them can see the brightness in them.

I don't care what else they have to say.

Whatever secrets the Ravenswyrd is whispering to Tyton, they're a message from the trees to him alone, but the song welcoming my return rings in my own ears as though I never left. An invisible string that connects us, pulling at me to bring me home to the trees, and my chest aches with longing to stand amongst them once more. The Fates have dealt me a cruel hand, to lead me so close and yet deny me that single hope I have left within my heart.

Tears prick my eyes, longing and relief mixing to choke me as I listen to the trees call out for us. Once, long ago, I thought the forest had forsaken us. I thought we'd done something to wrong the forest that had sheltered and provided for the Ravenswyrd Coven for generations, and that in return, it had withdrawn its protections.

I've learned better since then.

Thousands of refugees from the Southern Lands brought information with them to Sol City, and Pemba was meticulous about finding out what he could about our home. We learned what Kharl had done, that it was his treachery that cost us our family and our coven.

We know that the trees were betrayed.

My heart desperately craves to return to them and ease some of their pain, to show them that a Favored Child has come home, but it would be a lie. The coven is gone, the forest devoid of its ancestral caretakers, and my fate will take me into the Unseelie Court, where the high fae have forgotten the trees.

With the crackling fire and the small talk happening around it as the males begin to question everything the Fates could be planning, I might not be able to sleep where I am, but the more I can learn about the high fae while they assume I'm unconscious, the easier the coming months will be for me.

I'm woken in the middle of the night by the sound of footsteps.

I open my eyes but keep my body still, my back aching where it's pressed against the rough bark of the tree. These high-fae soldiers are experienced, and though not a word is spoken or even a limb moved, the camp is alert and ready for whoever is approaching. At the last moment, I feel a blanket of magic that isn't my own fall over me, a rudimentary and feeble concealment at best, but it does the trick well enough.

When the incoming soldiers break through the tree line around us, not a single one does more than glance in my direction, clearly seeing nothing other than the tree itself.

Muscle memory of the life I left behind kicks in, and I take stock of the situation. There are twenty soldiers, all of them high fae and well armed. They all wear the same uniform and fur-lined cloaks, but the blue tone is slightly different to those worn by the Savage Prince and his men, a shade or two off. I don't doubt it's intentional—nothing the high fae ever do is by accident—and it has me questioning their loyalty to their kingdom and the rightful heir.

One of the soldiers steps forward, his stance wide and cocky as he drops one hand to the pommel of his sword. "Prince Soren, we were not expecting to find you out here! We were unaware of your plans to travel so far from home."

The Savage Prince stares back at the speaker, who hasn't bothered to remove his helmet. If the Unseelie Court is anything like the Seelie, it's a clear act of disrespect toward the male who will someday be their king. The tension that radiates through the air is thick, like a force pressing against my chest.

A fight could break out at a moment's notice.

We're outnumbered three to one, and if any of them manage to kill the prince who is using magic to cover me, I'll be forced into action that I'm not sure I want to take to defend these high fae males who aren't worth the efforts. My scars prickle as the Fates send a warning—that same tugging feeling toward my chosen mate—but I have nothing but apathy to offer as I watch the confrontation play out.

"I was unaware that I'm answerable to you, Norok. Many things must have changed since I was last in Yris."

The soldier finally removes his helmet, and there's nothing to say about his appearance other than he's an Unseelie prince. The same ingredients, just stamped out in a slightly different face, perfection that does exactly nothing for an imperfect witch such as myself.

Norok looks around once more, his eyes sharp, and the corner of his mouth turns up in an arrogant way. "I was sent on patrol through the marshlands by the regent. Witches have been reported in the area, and it's my job to know who's traveling through the kingdom. You didn't send your ruler any information of such a plan."

He knows they're hiding something.

The Savage Prince stretches his legs in front of him, toward the flames, looking casual and unaffected by this line of questioning. The soldiers around the camp shift on their feet, widening their own stances a little, as though his feigned nonchalance is a sign of something to come.

I want to be as unaffected as he is, and yet, my years of

training kick in. I take in every little detail of Norok and his soldiers, noting which parts of them are tensing, watching their faces for signs of intent, squirreling away information to be used in the future—whatever is required to fulfill my fate and be done with it.

The Savage Prince shrugs and drawls, "My uncle rules the land as decreed by the Unseelie Courts, but he does not own my waking hours or dictate where I choose to go. I am a free male of this land, and certainly not answerable to the likes of you."

Norok doesn't like this response, and he definitely does not like the Savage Prince.

He takes two swaggering steps toward the fire before the surly Prince Tauron steps smoothly in front of him, his face cold and impassive as he stares him down.

He speaks softly, but in the dead of the night I hear him well enough. "You know what happened last time you started this fight, Norok. Do you really want to heal for months again? There are no healers left in the land to cut that time down for you."

No healers.

Possibly the saddest words to come out of any of their mouths so far, and my gut churns. There's no one left to help those in need, entire generations destroyed by this pointless and blood-soaked war.

Norok stares at him a moment longer before a slow smile stretches over his lips. "We're just passing through, no need for such fun and games. We heard a rumor that you picked up a prisoner, but unless you're hiding it under a rock, I suppose that's not true."

None of the soldiers move, not even the tiniest flinch in my direction, and Tauron flicks a hand around the area. "If you can find a prisoner, then you can have it."

Norok looks around once more, but his eyes skip over me

without noticing a thing. It's strange to me that none of them can feel the magic in the air, but the high fae of the Unseelie Court have fallen far from the old ways.

As the soldiers finally leave, melting back into the night as though they'd never been here in the first place, I suppose that worked out in our favor.

Long after their footsteps fade, silence continues to shroud the camp, and when I finally give up on sleep altogether and stare into the night with the murmur of the trees growing more desperate in my heart, I can still feel that magic pressing against my skin. It's there as clearly as my own, protection given only because there was no other choice.

FOUR

SOREN

The fire does nothing to warm the chill in my bones. It has nothing to do with the cold night that has settled around us, or the fact that my uncle's lackeys are closing in around me no matter how hard I planned otherwise. Someone in my household is reporting to the regent despite my best efforts to flush spies out of Yregar. The small talk around me can't draw me out of the depths of my fury, because nothing is going to change the fact that chained to a tree a few paces away from us and blanketed by Tyton's glamor is my mate.

Who happens to be a fucking witch.

I yearn for the problems of yesterday.

To be lamenting my lesson in patience and thinking it was the worst the Fates could do to me. As they are wont to do, the Fates have shown their fickleness, and clearly there's another lesson I must learn. Whether that lesson is how to take a throne without being married first—because there's absolutely no way in this realm or any other that I will ever touch a witch, let alone *marry* one and seat her on my mother's throne—that's another question.

As my friends and I sit around the small fire, Roan is the only one brave enough to broach this subject and, though he has been my best friend for our entire lives, I'm sorely tempted to kick him in the teeth.

"We can't afford to be stubborn about this, Soren, not with Norok and the other guards out there snooping after us. Put her on a horse and get us to Yregar. I shouldn't be away from Airlie this long, not in her condition."

It's the only thing he could say that has any chance of convincing me, and he knows it. Unfortunately for him, I've had a lot of time to think while we inched our way at a snail's pace, and I have an answer prepared.

"You can ride ahead tomorrow. The rest of us will get there when we get there. It's probably for the best that you warn Airlie of what's to come anyway. I don't want anything upsetting her right now, and this might be a breaking point for her."

Roan nods slowly, his eyes shifting to focus on something behind us but not quite looking at the witch, lost in his own thoughts. A deep line cuts around his mouth as he grimaces and the expression is common enough since Airlie announced her pregnancy that it isn't difficult to guess where his mind has wandered.

The rest of us have taken to doing everything we can to protect her, guarding her from not only physical threats but the mind games of the high fae. We've removed any opportunity for some idiot from the Unseelie Court to upset her. It's not easy, especially considering her mother is an active component of the court and a gossipmonger like no other, but Airlie's health and safety is our priority.

I'd expected that bringing home my mate would renew Airlie's hope, but instead, I'm bringing nothing but despair. Dragging a witch behind me, a member of the race responsible for her son's death and no chance of the curse being broken before her next child arrives, I've failed her once again.

I won't rest tonight.

"Get some sleep, Roan, and head out in the morning. Get

back to Airlie. I'll wake Tyton to take the second watch," I say.

I have no intention of waking anyone to take over from me. The longer I sit and stare into the crackling flames, the deeper the need to seek out the Seer digs into my mind. The rage simmering within me takes hold once more, intensifying the urge to climb onto Nightspark right now and hunt her down to demand answers. I need to ask her what the fuck the Fates could be thinking, to rage at that small female the way I stopped myself doing so long ago, and confront her about the false promise of the perfect mate for me.

As my cousins lie down on their bedrolls and get some sleep, I feed more wood to the fire and stretch out my legs. My sword rests on the log beside me, within reach at all times. The mercenaries said that they found the witch journeying from the port, so it goes without saying that she once fled to the Seelie lands.

All those years ago, when we'd initially linked through our minds only to lose the connection, I'd been so sure that she'd been taken prisoner. I'd agonized about the horrors she could be enduring, every last atrocity that I'd failed to protect her from.

She'd merely run away.

I have so many questions but no interest in discovering the answers from her. The very idea of removing the gag from her mouth and hearing her magic-soaked lies makes my skin crawl, every inch of my body rejecting the notion. For so many years, I longed to hear her voice in my mind once more, only for that wall to come down and my greatest nightmare to be realized, one so horrifying it never even crossed my mind as a possibility.

This is how the witches will win the war.

Their plan to put a witch on the throne of the Southern Lands is tied to my fate. The Seer told me that I would find my mate, marry her, take my father's throne, and bring about the end of the war.

I won't let it end like *this*.

Marrying this witch will bring about a peace treaty; it's the only path the Fates could intend that makes sense. Whoever she is, whatever stinking pit of a coven she crawled out from, she's been sent by Kharl. He hunted the Seers of the Southern Lands to near-extinction; he must have discovered my fate and found the witch. That would explain the soft and innocent words she manipulated me with, the web she wove around me to ensnare me, and why she disappeared, all of it intended to force me into submission and bring the high fae to our knees.

I'd rather turn my sword on myself and spill my own guts than do such a thing.

Kharl will have trained her meticulously for the throne as part of his plan to end the rule of the House of Celestial. I suppose she'll want to discuss a ceasefire, for the high fae to surrender and allow the witches to keep the Witch Ward and the lands they've stolen from us. The witches have much to bargain with now, but after a thousand years of bloodshed and death, I cannot yield.

I'd rather kill this witch myself than entertain such a fate.

As Tyton falls asleep and his magic falls away from her, I look at her again and find her staring back at me, the unerring color of her witch eyes like the flash of a dagger in the night. I'm used to seeing witches lost in their madness, the markings across their faces glowing and curses spilling from their mouths, desperation jerking through their limbs as they fight to the death.

She's too calm.

Her stare is unwavering. There is no fear in her as she looks at me, only surety and a sort of amusement that rankles. The innocence that was once in her voice, something that made me so sure of her identity as a sheltered high-fae princess, has been revealed as a lie. She wove a spell around me even then, one that sits tight around my neck like a noose now that I can see how fake it all was. Every interaction was a ploy, crafted to weaken me and destroy the kingdom with this war.

She wasn't kidnapped. She chose to prolong the war and keep me from my throne, keep my uncle in power, and weaken our ranks further and further to force my hand.

It's not going to work.

I don't care what I have to do. I'll take my throne without her.

I stay awake the entire night.

Tauron and Tyton each wake to take their shifts, but when it becomes clear I won't sleep, they each give up and head back to their bedroll.

Tauron, refusing to leave me to my despair, mutters under his breath, "At least one of us needs to be alert tomorrow, and it's clearly not going to be you."

The witch sleeps all night.

Roan wakes before sunrise and quietly packs his belongings, tying the bedroll to the back of his horse's saddle and riding into the darkness with nothing more than a curt bow in my direction. Worry bleeds off him; it has from the moment my cousin announced her latest pregnancy. I insisted on skipping him for guard duty, knowing he wouldn't have anyone watching his back on the ride home, but I doubt he got much more sleep than I did.

I doubt he ever truly rests.

As the first fragile rays of summer sunlight hit the grass around us, the witch's eyes open, fluttering as she comes back into consciousness. There's a single moment of softness on her features before she appears to remember where she is and why she's sleeping upright. Then the softness disappears. A hard look replaces it before that same blankness overtakes her, a small window of truth before the mask descends.

There are no markings on her face.

I've never seen a witch without them, and I'm tempted to search her to find where she hides them, but the idea of touching her makes my skin crawl.

She must feel my gaze, because she turns to look at me, but the mask stays secure as those silver eyes of hers pick me apart, dissecting every inch of my face and clearly finding me wanting. The distaste that dares to curl her lip burns me as surely as the iron is failing to burn her, a searing brand that blinds me with rage, and I'm forced to look away from her lest I risk the safety of the entire group. The fantasy of unchaining her from that tree, pinning her down, and flaying her alive is far too tempting. Maybe then she'd find something worth fearing in my scarred face.

"I need to find the Seer," I mutter under my breath, and Tauron sits up with a foul look on his face.

"She left years ago, you've no chance of finding her now. Not unless you want to risk a passage across the ocean to the Northern Lands. The Sol King won't welcome an unexpected visit from the heir to the Southern Lands, I'm sure."

He shoots an enraged look toward the tree before he stands and packs away his things, snapping out orders to my soldiers as we ready for our long journey.

I can't afford to leave my kingdom anyway. Whatever barbs my uncle has scraping at the surface of the Unseelie Court will surely dig deeper the moment I do, and the risk of the games he would play with my family is too great. Airlie's pregnancy complicates everything further.

I stand up and stretch, then pull water out of my pack before I walk into the forest to relieve myself. I go farther away than usual, more to clear my head than out of any sense of propriety.

I don't care what the witch thinks of me, but I can feel the heavy weight of her eyes as she watches me go, silent behind the gag shoved in her mouth. I've had centuries of learning to control my temper, endless lessons from my uncle's sadistic games and callous treatment of those I swore to protect, and yet I'm holding it back by a thread.

Her eyes will unravel the calm within me until I'm nothing but the savage my uncle swears me to be.

When I get back, Tyton and Tauron have overseen the rest of the soldiers as they pack away the bedrolls and saddled the horses. Tyton feeds them small handfuls of oats that he had stashed away, murmuring as he strokes a hand down his horse's nose. There's still an unbalanced look to his eyes and a frenetic movement to his limbs that speaks to how hard the magic of the forest is riding him.

I don't like how closely the witch watches him as well.

"Are you going to give her anything to eat? I'll get one of the soldiers to take her to relieve herself, but she's going to need water at the very least if we're going to continue dragging her back to Yregar on foot. If you want her to arrive alive, that is. I'm more than happy to return with a corpse for the fires," Tauron says.

The curl of his lip is damning, and when I force my gaze to follow his, I find the witch staring back at us. Every word passed between us has been weighed and measured by her now, I'm sure, every piece of information she collects going straight to Kharl's ear. I know almost nothing about the magic of witches, but anything could be possible.

He eyes her. "Could it be some sort of glamor? Some new curse they've cooked up for us? Because no matter how I turn this over in my mind, I can't believe the Fates would do this to you...to us all."

It certainly feels like a curse to me.

She's blocked me out of her mind again, so I doubt she'll answer me now, but I send a message through our connection regardless. *If you don't reassure me that you are in fact my mate and this isn't a ruse, I'll slit your throat right here and leave your body behind, Fates be damned.*

Nothing.

I step up to her finally, the closest I've gotten to her so far, and pull an iron dagger out of its sheath at my hip. The weight of it is heavy in my hands as the magic in my blood rejects it, but I'm comfortable handling it.

The witch eyes it then looks back up at me, and I press the metal to her throat. The smell of burning flesh fills my lungs as I push down my instincts to stop, to throw myself in front of the iron instead to save my mate from the pain. Hurting her goes against every moral I've ever held, the very male I believed myself to be, but the Fates are testing me.

As the iron sizzles against her skin, the witch doesn't react. She stares back at me, unflinching, until I want to gouge out those silver eyes of hers, a constant reminder of the blood running through her veins. I'm rough as I use my other hand to loosen the tie around the back of her head, pulling until the gag falls away from her mouth, murmurs of concern rumbling through the soldiers who look on.

She runs her tongue over the lush plumpness of her lips, and when she speaks, her voice cracks, hoarse from the dryness of her throat. "If you slit my throat now, all you'll achieve is breaking the Fates. I don't think that's a good idea, Donn."

Donn.

The single damning word feels like a noose tightening around my neck once more.

I've never told anyone the names we gave each other when I first heard her voice in my mind. I've never breathed a word about her to anyone for two hundred years, no details that could have been found out by the witches themselves, not from my lips.

That single name, and the insistent tug of the Fates in my chest, says it all to me.

My own voice comes out as a snarl, a deranged and dark thing. "What exactly do you think you're going to get out of me? What do you think you're going to achieve with this travesty?"

She stares at me, her eyes penetrating. She doesn't like what she sees, it's written clearly on her face, but as the worst of my fears is realized, even with the sickening drop of my stomach, I'm relieved. I relish her hatred, a mirror of my loathing for her.

The only fear I have left is that we'll be tied together with such spite.

"I want nothing from you. I'm merely doing as the Fates command me. If not for them, I'd be in the Northern Lands with my family. I didn't want to return. If I had *any* other option, I wouldn't be sitting before you right now."

The sizzle of her skin burning crackles between us, but she doesn't seem bothered by it at all as her eyes stay fixed on mine, cold and blank. There's no fear in her gaze, no panic or pain as the iron burns her, nothing. The more ice she feeds me, the hotter the rage inside me burns, until there's nothing but a renewed bloodlust for the witches left.

Tauron comes to stand by us, his gaze tracing over her before it flicks back to me. "Are we killing her or are we leaving? If we're walking again, we can't afford to lose much more light, Soren."

His voice is hard, but I can hear the mocking tone to it, the way that he's poking at me and inviting me into an argument. We've grown up together, trained together, gone to war together. If there's anyone who can tell just how close to the edge of madness I am, it's him.

He's willing to bear the brunt of my wrath to spare the

others, but I'm beyond that.

I let my lips pull into a cruel smirk before I finally gesture for him to refasten the gag. "We're not walking the rest of the way. Let's see if she can survive the fae door."

Even with the ground dry and lifeless beneath us, we easily follow the signs of Roan's journey to the fae door. It's the quickest way to Yregar Castle from here, though it means we have to pass closer to the forest of madness than usual.

When Tauron casts me a brooding look, I shrug, not engaging in an argument with him no matter how much he's itching for it.

Riding past the forest like this, it'll be a matter of hours that Tyton will have to endure the call of the trees. We could have been past it much sooner, but thanks to the slow pace we make with our prisoner, he's forced to stay close for three times as long.

Tauron bears the brunt of his discomfort, watching everything around us carefully while also murmuring quietly to his brother. His words are a steady stream of reassurance, a salve over Tyton's quickly devolving mind, but I'm not sure how much of it soaks in.

We will be on our way soon.

We're not ignoring the trees.

We're doing everything we can to return life and magic to the Southern Lands.

It feels like a lie.

Even yesterday morning I would've said we were working toward it and nothing was off limits. Now, one glance over my shoulder at the witch proves that's no longer the truth. I'm not going to honor that female the moment we get home. I'm not going to send word to my uncle, proudly decreeing that my marriage is on the horizon, my coronation only a matter of weeks away.

There'll be nothing joyful about our return to Yregar Castle.

The farther we travel in silence, the more of her I observe without laying eyes on her abominable form for longer than a moment. I've had many long years practice watching my enemies, inside the Unseelie Court and on the battlefield, and reading people is a keenly honed skill for me, one that has saved my life many times.

The witch is watching Tyton.

She was careful not to look at him as he gave her water from his spare flask but now her gaze never strays too far from his vicinity, and the icy depths of her eyes are so sharp, I'm surprised he doesn't bleed out in front of us all. She's good at hiding her interest and expressions, but even with the gag obscuring her face, I can tell. She looks anywhere but at his face, feigning ignorance to the madness that's claiming him. But his words about the forest have caught her interest, and if we had more time, I'd stop to question her about it.

I'd torture it out of her, if I had to.

But there's every chance we'll run into more of the regent's guards out here. Word will have traveled back to my uncle's ear, the next pawn in our never-ending game of chess moving in his favor.

We can't possibly have a king on the throne whose mate and queen is a witch.

When we finally make it to the fae door, the group is eerily quiet, as though we're holding our breath and waiting for an imminent attack. Even the witch is careful as she looks around the mountain, her eyes far too knowing as she takes in the barren wasteland the kingdom has become.

The door itself stands on the side of the mountain like a bad omen, everything around it dead and signs of an old battle nearby. One of my legs still aches from injuries I sustained here, thanks to our lack of available medical treatment.

I dismount from Nightspark's back, murmuring reassurances to him as he kicks up a little fuss. Holding his reins in one fist, I move toward Tauron's saddle and unclasp the witch's chains. The leather of my gloves creaks as I grasp the length tightly and tug until the witch has no choice but to follow closely behind me.

Fae doors are tricky, especially when moving prisoners through them, because as you cross, there's a moment of disorientation when you reach the very edge of what your mind can cope with, and if the witch were to work through that feeling faster than I do, she could get loose and flee. All the fae doors in the Southern Lands are connected, and if she breaks away from me and steps through with a different destination in mind, she could slip through my fingers once more. I can't be sure the iron chains will stop her, I've never transported prisoners through like this, but my anger at the dire situation I've found myself in has made me reckless.

We usually avoid using the fae door in these situations, but there's a part of me that hopes the journey will break her mind and render her useless so that she's no longer a risk to me or my kingdom, nothing more than a hollow shell to sit on a throne and meet the demands of the Fates.

A few of these old-magic structures still exist around the kingdom, mostly at high fae castles. There's even a fae door in the Witch Ward, the area of the Southern Lands that the witches have claimed as their own and the high fae castle there along with it. Yrmar in the northwest was once held by the Mistheart bloodline of the First Fae but is now the seat of power for Kharl Balzog.

Someday, when my fate is fulfilled and I win this war, I'll take it back.

The surrounding lands are now known as the Witch Ward, the villages within their control purged of lower fae and part-bloods. Each year, the witches push out the boundaries of their territory and claim a little more of the kingdom, like a disease spreading throughout the lands. Shortly after I stopped hearing my mate's voice in my mind, Prince Venyr of Yrebor abandoned his castle and Lake Hedgelock, which lies south of Yrmar, along with his entire household and the villages that surrounded the area. The moment a siege was imminent, he simply left it behind rather than defending his ancestral home and the land it lies on.

The next castle in the path of the witches' advance is Yrell, a day's ride from the current edge of the Witch Ward territory, and it's only a matter of time before Kharl begins his campaign to take it. I suspect he's building up his armies, playing a patient game as his people multiply over several decades. It's safe enough for him to wait; he's stopped the high fae from being able to do the same. If he succeeds in taking Yrell, the witches will hold three of our castles and a highly defensible area of the kingdom, an almost impossible expanse to take back.

There's apprehension in the witch's eyes as she stares at the fae door, but when I move us all forward, she doesn't hesitate to follow me, walking too close to my side for my liking. When her arm brushes mine, my stomach clenches violently, the Fates pulling me toward her so sharply I have to tear myself away, and I yank the chain. She stumbles but manages to catch herself before she falls to the frozen ground, surprisingly well balanced, like a soldier. She's had training.

I'll have to burn my cloak.

The fae door taps into the ley lines of magic that run deep within the earth and connect this door to the others spread throughout the kingdom. It once provided a fast way for the princes and princesses of my family to reach the Seer of the Augur Mountains and be given their fate. The Seer fell out of favor after she delivered mine, the high fae choosing instead to visit the Seer at Loche Temple until the witches destroyed it and killed her. The things they did to that Seer were horrifying and proved that witches have no conscience or morals to call their own.

The magic of the fae doors is slowly waning.

Long ago the doors could move entire courts from one end of the world to the other, but now there isn't much more magic than can move our group. It's something else for which I'm sure the witches are to blame. As I step through the structure, dragging the witch with me, everything goes dark and my mind hazes. My skin feels as though it's filling up and being crushed at the same time, everything pushing and pushing and *pushing* until I think I'm going mad.

Only when I'm about to lose the last vestiges of my sanity do I finally step out on the other side, pulling Nightspark and the witch along with me. Before my mind has a chance to adjust, I hear the shouts of the guards.

"Witch! It's a witch!" they yell, and I'm forced to stand in front of her, using my body as a shield, as weapons are drawn around us.

As impressed as I am by their swift action, I'm not happy at being forced to protect her.

"She's a prisoner, put down your swords," I snap, and for a moment I think the soldiers are going to swing at me to get to her, but then they realize who's speaking and the weapons drop away as their heads bow.

The captain steps forward. "My prince, my most humble apologies—"

I shake my head to cut him off. "No need, you were only following my command. Ride ahead of us and clear the path. She's going straight to the dungeon, where she won't be a danger to anyone."

The guard ducks his head again and moves off to give the order without question, but the others all stare at us squarely.

There's an unnatural sucking noise, and then Tauron steps through the fae door, his brother appearing behind him. The weary look in Tyton's eyes slowly eases as the deranged magic of the Ravenswyrd Forest finally releases him from its grip.

"Is it safe to have her in the castle?" one of the soldiers finally finds his voice to say, shifting uneasily as he stares at the witch.

I yank the chains again, enjoying the sight of her stumbling. "A few nights down there, and she'll be no use to anyone. We'll figure out what to do with her then."

The soldiers all look at each other warily before Tauron starts barking orders at them, directing them at his will. I finally glance over to see what the trip through the door has done to this ill-fated mate of mine, but she only stares back at me with those haunting, icy eyes. I turn away before my fury blinds me.

I think those eyes of hers will plague my nightmares until my last breath.

FiVE

ROOKE

Yregar Castle is every bit as heartbreakingly beautiful as my father once told me.

The first thing that strikes me is that the Unseelie fae live very differently from the Seelie, all icy perfection instead of the warm indulgence I'd grown accustomed to. The castle before me is carved out of white stone, a huge monolith of architecture and beauty as cold and stunning as the Unseelie fae themselves.

The second is how inhospitable the castle feels with the military presence here. Soldiers march along the tall outer wall in full armor, and watchtowers erupt from the stone at regular intervals, six clearly visible as we approach from the north side of the wall. The inner wall has them as well, a highly defensive design that is being utilized to its full potential—there's no route of approach to the castle for an enemy to take without immediate detection. While there are many gaps in my knowledge of the Unseelie high fae and the kingdom they rule, I wasn't expecting the scene before me.

The rumors of the Savage Prince made it clear that the Unseelie Court despises his warmongering ways, a confusing stance to take when Kharl declared war against the whole kingdom, and yet there are hundreds of high fae soldiers here under my Fates-cursed mate's command, loyal and obedient as any.

The castle is surrounded by yet another tall stone wall and there's a small village nestled between the two large stone walls filled with part-bloods and lower fae, all of whom stare at me as I walk behind the horses. The iron chains rattle with every step, which makes the silence of the crowd more obvious. Sneers curl the lips of most, their eyes either wide with horror or narrowed with revulsion as their gazes trace the robes I wear.

The closer we get to the castle, the bolder the crowd becomes. Soldiers wearing the colors of the Savage Prince murmur to each other and the villagers. I hear their words and understand them, the old slang of the Southern Lands a little clunky to my ears, but I decipher it well enough.

A witch brought here to burn.

They all assume I'll be disposed of on the funeral pyres, the way all my kind have been in such times. None of them are aware of the connection that I have with their prince.

I suppose it's for the best.

As I look around, I notice that although they are a mix of dozens of different Unseelie races—elves and goblins and banshees and even some humans all the way from the Deadlands in the north amongst them—there are no witches.

Not even the smallest hint of witch blood.

It's as though every last one of our kind has been wiped out. A mass extinction, a line in the sand between the high fae and the witches, immortal enemies. I'm sure there were once part-bloods with witch heritage here, but there's no sign of them now. Whether they joined Kharl or were victims of the prejudice this war has bred into the fae folk of the kingdom, they're gone. The icy casing around my heart grows a little thicker at the thought of it, another layer on the shell of numbness that I've come to call home thanks to the atrocities of the Fate Wars.

Part of me knows the persecution of witches regardless of

their stance in the war is wrong and evil, but I returned here for my fate, not to protest or join another war.

There's a second stone wall around the castle, one much smaller than the stone wall that protects the village as well, but this one is far prettier and clearly for separating the high fae from their subjects rather than for protection. Sigils in the old language are carved into the stone, decreeing the land and the castle as covenants of the Celestial Family, a royal bloodline dating back to the forming of this kingdom. Everything about the space is beautiful, regal, and a reflection of the prince the Fates have sold me off to.

My chest tightening at the sight of the castle is the same reaction as the one I'd had when I first laid eyes on him too.

He might be every bit the gorgeous high fae, but a cold heart beats in his chest, one that has no room for warmth in it toward me.

When we reach the castle courtyard, dozens of high fae courtiers are waiting for us, and gasps ring out as they spot me. Roan, the prince who left earlier to ride ahead of us, stands dressed in formal attire with a soldier at his elbow, watching the princes dismount.

The surly one, Tauron, unsnaps my chains from his saddle. The Savage Prince handed them back to him the moment we made it through the fae door, the old magic still strong enough to transport us all, despite my doubts. Disappointment had rolled off my Fates-cursed mate in waves—it's clear he was expecting the old magic to cause me some damage, the act of stepping through the ancient oak structure a test of mental strength and fortitude.

Little does he know...you can't break what's already broken.

"I thought you were planning on giving me time to prepare the castle before you arrived," Roan says to the Savage Prince.

He flicks a hand in my direction.

"I was hoping the fae door would solve our problems, but I suppose the Fates really have cursed me."

Tyton, the prince with magic in his blood, goes to the Savage Prince and murmurs to him, though I'm not sure why he's being so quiet as all the high fae have such good hearing, his low tone won't stop the crowd from listening in. "We should get her to the dungeon before any hysteria starts. I know the household is trusted, but I don't want any *accidents* happening."

The cold-hearted prince shrugs and hands the reins of his horse to one of the stable boys, who steps forward obediently and takes them. "You and Tauron can take her down there. I have more important things to deal with than a filthy fucking witch."

With that, he leaves, Roan striding along with him without so much as a backwards glance in my direction.

The ice around my heart holds, the numbness filling my limbs, and I stare at the high fae as a hollow shell of my former self. They're all the epitome of perfection, the same carving in slightly differing stones, the ice of their Unseelie blue eyes as cold as the steel their prince had pressed against my throat. Every last one of them is the perfect shade of moonlight as their bloodlines never deviate.

I feel nothing as they stare back at me.

Tauron shoos Tyton away, directing him to freshen up, and grabs one of the guards to escort me to the dungeon instead. They all seem to worry about the magic user, fussing over him like a healer over a fresh wound. The murmurs of madness he heard from the Ravenswyrd Forest have shaken them all.

My own heart aches with the loss of the trees, the only feeling I still experience, and I push it away now and wrap apathy around myself like a shield.

The song is quieter now but still there, coaxing me to return to the forest. My old home has mourned me, the same way that the loss of it has been an open wound in my chest from the moment my feet stepped onto the ship to the Northern Lands. Knowing the trees feel the same way is a comfort as much as a hardship. Someday, when I get out of this dungeon they're taking me to, I'll return and do what I can to ease the trees' suffering.

Even as I have that thought, a part of me whispers, *Will I ever escape this place?*

This is what the Fates had waiting for me—a fae prince destined to be my husband who cannot stand the sight of me. He's the heir to the throne of the Southern Lands; what's to stop him from marrying me and leaving me in the dungeon to die? All he needs to take the throne is a signed contract. He doesn't actually need a wife sitting beside him.

Tauron wraps the iron chains around his fist twice and tugs them firmly, dragging me into the castle. I keep up with him to let the chain slacken and take the pressure off my burned wrists, easing the pain there. I'm careful not to look around too much as we work our way toward the dungeon, dozens of eyes following me. No matter which way we turn, the hallways stay unobstructed, but that's the fae way. Large and quiet halls of grandeur and opulence while hundreds of workers toil away to keep up the perfection. Let there not be a single speck of dust to be found so that no one knows people actually live within these white, shining walls.

The formality and empty shell of the place makes my skin itch.

The practices of the high fae always have. Give me a mud hut in the middle of a forest any day of the week. Hell, give me a war tent in the middle of a burning battleground as the Ureen creep up on us. I'd rather that over the fake finery and subtle games of politics that come with high-fae courts, the way they charm you to your face only to cut your throat with a bejeweled dagger the moment you turn your back. I'd always preferred the company of the part-bloods and lower fae over the high fae of the Seelie Court, with only a very few exceptions.

In the Northern Lands, I met fae folk from dozens of kingdoms, including some I had heard of only in old lore and had assumed were long gone. All the high fae clung to their beauty and displays of grandeur. The Sol King may have changed the Seelie Court and some of its laws thanks to the war, but he couldn't change the hearts of the high fae.

They covet trinkets and riches; they crave the adulation of those around them and the power of ruling the lower fae. They spend endless centuries squabbling over bloodlines and birthrights, drinking fairy wine and gossiping over extravagant banquets. Dancing and laughing, all while plotting to further themselves for the sake of others' approval. I'd assumed it was a trait of the Seelie Court, the war ending and the status quo settling back into its old ways once more, but the opulent and cold hallways we pass through are an echo of those I left behind.

With the soldier following close behind, Tauron leads me to a staircase that plunges straight into the ground, the darkness of the opening a stark contrast to the white marble and light in the rest of the castle. The moment we take our first step down, the air becomes oppressive, growing thicker, hotter, and more damp as we descend into the earth itself. The Seelie high fae always knew the surest ways to torture their enemies, and that skill must span across their kind.

After a steady descent, when my feet finally touch the bottom of the stairway, my magic calls out for the air above us. The pressure against my skin fractures my numbness, a fine sheen of sweat breaking out on my forehead as I force my breathing to even out, deepen, slow...anything to stop panic from taking hold of my mind.

It feels as though we've been buried alive.

It's made worse because the land around us has been drained, and I'm experiencing all the desperate pulling and longing it feels at the presence of a witch.

Finally, you're here, save us, pour into us, sacrifice and give us what we need, it seems to whisper, and I grow unsteady as the pleas assault my senses.

Tauron tugs at my chains. He's less rough than the Savage Prince was, his pull more of a reminder to keep moving than an attempt to harm me, and when he finally leads me to a cell, I step into it without a word of complaint. He waits until the iron bars of the door have slid into place, locking firmly with a loud *thunk*, before he unchains my wrists through the bars.

I'm surprised he does. I was prepared not to have full access to my hands ever again. I'll admit it's a relief, one less trial I'll have to endure. The heavy earth crushing the air around me is more than enough to keep my mind occupied. It's distracting enough that I can't ignore the whisper in my mind, a scar from horrors I faced in the Northern Lands, telling me I deserve this and that's why I'm allowing them to treat me so cruelly without protest.

Tauron turns to the guard. "Get a bucket of water and whatever kitchen scraps you can find. We need to keep her alive, but don't waste provisions on her. Don't question her or interact in any way…in fact, don't speak while you're on watch down here. She carries no weapons, but I can't even begin to guess what magic this witch has."

I conceal a smirk. Their searches of me were thorough, the competent work of the most capable soldiers, but I would never travel without weapons. Magic is a good protection, but it isn't limitless. Seelie steel blades might be a luxury to some, but they're a necessity to me.

I'm better at hiding them than most, a trick I picked up from a friend now left behind.

The soldier dips his head and hurries out of the dungeon, his feet just a little too quick. He hates it down here as much as I do—they both do, but Prince Tauron is far better at hiding it. There's the smallest line around his mouth and tension across his shoulders, and his tone has reached a new depth of iciness.

He stares at me through the bars, wrapping the iron chain slowly around one gloved fist as his cold, hard eyes take in the sight of me. Walking behind the horses for two days has taken a toll on me, and I long for the bucket of water he demanded, my throat dry and itching. The high fae assume that I'll feel shame for drinking out of it, but they don't know the life I've lived.

I'm sure that's what they're hoping for—to shame me in every way possible—but I was raised in the forest as a wild little witchling then trained as a healer in the Fate Wars, called to take up a sword as the world ended around me.

I've experienced far worse things than a dungeon in the bowels of the earth.

"Whatever you're hoping to get out of my prince, you are not going to succeed. He'll do what he must do to become king, and then we'll kill you, just like we'll kill every last witch in the Southern Lands. Whatever we have to do to break the curse will be done. Enjoy your stay." He turns on his heel and walks out, leaving me to the feeling of being buried alive.

The air around me is hot and wet and feels even more so as the hours creep on. The only light in the dungeon comes from the burning torches, and the flames seem to increase the temperature as they burn. The burns on my wrists and throat throb, a demand for my attention that I ignore.

The guard Tauron sent for provisions eventually came back

and shoved a bucket of water and a tray of slops through a small hatch in the door, hissing curses under his breath at me for forcing him to be here. Reaching through the gaps in the iron bars, he loosened my gag just long enough for me to drink, the fabric still sitting over my chin and held in place by iron pins. I cupped my hands in the water and drank my fill of the clean, cold liquid, enjoying it as much as I could before I forced myself to sit back and take stock of the situation.

I'm stuck in this hellish cell until the Savage Prince deems it appropriate to let me out. I have my doubts that he'll ever do so, and I might truly be here forever.

During my time in the Sol Army, I was trained to withstand such torture techniques. Even though we were battling the Ureen, sightless and mindless monsters that killed indiscriminately without having the capacity to take prisoners, we trained as though we were facing the most intelligent of enemies.

The Sol King was selective about who he trained and where he placed them. I started off as a healer with the basic training that all within the Sol Army were required to complete. As time went on and the casualties continued to rise, my training intensified, and I took on more responsibility than just my healing duties. My previous life in the forest made me useful beyond my life-saving knowledge; it helped me to keep my mind clear even in the most trying of circumstances. With every new wave of attacks, I learned more about what it means to be a good soldier and a valuable asset within the ranks. I worked my way up until I was in a position where learning how to withstand torture and survive myriad adverse situations was necessary.

The answer to both is a strong and sound mind.

I'm not sure that I have one of those anymore—surviving the Fate Wars didn't come without cost, and while I paid a steep price, hundreds of thousands of others died. Sitting here in the dungeon feels like a paltry penance in comparison.

Once I drank enough water to quench my thirst and ate what small amount of the slops I deemed edible, I sat back against the stone wall. And here I still sit.

My eyes slip shut, and I take one deep breath, then another. It's hard to do with the gag in my mouth, but it's no use removing it now; it would cause panic and suspicion amongst the high fae if they realize that I can touch the iron pins holding it in place at the back of my head.

It might hurt like a Fates-cursed bitch, but being in contact with the metal is possible for a witch as strong as myself. I could heal the burns on my wrists and the charred skin on my throat, but I won't risk using magic right now. Healing magic is bright and conspicuous, even to those ignorant to the art of casting.

How far will the Fates protect me against my mate?

The man is beautiful and deadly and cruel in all the ways that the Fates wish to break me open. I've spent centuries in the company of high fae, both Seelie and Unseelie, from this land and many others, and yet it took only one look into his cold eyes to know that he was chosen specifically to bend me to the will of the Fates. My body reacted to him the second I laid eyes on him, and no matter how long I'd prepared myself to be unmoved by our meeting, a longing for him had opened up in me in an instant.

The hollow feeling within me is my only protection from the thread of the Fates that binds us together.

I can no longer afford to be reckless, not with the wheels of fate turning and the Seer's vision coming to fruition around me. My mate has found me and brought me back to his people, and his people have already started to discuss the next steps needed to secure him the throne, even if he's rejecting our union entirely. I have no choice but to surrender myself to the Fates and offer them my obedience.

I expected to return to a broken and scarred land, but I was unprepared for how sorrowful it would feel, the way that the earth and nature call to me. I'd forgotten what it meant to be a witch, a provider to the land, someone who protects and nurtures it. I'd forgotten what it felt like to be *home* and responsible for more than just myself and my brother.

The responsibility of the things that I abandoned when I ran from my fate hits me with the force of a Ureen's killing blow, the weight of the world pressing down on me all at once.

Thanks to the wounds on my wrists, it's easy enough to make myself bleed. I use one of my nails to slowly scratch away at the raw skin until a few droplets of blood land on the stone beneath my hands. It'll be harder to nourish the earth thanks to the stone floor, but I find a crack between two of the slabs and rub some blood into the dirt there, murmuring incantations under my breath, until the suffocation of the air eases just a little. The earth welcomes my offering, sighing as it absorbs my magic in a quiet and natural current. It takes only a few drops before the cycle of power establishes, passing through the dirt, into me, and then back out again.

It's a constant ebb and flow, as it should be.

You're home, Rookesbane. You're home finally to protect us all.

Magic that isn't my own sings underneath the scarred skin on my stomach and back, my connection to the Fates like the Seer's own, though it was never my intention to form one. It didn't occur to me that I'd become a conductor for such things as a result of my near-death experience. A calmness flows into my veins, easing away the last clutches of panic, and the song of the forest deepens within my heart.

The Fates approve of my actions.

When the earth pulls greedily at my blood, draining me even as it sustains me, it's easier to convince myself that I'm here as an act of service and not penance. It's clear that it's not going to be an easy task. I'll have to fight the high fae every step of the way just to restore the land they call theirs to rule. Why they don't care for it themselves is beyond me—maybe it's another tactic against the witches?—but even that makes no sense.

With the passing of the summer solstice, there's still many moons until the autumn equinox, but if I'm still trapped in the dungeon then, I won't be able to perform the rites required to breathe life back into the lands. There were no signs of the castle marking the solstice and the ache within the earth suggests it's been a long time since anyone practiced the fae folks' many traditions to honor the land and all it provides. Without the rituals of the summer solstice, the land cannot sleep deeply and repair itself over the long and harsh winter. As its magic and resources are continually drained, year after year, it's close to the edge of no return, devastation and catastrophe looming far closer than I think the high fae realize.

Will I still be in here for the spring equinox? Will I be here when the lands should be in a state of awakening and rebirth, flourishing and providing for us all?

This thought is one surefire spiral into madness, and so instead, I focus on what I can do now, pushing my life force into the earth and letting it take what it needs from me. Without a single drop of my own magic in the mix, my wrists begin to knit themselves back together. The minimal damage to my throat disappears as though it never was as the land pours back into me just as eagerly as I pour into it, gifting me this healing without my request.

I could give it every last drop of my blood and I still wouldn't die, because it sustains me as I sustain it.

The high fae might ignore the earth, and the witches might have turned their backs on it at Kharl's command, but I remember. The lessons my family taught me are burned into my mind, so even after centuries of fighting in a war, I can do what's necessary and honor the land the way my kind always has.

The sleeves of my jacket cover my wrists, and I'll keep my head low so no one will see that the damage has healed.

I fall asleep only to be woken hours later by the small hatch opening again. My plate of slops is pulled out and another bucket of water shoved inside. I keep my eyes closed as though I sleep, and I hear the guard curse and another voice answer him. Their words aren't censored at all.

They're not following their prince's order to stay silent around me.

"Why would they bring a witch here? It's a danger to us all."

There's a grunt as the other answers, "This one's different. There are no markings on its face. I wonder why that is."

The first speaker's voice is closer to the cell than the other's. "They never bring them back here alive, not since the regent found out. It's a risk to us all."

"It's only a risk if you open your fat mouth and tell someone about it. Are you loyal to the regent or the prince?"

The first speaker huffs indignantly. "I know who's supposed to be king around here, and I'm loyal to the Celestial line. Prince Soren would never allow me to stay if he doubted that, and you shouldn't either. I'm just saying it's risky, and I've never known the prince to act in such a way. Something is going on with this one."

The other speaker grumbles under his breath, subdued. "I suppose he could finally be getting close to taking the throne, and then we'll be able to stop dealing with the regent's guards."

There's a murmur of agreement. They both seem happy with this thought. They don't like the regent, the Savage Prince's uncle, who holds the throne for him in his stead, and it sounds as though the prince doesn't like him either. None of that matters for me, not for the purpose I'm here to fulfill. My fate is to save the kingdom with my marriage to the Savage Prince, and when I made up my mind to come back, I assumed the Fates were asking for my simple compliance. To meet him and submit to whatever horrors the Unseelie Court has in store for me.

The state of the kingdom is far worse than I imagined. Without magic and sacrifice, the damage will soon be irreparable. *This* is what I was brought back here to correct; I know it, even without the Fates chiming in.

As I work steadily, I listen to the soldiers gossip without concern for my attention. I learned a lot during my time within the Seelie Court, and ignoring politics would be dangerous for me.

I tuck the information into the back of my mind and listen as their footsteps echo through the dungeon and slowly disappear, the air no longer heavy as it blankets me. When I open my eyes and move to the bucket for another drink, I notice how much easier it is to breathe. The earth no longer suffocates; it welcomes me, cherishes me as it holds me.

It's happy that I'm here, even if the high fae are not.

SIX

SOREN

It takes an entire bottle of fairy wine and then another of fae elixir without pausing for a breath before I manage to get some sleep. Even after such a long trip home with no rest, the silver eyes of my Fates-cursed witch mate haunt my every thought until I have no choice but to find solace in the last of our meager supplies.

Is this my punishment for not submitting fully to the Fates? Did I bring this upon myself?

Centuries ago, I thought I could outsmart the Fates and find my mate sooner, her sweet voice filling my mind as she teased me and tempted me with nothing more than her presence there. I thought if I could just find her early, bending the fate I was given but not truly breaking it, I could save my people from the horrors of the war around us. I thought I knew better.

Eyes as silver as the threads that hold my cloak together, as silver as the Celestial Family crest on my shield...my stomach clenches every time they pop into my mind until I'm swallowing bile. With hair as dark as the Seelie fae and skin as fair as Airlie's, she looks nothing like the mindless, raving witches I've faced in the war.

The bile threatens to choke me the longer I think about her, sleep eluding me until deep into the night.

Breakfast the next morning with my close-knit circle becomes a form of torture.

I wake before dawn, as I always do, and pull my sorry self into the bathing room to wash away the evidence of my miserable night. If Airlie catches a whiff of the fairy wine, she'll put me on notice with her husband, and I won't hear the end of it from either of them.

She's so busy trying not to think about her pregnancy and what will happen at the birth that she's itching for any excuse to needle someone else. I'm fine with that as long as the person isn't me. I house dozens of high-fae nobles here in the riverside wing of the castle, leaving them to their own devices as the war toils on around us, and my cousin's irritation would be best directed there. The wing they occupy is spacious and guarded well, although far less luxurious than the accommodations at Yris Castle. They're safer here though, and that keeps them content. The families most loyal to me won't find comfort within the walls of my uncle's residence.

When the only sign of my insomnia-induced binge is the red hue of my eyes, I go into the small dining room, the intimate one where I entertain only my family members. They're already there, whispering and gossiping, though none of the gossip halts when I walk in.

I don't expect it to.

Although each and every one of my cousins is a member of the Unseelie Court, with bloodlines that date back as far as mine, I trust them all implicitly. Tauron and Tyton are brothers, though only their looks show it. They and our cousin Airlie look similar to each other and myself, with our Unseelie heritage of pale skin, white-blond hair, and crystal-blue eyes. We all descend from the Celestial bloodline, one of the four high fae royal bloodlines, and all of us are creatures of winter and sunless months, proof of what happens when an entire people spend all their time in castles tucked up in the snow.

Roan with his Seelie heritage is the only unique member of our group. His father is an Unseelie prince, but his mother was a Seelie princess, the Fates pairing them against the traditions of the Unseelie Courts. Roan is shades of warm summer nights, brown skin, black hair, golden eyes. He and Airlie make a striking pair, especially when you see their devotion for each other in their eyes. The Fates made a wise choice in their union.

Suddenly I want another bottle of fairy wine.

"You look miserable. We need to figure this out," Airlie says, her tone harsh even as she delicately puts together a hearty plate of meats and cheeses and holds it out to me. "You're hiding your hangover from exactly no one, by the way. If you're worried I'm going to shame you, rest assured I have other business to attend to."

I raise a brow in her direction and take the plate, then pour myself a glass of fairy wine as she raises her eyebrows back at me.

Tauron leans toward her. "It's called the hair of the dog, Airlie, and it's the only way to truly ease the headache. You wouldn't know, because you have something called 'self-restraint' that the rest of us lack."

She gives him a sweet smile, but it's laced with barbs and poison. "*Restraint* isn't a dirty word, cousin. You should learn some! Then maybe your mother would stop harassing us all about your future."

Their familiar bickering calms me more than anything else could, but I'd never admit it to them.

Roan gives me a knowing look. "Give him a minute to process what's happened. Once he's accepted his fate is real and unavoidable, then we can decide what we're going to do about her."

"Her? I thought we were calling the witch an *it*," Tauron mumbles.

Roan shoots him a look, his brows tucked low. "The Fates have decided that she's to be our future queen, whether you like it or not."

He says it to Tauron, but there's no doubt his words are directed to me as well. Roan has always been the voice of reason within our group, having been raised in a stable and loving household without the whispers of the Unseelie Court muddying his sense of self, thanks to his Seelie princess mother being shunned. His father refused to entertain the court, effectively closing the Outlands to any high fae who weren't friendly toward his family. It was a blessing in disguise, and now Roan doesn't have the same warped responses to things as the rest of us, none of the cutting humor and closed-off emotions to protect himself.

He's never had the need.

Since their marriage, Airlie has protected him with her wit and cunning the same way that he protects her with his sword and hands.

I take another drink. I don't want to think about putting a witch on my mother's throne, seeing my mother's crown upon that head of dark, matted hair. The situation becomes too much for me once again, and I drain the entire glass of wine in one go.

Roan winces, and Airlie shoots me a look. "Eat your breakfast, Soren. We can't afford for you to slip now, not when there are so many eyes on us."

So many eyes that we choose our words carefully, even within these walls. My home, the place I should feel most comfortable in the world, has been infiltrated by poison.

It's only a matter of time before my uncle sends word that he's heard about the witch. Then I'll have no choice but to make a plan. I don't have the luxury of sitting around drinking my woes away, no matter how tempting that may be.

Do I marry the witch to take my throne, or do I declare all-out war with my uncle and take it by force? Only one of those options sounds appealing, but even if I had the support to do it, the Northern Lands were almost destroyed by a broken fate. Do I think myself stronger than the Sol King? Am I so arrogant that I believe I could succeed where he failed?

No. But the other option makes me want to throw up, a sensation compounded by the headache still roiling in my skull.

When I reach for the pitcher of wine once more, Airlie shoves it out of my range, giving me a dark look and pointing at my plate again without a word. My lip curls in her direction but the filthy look Roan sends me on behalf of his heavily pregnant wife reminds me to hold my temper, my hand landing instead on the plate and dragging it toward me.

It doesn't matter that the curse is going to take their child from them; for now the baby in her womb is healthy and strong, and they'll protect it until the curse takes it. I've been in such a rush to find my mate that, in the chaos of discovering what it is, I forgot that small fact. My fate is to marry my mate, take the throne, and save my people. I believed that the curse would break at our union, or maybe my coronation, the intricacies of magic beyond my knowledge. I trusted the Fates to reward my patience and my efforts to save my kingdom, not to place an even greater obstacle in my way.

I'll never make that mistake again.

"I need to see the Seer," I mutter.

The words are just as futile now as they have been every time I've uttered them. Speaking to that female won't change the fate I've been given, and yet still I cling to the hope that I can convince her she's wrong.

That this union isn't my path.

Tauron and Tyton glance at each other before Tyton says,

haltingly, "Do you want one of us to cross the ocean and bring her back here? I'm not sure how we could persuade her, but we could...try."

The vessel of the Fates hates me, I'm sure of it.

I shake my head, picking over the wedges of cheese on my plate as though they can fix this problem for me. "I need you here for what's to come. There's no use splitting up when we're so close to the end. I'll just have to...figure out my fate for myself."

Tyton nods and rubs a hand over his forehead again. There's a tension in him that usually lasts only as long as the forest whispers in his ear, but even after a night at home, he looks haunted.

A cold sweat breaks out along my spine. "What's happened?"

He shakes his head. "The forest was in my dreams last night. I feel as though it has sunk into my mind, and I can't get rid of it, even with the distance. It's so *angry* at us all...so very angry."

We all stare at him. None of us are as tight-lipped as Roan, who once entered that forest and came out alive with his mind intact. No matter how much we poked and prodded him, he never told us what happened to him inside. All he would say was we wouldn't believe the truth. He barely believed it himself.

Airlie clears her throat and carefully moves food around the table until each of us has a full plate in front of us once more. "I understand that the identity of Soren's mate has been a great shock to us all, but there's no denying that we need a plan. *Nobody* wants a witch in this castle less than I do, especially so close to the baby's due date, but there's nothing we can do to fight the Fates. I know this just as well as the rest of you, so instead of bickering and arguing amongst ourselves, we need to decide what we're going to do about her."

It's a line in the sand.

A careful display of siding with her husband, and one I

was not expecting. When I sent Roan ahead of us yesterday, I expected Airlie to pack up and return to her ancestral lands to have the baby there, effectively tearing my family apart due to my ill-fated wedding and ascension. She's been so protective of her pregnancy, so careful, as if she did something wrong the first time around that caused the loss of her son. We all know that isn't true. The curse doesn't care how good of a parent someone would be. It takes every child.

And here she is, siding with Roan and the enemy in the dungeon.

I don't want to think about any of it.

The table falls silent as we eat, my mind churning through the responsibilities I hold over and over again until my hands are fisted around the silverware and my temper boils over. The curse is one horrifying problem, and the endless stream of lower fae and part-blood refugees who arrive at Yregar each week is another. We're struggling to house them, feed them, and offer them assurance for the future. Their plight fills me with an urgency that can't be talked away.

When I finish the plate in front of me, I set down the cutlery. "Enough of this. I'm going to the village to check how our people are faring. We have more to worry about than the twisted whims of the Fates."

Airlie nods her head sagely, a small smile creeping across her lips. "That's a good idea, Soren. Clear your head, come to terms with the fact that being angry about this isn't going to transform the witch into a high-fae princess, and once you've accepted it, we can move on to the tasks at hand. The only thing more difficult than getting the Unseelie Court to accept this union might be the wedding rites themselves. We can't just torture the witch into accepting you—the binding won't work, and your union won't hold without her full consent."

Now Tauron takes the fairy wine, ignoring the way Airlie

snarls at him, and pours himself a large glass before pouring me another one.

"We'll never get that far into this fool's errand!" he snaps. "The court will never agree, and we all know it. We'd be better off convincing them that the laws shouldn't apply to Soren because the Fates are shoving him off a mountain ledge right now with nothing but iron spikes to catch him." And he downs his glass in one go.

As tempting as the wine is, I have duties to attend that don't include losing myself in debauchery.

I leave my cousins behind and take stock of the castle. This duty is mine until I have a wife to pass it on to.

Over the long years of waiting, I imagined what my mate would be like. My fantasies were fueled by her voice in my mind, and every image I came up with is the opposite of the silver-eyed nightmare in the dungeon.

After the Seer's decree of patience, during almost a thousand years of waiting, I lost myself in grief for my parents and the war that raged around me. I entertained the affections of some of the high-fae ladies at the fringes of the Unseelie Court, always careful to steer away from anyone under my uncle's influence. For a time, I hoped that my fate would lead me to someone like Loreth, beautiful and cunning in the ways of our kind. She is a Mistheart, though far enough removed from the First Fae that the only title she now holds is Lady and not princess, but that didn't matter to me. If anything, it made spending time with her easier and though at the time I thought that what I felt for her was true, it was that ease that I was grasping so desperately at.

Loreth desperately wanted to stay in my bed, her affection for me known widely through all of the Unseelie Court, and I thought what I felt for her would be impossible to feel for any other. I ignored grave warnings from Roan and Airlie and their mounting concerns for the complication being with her would bring to my life.

Then I woke to the voice of my mate in my mind.

After just one single, faltering interaction with the shyly joyous female, and I couldn't bear the touch or sight of another. I craved her like nothing I had felt before, her existence igniting a fire in my blood that fueled an intensive search of the kingdom as I raced against the Fates to find her. I forgot about the throne, my responsibilities, everything. None of it compared to the longing I felt for her.

Now I suspect she used her magic against me, a curse or bewitchment, something that sank her claws into my mind. Every last word I treasured and coveted merely an act in the game of war.

When I realize my thoughts are spiraling once more, I direct my mind away before it sends me running back to the wine.

Down in the kitchens I find the Keeper of Yregar, Firna, standing over a large boiling pot of scrap stew for the soldiers. She was once a nursemaid for my mother, and she continued to watch over me during my formative years. She never overstepped her bounds as keeper, but she's been a motherly figure in my life ever since I lost my parents.

Unease holds her tongue, but the lines around her mouth say enough. It's treason to keep a witch alive, and yet we have one in the dungeon below, guarded but walked through the gates in full view of the entire household. It's only a matter of time until the consequences for this come calling.

When I do nothing more than check in on how the castle is running, she doesn't bring it up.

She waits until I've looked through the lists of the food stores myself before she says, "Provisions are low, Your

Highness, and it's only getting worse. The groundskeeper has said that the orchards are almost stripped. We're not going to make it through winter."

My mouth tightens, and I give her a curt nod. The kitchen hands and maids all scatter at the thunderous look on my face, leaving me a clear path as I move deeper into the sprawling kitchen toward the storeroom.

It's a bleak sight, rows and rows of empty stone shelving, cold and desolate everywhere my gaze lands.

We're still in the long days of summer. There should be a bountiful harvest to come, but the devastation of the war continues to whittle away my kingdom.

Firna meets my eyes, frowning as she murmurs to me, "The vintner has begun pressing what grapes he can, but with such a minimal harvest, he isn't sure what he can make of it."

I nod. "There won't be any recourse if this year's harvest doesn't yield. I'm already aware the male is trying to get blood out of a stone."

She nods back, but there's no sign of relief that the staff aren't going to be punished, because the reality of the situation isn't lost on anyone here. I glance around at the quiet kitchen staff, their heads bowed. Anticipation hangs in the air as they all hold their breath, the way they're looking at anything but me sending a ripple of frustration through my gut.

I snap, harsher than I should, "What else has happened?"

Ignoring my tone, she casts a stern look at the nearby maids until they scatter, and then with a dry drawl she replies, "There's no point in softening the blow. We've been sharing provisions with the village, but we'll run out before winter sets in if we keep it up. I've already had to send the princess to the nobles to stop their complaints about the rationing, and it's clear that we're not going to be able to keep the castle running like this throughout the winter. It might be time to reconsider the catering plans for the upcoming balls or, at the very least, cut down the guest lists."

I would throw every last simpering, whining member of the Unseelie Court out of Yregar Castle and lock the entire province down if I could, but I'm still answerable to my uncle. There's nothing the regent loves more than throwing a huge party with overflowing crates of wine and enough food to feed the entire kingdom, much of which goes to waste. I don't know whether Yris Castle is prospering with their harvest—it's one of the few fiefdoms in which I don't have allies, thanks to the regent and his station there. His lack of concern for his lavish lifestyle is yet another indication of his treachery, and the way that Unseelie Court blindly follows him says he's somehow convinced them of his ability to rule.

None of them care about the rest of the kingdom.

I've reached out to neighboring kingdoms about importing food, but I'm not holding out much hope for trade agreements. While the Fates have sat back and taught me their "lesson" in patience, my uncle's propaganda about my true nature has spread.

I nod curtly and leave before I can hear any more bad news. I don't have the heart to tell any of them that the rest of the territories in the Southern Lands are faring the same, if not worse, than we are.

There is no denying it. The land is dying.

The castle is subdued as I make my way outside to the barracks to check in with the commander. The soldiers all dip their heads in respect as I pass, loyal to the core, every last one of them. The sentries on the inner wall are sharp, a group of soldiers at the gate to scrutinize anyone passing through, and an escort walks with several maids to take food to hand out at the village temple. It won't be enough for everyone to truly eat their fill, but it's all we have to offer.

The commander, Corym, is directing the males into the sparring rings for the morning session of training, and when I stop at his side, he bows to me before murmuring, "No changes reported from the walls, Your Highness. The plains have been quiet since you rode out to aid the attack."

I nod and watch the sparring, Corym's gaze just as sharp as he calls out to fix footwork and sloppy technique. Overall, the soldiers are looking good. Better than good; under any other high-fae commander, they would be considered exemplary, but at Yregar we demand perfection. It's the only way we'll survive.

"Let's hope it stays that way. I'm expecting a visit from the court—move the soldiers around accordingly."

Corym nods. It's an order I've given him countless times before, and he pointedly doesn't ask about the witch. If only I could train all of my household to hold their tongue this way, maybe my headache would ease off. Airlie could never, Tauron wouldn't even try, and, though they both are far less rash with their opinions, Roan and Tyton will call me out at the slightest provocation if they think it appropriate.

I move on to the stables and take a moment to brush down Nightspark myself, enjoying the routine even as the stable boy fusses at the very idea of me doing the work for him. I flip him a small apple, one of the last meager crop from the failing orchard, and he gapes down at it for a moment before his cheeks redden. He fumbles over his gratitude, bowing deeply, and then bites into it in a rush as though someone might steal it from him.

I wonder how long it's been since he last ate fresh fruit, even a tiny and slightly sour apple.

He's a small kid from the village, and it still shocks me to think that people have continued to have children but, of course, the curse affects only full-blooded high fae. The village here at Yregar—and all of the other castles and villages in the Southern Lands—are full of part-bloods. There's never been a stigma within the lower classes for marrying across the lower fae like there is amongst the high-fae Unseelie Court, not until the war began and the entire kingdom became ravaged by the witches.

The longer I tend to my horse, the further my thoughts stray. Maybe the Fates don't intend for me to break the curse; maybe the next Celestial in line to take the throne is supposed to be part-blood.

The time of the high fae is over.

The words were spat at me by a witch years ago, a snarling and raving creature of madness we dragged down to the dungeon in an effort to uncover my uncle's true motivations, but they take on new life now. The prejudices of the Unseelie Court will be a nightmare to navigate but, if the curse holds and no high-fae children are born in our kingdom ever again, Airlie and Roan will never have the child they long for. None of the royal families already married by the Fates will continue their bloodlines, the fabric of our society will be inevitably torn, and who knows what will come of it.

"You'd think the boy would be happy you've groomed him—your horse keeps kicking the poor lad, and without a healer, he's been forced to endure the bruises healing the slow way," Stablemaster Ingor says, interrupting my somber thoughts. I smirk, watching as he grumbles at the boys under his command and sends them off to their duties.

The stablemaster is older and wiser than most, and I've watched him give lip to every prince and princess who ever stabled a horse here, confident in his ability to get out of trouble should he ever find himself in it. He's the best at what he does and loyal to his core, barely able to mask his contempt for my uncle whenever the regent comes to Yregar. Ignor will always have a place in my household, no matter which royal family he makes an enemy of.

The village is always lively and loud, but as I work my

way there on foot, I hear conflict ahead, and my pace quickens. It's not a friendly place for high-fae princes and princesses, and there's no one to blame for that but ourselves. Yregar was once a small, seasonal castle that the high fae moved in and out of at their whim. The village was once quiet and unassuming but, thanks to the war, it's overflowing with refugees, and my soldiers' presence is constant to mitigate any altercations centered around food.

I round the corner of one of the new sharehouses to the small square in front of the temple and find the crates the maids were carrying smashed to pieces on the cobblestones, dozens of bodies scrambling desperately to collect the spilled bread and soldiers barking orders as they wade into the fray.

Two steps forward, and I'm pulling people out of the crowd, shoving them behind me as I snap, "Get back to your homes and lock the doors!"

As I grab and move more of the onlooking crowd, more people notice my arrival. Some take one look at me and flee, but others hesitate, even in their fear of my presence. It takes me a second to realize they have no homes to return to, my command an impossible task for them to follow. I'm forced to change tactics.

I raise my voice, calling out to get more of them moving. "Return to your lodgings if you have them. If you're waiting on a bed, then step back now! Do not join the fight—we'll feed you without this madness."

I can't see the maids, females under my employ and protection, and if any harm has come to them there'll be grave consequences. Desperation is understandable, excusable even, but not at the expense of good, hard-working women who were sent here with aid.

There's wailing at my feet, and I look down at a small, filthy child huddled over a scrap of bread. There's a flash of movement at my side, and I step over the boy instinctively, my shoulder bearing the brunt of two grappling males as they fling themselves at each other without regard for who they might crush. They bounce off me and spill to the ground, shouting curses at me only to realize who it is they're calling the son of a pixie-whore.

The boy glances up, his eyes red with tears but his body safely sheltered beneath my stance, and a hush falls over the crowd. I shuffle backwards, far enough to scoop him into my arms, his bones digging into my hands and the weight of him barely registering as he tucks into my shoulder. He can't be more than two or three, starvation skewing my guess, and he's already wading into conflicts for the chance of a meal.

Soldiers step through the mess on the cobblestones to grab the two men, heaving them to their feet and yanking them toward me. Both bow deeply to me, blood running down their faces and spattered over their clothes. Terror thickens the air around us, the acrid stink of it clinging to me, and I have to focus to unclench my teeth, my jaw aching.

Alwyn, one of the soldiers, meets my gaze with grave eyes. "Your command, Your Highness?"

His words are firm and low, but they ricochet around the now-silent temple square. When I shift the boy in my arms around, I find him chewing on the bread, the layer of dirt it's covered in disregarded entirely as he consumes his prize in three bites. There's envy in the eyes of the villagers around us, none of them bothering to conceal it, and I turn back to Alwyn.

"Where are the maids? Are they injured?"

The solider shakes his head. "They're in the temple. We moved them soon after the fight broke out."

I nod and look around once more, but no one is looking at the boy with concern or familiarity. There's no sign of parents or relatives that I can see. "Escort the males to the gate to cool down. If no one else was seriously injured, they'll be let go with a warning."

Alwyn's brows inch up before he catches himself, nodding and moving at my command.

Still carrying the boy, I move past them and let the maids out of the temple, the crowd still watching. There's nowhere for them to go, nothing else they should be doing right now but waiting for food and hoping they'll get enough for their families.

I hand off the boy to Tyra to sort out and, once I've seen her and the other maids on their way back to the castle with a soldier escort, I address the crowd again. "There will be provisions for every person at Yregar, provided here at the temple each day. There's no need for fighting or stealing. We're handing out what we can, and you'll each get something. We'll have more provisions soon, but we're all going to have to make do with smaller rations until then. Any further fighting will result in far greater consequences. Now go, and come back tomorrow for food, *without* the fighting."

The crowd eases away, some moving back to their homes and others huddling against the buildings they're sleeping against for the time being. Irritation scratches along my shoulders. This is the best I can do for now. Hollow offerings, especially when I'm still not sure how we're going to make it through the winter, but I'll figure something out. I have no choice.

As I continue to the outer wall, the few remaining villagers flinch and bow so as not to draw my attention or ire. Hundreds of years ago, even the whisper of my temper wouldn't have changed the villagers' perception of me, but with all of the refugees and survivors who now live here as well, even after providing them food and assistance for decades, they fear me.

My uncle's sabotage is working.

The orphanage at the edge of town is overflowing, and the fight was far enough away that the children are playing outside without interruption. When she sees me coming, the female who lives there and cares for them shoos them out of the front yard and back into the building. I have no intention of stopping in or bothering any of them, and her action frustrates me further, the black cloud hanging over my head growing heavier.

To be given the opportunity to have children and to leave them behind is incomprehensible to me.

Many of them are the bastard children of high-fae nobles and have been left here as an embarrassing secret, which seems an even more shameful act. The obsession with fated bloodlines is ridiculous and harmful to our people and our kingdom. It's behavior that the regent supports, and something I intend on stamping out when I take the throne.

If I take the throne.

I curse viciously under my breath, startling a female carrying a large basket under her arm who then flees from me as though I'm a monster, blood dripping from my teeth as I eye her neck. I'm too preoccupied to worry about it.

I can't afford to think like that.

I *cannot* let my despair at finding that witch at the port win, because as I climb the guard tower at the outer wall and look back over the village, it's clear that we're in a do-or-die situation. My people are already dying, and I have to do something, even if it fills my body with revulsion.

Her haunting silver eyes flash into my mind once more, and my fists clench against the stone of the guard tower's hip-high wall.

I must wed her, remove my uncle from power, and change things, or my country will die. No matter how much my mind and my body reject the very idea of speaking with the witch, there's no other choice.

"No signs of the enemy, Your Highness," one of the soldiers says to me as he bows, a spear in his hands. The Celestial house colors wave overhead in the form of the Yregar Castle flag.

I've known this soldier a very long time and, if I were the type of male to make bets, I would place money that he's on my side, but still my eyes are narrowed as I take him in, picking over every inch of his uniform and weapons as though I might find some sign of the regent on him.

There's nothing to be found, as expected.

I stare at the rolling hills of decay before us and say, "It's been too quiet in the kingdom of late, and that's usually a sign they're about to attack us where we least expect it. Keep your eyes sharp and on the horizon. There are a lot of people here who depend on you for their safety."

He bows again before turning and staring shrewdly into the distance, his face set like stone as he follows my command. I continue along the top of the wall and take stock of any required changes and repairs. To walk the entire perimeter at a good speed would take most of the sunlight hours, and so it's not feasible for today. Instead, I go as far as the section over the river, where small grates let the water pass through the bottom of the wall.

I find a group of soldiers huddled up and speaking amongst themselves, hushed and frantic. They stop the moment they see me walking their way, jabbing at each other as they straighten and then bow to me. They glance at each other nervously, tension thick in the air, and my fists curl at my sides.

I speak through my teeth. "What's going on?"

One of them is shoved to the front by the others and, after shooting a filthy look over his shoulder, he faces me, words tumbling out of his mouth in a jumbled mess. "We were trying to decide how to come and tell you, Your Highness. We tried to stop it—we never thought this could happen."

I scowl at him and step forward. "Speak plainly."

He gestures over the side of the wall, and I glance down. All I see is the same death and decay.

When I glanced back up, he murmurs, "The fae flowers are gone. There was a patch there, always, every year, but this year only two bloomed. Overnight...they've died. There are none left. We stopped the villagers from coming here to pick them for their healing tinctures in the hopes that they would survive, but we woke up this morning to find the last two gone."

The last of the fae flowers.

Other words echo in my mind, repeating and blurring together like some sort of death omen until I'm forced to face the possibility of them. The *probability* of them, if I don't accept my fate.

The time of the high fae is over.

I have no choice but to marry the witch. Fates have mercy on my soul and my kingdom, but I'm going to have to do it.

SEVEN

ROOKE

The days begin to bleed into each other.

The only way that I know time is even passing is by the flow of my magic into the earth beneath me through the cracks between the giant, dirty stone pavers of the cell. My mind slips into a meditative state as I feel the day cycling above me. The sun's rays soak into the parched soil, the soft afternoon breeze rustles the bare branches of the now-dormant orchard, the mist of the late evening evaporates before it can soak into the ground…the land's magic shows it all to me as I honor the earth with my sacrifice of power.

To pass the time in moments of calm before battles while serving in the Sol Army, I played card games with Pemba until we were both more than adept at gambling, despite our reluctance to utilize the skill. We told old witches' tales to my friends and listened to stories from other lands. I wove the ribbon Pemba found the supplies for, at first trying to recreate the old patterns of our coven, and then using the task as a diary of sorts, a visual history of my time as a soldier with every pass of the shuttle as the ribbon grew. We tried many things to pass the time without thinking of the monsters that hunted us, but nothing was as effective as this magical connection.

The guards are a silent constant in the dungeon. They stay

away from me, laying eyes on me only when they bring me buckets of water and plates of the same meager scraps. The lack of food doesn't concern me.

My connection to the earth sustains me.

I don't feel hunger or thirst, though I'm careful about drinking the water. I don't need to push my body any further than this and, in the end, I'm still a prisoner in a high-fae dungeon. It would be reckless to act otherwise.

I find myself trapped within my own mind with nothing but my thoughts to keep myself occupied. It would be easy to lose myself in grief and sadness for the horrors that I witnessed during my time in the Sol Army. Instead, I murmur prayers to the Fates and perform a far smaller version of the old rites of my coven to honor this sacrifice of my power into the earth below, keeping my mind sharp as time creeps on around me.

Maybe the Savage Prince will just keep me down here.

Maybe he's found some way to marry me without my consent or participation, and maybe the Fates will be satisfied with that.

In my childhood, there were rumors of witches who gave themselves over to nature entirely. They formed a connection to the earth beneath them and let power flow through them and into the earth for centuries, becoming nothing more than a barely sentient power source.

I heard about them as a child and, as naïve as I was, I thought it would be a lovely experience. To be as one with the earth and give it everything I had. But I suppose that's the Ravenswyrd in me. Growing up in the forest with my family and our coven, we were a neutral zone and never entered into conflicts. Instead, we were known for helping anyone who approached us.

Any being wishing to enter the forest had to be allowed passage by the old gods who slumber there, the sanctuary the trees offered our coven lasting for generations of witches as far back as our histories go. We trusted that protection, and we healed any fae folk who came to us, replenishing them, doing whatever we could to help them, and then sent them on their way with no payment asked. People still left tributes and trinkets, bartered things and gave many gifts, especially to my mother.

She wasn't just my mother, she was the Mother of the coven, and I was the Maiden, readying myself to take over someday and make decisions for us all. I'd grown up wild and free, barefoot and dressed in hand-woven clothing made for me by my grandmother. I never did the things that I saw the younglings in Sol City do, like bathe regularly and be forced to take lessons.

Instead, I spent my days foraging in the forest and learning directly from my mother everything a witch could possibly need to know about how to heal, how to nurture, how to give every piece of myself away to the land itself, because we trusted the earth to give it straight back to us. A fate of giving myself completely to the forest was the only one I could see.

That was before death came for us.

Before the war arrived on our doorstep in the form of witches hungry for blood and power. Before everyone I knew and loved was murdered, my brother and I the only survivors, thanks to our journey to see the Seer.

That journey marked a lot of firsts for me.

My first time leaving the forest, my first time seeing a high fae, my first time taking a life…it was a journey of growing up and leaving behind the witch I'd hoped to be and the beginning of the jaded female I am now, someone who grew colder as my years in the Fate Wars marched on.

I hear the door open at the top of the giant staircase. I don't think anything of it. Not a lot of time has passed since the last plate of slops was thrust through the hatch, but I don't have it in me to question the goings on.

It's only when I hear the tenor of the footfalls that my eyes open. A female is coming down here.

The delicate sound of heeled shoes against the stone stairs is unsteady and slow, a careful descent. The oppressive air thickens once more, only this time it's magic and not the ravenous hunger of the earth that I feel. I don't move from my spot, but when a torch flares brighter, I open my eyes only to be faced with yet another heartbreakingly beautiful high fae princess.

A *pregnant* one.

She's a full-blooded Unseelie high fae with porcelain skin and white-blonde hair, and those icy-blue eyes that seem to pierce right through my flesh and leave poisonous barbs underneath my skin. Her resemblance to the Savage Prince is striking, especially as her cold eyes run over my haggard appearance. I haven't bathed since I left the Seelie Court. I haven't even been able to change my clothes since the morning I left the ship, and I'm sure that no matter how bad I think I look, the reality is worse.

"A witch mate. Part of me still doesn't believe it. I had to see you with my own eyes, and it's taken me a little while to muster up the restraint to come down here and see you."

There's no way for me to answer her, thanks to the gag between my lips, so I simply stare back, unflinching and unafraid. I'm sure that my eyes are unnerving, because her temper flares to life, her lip curling and marring the beauty of her perfect face.

Her voice drips with derision, cold and cunning as she chooses her words with care. "What a test my cousin has found himself facing! I suppose you and your filthy friends thought this fate of yours was a great gift, a sign of the Fates being on your side. Whatever you think you're going to achieve here, whatever plan you've made to manipulate the high fae once you're married, I can assure you, it's not going to work. Soren *will* marry you, of course, just as the Fates command, but you'll never gain his trust. You'll never have his ear or win his favor.

He loathes the very idea of looking at you."

I say nothing and continue to stare back at her, unimpressed. I don't know what it is about this prince that they all think that I would want so desperately, considering the rumors about him and the harsh demeanor I've been subjected to. The cold-hearted prince who hunts witches for fun, relishes torture, and desires blood. The only whisper proven wrong so far is the one about his scarred face.

The scar does nothing to detract from his devastating beauty. It's the loathing that burns within his Unseelie blue eyes when they meet mine that diminishes it.

The high fae are obsessed with power, no matter which court they come from. They incessantly need to have more, to *be* more, to get closer to whoever sits on the throne. I knew an exiled prince from the Dragon Lands, a male who despised the kingdom he could never return to, and yet he still spent his time in the Sol Army climbing his way up the ranks with a single-minded determination that was unhealthy, to say the least. When I questioned him about it, he simply shrugged and told me social advancement was the high-fae way. All of them are drunk on the need to climb the highest pinnacle they can.

Of course they would assume I want that too.

Every fiber of my being aches for the forest. I need to be with the earth once more, to pull off my boots and wiggle my toes in the dirt, to let my blood flow freely into the ground and give it everything I can.

I want anything but a throne.

Exhaustion nips at me, the type of tiredness that no amount of sleep can heal, and the magic in the air sickens me to the point that I want this female to leave and take this evil sensation with her.

"I suppose you're not as hideous as the other witches I've seen. You're not marked and spitting black bile everywhere.

I wonder if Soren's fate insists on there being children too? I guess your curse doesn't put *that* prospect in any danger, does it? A part-blood on the throne of the Southern Lands. The court is going to tear you to pieces."

Your curse.

Her tone changed when that word left her mouth, her lip curling even further at the very sound of it. One of her hands drifts down to rest over her belly. The magic that fills the space clings to her, clawing at her desperately as it seeks the life within her, and my stomach clenches violently as I realize it's waiting for the baby, reaching toward her womb and biding its time.

I heard the rumor that Kharl had laid a curse over all the Unseelie high fae, but I dismissed it as exaggeration. How could anyone cast such a curse over an entire people? The amount of magic required is inconceivable, the sacrifice required deadly. Yet the loathing in her eyes tells me it must be true.

The Unseelie high fae cannot bear live full-blooded children.

I spent my formative years learning about magic, the limitations of my power, and the power of my people. My lessons on wielding that power were cut short by the massacre of my people, but I had that foundation to help me master my magic over the following years. When Pemba and I crossed the seas and journeyed to the Seelie Court, I learned about the magic of the high fae and the lower fae in the Northern Lands. There were thousands of refugees from the Southern Lands, all of them fleeing from the War of the Witches. Straight into another conflict, yes, but one they felt they had a chance to survive. As a healer, I met thousands of fae folk, and I came to know them while fighting by their sides and listening to their histories and their experiences with magic.

I learned what it takes to curse someone, and I know *exactly* what it would take to curse an entire continent of high fae in such a way. Whatever other evil Kharl has wrought, none of it can compare to the blood sacrifice and power exchange of the curse. How many Mothers and Maidens chose to follow him? How many did he abduct when their covens refused his call? Generations of power and bloodlines, all of them bled out and murdered to fuel this curse.

I understand the source of the loathing in this female's eyes as she stares down at me, clutching her belly desperately, knowing that the child within will never take a breath due to my kind. I look upon her with far more kindness than she looks upon me.

The moment she notices that softening in my gaze, her face twists into a snarl. "Your pity is despicable. I will carve those eyes right out of your head for daring to look upon me. Your kind murdered my son and would take another from me. I'll see to it that Soren fulfills his fate and then tortures you endlessly, exactly as you deserve, because you're nothing but a filthy, warmongering, lower-fae cretin."

She turns on her heel and walks away with that unsteady gait that reveals she's not far from giving birth. The clock hanging over her head and the life of her unborn babe are ticking away, slowly counting down until their time together will end. The sorrow inside me only grows for that fierce mother. To know that the curse is clawing at her womb and to still long for a baby so desperately that she would try anyway…I don't blame her for her rage, her tiny frame shaking with it. She's right. I do pity her.

I pity them all.

As far as torture goes, a few days into my confinement, I decide that the Savage Prince needs to work on his methods because, after centuries of my sleep being interrupted by Ureen attacks and the demands of being a healer, I finally feel well-rested once more. My skin, though filthy with the dust and grime of the cell, glows with health, and even my cheeks have plumped out from the magic exchange, the skin no longer taut across my bones. I suspect that if I were to return to the Seelie Court right now, I would be unrecognizable to my friends.

Even after my wounds from the Ureen finally healed—a long and arduous process that drained much of my own power and that of the witches who worked tirelessly to save me—I remained in this numb state of being. At first, I thought my continued detachment indicated a wound of the mind, a trauma inside me that needed time to heal, but as time passed, the ice around my heart only grew thicker, and my mental health never truly recovered.

I longed for the forest.

I continued to live within my family's traditions, even in a land that was not my own. I performed the rituals of the solstices and equinoxes, took part in the sacrifices and the ways of the local witches, conformed to every last one of the ways in which the Fates required me to nurture the land, but the Northern Lands did not welcome me the way the land here does.

This land needs me.

I was born of the Unseelie lands, and my power and blood sustain them. No matter how far I traveled or the traditions I honored in distant courts, *this* is where I belong. I feel it in the way the earth devours my magic, as though it would take everything from me if only I would let it. It would consume me whole and still search for more, having centuries-worth of damage to heal. Here I'm a natural conduit. If I gave myself over to the exchange, I could live forever in this suspended state.

But it's not my fate to do so, no matter how much the land calls for me.

The longer I stay locked in this cell, the more I notice the patterns of the passing days.

Every morning a new bucket of water and a tray of slops appear through the hatch. The guards murmur as they confirm that nothing has changed within the cell, and then silence takes over the cavernous void once more. I have no doubt the guards are reporting that I do nothing all day, and the high faes' suspicions of my intentions are growing more obvious.

I make no effort to speak to any of them or to move, aside from drinking the water and eating a few scraps, but the guards' eyes are sharp on my body, watching it flourish.

None of it matters to me. I don't need their trust or their approval to complete my fate.

Instead, I continue in my meditative state.

I forget about everything happening around me and focus on the earth, letting magic take me over completely. This is the healthiest I've been since I left the forest; I'm in tune with nature, as I'm supposed to be as a witch. The Ravenswyrd witches were made from this earth, and I should never have forgotten that. And yet...I did.

It doesn't matter how I feel about my fate. I'll marry the Savage Prince just as soon as he gets past his futile rage at the Fates and gets on with it. He can take his throne and save his kingdom; I won't kick up a fuss, no matter how much the arrogant male deserves it. I'll do my own saving of the land from here without his meddling.

Of course, the problem of the curse begins to eat away at the back of my mind.

My fate says that I'm here to save the kingdom from the war and that my marriage to the Savage Prince will set off a chain of events to end the bloodshed, but I know far more about the Fates than I did when I fled the Southern Lands. I understand that it's not as simple as merely waiting for the Fates to use me like a puppet. No matter how much I want to sit back in this cell and retreat from the evils of this world, I must participate.

When I made the decision to come back here, I thought my tasks would be to find the Savage Prince and submit to the marriage, to be an opinionless figurehead and satisfy the laws of the Unseelie Court until it came time to face Kharl.

Now that I've seen the dire state of the kingdom, I know I have much harder work to do than only that.

I slip back into my meditation and, instead of emptying my mind, this time I look for the curse. There will be ways to weaken its magic, but I have a better chance of finding a way to unravel it if I understand the makings of the curse. The witches with that knowledge would be Kharl or one of his most loyal followers, but consulting them is clearly not an option for me.

I'd kill the male on sight, curse be damned, for what he did to my family.

It doesn't take me long to find the tendrils of the magic, which rests over the high fae like an oppressive blanket. It's invisible and undetectable to any of those who don't feel a strong pull to the power within them, but to me it's perfectly clear.

The strong and old magic is a form of contraceptive that's been twisted and pushed to an extreme, devastating for any high fae who comes across it. Dozens, hundreds, maybe even thousands of babies have been taken from the loving arms of their mothers, strengthening the power of the curse with their sacrificed lives and building its evil and potency.

The longer I examine it, the more I learn. It might be an old and powerful form of magic but it's also a weary curse, long overdue for a sacrifice to be poured back into it after so many long years without any high fae even attempting to fall pregnant. I might not be able to loosen its ties over the kingdom, but if I can manipulate it close enough to where it lingers over the princess before it takes the baby as a sacrifice, I might be able to break it.

I don't stand a chance of the high-fae princes letting me use magic around the pregnant female. In their ignorance and fear of my power, they'd kill me.

"Why haven't you just let yourself out?"

The voice tears through my concentration, my calm state slipping away as though it never was. My eyes slowly open, and I find myself staring at a high-fae prince once more, only this time, it's the one with magic. Tyton.

The one my forest speaks to.

That makes me want to trust him, the echo of the forest in his voice still ringing in my mind. If the trees have deemed him worthy, who am I to argue?

I stare at him, unwavering, but he only gestures at his face, his fingers flicking over his mouth as he glances at the gag in mine. "You can take it off. I know it, and you know it. I told Soren that you could, to make sure he's aware of the true danger that laid in wait for him here, and yet you keep it on just to fool us."

His voice is soft, sweet, like honey in a trap, but there's no doubt he'd kill me just as swiftly as the others would. I don't need the accusation in his words to know it—the sharp edge in his tone makes it clear enough. He's dressed in fine clothing, more casual than his armor but more formal than the clothing worn by the other princes so far. He's put this outfit together for…something. Certainly not to come down here and speak with the likes of me.

I stare him down, and then my hand rises, and I loosen the bindings and tug the gag from my mouth. My lips are cracked, and I taste blood when I try to wet them, my tongue swollen and sore. My body might be in good health, but it still bears many signs of my captivity.

When I don't immediately answer his original question, he

frowns at me. "Your silence grows wearisome, your inaction worse. Speak to me, witch."

My voice is cracked and weak but loud enough for his high-fae ears to hear. "Or what? Are you going to come in here and make me?"

His eyebrows slowly creep up his forehead as he stares at me. "Are you hoping I will? Are you trying to goad me into crossing the iron bars so that you can kill me?"

I don't need to cross the iron bars to kill this man

I don't need to cross the iron bars to kill *any* of them.

A smirk stretches over his lips. It's simple enough for me to read how confident he is in his abilities against me. I'm happy to use that confidence against him, and so I ask him the question I truly want an answer to.

"Tell me about the Ravenswyrd trees."

His eyebrows come crashing down into a scowl, and I let a smile pull up the corners of my own lips, happy that the barb hit him right in the center of his chest. "You want to talk to me, don't you? I'll tell you mine if you tell me yours. Tell me what the trees say to you."

He stares at me for a moment before answering, "You first. Why not leave this cell if you're not planning on lulling us into a false sense of security and then killing us all in our sleep?"

Bluntness delivered from the face of an ethereal creature. I'm glad I'm well versed in the games of the high fae, because I'd be tripping over my answers if I wasn't.

I rest my head against the cold stone of my cell and answer, my tone clear and sure. "I'm here to fulfill my fate. Whether you believe me or not doesn't change a thing. Unless you plan on going against the Fates and starting a whole new war here in the Southern Lands, then I know I am safe enough. Have you ever seen a Ureen? Ever learned the process it takes to *unmake* one? It's a terrible thing, and I've learned that it's better to leave my fate intact through my obedience. Now…tell me what the trees say to you."

He shakes his head, ignoring my request. "Why haven't you gone mad down here? Every witch we've ever brought here hasn't lasted longer than a day. How are you surviving?"

I shake my head back at him, a mocking display of disappointment, as though I really had assumed he'd speak to me. I know he won't, that none of them will give me anything. We're quickly reaching a stalemate that will end only with me being stuck down here forever, but I suppose telling him this truth won't hurt anything.

I close my eyes and let the power flow through me once more, my skin singing as the magic knits my damaged lips back together. "You'll always assume the worst because I'm a witch. What's the harm in acting the exact way that you all expect of me when you're going to treat me like this regardless? That's why I left the gag in. As for how I'm keeping my mind together down here, it's simple. I was born of this earth, and it cannot harm me. The others you brought down here—their markings were black, weren't they? Those witches turned away from who they are and what they're meant to be. I have not."

He scowls at me. "You're speaking in riddles. For all I know, you're attempting to cast some sort of curse against me, and only the iron bars are keeping me safe."

Around in circles we go.

I ignore his words and reply, "What did the trees say about the Favored Children? That's what you said to the Savage Prince, wasn't it? The Favored Children. What did they say?"

His lip curls as he snarls at me, "Don't call him that."

It's a sore point for them all, a wound I can poke and prod whenever I want to gall them into a tantrum. It's strange to me that Prince Soren's nickname is what upset him, but Tyton turns and leaves without fulfilling his part of the bargain. I'm not surprised or upset by it. I've learned a good way to dig under the skin of my Fates-blessed mate and his friends, should I need to.

The first true break in the pattern of my days is the door above opening in the middle of the night, the sound ricocheting off the stone walls like a clap of thunder. There's not supposed to be a guard shift change. There's not supposed to be anything happening right now, and so my eyes flutter open and slowly adjust to the darkness. It's always dark down here, but at night the guards let the torches burn out without relighting them, going down to the barest of essentials as though they're conserving resources.

It makes sense, given how dire things seem to be here.

I hold myself still and stare through the bars, taking in my surroundings only to find nothing has changed during the hours I've been asleep. The guard standing watch looks nervous though, straightening up carefully as footsteps on stone echo through the cells.

He shifts so that one hand hangs over his weapon, a stance he's supposed to hold the entire time he's watching me and not only when someone comes to check in. His eyes stay narrowed and steady as he focuses on the staircase. I can't see it from the cell, so instead I watch him, taking note of the tense lines of his limbs and the intensity of his gaze.

The moment the interloper arrives, I know it's not one of the princes, because the guard's body deflates and tension evaporates from him all at once.

A slow smirk stretches across his lips. "You're not supposed to be down here. We're not open for visitors."

There's a low laugh, a voice I haven't heard before, and then a new high-fae guard steps into my line of sight. His hair is pulled back from his face and tied with a crude leather strap, messy and provincial looking. His clothing is informal and shapeless, nothing like the tailored perfection of the princes I've been subjected to, a clear sign of his lower status. He's not here at his superior's command, and it makes me wonder exactly how the Savage Prince runs this castle of his.

The Sol King would burn this male alive, publicly and with no remorse.

"I've heard rumors about the witch bitch down here and I knew if I wanted to see her, I'd have to wait until you were on duty."

The guard shrugs and flicks a hand in my direction. "Well, there she is. Nothing much to see unless you like the look of dirt on witch-skin."

The newcomer chuckles again and steps up to the cell bars to look at me, his gaze flitting over me a little too eagerly for my liking. He has some scarring down his neck, an anomaly amongst the high fae. There are no obvious markings to tell me whether it was an injury from the War of the Witches, and yet my mind gets stuck on the possibility that he got it while murdering my innocent kinfolk, not those who had betrayed us all by following Kharl Balzog. I'm living proof that not all witches want this conflict and many have been caught in the crossfire, the tales of thousands of those deaths still spoken of widely in the Northern Lands by those who had fled there.

I hate the soldier on principle.

His tongue swipes over his bottom lip, and he simpers, "I wouldn't say *nothing* to look at. With some soap and water, she might even look like something worth bedding! Fates above, I didn't know witches came in any variety other than 'disgustingly crazed' and 'horrifically disfigured'. No wonder half the castle is talking about her."

A frown settles on the brow of the other soldier, and his

eyes turn toward the stairs. "If you get caught down here it'll be both our lives. They're taking her *very* seriously. Whatever she knows, it's big."

The newcomer slaps him on the shoulder, though he does so without taking his gaze off me. "I'm not going to get caught. It's the middle of the night, no one gives a shit about the prisoner. The princes are all *quite* busy."

The way he stretches out that word is unsettling, and I wait until he glances around, checking that no one followed him down here, before I move the sleeve of my shirt back over the small cut on my wrist to conceal the energy swap.

The guard tries to get him to leave, a futile task. "Seriously Merrick, you can't be down here. I don't want to lose this position and be forced back onto the frontlines. I can't go back there."

Gutless.

Merrick grins at him, this time slapping him on the chest before he pulls away and slips a key from his own pocket. He waves it at the guard with a grin. "Haven't you ever wanted to get back at them for what they've done to us? To destroy the witches as they've destroyed so many of us? I'll admit, the moment I heard from the other guards what she looked like, I wanted nothing more than to see tears running down that filthy face."

His eyes are icy blue and frenetic as they linger on me as though I'm nothing more than a piece of meat. A manic energy emanates from him. He's practically salivating, the prospect of violence exciting him into a frenzy, and I'm sickened by it.

I know what it's like to be stuck in the middle of a war and to loathe your enemy for every last one of the atrocities you've been forced to live through, to see, and to bear with no end in sight. I know what it's like to hate so blindly that you feel as though you will never know any other emotion.

I also know that males who take advantage of an enemy in the way this male is suggesting are using revenge as an excuse to hide their true nature. There's a darkness within their hearts, an evil that can't be explained away because, no matter how violent the battles became, the male soldiers I fought alongside—those I counted as friends—never once voiced such a desire to me. It never even crossed their minds.

"You can't go in there with her! Where in the Fates did you even get the key from?" the guard hisses.

Merrick grins at him, a sickening light in his eyes. "Come on now, Lysen, you don't want word to get around that you're a witch apologist, do you? That's certainly not something I'd want the Savage Prince calling me."

It's the first time I've heard one of the prince's own men call him that nickname. Lysen flinches, clearly far more loyal to his prince, but fear wins over honor. Enough, at least, that he doesn't physically stop his friend as Merrick opens the cell door.

Lysen says, feebly, "Her hands aren't bound and there's no gag in her mouth."

Merrick shrugs. "Prince Tauron has spoken with her. She can't have any talent with magic, so there's no danger. Do you think some witch bitch is going to be able to overpower me? Maybe we're not truly friends if you think so, Lysen."

I stay seated on the ground, my back pressed to the wall behind me, and watch Merrick duck into the cell, careful to avoid touching the iron bars. He's got nothing but cold arrogance in his face, complete assurance that he's stepping into a room with his next victim and not about to be caged with a monster.

I may not be what they all expect, but I'm also not defenseless.

Whatever assumptions he's made, they're wrong.

"Merrick," Lysen calls again, and Merrick barks back at him, "If you're so scared, then shut the door behind me and keep watch. I told Luren and Oslo that I was coming down. Both of them said they'd try her out as well, just as soon as their shifts end. We'll have her to ourselves for long enough to get the fun started."

Lysen doesn't shut the door, he merely stands in the doorway, clutching it with his protective leather gloves. His eyes can't decide if they want to focus on the horrors about to unfold in front of him or to keep watch on the staircase, his gaze bouncing between the two frantically. He does nothing more to stop his so-called friend.

I shift my attention away from the gutless high fae and back to the one advancing on me as if I'm his next meal. I stare up at Merrick and hope that a single doubt will permeate his skull, the slightest bit of understanding of this situation, to make him realize he shouldn't be doing what he's doing. But as one of his hands slips down to the front of his trousers and pops the top button casually, and his tongue comes out to wet his bottom lip again, it's clear to me he's not going to hesitate.

I idly wonder how I'm going to explain this to my Fates-cursed mate.

Merrick leans down and fixes a hand around the top of my arm, then yanks me to my feet. His other hand comes up to press at the clasps of my dress. The design confuses him, the fastenings nothing like those on the lace and silks of high-fae dresses or any of the fashions I saw in the villages on the journey here.

It's a traditional dress of Unseelie witches, one I had specially made in the Seelie lands, and it's held together with silver pins. I chose a sturdy fabric and a simple pin design, so it's easy to get on and off, but to the high fae, who prefer their ribbons and buttons, I imagine it's like a puzzle.

He grunts and fists the fabric at my chest as though he's going to rip it, and I decide to stop this before I lose the only outfit I have in my own style. There's a small flash of light as my dagger appears in my hand, and the surprised look on his face when he sees it is the same look he wears in death, my hand moving too fast for him to avoid. I slide the dagger into his gut as easy as butter, angling upwards and pushing my magic through the blade itself and into his body to magnify the damage. It's easy magic, small and undetectable to the untrained observer but devastating to the body, no matter which race it's used against.

Less powerful witches need their voices to cast spells, but as the Mother of the Ravenswyrd Coven and with the strength the earth has been cycling into me for weeks pouring into my magic reserves, it's easier than breathing to protect myself.

He's dead before I yank the dagger out of his gut, his blood splattering the ground and pouring onto the dirt like a sacrifice, the earth greedily drinking it in. Something wakes beneath us, something old and tired and *angry*, and it calls to me with a chant from the deepest recesses of the castle, the steady beat a mirror of the beat in my chest.

I press a hand against Merrick's chest and shove his body away. It falls backwards and hits the ground with a cracking sound from his skull. Lysen, who had only a view of his friend's back, yelps and startles toward the body. His instinct to help Merrick is instant, and he draws his sword as he moves, but realization of what's actually happened takes a moment longer— long enough that he walks straight into the cell without regard for his own life.

When he spots the blood pouring from Merrick's gut, he looks at me with a snarl and lifts his sword, and that's enough intent for me. I move faster than he does, fast enough that he's caught by surprise as I spin and slash my dagger across his throat with ease, a quick and practiced swipe. His sword swings downwards, narrowly missing me before it clatters to the ground, his hands clutching his throat but unable to stop the blood that pours through his fingers in an endless flow.

He falls onto his friend, more blood pooling around them both and seeping through the cracks of the stone into the earth. My eyes stay trained on him as he flails for a moment, choking and gasping, before I step past them both and pull the door of the cell shut. I reach through the bars and pull the key from the lock as well, then throw it across the room out of my reach so that it looks as though I had no choice but to stay in here.

I wait until my back is pressed against the stones once more before I pass a hand over my front and flick the blood onto the stones in sacrifice, my magic lifting all of the blood out of the fabric and my skin until there's not a speck of it left on me. When the earth accepts it greedily, I make another nick in my wrist and let my blood add to the offering. Then I stash the dagger away and rub my free hand over the tiny mark on my inner elbow to ease the tingling where the blade disappeared from sight. The earth sighs beneath me, happy for the extra blood it's been given.

I don't feel an inch of guilt for killing either of them. Not the would-be rapist nor the friend too gutless to say no and mean it.

I feel nothing as I let my eyes slip shut and sleep take me over, the bodies that are readily cooling only steps away from me already forgotten.

It's not my first time sleeping next to the dead, and as I savor the thrum of the Fates dancing underneath the scars of my back and my belly in their joy at my actions, I'm sure it won't be my last.

EIGI•IT

SOREN

Tauron wakes me just before dawn, the moon hanging low in the sky and a soft breeze shifting the open curtains at my window. I spent the day before training in the yards until exhaustion took over, and so, thankfully, I'm not soaked in fairy wine, my mind sharp the moment my cousin knocks on my chamber door.

No good news arrives at such an hour.

He doesn't waste time on pleasantries, his tone flat but simmering with fury. "Two of our soldiers have been found dead in the witch's cell."

I'm out of bed and pulling on clothing before he utters another word. In less than two full breaths, I'm buckling my sword at my side and slinging on my cloak, the fur warm against the cold of the night. Tauron is fully dressed as well, the dark circles under his eyes the only sign of his own sleepless nights.

"Why were two soldiers down there in the first place?" I snap, and he grimaces, the fury from his tone bleeding over his features until he's practically vibrating with rage.

"That was the first question I asked as well, and after some investigation, I have theories—none of them good. I'll let you take a look in the cell before I say anything else."

The castle is silent as we move through it, the lamps that light our way flickering against the frigid air of the early morning. Tyton meets us at the top of the staircase, the pinched look of his features the only sign of his anger, and when we reach the bottom, Roan is standing guard, arms crossed as he stares into the cell. He's dressed and armed to the teeth as though he's about to ride off to war, the large diamond on the hilt of his sword catching on the light from the torches as he dips his head respectfully at me. I ignore the tug I feel towards the witch, a far easier task than it usually is thanks to the scene before me.

There's blood everywhere.

It's seeped through the iron bars, and the stones outside the cell are slick with it. One of the guards' throats has been slit, his body draped over the other male, who wears casual attire. They've been left where they fell, sprawled out and not neatly stacked. The blood is undisturbed, no footprints or signs of a struggle, nothing but the single sword that lies still clutched in Lysen's hand. There's no blood on the blade, nothing to indicate he did anything more than draw it.

It's as if both of them stood there and allowed themselves to be killed.

There isn't a single mark on the witch, her eyes icy and cold as she stares back at us across the cell.

Unease pools in my gut, and my mouth tightens to mask it. She's been sitting down here without a word of protest, no reactions to the squalor or the scraps she's been fed, no requests to clean herself or even a chair to relieve the discomfort of the stone cell. She's been a model prisoner, and now two males are dead at her feet, locked inside the cell with her. Whatever I was expecting her first move against us to be, it wasn't this.

"Lysen was killed with a dagger. His sword couldn't make that cut. Where's the weapon," I say, and Roan shakes his head at me.

"As far as we can see, the sword is the only blade in there.

She must be hiding the dagger on her person somewhere, but the Fates only know where. We searched her before we put her in the cell."

Roan and Tauron share a look before Tauron shakes his head. "She wasn't given one. There aren't any missing from the stores. Everything is accounted for. She's never been offered so much as a butter knife."

Magic.

I don't even have to say it before Tauron responds. "She's in a cell in the depths of a cavern, deep underground, surrounded by iron bars, and has been fed the bare minimum. There's no way she could have used magic to kill them."

I look at Tyton, and when I see the glazed sheen over his eyes, I still. He glances around, his gaze continuously flicking down to the deep ruby pools of blood as he steps closer to the iron bars. "There's no magic in the air, no remnants of power from casting. None that I can see or feel. There's magic in her, of course, but we already knew that."

I step to his side and notice the witch staring at me, the icy depths of her silver eyes making my lip curl into a snarl. "How much magic? Can you tell me that?"

Tyton cocks head and purses his lips, but a confused look crosses his face before he looks at me a little nervously.

I give him a stern look back, flicking a hand in his direction dismissively. "Whatever it is, you can say it. There's no one down here but us, and we don't have the luxury of dancing around the truth right now."

Us, the witch, and two dead bodies already cold on the stone.

The pallor of their skin tells me they bled out over the past few hours. I know them both by name. I know all my soldiers by name, but Merrick and a handful of others have been monitored in the past as possible spies for the regent. In years past, my soldiers were ruthlessly vetted, and any question of their loyalty would have resulted in their immediate exile from Yregar. But as the curse continues to stop the birth of a new generation of high fae and our population has shrunk, I've had to make some reluctant exceptions.

Tyton takes a deep breath. "It's hard to explain, but my magic says 'mother.'"

"*Mother,*" Tauron says with disgust in his tone, his eyes flicking back to me in a twin horror to the sickening feeling in my gut.

Roan shakes his head at us all as though we're ignorant. "It's a status within covens, you idiot. It means there are people out there who belong to her and follow her. It means she has power."

I look at the witch, but she's no longer staring at me. Instead, she's fixed her attention on Tyton as though he's some great puzzle she needs to figure out. I don't like it and, from the look on his face, Tauron *loathes* it.

Roan steps past us both and slides the key into the lock, fixing a stern look on the witch before he opens the door. Tauron steps behind him with one hand on the grip of his sword, protective and ready to swing at a moment's notice, but the witch doesn't move.

She shows no interest as they remove the bodies from the cell.

I watch her carefully, the grime of the cell helping to hide some of the infuriating allure the Fates have cursed me to feel towards her, and it's only once the cell door is shut once again and Roan curses softly under his breath that I tear my gaze away from her huddled and filthy form. "What have you found?"

"Well, I'm pretty sure I know why Merrick is dead, and I'd wager Lysen was dragged into his friend's stupidity."

I look down and see the open button on Merrick's trousers,

a glaring declaration of intent. Rage numbs my senses for a moment, bile churning in my gut as I bite back a slew of curses at the son of pixie-whore stupid enough to think of touching her. The tug of the Fates in my chest only adds fuel to the burning turmoil within me, the soldier's actions forcing me to face the reality of an Unseelie high-fae male's reaction to someone daring to touch his mate.

The Fates might've made a serious misstep by commanding us to be together, but my body hasn't fully accepted just how wrong this witch is for me.

"He died because he went in there hoping to fuck her? Fates above, there's not enough fae elixir in the world for this," Tauron snaps as he pats down the bodies once more, careful as he shifts them around. Though he comes up with the standard issue sword Merrick would have been wearing when he was killed, there's no dagger to be found.

He scowls at the witch, sizing her up. "Well, this answers nothing! Merrick died first, and she certainly didn't stab him with his own sword then buckle it back to his side. There's not a drop of blood on the blade where it's sheathed, and the wound in his stomach is small. The angle of Lysen's slit throat is all wrong as well—she would have had to be standing right in front of him to make it, but there isn't a drop of blood on her."

Another sign that something isn't right.

Tyton walks around the dungeon slowly, eyes shut and one hand in front of him as he maneuvers by his senses alone.

Tauron growls at him, "We would know if someone else had come down here, Tyton."

His brother shrugs, his eyes still pressed shut. "How else do you explain the disappearing dagger? She won't speak, she didn't use magic, and yet there are two dead men."

Roan finishes his search of the body and then kicks Merrick's corpse. "He got what he deserves."

I grimace at him, but he shrugs back. "Your orders were clear. No one unauthorized was to come down here, and under no circumstances was the cell door to be opened. I'm not saying I'm happy the witch killed them, but if Merrick came down of his own accord, then he's a traitor. Any male willing to rape a captive and *supposedly* defenseless female isn't a male I want watching my back on a battlefield, no matter how strong his abilities as a soldier may be."

He's not wrong about that.

There's a good chance this was not Merrick's first time assaulting a female, and his death already means nothing to me. Now it seems like a good act of the Fates.

"From this moment on, until we find the dagger and any other traitors who might walk among us, no one watches her but us. Any soldiers who don't follow my orders are no better than the regent's guards, and are better off dead."

Things go progressively from bad to worse.

Every day I receive more information about the dying kingdom, and when soldiers are sent to the village to let them know rations will be cut again, there's an outcry amongst the part-bloods and lower fae. The desperation that comes from starvation is boiling over, and I'm forced to double the soldiers' presence to keep the peace.

Further inaction will only stack our funeral pyres higher.

I call one of my messengers, Hamyr, into my reception room. He bows deeply to me and then to Tyton as my cousin's magic stretches out around us to conceal our conversation. Roan is training with the soldiers at the barracks, and Tauron has taken a shift watching the witch, his spite for her fueling his surveillance. The witch's nose won't twitch without his assessment.

"Seek out an audience with the Sol King. I want to negotiate a trade agreement with the Seelie Court and the kingdoms further afield that require passing through his lands."

Tyton doesn't move an inch, but Hamyr cringes, his golden eyes flicking between us both before he asks, tentatively, "May I speak freely, Your Highness?"

I chose this messenger specifically for his loyalty, tested many times already, but also for his Seelie heritage. He's the bastard son of a Seelie high-fae lord and a part-blood of that court. His face is more selkie than high fae, but his eyes are as gold as Roan's own, a marker that facilitates his travels there at my command.

He trusts me as much as I trust him, and if he has something to say, I'll listen.

At my curt nod, he speaks plainly. "The Sol King has no love for the Southern Lands. Our gold won't be enough to sway him—if anything, he'll see it as an insult. We denied him aid in the Fate Wars—if we ask for it ourselves without apology or explanation, we could make a very powerful enemy with such a request."

He hesitates again then adds, "There's talk in the castle about the witch."

My gaze hardens, and he gulps, quickly adding, "I mean no disrespect, my prince, it's just...the Sol King offered his protection to *all* who answered his call. The talk said you found her at Port Asmyr in possession of Seelie gold. If the Sol King finds out you've imprisoned one of his soldiers, there will be no negotiation—there'll be war."

That strikes me dumb, my mind crashing to a halt.

She holds herself like a soldier. She killed two high fae with a dagger and no struggle. She hasn't cowered or flinched at the rough treatment she's received, and she walked behind the horses like the journey was nothing more than a casual stroll.

She hasn't tried to fight back, though, clearly outmatched, and I doubt that she was much more than a foot soldier or a sentry, nothing worth concerning myself with when the lives of my people hang in the balance.

I would do anything to save my kingdom and stop the suffering of my people. Nothing will change that, not even the truth of who my mate is. I won't let the witches win, not by spurning the Fates or by allowing her to twist my mind.

Meeting Hamyr's gaze, I say, "Go to the Sol King. Offer him my apologies for the wrongs of the past and assure him that things will change in the Southern Lands under my rule. Tell him I've found my mate and will take the throne soon, offer him our gold. Tell him we're eager to build a beneficial relationship with the Seelie Court once more. That the Snowsong heir also wishes to see his aunt and that, as Prince Roan's closest confidant, I'm determined to secure that meeting for him."

It's the truth, and one I'll wield now if it gets our stores filled once more. Roan has never met his mother's family, though he communicates with them often through messengers. They forbade his mother from returning to the Northern Lands during the war, the dangers of the Ureen far too great to risk the journey, and she died before the Sol King won against the monsters of the Fates.

Hamyr blinks at me, his mind sharp enough to understand exactly what I'm not saying, and he mumbles, "Your *mate*. If the Sol King asks about her, I'm to say…that the witch is your mate?"

I let out a deep breath. "Chosen by the Fates themselves. Whatever rumors reach his ears of her treatment, he can rest assured that I am obedient to the Fates' commands and will take her as my wife."

He leaves, and when Tyton lets down his magic, I see the task to the end. Hamyr will hold my confidence to his dying breath, but if I want the gossip mills to do their work, I need other ears to stumble on the news.

"Tyton, take over the guard shift from Tauron. See if you can get my Fates-cursed mate talking—she was watching you closely, and we can use that to our advantage."

My cousin bows to me, a smirk tugging at his lips as he opens the door and finds both soldiers stationed there scrambling to change their expressions, mouths gaping and eyes wild. The entire castle will know by nightfall, as will my uncle the moment a spy can reach him.

The regent's herald arrives one week later.

The high fae male is dressed in my uncle's colors, a mockery of the true Celestial family shades, with lighter blues and ruddy silver. The cloak around his shoulders is lined with ashy furs, and the Celestial crest is pinned at his throat. He stands with an arrogance that all the regent's guards display. He looks down his nose at Yregar Castle and my household with a contempt that he doesn't try to mask. I hate the male, and all of his ilk, but I know how to play these little games like the best of them.

By forcing him to stand before my desk as Roan and I ignore him in favor of discussing the progress of the soldiers' training for a full hour. It's petty, but as the herald's hold on his temper grows thinner, Roan's smirk grows wider. Galling these pathetic high fae is the quickest way to force them to slip up, a tactic that has worked for us many times in the past.

When it's clear the male is about to snap, I finally turn away from Roan but keep my eyes on the map in front of me, waving a dismissive hand at the herald and drawling, "Get on with it then, we have better things to do than trade gossip with a lowborn."

Color stains the male's cheeks, my words a very specific

blow. I don't care about bloodlines, but a high fae without a title or a place in a succession tends to be either resourceful or miserable. I cultivate the resourceful—those who want to channel that drive to climb higher within my ranks—with productive tasks. My uncle gives honeyed promises to the miserable, playing on their insecurities to gain their loyalty with the promise of *more* if only they side with him.

With his back straight and a sneer not quite concealed on his face, the herald declares, "His Majesty, the regent of the Unseelie Court and exalted ruler of the Southern Lands, travels with haste to Yregar. The entire Unseelie Court will arrive by nightfall to absolve you of the rumor that has reached Yris— that your mate has been found, and she is a witch. His Majesty, in his mercy, had proclaimed he will execute anyone speaking such treasonous lies about his beloved nephew. He is concerned about such slander against your reputation."

Roan scoffs and ignores the herald's dirty look. As the heir of Snowsong, one of the strongest and oldest families of the Unseelie Court, Roan is untouchable, and there's nothing the regent can do about his contempt. Not unless he succeeds in taking the throne from me.

I'll never allow that to happen.

I meet the herald's gaze with my own, and his eyes widen as he steels himself against the rage there, but I keep my tone level. "I look forward to hosting the court. My home is always open to the esteemed high fae of my kingdom."

The herald bows like he's taken a knife to the gut, clutching his stomach as his back barely bends, and then he stalks out of my chambers with viciousness echoing in his steps. He'll stay overnight and leave at my uncle's command, but if he thinks to lash out at any of my household with that demeanor of his, he's going to find himself sitting in the dungeon beside the witch.

Or bleeding at the end of one of Firna's kitchen knives. My

keeper doesn't suffer the tumultuous moods of any males, not even my own, though she's respectful in how she deals with me.

My stewing is broken by Roan jerking his head toward the door and muttering in the old tongue, "He knows it's not just a rumor. When the court arrives and finds out it's true, he'll use it to gain more favor."

Roan's been in a foul mood since he found out that Airlie went down to speak to the witch without a guard or her husband to protect her. Even with the thick iron bars between them, there were at least a dozen dangers for his heavily pregnant wife to face on such a task, and the two guards being killed with no weapon to be found only sent his mood to the very depths of Elysium.

I can't bear to go down there and lay eyes on the witch again myself, the tug of the Fates in my chest and my body reacting to her nearness a torture I won't suffer needlessly. My cousins have taken to learning what they can from her instead, and Tyton was the one to discover she can touch the iron implements we've been using against her without lasting damage, if any occurs at all. The cell contains her because of the lock and the guard, not the iron, and she isn't buckling under the torturous conditions because iron doesn't harm her as it should.

It's clear she isn't just a witch. Whoever she is, wherever she's come from, she's far stronger than any of her kind that we've encountered. The lack of witch markings should have been our first indicator, and I'm determined not to miss any further clues to her scheming.

"None of the families will change sides. If they haven't before now, our plan here will work," Roan says, coming out of his mood enough to offer his assurances, but I merely shrug. There's only one real option for me now, but the confrontation with the court will be easier if my closest confidants are in agreement.

I wait until I can no longer hear the herald's retreating footsteps before I answer, "Your focus is keeping Airlie safe and calm. Tauron and Tyton will guard the witch, and I'll play the games of the court. With any luck we'll satisfy them with one party, and they'll scurry back to Yris tomorrow, maybe the day at worst."

Roan curses under his breath and shakes his head, moving to stare out the window toward the horizon as though he can see the Unseelie Court descending upon us. He sticks with the old language but chooses his words carefully. "Tauron and Tyton will have to stand guard for her safety, not the court's. She's the missing piece to your ascension. Without your mate, the regent becomes king. He married his mate and produced an heir— Neyva's death doesn't impede his claim."

My aunt, Sari's mother, died in childbirth, a fact none of us want to consider right now, and the mention of her name brings another scowl to Roan's face.

My own gut clenches, over Airlie's condition, and at the thought of all these years of patience ending with the loss of my throne—and the kingdom with it—to my uncle. "We won't let him win, Roan, not after everything we've been forced to endure this far. Keep your focus on Airlie and leave the rest to me."

Roan rubs a hand over his brow as his entire body emanates stress, murmuring in a defeated tone, "I don't understand what the Fates are doing. I don't know how much more we can take."

I know he held out hope that finding my mate would break the curse before his child arrived, and now it's been snatched away from him. Every time I shut my eyes, I can see Airlie's face as she held the body of their dead son in her arms, and I can't blame him for losing faith. My own regrets continue to grow, guilt clawing through my gut at failing Airlie with this witch the Fates have thrown at me. Though I continue to do everything I can to protect our people, it's never enough.

We need to be rational and not lose our heads at the horrors still to come.

I take a deep breath and push aside the paperwork on my desk, then take the wine glass and empty it in one go. "The regent can't kill the witch without the backing of the Unseelie Court. Airlie's mother won't side with him, and neither will a handful of the others. To go against the Fates, he needs the support of the most established families, and he doesn't have it."

Roan mutters under his breath, "Too many games and guesses for me—it's a stupid way to live our lives, bound to the whims of others."

I step around the table and join him to stare at the withered pastures of Yregar. Even the palace grounds look dead and empty. There's no longer an orchard or a medicinal garden, nor any sort of garden for the kitchen. Nothing will grow in the Southern Lands, and if something doesn't change soon, my home will be renamed the Wastelands.

That's still preferable to it being ruled by the witches.

Shaking the frustration out of my limbs, I leave Roan and go down to the dungeon. My ill-fated mate never leaves my mind, the silver of her eyes the first thing I think of when I wake and the last thing I imagine before I slip into a begrudging slumber. The solid wall she's placed between our minds stands firm, but I'm convinced she's found a way to call to me regardless of the block. The Fates grow impatient with me, pulling at my chest at every waking moment, but I ignore them for now. I've been receiving updates of her quiet compliance within the cell but I haven't been able to bring myself to face the reality of my mate.

Until now, when I have no choice.

In a matter of hours, my uncle and the rest of the Unseelie Court will arrive at Yregar, and I will have to plead my case with them. I may have shown Roan nothing but confidence, but in reality I know there is every chance the regent will use this situation to make his next big move. Actually, I'm certain he will.

As I feel the earth envelop me and crush my senses, I expect to hear mumbling or another form of madness. It doesn't matter that, by all accounts, the witch is faring better down here than any we've brought before; my experience says that her sanity should be crumbling under the weight of the castle.

And yet there is nothing.

I meet Corym's eyes where he guards over the witch and nod to him in dismissal, waiting until he's disappeared before I step up to the iron cell door, finding my Fates-cursed mate sitting against the stone with her eyes closed. The bucket of water that was brought down to her this morning still looks full, and the plate of scraps from the kitchen has been picked over some. She looks in perfect health, better even than when we brought her here, a plumpness to her cheeks and a sheen to her matted hair. I've become adept at reading the condition of those living in squalor, and she's flourishing.

The hunt for the missing dagger came up empty, even after Tyton searched her with his magic. There's no sign that she returned to the Southern Lands with anything but the small satchel the mercenaries had taken from her. Clothing, a sleeping roll, and a small purse of Seelie gold—none of the contents gave us any clues about her life before she set foot back on Unseelie soil.

Her hair is in need of a good wash, and her hands are blackened from the grime of the cell, but there's still a quiet, serene sort of beauty to her. I catch myself leaning toward her, that thread pulling at me until I have to take a step back to regain control, muttering a curse at myself. It's a betrayal to my people to even notice such a thing, and shame curls in my gut until every inch of my body burns with it.

I want to crush her.

I want to spread her out on a torture table and pull her to pieces slowly, excruciatingly, until there is nothing beautiful left of her. I want to take every piece of frustration and grief and horror that has been given to me by this war and unleash it on her until there's nothing left.

I want to *destroy* her.

"If you want me dead so badly, Savage Prince, then maybe you should just kill me."

Her voice is too melodic. The way that it wraps around me and embraces me so wholly is like a dark seduction, a siren's call. It's different from the voice that haunted my mind for centuries, the one I still long for. She's not just more mature— the hesitance is now gone, the way that she once responded with wonder to my every encouragement. Long ago, through the connection of our shared fate, I could feel her drawing closer to me just as I reached for her, but there's no sign of her fighting the pull of the Fates as I'm forced to do. She radiates calm as I struggle to hold myself in check.

The leather of my gloves creak as my hands fist at my sides.

Her eyes finally open and focus on them, then shift up to my face. She's expressionless, seeming unaffected by me even as she wrecks every last wall I've built around myself, ruining the façade of a composed and rational prince who deserves the throne.

When I look at her, I am the Savage Prince.

Roan tried to convince me to clean her up before I take her to face the entire Unseelie Court, but the thought of showing her any sort of kindness fills me with rage, even though it would serve my own purposes.

"Tonight, you will be presented to the Unseelie Court, and a decision will be made as to what we are going to do with you."

She stares at me as though I haven't spoken. Her gaze is

unwavering, those magnetic eyes taking in every inch of me and finding me wanting. There's nothing inherently disrespectful about her expression, nothing terrorizing or combative, and yet it feels like another war that I am losing, as though my throne is slipping from my fingers the longer that she stares.

"You'll have to wear the gag again. It doesn't matter how much we teach the Unseelie Court about the dangers of witches, they only truly feel safe as long as you can't speak."

One perfectly shaped eyebrow slowly rises, and finally some emotion creeps onto her face as a smirk slowly tugs at the corner of her mouth. "They think I need words to be able to cast against them? My, how far the mighty Unseelie high fae have fallen from the way of the world."

My temper flares. I've had control of my anger and rage for centuries, and yet she has torn it down with nothing more than a few words spoken in her barbed-honey tone.

"You would do well not to speak like that, witch. It doesn't help your case to stay alive."

She shrugs at me, linking her fingers together as she clasps her hands in her lap. "I don't need a case to stay alive. I have the Fates on my side. If you want your kingdom to survive, you'll do as they ask."

Dual footsteps thump on the staircase, and I don't need to turn my head to know who's coming. Soft cursing confirms that Tauron has dragged his brother along to witness the spectacle of me facing down my Fates-cursed mate.

He studies me, and when he sees the scowl on my face, he says, "Are you getting any sense out of it, or just petulant looks?"

"She," Tyton corrects his brother, "You can't call her an 'it' in front of the Unseelie Court if we're going to convince them to let Soren marry her."

Tauron comes to stand next to me and shakes his head at us

both. "Do we want to convince them? What we should really be doing is convincing the Fates that this is a terrible fucking idea."

If only that were an option.

Tyton glances between us and steps closer to the bars. "Tell us your name. We can't very well stick you in front of the regent and his vultures if we don't know your name."

It didn't even occur to me that she has a name.

"Rooke," she says simply, and when none of us respond, that eyebrow of hers quirks right back up. "You're not going to ask me which coven I hail from?"

It doesn't matter. The only witches we know are the raving masses of Kharl's armies and the High Witch himself—any coven name she gives us would be as useless to me as the regent's guards.

Tauron scoffs at her. "Like we give a good Fates-fuck about witch covens. In the end, once we have what we need from you, you'll be dead and it won't matter which cursed womb you crawled out of." With that, he enters the cell and secures the chains around her wrists once more.

Tauron shows no hesitation as he drags her up the stairs behind us, but Tyton is acting strangely, glancing back at her every so often. Unease settles deeply into my bones but I push it out of my mind, just as I fight to push her out as well.

Now is not the time to question my cousin about it.

My uncle arrives as the sun goes down around us, darkness enveloping the castle windows as the halls begin to glow with the magic of the First Fae, the orbs of their making floating at the ceilings in a wondrous act of magic we no longer have access to. I hear the Unseelie Court flow into the Grand Hall, laughter sounding off the walls as though the harrying trip here through the fae door was an adventure rather than a risky endeavor. It galls me to know they use the waning magic so frivolously, so uncaring of the effects on our people once that magic finally disappears for good.

Yregar Castle may not be as big or as comfortable as the castle at Yris, but it's home for me and mine. I'd never leave it if I had the choice. When I take the throne my household is expected to move to Yris and, though I'd never step foot in that castle again if I had the choice, I'm looking forward to taking it from my uncle.

The floor of my parents' chambers were still wet when he moved into them, the maids barely finished scrubbing away the blood, and my gut clenches at the memory. I remember the feel of Firna's hand wrapped tightly around my arm as she kept my balance for me, her other hand wiping my forehead as I vomited on one of the ancestral Celestial rugs, as old as the castle itself.

Yregar Castle is my home now.

An entire portion here is occupied by high fae who are loyal to me, though outside of my trusted inner circle, and the riverside wing they reside in is large enough that they're able to live there, comfortable, secluded, and happy without much interference. Airlie will go over to the large reception rooms there every other week to check in on them and I'll go to sort out any grievances that have arisen, but I mostly leave them to Firna to corral. Most of those high fae avoid the Grand Hall and the village unless there's a spectacle they want to witness firsthand to fuel their gossip mill, such as the Unseelie Court coming to visit.

The castle is thrumming with extra bodies, with movement and life, and there isn't a single high fae within the walls of Yregar who is willing to miss this display.

I'm careful to lead my cousins and the witch through the service hallways to avoid any areas where the court might have strayed, and when we finally reach my chambers, we find Roan and Airlie waiting for us there. Roan steps in front of his wife, shielding her from the witch, but she scoffs at him playfully and slips her arm through his, placing herself firmly at his side once more.

"You're cutting it a bit close, aren't you? We're not going to be able to clean her up and get down to the Grand Hall before the regent demands to see her."

And throws a tantrum are the words she would normally tack on the end of that sentence, but we're choosing our words with care now that the court is here.

I shake my head at her, ignoring the creature entirely. "I'm not bathing her. None of us are—she can go down like this."

Airlie's petite nose wrinkles, and she stares at the witch sorrowfully, but only for selfish reasons. "I'm not asking you to bathe her for her sake but for mine! I don't want to suffer from that stench. Who knows how long the questioning will last, and I'm going to have to smell *that* the whole time?"

The witch's scent isn't actually that bad, and the idea of bathing her twists something in my stomach.

Memories flood back to me…the playful tone of her voice, the soft moans she sent to me through our mind link, her willing submission to every last one of my demands as she pleasured herself while she bathed.

My blood heats…and rage incinerates any remnants of the lust that once lingered.

I don't want to offer her any kindness or pleasantries. I want her to suffer in the worst way, and as the Fates have said I cannot simply kill her and end my own torture, this will have to do.

"You don't have to come down with us, cousin. You can return to your rooms, and I'll make excuses for you. If your mother has anything to say about it, I'll deal with her."

Airlie scoffs again, and Roan tucks her closer to his side, his hand gently rubbing her arm. He never touches her belly now that it is once again round with child, not the way he did before. It's as if he's detached himself entirely from what's to come to save his own sanity.

I still have no idea how Airlie convinced him to try again.

She stares down her nose at me like I'm an unruly child. "You're going to need all the help you can get in there, and we both know it. Besides, if you're going to use the curse to convince them you must marry her, having me with you will only help your cause."

Tauron grumbles under his breath, the chains clinking in his hands. "We don't need any help with that cause, they should all remember what's at stake, and if they don't, then they shouldn't hold a seat on the Unseelie Court."

His words are close to treason, and when I shoot him a look of warning, he bows his head respectfully. I know there's a part of him that would happily go out in a blaze of glory if only he could tell each and every last member of the Unseelie Court what he really thinks of them.

Sometimes I feel that way as well.

"She looks healthy, doesn't she?" Airlie remarks, bending down a little as she squints at the witch. "That's not going to help your case. They'll have just passed through the village and seen how starved the part-bloods and lower fae who are loyal to us are, only to find a plump witch waiting for them." She pauses, looking thoughtful. "I wonder where the witches get their food. Everything is dying—where are they finding provisions?"

Two questions I cannot answer and that we've spent a lot of time hunting for ourselves, but I can answer in this context well enough.

"She came from the Seelie Courts. The Northern Lands clearly still have food."

The real question is…why did she return?

Is it only her fate that brought her home, or does she have family amongst the sea of maniacal witches, some vendetta she is here to enact? I can imagine a dozen different options, and any of them could bring about our doom if we handle her the wrong way.

I'm aware of what's at stake if I get this wrong.

Roan stares at the witch with both distrust and apprehension, but there's no longer contempt in his gaze. He's well aware that, when I take the throne, if the Fates have their way, this will be his queen regardless of her heritage and the war we fight against her people. While Roan has never quite understood the complexities of the Unseelie Court, thanks to growing up far away from it, he does have an intense loyalty to the crown and to me. He's never faltered, not even before he and Airlie found each other and were blessed in marriage, thanks to the Fates.

"At least wash her hands and clean her face, Soren. It's not just herself and her race that she'll be representing. The Fates have chosen her as your mate, and that means something, whether you like it or not."

I have always listened to the advice of my oldest and most trusted friend, but for this, I can't even attempt it.

The witch is ruining everything.

We stand and stare at her a few minutes longer, and then the herald arrives once again. "His Majesty the Regent is eager to hear an explanation. He's calling for you now, Prince Soren."

The only thing that male is eager for is my downfall.

I nod my head curtly, and then I take the chains from Tauron and prepare myself to face my treacherous uncle and the salivating vultures of the Unseelie Court.

NINE

ROOKE

There's no sign of poverty or desperation within the long and spacious walls of Yregar Castle.

As the Savage Prince and his small, close-knit group walk me through the palace, I feel like an interloper on some sort of ethereal party ground. My feet scuff the glittering white marble floors, and I imagine a trail of dirt being left behind, thanks to the terrible state I'm in. My temper begins to wake down deep in my gut, like the slow smolder of a fire. It's not yet raging, but for the first time in a very long while, there's something there.

The royal colors of House Celestial cover every surface that my gaze touches, a deep navy blue with trimmings of silver like soft glimmers of snow on a clear winter night. Star motifs are painted and embroidered on everything, clearly marking the castle as an estate of the Celestial Family, and there's a tug of familiarity in my chest. The Seelie Court is ruled by the Sol King, every inch of his properties covered in gold and suns, the heat and the glory of the lands something to behold. The tug turns into an ache.

I miss my brother and my friends.

I let my gaze drift back to the Celestial finery, and the longer I look, the more my skin begins to itch. It's beautiful and luxurious, but at the sight of it all, that fire sparks deep in my gut like a breath of wind on embers and ignites. The high fae covet their wealth and their beauty, their thrones and their bloodlines, all while the land has turned to dust. Kharl's rhetoric would've never gained popularity with the covens if the high fae had remembered and honored their traditions. The resentments would never have taken root if the weight of the rites hadn't been carried solely by my kind.

Kharl might have been the one to shove the witches over the edge of madness, but the high fae led them to that edge.

There are oil paintings of past kings and queens, relics of times long since turned to dust. Beautiful faces all reminiscent of each other, a long and prolific lineage of high-fae rulers. The servants and maids we pass all look to be in good health, something that is usually an indicator of a good ruler but only makes the despair of the village even more stark. It's all a façade, a beautiful mask covering the truth of this land.

The high fae dance and drink and dine while the rest of the kingdom withers away.

The winding hallways slowly get busier as we work our way through the center of the castle to meet with the regent and the Unseelie Court. The Savage Prince stayed firm in his decision not to let me clean myself up, and I find the numbness that washed over me the moment I decided to journey back to the Southern Lands thawing out.

Shame curls in my chest until every breath shreds my lungs like broken glass.

The filth covering me might not be my fault, but my cheeks flush regardless, bile churning in my gut. The Savage Prince's loathing and ire is one thing, but parading me around in this condition might be his best attempt at torturing me so far. Fates be damned—I faced Ureen and survived the end of the world just to be forced to endure *this*? My magic tingles at the end of my fingers, my mind filling with the voices of all those I love who would gut this high-fae male for treating me like this, royal or not.

It's a futile fantasy to hold. Pemba, Hanede, Stone, Cerson, a hundred others—I left them all behind to fulfill my fate, and this is what I've been dealt. There are two options left to me, but I was never one to simply give up. Not without a fight.

I'm able to seep magic to hide the smell of my unwashed skin, but there's not much I can do about my appearance without rousing suspicions. I lift my head and take a deep breath, calm washing over me once more. This isn't my doing. Someday, the Savage Prince will have to explain his actions to his ancestors and mine when he's carried to Elysium on the smoke of the funeral pyres. I'd rather be cursed to walk the Fates alone for all time and never feel the peace of Elysium than bring such shame to my mother and father, and in this, my heart is clear.

I might be forced to walk through the castle on display as a dirty witch, but I hold my head high and unrepentant, never cowering from their derision.

I'm sure these people have forgotten what it's like to mix with lower fae outside of the Unseelie Court, the rituals and rites of the high fae and the lower fae nothing but a fable of the past. There are many things that go wrong when a society becomes insulated like this, and the starving villagers outside the castle walls are proof of that.

I think I'm about to get a vicious example of just what can go wrong.

We stop before a high-fae female who gasps at me and snaps, "You can't be serious! You can't bring *that* before His Majesty, the Regent. She's probably carrying diseases."

I look at the female who's spoken, the family resemblance like an echo across my mind. I'm quickly learning that all of the Celestials look far too similar to ever be mistaken for any other family.

"Mother," the heavily pregnant female says with a cutting tone, "the Fates have decreed that this is Soren's mate, and whether you and the rest of the Unseelie Court like it or not, we cannot go against the Fates. Not unless you're all ready to fight the Ureen." She rolls her shoulders back, and her perfect posture is a move of its own in this war of words. How she can stay calm and move freely with the curse wrapped so tightly around her body is a mystery to me, the sight of it sours my stomach.

Her mother makes the sign of the Fates against her chest, as if to ward off such a future, horror etched into every inch of her face. It's the first sign of intelligence I've seen at the Unseelie Court. I don't suspect we'll see much more today. A competent ruler would not have let his kingdom fall into this state.

"We're cursed. We have to be," she mutters.

The pregnant female laughs again. "Of course we're cursed, Mother. There's no question about that, but maybe if we try to *do* something about it, it won't be the end of the Unseelie high fae."

Her mother makes another sign of the Fates before slipping into the room in front of us, muttering under her breath about evil, disobedient children and the end of time.

I glance at the high-fae princes but it's as though they've become a solid wall around me. What I assumed about this dynamic before was clearly wrong, and my perceptions of them shift in my mind. They're shallow and thoughtless royals, cruel and selfish high fae, as most tend to be, but there's more under the surface.

I don't want to see it.

I don't want them to be an exception to the rule. I wanted to hold on to the whispers and assumptions of the lower fae and not look past the cold façade. I was going to hide in the dungeons of Yregar, licking the wounds my soul still bears from the Fate Wars, until the rest of my fate came to call. My heart aches, and I want nothing more than to rest down there in the cramped cell, to share my magic with the earth beneath me, to be nothing more than a creature of the dark. A root buried deep, sustaining the life above.

I don't want to be dragged into the light of day, to learn about the complexities of these people, to have any empathy in my heart. I went to the Seelie Court and learned better than the whispers; the same is more than possible here too, but they've done nothing to deserve that empathy from me.

I just want to be left alone.

The soldiers at the door hesitate before bowing their heads to their prince and opening the door. I'm struck by their behavior. Even the maids who move around us are tense as they glance our way, but not because of me. It seems that the Savage Prince isn't just whispered about in the Seelie Court; the rumors must run rife in his own kingdom as well. His family's concerns about him bringing home a witch mate go beyond the ramifications of the war; it's about his ability to take the throne with the support of his people. Without it, the regent may keep the throne for good.

Each of them seems calm now, as they haven't been staring at me with such loathing. The only sign of weakness is the way that the princess holds her husband's arm and the gentle way he cradles her against his side, his hand slipping around her to cup her hip.

He treats her tenderly, but it's glaringly obvious to me that he is purposefully avoiding the babe within her womb, a detachment that comes from a specific form of grief.

This is not the first baby they have lost.

Back in the forest, before my family was murdered, I trained from a very young age in the delicate art of midwifery. Before I went to the Seer to receive my fate, I assumed I'd stay in the Ravenswyrd Forest forever, healing anyone who came to us and specializing in midwifery care. There's nothing so incredible to me as helping bring new life into the world, and though my duties didn't allow for many opportunities, I did attend several births during my years there.

My mother told me I had a gift for it.

I can read a situation and tell exactly what a patient needs, preemptively providing for them in their most vulnerable hours. Mother said my gift of coaxing babies gently from their mothers came from the Fates themselves. I delivered my first baby by accident at thirteen, attempting to help when my mother was busy with another birth. I unwrapped the umbilical cord from around the little babe's neck and breathed life into its lungs, and the first cry almost brought me to my knees.

I wonder who attended the princess's previous birth and if they knew how to do such things.

As the doors to the Grand Hall open, I feel the circle close in around me. My shoulders tighten as I prepare for a fight, but they become an impenetrable wall. Each of the princes positions himself so that the princess and I are surrounded, cocooned within their protective stance. Physically, I'm not worried about any of the high fae. I can hold my own in hand-to-hand combat; I was a soldier in the Sol Army after all. But they're not an enemy to take lightly.

All of the high fae are tall. I'm at least a head shorter than the princess. I choose not to be intimidated; instead I pull myself up straighter, preparing for the battle that these males and females are clearly expecting to face.

I know what it means to stand my ground and defend it.

The herald announces the Savage Prince's arrival and, without a word, we move forward as one. The chains around my wrists clink as they knock together, the only sound our group makes even as whispers start up around the crowd. Stepping into the Grand Hall is like walking into a sheet of ice, and not just because of the freezing glares from around the room. Everything my gaze touches feels as if it's a reflection of the snow. Pale skin, blue eyes, hair so blonde it looks like moonlight. It's a sea of the same image, over and over again, and I feel as though I've been cast into its waters as I stare around at them all.

The more I study them, the easier it becomes to see who sides with the Savage Prince and who backs his uncle. They wear their allegiance in the colors they've chosen, the Celestial blue and the slightly off-shade version of it, and though the colors mingle together in the crowd, there's a clear divide in the way each side regards the heir to the throne.

There are dozens of groups bunched together staring at us with fear and loathing shining brightly in their eyes, and it's not just directed at me. They look at their own prince and heir to the throne as though he's a problem, one that needs to be dealt with viciously and swiftly.

The other half of the court stare with horror and pity, looking at the prince as though he has been given a death sentence, and their country right along with him.

Kharl's army has broken the spirit of these people—broken the high fae in a way I did not think possible. Starvation, death and the culling of an entire generation…they're on their last legs, and the Fates have decided to test them once more.

This time, I'm sure it will push them over their limit. The Savage Prince had said so himself.

I can't see the regent, but a shudder ripples down my body at the sound of a sinister tone. "Nephew, what horror have you brought before us now?"

The regent looks like his nephew in a physical way, but the longer my eyes spend picking him apart, the more my skin crawls. The Savage Prince is hauntingly beautiful; the Fates don't have to pull me toward him for me to recognize that, but there's something honest about his face. His eyes are cold but sure, and the scar cutting through his face is a testament to his abilities, every inch of his body keenly honed for the protection of his people.

The male sitting before us is beautiful in the way of a snow-capped mountain, waiting for a single word to bring down an avalanche of destruction. Everything about him is perfect and untouched, no scars or signs of hardship. He's never lifted a finger to do a day's work in his life, I'm sure of it. There's no sword hanging at his side, despite every other male in the Grand Hall wearing one, even if just for decorative purposes. He thinks himself above the defense of his people, or he's pretending to be.

His eyes narrow on his nephew, a smile curling his lips in a mocking fashion, and my jaw tightens.

There's something very *wrong* about him and the farce of him sitting on the Unseelie throne. The colors of his banners are off, and the way he's positioned his advisors is unintuitive— nothing about him sitting there pleases the eye. I don't need the uncomfortable energy that radiates from my Fate scars to tell me that this male is not a good person.

I've spent time in the presence of a lot of powerful men, males who, I would argue, are far more powerful than the regent sitting before me, but none of them lounged on a throne the way that he does. The Sol King has never been so disrespectful to his court, never held such that my teeth ache at the sight of it.

There's sarcastic air to him as he looks us over, a grating and belittling way that he stares down the future king of his country. Realization settles deep in my gut that this male has no intention of handing over the throne, and the Savage Prince's loathing toward me makes a little more sense. To be so loyal to the Fates and determined to marry at their command but so viciously set against me had seemed peculiar, and here is why.

I'm just another obstacle he must overcome.

The regent scowls down at us all, the platform that the throne sits on giving him the high ground, though he doesn't use it wisely.

His voice is rich and smooth, but it makes the itch on my body even worse when he says, "A *witch*? A witch you didn't kill immediately? We've had this conversation before, nephew. It's treason to keep them alive."

The Savage Prince doesn't cower from his uncle's scorn or his sharp gaze. I'm not sure of the royal etiquette for such a situation—the Unseelie Court is different from that in the Northern Lands—but the other princes and princesses around us lower their gazes to the ground respectfully.

I do not.

It's foolhardy and disrespectful in ways I have never been before, but if they're all going to hate me for no reason other than my being a witch, I might as well give them something of substance to hate. Seeing the land is broken as it is and feeling its desperate pull on my power has changed something inside me, despite the ice around my heart.

All signs point to this male being at fault for the destruction.

The Savage Prince's tone is cutting and truthful to the end. "I am a loyal servant to the Fates, as we all are. I don't imagine you're suggesting I go against them, are you, Regent?"

A smattering of murmurs rise around the room, small intakes of breath as people realize what he's saying.

Waving a hand theatrically, the regent replies, "Your fate is well known, nephew! To find your mate and save the lands... Are you so sure this witch has a part in that? The guards all said you brought only one female home with you—does the witch know where your mate is?"

The regent is forcing him to say it.

I hear the clinking sound of iron being ground together in the Savage Prince's hand, and I watch his movements closely. The high fae have extraordinary hearing; everyone in the room knows that he is holding on to his anger by a thread right now, and a hush falls over the crowd.

The rumors my brother heard of Prince Soren while searching for information about Kharl and the war had indicated that the moniker the Savage Prince came from his fighting prowess, that he'd become unbeatable on the battlefield and that his swordsmanship was unlike any other in the Southern Lands. In the Northern Lands, this was seen as a very promising sign of the ruler to come.

It's not hard to see that the Unseelie Court does not feel the same way.

Well, not entirely. There are definitely faces amongst the crowd who are staring at the regent with unease clear in their eyes, uncomfortable at this reckless display of power and social standing.

"The Seer was very clear about my fate, down to the moment I found her. There is no question that the witch is my mate and destined to rule this kingdom alongside me," he says. Another ripple runs through the scars on my stomach and back, the Fates chiming in to agree with his words.

I'm the only one who can feel it, of course.

"I would argue that that is definitely treason, Nephew. To even suggest such a thing."

I feel the fae princes around me close ranks without moving. It's in the way their senses heighten as they take notice of where the regent's guards are positioned around us. The only one who does move is the princess, who steps a little closer at her husband's urging. He's careful to position her out of the line of fire should things go as terribly as the malevolence in the room suggests.

The Savage Prince shrugs, playing along with the regent's nonchalant game. "Treason or not, I have never thought myself wiser or more capable than the Fates themselves. I'm surprised that *you* would suggest such a thing."

A scandalized buzz spreads around the audience hall. The Unseelie Court watches as the two most powerful males in the kingdom verbally spar, but I'm more careful about marking where the guards are and whether they're descending upon us. Not that I would do much about it, I'm here only because the Fates have demanded it of me. I'm going to trust that they'll get me through this alive, and if they don't, then I suppose it will be the Savage Prince's responsibility to clean up the mess.

I'm sure he could take on a few Ureen himself but I don't like his chances of pulling together an army from this crowd should the Fates open the sky here the way they did in the Northern Lands.

The regent leans back against the ornate cushions of the throne, the picture of relaxation, which only makes the forced urgency of his words even more obvious. "I would never suggest knowing more than the Fates. However, it cannot be denied that this is all quite shocking, to say the least. You can't expect the Unseelie Court to allow such a creature within our ranks. What if she has been sent by the witches? Will we be forced to surrender to them as some sort of parlay? Do you want to take the throne so badly that you'd give up some of our lands to our enemy after they've taken so much from us already, nephew? Which royal family are you going to leave homeless?"

A careful sidestep from the sweep of a sword, the regent is a master of bending the opinions of his court to his will.

He doesn't believe any of what he's saying, but he's coaxing his nephew further into the light, exposing his inner workings to the court in some grotesque trial. Whatever façade he's created for himself, he thinks it's more palatable than the truth of his nephew and, in the end, none of this is truly about me.

This spectacle is about the regent pointing out the flaws of his flesh and blood so that he can steal the throne from underneath him.

I should care more about this, and yet the same hollow feeling that got me onto the ship to return here still has my body in its grips. I have no sympathy for any of these people. Nothing for the rulers who destroyed the land I once called home, land that still cries out from underneath my feet. That's where I'll be focusing the finite reaches of my power. For all I care, the high fae can destroy each other while I do the real work.

The Savage Prince rolls his shoulders back, his voice unwavering as he says, "There's never been a question of my treatment of witches before, and I have killed more of them than everyone else in this room combined. I have no love for their race, nothing to offer them, not a kind word or a single inch of land."

He looks around the room at each of the princes and princesses, lords and ladies, every last one of the Unseelie Court, before his eyes finally flick down to me, loathing and distaste emanating from him.

"Were the Fates not involved in this situation, I would have killed her on sight, and should I find any opportunity to have a different fate, she will be taken care of. Swiftly and with no mercy."

The regent raises a blond, silvery eyebrow, happy to continue to spin his web of beautiful, confusing words. "That seems rather callous of you, nephew, to be so eager to be rid of a mate, especially one fated to you."

The Savage Prince himself is clear, staring at me, his gaze cold and hard on my own. "If there is any other path the Fates should choose for me, I'll be the first to drag a knife across her throat."

TEN

SOREN

The gazes of the court seem to burn my skin as I stare back at them all, unflinching. I hand the end of the chains to Tauron, ready to get the witch out of my presence and away from the prying, horrified eyes. He pulls on gloves before taking it, then walks the witch out of the Grand Hall without a word, followed by two of my most trusted guards. There's a deep frown on my cousin's face as he turns from me, unhappy about leaving my side when there are so many vipers poised and ready to strike, but he's the best option to take charge of the witch right now.

Roan will not leave Airlie's side, and Tyton is better at holding his temper than his brother is in these situations. He can also read the crowd better than anyone else, and we need all the insight we can get tonight; our options are running thin. The number of spies we've found thanks to the magic Tyton still can access is proof enough that he's needed in this situation.

There's also the small matter of the regent's guards who also make excuses to follow Tauron and the witch out.

He's the best person to protect her all the way down to the dungeons. He'll stay there and watch over her until we're sure that the guards won't make it to the dungeons, slip her poison, or try some other nefarious means to keep my uncle squatting on my father's throne.

I turn back to the regent and leave the monitoring of the room to my cousin and my closest confidant, trusting them with more than just my life. My uncle stares back at me, his eyes edged with a malevolent sort of victory.

He thinks he's won.

Only a few short days ago, I was sure he had won as well, but the last of the fae flowers dying reminded me what we're truly here for. This isn't about whether or not I can stand the sight of the mate the Fates have chosen for me. This is about my kingdom and my people. This is about who will make the best ruler, and I don't need to look around the room at the wanton waste of our very finite resources to know that I'm a better choice than my uncle.

The regent is letting the land die.

He's ignoring every last one of the signs that we're teetering on the edge of survival, and his arrogance—or stupidity— has him truly believing that being high fae is enough to get us through it. Countless people will die if I do not marry the witch, and I have a handful of months left to come to terms with what that marriage is going to look like for me. Royal unions are traditionally held on the winter solstice—only exceptional circumstances have allowed another date to be chosen, and my uncle wouldn't allow a majority vote to pass within the court to move mine. If the wedding is contested and we miss the solstice, I'll have to wait another year, but we don't have another year in us. Our provisions are gone, and the kingdom is at the breaking point. No amount of finery or wine can cover up that fact, despite what the high fae dancing around this room may think.

As the revelry starts up again, the regent smiles at me like a vulture circling an upcoming feast. "Such terrible news for us to return to Yregar for, Nephew. Tell me something positive, so that we might clear this terrible witch out of our minds. I suppose you'll be able to scrub her up and make her into something presentable by the time we see the two of you joining hands in marriage, though I'm not sure how."

Tinkling bells of laughter ring through the air.

I don't need to look to know that Airlie is taking note of every last person joining in, preparing a list of families who shall never be trusted again. We can't afford to lose any more favor, but letting poison into our midst is worse.

"It seems a shame that you have all come so far for bad news. I hate for you to return to Yris so let down but, rest assured, Regent, that I'll do everything in my power to fulfill what the Fates require of me without risking the safety or wellbeing of my people. Your dutiful service to the kingdom will end soon."

A hush falls again, a quiet in which everybody slowly turns toward the regent and readies themselves for the aftermath of my words.

I've always been so careful when dealing with my uncle and his fragile ego, so vigilant in the steps that I have taken in this little game of chess that we're playing. Never letting the court know that I'm aware of his scheming against me, never drawing my own weapons of wit and cunning, doing everything possible to lull him into a false sense of security while I waited for the Fates to deliver me my mate.

This is my first public move against him.

I move back to watch as the court takes to the dance floor, spinning and twirling around in all of their finery. It's easy to pick out those who are loyal to me—the colors of their clothing is the right shade of blue and trimmed with silver in tasteful and delicate ways.

Prince Meridian's voice rises above the crowd, jabbering on about irrelevant things, as always.

"Have you heard the latest news from the south? The Dragonriders have lost confidence in their king. They're attempting to dethrone him and place the prince in his stead.

There isn't an inch of the Dragon Lands that isn't on fire or crushed beneath the beasts they ride—the entire kingdom is falling apart! If those soldiers are allowed to decide what happens within the court, they're all doomed. That's not the way the Fates would have it."

It's a veiled threat, an easy way for the prince to voice his opinion of what's happening within the Unseelie Court without openly saying he thinks me nothing more than a brute, a soldier not capable of making decisions for the highborn. The lack of respect that he has for the males keeping him alive isn't a surprise to me, but it is disgraceful. His brother holds Yrell and barely leaves the castle there but Meridian always did enjoy my uncle's company too much to leave the Court and the endless parties that come with their travels.

His wife clutches his elbow, her tinkling laughter like the sharp point of a dagger to the eardrum. I want nothing more than to do away with them as well.

My aunt, Airlie's mother, Princess Aura, stares at both disapprovingly, smoothing her dress carefully as she looks down her nose at the silver color of Prince Meridian's suit jacket. She is my mother's sister, but they spent their early years separated, due to their age gap and my mother's fated union to the king. Aunt Aura's loyalty to me has everything to do with her obsession with the Celestial bloodline and her own proximity to it and nothing to do with affection for me. The only thing she loved about my mother was that her marriage to the king gave Aura their family seat on the court, the marriage removing my mother's claim to it.

Aunt Aura coveted the position and has fussed over it from the second it passed to her from my maternal grandparents.

She shrugs delicately, smiling at one of the ladies who crowd around and fawn over her. "I should think that the prince is the rightful heir to the throne, and if there are questions about his father's ability to rule, then they should be addressed, should they not? The Dragonriders have always been a reckless bunch—you'd have to be, to ride those beasts. We should hope they keep to their own kingdom and don't ever step foot in the Southern Lands without invitation."

Prince Meridian smirks at her, all teeth and pointed edges, and pushes his wife slowly to one side as he steps closer. "I doubt they'll step foot anywhere. Rather, they'll climb on those beasts and fly here. Have you ever seen a dragon before, Princess Aura? I certainly haven't, but I don't doubt that it would be a whole new challenge for our good prince and his soldiers to fight."

My aunt smiles back at him prettily, outmatching him on every front of this sparring match. "It's a good thing we have such amicable relations with them then, isn't it? A good thing the regent spends so much of his time on peacekeeping efforts to be sure to hold the kingdom safely for his nephew."

I lift my goblet to my lips to cover my smile.

My uncle's supporters have grimace-like smiles on their faces, sneering at the fact they've been forced to travel here to meet a filthy witch.

Aunt Aura may very well be a pain in the ass, but her loyalty is second to none, a trait she shares with her fierce daughter. My uncle doesn't like Aura, her loyalty to me, or the followers she's cultivated cunningly over the years.

He smiles at me, showing off a row of sharp white teeth. "We'll see how your marriage progresses. With your mate in chains, I'm not so sure how you'll convince her to take part in the exalted high-fae ceremony, but I look forward to attending such a *spectacular* event."

Royal weddings are elaborate and ornate, full of finery and rituals that have been handed down since the First Fae came to the Southern Lands. Nuptials amongst high fae are few and far between these days, thanks to the witches' curse preventing new generations of high-fae bloodlines.

I've attended two dozen in my lifetime, and the only wedding I remember fondly was Roan and Airlie's. It was the most extravagant ceremony that I've attended, but with Airlie involved I'd expected nothing less. Aunt Aura had been a nightmare as they'd planned it, the regent had spent countless months on a smear campaign against them both, and Roan's mother had fallen ill only weeks before the ceremony, fighting to stay alive long enough to see her only son wed. Through it all, Roan and Airlie never let anything come between them, each obstacle and trial only bringing them closer together. Their marriage is a testament to the Fates knowing better than anyone else who completes us.

The love that was so apparent between the two of them was something I'd hoped to share with my own mate someday.

The Fates must be laughing.

I step away from my uncle and go to the table of food, bypassing it all and finding a goblet of wine to drain instead. The crowd gives me a wide berth, even my supporters. No one wants to approach the Savage Prince after the spectacle they've just witnessed. I don't blame them; the bloodthirst within me is begging for a fight, anything to burn away some of this frustration.

The wine calms me some and, as I look over the sea of high-fae females and their fancy dresses, my chest tightens. A wedding between the heir to the Unseelie Court and his mate should be the most lavish and extravagant event of our lifetime, no expense spared, and the most joyous occasion the kingdom has ever seen, and yet, looking around the room, I know I'm not the only person who is considering the prospect with nothing but apprehension. My uncle is also right, though I'm loath to admit it.

How the hell will I convince the witch in the basement to consent to such a thing?

For the magic to seal us together and bond our souls, she has to agree to the marriage not only verbally but deep within herself, and the sly look in her eyes says that she's not impressed by me at all. If the witches have sent her here to take over the kingdom by marriage to me, they chose the wrong female for the job.

She hasn't protested our fated union yet, showing only resignation at the prospect and a contempt for me. If that changes and she unveils plans to use her fate for Kharl's war, I'll find some weakness within her to exploit, something to hold over her to ensure her compliance without giving an inch to the witches.

The laws of the Unseelie high fae are clear. I must be married to my mate to take the throne. But there's nothing in the laws that says she must sit beside me and rule as an equal. It doesn't matter what my parents did, or their parents before them—none of them were in this situation.

My fate also never said that she had to stay alive.

Many hours after midnight, I watch as the court devolves into its most debauched state. Their drinking and revelry seem to take on a new intensity, as though they're trying to use up the last of Yregar's provisions. The regent encourages the extravagance as he calls on each of the royal families and questions them extensively, until none of high fae feel safe to leave the hall lest they catch his ire. Instead, they drink until they're stumbling and eat until the tables lie bare, then they call out to the maids to refill the platters with haste, all while I sit at my uncle's side and endure.

There's a tug in my chest from the Fates themselves and I wince.

My magic lies dormant, but I feel it shifting there sometimes, reacting to the Fates' call. Right now it's pulling me toward the dungeon to watch over my mate myself, to be sure that none of my uncle's loyal followers attempt to kill her for him, but doing so would paint a bigger target on my back. Tauron is more than capable of keeping her safe, the iron bars immovable even if the metal doesn't affect her like the other witches we've held there, and my soldiers have the castle hallways as well as the walls covered.

Roan took Airlie back to their rooms shortly after I sent the witch back to her cell, but Tyton still lingers here with me, a goblet of fairy wine in his hands and a sour look on his face as his mother glues herself to his side. Princess Tylla Celestial is a cousin to me on my father's side but removed by several generations. I call her sons "cousin" as a sign of our friendship and not due to the strength of our blood connection.

Her voice is like a death knell to my ears, a pretty sound intended to lure listeners to their own demise. "I do wish your brother had stayed, it's been too long since I spoke to him. If I didn't know better, I'd think he was avoiding me!"

Tauron is absolutely avoiding his mother.

Elyra, one of the maids, steps over to refill my goblet with a bow, and I hide my smirk into the rim as Tyton sends Tylla a sympathetic nod, shielding his brother with a petty display of contriteness. "Of course he's not, Mother, he's just been busy fighting the war. He's an obedient son in all ways, and your loyalty to Prince Soren is reflected in his attention to his duties."

His mother glows at the praise, the crowd around them murmuring their agreement, and she stares at her younger son in delight. She's never figured out that Tyton's loyalties don't lie with her, his kind and loyal words a front to keep her from stalking his brother.

Tylla's ego is smaller than Aura's; she feels real affection for and pride in her sons, but she's still far too concerned with the gossips of the court for Tauron's tastes. She was overjoyed by the frivolity that overtook Tyton at his fate, seeing it as something she could mold into a useful trait for her, something to be bargained with, but Tauron was always headstrong, and his own fate only enhanced that quality, turning him into the surly and unapproachable man he now is.

Tyton's steadfast bond with Tauron means he'll endure their mother's whining and simpering presence as she pushes him for gossip about me and my witch mate. She'll learn all the details she can until she has everything she needs to manipulate the court for her own gain. Her loyalty is to herself, always.

I can't stand any more of it.

I make my excuses to my uncle, the wine he's downing like a dying male finally having dulled his temper, and I leave the Grand Hall behind, stepping out into the clear night and taking a deep breath to clear my head. I barely drank a thing, but the cloying presence of the court clings to my mind like a poisonous essence, influencing my every thought with a knee-jerk reaction of rage. It's not the way to navigate these circumstances—no good decisions can be made with such anger—and I center myself before I move off.

When I reach the barracks, I find them overflowing with bodies, extra males here thanks to the Unseelie Court's arrival. The soldiers' accommodations are tucked into the base of the castle on the east side, where they lie in the shadow of the wall for the majority of the day. It's a dark and gloomy place and one in which most high fae would hate to live, but those who've chosen to pledge their lives and swords to me don't complain. I've never had trouble filling the beds.

I have a room set aside for my own gear, and it takes a

matter of minutes to change out of the stiff and ornate court attire and into training armor. I have a replica of my own sword, weighted perfectly but with a dulled edge. I worked with the blacksmith to get it right, to make sure the swing is identical to my sword.

Forged of Seelie steel with a large blue diamond in the pommel, my sword is a Celestial family heirloom and was given to me by my father the year of his death. Calling it an heirloom makes it seem like nothing but a pretty object, as useless as the royals still dancing in the hall at my household's expense, but my great-grandfather carried the blade when he conquered the kingdoms and united them as the Southern Lands.

It feels like home in my hand and, while the training sword might be the perfect substitute to ensure I don't kill my own soldiers in the training ring, it doesn't sing the same way.

Two steps into the barracks mess hall, I know that the gossip about my mate has already reached the soldiers. Dozens of sorrowful eyes turn my way, these soldiers still awake after guard shifts or preparing to take over soon. They're no less respectful than they were yesterday, but every last one of them appears to be struggling to come to terms with the news.

The sorrow leaves their eyes the moment my own narrow at them. I turn to the commander, waiting there diligently for my orders. It doesn't matter that it's after midnight, that we're entertaining high-fae society, or that there are a dozen other things that the soldiers and I should be doing.

I need this.

My voice is sharp as I snap, "Training starts now. Get all the males dressed and into the yard immediately. It seems I've been away for too long."

ELEVEN

ROOKE

The surly Prince Tauron takes me back to the dungeon, the iron chain wrapped tightly around his fist as he yanks me forward. He doesn't attempt to use any of the side hallways or service entrances, instead walking me through the most populated areas and ignoring the way the entire castle stops to stare at us both. They look at him with pity, as though being so close to me is going to ruin his life, but he ignores them all as his hands jerk the iron chains to get me moving faster.

My memory is better than most, and even with the expansive footprint of the castle and the dozens of winding hallways we take, I map out the path. It's a subconscious habit that was trained into me and has become such an integral part of who I am that I don't even notice I do it anymore. I have no intention of escaping from the dungeon and the magic that flows within the dark and cramped space.

Though the Savage Prince threatened me with death, I don't truly believe he's going to kill me. The Fates have tied his hands; he just doesn't realize that mine are tied just as tightly.

Coming back to the Southern Lands was the last thing I wanted to do.

The high fae that walk the halls here do nothing to thaw out the frost around my heart and mind. None of them look deserving of salvation or mercy; they all look like the villains in this story. The Grand Hall has banquet tables overflowing with food and drink, a gluttony of provisions, when everyone else in the land is starving.

I pity them all a little more.

As we descend the staircase, I notice the taut lines of the prince's shoulders, the way that he's holding himself very carefully, and his gait as he walks me down to the cells.

He hates it down here.

The air must feel suffocating to him; unable as he is to tap into his own magic to understand what the earth is crying out for, it must feel like a vise around his chest. The high fae have fallen so far from the way of the world—as far as the witches of the south have, just in drastically different ways. The Unseelie witches chose to turn away from the Fates and the order of nature, but the high fae simply forgot what they're supposed to do. I knew this before I left the Ravenswyrd Forest. Generations have passed since the high fae stopped practicing their rituals, and even in our isolated home, the Favored Children knew.

If the high fae hadn't lost access to their magic, Kharl's evil would never have been able to spread the way it has.

After he shoves me into the cell, the prince unlocks the iron bands from my wrists. Then his gloved hand shoots out to grip one of my elbows hard enough to bruise and yanks the arm up so that he can inspect my skin.

Jerking me forward until he's looming over me, he snarls, "Why isn't it burning you? Why are you unmarked from this iron, even though Soren's dagger seared you? Tell me, witch."

He knows my name, and the gall of him to continue to ignore it bites at me. I owe this male nothing, not my truth or my respect, so I simply raise an eyebrow at him.

His eyes are icy cold and malevolent as he bends down to stare at me, his face close to mine as he inspects every inch of my dirty features. Antipathy curls his lip.

"We both know you can take the chains off—you killed two high fae soldiers without a scratch to show for it. You're down here pretending you're nothing but a meek little mouse, but I see through the lie. What other games are you setting up? Play them with me, witch, I'm not such an easy opponent. Merrick and Lysen were caught unawares. I won't be."

The absolute *nerve* of this high fae.

To keep me as a prisoner in these dungeons, parade me around the Unseelie Court unbathed and appearing broken, and still *he* accuses *me* of misconduct.

I take a slow step backwards into the cell and away from him, then another, and another, until my back hits the cell wall. His eyes narrow as I slowly slide down to sit once more, assuming the same position I've been in for the long days I've been held here. Ignoring him, I take a deep breath and settle into the dark embrace of the cell and the land beneath it.

When it's clear he's going to keep standing there, I answer, "You obviously don't know much about magic or witches if you're asking me stupid questions. Maybe you should read some history books…or is that beyond the Unseelie high fae? I suppose a royal like yourself would get someone else to read them for you."

His eyebrows creep lower and lower until he looks as though he's plotting my death at his own hands. "That's not the way to win my favor. You're our prisoner, you should be trying to convince me not to kill you, not pissing me off even more."

I shrug at him and then let my eyes slip shut, the ultimate dismissal and the only one I have at my disposal. "It's not my job to teach you about the ways of the world, prince. You'll have to figure it out for yourself."

He yanks the cell door shut and locks it before giving it a tug just to be sure it's secure.

I open my eyes just a crack to observe him. He's so sure that my ability to touch the iron won't aid my escape if the cell door is locked, and if nothing else had tipped me off to their underestimation of me and their ignorance of magic, that would have done it. He steps a little farther away and grabs the small, rough-hewn stool each guard has been sitting on and places it on the ground across from the cell door.

The surprising part is that he sits facing me, arms crossed, and continues to speak, none of the surly silence I prefer from him to be found.

"The mercenaries' chains burned you, so I'd wager it takes prolonged exposure to inflict damage. You have some sort of resistance to iron, but the bars here will keep you secure. Tell me where you hail from, witch. Convince me to keep you alive."

A smirk stretches across my lips. "I will convince you of nothing, and I've already freely given you my name. You've offered me nothing in return."

He looks around slowly, the torchlight outlining the silver-blond of his hair like a halo. He's as beautiful as the rest of them, but there's a cruelty inside of him. A dark and twisted fire flickers in the pits of his eyes, one that has burned long enough to do lasting damage. He's just as dangerous as the Savage Prince, of that I am sure.

"I don't have to give you anything. I'm sure that you'd rather not be tortured. How long do you think you'll last without food? I would rather spare your portion for someone who deserves it."

I'm not sure who could possibly deserve the slops from the kitchen, though I'm sure there's livestock or a kitchen pup that's missing out, thanks to me. His words don't hold any real threat, no matter his intentions.

The earth will not let me starve.

As reluctant as I might have been to come back, the land has welcomed me home. I might be more comfortable with a full

181

belly, but most of my life has been a test of my limits, and going hungry is not going to break me.

The more I ignore him, the hotter his temper flares. "You look like every other witch we've hunted down. I don't even have to close my eyes to know what you'll look like when we cleave your head from your shoulders. The moment the Fates have been satisfied, Soren will do it himself, but it doesn't matter to me whether it's my hand or his swinging the sword— being present at your death will be enough."

My head rolls back on my shoulders and my eyes open as wide as slits for him. "Aren't you a delightful creature? I'm not sure why I was expecting more from a prince of this land. I've been nothing but polite and genial to the lot of you, and yet that courtesy has been returned with threats of violence and deprivation. It's my own fault. I shouldn't have expected better of the Unseelie high fae."

I'm poking at him, frustrated to be trapped with him instead of his silent and—mostly—harmless brother. Tyton's questions are intrusive and petulant, but they're not a useless, never-ending attack with no intention of accepting my answers. If Tauron is to watch over me for the evening, I'm not going to be able to connect with the land in peace.

He cocks his head, considering me a little too keenly. "You keep pointing out that I'm Unseelie, but so are you. I guess you've spent quite a lot of time across the seas in the Seelie Court. You've come back to the Southern Lands with an idea of your 'right' to live here, but you have none. Every witch in the kingdom will be wiped out by the end of the war. You'll be nothing more than a footnote in those history books you mention. Perhaps you should have stayed in the Northern Lands with your precious Seelie fae."

For someone so friendly with a Seelie high-fae prince, he certainly doesn't seem to respect the rest of the Seelie much, but I shrug back to him. "I returned because my fate required me to. You should be grateful. That Savage Prince you're so loyal to can't ascend to the throne without me, can he? It seems as though I'm doing you all a favor by sitting here peacefully in this cell, and in typical Unseelie high-fae fashion, you have nothing for me in return, no gratitude or welcome. Nothing but selfish taunts and hollow threats of death. Pathetic, the lot of you."

As the night creeps closer to its end, the sun not too far away, Tauron calms the fury roiling within him, and some of the tension eases from the cell. His eyes never waver from me, no longer seething but wary all the same.

It's clear that he's not here to get information from me, merely to guard. Why he could possibly think I would try to escape with the entire Unseelie Court dancing upstairs is beyond me, but I let my head fall back against the stone once more and consider the insights the night has given me.

The animosity between the regent and his nephew was palpable, a living, breathing thing within the hall that no one could possibly ignore, and it answered a lot of questions I've had as to why the Unseelie Court would keep a rightful heir from the throne for the sake of an archaic law.

The Seelie Court upholds many traditions and has never lost the use of their magic, but they are quick to adapt in times of need. When the Fates tore open the sky and the high-fae soldiers took catastrophic losses, the Sol King changed the laws himself, no votes required, and the lower fae and part-bloods took up arms at his command. The lines of succession are at his discretion, and his court is not concerned with things like marriages and heirs.

It's peculiar to me that the Unseelie high fae are holding so tightly to this tradition and yet have let so many others slip, their use of magic being the most obvious and shocking. Magic is intrinsic to me, so deeply embedded within my flesh and bones that the thought of not accessing it is inconceivable. The high fae are built the same way. They use magic differently, of course, and they relate to it differently. They cast in stark contrast to the way that the witches do, tied to themselves and the Fates instead of being rooted to the earth and a connection to the land, but magic is just as vital to the high fae as it is to me. Their place in the cycle of nature might be opposite to mine, but it's still there, keeping the balance.

They're still partly to blame for the way that the earth is dying.

I feel the ground call to me, asking that I open a vein to bleed directly into it and to give to it so that it might give back to me, but to do so in front of the high-fae prince would only spark his suspicions.

He'd assume I was casting some evil curse against the whole castle, plotting some way of escape as though I couldn't simply open the iron doors and walk out if I wished. I could, but the Fates have put me in this cell, and so in this cell I shall stay, despite the guilt chipping at the ice inside of me.

Two hundred years I spent in the Seelie Court, fighting against the Fates themselves to prove to myself that I didn't have to surrender to their whims. I ran because I was scared, but, as I matured and grieved my family and found out who I truly was, I became determined to prove I knew better than the Fates. Surrounded by the devastation of the Ureen and the dire consequences of the Sol King's choices, still I fought to find a new fate for myself, and all that taught me was the futility of my actions. Millions of people die at the hands of the most evil and grotesque of creatures if we step away from what has been decreed for us.

When the Ureen laid siege to Sol City and the Golden Palace in the final battle of the Fate Wars, I was attacked by one of the monsters and nearly died. I was carried from the battlefield on horseback, desperate hands holding my wounds closed to be sure I didn't lose any organs or the last threads of my life as I was rushed back to the healers' quarters, the screams of the dying and wounded my last memory before I slipped away.

I woke, weeks later, with a scar connecting me to the Fates and ice around my heart. That battle broke the last of my resolve, and I submitted to the fate I was given and began planning my return to the Southern Lands, waiting only as long as it took to be discharged from the Sol Army and convince my loved ones to let me go before I sailed back here.

Shame curls in my gut, a stream of regrets bubbling in my mind. I can't let myself fall into them, but I can't ignore the simple truth that I ran away from the Seelie Court just as I once ran from the Savage Prince. The trauma I carry from the war is now greater than my fear of my fate, and so no matter how right or noble it is to do as I've been instructed, sitting here feels like I've failed.

I take a deep breath to center myself again, to calm my mind and clear away the shadows. These thoughts don't help anyone and, while I'm many things, a mindless, massacring witch is not one of them.

I'll do as the Fates have asked of me, even marry the Savage Prince, who wishes me a torturous death.

I keep my eyes shut and fall into a meditative state. Though I'm not bleeding my magic into the earth, I can still slowly let it seep from my skin into the stone beneath me. It's a far less efficient way to cycle it, but it isn't detectable to the high-fae prince with his sad lack of magical knowledge.

Many hours later, the door upstairs opens, and footsteps

J BREE

come down the staircase. I've learned the gaits of everyone who visits regularly down here, another trick learned from the Sol Army that comes in handy even when I'm not using it deliberately.

Tyton, the speaker of the trees, is coming.

He stops in front of Tauron and scowls at him for a moment before he murmurs, "You should get some sleep. I'll watch over the witch."

Tauron raises an eyebrow at him, unaware or uncaring that I'm observing them both. "I can smell the fairy wine on you from here. I'm staying to guard her, not to fall into a drunken stupor only to wake up to a corpse and a broken fate."

Interesting.

My assumption of them guarding me to ensure I don't escape was off. They're here to protect me.

Tyton grimaces and picks at his formal and fine shirt, holding it away from his chest with two fingers as though disgusted with it. "You smell fairy wine because Lady Essa was drunk enough to pour half a goblet down my shirt. I barely had a glass while I was listening to the latest gossip and distracting Mother from worrying about *you*. I'm not going to be able to sleep with all of them here anyway, you know that. One of us might as well be sharp. Go get a few hours and then come back...unless you doubt I can deal with the regent's soldiers myself?"

The surly prince stands up and hisses at him. "Why do you talk so openly? You know there are ears everywhere!"

Tyton only grins at him, holding up a hand that glows. "No one outside the dungeon can hear me, and I wanted the little witch to know that we're protecting her. She owes us for our kind act."

They both turn and look at me, and there's no point hiding that I'm listening. I stare back, but I have nothing to say to either of them, and after another moment, the surly prince claps his brother on the shoulder and leaves, murmuring as he goes, "A couple of hours, and I'll be back. I'll check on Soren to make sure he hasn't hung himself just to escape his fate and that filthy witch."

Tyton lowers himself onto the stool and listens to his brother's retreating steps, not looking in my direction or attempting to speak until the sound of the stone door shutting over our heads echoes through the cavernous space. There's another beat of silence, and I shut my eyes, ready to ignore this prince as I ignored the last, but his words break me out of my trance.

"Why are you giving your magic to the stones, little witch? What do you think they're going to do to get you out of here?"

My eyes snap open and meet his piercing blue gaze.

He doesn't sense only his own magic; he can sense mine, well enough to see exactly what I'm doing here. I study him before I answer him, honest to a fault but knowing he won't believe me.

"A lot of evil has been wrought here, and the earth is begging for help. Why wouldn't I attempt to repair that, since I can?"

His eyebrows pinch together, and it's the first sign of true familiarity I can see between the brothers. All the high fae look the same, but these two are so similar around the eyes when they scowl that their blood relationship has become glaringly obvious to me.

"Why should you care what the earth wants? Witches want nothing but power."

How very wrong he is. How warped and twisted the truth has become here, thanks to one man's maniacal thirst for power and his drive to change the status quo and wipe out the high fae altogether.

Kharl strayed from the true path of what it means to be a witch, from our place in the world, and he's led those who follow him away from our traditions. As much as I dislike the Unseelie high fae for their choice to abandon the magic that sustains our land and for the way that they treat the lower fae, I still understand my role in the world. I don't think it's as a subordinate to the high fae—I don't think anyone is truly subordinate—but I understand that we all play an important part in taking care of the kingdom and helping it flourish. If one of the pillars folds, the others should hold it strong until it can be rebuilt. Not only have the witches here turned their back on everything they know, they've taken a sledgehammer to the other pillars.

I choose to give Tyton the easy answer. "I'm a healer. I always have been, and I always will be. While the earth is suffering, I can't sit back and watch it die."

He cocks his head at me, the action the same as Tauron's down to the tilt, and his gaze runs over every filthy inch of my being before he nods. "A healer makes sense. I suppose that's what you did in the Sol Army, too."

It's my turn to knit my eyebrows together, but he shrugs at me.

"You stand like a soldier. Seeing you and Airlie next to each other made it obvious. I didn't see it when you were with only the rest of us, because you just looked like us, nothing out of the ordinary. Next to my refined and resplendent cousin, you stood braced for impact, and the healers within an army are soldiers, first and foremost. What a change it must have been to go from fighting against the Ureen to being a target here in the Southern Lands. I suppose you regret returning."

I shrug back at him and let my eyes fall closed once more. "I won't deny it, but who am I to question a destiny predetermined."

If I keep saying it, maybe it'll eventually sting a little less passing my lips. Maybe the lessons the Fates bestowed on me will stop throbbing like a wound in my mind. I wait for Tyton to question me further but whatever he's learned from me, whatever calculations he's forming to pass along to the Savage Prince, he's satisfied for now.

I let myself fall back into the connection and ignore his presence once more, a far easier task now that the wounds of my past are aching within me once more.

TWELVE

SOREN

The only good thing that comes from the Unseelie Court wreaking havoc on Yregar Castle is the information that Tyton shares after guarding the witch.

She was a healer in the Sol Army.

Our relations with the Seelie Court have always been fraught, and I don't have that many connections, thanks to the regent taking up space on my throne, but I still send a scout north with her information and description. Vorus is a part-blood, more goblin than high fae, but he has a small network in the Northern Lands and the Sol Army and he should be a good help to Hamyr in finding out *something* about this Fates-cursed mate of mine. Roan questioned him extensively before we sent him. The journey is a long one, but worth it if he finds out who she served with and the extent of her abilities.

I'm eager to find out whatever we can about the little witch the Fates have put in my path.

I want to know what her motives are.

As I sit on Nightspark at the edge of Yregar grounds near the large stone wall that protects the village and castle within, I catch sight of Roan's scowling face as he watches the scout step through the fae door.

He turns the scowl on me, and when he's sure none of the

soldiers are paying us any attention, he says, "I hope you're thinking straight here, Soren. If the Sol King finds out that we have imprisoned one of his soldiers, we'll answer to the Seelie Court. We're putting ourselves at great risk...it's a political nightmare in the making! The Northern Lands are no longer in danger from the Ureen, and they've rebuilt Sol City and the Golden Palace. If he's unhappy with our treatment of one of his soldiers, we'll be starting your reign as his enemy. If he wishes to come and free the witch himself, we have no army to protect us. Despite the losses of the Fate Wars, they have far more soldiers than we do. More than your uncle commands at Yris. Even with the Outland soldiers, we'd be at a disadvantage. The Seelie Court trained thousands upon thousands of lower fae and all those who heeded the Sol King's call for aid. You cannot take this lightly."

I stare at the old and decaying wood of the fae door, the magic leaching out of it the same way it's been leached out of the earth itself, as I mull over his words. Roan isn't saying this to be worrisome.

He knows better than any of us what the Sol King is capable of from the dozens of stories his mother told him throughout his childhood of her own upbringing in the Seelie Court. Some of that formed him into the male he is today. He's an Unseelie high-fae prince, loyal to his father's titles and lands, but he straddles the line between both courts in his thinking. It's a flaw in the eyes of most of the Unseelie Court, Aura's especially, but to me it's invaluable, a perspective that no other within the Unseelie high fae has offered me and one that has saved us many times over the long centuries of this war.

I glance around at the miles of devastation that surround us and sigh before I answer, "He's not going to come over here for one soldier. I was careful about how I spoke to Hamyr and Vorus and what I instructed each of them to say—he'll never suspect she's our prisoner. If the regent finds out and sends his own messengers over there to tattle and win favor, I'll say it's one of his twisted tales created to undermine my claim to the throne."

"King Rylle can smell a lie," Roan mutters grimly, nudging his horse with his knees and directing it along the cobblestone path back to the castle.

It's a well-known rumor, though I've never been able to confirm if he's just a very intelligent male who sees through the games and simpering of his court or if his magic can truly detect deception. It would be very useful to know for certain, but so far I've failed to confirm it.

Roan follows my lead as I direct us back to the castle, Nightspark snorting and sniffling at the soldiers we pass. I keep a tight rein to stop him from biting any of them and run a hand over his withers to try to calm his temper, but it only inflames him further. He's a willful creature, and his obedience to me doesn't change his true nature. I respect that about him, and I stroke his neck until he forgives me.

"Neither the official messenger or the scout is going to lie. Everyone knows about the war here, and Kharl's treason. The witch has been detained, but she hasn't been harmed. None of that is a lie, and the Northern Lands will know it. If anything, we might finally receive aid and provisions. If the Sol King sides with us, then the other kingdoms will answer my requests, and we might even coax some dragons over here to clear out the Witches Ward in one swoop."

It's a hollow hope, and we both know it. King Hex of the Dragon Lands has his own problems to deal with, and none of his dragonriders will journey here without his permission.

Roan shrugs, steering his own horse away from Nightspark when my mount's teeth snap a little too close for comfort. "They all think that we're a frozen wasteland, on our last legs before death. Why should they care if the witches win? Unless they suspect Kharl will turn his sights on their kingdom next...then they might act. Though you should put some thought into King Hex and the Dragon Lands. If his son is leading a revolt, we'll need to choose a side and hope it wins. If he's dethroned and we have his son's favor, we may find the Dragonriders coming to our aid."

I smirk and nod, an image forming in my mind of a battlefield full of raving, lunatic witches being burned to ashes by one of those giant beasts. It's a fantasy to me, an incredible magical image that I will no doubt dream about for many days to come.

A sobering thought overtakes me. "How is Airlie?"

Roan shoots me a bleak look. Airlie will never give me a straight answer on how she's feeling or the health of the baby, and so it's easier to ask her fretting husband instead. Roan doesn't sugarcoat anything. Nothing passes his lips but the cold and blunt truth.

"She's tired. Far more tired with this one than she was the last, and your uncle leaving Sari behind here for a *fun little visit* isn't helping matters."

I grimace at the reminder of Sari's presence in the castle, a strategic move by the regent that complicates things for me in the worst ways. We left Sari wandering through the castle and complaining about the furnishings when we came out here, and Airlie cursed us both to the ends of the kingdom and back for it.

Roan's expression shutters. "Airlie is struggling more than she'll ever admit. I've already told her we're not doing this again. I don't know how she convinced me this time."

Airlie could convince Roan to cut off his own legs if she tried hard enough. Thankfully, she adores her husband too much to maim him in such a way.

I keep that observation to myself. This subject isn't one to make light of, and we've all begun preparing ourselves for what's to happen in the coming weeks. Their last hope has been scattered to the wind, thanks to the arrival of my mate and her identity. An apology sits at the edge of my lips, but I can't quite get it out, the taste of it bitter on my tongue.

Roan and I have been friends since we were nothing more than faelings, spending the long winter months together in the frozen south and training to become soldiers after my parents' death. He was my rock in the storm during those years, and even when we were separated thanks to the regent's campaign against Roan's family and parentage, it didn't weaken our friendship.

He can read me as easily as a Seer perceives the Fates spread out before them. "There's nothing to be sorry for, Soren. The Fates are cruel and fickle no matter the circumstances. We knew it was a slim chance, but Airlie still wanted to try. This will be our last attempt."

His voice is firm, an argument he's clearly had with his wife and not one he intends to back down from. Roan's mild temper is deceptive to some, but that tone is the truth of him. When he's made up his mind, there's no changing it. It's why his acceptance of my fate and the witch when we first got back tore at my ego so badly—because hearing him call out my vicious response as useless and a waste of time was the brutal truth.

We all knew it.

Nudging Nightspark forward as I assess the devastation and the state of Yregar and my people, it's hard not to fall deeper into despair. The village is bursting at the seams, an endless supply of refugees arriving daily as they're displaced by the war. The crowds of homeless part-blood and lower fae have become ever more restless as the days pass and the rations tighten. We're building more houses and community spaces for them, but there's no way to overcome the lack of provisions. We're building shelters for people we can't feed.

The small boy who clung to me during the temple riot was cleaned up at the castle by the maids, but our search for a parent or a guardian was fruitless, the child abandoned or orphaned by the war. Firna has taken him under her wing, and when Tauron suggested bringing him to the orphanage to see if a bed was available for him, she scowled and told him to leave Sonny to her. It's not his name, but he's yet to speak to give us one, and Firna's nickname has stuck.

Each day when I check in with the keeper about provisions, I hear his giggles and a maid or two chasing after him as he runs wild, a welcome ray of glee in a bleak situation.

My family has a lot of gold, enough money to buy provisions from another kingdom for centuries to come, and yet I can't secure a trading route to bring in imported goods. Every last one of the connections I've tried to forge has failed, just as I am failing my people.

It's a sobering situation.

My thoughts stray even further into the maelstrom of our lives and those who have chosen our side, for better or worse. "Has Airlie spoken to her mother?"

Roan scoffs, his hands tightening on the reins as he attempts to control his anger. "If by 'spoken' you mean endured Aura's fussing even though she'd rather face off with a writhing banshee, then sure. She has a *lot* of opinions about this pregnancy, and none of them are helpful or her place to share. Airlie thinks Aura is trying to manipulate her into leaving Yregar before she gives birth, but we're not going anywhere."

We share a knowing look.

There's never been a day that Aura has considered anyone's actions to be about anything but herself, and she's been trying to drive a wedge between Airlie and Roan since the day the Fates put them together. Finding a way around the obvious demands of a fate is a dangerous endeavor, but others have done it. There are marriages within the Unseelie Court that are in name only. The unions were consummated and, until the curse put a stop to it, produced an heir before the mates chose to live separately. This was the path Aura tried to push on Airlie.

She wants her daughter home.

She's shallow, a female who wants nothing more than a pretty daughter to make her look better, hollow and shell-like so that she doesn't have to contend with a strong mind. Add to the mix that Airlie has one of the smartest and most keen minds I've ever known. It must have been torture for Aura to raise such an independent and beautiful child, knowing that she was going to eclipse her in every way possible.

I have no sympathy for my aunt and very little love.

The only positive I can find about her is that she's loyal to the true crown, standing up for me and my lineage as vehemently as she would if I were her own child, and it's enough for me to excuse almost anything my aunt can throw at us. She prefers the regent's lavish lifestyle and pandering over my own reputation and lack of concern for it, but she's a purist regarding the Celestial bloodline, through and through. Probably because she believes that any weakening of my claim to the throne might affect her own status, but it keeps her loyal all the same.

We need every last supporter we can find in this war.

The longer the silence stretches between us, the darker the cloud around Roan becomes. He frowns and rubs a hand over his chest as we continue on.

"What's wrong? Do you sense something?"

He glances at me and then sighs, his eyebrows drawing down tight. "Some of the regent's guards were overheard talking about traveling into the Outlands. I think the regent is going to try to intimidate my father again, and he hasn't been *well* since Mother passed."

Roan isn't talking about his father's health, but his state of mind and the obsessive bloodlust he's poured into the soldiers at his command to avenge his wife's tragic death. The Prince of

Snowsong holds the Outlands, the southernmost region of the kingdom, and lives in their ancestral castle, Fates Mark. The coldest territory in the Southern Lands, the Outlands always has snow, even in the height of summer, and though that deters many of the high fae from traveling there, it's one of the most beautiful places in my kingdom.

Fates Mark is carved into the peak of a mountain, marble and stone fused together with magic into a stunning display of the First Fae's power. It's breathtaking to behold, and even more wondrous within. The Snowsong bloodline has lived and guarded the area since the high fae came to these lands, and there's a deep pride in Roan to hold his title and be the next caretaker of the Outlands and his people there.

Fates Mark and the Outlands are now more heavily guarded than the Goblin Lands, but not always with the best tactics. Roan's father is reckless in his grief, and the regent knows it. He's exploited the weakness before.

Roan nudges his horse closer to mine, as close as Nightspark will allow, and murmurs even more quietly despite using the old language to conceal our conversation, "We guarded the castle and the witch too well for your uncle to kill her—this is his retaliation. If anything happens to my father, it will force Airlie and I to return to Fates Mark. Any of our circle leaving your side is a risk to you right now, Soren, and the regent is going to do his best to cut you off from the protections you hold. There are *very* few things that could force me to leave you exposed like that. My father is one of them."

I nod slightly. "I'll send soldiers tomorrow. We won't leave him vulnerable. No matter what, we will get through this together, like we always have. Your father will be safe—I'll make sure of it."

Stepping back into the castle, I scowl as the maids and servants who bustle through the hallways to clean up in the wake of the Unseelie Court's visit to Yregar. It was a colossal waste of food and time, and my temper flares until the entire castle is ducking their heads and running at the sight of me. The leftover food was taken to the villagers at first light, but the foods that are expected to be served to the court are wasteful and exorbitant and use up more ingredients than necessary, because the court is so fussy and eager to look as though they have a refined palate.

Our stores could have lasted until midwinter but, after a single night of enduring the court, we'll be lucky to make it through the end of summer. My sword hand begins to itch, a slow fire building in my veins as the fury builds inside of me, futile but unavoidable. And so it will go until the Unseelie Court wants to admit to themselves and each other that we're in dire straits, or I take the throne and force them to face reality.

Whichever comes first.

The only way forward is my marriage, thanks to the split within the royal families. Though shocking and a hot topic for the gossipmongers, the witch being revealed as my mate isn't going to change the decision of the court, and the stalemate of the court will hold. The reactions last night told me everything I needed to know, and the regent's display succeeded only in making the divide between the families wider.

Only two votes to overturn the Unseelie law that requires me to be married to take the throne are unaccounted for, but there's no use attempting to sway them. The Goblin King holds one, but he's never cast a vote, nor his father before him. He won't side with either of us, not really, and my best guess is that, if we force his hand, he'll back whoever he thinks he has the best chance of winning a war against. Someday, that male is going to break the treaty and take sovereignty of the Goblin Lands for the goblins.

I've had very few dealings with the Goblin King, an impudent male who can't even speak the common tongue. A few short weeks after my parents' murder, he came to Yregar, offering condolences as his excuse, but he was sizing me up. I was barely more than a child, pathetic in his eyes, I'm sure, and he left after a single interaction, never even dismounting from his horse. My strongest memory of him is of the disdain he had for me, which transcended the interpreter he spoke through.

He's known to kill indiscriminately if you should trespass on his land, and the justice within his own court is said to be equally brutal. When the Sol King sent out his declaration of open borders, after witches, exiled goblins made up the highest number of migrants to the Northern Lands. I once questioned the king about his feelings on the matter, and he gave me a measured look before simply replying, "They're no longer my people. Let the Sol King use them as bait for his monsters of the Fates' anger."

That sort of callous attitude is exactly why I've watched him for years. My father had warned me, even as a child with the many tales of my grandfather's battles in the civil war that had ravaged our kingdom for many centuries, that the Goblin King is a knife in the dark, waiting for my back to be turned to strike. He's as dangerous to me as the regent, and to forget that is to sign my own death warrant.

The Seer holds the other vote, a mark of respect to the Fates, and even before she fled to the Northern Lands she had never cast a vote, instead holding her neutrality in her own form of respect.

I want nothing more than to return to the training barracks and spend the day working through some of this frustration with my sword, but there's no chance of doing that without sacrificing the good of the household. Instead, I try not to take out my vicious mood on everyone around us as I go through the everyday dealings of being the head of a royal household. There are dozens of issues and concerns at Yregar, and though many are beyond my current capabilities to address, I'll hear about them all and resolve what I can.

Tauron and Tyton are still sharing guard shifts over the witch, in case my uncle has left a spy here to kill her. When they made up a plate of the banquet leftovers for her, intent on ensuring nothing was wasted, the food was tested and tasted before the plate was slid across the filthy cell floor to her.

Tyton has been the most successful in getting information out of her. Something about his magic calls to her; she watches him a little too keenly for my liking, and I've spoken to Tauron about keeping her away from his brother. The acts of magic that witches are capable of are horrific. The curse to stop high-fae babies from being born alive is only one of their many magical assaults, and there isn't a high-fae soldier under my command who doesn't know of the death curse that took Yrmar from us. I don't know for certain that it's even possible, but if the witch finds a way to take Tyton's magic and use it to get herself out of the dungeons, I'll never forgive myself.

Although Tauron would destroy her before I had the chance.

Within a week of the Unseelie Court departing, a messenger arrives in the early hours before dawn, the air wet with dew from the mists that linger over the dead fields surrounding Yregar.

I'm awake before his arrival, sleep slipping through my fingers like sand most nights, and I meet Fyr in my reception room. As the entry room of my chambers, it holds my desk and chairs but nothing else, and two soldiers guard the doors at all times to ensure no one enters the small sanctuary I call my own. My chambers aren't the opulent extravagance of the heir's suite at Yris, but they're more than enough for me.

Roan and Tyton join me, Tauron in the dungeon on his shift to guard the witch, and my cousin casts a barrier to ensure no one can listen in, rubbing at his reddened eyes after a long night of his own guard shift.

Fyr has returned from the most dangerous and complicated of my commands, riding to the Western Fyres to negotiate with King Salem, the high-fae ruler there. Traveling through the Goblin Lands is prohibited without the Goblin King's permission, and it took years for Fyr to reach an agreement of safe passage. He alone is allowed to pass through, and under strict rules, never straying from the path he is authorized to travel.

He takes off his cap and bows his head respectfully as he delivers his news. "King Salem is happy to barter and trade, but we would have to ensure a safe trade route for the goods."

I let out a breath, but when I shoot Roan a look, I find him grimacing.

A small step forward only to face yet another obstacle. The only viable route is through the Goblin Lands. The overpass that we used in years past was destroyed by the witches, and it could take decades to clear it and build new foundations through the mountains to open it back up.

Both options are impossible.

The very idea of a pipeline through the Goblin Lands is laughable. The regent has yet to send guards there to speak to the Goblin King without losing them.

I nod and thank Fyr. He rode through the night and looks haggard, but he's done a good job. My messengers are just as important to me as my soldiers, and they bunk in the same area. I train them to be able to defend themselves but their greatest assets are their speed and their secrecy—the way that they're able to blend in with the lower fae and part-bloods.

Fyr is Keeper Firna's only child, both of them mostly high fae, with a human ancestor somewhere in their lineage. Enough that most high fae don't look twice at Fyr, but it gives him an edge in passing through certain areas. The lower fae are wary of him and don't want to mess with him, thanks to his mostly high fae blood, but the high fae don't take much notice of him because, to them, the human blood makes him a part-blood.

He is the perfect spy for me.

He's also incredibly loyal, paying back my own loyalty to him in spades, and I trust him with even the most sensitive of messages.

I wave Fyr off to find refreshments and get some sleep, but he glances between all of us and says, "There's more. A group of the regent's guards was seen crossing into the Outlands, and they ride to Fates Mark."

Roan curses viciously under his breath, turning away from us all as he runs a hand down his face. Tyton's eyes glaze over, his magic taking hold of him, but there's no questioning him about it until his trance is finished, so I focus on Fyr and the problem at hand.

Fyr glances at Roan before he continues, steady and sure. "There are groups of exiled goblins in the area, and more raiding parties of witches along the border. Both followed the guards through the break in patrols. I had to double back and use the fae door to avoid them. I don't know whether they'll make it to Fates Mark without detection, but for as far as I saw them travel, they moved unimpeded. Prince Roan was reported to be in the Stellar Forest, and many of his soldiers too."

He's not talking about this Roan, of course, but his father, the family tradition of passing on their name both old and confusing for us all. Fyr continues giving us the facts, and though he's good at never adding his own speculation, I can add my own well enough. My uncle is committing treason. This is all too convenient for the witches, to be led safely through the icy plains into the most guarded territory of the kingdom with ease.

Thousands of fae folk live in the villages at the base

of the mountains, and hundreds more in Fates Mark; if the witches make it there without contest, the devastation will be catastrophic.

I dismiss Fyr with my thanks, and the moment the door is shut I turn to Roan. "I'll go to Fates Mark with a company of soldiers. We'll deal with the witches, and the goblins too. If we use the fae door, I can get to the village first and have the situation under control before there's any chance of an attack."

Roan shakes his head. "You can't. The Unseelie Court is deliberating over whether or not you're going to be crowned after your wedding, it was all the court could talk about while they were here. You can't afford to play this game with the regent, and he knows it—that's exactly why he's chosen to do this now. He'll draw me out and weaken your defenses, then he'll strike. He knows his hold is tenuous at best and he can't face you at full force."

Tyton's eyes clear as the hold of his magic on his mind eases away. He glances between us. "Tauron and I will go. Roan can stay here, watch your back, and protect Airlie."

Roan shakes his head. "We can't afford to have both of you go, and neither of you know the area well enough to redistribute the Outland soldiers. Father will argue with you both—he's too stubborn to accept direction from anyone but Soren and me. I don't have time to make plans or explain terrain conditions—I need to leave now, or even going by the fae door won't make up enough time to beat them there."

I shake my head. "You can't leave Airlie right now."

The storm that passes over Roan's face is testament to the trust that he has in Tyton and me, the vulnerability he's willing to show because he knows there will be no judgment from either of us.

"I would rather march to my own death than leave her right now, and were it anyone else, I'd let them fight their own battles, but I can't leave my people to die. Not after what the witches did to my mother—my father would never recover from the failure. Airlie still has a few weeks left, maybe two full months if she goes late like last time. I should be able to get there, stop the attack, place soldiers in the right places to shore up the territory's defenses, and then return before the baby arrives."

He holds my gaze, then Tyton's, his expression showing resolve and the determination of a high-fae prince facing down death. "I trust the three of you to keep her safe and…if the baby comes early, I trust you'll see her through it safely. I'll owe you all a life-debt—she's going to hate this."

I rub a hand over my eyes even as a rueful smile tugs at my lips. "Maybe I'll go with you just to escape her wrath."

Roan laughs quietly under his breath, a hollow sound. "You know as well as I do the moment I tell her, she's going to pack my bags for me. She's stronger and fiercer than any of us. She just hides it well under the pretty dresses and that perfect face of hers."

She's had no choice but to be strong, we all have, but this will be a test for us all. One we cannot afford to fail.

THIRTEEN

ROOKE

Tauron and Tyton spend their days taking turns in watching over me, and I notice how quickly they both devolve into boredom-soaked restlessness. I remain unaffected, my mind kept busy as I feed the earth and listen to all it has to say back to me.

I learn how long it's been since anyone took care of this land—one hundred years since someone marked the equinoxes and solstices. One hundred years since someone gave willingly without expecting anything in return, and my heart bleeds for the land that has been so neglected. It was a witch, and I have my guesses about which coven she hailed from, the land offering me a few clues, but not enough to be sure.

Tyton watches my every move, his magic pressing against me as he monitors what I'm doing, but even as they pass each other like ships in the night, he never passes on this information to Tauron. Neither of them speak to me, but the food does get markedly better, which is good, considering they insist that I eat.

When I did little more than graze from the first plate, Tauron stood up and came up to the bars on my door, glaring down at me as he snapped, "If you don't eat that food, I will come in there, force your jaw open, and shove it down your throat myself."

In my past life, I would have ripped the man's arm off if he tried such a thing, but that's not my purpose here. Docile and sweet little Rooke from the Ravenswyrd Forest—the girl I left behind—that is who I am now. I'm hiding my Northern Lands self behind compliance to survive this confinement.

On the third day after we confronted the Unseelie Court, I notice a frenetic sort of energy around Tyton, a jerky manner to the way his limbs move and a curt tone to his voice as he sends Tauron on his way.

I study him carefully from the corner of my eye and, when he senses my attention on him, he shifts his ire to me. "I don't care how bored you are in there, witch, stick to your tinkering with the earth and keep me out of it."

I shrug at him and pull myself to my feet, then pace the cell to stretch out my limbs. They crack with disuse, a tautness in them I have not felt in some time, and I bite back a groan.

I distance myself from the pain by prodding at him. "You should drink some honeysuckle tea. Brew it with peppermint to hide the bitter taste, and it'll ease your headache."

His eyes narrow at me. The vicious look on his face is common to Tauron but an anomaly for Tyton.

"Are you trying to poison me, witch?" His voice is scathing. "Are you trying to use your magic against me now that you have shown yourself to be nothing more than a docile little lamb caught in a deadly trap? I won't fall for it."

I bend at the waist to stretch down and touch my toes, feeling relief as my back finally pops audibly, the sound ricocheting off the stone walls. "It's not magic, it's medicine. Any healer worth their salt would give you the same recipe. If you want to walk around grumpy and in pain for the rest of the day, be my guest. It's no bother to me."

He scoffs and rolls his shoulders back, finally shifting his eyes from me as he inspects the roughly hewn stone above our heads. The blocks still show the markings from the primitive tools that were used to build this dungeon in the first place, and I often find my attention pulled to the deep, systematic grooves.

"I suppose you spent a lot of time in the Sol Army giving out tinctures for headaches, did you? I'm sure that helped greatly against the Ureen."

I don't like hearing those words out of his mouth, the way that he trivializes the horrors I endured for almost two hundred years, but I've had enough time to recover from the Fate War and the devastation of the Ureen to keep my face carefully blank. "You'd be surprised at the things I learned in the Northern Lands. A lot of things you wouldn't think were useful saved countless lives."

There's a booming sound above us, voices thumping. His gaze darts to the stairs, and he frowns. The noises are loud enough that even my hearing can pick them up.

I wonder what extra information he's getting right now.

When the thuds ease a bit, he speaks again. "Describe the Ureen to me. If I'm going to be stuck watching you for the rest of my goddamn life, I might as well get a story or two out of it. Tell me what it was like to see one of those creatures."

I would rather strip myself naked and sun myself on the decks of the castle in front of the entire Unseelie Court than have that conversation with this man. He's the only one who will speak to me though, the only one who giving a little information to might get me some in return.

His eyes are sharp and calculating as he watches me, seeing far too much of me even as I work to keep my face blank. I suppose the numb feeling within my chest is helpful, because it's easy to say the words clinically, as though I'm reciting from a history book and not from the worst memories I have ever had the displeasure of making for myself.

"The Ureen are monsters that guard the Fates themselves.

The Seelie Court had no idea what was coming for them. When the Fates tore an opening in the sky above Sol City, they thought it was a warning."

I keep the details to myself, the things that only someone who was in the Northern Lands during the Fate Wars could truly know. The Sol King had been desperately trying to fix his fate; he hadn't meant to break it in the first place, though no one outside of the Seelie Court believes that.

I know it better than most.

Tyton motions at me to continue and, for some reason, I do. "The Northern Lands are bigger than our kingdom, with a larger population than the Southern Lands has ever held, and their castles are surrounded by cities that were bursting with life. By all accounts, the Northern Lands were flourishing before the war started.

"The first night that the Ureen came out of the tear in the sky, there was nothing that the Sol King or anyone else could do to stop them. They killed hundreds of thousands in a single night. They're creatures made of shadow and light, so unnatural that your eyes don't want to focus on them. Your mind falters at the prospect of describing what they look like…they're everything and nothing all at once, and they reach into the deepest recesses of your mind and pull out your nightmares and *become* them. They consume *everything*—they're unstoppable, insatiable, and the chaos of war is a glut to them."

I stop just to take a breath, to rein myself back in, because I can feel the panic and hysteria creeping up my chest at the memory. Two centuries of war did nothing to numb me of my fear of them.

I found out in the hardest way what would befall me and my home if I didn't return to face my fate.

Once I've collected myself, I finish with, "They can't be killed or defeated the way that normal creatures can. They have to be unmade, like a promise unraveled. It took dozens of soldiers to kill even one of them, and the death toll in the Northern Lands was catastrophic."

Tyton stares at me for a moment, looking shocked at the tumble of words that streamed out of me, and his head is cocked as if he's reading the truth in my voice. I've met other high fae with the power to read the truth and intentions, and even witches with the ability, and there's a curiously vacant sort of sheen to their eyes as they do it that's reflected into Tyton's expression now that prods at the back of my mind.

I can't be sure that's what he's doing, but he nods slowly, regardless. "You've seen one with your own eyes, I can tell. The stories we've heard down here have always been second- or thirdhand. People have described them, but they're not afraid of them like you are. You saw one up close."

I saw thousands.

Hundreds of thousands, but to say that would reveal too much—it would get too close to a truth I don't ever want to speak again—and so instead I let the quiet settle over us once more. The bad mood that plagued him when he first arrived seems to have dissipated. I don't expect this peace to last, so instead of pushing my luck and engaging in more conversation with him, I simply sit and open up my magic to the earth once more.

I haven't eaten—the one meal I get each day hasn't arrived yet—but I feel no hunger. The earth doesn't let me feel hunger, not when it has so much sustenance to freely give back to me.

Tyton speaks again, but his scathing tone is absent. "Why return here? If you knew that the War of the Witches was raging, why come back? Tell me the truth now, witch, and maybe I can get you out of the cell. Not freedom, of course, but if you'd like to see the sunlight again for a few moments, breathe some fresh air, tell me the truth, and I'll see what I can do for you."

I don't need sunlight or fresh air—he should know that better than the rest of them.

My eyes roll in his direction, disbelief coloring my tone. "Isn't it obvious? You just asked me what the Ureen look like up close. Do you think after spending centuries in the Northern Lands, helping to defeat them, that I'd just ignore my fate and risk another tear in the sky? Death at the hands of your Savage Prince is far preferable to me than another war with the Fates. There isn't much I won't do to stop that from happening."

He stares at me, his face carefully blank, before he nods slightly. "That's why you're not worried about what's happening, isn't it? You think this is the path of your fate, and there's no other option for you."

I splay my hands on the dirty flagstones, pressing my palms flat as I feel the power of the earth flow into me. It's as though his questions have opened up a wound deep inside of me, and now nothing but the truth, dirty and raw, pours out. "Everything that's happening is another step toward my fate. It doesn't matter how poorly the Savage Prince treats me, how long I go without a bath, what little insults the lot of you have for me—we'll all end up in the same place, regardless. The Savage Prince's hands are tied—you all know it—but mine are too. The sooner you accept that, the faster we'll get to where we need to be."

Tyton exhales before he murmurs, "A marriage between two enemies to unite the land and save our people."

I'm not so sure they're worth saving, but I know the cost of failure.

Despite his easier temperament, I decide I prefer sitting with Tauron over Tyton. At least the scowling and seething brother doesn't slit my chest open and expose my bleeding, bruised, and broken heart to the ruthless light of the day.

I'm woken by the sound of more footsteps and tug in my chest, a quiet murmuring that is too low for my ears to distinguish words filling the empty cavern of the dungeon, and then the scrape of a key sliding into place in the iron door. I've become accustomed to sleeping sitting up, not wanting to lie on the filthy floor any more than I have to, and when my eyelids peel back, I find the Savage Prince staring down at me. Distaste rolls off him, seeping from his very pores as his gaze flits over my hunched form.

Tauron and Tyton stand behind him, talking quietly between themselves. I study my Fates-cursed mate closely as I wait for whatever the next round of his temper will bring to me. My breath catches in my chest at the intensity in his eyes, the blue flashing as he looks around the cell as though he's expecting to find a weapon lying around, or some sign of my nefarious plans.

When his mouth tightens, my own gaze gets caught on the perfect bow of his lips. If I could ignore the indignant fury in his words, I'd say that his voice sings to me in an echo of the song of the forest, a call to the most innate parts of me in a cruel tactic of the Fates to win me over to their whims. Not that they need to, I'll submit to them regardless, but it feels like a particularly cruel twist of a dagger in my gut to know that he can affect me without even trying.

In the handful of times I've seen him since the port, I've done my best not to look too closely at him, meeting his eyes without flinching but never lingering on the breathtaking beauty of him. The sound of his voice was bad enough but now that my gaze has strayed from the burning azure depths, I'm stuck basking in all of his glory. How has the shine of the Unseelie high fae dulled for me in every last one of them except him? Why does my reaction to him only grow stronger, even as my fury becomes an untamable beast?

The Fates are cruel to bind me to this male.

He stares back at me, eyes full of resentment, before he

211

reaches up to grab the iron chains from where they hang by the cell door waiting and then he clips the cuffs into place on my wrists. It's the closest he's ever been to me, so close that he almost touches me, and there's no missing the curl of his lip.

"You stink," he snarls, and I wait to have some sort of reaction to his words, some shame or embarrassment, and yet I find I'm still numb. I've been hoping that my return would ignite some emotion in me once more, ease away some of the numbness that has taken over my body, and yet I stare back at him with nothing.

I shrug, "If you don't like it, then you should do something about it, because it makes no difference to me."

He stares for a moment longer, just a heartbeat of stillness between us, then he jerks on the iron chain until I have no choice but to stand with him or risk him ripping my hands clean off. My arms stretch before me as he drags me behind him, and my gaze drops to the blackened skin of my palms, dirtied by the filth of the cell.

I've lost track of how many weeks I've been down here, but I can feel the filth coating my skin. It's not particularly comfortable, and I would like to take a bath and scrub myself raw, but that has nothing to do with the delicate sensibilities of my mate. The life I left behind dances in the back of my mind, an echo of a time where I knew the love of friends and the respect of fellow soldiers, and the true terror of war and displacement.

The last time I was this dirty and went this long without a bath, my brother Pemba and I were scouting, pushing hard to try to make it to the outer villages in the Northern Lands to provide aid and recruit more soldiers after the latest attack of the Ureen. We were chosen, along with a handful of other soldiers, for our healing abilities, and we'd traveled for weeks through the unforgiving mountainous north of the kingdom only to arrive at the most remote reaches of the Sol King's land to find that the villages no longer existed. Nothing was left behind, not a male, a female or a child, not even the buildings they had once dwelled in.

Everything had been consumed.

It was the first time in the war that I truly felt despair, as though we could not win, and though Pemba had put on a brave face and murmured quietly to me old stories of our parents and our home and all of the wonderful things in our lives that we still clung to like the children we once were, I could not find any hope in my chest.

I'd almost given up that day. Only the thought of what such a thing would do to my brother had kept me going. He had already lost so much, as much as I had, and yet he pasted a smile on his face every day for me. I could be selfish toward myself, but I would never do that to him.

I follow the Savage Prince up the long flight of stone steps, and when we reach the top, I find that it's still dark outside, the huge glass windows that line the hallway show a black night sky. There's light everywhere thanks to the glowing orbs of magic, a remnant of the First Fae and their power that has lasted millenia, and my eyes tear as they adjust, but my vision soon clears and I follow silently as the Savage Prince drags me through the castle. When we exit through one of the castle's side doors, I realize that this could be my end, that he could be taking me outside to kill me and spread my ashes over the deadened earth, but still, it doesn't matter to me at all.

I follow him as patiently as I follow my fate.

When we reach the barracks, I see rows of high-fae soldiers sitting on horses as they wait to ride out, thirty males in full military regalia but without any house colors, bowing in their saddles as their prince arrives. Only one waits on foot for our arrival.

Roan, the Seelie-blood prince, steps forward from the front

line, his horse's reins in his hands as he greets the Savage Prince. We meet him by Airlie, the heavily pregnant princess. She's in a nightgown with a fur-lined cloak thrown over the top, casual and discreet about this early morning meet-up.

The moment we stop alongside her she snaps, "You're taking too long. We're supposed to be moving with haste, not dragging things out. Every moment could be Prince Roan's last!"

She seems annoyed but not particularly concerned, a weird sentiment for a female who clung to her husband so lovingly last time I saw them, but the male in question runs a gentle hand over her cheek. "He's going to be fine, my love. I'll sort this mess out, set up a patrol, and I'll be home to you before the baby arrives. I promise."

A different Roan then, one who is important enough to tear an expectant father away from his beloved wife in such a dark hour. The curse lingers around her like a poisonous halo, muddying the air so much that even with all the despair that I feel from the lands, it's still the strongest presence here. It makes me sick to my stomach.

Roan steps away from his wife to bow to the Savage Prince, formal in a way I haven't seen before in their interactions.

The chains clink together as the Savage Prince claps his friend on the shoulder, murmuring to him, "Don't worry about Airlie and the babe, just get your father to safety and protect your ancestral lands. Everything will be okay."

None of the soldiers move or make a noise, they stand well trained and obedient as they wait for his command. It gives me an insight into who my mate is as a prince and ruler. He demands respect from his people, but he's taken responsibility for them as well.

Which the regent clearly has not.

I suppose this could be another move against his uncle to shore up his claim to the throne, and yet there is an energy around us, a desperation that cannot be faked. They all care about what happens to Roan's father and his lands. There's a lot at stake here; their somber faces speak to that.

Roan gives the Savage Prince a curt nod before turning back to his wife and leaving her with one last kiss, nothing more than a chaste press of their lips together. He doesn't attempt to touch her belly in any way, no connection between him and his unborn child, though Airlie's hand rubs the mound gently as she watches him mount his horse. He swings up with the practiced ease of a proficient rider, without any sort of pomp.

He kicks his horse and leaves us, the soldiers moving into formation behind him without a word. We stand together and watch as the company moves through the castle grounds and exits the first of the walls, and then rides through the village. There's no sound other than the clopping of hooves against stone, and I find myself sending them well wishes.

Roan is the only one of the fae princes to offer me any sort of kindness, and even if it came from a sense of duty and loyalty to the crown and the Fates themselves, I still send a silent prayer for him to the Fates.

Let him come back safely. Let him return to a wife and a child, let his father survive whatever horrors are happening out there, let this mess that we have found ourselves in unravel and the high fae return to their true purpose once more for the sake of the entire kingdom and those most vulnerable within.

Airlie waits until her husband is no longer visible before she turns to the Savage Prince, her nose wrinkling. "The witch stinks. If you insist on having her up here with me, then you *have* to wash her, because I'm not going to sit around and wallow in that thing's filth. You're asking too much of me, Soren. I won't do it."

His gaze drops to her belly and hardens, until I wonder if he can see the tendrils of blackened magic that dig into the swell there. "She's staying in the castle until we sort out the latest issue. Fifty lower fae arrived at the gates this morning just after the messenger—their village was leveled by Kharl's raving forces, and the death toll is already in the hundreds. I need Tauron to assess the damage—guard shifts will have to wait."

FOURTEEN

SOREN

I've left the guarding and daily care of the witch to my inner circle until now. It's been both a simple choice and an easy out, thanks to my duties and the ever-present eyes on me, but with Roan leaving and the witch attacks coming closer to Yregar, I have no choice but to take matters into my own hands.

Tyton escorts Airlie back to her chambers so that she might get a few more hours sleep, a weariness settling over her body now that her husband has left the city walls. Tauron waits a moment before collecting his own band of soldiers, bowing his head and sending me a decisive look as he leads them out through the village as well, only instead of passing through the fae door, they ride through the gate of the outer wall toward the remnants of the village, the smoke on the horizon still curling into the air as the sun begins to rise.

With the increase in attacks and movement from Kharl's forces, I'm careful about how I move my forces to ensure the castle's defenses aren't weakened. If there are more calls to aid, Tyton and I can still ride out and know that the castle is safe under Corym's command. I'd rather avoid such a prospect, and there are other soldiers I could send out in our stead, but we've survived many other years of constant attacks and I'm well prepared for the prospect.

The baby complicates things this time around, as does the witch.

The iron chains weigh heavy in my hand as I wait in the small courtyard by the barracks for a few minutes longer, lost in my thoughts of plans to come and listening as the horses reach the fae door. I hear the moment they cross through, the sudden disappearance of them all as they travel through the old magic.

I've never been quite so aware of how finite my resources are. Three hundred and fifty soldiers under my command, and thirty more scouts out patrolling in the kingdom. There's a constant balance to ensure we're protecting Yregar while still offering aid to the fae folk left defenseless throughout the kingdom. There's no question of how much I'd prefer to ride out and hunt the witches responsible for the attack myself, but everything is about compromise and strategy.

We need more soldiers.

Turning on my heel, I jerk the chains to move the witch behind me. But she walks without need for coaxing, staying one step back the entire way as I weave through the castle. The compliance irritates me, eats away at the edges of my sanity, proof of the game that she's playing with us.

I prepared myself for decades for what our lives would look like once I rescued her, for the gentle way I'd have to handle her to help her heal from her ordeal. I prepared myself for kindness and understanding, yet none of that was needed.

Instead, I found out she's my enemy and the Fates have bound us together regardless of the ruin the witches have wrought upon my kingdom.

I set off for my chambers and ignore the curious and sympathetic looks of my household as they watch us pass. In the time since Roan left, the castle has woken up and become a flurry of morning activities.

I attach the chains to one of the anchor points in my reception room, put there years ago to detain prisoners while I questioned them personally. I'm already dressed and ready for the day, but I strip off the protective gloves and tuck them into my belt, then go through to my chambers to wash up before I eat breakfast. A phantom oily feeling crawls over my skin, a layer of filth that has somehow shifted from the witch to me, even though I've avoided touching her entirely, and I scrub at it.

No matter how hard I scrub, the sensation doesn't change, and the tug in my chest remains as demanding as ever.

I mutter a curse at myself, then at Kharl and his war, my uncle's treachery, and the Fates themselves in the old language. It does nothing to lighten my mood or change my tasks for the day. Moving back into the reception room, I sit behind my desk and go through my correspondence, a large plate of food in front of me and a vicious temper growing within me.

The witch's gaze follows me.

I want nothing more than to pluck her eyes out, stop the way she takes in everything like a sponge soaking up every detail around her. I warned Tauron and Tyton to be careful what was said around her, and I remind myself of the same thing. Every piece of information fed to this creature could be our undoing, and keeping myself away from that silver gaze could very well be the trial that the Fates require me to complete. I spread butter over a slice of the fresh sourdough, baked in the kitchen early this morning just for my table, and eat it in front of her without a thought.

I study her just as keenly as she studies me.

She's been here for weeks, trapped underground without sunlight or fresh air, and yet there is no change in her demeanor or physical appearance other than the layer of filth that now covers her. She's barely eaten, subsisted on a few scraps here and there, yet there is no thinning to her body. Her hair, so dark and unruly, hangs over her face and I find myself grateful to have it obscuring those silver eyes from my own assessment of her. The poor state of her clothing helps to keep my own reactions to the insistent tug of the Fates to myself but still frustration simmers within me at the anomaly of her sound mind and state despite her imprisonment. She's been searched a dozen times and has nothing but the clothes on her back, no clues about who she is or where she's been except the small pouch of Seelie gold that the mercenaries took from her. Trapped under the earth and surrounded by iron and stone, she has not wavered.

If anything, she looks better than when we first found her.

It's not just suspicious, it's frustrating. Everything about her is—the calm demeanor, and the way she looks down on us all as though she's superior to the high fae. The barbs she's thrown out, always in retaliation, are indignant at the state of the kingdom and the actions of the high fae whom she's deemed a factor in it. The worst of it is, I can't deny what she's saying, and my anger at her intensifies until I'm blinded by my need to prove her wrong.

To ruin her as she's ruining me.

Her expression doesn't change as she watches me eat. There's no hunger in her eyes, or anger that I haven't offered her anything after dragging her out of the cells before dawn. The shackles on her wrists have no slack in them so that she's forced to stand rigidly in the corner as I settle into the plush cushions of the chair and eat my fill.

I dismiss her, determined to ignore her presence and the pull I feel toward her so that I can focus wholly on the letters in front of me. As I work through them, my temper pulls tighter and tighter until I'm an arrow on the string of a bow, nocked and ready to kill someone.

The Goblin King has declined my request to negotiate, claiming to be busy with his own acts of war against the witches and protecting his territories.

It's a lie, bold faced and presumptuous, but without evidence to refute it I can't force him to see me. The Dragon Lands want our gold, but King Hex's letter fills me with unease, his words far too eager all of a sudden. For the king of the Dragonriders to suddenly accept my request for trade is suspicious and, even as desperate as we are, I'll push forward with the Western Fyres negotiations instead for now.

The Northern Lands won't speak to me until I ascend to my throne.

I drop the parchment from the Sol King on top of the pile and sigh, rubbing a hand over my face as I consider how in the Fates-good fuck I'm going to get the Goblin King to reconsider. I send Darick, another of my messengers, back to the Goblin Lands with my hopes to meet with the king in person.

A part-blood of high fae and elven descent, Darick grew up in an elven traveling group. With his mother, he traveled in the wagons throughout the lands, selling their wares to survive. She was particularly good at brewing elixirs, and many villages looked forward to purchasing them from her when they traveled through.

Darick came into my service years ago, after the traveling band was attacked by the witches. His mother was killed, and his grandfather, too old to take care of him properly, brought him to Yregar and left him at the orphanage.

Within a year he'd aged out and started on as a stable hand at the castle, where he'd worked harder than all the others combined. When he overheard my soldiers discussing a war strategy in an area he knew well, he sought me out himself. He was so thin and haggard looking, his entire body shaking as he addressed me, terrified of the rumors but still brave enough to speak up.

He knew exactly where the witches would lie in wait.

A keen mind, he recalled every route his people had traveled and knew the spots that were most vulnerable to an ambush. It saved the lives of hundreds of my soldiers, Tyton included. From that moment on, Darick was one of my messengers, with a horse of his own and the freedom to roam with the protection of my shield pinned to his coat.

He'll get closer to the Goblin King than any other messenger can, even Fyr, simply by knowing a different path to take, and as every avenue slowly closes before me, it's clear I'll have to give the Goblin King whatever the hell he wants to get a trading route through his land. Until our own land is fruitful again, I have no choice.

No choice but my fate and the little witch in the corner who watches everything with her knowing silence, like one of my uncle's guards lying in the dark with a sharp blade.

As the hours creep on without news from Tauron, I begin to find the witch's silence and the frenetic hum in my blood at her presence maddening. She stands with perfect posture, head up and shoulders back, her feet planted squarely on the rug as though this is nothing to her. Whatever training the Sol King puts his soldiers through, it's gotten her in better condition than even my best males.

It makes me rash.

Without looking up from the letters in front of me, I say, "What's to stop you from murdering us all? The iron cuffs don't seem to be doing much to you."

She stays silent, and when I glance up to make sure she's not ignoring me, I find her staring back at me with that unwavering gaze of hers, the cold steel of her eyes slicing me to the bone. I'm tempted to hand her a sword to see just how much she learned in the Sol Army, to put all of those promises of death in her eyes to the test.

She shrugs, her posture still frustratingly sharp. "What's to stop *you* from murdering everyone? It's a stupid question to ask, one of my morality, and though you've treated me like a criminal, I have no real reason to wish you dead. Other than avoiding our entwined fates, and I have no intention of ever facing a Ureen again."

I lean back in my chair and look her over once more.

She's nothing like the witches I've met before, and not just because her face is free of any markings. There's no fanatical ideation spewing from her lips, no manic look to her eyes as she stares at me. She's far too calm, given the circumstances and her treatment here. I would wager that she's in the upper level of the witch rankings, perhaps even directly under Kharl himself.

I've never come face-to-face with the leader of the witches, the male who weaponized his entire race under the guise of freedom. His name has been on the lips of hundreds of witches I've fought and killed, screamed out and exalted as though he's a higher power than the Fates themselves. I once laughed at them, ridiculing their delusions, but I don't find humor in it anymore. Kharl Balzog has crippled our kingdom with the madness he's fed his armies.

My tone is icier than her eyes. "Witches have no morality."

A single eyebrow rises, and one corner of her lips curls slightly upwards, as though I'm amusing her. A ripple of frustration works its way down my limbs at the sight.

She soaks in my furious reaction without so much as a flinch. "If the rumors are true, there's no morality in the Savage Prince either. I must believe you are every inch the monster that they say you are."

The lower she aims, the lower I'll descend right after her, to the very depths of Elysium should I need to. "And yet I've heard nothing of you. Suspicious, considering how much power you have."

The corner of her lips only quirks up a little further, until there's a proper smile on her face. I find myself eager to reach forward and break it, to wipe it from her features, to have them slacken forever in the cold embrace of death.

She nods at me slowly, the smile slipping away as she watches me as though watching a circling dragon. "I feel as though we should attempt to reach some form of compromise, or we're going to do nothing more than this. Don't you want your throne?"

"I don't compromise with my own people—why would I ever compromise with a filthy witch?"

She shakes her head slowly, her gaze tracing the scar on my face. "You're not going to be a very good king."

"How would you know what a good king is?"

She shakes her head at me once more. "I just returned from the Northern Lands, didn't I? I watched a high-fae king give *everything* for his people. You don't have an ounce of his integrity or backbone, Savage Prince. You're nothing but a pouting royal demanding what you suppose is owed to you by blood, forgetting that it's not just a crown but a position of power."

My temper flares once more, and with it, a ripple swells under my skin, tingles shooting down my arms, and I watch as her gaze drops to them as though she felt it too. My hands clench into fists to hide the way they shake as a killing rage bubbles inside me. I want the witches gone from this earth, and so I must submit to my fate, no matter the price I must pay.

There's a knock at my chamber doors, and I take a moment to collect myself, to stop the heated rise of rage from bubbling over even as a dash of frustration adds to the mix.

There's only one person who knocks like that, a delicate rapping of knuckles against the wood in a particular pattern designed just for me. It sounds as though she's trying to make music with it, every part of her life fanciful and pretty, and I have to remind myself that she doesn't know better. She's the product of her upbringing, and I shouldn't blame her for that failing—her heart is better than most.

My eyes flick toward the witch, but there's nowhere to hide her, not without moving her into my inner chambers, and my reception room is as far as I'll allow her to go. The pull of her magic on me—or maybe it's the threads of the Fates insistently binding us together—fills the space around us both. I know the feeling will linger after she's gone; the other times she's been let out of the cell, I've been stuck feeling her absence for hours after we parted, and I don't want that magic following me to bed.

I pointedly never think of the witch in my bed and what a betrayal of my kingdom it will be when the fires of my anger for her twist into something different. If the Fates would allow, I'd find someone else to pour that rage into and maybe finally get some sleep, but the thought of touching another female also curdles my gut.

The only speculation worse to me than that is the one I have about the witch's life in the Northern Lands and with *whom* she shared it.

The darkest, most vicious depths of my mind keep whispering that it's Kharl, that she's been sent here by her lover to fulfill our fates and bring him the throne by a knife to my gut the moment she earns my trust. I have no evidence of him traveling to the Northern Lands but there's nothing to say that she hasn't traveled between the two kingdoms, or that he's found a way to open his own fae door to stay in contact with her.

It takes a very deep breath to clear those thoughts away and fix a blank mask over my face.

"Come in," I call out, shuffling some of the papers to ensure that Sari—and whatever guard her father left behind with her—can't see my correspondence.

My cousin flounces in.

There's no other word for the way her entire body bounces with glee and her skirts ruffle like frothy nightmares. She has one of her maid servants with her, a half-sister who doesn't look up from the floor even as she walks alongside her mistress, and of course there's the guard her father left behind with her. I don't recognize him, but that's not unusual. The regent picks his guards for their loyalty to him and their hatred of me, none of it earned from firsthand experience. They're fed a stream of his propaganda until they're molded into the sneering form in front of me now. Watching over the regent's beloved daughter means the guard doesn't have to hide his contempt for me—there's no law or social reason for him to pretend to feel anything else.

Only the risk of the consequences once I become king, a probability he foolishly rejects.

I shift my gaze back to my cousin and find a vacant sort of joy in her eyes as she smiles across the desk at me. There are only a few decades between Sari and Airlie, and yet there might as well be thousands of years, all of Airlie's maturity and sophistication in stark contrast to Sari's naïvety.

Despite our opposing sides of the court, she's always sought me out and spoken to me with affection, more insistently as the years have gone on. I've handled her carefully but never turned her away either, and not just because her father would twist my action and every last word I've ever spoken to her. There's something about her that I question—something behind those vacant eyes and childish demands that has never sat right with me—but no poking or coaxing has revealed an answer.

Sari looks around the room carefully, her eyes flitting over the witch as though she doesn't care about her any more than she cares about the color of my drapes.

"We've been holed up in here all day, Cousin! Father said that you'd take me for a walk around the garden while I was here, if only I asked, but every time I've sent Malia to find you, your soldiers or the servants send her away."

She pouts and bounces forward to take a seat in one of the chairs across from me. Malia and the guard step forward so they're still within an arm's reach of her. Malia drops onto her haunches to fuss with her lady's dresses and skirts, always ensuring she looks perfect enough for a portrait.

She doesn't ever look up.

"Have your guard escort you there. I have an entire castle to run, Sari, I'm sorry. I'd take you there now if I didn't have pressing issues. Maybe Airlie can go with you—she's supposed to get some exercise each day, and I'm sure she'd love the company."

Airlie can barely tolerate Sari, seeing far too much of her own mother's vanity within the female, and I mentally make a note to apologize profusely to my cousin for putting her neck on this chopping block.

Sari only sighs at me, the pout on her lips growing bigger. "I don't want to walk with Airlie. She bumbles along too slowly, and she spends all her time telling me off. I suppose that's what my life would be like if I had a mother."

For all her innocence and naïvety, she wields guilt like a sword. She knows her pretty face and everyone's perceptions of her as the poor orphaned princess are the best weapons she has to get what she wants. Her life with the regent hasn't been an easy one, and though he showers his heir with every pretty trinket and luxury she could possibly want, I've never seen them interact with any sort of warmth.

She's a lonely and spoiled child, no matter how old she is.

"Airlie worries after you because she cares, not because she wants to be mean. We all worry about you."

I feel the guard's gaze burning into my skin, but my focus stays fixed on Sari. The neckline of her dress sits firmly at the base of her throat, and her sleeves cover her arms to her wrists, but there are no lace panels or ribbons woven through the fabric like most high-fae females wear, only a single line of pearls stitched around the flattened collar. They're misshapen and small, an odd choice for my cousin, but against the off-tone blue of her dress they're an elegant touch, and they match one bracelet on her wrist, hidden amongst stacks of white gold and sapphires.

She sighs at me again and shrugs, leaning back in her chair, and Malia once again fusses with her appearance. I find it suffocating, the idea of someone touching and poking and prodding me at all times, and yet the level of perfection Sari is forced to live under has paved the way for this.

"Can I talk to the witch?"

My gaze snaps back up to her, my mouth drawing in tight, and the smile across her lips grows bigger, just a few too many sharp teeth shining through. There's the Unseelie high fae in her, the ability to wheedle and nickel and poke until she gets what she wants.

"Absolutely not, Sari. She's not docile, don't let the chains fool you."

Slowly, as though giving her best performance, Sari turns in her chair and looks over the witch once more, her head cocking and displaying a long line of white, unmarked skin. Her neck looks fragile, like porcelain, as though she's made of something different than the rest of us.

"I don't know how you can stand being in the same room as a witch, especially one as disgusting as *that*. However are you going to marry her, Cousin? My heart feels sick thinking of it."

Pretty words, but with nothing behind them, they ring hollow. Her face didn't change as she said them, going through the motions as she's been taught to do by courtiers and instructors.

Still, there's something about her that makes us all worry about her, and I change my mind.

I wave a dismissive hand in the witch's direction and say, "Airlie is coming to collect her and get her cleaned up now that she's met the Unseelie Court and we've considered my options. It's clear what the Fates are asking of me, and we're going to begin the preparations."

Sari's face snaps back toward me. "You're not truly going to marry it? Surely not!"

I cross my arms and lean back in my chair as I regard her. "And what do you suggest I do instead? I'm sure even in the gilded chambers of the regent's heir you must've heard of the Ureen."

She shudders, and it's real, the little sign of the intelligent mind hidden underneath the pretty jewels and luxurious fabrics. "Maybe you should speak to the Seer again? If you can find her, that is. Maybe there's another way."

I shake my head. "I've been to her many times. I spoke to her many, *many* times, and the witch has confirmed our joined fates."

She looks back at the small, filthy figure. "And you believe what the witch says? Why should we believe that the Seer gave your fate to you as the Fates commanded? All Seers were once witches—why wouldn't they side with their own people?"

Long ago, I considered that, but the vehemence with which Kharl hunted down the Seers convinced me otherwise. I lean forward in my chair with my gaze still fixed on Sari, but her own stays on the witch. There's something in it that isn't quite right. She's not scared of the witch at all. There's curiosity in her eyes, but something else as well. If it were anyone else, I'd pry into that look further to find out exactly what it was for but Sari is not someone I'm willing to push like that. Her bloodline

229

complicates everything.

"How long are you staying with us? I'm sure that the empty hallways of Yregar Castle aren't to your liking."

She turns back to me, and the pretty smile melts back over her features. "I missed you, Cousin. No one speaks to me like you do. That's why I'd like to go for a walk with you, but... if I'm in your way, I'll go home to my father. He was hoping we could spend some time together, but I see that you're very busy."

My gaze flicks back to the guard, but he doesn't look worried. Whether she knows it or not, her father left her here to collect information, and in his Fates-cursed wisdom, he sent the right person.

Sari has always wriggled her way beneath my defenses, and the guard watching over her with the permanent sneer can take note of whatever slips from my mouth as the princess talks circles around me, unknowingly endangering me with every second that passes. It's always been this way with Sari. No matter how bad things get, all she can see are the pretty pictures her father paints around her.

I rise from my desk and hold out a hand to my cousin, determined now to distract her curiosity. "Come. We'll find Airlie to deal with the witch, and I'll leave some of this work to Tyton so I can take you to the orchards. They look a little grim at the moment, but I'm sure that will change soon, with the upcoming nuptials."

The words hurt to grind out from between my clenched teeth, and the witch sees it all with those silver eyes that notice far too much. I don't like the way she's looking at Sari, the interest she's taking in our interaction. It reminds me of the way she looks at Tyton, and my temper lights.

If I can send Sari back to Yris with a story of my obedience to the Fates and my efforts to make the witch presentable, then this snooping will be worth a walk around the orchard. Sari moves through both sides of the Unseelie Court with ease, everyone pandering to her and encouraging her free-flowing opinions to satisfy their own need for gossip. If I can get her to say the right things, maybe my wedding won't be such a divided event. And if the game distracts me from the stack of letters, Roan's race to Fates Mark, and the villagers Tauron has gone to offer safe passage to Elysium on the funeral pyres, then all the better.

Sari slips her hand in the crook of my elbow and stands, ignoring Malia as her handmaiden jumps into her fussing. It's only when the guard turns away that I see Sari's other hand slip into Malia's to squeeze it for a brief moment, a tiny reassurance and sign of affection to her sister that's over before I can blink.

She sees me notice and blanches a little, glancing at the guard as if to be sure he didn't see it as well, and her voice is a little too bright as she says, "I don't care if it looks grim, Soren, none of that worries me. You're going to invite me to your wedding though, aren't you? I wouldn't miss it for the world."

The suffering of the kingdom might not worry her, but her guard certainly does. Or maybe it's her father's image she's worried about, her affections for her sisters a closely guarded secret.

I ignore Malia, though I hate doing so, but when I don't draw attention to the female, Sari relaxes, and I lean into the act, playing the part well and spurred on by the fact that it's for Sari's benefit as well as my own. "You're at the top of my guest list, Cousin, second only to the regent, as is respectful. I'm sure Airlie will make the witch presentable, and the wedding will be to your liking. Which tiara will you wear? I'll be sure to have the temple decorated accordingly."

FIFTEEN

ROOKE

The Savage Prince is true to his word, and I'm taken to a different wing of the castle by two of his soldiers, one far less fine than his chambers, and stripped naked by two maids under Airlie's watchful eye. I stare back at her defiantly, my mouth pressed into a thin line as I endure their eyes on me and the press of the curse in the room.

I'm dragged into a large wooden tub, one that I'm guessing the maids and servants use. There's another iron loop embedded into the marble flooring here and I'm chained to it with only enough slack that I can get my arms into the tub but not relax them fully. It's awkward, but I enjoy the way the chains complicate the process, the maids both having to fumble and fuss to get around them. They both treat me like I'm a cornered wraith and they're being forced to serve their worst nightmare.

Airlie stands over me as they dump a bucket of frigid water over my head, a self-satisfied smirk on her face as she watches my skin erupt into goosebumps and the shakes take hold of my bones. She stares at me as they pull my arms out, the leather gloves they wear to avoid touching me soaked through, and begin to scrub my skin, the water quickly turning gray with the layers of filth they strip away. The long days that turned into weeks in the cell have not been kind to me.

I'm surprised the princess stays in the room with me, although there's far more maids in the room than are required for this task and they're positioned to stand between Airlie and I like some sort of fae barrier. Between the iron chains at my wrists and my naked state, someone has decided that I'm incapable of harming any of them in this state.

Idiots.

"Are all witches shaped like that?" Airlie says, waving a hand at my naked body as though I'm a spectacle to her.

The maids washing me share a look at her blunt question, but I stare at her blankly.

"Are all high-fae females dense and shallow? I'm surprised your husband isn't walking around bleeding at all hours from that tongue of yours."

Her eyes narrow and she crosses her arms over her swollen belly, threading her fingers over the peak of it. "I don't think I've ever been called dense before, that's a new one. Shallow is one of my favorite insults though—it proves to me that you're far stupider than you know. I don't know why you're acting so defensive about my opinions—only your mate's matter. Though if Soren has any questions about what his wedding night has in store for him, I suppose I have disappointing answers for him."

I'm not so concerned about my marriage.

For one, I'm not inexperienced with high-fae men. I doubt that the Savage Prince will be so different from those I've been with in the Seelie Court, but I'm sure there are Unseelie wedding customs I don't know about that will prove...*challenging.*

"The skin on her stomach and back is horrifying," one of the maids mutters, and Airlie steps forward to peer at my scars.

She gives me a haughty look. "Damaged? I suppose you got those in the Northern Lands. Roan told me the Sol King offered protection to all fae folk who served in his armies. What a failure you must've been as a soldier that you came back here without any protection."

She's digging for information, and my honor stings from her vicious swipes, but I shrug back. "I don't suppose any of you know anything about me or my kind, and I'm not going to waste my breath telling you about such things. It would go in one of your pretty little pointed ears and straight out the other one, coming up against nothing but air."

The maids all gasp and murmur amongst themselves at my gall, but the smile on the princess's lips stays put.

"Such a sharp tongue, and after I've offered you some decency. Who's the dense one now? You're getting clean, aren't you?"

As though all I could possibly care about in this world is the state of my skin. They're all fixated on the surface—on my scars, the color of my eyes, the curve of my hips, the way my hair stays in dark curls even soaked through like this—on all the ways that I'm different from them and their idea of perfection. I might hate being dirty, but it's the loss of my clothes that concerns me more.

"What are you going to have me wear once you get me out of this tub—or am I to be paraded around the castle naked? I suppose the Savage Prince cares so little for his reputation that he would subject his future wife to being such a spectacle."

She stares at me. "There's no point trying to clean those rags. We'll never be able to get the stench out of them. We'll find you something from the seamstresses, though I'm not sure any of our clothing will suit your *tastes*."

She pulls a face and moves haltingly over to a pile of dresses draped over one of the chairs. As she sizes them against me, she mutters unhappily, as finding a fit proves to be a difficult task and she's forced to move onto the maids' dresses which are far more accommodating to my proportions. The high fae are all tall and long, firm and refined, and I'm a witch of the Ravenswyrd

Coven with a far more curvy figure. It's nothing I'll ever be ashamed of; as a healer, I've seen a thousand different shaped bodies, and I'm sure I'll see many more. But the high fae are obsessed with themselves and always have been. I'm sure the princess has a lot of cutting opinions of my appearance even now that I'm clean.

I wince as another bucket of ice-cold water is dumped over my head. The oils the maids rub over me have no real fragrance, and they leave behind a residue that makes me want to peel off my skin. It's not painful, but the oil is poorly made and achieves nothing, a waste of time and resources.

Airlie peers dramatically at my soiled dress, her nose wrinkling as she pokes the toe of her boot through the folds of fabric as though she's expecting a swarm of bees to burst out of it. "There's no making sense of any of it."

One of the maids comes to her holding out a handful of the little silver pins. "These were holding it together. It must be some sort of Seelie fashion."

Airlie glances in my direction before she picks up one of the pins and squeezes the tines together. She blinks as it springs back into place. "I've never seen such a thing before, but I've never traveled to the Seelie Court either. I suppose this is what the villagers there wear. The fabric is too filthy to clean. We'll have to dress her in something else."

The maids all stare at each other before one of them pipes up, "A dress, Your Highness? Something fit for Prince Soren's future wife?"

Airlie grimaces, her lip curling a little as she stares at the silver in her hands. "Once we've shown her off to Sari, she'll be going back into the dungeon, so nothing too fine. There's no need to waste good fabric on her."

I meet her gaze and gesture to the water. "I'm happy to scrub my dress in there and wait for it to dry. I'd rather wear it than something of yours."

One of Airlie's hands clutches her dress, and she mocks me, her voice sickly sweet, like poison hidden in honey. "You certainly won't be wearing anything of mine. There's more than enough clothing from the servants and maids—they'll find you some form of decency. I'm not going to waste my time waiting for those rags to dry."

She's being dramatic. My dress is filthy, yes, but certainly not rags. I chose the fabric specifically for how sturdy it would be, and there's nothing about the dresses and finery of the Unseelie high fae that I wish to be subjected to. Even the maid's clothing is too fussy for my tastes.

Airlie notices my expression. "Some true emotion from you, finally. I'll have to tell Soren you don't approve of our fashions. Perhaps that's how he'll torture information out of you—forcing you into a dress or two. To think, a filthy witch looking down her nose at the craftsmanship and skill of the high fae."

A pained look crosses her face, and one of her hands slips down to rub her belly, the underside where the baby grows looking heavier by the day. As sharp as her words to me have been, there's a pang of sympathy in my chest when the curse tightens around her until a small grunt ekes out from between her clenched teeth. The maids falter in their work and share another look, but the pain passes and the princess straightens once more, the tension carefully released as she gets back to her task as though she never stopped.

The doors open, and another servant walks in, an older female part-blood who is larger and broader than the rest. She looks formidable, and under her stern gaze, the other maids all lower their eyes, indicating she holds a position of power over the rest of them.

Airlie smiles at her warmly. "It's good to see you, Firna. How fare things in the kitchens? I'm missing out on all the fun, thanks to Soren's interference."

I can't make much sense of what she's saying, but Firna simply moves the pile of clothes from the chair onto the floor and points at the seat. "You shouldn't be on your feet and you know it. I'll get you something to eat and a glass of water to tide you over."

I'm expecting the same scathing reprimand I've been enduring, but the princess looks at the female with respect and affection. She laughs, the sound like tinkling bells and beautiful now that it's directed at someone she clearly likes.

Her cruelty towards me stems from a twisted mess of misdirected emotion, loyalty to her cousin, and the curse that haunts her every move. I regret some of my own sharp retorts. Not because I said anything that wasn't true, but because there's no good to come from pressing on someone's wounds and then judging them when they lash out. I've made my fair share of terrible decisions while stuck in my own grief, and if this high-fae princess can smile softly and share confidences with those she holds power over, then I'll work to keep my temper in check.

For now.

Taking the seat obediently, she says, "I swear you spend all your time trying to fatten me up. I'm not hungry, but I'll sit because you asked me so nicely."

The maids share a look between them, but Firna isn't holding back, her words indifferent to the princess despite her royal station. "You're never hungry these days, Princess. You can't let the queasiness of the baby stop you from keeping you both fed and healthy. Sit and let me do this for you, or I'll go straight to Prince Soren and see what he has to say about it."

Airlie leans back in the chair and settles herself, her hand again resting over her belly, the baby clearly never far from her mind. As Firna steps back out of the room, she casts the princess a long look, one full of worry as her gaze traces over her. I follow it and find not only a swollen belly but ankles to match. Not always a danger, but something to watch out for.

I wonder if they know this?

As Firna's gaze flicks over to land on me, her eyes harden, and all the leftover warmth leaves the room once more as another bucket of icy water gets dumped over my head.

The dress that I am poked and prodded into is too tight across my shoulders, and the skirts pool at my feet. It's made of a rough cotton, the weave of it itchy on my skin, and I want to rip it off my body and just forgo clothes altogether. I'm so uncomfortable that I want to scream, and yet I'm careful not to let the princess know how close to snapping I truly am.

She watches me with a careful eye as the maids force my feet into a pair of shoes that pinch my toes as they lace them up my ankles and over my calves.

This the real form of torture that the Savage Prince could use to break me.

I was forced to get used to wearing shoes every day in the Northern Lands, but after years of pain and suffering, I found a style I could cope with having on my feet, even if I never truly acclimated to wearing them. Give me dirt and moss under my bare toes any day of the week.

The restrictive heeled boots that the working class of the Unseelie high fae wear are far from tolerable.

My mind blanks out as I try to forget about my feet, to wipe the pain of their current existence from my consciousness altogether, and I have trouble following the maids' conversation as they talk amongst themselves.

It takes me a moment to process what they're saying.

"The scarring is terrible."

"She's been tortured; the scars are in layers. Unless something…tried to tear her in half? Surely not."

"A wound like that should've killed her. Whatever she did to deserve that must have been terrible."

A cold sweat breaks out over my forehead, and I turn away from them abruptly, running my hands down my skirts in a nervous gesture.

The princess raises an eyebrow at me. "Parading around the castle covered in filth means nothing to you, and yet a few words about your ugly scars has you twitching? My, my, what an interesting nerve you've exposed to us."

Ugly.

As though I could possibly care what my scars look like. As though it's their opinion of them and not the source of them that has me feeling this way. Typical arrogant and shallow high fae, caring only for how they look in their stupid dresses and Fates-fucking-cursed shoes.

I swallow my reply, my resolve to remain indifferent to her seething attacks already sorely tested as I tuck my chin into my chest to avoid looking at her smug face. As I look down at the boots, I'm careful not to let my gaze linger for too long, but I do check to be sure my feet are covered with leather and laces and I haven't been fitted with iron cages by mistake. I can't even wiggle my toes, which are restricted to the point of stinging pins and needles under the shoes.

"You have nothing else to say to me then? Nothing to say to any of us for helping you tidy up? Rhya and Lily worked hard to get you clean."

It will come off as petty, but I ignore her question, exhausted from dealing with this female and the stupid games of the high fae. I almost regret sending my prayers to the Fates for her husband's safe return, and I hope they all expire somewhere very far away from me for clothing me in the Fates-cursed dress and boots.

With a deep breath, I remind myself that I'm better than such sentiments.

I feel a tug in my chest as Airlie gestures at the maids with a huff, and they both stand up abruptly and brush the dirt from their aprons, then rush to the door. Opening it, they let the guards back in and the Savage Prince with them. The lengths of the iron chains hang from his hands and, without a word, I hold out my wrists to him.

He doesn't waste any time reaching out to take the length of chain, his eyes averted from me as though I'm not worth a moment of his time. His lips move, but whatever he says is too soft for me to hear. Airlie nods back but stays seated as he tugs me down the hallway once more, leaving the princess behind without a word.

I gaze around the castle as we walk, no longer hiding my interest in the layout and workings of the household and struggling not to wince at the pinching of my toes in the terrible shoes. Prince Soren is silent as he drags me along, and the two soldiers murmur to each other as they flank me. I don't know if they can sense the tension that seems to grow thick in the air around their prince and I but with every step it chokes me, gripping my throat tightly and squeezing until I can barely breathe.

I'm led to the floor above the Savage Prince's reception rooms, my orientation of the castle getting better the more of it I see. With a knock, the Savage Prince walks into one of the chambers, and we're met by the sight of dozens of bags covering a sitting room, every lounge and table holding luggage with its contents spilling out, acres of fabrics that look luxuriously soft in stark comparison to the cotton that's scratching my skin.

"Cousin! I was getting worried you'd forgotten about me! I was hoping we could visit the library together. I haven't been there for centuries."

I turn to see Princess Sari standing at the doors that lead further into the chambers, color on her cheeks and a smile on her mouth that doesn't reach her eyes but does show off some very sharp teeth. Her own perfectly blue eyes widen as she does a double take at me, her mouth falling open for a moment, and the chains pull on me for a second as the Savage Prince's hands fist at his sides.

"Soren, she's…I didn't think witches could be beautiful like that! Well, the court can't argue about your heirs—they'll be blessed with stunning looks from the two of you."

The ground tilts beneath my feet, and—thankfully—my training kicks in, my stance widening and saving me from toppling over. I'll blame the pain in my feet and not the mention of heirs, a part of this fate that has never factored into my plans. Airlie made a snide comment about it to me, but there's something about the approval in Sari's tone that rocks me, bringing that possibility to the very forefront of my concerns. My fate never mentioned children, but the Savage Prince doesn't appear to have been blindsided by this statement, only furious that his cousin is complimenting me in the first place.

Sari's eyebrows slowly rise, but when the high-fae guard steps up behind her, the Savage Prince's anger melts away and he says, "There are still many, many details to work out before we need to concern ourselves with heirs. The safety of the kingdom is my priority, and we're still being cautious with the witch, even as I obey the Fates' commands."

She smiles back at him, but she's holding herself rigid, as if the male standing at her back is a threat to her. If he's her guard, that can't be the case, but the longer I stare at her, the more sure of it I am. She's scared of him—terrified.

She steps forward, ignoring her cousin's scowl, and murmurs to me, "Soren told me your name is Rooke. Mine is Princess Sari

Celestial, Heir Apparent to the Regent of the Southern Lands. If you prove yourself, we'll be cousins soon too. I never thought I'd call a witch a friend."

I look down to find her hand extended, an offering of peace. Bemused, I glance at the Savage Prince before I clasp it, the chains rattling as she gently squeezes my fingers with her own. I murmur a greeting in the old language, a habit when shown these respects, and her eyebrows flick upwards.

There's a rustling noise from the corner, and I glance over and see the tiny, cowering female who accompanied the princess earlier. She works quietly to straighten up the room, and Sari ignores her, but I saw their earlier interaction. The princess is ignoring her with every fiber of her being in the way that only someone desperately protecting a loved one can. I look past the princess and take a long look at the guard, sure to memorize his features as I mark him for death. I didn't catch his name, but I'll never forget his face, no matter how similar the Unseelie high fae look to me.

The Savage Prince moves me backwards and away from Sari as he says, "I'm taking her back to be guarded. Tauron will return soon, and there's much for me to do to pass it all off to Tyton. I'll see you at dinner—stay in the castle until then."

She wrinkles her nose at him but bows respectfully, a smile back on her lips as she sees us on our way. The meeting was a carefully orchestrated display, none of it for my benefit, and now I have a new puzzle to piece together while I languish in the cell. Why is the Savage Prince friendly with the regent's daughter, why was she so kind to me, and how in the Fates good name have none of them noticed she's so scared?

There are no answers for me in the tense lines of the Savage Prince's back as he directs me back down the staircase.

When we go through the kitchens, I see a large group of females toiling away at a bubbling pot and others who are kneading loaves of dough. Firna is rushing around the room with a deep scowl on her face, checking the amount of ingredients that the maids are using and their techniques.

"You need to halve the flour, Mirym! Yregar will starve if we use it all now," she admonishes, and the girl scowls down at the mixing bowl.

"I've already cut out as many of the ingredients as possible! The bread won't rise if I don't add the yeast and the right amount of the flour."

Firna mumbles under her breath, "Better to have flatbread and enough to feed the villagers. They're not going to complain about whether or not it's cooked right, they're going to complain if their bellies aren't full and their children are starving! We do the best we can and hope that it's enough."

I don't realize that my feet have slowed until the tug of the chains drags me forward again. Prince Soren doesn't bother to glance back at me to see what slowed me down, but one of his soldiers does, his features pinched together as though he's terrified of the prospect of having to force me to go down to the dungeon. Whether he's terrified of witches or the deaths of the guards rattled him, I don't know, but I'm good about getting back on our path.

When we reach the top of the stairs to the dungeon, Prince Soren turns to one of the soldiers and holds out the length of chain for him to take.

"Take her straight down and lock her in the cell. Tyton will be there in a moment—*don't* take your eyes off her until he arrives."

The soldier bows to him as he takes the iron links and Prince Soren leaves without another word, simply turning on his heel and disappearing. The soldier glances down at the chain as though they're about to bite him, but then his fist tightens, the leather of his gloves creaking a little, and he starts down the stairs. I follow.

I wait until the door above us is firmly shut and we're well on our way down into the cavernous space before I speak, breaking the rules myself for the first time. "Why are the kitchens cooking for the villagers?"

My question is met by a stunned silence. The soldiers glance at each other as if they have no idea what to do, and I wait a few steps before I try again. "Is the Savage Prince selling bread and stew to them? How much money do they have for such things?"

The soldier holding the chains jerks on them, and my feet slip on the stairs, the boots making me clumsier than sitting on the floor ever has. I catch myself just before I slam into their backs. I'm sure that would terrify them more than anything I could possibly say.

"Prince Soren takes care of his people. The villagers have no money to give him. Your kind has killed everything. Don't act like you don't know that."

Silence falls over us once more, only the sounds of our shoes against the stone to be heard.

I mull this over. The choice of rulers for the Southern Lands is a regent who happily wines and dines as his people starve and a prince who gives away food for free but has a terrible temper and a scarred face, a drawback for the vacuous Unseelie Court who don't value the story it tells of a future king who fought on the front lines of the war for his kingdom. It seems like a no brainer to me, but the Unseelie Court is incredibly stupid.

That's nothing I didn't already know.

When we reach the cell I find a chair waiting in it for me. Nothing fancy or comfortable, just simple wood carved into a makeshift seat.

"The princess had that put in there. She doesn't want you getting dirty again, in case the Unseelie Court comes back. Now that they know what you are, you're not to shame the prince any further. You should thank the princess for her kindness," the soldier says. He slides the door shut again, his voice formal and practiced.

The sound of the lock slipping into place ricochets through the cell as loud as cannon fire.

I don't feel even the tiniest bit of gratitude within myself. I feel nothing but spite and an awful tenderness in my toes, knowing that, as the negotiations for my marriage begin, the only opinion not being taken into account is my own.

SIXTEEN

SOREN

I wait in the kitchens for Tyton to take over from watching the witch for me and then flee back to my reception room to bury myself in my work there until the shame curling in my gut dissipates.

I couldn't stand being in her presence any longer, the grime scrubbed away from her skin and the beauty of her that had struck me dumb at Port Asmyr once again unavoidable. It was easier to convince myself that the pull I felt towards her was nothing but the Fates when she was dirty but not even the silver flash of her eyes could cool the fire now raging within me, fury and longing stoking higher with every second with her walking behind me.

At my command Sari stays in her rooms for as long as it takes me to walk the witch to the dungeon before she sneaks down to the riverside wing to meet with the lords and ladies who live at Yregar under my protection, the maids and servants quick to report her movements to me.

Tauron and the soldiers don't return from Mirfield. There's no word from them even as the smoke dissipates from the horizon. Hundreds of fae folk are dead or need to be accounted for, so it's not concerning.

Yet.

The next morning, Sari appears in my reception room at dawn with another bright smile and a determination that won't be swayed. She insists on shadowing me for hours, wandering with me through the castle and the grounds and making all sorts of sad sounds about the state of things. Her guard grows more and more tense as the day goes on and my answers stay vague and banal, neither of them getting any sign from me about my true state of mind.

When Tyton finally comes and collects our cousin with the excuse of wanting to see her new pony, leaving Corym in his stead with the witch, I'm ready to throw myself into a writhing pit of witches with nothing but my practice sword just to get out of the never-ending spiral of questions and comments.

Why aren't you growing any begonias, cousin? They're my favorite.

The ground doesn't just die, Soren, get the gardeners to fix it.

Your guards are patrolling too much, it spoils the quiet of the garden. How are we supposed to enjoy our walks if they're marching about covered in weapons? Ghastly.

She scowls at Tyton for interrupting us, but he reaches out and tugs on one of her perfect blond curls, an echo of their shared childhood of long ago, before we'd seen the pain and horror of war. When her scowl transforms into a pretty grin, Tyton's face clears in return.

I make it back to my chambers only to find Firna waiting for me with a long list of problems in the kitchens that I have no solutions for. When she sees the look on my face, she merely nods and says, "We're doomed if there isn't swift action soon, Your Highness."

She's the only servant in my household who would ever speak to me so plainly, but as my mother's most trusted maid who then became my nursemaid, nanny, and then the Keeper of Yregar, she's as close to family as any non-royal can come. If she says we're in trouble, then we need action, now. I can't wait until the winter solstice. Yregar and all who live within our walls will starve long before then.

I must go to see the Goblin King myself.

I meet Firna's eye over my desk. "Roan will be home in a week, maybe two. Once he's back with Airlie, I'll do whatever is necessary to open a trade route."

Fiona bows her head at me, respectful but no-nonsense to her very core. "I also need to talk to you about the witch."

The pressure building inside me leaves my bones feeling restless and frenetic, but I force myself to sit still. "What about her?"

Firna's mouth turns down at my sharp tone, but she speaks through her discomfort. "There's too much talk in the castle about her. If she's the mate the Fates have given you, and you intend on marrying her, you need to get her out of the dungeon. Not for her own good—the witches made their choices, and they can suffer the consequences—but for you. You're the rightful heir, and you can't let your fate with that female tarnish your reputation."

She doesn't voice the true ending of that sentence—*more than your uncle already has.*

Those words hang in the air around us just as heavy as the ones she did speak. There's no need to play games with this female to attempt to save face; she's known me longer than any other. She held my mother's hand in the birthing room and supported her through my earliest days. If she's saying this to me, there's no denying the truth.

I give her a curt nod. "I will make some changes."

She leaves me to my desk full of letters and half-baked plans of the future, the lives of the people of my kingdom in my hands. The day drags on into the late afternoon, and I plan and strategize until I'm certain I've thought through every possible scenario to ensure the best outcome.

I'll fight my way into the Goblin City if I have to.

As the sun begins its slow descent in the sky to make way for a clear and cold evening, the scent of fresh smoke arrives before the soldier does. Riding as though the Fates themselves command him, one of the males who rode out with Tauron doesn't slow his pace until he reaches the castle and flings himself from the saddle. He tears off his helmet, ash and dirt streaked across his face as he bows deeply to me.

"Prince Tauron calls for aid. As we finished the last of the funeral pyres at the village of Mirfield, we saw more smoke on the horizon. Havers Run has been attacked, possibly by the same witches. The prince rode there immediately and sent me to you."

My soldiers are always ready to ride out, so it's as simple as giving my command, and a troop is waiting for me outside the stables, covered in weapons and already in their saddles. I leave Tyton behind to keep an eye on Airlie and Sari, my order to stay in their chambers now a direct one, and Sari meekly ducks her head into a bow as she obeys. Airlie scowls at me, concern rolling off her, but I squeeze her hand reassuringly, the only gesture I can give her in my haste to get to Tauron and the witches pillaging my kingdom and murdering defenseless fae folk.

Havers Run is a small village northeast of Yregar, one of the few still standing. Most of the villages currently bursting with fae folk are within the walls of the castles, but there are a few, such as Havers Run, that built walls of their own early on in the war and have survived the attacks so far. While Mirfield was unprotected and almost fully abandoned, Havers Run should have been able to withstand an attack.

Part-bloods and lower fae are the only fae folk left in these free-standing villages and towns that are scattered throughout the kingdom. Before the war, the villages were filled with witches and high fae as well, a cultural melting pot as everyone came together to carve out a life for themself. I was only a faeling then myself, and many centuries have since passed and taken with them the communities that once thrived. The last time I came through Havers Run, doing a welfare check on the villagers as we hunted another raiding party, it was clear that desperation had taken hold and the challenges we faced at Yregar were taking lives in the less fortunate areas. Homeless fae crowded the streets, and the market stalls were mostly bare of food.

The soldiers ride in formation, fanning out in case the witches have laid a trap for us, but I see nothing of concern as the smoke thickens in the air around us. When we see the walls of the village, we find the first of the dead witches. They're strewn around in pieces, lying wherever they fell as their blood seeps into the ground and begins to poison it.

Grim satisfaction courses through me at their deaths, and I hold on to that when we see the carnage ahead. Blackened bodies line the village walls, hanging from the top as though sacrificed by the witches. It's a gruesome sight, and no matter how many battles I've fought or villages I've seen pillaged like this, the sickened feeling never leaves me.

Men, women, children…age doesn't matter to the witches. They might not hunt the part-bloods and lower fae the way they hunt the high fae, but they kill them all the same, especially if they believe that they're taking our side in the war.

I push Nightspark into a gallop, riding around the wall as I follow the sounds of battle ahead.

At the far side of the village, facing the Lore River and the trees beyond, we find Tauron and my soldiers as they cut down the last of the raiding witches. There are bodies everywhere, and I draw my sword and ride into the chaos, swinging without hesitation as I cut my way to Tauron.

When he sees me, relief blooms on my cousin's face. Blood runs down one of his cheeks, and blackened witch blood splatters his armor and his horse as he cuts down the raving enemy in front of him. The battle is over in a matter of minutes, the last of the enemy fleeing at our arrival, and I call out orders for soldiers to follow them and leave no survivors.

"You're late," Tauron mutters as he grimaces and sheaths his sword.

I shrug back at him. "I came straight away, and you had it handled. Any losses?"

He grimaces again, lifting his sword arm as though it pains him, and jerks his head at the wall before us. "The village had plenty, but we arrived in time to save some. Not enough."

His tone is bitter, and I turn away, giving orders to get the witches piled up and burned before their blood can do any more damage. The soldiers move swiftly, and I ride around the wall toward the gate to witness the witches' handiwork inside for myself, my cousin and two other soldiers following behind me.

"Barbaric fucks," Tauron mutters under his breath as the smell of the rotting enemy crawls down the backs of our throats, permeating everything until it's all we know.

They smell vile even before they're dead, and when I look down, I find one of them splayed on the dirt in front of the gates, torso cleaved open by a high fae sword. Black spittle still stains the witch's lips and teeth, its mouth open wide in a final scream, the ground surrounding the body already showing the charred effect from the toxic blood. Sightless silver eyes stare at the stars above us.

My stomach clenches.

I have to force my gaze away from those eyes, another set of silver irises flashing through my mind as I rub a hand over my face to clear away the anguish haunting me.

The village gates are open, the paneling of iron-lined oak hacked to pieces during the siege, and I stay in Nightspark's saddle as we pass through. Everything is smoldering around us but the air is clear enough to see the blood and signs of the massacre. The flames have dampened to embers, thin streams of smoke still streaming around us and polluting the air. The dead grass was easy kindling, and there's a fine layer of ash and soot underfoot. The thatched roofs of the houses have all burned away to nothing, and there isn't much for us to see.

I direct my soldiers to dismount and look for clues, any small semblance of proof that my uncle had a hand in this, and Tauron goes with them for his own search. Though all of my males know what signs I'm looking for I've always been careful not to discuss openly what the witch marks are proof of, treason a marring of my reputation I won't help feed into. Especially not where my uncle is concerned. All I have so far is circumstantial evidence and my own gut feeling, which is more than enough for me to know that he's guilty of my parents' deaths, but without hard evidence, there's little I can do to stop these senseless attacks on the kingdom's most vulnerable people from happening again and again.

The regent's treachery and greed has dragged my kingdom into despair.

"The survivors are in the temple—we'll escort them back to Yregar when the pyres are burned through," Tauron says. He steps toward me and lifts one hand, showing me a small piece of charred and broken wood.

An arrow shaft with black raven feathers for fletching. We've seen thousands over the years; they're a marker of Kharl's armies. The wood creaks in Tauron's hand as he closes his fist around it once more.

"There are children everywhere," he mutters, his jaw clenching as he turns away.

The fae folk all practice different belief systems relating to the Fates and the ways we honor them, but we all agree on one practice, no matter our station or where we call home.

We burn our dead.

As the soldiers build a funeral pyre for the villagers, I join in to help move the bodies onto the massive structure. It's nothing fancy, unlike the pyres in the ornate rituals the high fae perform to send our own dead back to the Fates and the comfort of Elysium, but it's what little we're able to offer them. It takes hours, and by the time I lift a torch to set the kindling alight, the sun has long since set and the flames glow bright in the darkness.

There are small pops and crackles as more and more of the wood is engulfed in the flames, until the fire ignites the entire pyre. The smell of burning flesh takes over the air, and the heat bites at my face, my eyes stinging and watering until tears run freely down my cheeks. No matter how painful it is to keep them open, my eyes do not waver from the sight of the dead as the last of Havers Run burns away to nothing.

Another failure in a long line.

One of my soldiers approaches, a messenger with him looking around with wide eyes and a tremor in his voice as he speaks. "Your Highness, we found more survivors. They ran toward the Brindlewyrd Forest as the wall was breached, but we found them as we cut down the last of the fleeing witches. Should we take them to Yregar Castle?"

I turn to the soldier, Calys, his helmet off and tucked under his arm as he bows his head at me. Relief wars with frustration inside me, because there's nothing I can offer the victims of this attack but the overflowing streets of Yregar. Our rations are already stretched beyond breaking point, but we'll have to make it work.

I can't keep failing them all.

"We'll bring them back with us along with those who took

shelter in the temple. We can get them settled into the Grand Hall for now and offer whatever assistance we can. Send word to Yrell for a healer."

Calys bows deeply and moves away without another word, calling out orders to the soldiers around us. He waits as long as it takes to know they've heard him and are getting to work before climbing onto his horse to ride north himself, to Yrell Castle and its surrounding city, held by Prince Mercer. I catch the look that Tauron sends me but hold my tongue, no point saying what we all already know. It's a fool's errand, one I'm sending Calys on to warn the prince rather than in true hopes of gaining aid.

There are no healers left in the Southern Lands—none but the witch in my dungeon with cold silver eyes and a fate to match mine.

We ride through the night.

With the survivors on foot, we have no choice but to walk at a snail's pace, our attention on the eerie quiet of the dead plains. Some of the soldiers walk and carry the more gravely injured on their horses, and it's a long night for us all.

When we arrive back at Yregar with the first of morning light at our backs, crossing through the first gates and then the inner gates to the castle itself, my gaze catches on something, and I pull Nightspark to an abrupt halt, sure that my eyes must be tricking me.

Thinking that it must be a scrap of fabric or the effect of a long night with no sleep, I can barely believe it, but as I blink and stare again, there's no denying what I'm seeing. There, at the edge of the orchard where I was walking with Sari only hours ago, are new shoots of grass.

Grass hasn't grown here in almost a decade.

The few plants that we still have are protected within the garden grounds and fretted over by the gardeners, and even with all their labors, the greenery is dwindling. Their efforts to turn around the death and decay of our land has become fruitless work, quite literally.

Yet here is something new, a rebirth that has no rhyme or reason.

Tauron stops at my side, and his gaze slowly follows my own until it pauses on the grass. "What the hell is that?"

I shake my head. "Call for Tyton. Send a soldier for him, and quickly."

There's no reason for the urgency—the grass isn't withering away as we speak—but Tauron rides to the castle himself to find his brother and drag him down here. The soldiers continue to direct the survivors around me, sending curious looks, but I can't tear my gaze away for long.

Tyton has barely come to a halt at my side, a harried look on his face, as I say in the old language, "Can you feel any magic? It must be a trick, some illusion of false hope."

He hesitates, silent as he looks around us, and when he doesn't seem to find anything alarming, he slides slowly from his saddle. I swing down from Nightspark as well, handing the reins off to Tauron as I follow his brother, at his back in case it really is a trap. Tauron curses when Nightspark snaps at his horse but I leave him to sort out their bickering for himself, all of my focus on those green shoots.

Tyton walks slowly, haltingly, as though he's approaching a rabid beast and doesn't want to startle the small sprouts of green on the ground. When he falls into a crouch, I do the same next to him.

I can smell the difference. There's life in the air here. The undeniable rich smell of the earth beneath us, the smell of growth, of prosperity, of *food* and nature reclaiming what it lost.

It's a scent I didn't even realize that I missed, though now I feel it like a hole in my chest.

Life has slowly leached away for us all, slow enough that I didn't notice the absence of the fresh scent until now, as it's waved in front of my face once again.

Tyton slowly pulls off one of his leather gloves and then, moving so quickly I couldn't have stopped him, he plunges his hand into the earth. The fact that he can do so—that the ground beneath us is soft enough to welcome him—has me rocking back on my heels.

Even a few meters away, the ground is rock hard, cracked, parched, and dead, and yet here is a small patch of fresh and live earth, no greater than my arm span.

"Well, what magic is this? What trap is laid out for us?"

Tyton turns his head slowly toward me, until I can see the glowing nature of his eyes and an unsettling sensation washes over me as it always does when he loses himself to the power within him. My hands drops to the grip of my sword, as though I could fight against such a thing taking him over. I couldn't, of course. There's no way to wrestle its grips from his mind and to stop the magic would require killing my cousin along with it, the power a part of him just as intrinsic to his being as the blood in his veins.

"Home," he says in that voice that shakes with power. "They've come home."

I don't know what that means, and I definitely don't like the sound of it. "Who, Tyton? *Who* is home?"

"A Favored Child has returned. A Favored Child has returned to us. It fixes, it gives to us, it bleeds for us."

If I wasn't positive that we were standing on Yregar land, I would swear we were standing at the edge of the Ravenswyrd Forest once more. He speaks with the same possessed voice that he always does near the forest, sounding so urgent and desperate, racked with grief, and yet…this time there's an undercurrent of joy, of relief.

Of hope.

Hope is a dangerous thing. I've learned that a hundred times or more, and still I'd let myself hope for my mate. If I hadn't learned the lesson before, finding the witch staring back at me had certainly done the trick. I'm not feeling hope now.

I glance around, but none of the villagers stopped when we did, the soldiers directing the small stream of beaten and broken folk through to the castle and into the Grand Hall. I nod to Tauron to get the horses stabled with Ingor with haste, keeping his brother close to me as I plan a route to move without the entire household hearing what is spoken in his magic-soaked madness.

I'm aware of all the high-fae ears within the castle, especially Sari's guard, but I have no choice but to walk Tyton through the service hallways and past the maids there to reach my chambers. Airlie is already in my reception room, set up with her breakfast in one of my more comfortable chairs, and Tauron goes over to stand by her with a scowl on his face that only deepens when he sees the meager amount she's eating. She ignores him, her nose wrinkling at the smell still clinging to us all. She pushes the plate away.

I take both of Tyton's arms to keep his attention. "Who is the Favored Child? Tell me."

He cocks his head slowly, and the sinking feeling in my gut only gets worse. "We want more. We *need* more. They must all return to us."

I don't like the sound of that.

Tauron stares at us both as though we're fools, and with a single finger pointing down, he says, "We have a witch in the dungeons. She's spilled blood. What's to say that she isn't a *Favored Child*?"

My eyes narrow at him, but he holds my gaze unflinchingly, one eyebrow slowly rising. "It makes sense, doesn't it? The Fates have given her to you for a reason."

Sightless silver eyes flash through my mind, and every inch of my body rejects that notion.

The smell of the dead still lingers in my nose even as those silver eyes of hers flash in my mind, and I shake my head to clear it, my teeth bared at him as though I would rip his throat out for suggesting such a thing. "It says it wants more Favored Children, that they need to return. If it is the witch, then I'm right in my suspicions and she's here to further the witches' reach in the kingdom."

Airlie tilts her head, carefully perusing each of us from her seat in the corner with her feet propped up. Her ankles are a little swollen, and a dish balances on her belly, covered in biscuits and freshly cut fruit that she pokes at half-heartedly. She's been queasy and struggling to eat the meager rations, but it hasn't dulled the sharp edge of her tongue.

"You really need to make a decision about her, Soren. Either you trust the Fates and marry her as you have been instructed to do, or you go against them and we prepare ourselves for the consequences."

Tauron spins on his heel to glare at her. "It's not even possible to defy the Fates! The Sol King was at the pinnacle of his strength when he broke his fate, and it almost killed him. Then the *consequences* almost killed his entire country, wiping out an entire economy *and* generation. The entire kingdom would have perished if they hadn't taken on soldiers from other lands."

Airlie shrugs and says, "Why shouldn't we do the same? The witches are going to kill us all if we don't put aside our pride."

I'm not so pigheaded that I haven't thought of such a thing, but my uncle is still in power. Until I take the throne, I can't put out such a request for aid, and she knows it. The other kingdoms have barely replied to my offer for trade—an offer any prince could make—they will never answer a call for aid from an heir.

Something has happened between her and the witch, and now she finds herself in a mood to argue the point.

"Do you want me to marry her or not?" I say, and Airlie glances at me before her gaze drops back down to the small slices of apple.

Even from here, I can see that it is not the greatest of specimens, the rosy blush and crisp flesh dulled, but she nibbles at it all the same. "I hate the female. I wish nothing but a violent and painful death for her."

One of her toes taps in the air as she thinks, her delicate slipper embroidered with pearls catching the light, and she goes on, "I wouldn't go against the Fates, though, and not just because we've seen what happened to the Sol King and the Seelie Court. If we forsake the Fates, then who are we? They've never led the Celestial line wrong before. We have to believe that they're steering us right in this as well. Tell me again, Soren, exactly what the Seer said to you. There has to be an option that we're not understanding right now."

I sit in the chair across from hers and lean back against the plush cushions, rubbing a hand over the scar on my face as it aches. "The Seer said that my mate would be at Port Asmyr the day after the summer solstice. She said I had to learn patience, and the nine hundred and eighty-eight years of waiting would teach me that. We would marry and I'd claim my crown, and only with our union could I restore my lands and defeat my enemies. She said that the high fae would flourish under my rule."

The words come out as plainly as they always have, falling out of me as easily as a recited poem for how long I've worked them over in my mind, but I see them a little differently now. The witch had watched Tyton closely as we moved past the forest of madness. At the time, I assumed that she was taken aback by his comments, or that the magic was calling out to her in some way, but now Tyton's words come back to me.

It needs the Favored Children.

Was it her that the forest was calling out for? Was she surprised to hear a high fae mentioning such things? Is she going to lead an army of witches through my kingdom to steal the throne with the blessing of the land because their kind have somehow fooled it into thinking that she alone can fix the damage?

I'm tempted to go back down to the dungeon and question her myself, but those silver eyes flash back into my mind once more, and I cannot bear the thought of looking into them. The way that she peers into my very being, the solemness with which she has withstood and accepted everything we've done without question... I assumed that she was helpless, that she knew she was outnumbered and could not risk fighting back, and yet…she killed two of my soldiers.

If I could access magic myself, I would use it to learn what transpired in that cell, how she overpowered two fully grown and well-trained high-fae soldiers. I want to know *exactly* what they did, how far they had to go to cause such a reaction in her, how far they pushed before she snapped.

I want to know what I have to do to break the witch and the hold our fate has over me.

Tyton has been the only one to truly coax information out of her and only when she was questioning him about the kingdom, an exchange taking place between them. I'd rather be forced into inane ramblings about pretty trinkets with Sari than utter a word to the witch with the ash of my people still clinging to my clothes, their deaths just one act of war out of hundreds of thousands by her kind, but there are other ways to lure her into revealing her true plans here.

Other ways I can find her weak points and drive an iron blade into them the moment the Fates have been satisfied, regardless of how they call me to her.

I meet Tauron's eyes. "Bring the witch up to the Grand Hall. Call the household together to hear the survivors' tales and we'll see how the witch fares holding onto her unaffected state while the spoils of Kharl Balzog's war is laid out for all to hear."

A slow smirk stretches over Airlie's lips and she stands carefully. "I'll collect her. Corym is still down there with her, I'll be safe with his escort and I'm getting adept at finding the witch's sore points. I refuse to sit by and wait while the rest of you deal with the female. I'll go insane if I don't do something useful."

SEVENTEEN

ROOKE

The addition of a chair in a cell might seem like a small comfort to the high fae, but it's nothing but a piece of clutter to me. All of the finery and material possessions they're so obsessed with are useless objects, trinkets that they keep and hoard. What use is a chair to me when there is already the ground on which I can rest?

There are many things I would have preferred in its place, the first of which are the shoes they took from me.

Tyton had left me behind with the commander and another of the soldiers, the male clearly trusted enough to be their backup when resources are stretched thin, and when Airlie finds me sitting on the ground her mouth turns down at us all. She snaps at the soldier to unlock the cell and fasten the chains over my wrists once more, and the commander moves to stand between the princess and I as the soldier obeys her demands.

I stare back at her, unflinching, as the chains lock into place on my wrists, rising to my feet only when it's clear they'll drag me out if I don't go willingly. If these guards feel any hesitancy about touching me, they don't show it.

Airlie huffs and waves a hand at me, her tone scathing. "All of my good work is undone! If you want to lie around in your own filth, then we should lock you up with the pigs we're fattening up for winter, though you seem to be doing a fine job of that all on your own."

I hold back a flinch at the pain in my feet, letting the ripple of discomfort roll down my spine as I straighten carefully to hide it. It's always a shock to my system to realize that, no matter what horrors I've endured in my life, the little things can still be so upsetting.

I never got used to wearing shoes.

Hundreds of years in the Sol Army marching and fighting did not cure me of my hatred for them. My time spent in the Seelie Court once the war ended only made me hate them further but, no matter what my upbringing in the Ravenswyrd Forest was like, the Fates destined me for a life of wearing uncomfortable items on my feet. I have no choice but to accept that.

The commander holds the lengths of chain as we follow the princess up the stairs, Airlie berating me all the way.

"After everything I did, you went and threw it away. Look at you! Filthy! You could've just sat in the chair—do they not have *seats* in the Seelie Court? I've never heard of anyone sitting around on the floor—or is it a witch thing? It wouldn't surprise me to know that you all roll around in the mud like the filthy cretins you are."

She's not expecting an answer, and I have no intention of giving her one.

The moment we reach the top of the staircase, I feel a change in the atmosphere. The tenor of the glances the maids and servants are stealing in my direction has changed. It's no longer simple fear and morbid curiosity—there's loathing in their eyes now.

The high fae have always looked at me like that—but not the servants.

We make our way to the Grand Hall, and I find myself hoping that the Unseelie Court isn't here again. I don't have the stomach for their particular type of spectacle today, or any other day, I'm sure.

How anyone can live their life so obsessed with their own reflection while the world around them withers is baffling to me.

Flutters begin to build in my stomach and I curse my body's reaction silently, the way that no matter what my own opinions of the high-fae prince the Fates have chosen for me are I'm forced to endure this connection and awareness of him the moment we're drawn closely to one another. When the large doors open in front of us, the Grand Hall is almost empty compared to the last time I was here. Soldiers and servants mingle as we walk through, and I realize I'm seeing more of the household of Yregar Castle, those who live here and serve the Savage Prince.

As we get closer to the thrones, I see high-fae families as well. Not just the inner circle of the Savage Prince but other nobles who wear the right shade of Celestial blue. It's the only visible sign of their loyalties I can trust, because their facial expressions are often a calculated façade, a lesson I learned from the Seelie Court that holds true across the high fae.

Princess Sari and the guard at her side are the only two in attendance wearing the wrong color, and my curiosity deepens about the female. There's a crowd around her, accepting her into the fold, and yet she's marked herself as the opposition. I'm adept at navigating the political sphere of the Northern Lands, but there's clearly much for me to learn about the Unseelie Court.

A gaggle of males and females stand with a perfect view of the prince. He isn't taking the throne, but there's no doubt he's the head of this castle.

The females all smile and blush in his direction, stealing glances and acting as though they're attempting to win his favor. The Fates have clearly chosen the wrong male for me, because I feel no jealousy or sorrow at their fawning over him, nothing but derision and the itch of frustration—and poorly woven cloth—across my shoulders.

I want to ignore him while I pick apart the room and discover what I can about these people, and yet every inch of my body has come alive in his presence. A hum of power dances along my skin, as though the influence of the Fates is no longer centered on my scar and instead runs riot in my blood until there's no escaping it. I keep my gaze away from him, but every step brings me closer to the inevitability of looking upon him, just as our fates loom undeniably.

When I finally stand before the Savage Prince, one of the soldiers yanks down on the chains until I fall to my knees, bowing before their prince as the soldier locks the ends of the chains into an iron loop on the ground and traps me there before my Fates-cursed mate. I grimace at the pain shooting through my knees.

When I glance up at the Savage Prince, I find him still dressed in his fighting leathers, his armor removed but the formal attire he usually wears in this hall absent. There's dirt and blackened witch blood on his boots, as though he just arrived at the castle and immediately called his household into attendance.

These circumstances can't be unusual—none of the high fae seem concerned about his attire, and it's the first time I've seen any of them disregard their delicate sensibilities regarding appearance so easily. There's a low murmur through the crowd as everyone watches us both avidly, but the words that stand out to me don't center around the state of their prince. Instead, their derision is directed firmly at me.

Killed them all.

It doesn't take a genius to work out there's been an attack and the Savage Prince intends to hold me responsible for the crimes.

I idly wonder if the Fates are about to let me be whipped for something I took no part in, if they care about such things. Then I remember what the Fates have in store for me, the future I ran from, and being whipped doesn't seem so harsh anymore.

"Mirfield and Havers Run are gone."

Gasps ring out amongst the crowd. The high-fae females murmur amongst themselves, but they clearly already knew this. It's the servants and maids who are horrified, and I realize some might've had family in those villages.

The Savage Prince waits until the room quiets some before he continues, "The survivors have been brought here and are being treated, and we're seeking appropriate lodgings for them in Yregar. We can't find a motive for why the witches chose to attack these villages, but as we have one among us, I thought it would be simple enough to ask."

He takes two steps toward me, and I look into the icy cold depths of his eyes, his lip curling the moment our gazes meet. The scar across his face stands out, slashing through his features cruelly as his mouth snarls in rancor at me. Why the Fates believe a union between us will work is beyond me, but it doesn't really matter what I think.

Nothing about today is going to change that.

My own voice is clear and strong, carrying through the room with ease. "I have no affiliation with the witch armies terrorizing the kingdom. I fled to the Northern Lands as barely more than a witchling and have never interacted with Kharl Balzog or any witch under his command. I have no loyalties to them or their barbaric aspirations, only to the land and the peaceful people here."

Disbelief rings out. No one attempts to hide their reaction to my words, and one of the soldiers to the side of me scoffs and scuffs his foot on the ground as he hisses out to those standing next to him, "All witches lie, there's no honor among any of them."

Careful to look casual as I scan the crowd, I catch Sari's chin lift toward me, her own mouth clamped firmly shut. She knows I speak the truth, but the guard at her side has a hand on her elbow, deceptively gentle in the presence of the Savage Prince and his household.

When I turn back to the Savage Prince, he shakes his head at me. "You must take us all for fools. Clearly I've been too kind to you if you believe you can trick us simply by sitting in that cell without protest. Do you think acting submissive will endear you to us? That you can simply wait me out, and I'll change my mind about you over time alone?"

Something he said on the long walk here from Port Asmyr drifts into my mind, and I raise an eyebrow at him. "Have you finally learned some patience?"

Gasps again hiss throughout the hall and a low murmur of shock at my lack of groveling and respect to the prince, but Airlie and Tyton both flinch and look away from the spectacle we both make.

Tauron's eyes snap in my direction, and a thunderous look overtakes him, his hands fisting at his sides as though he's holding himself back from meting out his own justice on my flesh.

The eerie calmness that has overtaken me is like an old and forbidden potion of gorgon root and elf blood, numbing me completely. With detachment, I watch as the prince bends toward me until one hand snaps out and wraps around my throat. His hand is as cold as ice, as cold as his eyes as they bore into my own, and the chill they leave behind seeps into my bones. He jerks my body toward him as he crouches over me like a predator pinning its prey. Silence takes over the room, not a rustle of fabric or the clearing of a throat to be heard as the court watches their prince and his Fates-cursed mate.

The smell of the toxic witch blood clings to him, bile

creeping up my throat at the stench of it and my nausea made worse by the feel of his skin against mine. The Fates rejoice at the connection between us even as I hold myself rigid, desperate to fight my pull to him but unable to get away without causing a bigger issue.

The Savage Prince's eyes narrow at me. His tone remains level and low, but the high-fae ears around us will no doubt hear every single syllable perfectly. "I have learned enough patience to wait this fate out. The moment I've fulfilled it, I'll feel the warmth of your blood run down my arms as your life leaves your body. I'll sacrifice *everything* for my people and my land, but the ending will always be the same—your blood spilled and your life forfeit. Nothing will fill me with greater joy."

I stare up at him, my words matching his in tone and intensity. "I have no doubt of such a thing, Savage Prince."

When the Savage Prince turns away from me, dismissing me without a word, I'm not taken back to my cell like the last time he put me on display to the high fae. Instead, the gathering continues around me as though my arrival never interrupted it in the first place. Everyone ignores my hunched form, and I remain chained to the ornate floor in front of the throne, an ache spreading from my knees down to my toes where the guard dropped me.

I can't use my magic to heal the muscles and bruises from the fall and the rough treatment, not without sparking new suspicions and possibly losing my head to one of the iron swords buckled at the hips of the soldiers around me. Healing like that glows brightly, and the high fae have already proved to be terrified of any power I might wield.

Unlike last time, there's a large military presence in this room. Keeping my head ducked and my gaze on the pristine marble before me, I let my magic out as carefully as I can to sense what my eyes and ears cannot. Tyton is in the room only a few paces away, laughing at something his surly-faced brother said, and there's every chance his magic will feel mine if I'm too bold about casting it out.

I observe what I can, soaking in the atmosphere and dynamic of the Unseelie Court that the Savage Prince rules and noting the differences between this evening and the previous raucous affair when I was brought before the regent.

These high fae are subdued. There's no wanton drinking or gluttonous eating. Everyone in this room appears to be aware of just how dire the food situation is, and though there is laughing and revelry around me, it's restrained, as if they all know they're teetering on the knife's edge of ruin.

The Savage Prince never takes a seat on one of the thrones.

He never so much as looks at the perfectly polished, silver high-backed thrones, sapphires and diamonds set into their ornate filigree designs, a plush Celestial-blue cushion on each of them. He works his way slowly through his people, the stern look never leaving his face. All who approach him are reverent and respectful, bowing deeply and speaking to him as they should to the heir of our kingdom.

I watch grudgingly as he averts conflicts and suggests solutions, as he praises the efforts of his soldiers, congratulates them on their victories and upcoming nuptials, and blesses a part-blood couple amongst the group of servants who announce they have a baby on the way.

The couple is shy about it, glancing nervously toward the stone-faced Princess Airlie, who is sitting with Sari and protectively clutching at her belly as she studies the Savage Prince's interactions. She doesn't react to the news of the pregnancy, even when the other female murmurs something to her quietly, though she does grimace when Sari pats at her swollen belly and the child she holds so dearly.

She doesn't stop her.

There's a lot of love and respect in the room for the Savage Prince, and sorrow hangs in the air. The true trials of his fate are fast approaching, and they all know it, a clock ticking over his head as the summer days grow shorter and autumn takes hold. It's clear this household is of the opinion that the only fate worse than a slow death by starvation is the prospect of a witch queen.

Some of the servants and lower fae in attendance share haunted looks, a scarred hand here and the remnants of a burn there, and I can't blame them for their opinions of me. I might not be ashamed of my witch blood, of my family name or the coven I hail from, but only a blind person wouldn't be able to see the damage my kind have done. Not just to the high fae but to those they rule as well.

They don't sit down for a proper dinner, instead eating by the buffet tables and mingling around the room, and it's only once the empty plates have been cleared away and the jugs of wine handed out that the Savage Prince calls for a chair to be brought over for him.

He sits an arm's length away from me, never once glancing in my direction, before he calls out to one of the soldiers to come forward.

The soldier is covered in ash, streaks of it coating his white-blond hair. His eyes are hooded and bleak. His hands have been washed, but when he removes his helmet and tucks it under his arm, bowing his head respectfully at his prince, his face is still marred with the grime of the battlefield. It doesn't take a genius to figure out this is a display for the high fae, a reminder of the reality of what the kingdom faces outside the walls of Yregar.

The Savage Prince stares at him with far more empathy in his eyes than I've seen before, calling for a goblet of wine to be placed in the man's hands and waiting patiently until he's drunk his fill.

The soldier hands the goblet back to one of the servers and clears his throat, his voice hoarse as he addresses the Savage Prince. "My deepest apologies for appearing before you in such a state, Your Highness. I was escorting the last of the survivors into the village and seeing to their care. Please know that I would never keep you waiting for the sake of my own comforts."

There's a murmur of approval around the room, a respect that he's saying the right things to their prince. Sari wrinkles her nose at the state of the soldier, but when she looks around at the rest of the crowd, she shakes off her reaction, only the tense lines of her shoulders showing her disgust. My gaze drifts over her shoulder to her guard, and when our eyes meet, I see contempt written all over him.

The expression doesn't change when he looks at the Savage Prince. If anything, it deepens.

"Well met, Byzir. You can report to me now. It's important that everyone here understands just how extensive the damage from these raids is."

Byzir does a double take when he sees me kneeling on the ground. His face twists into a mask of anger before he catches himself and ducks his head in shame. "My apologies, Your Highness."

The Savage Prince merely shakes his head. "There's nothing to apologize for. Tell me what happened, what you found there."

Byzir lifts his head again and stares rigidly at his prince. As he speaks, his eyes never stray to the crowd, no matter how loud and distracting the gasps become. "We rode through the night, following the tracks the witches had left behind. They led to Mirfield, one of the last elven villages still standing. It had been attacked, the fae folk murdered and the houses gutted. We searched for survivors and found none, and so we built the funeral pyres. We stayed while the entire structure was consumed by flames and the souls passed on to Elysium, but before the last pillars turned to ash, we saw smoke on the horizon as Havers Run was hit next."

Murmurs grow loud again in the crowd, and Byzir waits until they quieten once more before he continues, "Prince Tauron sent a soldier for aid while the rest of us rode out. The scale of the damage at Mirfield spoke of a large group of witches, and we didn't want to leave any of them alive. I went with the hunting group as we split off at the wall. The witches had already infiltrated the village, and forty of their numbers fled at our arrival. I was in the group that hunted them. We killed them all on the path to the Brindlewyrd, and it was there we found signs of the villagers who were able to flee before the witches attacked. Most of them were children old enough to run without aid, and a few younger ones they carried with them."

He drops his head and clears his throat once more as he collects himself. "We offered to escort the survivors to one of the other villages, many have family nearby, but most wanted to come to Yregar. The villagers know that Yris isn't accepting any displaced folk, and their safest bet is to be here with you. We all know you're the one protecting the kingdom."

He dances around the line of treason but no one in the room questions it, almost universal pride and admiration shining in their faces as they stare at their prince. There is no love lost for the regent here, except for the guard full of loathing and Sari, whose own face is carefully blank.

"How many survivors? You said a small group, how small?"

"Two males, eight females, and fifteen children. The youngest, only a few weeks old, was carried out by her grandmother. Her parents were both killed helping the rest flee."

The Savage Prince nods slowly, motioning with his hand to dismiss Byzir, and the soldier melts into the crowd without another word. The court accepts him without reproach, another stark difference to the night with the regent. No one here cares about the state the man is in; appreciation shines from them all.

The Savage Prince gestures to one of the maids, and she steps forward with a chalice of wine, refilling his cup as he murmurs a quiet thank you to her. I see as an idea strikes him, his hand catching her wrist gently as he stops her from stepping away.

"Tell me, Shyla, how does your father fare now that he has lost both of his hands to the war of the witches? Tell my Fates-*blessed* mate."

The female startles, and then her eyes flick down to where I'm kneeling on the floor. She frowns as she tries and fails to keep her contempt from showing. "He cannot work, Your Highness, nor can he help my mother with my siblings. He's no better than a beggar on the street. Were it not for my work here in the castle, my family would starve. I'm very grateful to you, Your Highness."

He nods sagely and continues to call out to several of the servants, all of them part-bloods from villages similar to Havers Run and Mirfield, and each of them with a terrible story of what the witches did to them.

I kneel there, my knees screaming with pain, as I listen to the horrors the Southern Lands have been subjected to. Yregar Castle has become a sanctuary for those who have been maimed by the witches. This conflict wasn't perpetuated by the part-bloods and the lower fae, and yet here they stand as victims of the war.

The consequences of Kharl Balzog's deceptions are thick in the room.

Slowly but surely, as the stories of horror and pain weave around me like a spell of their own, the ice that surrounds my heart chips away, a small fire in my gut melting it until, *maybe*, I consider doing something about Kharl and this war he's waging.

This Fates-cursed mate of mine might not deserve any of my help after all of the terrible treatment he's dealt me but the people of this kingdom are blameless and it's clear he's done what he can to help them. How much longer can the Southern Lands withstand Kharl Balzog? How much longer can I sit and wait for my fate to occur while others wither and perish?

It's not my fight.

It's not my fate to step in now, not before my union to the Savage Prince…but when has that ever stopped me?

EIGHTEEN

SOREN

I rise before dawn after a restless night, the bodies we cut down from the walls of Havers Run still haunting me. I barely touched the wine in the Grand Hall, my stomach already soured, and the testimonies of my people only making the revolt worse. The display worked better than I had hoped though, the seething antagonism in the witch growing quieter with every horror woven around her. By the time the guards dragged her away to return her to the cell, she was an empty shell once more, the same blank look on her face as when she walked into Yregar.

She doesn't seem like the naïve type, not with the way she holds herself or the vitriol in her tone when her temper flares, and yet she listened to the survivors as though the reality of the war just hit her as hard as one of the Ureen that once plagued the kingdom she ran off to. There's no way she didn't know about the attacks and the victims left behind in the ashy wake of her people and yet as the evening went on she paled further as the bleak stories wove around the Grand Hall until we were all suffocated by the grim outcomes.

The cacophony of the village outside the inner walls is loud enough that I hear it the moment I step into the courtyard. The survivors of the witches' attack were settled into the Grand Hall once the audience there was over with, but a stream of refugees from other towns that were hit farther away started trickling in the following day and night.

In years past, they would have traveled to the closest castle to seek refuge and gain support to rebuild their villages. Some would choose to secure what was left from the ashes, comfortable with the familiar, while others would relocate and start a new life, hoping to leave the war behind.

They no longer turn to my uncle or any of the high fae royals who back his claim to the throne.

It's been a long time since I last traveled to Yris Castle and the village that surrounds it. It doesn't matter that it was once my home, it's now nothing but a place of pain and heartache for me. A blood-soaked reminder of the betrayal that took my parents' lives.

Tauron and Tyton have both been to Yris in the past few decades at my uncle's request, and both have said that there's no sign of the refugees who originally migrated there. Whether they've been relocated or disposed of, we don't know, but as my cousins walked through the perfect village, there was no sign of the desperation, death and decay that surrounds Yregar. The villagers are those who've lived there for generations, and they looked well taken care of, though they averted their eyes the moment my cousins passed.

Rumors about Yris, some secrets about the missing lower fae, have reached the ears of the rest. They would rather join the desperation of Yregar than take a chance anywhere else. The laws that protect the fae folk from abuse by the high fae are limited, to say the least, but although the Unseelie Court has never overtly allowed blatant tyranny from the royals, without going to Yris myself, there's no holding my uncle accountable. Even if I did, his sway within the court would spare him.

I leave Tauron in the castle to watch the witch. He accepts the duty without a peep for the first time since we brought her home, but only because he'd rather watch her in silence than entertain Sari and her every whim. Tyton stays with Airlie, keeping her company and encouraging her to rest. Firna had brought concerns to me about the baby lying low in her belly far too soon for the keeper's liking.

The roles within my family at this castle aren't as strict as they are within other households. Each of my inner circle have risen to whatever occasion has been sprung on us over the long centuries, always with our kingdom's welfare in mind. Tauron, Tyton, Roan, and I spend most of our time with our soldiers out in the kingdom, leaving Airlie here at Yregar in the relative safety of the castle's heavily guarded walls, where she oversees the running of the household in my stead.

She's never been interested in fighting hand to hand; though a rare occurrence amongst the high fae, there are still some females who take up arms.

Duties that were once straightforward—consulting with Firna as the Keeper manages the many servants and workers, hearing disagreements, and sourcing provisions for the wellbeing of all—have grown far more complex during the war. Airlie has spent years rationing the meager produce that we've been able to cultivate on the dying lands and desperately searching for supplies to improve the homes of those we shelter. Airlie would oversee and give approval as Firna moved workers throughout the castle, employing at least one member of each household from the village to ensure no one slips through the cracks, sending food to the orphanage. Airlie would tend to the wounded as best she's able—it hasn't been an easy job, but Airlie has always done it with grace and a clear head.

Now that she is so far along in her pregnancy, and without Roan here to watch over her, I choose to go to the village and take stock of the situation instead. This morning, soldiers have escorted some of the maids down to hand out food at the temple, and another group have taken crates of bread to the orphanage for the children there. On days with such a large increase in refugees, I keep more of a presence in the village to be sure that riots don't break out. The villagers might be meek around the high fae, but they're outright terrified of me, especially those who are new to the area.

Desperation gets the best of even the calmest men.

The first obstacle of the day is waiting for me at the bottom of the stairs, despite the early hour.

Sari, Malia, and her bodyguard, the sneer still fixed on his mouth, all watch as I stomp toward them, fastening my thick cloak over my shoulders. They're dressed in riding clothes, which offer a far more sedate version of my cousin than I've seen for her entire stay, and I shake my head at her before that wheedling smile of hers stretches over her rosy cheeks.

"I can't take you for a walk today, Sari, but Tyton is upstairs, and I'm sure he would love to."

Sari bats her eyelashes at me and runs a hand dramatically down her charcoal-colored skirt. "I heard you were going into the village. I thought I would come to you and see what wares are down there. I like collecting pretty little things."

I'd like a stern word with whoever is informing Sari about my plans, and I smother the grimace and the sigh warring within me. I have no doubt she has a large collection of pretty little things, likely gifts from those around her to distract her from what's really going on.

"There aren't going to be *wares* for sale, Sari. There hasn't been anything for sale for a *very* long time in Yregar. It's much safer for you to stay in the castle."

Her eyebrows pinch in just a little, her head cocking as it always does when she's focusing every ounce of her mental ability on a problem. "How do people make money if they don't sell wares? Never mind—I've found myself bored of the sourdough and cheeses here. We can go to the food market, and I can find something else. I like the foods of the lower fae. It's interesting to see what they do with such few resources."

Clenching my teeth, I walk down the last of the stairs. Malia cringes away from me, tucking behind her mistress as though she's hiding. I don't know whether it's me specifically that she's cowering from or just the idea of a high-fae prince being near her. I share as much blood with her as I share with Sari, and yet propriety and royal etiquette say I am to ignore her entirely. While the regent holds the throne, there's nothing I can do to change this either, no matter how badly I may wish to.

The guard shifts forward the closer I get, as though I'm going to lay hands on a female, let alone my sweetest little cousin who couldn't hurt a fly if she tried, and I stare him down until his gaze finally averts and he gulps at the savage gleam in my eyes. It's a shame—nothing would make me happier than taking a swing at him right now. Even better if my sword were in my hand too.

It's hard to sneer when your throat has been slit open.

I turn back to my cousin. "Sari, there isn't a food market in the village either. There's nothing but refugees, poverty, and danger for someone like you, wandering around without protection. I'm riding to the outer wall to check in there as well—this isn't a little walk to stretch my legs. Please stay in the castle."

The pinch between her eyebrows grows deeper, and she stomps her foot, clad in a silk slipper. She didn't even bother with proper riding boots, another strike against her plans for the morning.

"Soren, I'm bored, and I'm about to make myself a problem for the whole castle to deal with if you don't let me out of these gloomy walls for a little while. I have a guard for a reason, and I'll be perfectly safe going down there with you! I travel with

Father all the time, and I'm a high-fae princess of the kingdom. If I want to go down, I can. Either you bring me with you, or Malia and I will just follow along after you until you speak to us."

My eyes flick toward Malia, though I doubt the handmaiden has anything to say to me. The more I consider it, the more certain I am that I've never heard the female's voice, much less seen the color of her eyes. Her eyelids are always covering them as she stares at the floor in my presence.

An idea strikes me, cruel but safe enough. "Fine. You may come. But you will *listen* to me down there and always do as I say—none of this acting up—because if it gets dangerous, your safety will trump your wishes."

The sneer on the guard's lips only grows wider as I back down to her tantrum, but Sari smiles at me, her shoulders wriggling a little with excitement that is entirely misplaced.

There is nothing exciting about where we're going, nothing to rejoice over in the streets of Yregar.

I lead them to the stables, watching as Sari smiles at each of the soldiers and tilts her head in regal greeting to those she recognizes. Some of the newer soldiers duck their heads and turn from her as we approach, as though they're ashamed to be seen, or maybe they've met her and know of the capricious temper her smiles hide.

A stable hand brings out Nightspark and Sari's small pony, which was bred to be sweet and well-behaved, not to carry her swiftly and safely to wherever she needs to be. Even the saddle is ornate, with ribbons and fine embroidery on it, every inch adding to the spectacle of a spoilt girl. She's only a few decades younger than I am, and yet everyone around her treats her like a child, one to be protected and worshiped and loved, never to be exposed to anything that might upset her or endanger her.

Coddling to the point of stupidity.

Whatever fate the Seer revealed to her, I've never heard so much as a whisper about it. No speculation, no snide comments, nothing. Airlie once told me she thinks the regent stopped Sari from traveling to find out her fate, but I can't imagine him doing that. It might be only guidance for her, but it would be valuable information for him, a peek into the future for him to manipulate and prepare for to ensure it works out in his favor.

There's no questioning her about it without the guard reporting the conversation, an endeavor too risky simply to satisfy my curiosity.

Malia gets Sari into the saddle and fusses with her until she's satisfied that the princess can't look any better where she's sitting, her skirts plumped out and draping over the flank of the pony. The guard collects a horse and mounts as well, but there isn't one for Malia, so the handmaiden walks behind the rest of us.

The horses are more for show and a quick getaway should Sari need it. Nightspark is also far more useful in a fight than I have any hopes the guard will be, the large force of the horse's body like a barricade between us and the townsfolk.

Those families who have been here for centuries are compliant and grateful, but the refugees have come from great trauma and they don't know who I am as a ruler. They look at me and see the Savage Prince, a monster incarnate, the high-fae prince who went feral after his parents' deaths and now craves nothing but blood and war. The heir who rules over his castle and soldiers with an iron sword and unquenchable bloodlust. The rumors that my uncle has been so careful to spread have reached even the ears of the lower fae folk who live simple lives in faraway fields that no longer bear crops.

They may see Yregar as their only option, but they'll find safety here and provisions, no matter what lengths I have to go to. I'll make sure they don't regret the journey here or the life they build.

Sari makes a happy noise and wriggles in her saddle as we cross through the gate. Her joy falters only when the sounds and smells get closer, when she sees the desperation and the state of the people living in squalor while we do what we can to find them shelter and food.

This is the real reason I let her come with me—the reality check that things in the kingdom are far worse than her father would ever let her believe.

Her stay at Yregar Castle is not one she'll soon forget.

"How can you stand the smell, Cousin? Can no one come down here and clean the village up a bit?" Sari murmurs.

If her voice were any louder, the villagers would hear as well, and I'd rather not shame them in such a cruel way. They were attacked by witches, hundreds murdered in a single night, and they lost everything when they were forced to flee here. They're not so concerned about finding a bath as they are food and shelter.

My thoughts filter back to the witch in the dungeon and the state that she's been living in, and my gut clenches. She's not a victim of anything, and she deserves every inch of derision and discomfort that's thrown at her.

These people do not.

"Can't you send the maids down here to tidy them up a bit? This is a Celestial holding, one of the royal family's most sacred covenants. You can't have people standing around stinking at the bottom of the castle. I mean, it smells no better than a goblin mud hut! The court will talk if you're not careful."

Her disgust is directed not only at the refugees but goblins as well, so whatever *additional* loyalties she has picked up from her father, they do not extend to the Goblin King. I'm also certain she's never seen a mud hut in person, let alone smelled one.

Many goblins journeyed to the Northern Lands to answer the Sol King's call. Once exiled from the Goblin Lands, a goblin would find no place of safety and acceptance within the Southern Lands. Part-bloods might blend into the villages and cities, but a full-blood goblin is met only with scorn from the high fae, the contention within the royal families running deep, and villagers often feared what might happen to them if they accepted goblins willingly.

I glance back with the ruse of offering her a reassuring sort of grimace, but I'm more interested in what's happening on her guard's face than in the turn our conversation has taken.

There's a smirk on his mouth and contempt in his eyes as he looks around at the masses of folk squeezed into the village grounds.

The maids and servants have already brought the food to the temple, and the line of villagers reaches all the way to the gate. Females and children huddle together as the line creeps forward, worry in their faces as they try to look ahead. They all fear missing the meal, or their children missing out, and only the strong presence of soldiers monitoring the line keeps the peace.

I spoke with Firna again early this morning, and she's sure that we have enough to feed everyone at least one meal a day and still make it to the end of the summer.

It's up to me to solve the food shortage and keep us fed after that.

"Are there really no shops down here, Soren? What do you and Airlie do for fun? No wonder she's so grumpy all the time. Do only the seamstresses in the castle make her dresses? What about ribbons and jewels, does Airlie just…never purchase new ones?" Sari sounds baffled by the prospect, her eyes sharp as she watches the long line of villagers and refugees.

Her hands are tight on her reins, the only sign that she's deeply uncomfortable, and the pony nickers in protest, yanking his head down as he walks alongside Nightspark. I wait for her to get him back under control, slowing further when Malia stumbles on the cobblestones. The roads are worse for wear with so much traffic on them, as old as the castle itself, and I take note of the worst spots, intending to send workers down to make repairs.

As we continue the tour, I lead Sari past a small bakehouse that was once popular. The baker was forced to shut her doors at the end of the last summer, after they could no longer have any supplies brought in.

The family has lived at Yregar for longer than I have, and with a plentiful bounty of children to feed, they were forced to find work in different areas. One of the daughters works in the castle as a maid and chooses to be paid in food rather than gold.

Most of the servants and staff choose that option these days. Gold means nothing when there's nothing to buy.

I nod to a few of my soldiers as we survey the area, but there doesn't seem to be any conflict. Whether that's due to our presence or that the refugees are too tired to worry about anything but getting food into their bellies, I'm not sure. None of the villagers were in a good state even before more refugees came to Yregar.

"Is there a healer who can come down here? Maybe I'll speak to Father about sending you one. Some of these people could really do with medical assistance."

I stare at Sari again, surprised by the hesitance in her voice as she looks around at the crowd. The smallest glimpse of empathy shocks me, but it also feels like a victory against the regent. She might not fully grasp the situation we're in, but it's good to know that her father's scheming hasn't ruined the soft heart inside her.

Not yet anyway.

I do my best not to choke on the words as they come out. "I doubt your father will want to send Volene here for villagers. He's the king's physician, after all."

The high-fae healer is older than the entire Unseelie Court combined, and he knows how to wrap a bandage and clean a wound, but there's nothing he can offer the people here. He's been one of my uncle's supporters from the beginning and, while he doesn't have a seat on the court, the healer is adept at twisting the truth to work in his own favor.

Sari doesn't notice my struggle to keep my tone from being too dismissive, and she frowns at me, her voice dropping as she says, "Do you really have no one here that can help them, though? Father is in good health, I'm sure he could send him for a few weeks…just until everyone is back to normal after this tragedy."

I hesitate, weighing the price of the truth versus deflection, and a fight breaks out ahead of us. There's a small space of empty land between the orphanage and one of the bunkhouse-style buildings we've been building to house the displaced masses. Even through the piles of belongings and rubbish littering the area, the small, huddled forms of sleeping lower fae are easy to pick out, and when the fight turns into a brawl and three soldiers run over to start picking folks off of one another, the lower fae all jump into the fray. Whether they're attempting to break it up or join in is impossible to tell.

I use Nightspark's body to push Sari and Malia both back. The guard does nothing to help, simply directing his own horse away from the fight and leaving my cousin's safety to me. Worse than useless, he's getting in the way, and again I consider killing him. The fight quickly escalates, growing and worsening, until finally a long stream of soldiers arrives to help.

Sari clutches my arm until we can move again, her face pale as her eyes take in the blood and broken bodies left behind.

I lean toward her in my saddle, the choice made for me. "This wasn't a tragedy, Sari, none of it. This is an everyday occurrence. If your father sends his healer down here and instructs him not to leave until everyone is healed, he will be without a physician. We've just finished building the latest set of bunkhouses. We built them twice as big as we thought we needed, but the unrest in the kingdom has only escalated, and still there are people sleeping on the streets. The castle is employing as many as we can, but it's overflowing.

"You need to return to Yris, Sari. It's not safe for you here, and quite frankly, this isn't the right place for you. Your father has protected you from a lot of what's happening out here, and I guess that comes from his deep love for you, but the rest of us live firmly in the reality of this war. I don't have time to wander through gardens or explain to you why Airlie can't buy trinkets from people who are starving to death down here. I need to get back to work."

Her eyes widen, and she hesitates as she glances at the guard, who is listening to our every word. It's the first time since she's been here that she's openly indicated he's here to listen to us, another sign that there's more going on underneath her perfectly curled mop of high-fae blonde hair than could be assumed by her usual comments.

Once the fight has been disbanded and we're able to move once more, we complete the loop and head back to the castle.

Sari waits until her shock and fear have settled before she speaks again, her voice soft but strong. "I will speak to Father about this and see what assistance we can offer. We haven't been hit so hard up in the north. Perhaps it's the cooler weather down here that inhibits the crops so badly. I will do what I can for you, Cousin. I don't want to see our people living in such despair and you with so much on your plate. It hurts my heart to see Yregar like this."

We pass the line for the food once more, and it's as long as ever. The fight didn't deter anyone, not even the maids, who continue to carefully ration the bread and paltry stew.

I take a deep breath to find my patience with my cousin, but I keep hold of my temper. "It's like this everywhere, Sari. Why do you think Roan left Airlie to return to Fates Mark when she's so far along with the baby? Yris is the only castle left in the kingdom without refugees arriving daily. It's the only place that isn't under threat of attack on a daily basis. The rest of us are living a completely different story."

She glances at a small child, huddled in line with his mother and clinging to her arm as he stares up at us with the deep brown eyes of the lower fae, flecked with green and looking like the rich depths of the earth as it once was.

"I suppose you'll marry the witch and take the crown soon, Cousin. Will you be moving to Yris, too?"

Each word is measured and spoken softly and carefully. For a moment, I think she's speaking quietly so that the villagers around us won't hear her, but the guard's gaze lands on me and digs into my skin as though he's reading me to detect a lie. I would need to know what family he hails from to know if he can actually discern deception, but I speak the truth, so it doesn't really matter.

"I have no intention of moving to Yris, Sari, not now, not ever. Yregar is my home, and I won't leave the people here behind, no matter how prosperous the fields may be elsewhere."

NINETEEN

ROOKE

After the encounter with the Savage Prince and the Unseelie high fae under his rule, I'm escorted back to my cell by Tyton. My knees ache with such ferocity that I'm eager to get back down into the dingy area to open myself up to the earth once more and let its healing energy wipe away the pain.

I wait until my wrists are unchained and the iron doors are firmly shut behind me before I undo the shoes and wriggle my feet out of them, wincing at the state of them. To the fires with the lot of these people, I hope they all dance their way to the pyres right now and leave me to my peace!

Tyton watches me without a word. I'm not sure if he can see well enough through the dark to note the blood that drips from the blisters that line my toes, but the earth takes the sacrifice willingly, greedily as it drinks it up and my power with it.

The soles of my feet are black within minutes from resting on the stones, but it doesn't bother me one bit. I've come to accept the power exchange with the earth, even when Tyton is present and watching keenly, though only him. I want him to see it, to know that I can speak to the earth the way that the trees have spoken to him. I want him to start a conversation so that I can question him to my heart's content about the Ravenswyrd Forest and everything I left behind there. I can hear the trees in my heart, their welcome and joy still ringing through me, but I'm curious to know what secrets they whisper to him.

What lessons they've chosen for him alone.

As if he knows my intentions and wants to deny me, he watches me in silence as the power drains from my blood into the earth and as the earth pumps it back into me. The aches and pains drift away, the blisters healing over, my stomach no longer feeling empty, my tongue no longer dry as it's sustained. When the connection strengthens, I forget about him, giving myself over to the magic and feeding the land as it aches to be fed.

I stay in the exchange for an immeasurable amount of time, hours, days, months, I do not know, but I become aware again to a low murmur. My eyes stay shut as I take stock. Tyton is still here, but he's arguing with Sari as she tries to wheedle her way past him.

"It's not safe for you down here, Soren will be *furious* when he finds out."

There's a whine to her voice, a petulant sort of tone that itches at my skin. "I just want to see her once more before I leave! He's taking me home in the morning, and I'll be stuck up at Yris for months by myself again with no one to talk to. Why shouldn't I get to know the newest member of our family?"

I open my eyes in time to see Tyton cringe, repulsion etched into his features, and he doesn't even attempt to mask it. "I wouldn't call her that, Sari, and certainly not in front of Soren. Where's your guard? Where's Malia? Why did no one stop you from coming down here?!"

She giggles, pressing the back of one of her hands against her forehead in a mockery of a faint. "I told them I have a headache and to leave me be. It's the only time they ever do! Then I snuck out down one of the servants' staircases, the ones you all seem to forget that I know about. I spent my summers here as a child too, you know. I remember it all, even though you all forgot about me."

There's real hurt in her voice, though her tone dances around melodically. It's fascinating, watching her interact with him, like watching a different female to the one who offered me her hand in greeting. There's nothing about this female that isn't put together perfectly, as if intended to be pleasing to those around her. She has the same beauty as all the Unseelie high fae, but there's a reckless edge to Sari's words that doesn't fit with her appearance.

The most interesting part of this exchange for me is the hue of her dress, which is still the wrong shade of blue. The Unseelie high fae play their games the same way that the Seelie high fae do, and the color choice is a clear declaration of her allegiance amongst the royals and one I've noticed every time I was dragged before the court.

Despite her welcome here in the Savage Prince's household, she's siding with her father.

Yet here she is, discussing family and loyalty with Tyton. Given Sari's ties to the regent, the softness with which Tyton regards her is another surprise, not just an anomaly of the Savage Prince, and the care with which he chooses his words as he attempts to cajole her back upstairs and far away from me is striking.

"Things aren't what they seem. Soren isn't sending you away because he doesn't want to spend time with you. He's taking you home to keep you safe—that's all he worries about."

There's a tightness around her eyes, but the smile stays there, her words still dancing gaily out of her mouth as though none of this is hurting her. "Yes, I saw the danger down at the village. But whatever the reason, I have no choice but to submit to his whims, do I? Please, just let me speak to her again for a moment. I promise I won't tell anyone about it. Not Soren or Airlie or Father. She's the first witch I've ever met."

Tyton reaches up and places both of his hands on her cheeks, leaning forward to meet her eyes. It could be taken as an act between lovers, but the way he regards her is brotherly, as though he's speaking to a small child and trying to make sure he has her full attention. "And thank the Fates for that, Cousin. We've worked hard to ensure that you've been kept out of the war, and here you are, desperately throwing yourself at danger. That's not very appropriate for a princess of your stature."

She pulls away from him with a pout, turning in his arms, and her skirts swirl, forcing him back a little as if she's erected a barrier between them. They're a dramatic length and volume, far more elaborate than I've seen the other females wearing, and yet the look suits her perfectly. Her hair is delicately curled and carefully pinned in place, and the long sleeves of the dress cover the backs of her hands, secured with a loop around each hand's middle finger, making her limbs look even longer than they already are.

Her gaze collides with mine, and her eyes widen as the pout disappears, her bottom lip sucked between her teeth as the first sign of nervousness crosses her face. For one so desperate to speak with me, she looks downright terrified now that we're face-to-face. The smiling girl I met is gone, and there's no sign of what happened to change her attitude so firmly.

I lean back against the wall and plant my feet on the stones, my position as nonthreatening as I can make it. My hands fold in my lap and I attempt to look as docile as I can, feeling compelled to behave well due to the naïvety of the princess.

She watches my slow movements and takes a halting step forward. Her voice is careful as she says, "I wanted to speak to you without Soren here. He said you came from the Northern Lands but that you're plotting with the witches. He said you'll kill us all if given the chance."

Her small offer of kindness and friendship must have really

galled the male for him to scare her like that.

I shake my head, keeping my eyes trained on her hands as Tyton begins to fret behind her. "I have no interest in harming you or any of the rest of the high fae here."

Her eyes flash white in my direction before sliding toward Tyton. "She's telling the truth."

A small line forms between his brows and he glances at me. "She could be using her own magic. She can hide a lie from your senses, Sari, I'm sure of it. She's fooling you into believing her until she can use your trust against you."

She's steps forward again, more confident now. "Can you feel her using magic? Because I can't, but you've always been better with that than anyone I know."

I let my gaze slide away from her to Tyton. He's looking at my feet, still smeared with remnants of my blood and keeping my connection to the earth, less urgently now but continuing nevertheless.

"The witches are better with magic than we are. It's how things have gotten so bad in the war in the first place! I'd never risk our lives on such a guess."

I grow tired of their bickering and interrupt them. "You wanted to speak to me, didn't you? Speak and then be on your way before you get yourself into trouble for nothing. All this arguing is doing is upsetting Prince Tyton, and I'd rather not be on the receiving end of his bad mood."

The corners of Sari's lips twitch as though she's fighting off a smile. "Tyton doesn't have bad moods. Soren said you were more observant than that."

She puts a lot of stock in the Savage Prince's words.

She may wear the color of the regent, but there's a bit of reverent admiration within her for the true heir to the throne, a worship of him that feels almost invasive to witness. How she came by it is a mystery to me—his impatience and frustration with her had rolled off him in waves when I saw them together.

I hold my tongue and wait for her to continue. It doesn't take long, her patience clearly terrible. "How is my cousin going to convince you to marry him if you're down here in this disgusting dungeon? He said he was guarding you, but this is imprisonment. You have to consent to the union, or the Fates won't bind you together. If you're not married in true high-fae tradition, Soren can't take the throne. That's why he's waiting until the winter solstice instead of just doing it now. If you say no, my father will stay regent, and nothing will change."

Another inconsistency—she doesn't sound happy about that prospect. I look her over once more, but the perfect porcelain features of the high fae are too similar for me to easily see any unique family resemblance to her father.

I nod at her slowly. "You're the current heir to the throne? I suppose you're the one with the most to lose if the marriage goes ahead."

Her eyebrows rise a little, her gaze shifting to Tyton and then back to me as she takes another half step towards the cell, walking as though she's drawn by some secret melody.

"I'm the Heir Apparent to the Southern Lands, as I told you, but I've always known that Soren will take the throne someday. It's his birthright. My father only holds the kingdom in safety until Soren completes the Unseelie Court's requirements. Look me in the eye and tell me that you're not going to hurt Soren. I'll believe you, even if the others won't."

My own eyes narrow at her. She's impossible to read, more difficult than any of the other princes or princesses who've ventured down here to speak to me. There's admiration for the Savage Prince but loyalty to her father and the Unseelie Court, a joy even in the time of war, though she's hesitant to speak to a witch. She ignores the maid in her employ even as she radiates love toward the female, and laughs with her guard despite the terror clawing at her perfectly blue eyes every time the male's gaze turns her way. She's a walking embodiment of contradictions.

I make a guess, and her eyebrows tell me I'm right when I murmur in the old language, "My fate is to marry the prince and end the war. With your cousin on the throne, the lands will flourish once more. If you're choosing sides, princess, make sure you're on the right one."

The princess turns on her heel and steps toward Tyton, flustered, but as she does, I offer her one last parting gift. One small piece of knowledge for speaking to me without any of the vitriol I've become accustomed to and for the olive branch she extended.

"You should strap your knee. Try to find some rosemary oil as well—it'll be hard to come by with the healers gone and the land destroyed, but you might get lucky."

Tyton scowls at me and crosses his arms, but Sari shifts a little to look back at me, her eyes wide.

I gesture at her leg. "Your injury. Whatever happened, rosemary oil will help speed the healing, and strapping it will ensure it will stay strong if you're not able to rest it."

Tyton scowls at her. "What happened? You didn't say that you were injured; what the hell are you doing coming down all those stairs if you're hurt!"

A blush creeps over her cheekbones, and she ruffles her skirt, her voice sharp as she snaps, "I'm not injured. She's lying."

She leaves without another word, the limp I noticed in her gait more pronounced in her anger, so much so that Tyton sees it as well. He can't chase after her and question her further without leaving me, and his orders to guard me trump all.

When the door at the top of the staircase slams shut, I lean down to slip the nightmarish shoes back on, grimacing at the firm bindings of the laces. I'd prefer to leave them off forever, but I'm sure the consequences of this conversation will result in me being dragged out once more. I'd rather not be caught unaware and barefoot around the Unseelie Court, not when they're so desperate to find my weaknesses and destroy me with them.

Falling asleep with the pain in my feet is difficult, but I manage it, my back pressed against the stone, and my magic carelessly leaking out everywhere.

When I slowly come back to consciousness, down in the cells of Yregar Castle, I feel a deep, foreboding sense of doom.

At first, I brush it off as nothing more than a delayed reaction to the stories I'd been told last night while being forced to kneel and endure by my Fates-cursed mate. My dreams are usually filled with the sickening nightmare of the Ureen and the horrors of the war I lived through. But last night, I dreamt of witches lost in the madness of Kharl's war. I saw black markings, manic eyes, and vicious desperation in their limbs as they attacked the vulnerable.

Not all witches were like the Ravenswyrd Coven. There were plenty of covens that sold their skills to the highest bidder, and whose morality was far from my family's and my own, but all of them cared for the land. All of them wore white markings, and they cared for the earth and the Fates that wove our lives together the way we were created from the land to do.

The blackening of their marks is the result of turning away from our purpose. A grave warning that was drummed into me as I grew up in the forest, the consequences of defying the way of the witches and the purpose of our kind within the kingdom. I thought it was nothing more than a cautionary tale told to scare children until I learned better from the witches of the Sol Army.

The blackening of those ancient and once holy symbols shows the unnatural state of the witch and the power within them, the corruption of their magic into something horrifying.

All night, my mind was filled with them.

Letting my head fall back against the stone, I clear my mind once more. Chasing the dreams away doesn't shift the feeling of doom—if anything, it grows stronger. My skin crawls with it, my magic rejecting the feel of the curse as it hangs low in the air.

I open my eyes and find Prince Tauron standing guard over me, silent and scowling at the stairs as though this is the most boring place he could possibly have found himself in. His loyalty to his cousin and the crown is commendable, even if his attitude and opinions are deplorable.

"I need to speak to the Savage Prince."

His head snaps in my direction, his shock at my words so evident that he doesn't have a chance to keep the surprise from his face. "What makes you think you can demand anything of me or him?"

I stand up slowly, attempting to wiggle my toes in the cursed shoes, but they pinch too tightly. "It's important, I need to speak with him now."

Tauron straightens and stalks toward the iron bars, stopping just before his feet touch them, and he stares at me as though I'm the most grotesque creature he's ever laid eyes on.

"So, Airlie gave you a bath, and suddenly you think you're allowed to make demands down here? I don't do your bidding. The only reason I'm speaking to you now is because I enjoy nothing more than putting a worthless, stinking witch in her place."

I stare him down, my gaze unrelenting, though unlike the other high fae, he stares back at me without dropping his eyes, hatred and loathing rolling off him in waves.

Whatever my kind has done to him, it was personal.

"The Savage Prince—"

He cuts me off, "Why would I bring you what you ask for when you're addressing your *Fates-blessed mate* by that name? As far as the treatment of witches, he has been good to you. He hasn't let any of the soldiers down here torture you. You've been fed, given fresh water and a bath. If anything, this has been a little holiday for you, and yet you still speak of him with such disrespect? No, I think you can sit down here and rot. We'll leave Soren to his work of undoing the damage you've done to this kingdom."

Fates curse this pig-headed, surly male!

I almost break my resolve and reach out to the Savage Prince through the mind connection just to be done with this, but the consequences if he manages to push back into my mind himself are far too great to risk it. I'm sure he's incapable of doing it on purpose, but the Fates tug insistently at me every time he's near me, and if they were to help him to stumble into my mind, it would be far too easy with me opening it up to him.

I step closer to the bars, but Tauron doesn't move. There's no more than a single hand span between us with only the iron caging me in. "I haven't done anything to this kingdom, not its people nor the land. I need to speak to Prince Soren. It's urgent."

I almost choke on his name, the sound of it covered in barbs as it slips from between my teeth. After centuries of holding his name inside my chest like an ache, to be forced to prod at that wound like this hurts me more than I would ever like to admit.

Tauron's gaze roams over my face and down my neck, the icy depths of his eyes colder than the highest reaches of Fates Mark are rumored to be. "I will give you *nothing*, witch. Nothing but an iron blade across your throat. I count down the days until Soren is free of you, and the rest of us along with him."

He turns from me on his heel, his back straight and the

breadth of his shoulders blocking out the light from the torches.

One last try, and then my conscience is clean, no matter the outcome.

I take one last deep breath before I blurt it out. "The curse has come to Yregar. Princess Airlie is in danger. If you don't bring Prince Soren down here to speak to me, the baby's life will be forfeit."

He freezes in place, the taut lines of his shoulders turning to stone, and I find myself wishing that it was his brother here and not him. Tyton hates me as much as they all do, there's no question of that. He isn't a witch sympathizer. But there's a balance in him that is lacking in Tauron, and I don't have to wait for this prince to turn back to me to know that my explanation has only enraged him further.

"Sit *down* and shut *up*, or I will make you, witch," he says, drawing out each syllable carefully so there's no doubting the seriousness of his threat.

I haven't seen this male—or any of them, for that matter—swing a sword, but the confidence that he holds himself with says he's more than competent.

Should I risk my life and my fate to fight with this male over a female who loathes me? Should I risk it all for her unborn child, completely innocent of any of this mess?

I step back until I find the chair against my legs and drop onto it, pressing a hand over my chest as I try to breathe through the suffocation, the curse pressing into my skin so hard that I feel faint. Whether it's my own power calling to it or the curse feeling my contempt for it, it wraps around me until I feel as though I'm dying alongside the baby.

I sit in silence until the guard shift changes at its usual time, Tyton walking down the stairs and relieving his brother without much passing between them. Tauron doesn't look my way once, doesn't mention what I said about Airlie or the baby. He simply leaves the dungeon as though I never spoke to him in the first place.

I could bring it up with Tyton, could push it further, and the healer in me desperately wants to, but the high fae don't want my help. They don't want me *breathing,* so I settle into my seat and wait for the tragedy to unfold in the castle above. The ice around my heart melts a little more, the sorrow burning hot enough to break through the chill that took hold of my bones.

I try to distract myself from the pressure, my gaze landing on my guard and taking stock. Tyton's appearance is the same as always, dressed in the casual attire of the Unseelie high fae, though he's wearing a softer blue color today, one that makes his eyes stand out even further. He still has his weapons, and there's a sharpness to him as he looks around the room and more tension in his shoulders than there normally is, but there's no doubt that whatever chip his brother bears on his shoulder, Tyton escaped it unscathed.

A short time later the door opens once more and footsteps thud down the staircase. I sit up a little straighter, because I can pick out the pattern of those footfalls, strong, confident, not concerned with falling, but at a speed that says he has no interest in being down here. My chest tightens in anticipation and my body comes alive at his arrival. My eyes slip shut as I take a deep breath, forcing the flutters of my stomach to quiet down. When will this reaction dampen? I can't live like this forever, not with a male who questions and belittles every part of me.

Prince Soren appears at the bottom of the staircase and strides over to my cell, staring in at me. Tyton ducks his head a little in greeting but doesn't seem concerned by his cousin's sudden arrival. The two of them don't bother to exchange pleasantries, and Soren steps up to the iron bars without preamble.

"I'll admit you're better than I thought you'd be. All of that sitting and watching came in handy to figure out when you would attempt your first blow, but whatever magic you've been pouring into the earth, it's not working."

I stare at him, my hand itching to rise and clasp the soft skin of my throat, the only place this male has ever touched me. My skin there tingles as though he pressed an iron glove there instead of his hand, and I feel the Fates dance in my scars, joyous at simply being in his presence.

I hate it all.

"The curse is here. It's come for the baby."

He stares at me for a moment before he slowly shakes his head, one corner of his mouth tucked up into a smirk. "You guessed that Airlie would be the weakest link, the easiest way to burrow into my good graces, but you're wrong."

My eyes stay fixed on his, never wavering because I need him to believe me if I want to give that child the chance at life. "Only an idiot would think she's the weakest link in this household, and I'm not trying to burrow into anything. Your opinion of me is the least of my concerns. The curse is filling the castle, how can none of you feel it? She needs a healer and protection, immediately. Call for one, you must know *someone* who can assist her!"

Tyton glances between the two of us before settling on Soren. "Is the baby coming?"

Soren shakes his head, his eyes still hard as he stares at me unflinchingly. "Airlie hasn't felt a single pain. If anything, she looks stronger now than she has in weeks because she's been resting more. No doubt the witch wants us to let her out so she can examine her, use her magic to start the labor early, and then pass it off as the curse. I've already forbidden Airlie from coming down here anymore. Over my dead body will you set eyes on her again."

The weight of the curse presses on my chest, as ugly and grotesque as any act of war I've ever seen. To go after the most vulnerable of the high fae in such a cruel way might be a clever tactic to cripple a race notoriously stronger and far more resilient than the witches have ever been, but it's disgraceful. I can't think or form an answer to argue my case against this immovable male, not while this pressure threatens to break me open.

Soren glares at me, and when I don't have an answer for him, he turns back to his cousin. "Watch her carefully. She's not to move from that seat for anything until the kitchens bring her scraps. I swore to Roan that I would keep Airlie safe, and I will not let some false claims endanger his wife and unborn child."

Tyton nods and settles back into his stance, his eyes more sharp as his gaze bounces around the cell. There's nothing for him to find, no nefarious traps that I've been constructing for them.

Soren nods at him. "I'm escorting Sari through the fae door in the morning. Tauron will ride out with me and Corym will assist in the guard shifts here. When I return, I'll deal with the witch."

TWENTY

SOREN

Tauron stays with Airlie all night, watching over her as she sleeps, despite her protests, but there's no sign of labor. Other than the baby bouncing on her bladder and her scathing attitude about Tauron's offers to help her to the bathroom, the night is uneventful. When I stopped in to check on them both in the morning, Airlie looked in the best health she's been in for months, with more color in her cheeks and her ankles back to a reasonable size.

As I expected, the witch's words were an attempt to goad me into letting her out of the cell with promises of her experience as a healer. She's far more patient than I would've guessed, more than I thought a witch could be. My perception of their race as a whole may be skewed by the manic soldiers I've been facing on the battlefields, and this is a good reminder that they aren't all like that.

The handful of witches I met in my early faeling days before the war started were more like my Fates-cursed mate in temperament. Calm, reasonable, and with a quiet power in the way that they held themselves. The few who lived at Yris in my father's household were deeply respected and well-versed in the healing arts, the skills that their people usually traded with the high fae. I'd almost forgotten that it was possible to speak to

THE CROWN OF OATHS AND CURSES

them, to understand them, and, worse of all, to be fooled by their calm and passive demeanors.

A monster lies beneath my witch mate's skin.

It hides itself well in her smooth movements and long, unblinking stares, but I can see it. With the right pressures, I've provoked a fiery anger out of her, and I found the monster within staring back at me. The moment I show her weakness, bare my throat for even a moment, she'll go in for the kill.

After sending out orders for a small group of soldiers to prepare to ride out, I sent a maid to collect Sari for her journey home today. We'll be traveling through the fae door to get her home to Yris Castle, a full day to ride there and back even with the help of the old magic. I wouldn't be so worried if it weren't for the witch's trick, Airlie's health at the forefront of my mind.

I would put off the trip if Sari hadn't become such a taxing guest, snooping around the castle with her guard at her heels.

I ready myself for the day and check in on Airlie one final time to be sure she's safe. Once she's cursed me and my meddling ways thoroughly, and I'm assured that she's in perfect health, I go to my reception room to meet with Tyton and the two messengers who arrived at the castle in the early hours of the morning only minutes apart, their messages important enough to delay our journey until I've heard what they have to say.

I'll push the escort group hard on the ride home to make up for it.

Fyr bows deeply to me as he steps forward, and nods his head at Tyton, who stands at my shoulder as well, before he reports in.

"The witches and rogue goblins arrived at Fates Mark, but thanks to the fae door, Prince Roan beat them there. He was able to defeat the witches and meet with his father. The Outland forces have secured the borders once more, and Prince Roan is confident he will be returning to Yregar shortly. The Outland soldiers found more witches about to travel into the Goblin Lands, but they fled to the Brindlewyrd Forest when Prince Roan arrived to deal with them himself. They've set up camp in the temple at Loche Mountain, but Prince Roan has stayed within the Outlands for now, sending scouts to monitor them instead."

Roan knows better than anyone that our kingdom is infested with raving witches, striking us at every opportunity, and if we can keep the scouts there to track their movements, we have a better chance at cutting off their attacks before we lose more innocent lives.

The temple at Loche Mountain was ransacked the night they murdered the Seer there centuries ago, killing her for whatever future she was instructed by the Fates to speak. Though the words were never her own, Kharl killed her for them just the same. To insult the Fates by brutalizing and murdering one of their vessels is unthinkable, and it's more glaring evidence of the madness that Kharl has dragged his entire race into.

We've given up trying to eradicate the witches from the forest.

It makes the journey to Fates Mark and the Goblin Lands fraught with danger, ambushes possible at every ledge and cliff. Roan spent most of his formative years in the area and can usually travel through unscathed, but larger groups need to be heavily armed and constantly guarded to have a chance of getting through.

The Goblin King has never called for aid.

I nod to Fyr and dismiss him, waiting until he's ducked out of my rooms before I turn to Darick, the other messenger. Tyton raises a hand to put up a sound barrier, covering us so we can discuss the more complicated and sensitive mission he'd been sent on without any prying ears picking up on the details.

The fact that Darick has arrived back to me alive and in one piece, still of sound mind, is a good sign. I'd begun to worry I'd sent him to his death. He's been home long enough to wash up, though the smell of his horse still clings to his clothes and fills the room. It doesn't offend me, in fact, his urgency is the reason I sent him in the first place.

"I made it across the border and a full day's ride into the Goblin Lands before the soldiers picked me up. They held me captive for a few days before we got a translator to pass on your message and get an answer. The Goblin King has agreed to speak with you and only you. He will kill any representatives sent in your stead and consider it a grave insult."

If I were king, that would be a treasonous threat. As the heir, it rides the line, but I'd have to get the Unseelie Court to agree with me to do anything about it.

Opening the trading route is more important than having his respect right now.

I exhale deeply, glancing at Tyton before I nod at Darick once more. "You did good work. Go down to the kitchens and get some breakfast before you hit the bunks. You've made your parents proud."

I'm expecting him to grin and duck his head like he always does, praise being his favorite reward, but instead he looks at me with a grimace on his face and shifts uneasily on his feet.

"When I was riding back through the Shard, I came across some of the regent's guards. They were transporting prisoners… *live* witches."

I scowl, my eyes flicking down to the map laid out before me. I know every inch of my kingdom like the back of my hand— every inch except the Goblin Lands, which are impossible to enter without express permission and the guidance of the Goblin King himself. The Shard is a mountain range that lies directly between Yregar and Fates Mark, the gateway to the Outlands, where the snow never stops and the icy wasteland is deadly to any who attempt to cross it without a knowledgeable guide.

"Why did you go through the Shard in the first place?"

Darick wrings his hands. "A band of witches came out of the Brindlewyrd. They caught my trail on the way back from the Goblin Lands and followed me for miles. I knew I couldn't fight them off by myself, and so I rode into the Shard, knowing they weren't likely to follow me."

It was a smart plan, one that probably saved his life. With cliffs made of ice and razor-sharp rocks, the formations in the Shard change throughout the year, thanks to the unpredictable weather in the Southern Lands, and it makes navigating them almost impossible. Still, I'm surprised Darick chose to ride through the treacherous mountains. There are a few places in the kingdom he chooses to avoid, and the Shard is one of them.

It was there that his mother lost her life to the witches.

He scowls down at the map before me. "The guards knew the way through the Shard—it wasn't an accident that they were traveling through there. Whoever the witches are that they had hostage, the guards didn't want anyone to know they were moving them, and certainly not alive."

It's speculation, but I'd wager he's correct. My fingers press into the embossed mountains of the Shard, then run across the map until they hit the symbol for Yregar.

Three days from here.

Only a three-day ride away, my uncle's guards are transporting live witches through the kingdom. To where and why, I cannot guess, but I know that Darick has done me and the rest of the kingdom a great service by bringing me this information.

"Good work. Now off with you to rest up. I'll have more work for you soon."

He bows again deeply, long fingers clasped in a fist over his heart, before leaving and shutting the door quietly, his cloak swirling behind him. He barely ever takes it off, his pride at having it in the first place deeming it impossible to part with.

"No one goes through the Shard, not unless they're desperate," Tyton murmurs as his eyes shine down at the map, his magic still protecting us from any high-fae ears.

My mind is never far away from the guard my uncle left behind with his daughter, the contempt on his face an admission of guilt, as far as I'm concerned. All of the high fae who are loyal to the regent are confident that he's going to keep the throne, but those who serve him as guards can't claim to be unaware of his treason.

They're the ones doing his dirty work.

I stand and lift my sword from where it rests against my desk, buckling it to my hip as I answer, "The real question is whether he's trying to hide the prisoners from us, or from Kharl. If I'm right about them working together, which I'm sure I am, he's not going to give up the throne to the witches either. If I were Kharl, I'd be questioning every move the regent makes, because one of them will surely lead to the High Witch's demise."

Tyton reaches forward and taps his own fingers against Fates Mark. "The important thing for now is that the Goblin King will see you, and that Roan is almost finished securing his father's lands. If we can get him back to Yregar and open a trading route through the Goblin Lands, that's two major obstacles taken care of. If we can get both of them done and you married by the winter solstice, we have a chance of saving our people and stopping your uncle from dragging us all to our deaths."

With a sharp nod, I get out from behind my desk, clapping him on the shoulder as I take my own cloak and buckle it on, letting the thick fur settle around my shoulders. "I need you to take over from Tauron downstairs. He's coming with me to escort Sari back through the fae door. Once she's safely secured at Yris and the regent's ears are out of Yregar, we can send word to the Goblin King and arrange the meeting with him. With any luck, Roan will be home with Airlie once more, and you can both guard the witch while Tauron and I see the Goblin King."

Tyton lets out a slow breath, reaching up to scratch the back of his neck with a sheepish look on his face. "Are you sure that Tauron's the right person to take to the Goblin King? Better to leave him behind with me and take Roan. We both know my brother's temper is too quick for such delicate diplomacy, and at the first sign of disrespect, he'll start a whole new war on your behalf."

I might start a war myself.

Tyton isn't wrong about his brother. He's had centuries of complaints about the Goblin King and his refusal to help with the War of the Witches outside of the borders of his own lands. There's no law saying he must, or even social reproach, thanks to the other high-fae families that are too terrified to do anything but chase the regent around and hope for his protection. That doesn't mean that Tauron and I don't have our own opinions about it, though.

"Everything will be fine, Tyton. This is good news, and we need to hold on to hope after so many years of despair. Let's not spit in the face of the Fates when they finally give us a break."

Tyton's eyes shine a little too brightly to be nothing more than a trick of the light, and the apprehension stays firmly stamped across his face as I leave him in the reception room.

A small seed of dread buries itself in my gut at the sight of it.

I'm relieved to find Malia on the back of a small pony at Sari's side, the princess flanked by her guard, who watches her like a hawk.

The etiquette of my cousin and her half-sister has always confused me, and there's a small part of me that thought she might force her handmaiden to walk just to be sure the guard never suspects she shows affection to her half-sister. There would be dire consequences if word of that got back to the regent.

There are other bastards of his at Yris, all of them tending to Sari and living with the stigma of being his bastard children, but Sari only ever travels with one. Malia has been her close confidant for many years, not that you could guess their closeness by the icy way that the Sari treats her handmaiden in public, or the way that Malia's eyes stay fixed downward.

Tauron takes up the rear of the escort, his gaze sharp and shrewd, and the group of soldiers fan out around Sari in a protective circle.

I start off in the lead but am forced to drop back when Sari continues to ride alongside me asking questions about the landscape and the state of the kingdom as we pass through the inner walls of Yregar, then toward the outer wall and our destination.

Sari pouts at me. "Do we have to go by the fae door? I hate using them, and I would much prefer to simply ride to Yris. I packed enough supplies to camp for a few days along the way. Malia even packed my tent."

I cast a long look in Malia's direction, but her horse steers itself, following docilely behind Sari as the maid fixes her gaze on the dead earth before us.

"This isn't a fun camping trip, Sari. I have tasks to get home to. I'm leaving now only because your safety is so important to me."

She beams at me, happy with even the tiniest scraps of affection thrown in her direction, and she settles back in the saddle a little more securely.

Her cloak is fastened low at her throat by a clasp with the Celestial House insignia on it, stars and branches cast in a beautifully polished silver. The stars are embedded sapphires that shine as the low morning sun hits them. She's dressed more plainly than her usual attire, but there's still a large blue bow pinned to the back of her head, the curls tucked around it as though she is riding out to impress the Unseelie Court and prove herself to be the perfect princess.

Everything about her is functionally ornate, perfectly designed to keep her warm and secure while also proving her wealth and status as the heir apparent to the regent. I often wonder how different her life would be if her father was a little less obsessed with her image, but it's never a good idea to get stuck on what-ifs. I know that better than most.

As we approach the fae door, the soldiers tuck into a tighter formation until we're forced into a single file, slowly moving through the fae door in a predetermined order. The soldiers cross through first to ensure the safety of Sari and her handmaiden on the other side while Tauron stays at the rear to be sure that we all get through without a hitch. The feeling of being transported through the fae door is uncomfortable, but over in a few short moments.

Sari makes it through with nothing to show for it but a trembling bottom lip, bitten tightly between rows of sharp white teeth. She's unusually stoic about the ordeal, refraining from her habit of complaining at the tiniest of inconveniences.

Malia moves through the fae door and shakes herself a little in the saddle, her eyes lifting just enough to be sure that her mistress is here safe before they focus back on the ground.

Looking over the Augur Mountains, I find them as lifeless as when we passed through them weeks ago with the witch in tow. There are no signs of new life, no glimpses of hope around us, just dirt and rocks as far as the eye can see. My thoughts drift back to that small patch of grass that we found just outside of the walls of Yregar, lush and green with life.

It's still there.

I send a soldier to check it each morning and, despite our initial shock, it's continued to grow—at a snail's pace, but still a sign of life and the possibility of hope.

"Do you think the Seer will ever come back?" Sari says, her eyes squinting up toward the temple at the top of the hill.

Those cursed stones lead up to the temple that once held the Seer who gave me my fate. She left the Southern Lands for her own safety shortly after my last visit, walking all the way to Port Asmyr and sailing to the Northern Lands, where the Fates War is over and witches are treated with less violence and suspicion. Word arrived later that the Sol King offered her residence within the Golden Palace, the shining centerpiece of the Sol City and, if rumors are to be believed, a sight like no other.

I wonder if she met my mate while she was still there, if she told the witch about all the times I visited her and begged to learn my mate's location. My theories of her having been stolen from me, abducted and held captive, all of it a fantasy compared to the reality of things.

"It's not safe here for Seers. You know what the witches did to the one at Loche Mountain. The protection wards laid over her temple for millennia couldn't hold up forever. She knew she was safer somewhere else."

Sari's delicately gloved hands tighten on her pony's reins. The animal barely reaches Nightspark's shoulder, but it's obedient and carries her well enough. It's not like she needs to ride into war, and with the guard at her side, she should be safe.

She hums under her breath, taking in the bleak view of the kingdom around us. "I sometimes forget that the Seers were once witches too. I got my fate from the witch at Loche Mountain. She was kind to me. Strange in the way that all Seers are, but kind."

Sari has never told her fate to me, I wasn't even certain she had made the journey to receive one thanks to the turmoil in the kingdom after my parent's murder. The regent once mentioned that it would be some time before he'd be getting any further heirs, so she must be waiting for her mate like I had to. I wish now that I'd asked her without the guard present, because her sad look underneath her pinched brows strikes my curiosity.

"We don't have time for that. Your father's males are meeting us at the northern bridge on the Lore River. If we don't get going now, Cousin, you won't be back at Yris before nightfall."

She sighs and urges her horse on, clicking her tongue at it until we're moving swiftly down the north side of the mountain. Fields that once were filled with crops and livestock lay barren before us, but the path north to the bridge is quiet. I'm expecting it to stay quiet until we see Sari safely into the arms of her father and his guards.

It's on the ride home that we'll be ambushed, another so-called coincidence in a long list of attacks that never impede the regent or those who follow him but always happen at my expense.

Sari holds herself stiffly in the saddle, her posture growing tighter the farther we ride. She could brush it off as simple discomfort, but she's favoring one side.

Tyton questioned her about an injury last night, before she retired to the guest wing, but she swore that she was in perfect health. The way she tenses and leans toward the left, I would guess that she's hiding a wound from us all.

The witch was the one to spot the injury and point it out to Tyton. Sari denied it vehemently, but once he spoke to me about it, I could see it as well. Loath as I am to admit it, I find that I'm jealous of the witch's ability to observe more than the usual naked eye, her searing gaze never missing a thing.

From the moment we first made camp with her, I said that

we'd have to watch out for her. There's never been a doubt in my mind that she listens to every word spoken within her earshot. Her attempt to use Airlie against us was fumbling at best, but proof of that.

"Your Highness!"

I snap myself out of my thoughts and look over at the soldier who called out, standing in his saddle as he peers down at something on the edge of the path, dead underbrush thick all around us.

I motion to Tauron, and he nods as I ride forward, snapping at Sari to stay put when she attempts to follow me. The guard and Malia both move to stop her as well, pigeonholing her in the safety of the circle of soldiers, and when I reach the soldier, I look down and see the dead spot.

It's a sign of a battle fought here, and witches dead but not burned up. It's still fresh enough that the ground seems to ache from the acid left behind by the magic. Even with my distance from magic, I can feel it, the way the pain radiates into the air around us, and though I can't describe exactly how I know, there's no doubt in my mind that it's real.

The earth is in agony.

Thanks to high-fae hearing, I don't need to raise my voice to get my orders out. "Fan out and keep your eyes sharp. This is only two or three days old, and there's every chance they're camping nearby or lying in wait for us."

Cursing under my breath, I direct Nightspark back into the lead position and get us moving. Having Tyton with us would've been useful, blanketing us and masking our presence with his magic, but Tauron has his own skills to contribute.

When Sari opens her mouth to question me again, he snaps at her, sharper than usual, "We're in danger, Sari. I need you to stop talking and keep your pony moving. We're an hour away from the river at best, and every word out of your mouth could bring us closer to our deaths. Not another word, or you might as well wave a banner for the witches to come get you for their next meal."

Tauron never flinches from the killing blow, no matter the consequences or the recipient. If it must be done, he never hesitates or wavers.

Sari's teeth crack as she snaps her mouth shut and glances at Malia, but when her maid doesn't return her gaze, her eyes flick toward the guard.

The contempt on his face doesn't melt away as he looks at the regent's daughter. Instead, his hand drops down to rest on the hilt of his sword, and he jerks his head to direct her forward. She gets moving, her lips pressed tightly together and every last trace of joy wiped from her pretty features. As the group continues forward, the dead spots appear more frequently until we're forced to ride over them, no longer able to maneuver around them.

The ache of earth becomes so loud in our minds that Sari begins to clutch at her cloak, wrapping it tighter around her shoulders as though she can chase the terrible feeling away if only she can get warm enough. The soldiers are primed and ready to fight, silent through the carnage until finally we find the first dead body on the ground.

The witch's eyes have been plucked out by some opportunistic bird of prey, its mouth open in one last scream, forever gaping up at the sky.

Sari tries to smother a gag, but it bubbles out of her regardless, and she gasps and chokes as she presses a handful of her cloak against her mouth.

I'm drawing my sword before I hear the first war cry ahead of us, only minutes away from the river and no way to get to the regent without first facing the enemy between us.

TWENTY ONE

ROOKE

Hours after Prince Soren bids Tyton farewell and leaves him with the command to watch me while he's gone, I'm startled by the door at the top of the staircase bursting open but no footsteps following.

Tyton straightens with a scowl and strides over to see what the hell happened, but he stops abruptly just out of my line of sight. Whatever is said to him is too quiet for me to hear, but I catch his answer perfectly.

"Send a messenger out to Prince Soren immediately and one up to Fates Mark to Roan. Clear the castle of any visitors and triple the guard duties. I'll remain here until Soren arrives, unless Airlie needs me. Keep me updated."

The labor has begun.

I squeeze my eyes shut before Tyton returns to his post, my gut churning as bile creeps up the back of my throat. This might be the most effective torture so far, to be forced to sit here and wait while tragedy unfolds in the castle above me. I can't open a connection to the earth, not while my mind is in such chaos, and it takes all my focus not to vomit.

The minutes crawl past, slowly ticking into hours, and nothing changes, not the loaded silence in the room or the violent revolt of my gut, not even the intensity of the curse as it sings its bleak victory in the air around me. I wonder how long it's been since a high-fae baby was taken by it. By the hunger within the magic, the glee of the evil around me, it must have been years, if not decades. The curse aches for life the same as the earth does, though for unnatural and unconscionable reasons.

It's impossible to tell what the time is here in the dungeon, but as I let my own magic out around me, I find the sun is still sleeping, hours away from rising. There's nothing else here that could have woken me, no signs of changes in the dungeon, but the slick feel of the witches' malevolent magic on all high fae within the kingdom is so thick in the air that it chokes me, and all I can hear is despair.

It's here to take the life of the baby.

I could stay right here in the dungeon, where I've been left to rot by my Fates-cursed mate. I could do what I set out to do when I returned to the Southern Lands, merely sit back and let my fate come to pass around me, as the Seer had told me.

The words that were spoken to me repeat again in my mind, and the Fates begin to play wildly under my scar once more. Saving the kingdom could mean that I pour my magic into the earth to give back to it…and it could also mean breaking the curse laid over the high fae.

My treatment here in the castle says I should stay here and leave them to figure it out on their own.

I look at Tyton and find him staring back at me, his face drawn and guarded as he listens to the chaos above us. My own ears aren't sensitive enough to pick anything up, but the curse is running riot with my senses, my magic leaking out all over the cell, until the picture in my mind of what's happening is so clear that I might as well be up there in the room with Airlie.

"Soren will kill you for doing this to her, Fates be damned," Tyton spits at me, his face a vicious replica of his surly brother's, but whether I want to admit it or not, I've made up my mind.

His raw magic might be strong by high-fae standards but it's nothing compared to mine. I push into his mind in a rush, breaking past the barriers he's so feebly erected there, and put him into a deep sleep, as simple as blowing out a candle. A net of power catches his body as he slumps, easing him onto the ground and positioning him to be sure he won't do something stupid and inconvenient for me like choke on his own tongue while I'm busy upstairs.

I stand and brush the dirt from my pants as best as I can and let my magic flow out of my body, wrapping around the iron bars of my cell, and then I pull it back into myself in a sharp action, breaking the cell door until I can push it gently with my hand to open it, ignoring the slight sting of it as my bare skin touches the horrid metal.

My legs ache a little from sleeping bunched up against the stone wall, and I take a moment to shake them out before I climb the treacherous staircase back up to the castle. There's every chance I'm going to be discovered by maids or servants, and I'll have to decide then how badly I want to intervene with what evil is about to take place here.

The princess may still refuse my help.

My guess is she will, but I was raised in the Ravenswyrd Forest as the Maiden of the coven, to someday be the Mother, and to give help to any who need it, selflessly and without ever asking for payment. Nothing has taken that away from me, neither my time in the Seelie Court nor my mistreatment here at the hands of my mate and his family.

I won't wallow in my misery when there's a chance I can help her.

My feet on the stone staircase are silent to my own ears, but the high fae can hear a mouse's footsteps from ten miles away if they try hard enough, so I move quickly. I know the basic layout of the castle, thanks to my rare trips out of the dungeon, but I don't need to know the exact way to know where I'm going.

I let the curse lead me.

Three long hallways, another set of stairs, through two more doors, and then finally I'm led into a wing of the castle that looks like a home, all while using my magic to side-step and hide from the inhabitants. It's slow going, and my skin itches with impatience, but I find myself staring at a large set of wooden doors, white oak and inlaid with silver filigree, beautiful and throbbing with death.

The princess screams within.

Productive screaming—she's working through the labor and sounds as though she still has her strength. It's a good sign, considering how heavy the curse lies in the air.

My hand pauses over the door handle.

This is the most vulnerable state a female can find herself in. Is it wrong of me to barge in there and demand to help her, even if I'm the only one who can? If she would never have agreed before the labor began, is it wrong to ask to help her now while she's in such pain? Is the child's life worth the invasion of privacy?

The hand she constantly held over her belly in my presence flashes into my mind, and I murmur a quiet prayer to the Fates. Not for their forgiveness, I'm still too numb to think about that possibility yet, but to give me the strength to leave this room if the princess throws me out. I shove the door open without another second of hesitation and step through the frame with the confidence of a healer who has attended hundreds of births and seen it all.

Three maids, a soldier, and the princess all turn to me in horror.

The soldier reacts first, his back turned away from the scene on the bed, and charges toward me as he moves to draw his sword. I knock him out the same way I did Tyton, letting him fall on his face in front of me and then stepping around his prone form.

One of the maids screams and runs, dropping the bundle of cloths in her hands in her haste. The youngest simply gulps, her eyes glued to the soldier as she trembles, her feet rooted to the floor.

Firna steps in front of the bed as though shielding the princess, her own gaze steady on mine. "Leave now and I won't send the soldiers after you. I'll give you a head start back to the ports and, if you're quick, you'll beat Prince Soren there."

Airlie's breathing changes, and she grunts under her breath as the next wave of a contraction descends upon her. Her back arches up as she works through it, oblivious to anything but her labor. The younger maid finally takes control of her own limbs and leans over the princess, mopping her brow with a cloth and trembling hands. The smell of incense and herbs is strong in the air, but they're the wrong types, fragrant and pleasant but achieving nothing toward a healthy birth or pain management.

None of them have magic, at least not enough to feel when I reach out to the princess and wedge my power between her and the curse. It's not enough to save the baby's life, but it will buy me some time to convince them I mean them both no harm.

Firna doesn't move, unblinking as her offer of a chance for freedom in exchange for the princess's life stands.

I shake my head at her slowly, carefully, so I don't startle any of them into doing something stupid. "I'm here for my fate."

Firna swallows at my words, fear creeping into the tense lines of her shoulders as her eyes flick to the soldier's sleeping body, but I shake my head again. "I'm not here to hurt them. I'm offering my help to them. The curse is here for the baby. I can feel it, and with how strong it's pressing down on me right now, I'll wager you all can too. I'll help get the baby out without the curse touching it."

My words are met with silence, Airlie's breathing even once more as she rests between the pains, and I begin to count. I couldn't forget the timeless processes of labor if I tried, my mind already moving through the teachings my own mother once gave me to properly attend births. The contractions are strong and long, so depending on when the next one arrives, I'll know how long the princess has to make her decision.

Holding my head high, I stand and count calmly as I wait for them to decide. The young maid looks anywhere but at me, clutching the bowl of water and cloths as though they'll save her from the evil witch. Firna waits, as still as I am, conflicting emotions warring over her features.

Finally, Airlie's mind seems to clear, and she snaps, "*Get out*. Get out and go back to the cells to rot where you deserve to be for what you've taken from me!"

Firna's eyes widen, but I ignore her, speaking only to the princess. "I have taken nothing from you, Princess. I'm here to help you and your baby."

Airlie begins panting again, and I haven't yet made it to one hundred. The baby is almost here, and if her body hasn't begun pushing yet it's only a matter of time before it will. We don't have time to argue about this.

A truth to ease the way, one I would give only under such circumstances.

"I've attended hundreds of births, both here in the Southern Lands and during my time in the Northern Lands. I've helped every race—it never mattered to me who was birthing, only that they needed help. I'm your only option."

She moans under her breath, tears streaking down her face, and that's what forces the next words out of my mouth. "The last birth I attended was for the Sol Queen. Her son, the heir of the Seelie Court, was breech. She labored for three days, but I helped her deliver him safely. I will use my magic, but only against the curse, I swear it on the Fates themselves."

That's enough of an endorsement for Firna.

She steps aside, moving back even as she watches me closely. I have no doubt that she will step in if at any point she thinks I'm endangering the princess, but I'm also aware that I'll knock her out if that moment comes.

I step closer to the bed, finally getting a good view of Airlie and the state she's in. The bedding has all been removed, and she's wearing a linen shift, her hair in a simple braid to keep it away from her face. I wait and watch as she writhes through the next contraction, silent until the calm falls over her once more.

"Do you want this baby or not?"

She looks at me with loathing, but there's a fierceness to her that I haven't seen before. A lioness crouching over the life of the babe in her belly, alive for now, and any doubts I may have had about her vanish. She's not only strong enough to do this, she is determined enough to accept nothing less than the best for her child.

I pitch my tone low, calming and sure. "If you trust me to help, I will get him out alive."

Her lip trembles, her composure wavering for just a moment, but then she says in a small voice, "Him?"

I nod. "I can feel him there. He's healthy, and he's fighting to get out and be here with you. Are you going to fight for him as well? I will fight at your side. I'll help you break this curse once and for all."

Firna gasps, but I ignore her, my eyes trained on the princess. She stares back at me, afraid and strong in the way that only mothers can truly be. To feel all of the possible futures in their hearts and to grasp at the best one for their child, holding on tight with everything they have.

The baby is a lucky child to have such a mother fighting for him.

"What will it be, Princess? Are we going to break this curse together, or will you leave it to the Unseelie Court, hoping they someday get around to doing something about all this pain and heartache?"

She swallows, her brow still slick with sweat and her cheeks flushed from the pain she's in. Small wisps of hair that have come loose from the braid stick out in every direction, framing her face, her limbs bare and shaking a little, but she's never looked more beautiful or powerful to me.

She is female incarnate, and the moment her eyes meet mine, clear and sure, she nods.

"I won't be burning another son on the funeral pyres. If you get him here safely, alive and unharmed, I'll help you. I'll get Soren to let you out of the dungeon."

I shake my head and grab the burning bowl of incense, prying open the window and shoving it out to clear the room of its useless scent. "I'm not doing this for your favor. That's not how I was raised. I'm doing this because you have a need for a midwife and I'm capable. That's it. We can discuss your opinions on my treatment later. Let me get the room cleared first while I track the pains to be sure of how far you are into your labors."

Her eyebrows stay bunched up, but she nods and slumps against the pillows while I work around her. Firna's gaze follows me, but she doesn't attempt to step in as I remove all of the useless herbs, oils, and flowers from the area.

Once I have fresh air in the room, I scrub my hands in the adjoining bathing room until I'm sure there isn't a speck of dirt left on them. Then, sitting at the end of the bed, I watch the princess as she breathes through the next wave of pain.

She's strong and focused, far more so than she was when I arrived. She truly believes I might be able to help her, and I'm glad for it. This will be much harder if she's lost all hope.

"There are herbs that can help with the discomfort; I can give the maids a list to find for you," I say but she shakes her head.

"I welcome the pain. The pain says he's coming finally, each one a step closer to holding him in my arms."

Her words are strong, but she still sounds sorrowful, as though she's already preparing herself for failure. He's coming soon, working his way out of her womb with every wave, and she's trapped in the winding mess of the curse pressing on her body like an iron slab, held up only by my own magic. Curses are fickle beasts to best, but this one has been stretched thin. To cover an entire kingdom, it needs to be fed. I'd wager in the first centuries, there were many lives lost as the high fae came to understand what the curse was doing to them, and those unwilling sacrifices fed the evil and strengthened it.

I doubt there've been any sacrifices since the last baby Airlie lost, and before that baby, many centuries may have passed. The grips of the magic feel desperate, the clawing vicious as it digs to claim the baby. If I get the baby out alive, I can break the curse.

Shields have always been my greatest gift.

I build a wall around that little boy, pouring every drop of power the earth has been sharing with me into it until I've woven together an impenetrable cocoon to hold him. The curse fights me; it's older than I am and a malevolent thing as it claws at me, but I've fought off far worse than this. If I can travel to the Northern Lands, become a soldier there and fight the Ureen for centuries of heartache, if I can take the little girl from the forest and form her into the female that I am now, I can protect this small babe.

I'm sick of watching everyone around me die.

"I feel as though I need to push, but it's too early for that," the princess moans, her hands clutching the bedsheets, and I send a warning look to Firna when she startles toward the bed in fear.

My tone is low and soothing, calm against the storm of Airlie's fear and desperation, as I say, "Babies come when they're ready, not on our timing. If your body says to push, then listen to it, I'll do the rest. Princess, look at me and hear the truth in my words. I will do everything else, you just focus on getting him out."

She chokes on a sob, another small sign of despair, but then the pains begin again. She grits her teeth, a low grunting noise tearing out of her unbidden as she pushes with every last fiber of her being.

The curse digs into the shield I've protected the boy with, and pain bursts behind my eyes as I force myself to ignore it and keep working. I cast my magic over her womb and feel the baby continue his descent, working with his mother to join her. The cord is coiled around his neck, and my magic eases it away a little as I ready myself to free him, a natural occurrence that I won't let take him after everything else we're doing to get him here safely.

The princess lets out a scream, and I have to stand up to get her attention before I can get back to work, a sweat breaking out over my forehead as the curse fights me with all of its might. "Stop pushing for a moment, just breathe, that's it, short breaths, I'm getting his cord away from his neck, just a moment—okay, push again, Princess, we'll get his shoulders out next. He's beautiful, looks just like his father, one more push…there he is!"

I look down to find the baby staring up at me, his golden eyes bleary but curious in the way of babies, and he blinks at me as I catch him, one last scream tearing out of his mother as she feels the relief of his birth, the effort and pains over with in one final mighty push. The pressure of the curse feels as though it's about to break open my skull, the final desperate push to hold onto the baby's life and consume it, but my magic holds strong. Even as my vision blurs, I hold true. The princess fought hard for her son, and she's *won*.

The curse shatters around us.

Blinking away the last of the stars from my eyes, the pain disappearing in an instant but my body struggling to catch up to its absence, I grasp the baby's slippery form firmly in my hands. He's small and a little limp with exhaustion, but alive. I move him quickly onto the bed to clear his airways, rubbing his back and then giving him a quick breath to get his lungs working the way they need to. He's so small, maybe a little early in his arrival, but his arms are strong as he flails them in the air, searching for his mother's warmth.

The princess collapses onto the bed with a sob, her entire body overtaken by grief as she mourns her son.

But he's alive and well in my hands.

With one last breath from my lungs into his, he sputters out a cough and then makes the most beautiful sound a mother could wish for in this moment.

He screams for her.

TWENTY TWO ✦

SOREN

Tauron screams my name, enraged, as I kick Nightspark and spur him forward into the fight. I bark out orders to the soldiers to cover Sari and her handmaid as I leave them behind, all of my focus on the war band.

Whoever they were fighting is gone now, leaving behind this small battalion of witches, but the moment I charge, riding Nightspark toward them like a monster of the Fates, they spring into action.

Screams rend the air as they cast their magic, arcs of light and power surging at me until the air around me is thick with it. I lift my sword toward my face, blocking what I can even as a ball of power as big as a fist strikes my shoulder. It glances off my armor but still does damage, a crater left behind on the iron plate.

When I lift my sword again, the muscles scream, but I ignore the pain and swipe at my enemy as they flock toward me in a swarm, the same battle plan they always have. Dozens of witches against a handful of high fae, their numbers are the only chance they have to win against us, but the magic in this group is stronger than the simple raiding parties I've been dealing with lately. It's a timely reminder of the true threat they are, biding their time until we're at our weakest before they go in for the kill.

Nightspark whinnies and rears as the ground around us

lights up, the dead grass like a tinderbox the moment the magic hits it.

"Get Sari to the river," I yell as I swing my sword again, grunting as it slices through the witch in front of me.

My injured shoulder takes the brunt of the impact, but my arm slowly begins to numb out, the pain pushed to the back of my mind as the swarm of our enemy rides around me. The markings on their faces glow black as they become an advancing wave of destruction.

The witches all hold swords of their own, pathetic in their technique but hard to fight off when there are so many of them. I hear my soldiers fighting around me and can only hope some have done as I've instructed and gotten Sari away to safety.

The screaming, ranting madness of the spells chanted in a foreign tongue blocks out all other sounds, and I'm forced to clear my mind of anything but the swing of my sword so I don't get hit by their magic.

Swing, hack, stab, and block. I push Nightspark forward into the mass of bodies and use him as a weapon of his own, trampling witches as the magic bounces off the iron breastplate hung high around his neck.

Swing, block, hack, swing, the witches don't even bother to lift their swords as they desperately throw their magic at me. They're exhausted from their earlier battle, and their magic is depleted, stopped by the iron surrounding me. Limbs go flying as their screams drown everything else out. I fight through muscle memory and reflex alone, becoming nothing but cold rage even as my enemies' fury burns around me.

My senses scream, and I turn in my saddle just in time to raise my sword and impale the witch flinging himself at me, silver eyes manic and rolling with black spittle running down his chin. The black markings on his face throb with power, even as he chokes on his own blood. His limbs are still jerking in the throes of death when I yank my sword away, and the body drops from it and crunches as it hits the ground.

There's more jeering and yelling, and Tauron comes alongside me, swiping and maiming as he goes, cleaving the head off one of the raving witches with a single swing of his sword. The sapphire in the hilt glows with power as it absorbs the magic of the witch's blood, neutralizing it and sending it back into the earth. It's the advantage of using my grandfather's sword, passed down the Celestial bloodlines from the First Fae and infused with their power, now long forgotten.

We work together, and the last of the witches who swarmed me falls away from Nightspark, its chest cleaved open by my sword and its black blood oozing into the earth beneath us. I take stock of the situation.

Three of my soldiers stand with Tauron on foot as they deal with the remaining witches. Many were too injured to join the fray with no magic left to protect themselves.

With nothing more than a grimace on his face, Tauron works his way through them all, shoving his sword through their throats and into the cracked earth beneath them to sever the heads from their bodies, both hands grasping the hilt of his sword as he works. There's a grim satisfaction etched across his face, even as he curses under his breath.

"A simple escort, you say, just getting the princess to the river. Nothing to worry about, no chance of an attack this close to Yris, and yet here's an entire war band waiting at the bridge for us. Thank the Fates above we decided to bring the extra soldiers because, without them, I would've been forced to choose between my sobbing, terrified, cousin who wouldn't know which end of the sword to pick up or my impulsive, pig-headed cousin who rides headfirst into a raving mess of witches as though he isn't the heir to the throne of the Unseelie high fae, our future, and the only chance this kingdom has of getting out of this fucking mess!"

It's better to leave Tauron to his furious ranting than to reason with him, to point out to him that my death toll is a mountain of the strongest witches, whereas the soldiers we brought merely picked off the weaker ones who broke away from the rest.

I have never taken my position as the heir lightly, and if I wasn't so sure of my abilities, I would have been far more hesitant to throw myself into the fray.

Tauron's lip curls at me, and he stabs a finger in my direction. "I don't want to hear it, Soren, don't tell me about the things that only you can do right now, because I will shove you out of that fucking saddle and beat you to death myself."

Any other male would die for speaking to me like that, and a look around at the soldiers says they know it too, none of them meeting my eyes as Tauron fights to calm himself down.

I sheathe my sword, wincing at the blackened state of the blade, before I swipe the back of my glove across my forehead. "You're lying, but it's good to know you care, cousin. If you're so worried about me being your future king, then perhaps you should tone down some of the threats you're throwing at me."

It only enrages him further, the vitriol growing louder and more colorful as I walk Nightspark back to Sari and the group surrounding her.

Her eyes are red, and her makeup is smudged as she wipes furiously at her cheeks, tears in her voice as she snaps, "I thought you said it was safe, Soren. This doesn't look very safe to me."

I shake my head at her and glance over my shoulder to be sure that Tauron and the other soldiers are getting back on their horses and heading this way. We won't be able to burn the dead until we've seen Sari safely across the bridge to her father, and it's imperative we do that as quickly as possible.

"I said you were safe with me, cousin, not that the trip was safe. I would *never* say that. There's no path I could take you on in our kingdom during this war that is truly safe. There's no castle you can live in that's immune to this danger. The regent has worked very hard to shelter you from such things, but the truth is that, regardless."

If the guard wasn't standing with her, listening to our every word and untouched in his saddle as he never bothered to draw his sword, I would tell my cousin that the regent has crippled her by doing so. She was so unprepared for the witches today that she's a danger to herself and everyone around her.

Even such a slight criticism of the regent would be twisted though, so instead, I command the soldiers to get back on the road to the bridge, and I direct Nightspark to walk calmly alongside Sari's pony until her quiet sniffling eases up.

When we arrive at the bridge, a group of the regent's guards are waiting for us, though my uncle himself is absent.

Sari doesn't look surprised to see her father missing from the group, but when she leans forward in her seat to hug me, her arms bending tightly around my waist without a worry of the black blood covering me, I'm too shocked to deny her. I grunt a little as she jars my injured shoulder but let her squeeze me until the last of her tremors subsides.

"Thank you, Cousin. I hope to see you again soon. I look forward to your nuptials—make sure you send messengers, because I wouldn't miss it for the world."

As I watch her pony walk carefully across the bridge, the sneering guard and Malia close behind, her words spinning uselessly in my head. She meant them, there's no doubt of that. She looks forward to my wedding, no matter what it means for her and her father. I hate that she's been forced to witness such violence and bloodshed, but it might have served a purpose.

Sari Celestial, Heir Apparent to the regent, just woke up to the world as it exists around her, violent and on the edge of total ruin.

We're less than halfway to the fae door when the sound of horse hooves thundering toward us carries on the slight breeze.

I share a look with Tauron, but it's only a single horse and far more likely to be a messenger or someone fleeing conflict than a concern for us. Just to be sure, we pick up our pace and ride in the direction of the sound. It's the same path we're already on, slowly curving to the east as we follow the river.

By the time Darick's form becomes visible on the horizon, the seed of unrest I felt within me this morning has taken root, dread choking me as I feel the Fates laying down a path before me.

I've felt this before, and the outcome was never good.

The messenger doesn't bother to wait until he approaches us, or attempt to stop the horse, merely calling out the moment he's sure that we'll be able to pick up the words over the sounds of our horses' hooves.

"The baby is coming. Princess Airlie has gone into labor. Prince Tyton has sent for you to return as quickly as the horses can carry you."

I don't need to hear anything else.

I spur Nightspark on until he's galloping, pushing him as fast as his powerful body can go. Some of the other soldiers will inevitably fall back, but Tauron and his own horse keep up, as determined to make it home as I am.

When we get to the fae door, only Tauron, Darick and two of my soldiers have kept up with my brutal pace. If this were any other situation, I would have slowed down and kept formation, but not now, not for Airlie. Even without the promise I swore to Roan, I wouldn't leave her to endure the curse alone.

Tyton is either by her side or still guarding the witch, and one option is as bad as the other. Airlie left alone to endure the death of her son, or the witch unguarded and finally able to strike.

I was arrogant. I was confident that, if nothing else, the iron would keep her contained.

Tyton told me that she's been using her magic, but only in exchange with the earth. She never crossed the iron bars, that he could tell, not physically or with her magic. I made every excuse, told myself that it was fine because the small patch of grass we'd found was worth the risk of the witch being unbound in the cell. She was guarded at all times, what could she do? I rationalized it until I believed it, I left the witch to rot in those cells, and now my cousin's life may be forfeit to my arrogance.

I will never forgive myself.

The trip through the fae door is slow, there's no way to gallop through it, but the moment we make it through and the walls of Yregar are within sight, I kick Nightspark and we take off at the same breakneck pace. I'm not waiting for my cousin or the soldiers behind me, and Tauron curses as he gallops through after me, but I'm single-minded in my desperation to get back to the castle.

The soldiers are waiting for my arrival, the gates opening without me slowing my pace, and I note with approval that every male is armed and on watch. The entire area is on lockdown because of the baby, a solemn vigil as they wait for the news. It feels the same as the last time Airlie gave birth, everything except for Roan's absence.

I can't build a funeral pyre without him here. I can't send his child to Elysium if he's never gotten to see the baby.

The messenger said Roan was almost finished with his work at Fates Mark, but even traveling alone and at his fastest pace, he's still at least a week away. There's no chance of him arriving here in time to be with his wife, his Fates-blessed mate, to mourn their child. At best, he'll see a small bundle of cloth on the funeral pyres, wrapped in the finest of linens by his mother as we send the baby to Elysium to join their first son.

This is going to break Airlie once and for all.

The villagers all stare as I ride past, ducking and scrambling to get away from Nightspark. I don't ease up until I reached the stables, throwing myself from the saddle and snapping to Ingor to take the reins before I storm up the staircase at the side entrance. The stable hands all scatter, cowering away from the thunderous look on my face.

As I reach the doors, Tauron and the other soldiers arrive at a gallop, my cousin cursing me all over again as he scrambles from his horse to follow me.

The castle is silent, the maids and servants going about their daily tasks in a somber dance as the mourning begins.

"You can't just charge in there like this, Soren, you need to stop and take a breath. You'll be no help to Airlie, and she might not even want you in there. She threw Roan out three times with the last baby, what's to say she'll be any different this time?" Tauron says, his voice pitched low, but his feet never faltering as we weave our way through the castle to Airlie and Roan's rooms.

When we reach the second flight of stairs, we find one of the maids there trembling, her hands pressed over her temples as she mutters unintelligibly. I'm striding past her without a glance when amongst the nonsense words, I hear *witch*. My head snaps toward her.

One step, and I'm looming over her, my hand closing around her arm as I pull her to her feet. Her eyes are wild as she tries to scramble away from me, seeing my face only at the last second and then freezing.

"What did you just say?"

She bursts into tears, words tumbling out of her in a mess,

"The witch, the witch came for the princess, she killed the soldier, the witch is going to kill us all—"

Without hearing another word, I drop her and run, the sounds of her sobs following me as I sprint toward the bedrooms. My hand is on the hilt of my sword as I burst through their living room chambers, and I get halfway to Airlie and Roan's bedroom door when I'm struck dumb, my feet forgetting how to work as I come to an abrupt halt. Tauron stumbles to stop at my side, his mouth gaping open.

A sound rends through the air that must stop everyone in the castle dead in their tracks, a hush falling like a blanket over us all. A sound so familiar, so longed for, so foreign now for however many centuries it's been since we last heard it, and yet there's no denying what it is.

A newborn baby screams.

A high fae baby.

Living and breathing.

PART TWO

J BREE

TWENTY THREE

ROOKE

Princess Airlie looks down at the baby in my hands, tears still running down her face, but the shock at seeing him alive and squirming seems to render her senseless, unable to do anything but stare. He screams again, his lungs working perfectly now with some practice, and I move around the bed with him carefully bundled in my firm grip, the cord still attaching him to his mother.

"Listen to that beautiful sound. He wants you, Princess. He needs his mother. Firna, I need you to open up her gown so we can get him settled in his mother's arms."

The young maid staggers away from the bed, looking at the baby as though he's a banshee scrambling her mind and rendering her unable to fight back, but the moment I speak, Firna jumps into action. She steps over to Airlie and, in her no-nonsense way, opens up the princess's linen shift and helps me to lay the baby on his mother's chest. His cries instantly quiet down as he sighs and finds his fist to suck on, preparing himself for his first meal.

Airlie doesn't move to stop us or help us, she simply lies there and lets us shuffle things around until the baby is secured under her chin. Firna starts to tuck blankets around her, but I haven't yet cut the baby's cord or begun any of the afterbirth process. I'm still worried about the princess's state of shock, the pallor of her face a concern. I check, but her bleeding is normal, nothing to be worried about.

"Why isn't he crying?" Airlie says, her words stilted and shaking, and I reach forward to place a hand over hers where it cradles him.

"Because he's safe with his mother. He doesn't need to cry, not until he's hungry and wants to let you know."

She blinks at me and then back down at him. "He's alive."

I nod, and at her grimace, I move back down to the end of the bed and ready myself to see her through the last of the birthing process. There's still much to be done before she can rest with her baby.

The hard work isn't over yet.

Airlie follows my instructions without question or complaint, nodding and grimacing through it all. By the time I have the cord cut and the afterbirth dealt with, Firna has found baby blankets and cloths for diapers, all of them too large for the tiny prince but will do for now.

After changing the sheets and cleaning up, we get the princess tucked back into the bed, busy acts of service that have always warmed me. The ways in which women come together to help each other during this sacred time…it's as the Fates designed us, and though my presence was never requested, I still feel the weight of that honor on me.

The princess doesn't say another word, not to me or Firna. Her eyes stay fixed on her son. It's as if she fears the simple act of blinking will make him disappear from her arms. She watches the baby as Firna tucks a diaper on him and bundles him into some blankets. The older woman moves to hand him back to Airlie, who is now propped up comfortably on the bed, and I move back to them.

I murmur to Airlie, careful not to startle the baby, "You should place him on your chest, his skin against yours without all these blankets in the way. Birth is a hard process and he needs his mother close."

I don't know how the high fae of the Unseelie Court once went about the early hours of life and caring for infants—the cultural differences in each of the different fae folk are usually quite stark—but Airlie nods her head and opens up her gown again, unquestioning, as Firna unwraps the baby once more. The cold air washes over him and he finds his voice again, letting out a squeal of discomfort that quickly strengthens into a beautiful, healthy scream.

Airlie's eyes water again, but a smile stretches across her lips.

"He's alive," she says again, and I nod.

"Alive and hungry. He's doing beautifully, Princess."

With a reassuring smile, I move around the bed to assist her. She doesn't question me or protest as I help get him settled and feeding at her breast. She doesn't need much direction, just a few little adjustments I can offer from a lifetime of experience with babies of all shapes and sizes.

Her eyes snap to the door seconds before it bursts open, but the tug of the Fates within me is the only warning I need to know who has arrived home.

Firna jumps up, ready to scold whoever is interrupting the princess or perhaps to protect her with her life once more, but the moment she sees Prince Soren and Prince Tauron storming in, her head drops into a bow.

I keep a good hold of the prince on his mother's chest, ignoring their arrival as I work to help Airlie tend to her small son's needs. Egos and the fruitless war between our races can stay out of this space.

"Get your hands off her," Soren snaps, his own hand

dropping to the hilt of his sword, but as he begins to draw it, I find my temper once more, my magic lashing out to wrap around his wrist and stop his hand, then wrapping around both princes' legs to stop their advance into the room. If either of them attempts to grab me right now, it could harm the baby or his mother, and neither of those possibilities are acceptable to me.

"This is a birthing room. You *will not* draw a weapon in the presence of a mother and a baby, not while I breathe."

Airlie's eyes finally move away from her son, snapping up to meet my gaze. She doesn't look scared or worried at the command in my tone, or the way my silver eyes are now glowing with magic. Her resolve is steady as I resume gently directing her son to eat, moving him and adjusting him until the latch is good and he begins to suck greedily.

He's small, definitely early, and she winces for a moment before we get him in the right position and settled comfortably. I ignore the commotion by the door, magic settling around both princes to ensure they cannot step even a single foot closer to the bed, and it's not until the baby is secure and suckling that Airlie glances up at her cousins.

"He's alive," she says again, her words barely more than a breath.

The wonder in her tone forms a lump in my throat. This isn't her first baby, but it is the first one she's been able to hold close to her heart with nothing but joy.

"Cousin, what has happened here?" Tauron demands, and Airlie grins back at him.

"My son was born alive."

I sit on the bed and watch them both, my mind already moving through the necessary actions that come after a baby. Airlie needs to eat. There are herbs we need to find to help her milk supply come in strong. Clothing and blankets, and we need to warm up the bedroom, because the baby is so small and will struggle to stay warm.

I glance around, but there's no cradle for the baby, no sign in this bedroom that they were preparing for a new life, and the lump in my throat only grows bigger. They were so sure that this was a futile attempt, and yet they still tried, this little prince so wanted and so loved.

I look at Firna, meeting her still-awed gaze. "The princess needs food and water. I know you all drink a lot of goblin wine, but is there any ale? We need the darkest brew you can find."

Firna's brow furrows a little more, but she nods. "We do have some, but it's been stored away for the Unseelie Court when they visit."

I glance at the princes, whose eyes are fixed on me, before I glance back. "She doesn't need a lot. Just a glass a day to help the milk come in until I can brew her some tinctures and teas. I'm assuming there aren't any wet-nurses available for the prince and our options for feeding him are very limited. Her milk is the most important thing for his survival."

She nods at me firmly, then steps around the bed before her gaze lands back on the two princes. She bows deeply before addressing them, no nonsense in her tone or words.

"Princess Airlie asked the witch to stay after she offered her help. She saw the baby here safely, and she broke the curse. I'll do as she says, for the sake of the prince's health."

It's not a question, but she doesn't move from the spot until Soren finally gives her the tiniest of nods, a jerking of his head that I'm sure cost him dearly.

His pride must be in ruins.

The keeper walks out of the room without another word, feet moving quickly in her haste to do as I say, and I turn back to the princess.

The tears have dried up and her eyes are sharp once more.

"What else can I do for my milk? After everything we've gone through, I'm not going to risk him now."

I nod and reach out again, my hand clasping her shoulder. The empathy I feel for her is a shock, my mind reeling at the emotions bubbling up inside of me once more as the last of the ice around my heart melts away. I thought I'd lost my ability to feel such things. My time in the Northern Lands may have hollowed me out, but maybe my connection to the land here has filled me back up again. Maybe all I truly needed was to return to my ancestral home and become a simple witch of the woods once again. That's all I truly am, no matter what new responsibilities and titles I may hold.

"There are herbs that we can get for you, but eating and drinking regularly is the most vital part to a good supply. You need to eat well—no more picking at small bowls of fruit. It may have sustained you in your pregnancy while you felt sick, but it won't be enough now. You must eat for the both of you. Breads and cheeses, produce and meat—you need a good variety, and you need to eat often."

Her brow furrows again but she nods, glancing at the young maid who still cowers in the corner, and her mouth firms into a line but she addresses the girl kindly enough. "Veera, I need you to get me a glass of water and then go down to the kitchens and help Firna."

The young maid nods at her, her shaking hands fumbling a little as she moves around the room to do as the princess instructed. A glass is placed on the small table by the bed before she scurries out of the room, stumbling over her feet as she bows to the princes. Only once the door is shut behind her does Airlie look back at her cousins once more

"You're using your magic on them now, aren't you," she says to me, her lips tight in disapproval.

I nod. "I don't care who they are or the circumstances. *No*

344

one draws a weapon in a birthing room, not while I live and breathe."

Her gaze traces my face, her stare serious, as a single finger gently caresses her son's temple and strokes the tiny cap of dark curls at his crown. One tiny, pointed ear is visible over her arm, and my heart clenches at the sight of it.

The curse was denied him, but how many other infants just like him were taken?

Airlie murmurs, "And if I get them to promise they're not going to draw their swords, you'll remove your magic bindings from them?"

I raise a brow at her. "I don't care what they do to me, princess, what words they have to say or what punishment they deem necessary for my actions today, but *none of it* will happen in this room. I'll take the magic off them, but they'll have to restrain themselves until I've seen you and the small prince through these first few hours. Your safety and health are my priority."

She nods curtly and when she looks at the men, still trembling with rage and contained only by the power that's wrapping around them, her steely gaze doesn't soften. She may love them both and respect them, she might be loyal to the Savage Prince and his claim to the crown, but in a few short minutes, she's transformed from Princess Airlie into a mother. It's a fearsome sight to behold.

"She came here to help me, and she did exactly that. We can discuss her motives later. Right now, all that matters is my son, and neither of you will bring her harm in this room. Not unless she strikes first."

I ease my magic away from both princes and the soldier still lying prone on the ground by the door. The moment I do, the soldier groans, and both of the princes startle as they glance down at him, but I ignore them all. Instead, I help Airlie swap the baby to her other breast as he fusses.

Her eyebrows pinch together. "Is that bad? I don't think I have any milk, is he going to starve?"

I smile at her, sure to keep my tone calm and low. She's in a heightened state of concern after the birth and from all the extra emotions that come with a baby. Treating her gently and kindly right now is the only course of action.

"He's working to help your milk come in. He'll be fussy for a little while, but he should sleep through most of the wait until it comes in. With the extra help we'll get you, it won't take long. He's perfectly healthy, I've already given him a look over, and there's nothing to be concerned about."

I hear footsteps and a shadow falls over the bed, but I don't look up, not until I have him latched properly and the wince is gone from the princess's face.

"Is it supposed to hurt?" she asks quietly, almost shy.

I shrug carefully. "A good latch doesn't hurt, but he's on the small side, so it might take some growing for him to learn how to do it properly. Everything is going to be fine."

She nods and runs a finger through his hair once more, eyes misting before she glances up at the looming high-fae prince. "I need Roan, has someone sent for him?"

I glance up, and Prince Soren is staring at me as though it's taking every ounce of restraint within him not to wrap his hands around my throat and squeeze until my last breath is finished. It's clear he's not going to answer her, so I do it for him.

"Prince Tyton sent a messenger for him at the same time that he sent one for Prince Soren and Prince Tauron. Trust your family to find your husband—you need to stay focused on your son right now."

My words are a gentle but firm reminder to her of the task at hand, so she doesn't lose herself in the pain of Roan missing out on this experience. I have no idea how long it will take to find Prince Roan and bring him back here, but there are many emotions that come with the early days after a birth, and whatever we can do to keep the princess focused and healthy right now is vital.

She nods and looks back at her son. The small prince falls asleep at her breast, his mouth suckling for comfort but not much more.

I move away from the bed, carefully skirting both princes as I make my way to one of the seats in the room, leaving the cousins to their reunion and celebration of the baby.

Both princes watch me until I'm settled against the plush cushions. I try not to wince at the state of my dress. It's been only a few days since the icy bath, but the dungeon cell isn't the cleanest, and the dress is covered in black streaks. I've been careful not to let the fabric touch the princess or the baby, but the silver and blue cushions of this ornate chair might very well be ruined.

"What were you thinking?" Soren murmurs.

Airlie snaps her gaze to him, her eyes narrowing dangerously. "I was thinking that it was worth a try, that I would do *anything* to give my son a chance to live."

Soren scowls at her. "And if she had killed you, Airlie? She was probably the one to bring the labor on in the first place."

Airlie moves the baby higher up on her chest, his mouth releasing her nipple and a small sigh escaping him, a happy and content sound as he nestles against her. The sound draws all eyes, no small amount of wonder in this room as they watch him.

"Soren, by the time she came into this room, I had decided I'd rather die with him than burn another son on the funeral pyres."

I swallow around the lump in my throat, glancing away from

the three of them. This conversation seems too intimate for me to overhear, and though I'm used to the secrets and confessions of a birth room, the sacred space always bringing out such things, it feels invasive here.

I didn't cast the curse, and I certainly had no part in this war, but I'm still the enemy in their eyes. In any other circumstance, it wouldn't bother me, but the loss of a child is something I would never take lightly. I have helped bring too many into this world and out, the Fates choosing our paths but never with mercy.

The soldier groans again and rises carefully to his hands and knees. I remember that the third high-fae prince downstairs will be doing the same and no doubt charging up here soon, ready to kill me. In the shock of finding Airlie and her son, they seem to have forgotten about the missing prince.

"Prince Tyton is downstairs in the dungeon asleep, but I've released the magic on him. He'll be waking up now, but rest assured that he's fine."

Tauron's eyes snap toward me, his lip curling into a sneer. "What did you do to him?"

I shrug. "I just said I put him to sleep. There isn't a scratch on him or anyone else. He did exactly as he was ordered and had no intention of letting me see the princess."

"Why did you come then? If every person in this castle said no, why did you come?" Airlie asks, a hand stroking down the baby's back. An innate part of her has transformed into a mother, now that she has the baby she so desperately desired, and it's a beautiful sight to see.

In my despair, I had almost forgotten about such things.

I sigh, tired of arguing this point only for them to remain unchanged. "I was born a healer and I'll die as one—nothing that happens between those two events will change that. I told you it's a responsibility I carry, and I wasn't lying. If a woman needs me, I'll tend to her."

Airlie glances at Prince Soren. "She delivered the Seelie Court's heir. She saw him safely into the world even after a long labor. Whatever she did in the Northern Lands, they trusted her with their queen."

Prince Soren stares at me, his eyes cold and hard. Nothing about today has changed his opinion of me, but that wasn't my intention in the first place.

Our fate will unfold whether he likes me or not.

The chamber's outer doors open and we hear the clink of china before Firna enters the bedroom with a large tray of food. It's not as much variety as I would like for the princess, but I'm sure it's the best they can do.

Firna places the tray on the small table and glances at the princess before looking over to me. "Is this all okay?"

The princes both snarl with irritation that she has consulted me, but I nod to both women, more than happy to ignore them both while we get the important work here done. Men's egos have no place in such matters, and I'll kick them both out of here if they attempt to intervene.

"That's good. Eat as much as you can, Princess, and leave the rest for snacking."

Firna nods, her mouth drawing up in satisfaction that she has attended her princess well. She fusses with the bedding and moves things around as she puts together a small plate for Airlie. Once the princess is munching on some bread, she straightens back up, turning her back to me so she can address Prince Soren and Prince Tauron once more.

"The witch said that she can help us get herbs for the princess. She wasn't wrong—we don't have a nursemaid available. There aren't any women in the village who can help either, even if we were able to find someone suitable."

I hate to think what the high fae would deem suitable for a nursemaid, and I stay out of the conversation.

Prince Soren turns to Tauron and says, "Go down and get Tyton. Make sure that he's alive and unharmed."

His cousin nods and leaves the room without another word. As he passes, the soldier finally staggers to his feet, his brow furrowing at the scene before him, but he snaps to attention when Prince Soren addresses him.

"Go back down to the barracks, Renly, and join the watch there." His tone is cutting, as though the soldier did something wrong.

He was always going to be outclassed by me. I could feel pity for him, but I don't have that much empathy left for these people. I'm too certain there's innocent witch blood on their hands from those caught up in a war they never wanted.

"What's to say that the list of herbs she has for you aren't going to poison or curse you? We have no knowledge of these things, Airlie; she could do anything to you."

We're going to talk around and around in circles forever, and I don't have the patience within me for such things, not when there's a baby's life at stake. I curse under my breath and roll my eyes, but he ignores me, intent on dancing around this topic all the way to Elysium and the Fates themselves.

Airlie shrugs. "We don't have much choice, Soren. There are no nursemaids, and that isn't true of only this village. You can't have a nursemaid in a starving population. You heard what the witch said—I need to eat to bring my milk in and keep a supply."

I wouldn't be surprised if there are babies in the village with mothers struggling to keep them fed too. "What we need is food."

Airlie turns back to me. "Tell Firna the list of herbs, and she will do what she can to get them."

When Soren's jaw clenches, Airlie sighs, the baby rousing a little on her chest before settling once more. "You all kept asking why I was trying for a baby when the curse was on us... my fate was Roan, you all know that, but the rest of my fate was that my son would break the curse."

My eyebrows slowly inch up my forehead. I wasn't aware that the high fae often got a longer fate than just who they were meant to be with.

I thought that was just Soren and I, bound together in a fearsome destiny.

Soren looks as taken aback as I feel. "Does Roan know this?"

She nods. "I won't tell you his fate, not the rest of it, but my fate said my son would break the curse and become the Prince of Fates Mark. He will survive this. He'll grow up strong and into a loyal prince of the crown, like his father and his father before him. I felt the curse pressing down on me and reaching desperately for him. I felt the witch protect him, felt her magic hold him and ease him into the world untouched. I felt the moment the curse broke, a war fought over my body, and we won, Soren. Your fate is to marry her and win the war. I do not doubt the Fates. I did for a moment in my grief, but they didn't falter, and my trust in them has brought my son here. You need to let her out of the dungeon to help Firna. You need to let her care for me and my son and see us through these first few weeks, at the very least."

She looks down at her son and then swallows, determination settling across her face as she continues, "I know you would do anything for your people, as I would do anything for you, but sometimes the right path looks far more dangerous than the one that leads to ruin. Trust in the Fates, Soren."

TWENTY FOUR

SOREN

After I leave Airlie and the witch under the seething guard of Tauron, I call Firna and Tyton into my reception room to question them about the full extent of the damage the witch had done.

Tyton was unharmed and had very little to say. One moment he was staring at the witch, enraged as he was forced to listen to the sounds of Airlie in pain, and the next moment he was waking up on the ground, staring at the cell door blown open by magic.

She was strong enough to break through the iron door, knock two high fae unconscious without harming them, and then break the curse. She's been sitting in that dirty, dark hole under the ground for weeks, pretending to be at our mercy, and all the while she was playing a game.

It took three attempts before Tyton believed that the baby was alive.

When the realization finally set in that he couldn't hear Airlie crying, that her labor had ended but no one was preparing a funeral pyre, he fled the room without waiting to be dismissed, eager to see with his own eyes a living high-fae child. Airlie and Roan's son.

Firna stands before me with a resigned look on her face

as she bows her head, prepared to take whatever punishment I might deal her for the events that transpired. For any other, I might have more doubts or questions to be answered, but I know my keeper and her love for Airlie, I know how loyal she is to me and my household. If there's any anger in me about what happened here today, it's not directed at her.

My tone is firm but low as I say, "There wasn't anything else you could do."

Her head snaps up, her gaze meeting mine, and she nods slightly. "I saw the dungeon. I'm aware of the danger she truly is, but she fought for that baby. She was willing to do anything to be in that room and help the princess. The Fates chose her for you for a reason."

I'm getting quite tired of everyone telling me the same thing as though it's as simple as agreeing and taking her to my bed.

I fix her with a hard look. "The entire kingdom relies on my decisions, and though the Fates have told me what they intend for me, it's still my responsibility to find my way there and I won't be questioned about my decisions."

Firna glances at the door as though she expects someone to burst in, or perhaps a guard to be pressing his ear against the wood, but when she turns back to me, there's a determined set to her mouth. "My apologies, Your Highness. The most important thing right now is feeding the princess and her baby. This isn't just about Princess Airlie but the kingdom as well. The Unseelie Court will see that the Fates are with you, that you've been the one to lead us out of this war, and that baby is the first sign of the tide turning. We need to find the herbs and provisions."

"Show me the list of things she gave you."

Firna pulls out a small scrap of parchment with her own handwriting, rough and smudged as she'd taken down the list in haste. "There's nothing on it that's dangerous, but I've never claimed to be an expert on such things."

She might not claim it, but she's been Keeper of Yregar for many years and knows more than most. I read the list, but it doesn't mean much to me. "Do we have any of this?"

Firna's mouth turns down at the corners. "Some but not all of it. I checked the stock of the ale that she requested, and we have enough of that to get through the first three months. The herbs are harder. The fae flowers have stopped growing, and we have only a small amount left of what we were able to preserve. The witch says we must find the milk thistle. There's a tincture she can make with it, the simplest of all her remedies, and so if nothing else, that one is vital."

I don't even know what milk thistle looks like, but I'm sure I haven't passed it on the barren plains in centuries. Nothing grows there.

I dismiss Firna, sending her back to Airlie to continue tending to the princess. She spent the morning collecting as many baby items as she could find around the castle, but it has been many long centuries since the last royal baby was born. The seamstress has been put to work to ensure the baby is clothed and warm, and the kitchens are working hard to find variety in her meals, as the witch had instructed.

A cradle, once used by royal families visiting Yregar long before I called it home, has been brought down from one of the storage rooms, and the maids are scrubbing it clean for him, awe in their every move.

Airlie did all of this herself during her first pregnancy, preparing for a baby she was so sure would live. Her fate had instilled a confidence in her that had defied all logic.

It makes sense to me now, why she chose to fall pregnant and the long months she spent ignoring everyone's concerns as she built a nursery for her unborn baby. She filled it with all the things she wanted for her son, everything made just for him, with all of her hope and love woven in.

Roan had gotten rid of everything during those first weeks of their mourning. Airlie couldn't bear to look at any of it, and so he took the clothes and blankets down to the orphanage, telling the women there to dispense them to anyone in need.

When they thanked him, he simply turned on his heel and left, furious that the Fates had forced this nightmare onto his family.

Back in Airlie's rooms, I find her sound asleep and tucked in her bed with extra blankets. The tray that Firna brought her is mostly empty on the table beside her bed, a few small bowls with fruit in them remaining, in case she should wake hungry. The large pitcher of water has been refilled, and it's clear that the maids left everything she could need within arm's reach.

The baby is wrapped in blankets and nestled in the bed beside her, sleeping peacefully. The witch sits in the armchair and watches them both carefully, her eyes never straying from the infant.

Tauron and Tyton are there, both watching the witch. How Airlie can sleep through such animosity is a testament to the exhaustion she must feel after the labor.

Tauron turns to me and murmurs, "Is there any news of Roan?"

I shake my head. "The messenger won't have made it to Fates Mark yet. The frozen plains of ice will add at least another day to the trip."

The ice never truly melts in the Outlands, even in the peak of the hottest summers the Southern Lands have seen. The terrain is impossible to navigate if you're unfamiliar with it, and though the commander sent Fyr, with his vast knowledge of the Outlands, it still could be days before he finds Roan. The last we heard from him, he was securing the patrols and checking in with the villages to be sure there were no other witch sightings or potential for danger before he returned to Yregar.

"Are we just going to leave her here with them forever? I can't stand the sight of her watching the baby," Tyton mumbles, softly enough that the witch can't hear it.

I shoot him a look for the tone he's using, but his eyes are fixed on the witch. "It's an impossible decision. If I take her out of here and something happens to the baby, no one else will know what to do."

Tauron scowls. "Firna was once a wet nurse. She helped your mother through her labor with you and helped her raise you. We can leave Firna with Airlie and get the witch out of here."

I shake my head. "The baby came early. Firna is worried that without a healer he'll struggle and weaken. All of the herbs and remedies Firna knows of are lost to us now. The herbs the witch listed for her were once commonly used by the women in the village—Firna spoke to some of the maids to confirm it. The fae flowers are gone—we have no choice but to find the milk thistle."

Tauron curses under his breath. "Is there anything at Yris? I will go and face the regent and the Unseelie Court myself if it gets Airlie what she needs."

I shake my head. "I don't want my uncle to know about the baby yet."

I don't want *anyone* knowing of the baby until Roan arrives, but there's no way to stop the gossip. Everyone heard Airlie's labor and the baby's cries, and now the castle is alive with speculation, wonder, and a healthy dose of fear at the witch's actions. After some panic at the exaggerated details of her escape from the cell, I was forced to send extra guards into the high-fae wing to put the castle into a true lockdown.

Whatever we need to do to keep this baby safe, I'll do it.

I scowl at Tauron and shake my head. "To ride to Yris is a futile mission, regardless. The regent won't just hand over any supplies they have there without questioning us and then demanding to see the baby. He'll drag the witch in for questioning, and he'll use it as an excuse to take her from us and stop the wedding. Going there is not an option."

Tyton stares at the witch for a moment before he raises his voice to her hearing level. "Where would you get the herb from? If we let you out of this castle to collect it, where would you go?"

Her eyes flick toward him but move right back to the infant as she continues her watch.

She speaks quietly so she doesn't disturb him. "Is there anywhere in the kingdom that isn't barren like the plains here? We could go to the forest. The Ravenswyrd was still lush when we passed it."

Tyton recoils as though he's been struck, and Tauron snaps at her, though remembering to keep his voice low, "You want to lead us to the forest of madness for herbs? Over my dead fucking body."

She sighs and rolls her eyes at him, then speaks slowly as though to a child. "Milk thistle grows rampantly wherever there's life. That's why I put it on the list. There are other herbs that work better and with less preparation, but they're harder to come by and we would need to mix them. Wherever there's life, we'll find the milk thistle. I haven't been to the Southern Lands in two hundred years, and before I left, I spent all of my time in the Ravenswyrd, so I'll have to leave figuring out the location up to you."

I never knew there was a witch coven in the Ravenswyrd Forest.

Tauron turns to look at me, his eyes wide.

Two hundred years ago, the witch left her home. Through our mind connection, I'd felt her terror and aching sadness, though she never told me what happened, no matter how much

I tried to get her to confide in me. Something *had* happened to her, and she'd fled on foot, walking for days with her brother while I searched the kingdom desperately for her.

She grew up in the forest of madness.

It's been called that for more than a millennium, far longer than I've been alive. Any high fae who dared to cross the threshold of those trees would lose themselves there. If they made it out alive, a madness had taken root in their minds far more terrifying than the brief clutches that Tyton finds himself in whenever he ventures too near.

The victims never recover. The only high fae to have walked into the trees and left again sound of mind, that I know of, is Roan. We were attacked by a horde of witches, and he took an arrow to the chest before being separated from the rest of us in the melee. I was sure he was dead, and after hours of searching for him, we found him at the edge of the forest, his wounds healed.

He's never spoken of what he saw in there.

"The Goblin Lands," Tauron murmurs, and I glance at him.

"You need to meet with the Goblin King to open a trading route through his lands. You already need to negotiate with him, but now Airlie needs you to go as well. If you take the witch with you, she can collect the herbs there and hope that the Goblin King doesn't mind you foraging on his lands. It's the only part of the kingdom with green earth left."

Tyton huffs, his fists clenching as he struggles to keep his voice low. "So those are our options? A forest of madness or stealing from the Goblin King, the same man who's already threatened to kill any high fae who crosses his lands without his consent?"

The witch's eyes flick back to us as she rises and steps toward the bed. She moves the blankets away from the infant's face as he begins to fuss, grunting and letting out a tiny whimper.

Her hands are so careful and gentle, treating him as though he's made of glass as she soothes him back to sleep like the most competent wet nurse.

She whispers to us without looking away from the small gift on the bed, "The goblins won't mind parting with the milk thistle. It's practically a weed."

The fae door outside the walls of Yregar was once most commonly used to travel to the Augur Mountains and the Seer who lived in the temple there. Generations of my family made the journey to hear what the Fates had planned out for our lives.

It can also transport people to the other fae doors within the Southern Lands. A very valuable resource, except that there are fae doors in the Goblin Lands and Yrmar. Both are the reason the fae door at Yregar is so heavily guarded, night and day. It doesn't matter that neither the goblins nor the witches have ever attempted to use it; it's still a crack in our armor, and someday I know they'll come calling.

The reason we don't commonly use the fae door to the Goblin Lands is that the Goblin King has warned the high fae about entering his lands without his permission, and he's proved he'll keep his word. Dozens of the regent's messengers have disappeared in the Goblin Lands over the centuries, never to be seen again, though mine are merely escorted to the edges of the land and told not to return.

We'll use it today and hope his agreement to speak with me is enough warning for him. It'll be the quickest way to meet with the Goblin King, collect the herbs the witch needs for Airlie, and return to the castle.

"You could just describe this herb to Prince Soren, that way you don't have to travel with him," Tyton says, his arms crossed and his face uncharacteristically stern as he regards the witch.

She doesn't relent, calm as ever. The unflinching way she stares at us all sends a ripple of irritation down my spine. She knew all along that her magic was strong enough to get past our defenses, and yet she played her game with us, to what end I still can't guess.

"If I do that, there's every chance that Prince Soren will come back with a handful of brandy weed and the entire trip will be a waste of time. Is there anyone in here who has knowledge of plants and magic properties?"

Tauron's jaw flexes as he grinds his teeth, loath to admit any failings to her. His hand twitches like he's imagining her death, blood-soaked and so satisfying. I can't blame him.

It doesn't change the fact that she's right.

We have gardeners, but none of them are experts in medicinal plants. They've cared for the orchards, but there's been nothing they could do to stop the slow decay of our land. Their job has always been to keep the gardens at Yregar pretty and pleasing for the Unseelie Court's arrival, relying on the healers who once kept the garden in their own quarters to grow their own ingredients and mix their own tinctures for the castle and all of those who live within Yregar's walls. That knowledge is lost to us now.

Without a word passed between any of us, the witch nods firmly. "I'm the only choice, and before you start on your usual tirade of speculation about my motives, you should know I'd rather not leave the princess or the baby."

I raise an eyebrow at her. "You don't trust Firna with them? Your arrogance is shocking, considering your position."

She raises an eyebrow right back at me, turning from my cousin to face me fully. "And what position do you think I'm in, Prince Soren? As far as I'm concerned, the high fae are in dire need of aid and, though you've all treated me appallingly since

I arrived back in the Southern Lands, I'm still standing here and offering it. Perhaps you should learn some manners and stop insulting the healer who just saved the future of your race."

Tauron isn't the only one who'd like to slit this woman's throat, and the taunting gleam in those silver eyes of hers says she knows it too. Never have I hated the position we're in more than now as this witch looks around at the high fae and finds nothing but desperation.

Firna steps into the room, a bundle of clothing in her hands, which she holds out to the witch and says in an urgent tone, "I'll take you to the guest rooms and get you cleaned up so you can head off with Prince Soren now. You must make haste and return to the princess."

The witch takes the clothing and looks back at me, an eyebrow raised. "Are you going to send a guard with me, or am I safe to step out of this room without you all assuming I'm going to stage a coup?"

I flick a hand at her, ignoring the incredulous look that Tauron shoots me, and Firna hurries her out without another word.

The moment the door shuts behind them my cousin turns on me, his lip curling as he snarls, "So we're just going to let her wander around the castle as she pleases now?"

My temper finally boils over at his pig-headed insolence. "She destroyed the iron door of her cell. There isn't much we can do, short of cutting off her head and forsaking my fate all together."

He growls back at me, but my own gaze hardens, my words a command. "Find Darick, put an escort together, and get ready to ride out. We'll cross at the fae door."

As Tauron leaves, Airlie calls to me softly from her room. I go to her, blinking in the darkness until my eyes adjust.

The space has been cleaned, everything back to the very

precise setup that Airlie prefers, with the addition of the few items Firna has been able to find for the baby. The small crib has been cleaned and placed beside her bed, white oak carved with the Celestial family crest and lined with silver and blue blankets.

The baby is already sleeping in it, sucking on his fist and grunting. He's dressed in a tiny blue suit that's still too big, with polished silver buttons and embroidered snowflakes on the sleeves. Where Firna found it, I couldn't guess, but he's warm and content.

It strikes me that Airlie hasn't told us his name yet, but until Roan gets here to see him, I won't ask. Names are important to the high fae, a tie to family and the Fates, and to ask about it now would be a great insult to them both.

Airlie stands next to the crib, bathed and looking more like herself. She's dressed in comfortable clothing, another simple shift dress with buttons down on the front so she can feed her son with ease, and her hair is brushed and braided back. With the color back in her cheeks, you can't tell that only hours ago she was desperately fighting for her son's life as the curse loomed to send him to the funeral pyres.

"Thank you for doing this, Soren," she says, a hand wrapping around the crib as she smiles up at me. "I'll be safe with Firna until you both return."

I nod to her, the decision made, and step back out of the bedroom, leaving Tyton to watch over them both until her husband returns.

The air in their rooms is too hot and presses against my skin, suffocating me as the weight of the entire kingdom falls on me. Every step I take needs to be calculated and perfect, never erring from the right path, or else we'll all die in this endless cycle of suffering.

The witch steps back into the room behind Firna, having

quickly cleaned herself and dressed in riding clothes, charcoal-colored pants and a linen shirt with a cloak over her shoulders. Her hair is brushed and braided back, long tendrils framing her face where they've escaped from the ribbon. Her steely eyes are as sharp as they always are, but there's color to her cheeks as she smooths a hand down the fabric, a furrow between her brows.

At the sight of her, my stomach churns and I grimace. She's clean and confidently prepared for the ride ahead of us. It was easier to think of her as a mindless, raving witch when she was filthy, but now I'm struck by the quiet beauty of her. There's no finery or fussing necessary to make her shine; if anything, those things would be a detraction. No matter how hard I fight against them, the Fates have wisely chosen me a mate who will make me question everything.

Including myself, for daring to find something I crave within her, the sensation only growing more insistent as I fight it.

My tone is cutting as I snap, "Can you ride a horse?"

She sends me a sardonic look. "I'm not sure I would've lasted in the Sol Army if I couldn't, but rest assured, I won't be left behind."

Firna glances between the two of us and then bows her head at me. "I'll take care of the princess while you're gone. The witch has instructed me on the prince's care, and I won't let any harm come to them."

It's a solemn vow, and one I am staking their lives on. Firna would lay her life down for either of them, I knew it before she dove between them and the witch.

With a scowl, I nod. "No one is to talk about the baby until Roan arrives, not a single whisper. The maids are all to stay in the castle until then. No one is allowed in or out of the castle walls until we return, not even the regent or his guards. Make sure it's known that to speak of Airlie, her son, or anything that has taken place today is to die."

A single detail could be used against us, the pretty tales and dark seductions of my uncle needing only the spark of an idea to wrap around your throat. I've watched him cleave families and bloodlines apart with nothing more than a single grain of truth, his cunning too great to be dismissed.

The witch watches me carefully, weighing my words, but Firna only bows her head once more. "I'll be sure they all know, Your Highness."

I turn on my heel and walk out of the room, not looking back to check if the witch is following me. I don't need to, her silver gaze presses against my back like a ball of iron as we make our way to the stables. Tauron and three soldiers wait for us there, already in their saddles and ready to ride out.

The stable hands startle at the sight of the witch, their gazes dropping to her wrists, where no lengths of iron chain hang, but I ignore them as I address Ingor, taking Nightspark's reins as he holds them out to me. "Bring me Northern Star as well—the witch needs a horse."

I need her to be able to keep up with me, and there are few horses in the stables who can ride alongside Nightspark. Northern Star has a temper to match my mount's, but if the witch says she can ride, then she'll have to manage the beast.

Ingor doesn't question me, not even when he flinches at the steely gaze of the witch, and he strides into the stables and barks orders at the stable boys. The horse is saddled and led out in a matter of minutes, my people efficient as always.

The witch doesn't need help as she mounts Northern Star and settles herself in the saddle, her back straight and in perfect posture as she directs the beast. One of her hands strokes the mare's neck as she settles her, Northern Star snorting a little but keeping calm. She's unaccustomed to carrying a witch, and becomes flighty at the feel of her magic.

Horses can always feel it.

Nightspark snaps his teeth in her direction as I climb into my own saddle, but with a simple nudge of my knees, we're off through the village and riding toward the fae door.

TWENTY FiVE

ROOKE

When I first arrived in the Northern Lands, I was terrified of riding a horse.

It wasn't the animals themselves—I gravitated to them as though pulled by a siren's call—but the feeling of being at another creature's mercy was terrifying. Pemba laughed at me the whole time; he had climbed into the saddle and taken off at a canter without blinking, and I was furious at the ease he felt while I was a panicked mess. I spent weeks building up the courage to even get on a horse only to fall off the moment the horse bolted from beneath me, spooked by my fear.

Pemba didn't find that so funny.

Hanede was the one to heal my dislocated shoulder, giving Pemba a very long and harsh talking to, which everyone within the healer's quarters found most amusing. Mostly because Pemba let him, the two of them as close as brothers within weeks of knowing each other. I was mortified and refused to go back to the stables, insisting that I'd stick to being a healer and maybe learn how to use a bow if absolutely necessary.

Eventually, a high-fae prince taught me to ride in the dead of night, when everyone I knew and loved was sleeping. He was an exiled dragonrider and understood better than anyone the fears I faced.

Stone took one look at me and demanded, "Are you going to let a horse stop you from protecting your brother? Your friends? What are you going to do if the Ureen arrive here and the children of the city are depending on you to get them out? Are you the Ravenswyrd Mother or just a scared little girl from the forest?"

I was riding better than Pemba in less than a week, better than Hanede in a month, and Stone was a very smug instructor until I bested him as well.

Looking around the village of Yregar, the state of the villagers is far more concerning now than it was the day I arrived. Countless bodies in haggard condition litter the streets, children starving with sunken cheeks and filthy clothes, folk of every lower fae race staring at me as we pass, desperation in their eyes.

My mind was so focused on the young prince's health and Princess Airlie's safety that I'd forgotten there are countless other children suffering here, all of them without high-fae royal bloodlines to keep them fed and cared for. I have many questions for this Fates-cursed mate of mine, especially as the mounted group keep their heads held high and ignore the fae folk around us as they focus single-mindedly on getting to the fae door.

I wonder if it's only the high fae that Prince Soren cares so much about. Were the stories of the refugees he brought me in to listen to nothing more than a way to throw barbs at me? Does he care for none of these folk?

As we get to the small village square, there's a long line at one of the temples and I see some of the villagers walking away with small packages of bread tucked in their hands, a sign of the high-fae prince's mercy, even as he ignores them now.

That's a lot of conflicting information, all of it a puzzle I'm not sure I have the energy or focus to unravel right now.

When we get out of the village and near the outer reaches

of the castle walls, the horses speed up, galloping as though the Fates themselves command them. My horse, though prickly at first, doesn't falter, keeping up with the giant ebony beast that Prince Soren rides. *That* horse has a temper on it, something to behold, and I'm glad I'm not sitting on top of it.

When we arrive at the fae door, one of the soldiers dismounts and hands the reins to one of the others, then takes Northern Star's reins from me. He doesn't meet my eyes or say a word, simply watches as Prince Soren steps through the fae door ahead of us. He then leads my horse through as well, ensuring that I don't use this moment to travel somewhere else instead. I'm sure these precautions are all very logical to the high fae, but they're nothing but foolish to me.

I risked my fate to leave the dungeon and help the princess. They're all now very aware of the magic that lies in my veins— not the true extent of it but the potential—and Prince Soren could choose to delay our union until he's satisfied I'm not a danger to his people, an impossible task to achieve. The idea of missing the ceremony at the winter solstice and this entire debacle stretching out for another year or more makes my skin crawl, but I did it to get that baby out alive. I broke the curse so no more children would be lost.

Why would I leave him now to an unknown future and in the care of a race who have forgotten so much?

Traveling via the fae door is just as unpleasant this time as the first, and my skin pulls too tight over my bones as we finally step through and into a white landscape. We're in the depths of a kingdom where winter never truly ends.

I scowl and turn to Prince Soren. "Are we in the Outlands? We need to be where there's *life, not* in the middle of a blizzard."

The prince ignores me, waiting until Prince Tauron and the other three soldiers are settled on their horses with us before he leads us deeper into the snow. My fingers itch with power, desperate to blast him with my magic, but it would only complicate things more.

Only his obvious affection for his cousin and that baby keeps my mouth shut as we take the slow journey through the snow.

With it falling so heavily around me, it takes me a while to make some observations about the area. We're heading downhill, not drastically down a mountain but definitely an incline, and the snowfall slowly lessens around us.

When the sun finally peeks out from the clouds and hits us with its warmth, the first signs of a lush forest appear on the horizon. As we get closer to the greenery, I begin to smell it too. As the snow begins to melt, life springs forth from the ground. It's as rich and sumptuous here as the land I'd once known, alive and thriving the way the Ravenswyrd Forest always flourished.

The deep ache within me that came from the earth itself the moment I stepped foot in the Southern Lands at the port is still there but now just an echo, a reminder that even while this area flourishes, as a whole, the land is dying.

When the hooves of my horse finally hit grass instead of snow, I take stock of what I can see around me. Clover, brandy thistle, a smattering of wildflowers and mosses…it's not what we need yet, but I have no doubt we'll find it.

Prince Tauron urges his horse forward to walk alongside me. "Where is it?"

I look at him sternly from the corner of my eye. "I said we would find it where there is life, not that it's the only thing that would be growing here. This is the very edge of the snow—another hour of riding and we should find some."

Tauron scoffs under his breath. "I knew you were lying. Anything to get out of the cell."

It's a struggle to hold my temper. I have to be careful not to give them any reason to believe I'm one of those raving witches they described, but I have long since let go of the little girl who listened blindly to those with authority around me, trusting what they said to be true simply because they were in power.

I sat in that cell because I chose to, not because I had to. I stayed there as a form of penance, one these people would never understand, not even with their own experiences of war.

One of the soldiers rides forward. He's smaller than the rest and very clearly lower fae, an anomaly in their ranks. He's armed but not as heavily as the rest of them, and he steers his horse with his legs instead of the reins, far more competent in the saddle than most of the others. It's clear he spends more time riding than the rest do.

"The Goblin King said that we could approach the outpost and he'd travel to see us. I asked him if there was a specific time, but he said if you come, he will know and meet you."

The Goblin King.

I've never met the male of course, but hundreds, if not thousands, of goblins and part-bloods, exiled and free, had journeyed to the Northern Lands on the Sol King's promise of a good life after the war. I have many friends with goblin blood and heard many stories of their fabled and beloved king. Even those who were exiled had a respect for the male that could not be shaken.

Their love for him always confused me, considering they were willing to leave him and die for a high-fae court, but the explanations they gave me were always complicated, nuanced even in a time of desperation. The goblins have their own struggles, just as the high fae do.

Prince Soren allows the soldier to take the lead, nodding to him and jerking his head forward even as they ride side by side.

He refuses to speak to me or any of the others, riding in a surly silence that carries through the group as he sets the tone of the trip. I prefer it this way, focused as I keep my eyes sharp on the ground. I make note of dozens of plants that would be of great assistance not only to the princess but the people within the village. Their poor conditions hover in my mind, and I know exactly how delicate this meeting is going to be.

There's a tension in Prince Soren's posture that doesn't bode well.

I nudge my horse a little to the side, stepping off the path for a moment, and Tauron shadows me, moving so he's always within arm's reach of me. I find a small patch of the plant we're looking for, but I don't dismount to collect it, steering my horse back toward the group instead.

Tauron scowls at me even as he follows me. "Well? Was that it or not?"

I nod but when he moves to pull his horse up short, I turn to face him. "Do you really want to go before the Goblin King with a handful of his property without having asked to take it in the first place? I'll collect it on our journey back to the fae door."

He raises an eyebrow at me even as the soldiers riding on either side of us share a concerned look. "I thought you said he wouldn't notice?"

I shrug. "He won't, but, nevertheless, we should take it on the way out."

I have no intention of taking anything without permission, but the high fae don't need to know that. It's not the Ravenswyrd way, and though they're all approaching this meeting with apprehension, I'm less concerned.

Tauron turns back to his prince, and they speak, their lips moving, but I hear nothing, their voices pitched so only high-fae ears can hear, probably to spite me.

As we reach the top of another small incline, the ground a rolling untouched mass of greenery, I see a stunning patch of fae flowers. My heart clenches in my chest, and my throat closes at the sight of them. The fae flowers that grow here are unique to the Southern Lands. There's a variation of them in the Northern Lands, golden as they bloom and follow the sun's path through the sky as they thrive in the heat of the Seelie Court.

My heart always ached for the stunning silvery-white and blue flowers of home.

My time at Yregar has lessened some of that longing. I was unaware that the Celestial family wears the exact shades of those petals and claims them as their own. It's only now, staring down at the blooms, that the origin of the high-fae colors becomes clear to me.

Fae flowers once grew in abundance throughout the Ravenswyrd Forest, a blessing and a sign of our status as the Favored Children. The medicinal properties of the flowers were boundless; dozens and dozens of tinctures and ointments and teas could be prepared from them for hundreds of ailments. These very flowers sustained the Unseelie population for millennia in the Southern Lands.

I didn't see a single petal on the journey from the port to Yregar, and their absence hurt me more deeply than the barren plains. The damage done to the earth and the consequences of the war are a stark reality I can't ignore.

The rest of the group have a similar reaction to seeing the flowers, their eyes trained on them as though it pains them to turn away, but we make it to the outpost and turn our attention to the matter at hand.

It's a brick building, small in diameter, that climbs into the sky, a group of goblin soldiers standing at the top watching us approach. We stop the horses a few paces from the bottom of the tower facing a small wooden door.

Our lead soldier calls out, speaking in the common tongue, "Prince Soren Celestial, heir to the throne of the Southern Lands, is here to see the Goblin King, at his invitation."

There's no reply, at least not one that I can hear, though the high fae all grumble and groan around me.

Tauron mutters under his breath, "They're too primitive to speak the common tongue. It could take hours for a translator to arrive, and we don't have that long."

I glance at each of them, a frown on my face, before I sigh. I shouldn't be surprised to find out that Prince Soren doesn't speak the languages of his own kingdom, especially with the derision on their faces every time the word *goblin* passes their lips.

The princess and her son are in good health and could wait for however long this mess of a meeting takes, but I'm not patient enough to endure it.

Speaking in the goblin tongue, I call out, "*Prince Soren is here to see the Goblin King at his invitation.*"

"You are *not* to speak on our behalf."

Prince Soren doesn't even stop to question my abilities or thank me, he just turns in his saddle to snarl at me.

With a sigh, I call out to the goblin soldiers once more.

"*Prince Soren humbly requests that you bring a translator with the Goblin King's arrival as we have need of one.*" I don't think Prince Soren has humbly requested anything in his life, but I'm not as arrogant and rude as the rest of them. The goblins deserve our respect and good manners, and I'll be damned if I don't give those to them.

At my words, the soldiers above move about as Tauron's hand clamps on my reins and jerks the leather out of my hands.

"What have you done?" he snaps.

I roll my eyes at him. "I requested a translator so Prince Soren can rest assured I'm not tarnishing his wonderful reputation to the Goblin King without his understanding."

Tauron yanks on the reins to pull my horse toward his, looming over me in his saddle. The breadth of his shoulders is twice that of mine; physically, he could crush me, but I stare at him unflinching and unafraid.

"This isn't the place for your little tricks. I will slit your throat right now, Fates be damned, and face the consequences."

I've never held this high-fae prince in lower regard than I do now, my opinion of him reaching the deepest pits of Elysium the moment those words slip from his mouth, uncaring of the hundreds of thousands lost to such actions across the ocean.

I turn to Prince Soren, but he ignores us both, confident his cousin can reel me into line as he watches the goblins move around at the top of the tower. A few of them disappear, but they don't come out of the door at the bottom of the tower.

Without the knowledge I have, I would assume they were ignoring us and simply going about their duties, but the goblin city is like no other. I know its actual name—Aysgarth—but the high fae don't use it. Every part of this territory is simply called "goblin," instead of acknowledging the culture and people behind that word. It's dismissive in the most abhorrent way.

The city is rumored to be a mix of sparse buildings and gardens on top of the land and a much larger warren of streets and cavernous buildings beneath the earth. This tower no doubt connects to that city deep beneath our feet.

I wonder if the high fae know this or if they can hear the sounds of life beneath us. There's no sign on their faces as they stand in silence, watching the soldiers as we wait.

It becomes clear to me that the soldier who led us here is, in fact, not a soldier. He doesn't sit motionless like the rest of us do in our saddles; instead, he fusses and twitches as he waits. He hasn't experienced the intensity of waiting at the edge of battle for hours, poised and ready to strike and yet enduring a seemingly endless expanse of nothing. It takes more control than most people naturally have, something that's trained into soldiers over decades until it becomes second nature.

The fact that both princes have that discipline would be admirable if I could muster up that sort of feeling toward them.

The door at the bottom of the tower finally opens, and a group of soldiers spill out, marching and forming a wall before us. They're mostly full goblin, with green skin and horns protruding from their heads. Two white tusks grow from beside their mouths, which makes them look vicious as their tails whip and dance at their sides.

They're heavily armed, swords buckled at their sides, shields and spears in their hands as they stare out as though we're not standing before them, seeing everything and nothing as they wait for orders to strike. We're outnumbered, five-to-one, and Northern Star begins to fidget. I stroke a hand down her neck, steady and sure, until she settles.

The door is held open by another soldier, and the threshold darkens as the Goblin King himself steps through it without any announcement, a mountain of a man.

He's a part-blood himself, a mix of goblin and high fae, though only the smallest amount of goblin shows in his features, the slight green hue of his skin, and the dark hair on his head. He's taller than his people, as tall as Prince Soren, and his eyes are as cold and calculating as any royal I've ever seen.

He's dressed formally, with scaled armor plates over his shoulders and a modified breastplate covering part of his chest. It's more ornate than functional, a symbol of his capability on the battlefield as well as his station. His clothing is black and trimmed with silver, and he wears a royal family crest on his chest that's so similar to the Celestial crest that there's no denying the connection between the two houses. The Goblin King descended from the First Fae the same as the Celestials did, regardless of their animosity.

A female steps around his side, a part-blood with pointed high-fae ears, a pixie-like tilt to her nose, and the green-hued skin of the goblins. She has a keen gaze, hinting at the sharp edge of an intelligent mind.

The Goblin King waits until we all dismount from our horses and fall into position before him, a few paces between him and Prince Soren, before he addresses us.

"You have come to speak to the Goblin King, and he has met you as requested. This is a sign of respect he has graciously given you."

The woman translates his words perfectly, and though Tauron and the rest of us bow our heads respectfully, Prince Soren does not. His eyes are unblinking and steady as he stares back at the Goblin King, his face carefully blank.

"I'm here to negotiate a trading route through the Goblin Lands to the Western Fyres. The witches have destroyed the old path, and we can't repair it until we take back Yrmar Castle."

The translator passes this on, and the Goblin King frowns, speaking sternly as the translator relates it back. "We will not have the high fae traveling through the Goblin Lands. There's too much animosity between our people, and I will not risk goblin lives for the high fae to collect their pretty trinkets."

My gaze moves around the group, their faces as impassive as ever. There's no chance the Goblin King is unaware of the desperation in the rest of the kingdom. He's baiting Prince Soren and forcing him to admit the truth of the situation.

Prince Soren's jaw clenches hard, but he's obviously prepared himself for this response. "The trading route is for food and supplies. It will never be used for such frivolities."

The Goblin King cocks his head, his eyes searing. "I would think with the war, you'd have fewer mouths to feed, not more. Are your farmers so lacking that they cannot keep up?"

If Prince Soren loses his temper, I'm going to be forced to

step in just to stop our fates from being broken, and the very idea of such a thing eats at me. He doesn't deserve my help and, as far as I'm concerned, he deserves every bit of the Goblin King's taunting. The derision in the princes' tones when they've spoken of this male was enough to reveal to me their prejudices.

"The witches have destroyed the lands and nothing grows. I'm working to win the war and set things right once more, but I cannot let my people starve while we fight to rid the lands of Kharl and his forces once and for all."

The Goblin King nods slowly before looking around at the lush land he stands on. "I don't think the earth dies everywhere, Prince, only where the high fae rule with arrogance. Your kind have forgotten much of what it means to be a caretaker of this kingdom."

The censure in his voice is clear, no matter the language he uses. Even with the translator softening his words, there's no denying he's appalled by them all. The Goblin King studies our group with a sneer on his lips, only this time his gaze catches on me.

His eyebrows rise slowly, incredulously, as he snaps, "*A witch amongst the high fae. Have you brought her here as a threat to me?*"

Before the translator has the chance to relay the information, I bow deeply to the Goblin King, ignoring Tauron's curse and the hand that wraps around my arm to drag me back up.

"*My deepest apologies, Your Majesty. I'm here only to speak with you about an herb I would like to collect on our return home, just a few bushels, and one that grows in abundance here.*"

The translator begins to translate both his words and mine, but the Goblin King doesn't wait for her as he addresses me. "*You're here with a high-fae guard to collect herbs from my lands? This is most unexpected. What is your name, witch, and what coven do you hail from?"*

A smile tugs at my lips, even as I try to smother it. He's the first high fae to ask me that since I returned, a show of respect and a good sign for this conversation.

"I am Rookesbane Eveningstar, Mother of the Ravenswyrd Coven."

His face slackens in shock. He takes a single step forward before he sees the ripple of unease among my group at his approach, that they don't understand what we're saying and see his approach as a threat. Prince Soren is probably assuming I'm conspiring with the king, but before I can offer him any reassurance, the Goblin King speaks.

"A Ravenswyrd witch? You're the Favored Child returned."

Unable to fight it, a grin spreads across my face. *"You speak to the trees? I'm delighted to hear such a thing, Your Majesty! I hoped someone was still listening to their stories after my brother and I left for the Seelie Court. It's a relief and a great honor to know that a king such as yourself hears their songs."*

He scratches his chin, a knowing look passing over his features, and murmurs quietly to the translator, low enough that I don't catch their words. She stopped translating our conversation to the group when she heard my coven's name, the Goblin King's shock making her cautious.

She nods to him, and he looks back up to meet my gaze as he addresses me once more. *"The goblins never stopped speaking to the trees. The Ravenswyrd has missed you for a very long time, and the sorrowful melody it sang for you reached far across the kingdom. I hope you return to the trees again soon, they have mourned your loss."*

Tears prick at my eyes, unbidden, and I nod, unable to find words.

He takes pity on me and changes the subject, steering away from such painful admissions. *"What herb do you require? I would not so easily dismiss a request from you."*

"The herb I am looking for is milk thistle, nothing valuable or rare. I would never insult you or your people by asking for something precious."

There's a knowing look in his eye as he nods to me, his reply a statement not a question. *"The curse is broken. A high-fae baby has been born."*

Prince Soren's concern for the baby's safety rings in my ears, but when I hesitate to answer, the Goblin King holds up a hand. *"I felt the moment the curse broke—you've shared no secrets with me. You can take as much of the thistle as you can carry, but only you. The high fae have found no favor with the goblins and will get nothing from me. Tell me, witch, are you being held against your will? Let me offer you sanctuary here among my people. Ravenswyrd witches are always welcome on goblin lands."*

I bow again deeply, ignoring Tauron's furious muttering as I reply, *"Thank you for such a generous offer, but I returned to the Southern Lands to follow my fate, and I must now stay with the high fae."*

His brow furrows, his gaze tracing over my group once more. *"Your fate demands you stay with them?"*

His eyes fix on Tauron's hand, wrapped tightly around my arm, his fingers biting into my flesh and sure to leave behind a bruise.

"My fate is Prince Soren. He is my mate, given to me by the Fates themselves, and our union will end the war. I have no option but to stay with them."

TWENTY SIX

SOREN

There's nothing that we can do as the witch charms the Goblin King, speaking to him in the goblin tongue while the translator remains silent at his side. She continues to bow to him and smile, the picture of a gracious guest on his land. He doesn't look away from her as she speaks confidently, never slipping on the harsh and monosyllabic language. His eyes hold more respect in them now than they ever have for me.

Tauron and the soldiers shift on their feet, desperate to put an end to this, but I wait it out. We're not here to stroke my ego or force loyalty from this man, we're here because there's no other option. The rows of soldiers might look fearsome, but I'm confident enough to know I'm not in danger here, not the lasting kind anyway.

When the translator finally looks up at the Goblin King, he nods to her, speaking one last time to the witch alone. She startles and then clasps a hand into a fist, pressing it over her heart in a mark of respect to the Fates as she bows one last time.

The translator calls out to us, "The Goblin King has decided to allow a trading route through his lands to the Western Fyres but only under his conditions."

My breath freezes in my chest and my limbs slowly numb out, but I don't let it show on my face.

I meet the Goblin King's eyes as I reply, "And what are these conditions he demands?"

The Goblin King answers, the translator speaking for him, "The supplies must be only provisions as you have claimed them to be. The high fae who make the trip must follow the exact route the Goblin King chooses. You will have only three trades between now and the winter solstice. The Goblin King will meet with you again then to discuss if he wishes to keep the routes open and what compensation he should receive for allowing your people onto his land."

Three trades.

It's going to take a huge amount of planning and negotiation to get enough food through the goblin lands to feed all of those under my care. I was hoping for a constant stream of supplies, far easier to recover from raiding witches if there's more to come soon, but it's still a better deal than I thought we were going to be forced to agree to. Meeting with the goblins again, even hosting them at Yregar, is the lesser of many evils.

I nod once, a sharp jerk of my head, and the Goblin King does the same in return, without a word spoken between us. It's customary for the high fae to clasp palms to seal an agreement, but neither of us moves toward the other. There are too many years of animosity between the goblins and the high fae for that.

Finally, a slow smirk stretches across his lips as he ducks down to speak to the translator once more. His eyes flick to the witch as he speaks to her again, and she startles at my side, sending a long look in my direction.

When she replies to him, apprehension colors her tone and the words drag out of her as though by force.

I look at the translator, my eyebrows raised, and she also smiles back at me. "The Goblin King sends his congratulations to you for finding your mate and honoring the Fates by walking the path they have chosen for you. He has offered such congratulations to the honorable Rookesbane, as well. He looks forward to seeing you both again at the winter solstice to join you for your nuptials—he assumes you'll be marrying in line with Unseelie law."

My skin crawls at the very idea, but it's clear that the Goblin King has taken a very specific liking to my Fates-cursed mate, his eyes sharp as they watch my reaction, and I nod sharply to her as though signing my own death contract. "I look forward to meeting with him again then and discussing renewed terms to our agreement. I'll leave behind Darick to make the journey to the Western Fyres."

The Goblin King nods as the translator relays this to him, murmuring something back to her before turning on his heel and leaving, barking orders to his soldiers over his shoulder without a glance in their direction.

The translator smiles at the witch before she turns to me, face impassive once more. "The Goblin King says well met. He looks forward to seeing you again."

She turns to follow him back into the tower, but the rows of goblin soldiers stay where they are, facing us, as unblinking and unmoving as a wall. We have no choice but to mount our horses and turn our backs on them.

I despise showing my back to my enemy, but I ride out without another word, eager to return to Yregar through the fae door.

As instructed, Darick rides with us for two hundred paces and then veers off to the west, with nothing more than a respectful dip of his chin in my direction. Following my orders, he begins his journey to finish the negotiations with the Western Fyres, the lives of our people resting on his shoulders.

The witch doesn't speak a word as we ride back through the living territory and past the fae flowers, an echo of the beauty our kingdom once held.

She doesn't attempt to harvest any of the other plants that catch her notice, her gaze tracing over them all, but when we finally approach the patch of milk thistle she spotted on the ride in, she pulls her horse up short and dismounts to begin picking bushels of it.

Tauron swings from his horse as well, grabbing the reins of Northern Star. The sneer on his face has lifted, nothing but a calculating sort of curiosity left behind as he watches her work.

She doesn't simply tear the plant out of the ground or break off the stems.

Instead, she murmurs quietly under her breath in the old language, a reverent thanks to the Fates for providing exactly what Airlie and the baby need in such abundance, for leading her to it and giving her the skills to find it. She prays to the Fates that the plant will do exactly as it needs to, that the baby will grow and prosper, that he'll be safe and healthy and loved, and Airlie will flourish alongside him.

I feel the magic in the air, the way that she wraps these healing words around the plants to preserve them as she takes a bountiful harvest with such care.

There's a calm sort of confidence in her as she moves about the task, the exact sort of healer you'd want to tend to your wounds. Dark wisps of hair fall in curls around her face, her lashes dark as they fan out over her sun-kissed cheeks, every inch of her serene as her hands move swiftly in her harvest. Though I'm struck by the sight of her all cleaned up, her demeanor hasn't changed. She's been far too calm about her treatment at our hands, too confident in her own path, and my suspicions grow stronger.

There's more to her fate than she's telling me.

Tauron reaches into the pack on the back of his own horse and pulls out a small leather satchel, large enough to fit the bushels in the witch's hands but not much more.

When he moves to take the plants from her, she shakes her head. "The Goblin King was very specific about his agreement for me to take the plants. We can take only what *I* can carry."

Tauron's eyebrows pinch together, and he glances at me. "You told the Goblin King what you were doing here?"

She nods sharply. "He has eyes everywhere in his kingdom. It's not as simple as taking a few plants and riding to the fae door without drawing attention. We'd have a swarm of goblin soldiers waiting for us. They're ready to kill us all and be done with it if we take anything without his permission."

She ties the satchel securely to her own saddle and, without preamble, swings on top of the horse and steers Northern Star back onto the path. We set off once more, and after a few paces I nudge Nightspark until I fall into line next to the witch. She doesn't react except to send me a sidelong look, distrust woven into her features as she readies herself for an attack.

"What did you speak to the Goblin King about?"

She's expecting this question and has had more than enough time to prepare her answer for it.

The cold and empty smile that stretches across her lips is very different to the one she gave him. "I don't know why you ask, Prince Soren, when you have every intention of dismissing my words as lies."

I watch as the green fields around us sway and murmur with life. The peace I feel in these fields is an insult to the rest of the kingdom, the damage wrought there by her kind. "Tell me anyway, and I'll see if I can find it in myself to believe you. Swear it on the baby and maybe I will."

Her eyebrows rise but her focus doesn't stray from the path ahead. "He asked me who I was and where I came from, and I told him. The goblins haven't forgotten the way of this world, and my name means something to him, enough that he offered me sanctuary in Goblin City."

My head snaps toward her, but she ignores my reaction, her tone unchanging with her calm delivery. "I told him that it's my fate to stay with you and that I wished to take the milk thistle. He already knew the curse was broken—he felt it. When he asked about it, I didn't answer for fear of the princess's safety. I don't believe the Goblin King would do anything to harm her or the baby, but there are too many ears in the kingdom to risk such words."

I have no doubt of her protectiveness toward Airlie and the baby. She wants them alive. My concerns are her motives behind that desire, but for now, I'll use her knowledge and skills to ensure their safety.

We fall into silence once more, and it's not until the horizon before us turns white and the horses begin to climb the beginnings of the mountain that the fae door rests at the bottom of that she speaks again.

"He offered me some marriage advice as well, but I told him it wouldn't apply in our case."

My gut clenches, my tone harsh as I snap, "You truly believe I'm going to marry you?"

She huffs out a chuckle, adjusting her hands on the reins so she can stroke Northern Star's neck. The beast is bewitched by her, calming under her sure touch.

"I believe you have no other choice, Prince Soren. I went to the Northern Lands in search of a different fate and found nothing but disappointment and heartache, a glimpse into the future if we choose to ignore their demands."

She speaks in riddles, the worst sort of conversation, because she knows more than I do, or at least she thinks she does. No matter what else she does, whatever acts of service and loyalty she shows, I can't trust her for this reason. Her motives will always be her own, while mine must always consider my people, my hands tied from birth.

When I can't bear her silence any longer, I ask, "Why won't it apply to us? If you're so sure of this future, why does his advice not apply?"

The horses' hooves crunch on the ground as we reach the edge of the frozen land, the green disappearing under the slurry of snow that's begun to build until it's all we can see once more.

"He told me the Fates know better than we do, and if they placed us together, then we can trust in that. He's sure that someday, we will find our way to one another, not just in our physical forms but in our hearts as well."

She turns to me, her silver eyes flashing in the icy, white depths of winter's hold. "I don't see any danger of that happening here, do you, Prince Soren?"

The witch is silent for the rest of the trip through the Goblin Lands and doesn't speak again until we have made it through the fae door and back to Yregar. The soldiers that wait for us there all bow their heads in respect to me as we pass through.

The soldiers' presence here has tripled, just as I instructed, but the horses are slower as we work our way back toward the village in the darkness, only the stars above to light our path.

I watch the tense lines of her shoulders grow even more taut the closer we get to the castle, her apprehension of what we'll find there a mirror of my own. I have no idea where I'm going to put the witch now that the dungeon is no longer an option.

I'm busy considering this when she breaks the silence. "The trading routes will feed the castle and the villagers until the winter solstice, but what are your plans after that? Are you going to trade with King Salem forever?"

Tauron huffs out a breath at her presumption, questioning the heir to the Southern Lands on his plans for the kingdom, but the small scraps of information that we've found out about her have come from Tyton's open questioning, from Airlie accepting her help, and from the Goblin King, his eyes filled with respect as he hung on her every word.

Conversation isn't so difficult, not when the welfare of my kingdom rests on my shoulders.

"With three trading passes until winter solstice, if we are able to purchase enough and transport it through the kingdom without the witches taking it or destroying it, we'll be able to survive until the spring. The Fates have decreed I'll have the throne by then, and many things within the Unseelie Court will change."

Her eyebrows furrow. "How will they change? Do you know why the kingdom is withering, and do you know how to bring it back to life?"

The guards at the inner wall bow at our approach and open the iron gates to let us through to the village. Night might have fallen around us, but the streets are still bustling, littered with the survivors of witch attacks who don't yet have lodgings as they move at my soldiers instructions. It's cold out—the Southern Lands always are at night—and they're eager to get out of the chill.

I'd taken to opening the Grand Hall and letting them sleep in there, warm and safe for the night with the soldiers looking over them all. With the birth of the baby, I instructed Tyton to keep the castle doors closed for now and to open the temple instead. We try to keep the sacred space free for worship and for giving out the rations, but it's the only other building large enough to house the displaced fae folk who've found their way to Yregar.

"When I'm king, I'll have control of the entire Unseelie high-fae army, and I'll lead the attack to end the war, to kill Kharl, his generals, and every last witch who fights for them.

Without their magic decaying the kingdom, it will recover, and the fields will prosper once more. We'll be able to fix the original trading route and leave the goblins to their own devices once more. When I'm king, I'll restore the lands to the glory of my father's reign."

Even in the darkness of the village I can see the flash of silver as her eyes pick me over, unblinking as she weighs up my words. I see the internal battle warring within her, the way she fights with her own best intentions over her answer.

Ultimately losing, she says, "The lands aren't dying because the witches are poisoning them. The lands are dying because no one is caring for them anymore."

An easy fix. "When the witches are dead and gone, I'll move the villagers back to the plains. The farmers will feel safe tending to the land once more and everything will be right again."

She lets out a long breath and shakes her head, as though dealing with an unruly child, ignoring the warning growl that Tauron lets out at her disrespectful attitude toward me.

"Farmers don't care for the land, they cultivate it. They *take* from it. What do the high fae do at the equinoxes and solstices? I didn't see any celebrations or offerings for the summer when I arrived here. When do the high fae ever give back?"

I scowl at her, leading the group through to the stables and dismounting the moment we get there. I hand my reins off to Ingor and then take Northern Star's reins from the witch, watching as she carefully dismounts and retrieves the leather satchel.

She opens it and carefully looks over her bounty, her eyes shrewd as she checks its quality, nodding to herself when she finds it suitable.

Tauron moves to take it, intent on leading her back through the castle, but I shake my head and wave him off. "I'll take her.

Go check in with Tyton and Airlie, make sure nothing happened while we were gone."

He frowns, his eyes flicking down to the witch before he bows and leaves, taking two steps at a time in his haste. I dismiss the two soldiers as well, sending them to the barracks to clean up and prepare for their scheduled watch, before I lead the witch back through the castle.

When I veer away from Airlie's rooms, she doesn't say a word, simply follows me down the long hallways and down a set of stairs until we reach a small workshop. The door is stiff as I pry at it, the hinges needing a good oiling, but once it swings open I gesture inside with a dismissive hand.

"This is the healer's quarters. You'll stay here from now on."

Her eyebrows rise a little, but she steps into the room confidently.

There's a small bunk carved into the plain stone wall, the mattress old and dusty from many long centuries of disuse. The entire area needs a good scrubbing, but there are shelves and shelves of vials and jars, an old mortar and pestle sitting on a work table, as well as a washbasin and a small fireplace.

Cupboards line one of the walls, and as she steps into the room and places the leather satchel on the workbench, the witch stares at them. Wasting no time, she begins digging through the cupboards, humming under her breath in concentration until she pulls out a large bowl, a sharpened knife, and a brewing pot. There's a determined set to her face, a stern expression that leaves no room for arguing.

Whatever her life was before her return, she's not accustomed to being told no.

She glances at me, her tone firm and her instructions clear. "I need cleaning supplies. I can't brew the tincture with dirty tools, and I need ingredients to mask the bitter flavor, otherwise the princess will struggle to ingest it."

I step out of the room and motion to one of the soldiers, ordering him to bring down a maid with cleaning supplies. Then I think better of it and call for Firna herself. There's no one else I trust with this task.

When I step back into the room, the witch already has her sleeves rolled up and the washbasin filling with water, steam rising from it as she ducks back into the cupboards to rummage for more supplies. The hot springs under the castle heat the water naturally, and I often send my thanks to the First Fae for their foresight. Without magic, heating water for an entire castle and the village surrounding it would be a challenge, to say the least.

"Firna will bring you whatever you require for Airlie and the baby. She will also bring your food to you here, and you will instruct her on every part of the process for making the tincture so that she can give it to Airlie in your stead."

She casts me a look and shakes her head slightly. "I'm going to watch over that baby for the next few weeks myself, just until we're sure he's growing as he should. That isn't for my own nefarious plans, or whatever other fantasies you have dreamed up in that mind of yours. I'm doing it so he lives. The curse might have brought him here early, but I won't let it stop him from thriving."

I nod and step out of the way as Firna arrives, arms full of cloth and soaps that she sets out on the large workbench without ceremony.

The keeper grimaces as she looks around the bleak room. "I'll call the maids down to get this cleaned up."

The witch shakes her head. "There's no need. I'll do it myself. I need you to bring me some honey and any plain teas if you have them. Does Princess Airlie have any preferred tastes? A sweet tooth, perhaps?"

Firna nods. "She drinks a chamomile brew in the morning

with her breakfast. I can bring it to you with the honey and some supper—it's been days since you last ate, and you can't waste away while we're caring for them both."

The witch places a hand over her stomach and looks down at the stones beneath us as though looking for the green earth we just passed on our journey. She's a peculiar fae, unlike anyone I've ever met, but she doesn't seem to notice or care.

"Thank you, Firna," she says, and the keeper nods, turning back to bow to me as she leaves the room with her busy work.

"What offering would you give the earth to have it aid you?"

She doesn't stop her work at my words, her hands busy as she soaps up the water in the basin and begins to scrub the tools she's selected. Her gaze drops to the fireplace and, from out of nowhere, flames burst into life there.

It's a small act of magic, but still more than many witches have ever had within them. She shows more control of her magic than any high fae I've ever known, at least here in the Southern Lands, and she does it as though it's *nothing*. A simple act to make her life easier as she sets the now clean pot on top of the stove, water boiling within it.

"You asked what I was doing in the dungeon and how I sustained myself? I gave a blood offering to the earth and, in return, it sustained me. It doesn't want to take from us without giving something in return, so why should it give to us if we don't offer the same?"

We watch as the water on the stove begins to boil, and she places each of the tools within the pot as the bubbles engulf them. I don't understand this practice, but none of it appears dangerous to Airlie or the baby. Still, I watch it all.

"The Goblin Lands…you think the king makes an offering to the land and that's why his land flourishes?"

The corners of her lips tug up as she replies, "I know he makes offerings to the land. I could hear it in the earth as we rode through, couldn't you? Have the high fae forgotten *everything*?"

The skin at the back of my neck itches as a snarl curls my lip. I hate the way she says that, the superior tone of her voice... and I hate the way it's true. We *have* forgotten what it means to take care of anything but our own affairs, starting with our magic.

The high fae forgot how to use it long ago—long enough that my father didn't have access to his own magic, nor his father before him—generations of high fae with a power within them they don't know how to touch.

Firna steps back into the room, balancing a tray in her hands and a satchel tucked under one of her arms, never once faltering as she places everything on the workbench that's now been scrubbed clean by the witch's own hands.

I turn to her and wait until she bows, her task clear, before I leave them behind. Firna will watch the witch's every move, both learning and guarding to be sure she's true in her intentions to help, while I move my focus back to finding out where in the Fates-filled *fuck* Roan is.

TWENTY S·EV·EN

ROOKE

Three Unseelie high-fae princes hover around my seat at Airlie's side, glaring and savage, as they watch the princess drink the tea I brewed for her.

She doesn't sip it slowly, instead downing the glass in two goes, as if she's desperate to get it in her body and working as quickly as possible. She sets aside the cup on the small table by her bed as her hand strokes the back of the sleeping baby, who's content in her arms as he dozes. There's a tug in my heart at the sweet and gentle noises he makes, a small reminder of the other babies I've seen into the world and honored in this way.

The princess's gaze is sharp, but she keeps her voice low, conscious always of her son. "How did the Goblin King know that the curse was broken?"

I take a seat in the small armchair sitting by her side of the bed, moved there by one of her cousins as they've kept a vigil over her and the baby. I doubt it will end until Roan's return, each one of us holding our breaths as we wait.

Watching the steady breaths of the sleeping baby, I keep my voice low. "The goblin lands are still green and lush, their people are unaffected by the curse, and so their land prospers. If I were to guess, I'd say the Goblin King still has access to his magic, and his family never forgot such things. He speaks to the trees."

Her lips purse as her brow furrows, and I search for the best way to explain. "Magic like that doesn't hide itself— it's too powerful to be a secret. The curse covered the entire kingdom—I could feel the reach of it the moment I stepped foot back in the Southern Lands. It's an old power that might've waned over the years without new deaths to sustain it, but it was still strong enough to linger over your son like an executioner's blade. I didn't know the specifics of what it did to the high fae until I spoke to you, but I knew the magic was there. A lot of power went into casting that atrocity, sacrifices made and then reinforced with every death of the innocent high-fae babies. I'm not surprised that the Goblin King felt the moment it broke."

A soft frown settles on her face, and she nods slowly. "I can feel its absence, but I passed that off as relief. Tyton says he can feel it too, but I thought that was because he was so close to where the curse was undone."

I shrug. "His magic is more...*wild* than that of most high fae, enough that it bubbles out even without training. I think no matter where in the kingdom he was, he would have felt the curse break if..."

Airlie sends me a sidelong look. "You mean if he'd been conscious to do so?"

There's unhappy grumbling behind me, but I nod, not about to apologize. The baby is alive because of what I did, and if he really wants to hold a grudge about it, then I suppose I'll just have to deal with it.

Airlie's hand is gentle as it runs down the baby's spine, comforting herself in the petting, the small way she enjoys the feel of his steady breathing on her chest. No doubt it's a reminder that he's here and safe. There's been no mention of a name yet. No one has asked her in my presence, either, so I take their lead and leave such things for later.

The quiet of the room stretches out, and when the princess

yawns delicately, I ask her, "Do you have someone staying here with you tonight? Firna or one of the maids? Your son is perfectly healthy, but you shouldn't be alone while you recover."

Airlie shoots the princes a stern look and then says, "I was hoping you would stay with us for tonight, and then Firna can stay tomorrow. Roan should be home after that, and I won't need any more assistance."

There's no protest at her request, so it mustn't be new information to Prince Soren. I nod, settling back in the seat, ready to take up watch without another word. When her eyes begin to grow heavy, I help the princess move the baby back into the small crib and then encourage her to rest.

I haven't slept, but I have more training than most in going several days in a row without a moment of sleep.

Tauron and Tyton both disappear, but Prince Soren pulls another chair into the corner of the bedroom, far enough away from the princess and me that he won't disturb us, and takes up watch there. His gaze follows me as I go through the routines of early child care and tending to a new mother, his presence impossible to fully ignore no matter how focused on the tasks as I am. He doesn't say a word or interrupt in any way as the night goes on in a blur of tasks and it makes the work easier for me. The baby wakes, his diaper is changed, his mother feeds and burps him, smiling at his grunting as he works through his wind, then settles him back in the crib for a few hours only to start all over again.

Prince Soren watches it all and never once closes his eyes. Neither do I, the two of us standing guard over this precious gift of life as we see Airlie through her first night, the biggest adjustment to the constant demands of a small one, all while her body heals from its incredible journey to motherhood.

Around dawn the baby stirs again, and before he wakes fully, I take him from the crib and walk around the edge of the bed to set him on the other side and change his wet diaper.

When I find that he's wet all the way through, a fantastic sign of the princess's milk supply, I do a full inspection of him as I get him changed into clean and dry clothing once more. I check his reflexes, his breathing, the pallor of his skin, and the small section of the cord still left on his belly from where he'd been connected to his mother.

There's no sign of infection; his limbs are strong and his temperature is perfect. By all accounts, he's perfectly healthy, just a little bit small. By the time I have him dressed once more, happily bundled up, his grunts and whimpers have turned into a proper little cry as he calls to his mother for more food.

Airlie wakes, her eyes popping open as she sits up in the bed in a rush. The same moment of panic is on her face every time she wakes, so terrified it's all been nothing but a dream. When she spots him in my arms, a sigh of relief expels from her lips as she reaches for him, and I help her get him settled once more.

She never questions my critiques or adjustments, simply listens to me and nods. She's not at all what I was expecting her to be as a patient. I assumed the moment the baby was born alive and well, she would throw me back into the dungeon, refuse my help, and spurn any suggestions I might have. Instead, she soaks up every bit of the knowledge I give her, steady and confident in herself. She hasn't just yearned for this moment for a long time, she's prepared for it as well.

"Is the sun up yet?" she asks quietly as he drinks, his little grunts loud in the otherwise silent room.

I nod. "He's been with us for his first day, and many more to come."

I murmur a quiet thanks to the Fates in the old language, a custom of the Ravenswyrd Coven, and the princess's eyebrows rise. "How many languages do you know? I thought only a few of the high fae remembered that one."

I stand and walk to the window to pull back the heavy drapes, letting in some light and freshness to chase away the last remnants of the long night. I'm aware that Prince Soren is listening to our every word, weighing up my actions and my truths for his own assessments of my character and motives, but in this I have nothing to hide.

"My father taught me every language spoken in the Southern Lands and a few others that might come in handy."

Airlie smiles and says, "The Seelie tongue certainly did, what a stroke of good fortune. What happened to your father?"

It's an old wound, old enough now that when people ask, it doesn't hurt me like it did when my brother and I first crossed the seas. Back then, every question was like tearing open my flesh, my heart sore and exposed. Now it's the memory of an old ache.

"He died a very long time ago."

I don't offer her anything else and, whether in payment for my services or simply because she doesn't care to pry any further, she leaves it be as she adjusts her son on her chest. He makes happy baby noises and finishes his morning meal, content in his mother's loving arms.

I step back to the bed to pour another glass of water, and then look over to where Prince Soren sits, his body tense and his eyes as sharp as they were when we returned here yesterday evening. He clearly has experience with sleepless nights as well.

I glance at Airlie. "I'm going back to the healer's quarters this morning to brew up more of the tinctures. I'd like to have an ongoing supply ready for you."

She nods once more. "Were you able to pick enough herbs?"

I nod, fussing with the blankets around the prince until I'm sure he's warm. "More than. Your supply should even out around the winter solstice, if not before, but I collected some cuttings to grow milk thistle here as well, just to be sure."

Her brow furrows. "It won't grow. Nothing here does."

A smile tips up the corners of my mouth, and I pat the back of one of her hands gently. She startles at the familiarity of the action, but she doesn't protest.

"I have a great skill with such things, and there's no reason the milk thistle won't grow for me. The land has always provided for me as I provide for it. Now, I'll settle the prince back in his crib, if you'd like to get some more rest?"

Airlie shakes her head and pulls back the covers of her bed, shaking out her long and graceful limbs as she stands in that easy way of the high fae. "There are many things I need to be doing today, and none of them are lazing around in bed."

I shoot her stern look as I take the baby, rocking him gently to settle him in my arms. "As your healer, I should remind you that lazing around is not what's happening here. It's called *resting,* and you need to do a lot of it in these early days. In fact, it's all you should be doing."

She nods and waves a hand at me as she steps toward the bathing room, her eyes fixed on her son before she goes in there.

I'm sure she trusts me with him only because Prince Soren is sitting in the corner watching us both, his gaze like a hot brand across my skin that I can't truly ignore, but it feels like the smallest of victories. A tiny step toward a less tumultuous path to my fate, and relief warms my chest. If I have to be here with these people, I might as well find some peace.

The healer's quarters are a modest and long-abandoned area of the castle, tucked away near the kitchens on the lower level. There's a small stairwell to get to them and a side entrance to the castle at one end that leads to a small, equally long-dead garden. There are remnants of a large medicinal crop of herbs and flowers where the previous healers once tended to the garden themselves, a tantalizing prospect.

I spend the rest of the day scrubbing the entire area clean, hard work that keeps my mind from delving too far into the what ifs of the changes I find myself in. I have to keep stopping to check on the tinctures brewing or to receive supplies from the maids as Firna sends them in throughout the day.

At first, it's only supplies for more tea for the princess, but then a maid arrives with armfuls of blankets and pillows and deposits them on the small bunk I just scrubbed out. She doesn't speak to me, ducking her chin shyly as she walks past, but she begins to make up the small bed.

I've seen the plush bedding in Princess Airlie's room; I'd even stripped and made the bed for her after the prince's arrival. This bedding is far more humble than the ornate and luxurious fabrics used there, but it's warm and it's clean, and far more than I've been offered so far in the castle. I thank the maid, sure to meet her eye, and she swallows roughly as she dips her head a fraction, her feet moving quickly as she flees the room.

Hours later, Firna herself comes to see me with a small tray of food in her hands. It's simple fare—bread, cheeses, and some fruits, but it's not the slops I was given in the dungeon.

"I'll take the tea for the princess with me now and care for her this evening. If there's anything we should need you for overnight, I'll send one of the maids down to collect you."

I hum in agreement, pouring out the mixture for her, and she removes the plates from the tray and replaces them with the items for Airlie.

"I don't think you'll need me—Airlie is adjusting beautifully, and she was perfectly fine when I left them both earlier. Is there any sign of Prince Roan yet?"

Firna sighs, pressing a hand into her forehead and looking weary for the first time since I've known the woman. "Nothing yet. Prince Soren sent messengers and extra soldiers to the Outlands, but there's been no word."

In times of war, no news is definitely not good news, and my lips tighten as I give her a firm look. "If the princess asks, tell her the truth but keep the focus on her son. She's not one to accept pretty lies to cower from reality, but there's no use in her worrying just yet. Stress will only make things harder for her body as she heals and adjusts."

Firna nods, taking the tray and leaving the room with the confidence of a woman who runs the entire household.

Moving to the window frames, I check the small jars of milk thistle cuttings I placed carefully on the sills. They're already showing signs of life, thanks to the little extra boost my magic gave them. It helps that milk thistle grows like a weed, rampant in the climate of the Southern Lands so long as the ground isn't frozen or sucked dry of life. I won't struggle to cultivate it in the small garden plots outside, a task for tomorrow after I've cleaned the area out.

It's not going to be easy, but I've never been afraid of hard work.

Removing the dress and awful Unseelie high-fae boots, I set them on the small wooden chair next to the sleeping bunk before I climb onto the mattress wearing nothing but the small shift Firna had given me as underwear.

I'll have to see later if the keeper's kindness toward me will extend as far as more clothing, but for now, this will do. I fall asleep quickly, secure and blissfully unwatched for the first time in months.

I'm woken by a rough hand on my shoulder. My magic flares to life, snapping out in protection as I'm caught unaware, and it reaches out to grasp whoever is attacking me. Only at the last moment do I see a maid staring down at me, terrified as she feels the tendrils of power wrapping around her arm.

I curse under my breath, pulling it back into myself, but before I can form any apologies in my sleep-hazed mind she stutters, "The prince has called for you. You must make haste!"

She doesn't specify which prince, but I can hazard a guess.

It takes me a few moments to get back into the dress and pull the shoes onto my aching feet. The maid wrings her hands by the door in panic as she waits, and when I finally gesture for her to lead the way, she bolts out of the room like a terrified rabbit.

I feel bad for scaring her so badly, but she doesn't want to be in my presence long enough for a sincere apology. When we get to the ground floor, I'm surprised when she veers away from the staircase that leads to Airlie's rooms and instead takes me to the Grand Hall. My stomach drops. Midnight meetings in such places are never a good sign.

Lamps glow everywhere, the castle lit up like there's a ball underway, and the marble floors sparkle as though by magic as it reflects the light. When we approach the door, it's opened for us by two soldiers, both heavily armed as though braced for an attack. The maid steps into the room, her head bowing instantly before Prince Soren and the woman with him. She turns to me, her mouth opening and her eyes widening in horror.

This is Princess Airlie's mother. I met her when I was dragged before the Unseelie Court. She didn't make a great impression on me then, and the drivel pouring from her mouth now only makes matters worse.

"How could you do this to her, Soren? How could you let one of those filthy creatures touch my daughter! You were supposed to take care of her. *Roan* was supposed to take care of her."

Prince Soren holds up a hand, ignoring her indignant protests, and calls his orders to me, "The castle is on lockdown, no one in or out. You will tend to Airlie in my absence."

I nod, moving to leave the Grand Hall, but the soldiers at the door don't open it, standing like a wall in front of them, so I'm forced to listen as the woman's shrieking begins anew.

"You would deny me access to my daughter but send a *witch* into her rooms instead? Soren, have you gone mad? After everything we've done to keep you safe and a prospect for the Unseelie Court to place upon the throne, you're throwing it away for that witch? Has she cast a spell on you? I'll have to ride out and speak to the regent myself!"

I step forward again but the soldiers stare past me, unblinking. I huff, not eager to listen to the same tired hatred and distrust for me, and the maid steps up to stand at my side. She's been assigned to me, clearly, and I turn back to watch the disastrous scene play out before us.

Prince Soren steps toward the woman, a relation of his somewhere along the line, but his eyes are cutting as he stares at her, none of the warmth he shares with her daughter present. "Airlie doesn't want you to see the baby before Roan does. You'll wait until she calls for you. Your daughter was offered help by the witch to break the curse and she chose to take it. The Unseelie Court passed the law that I must marry my mate before I can take the throne, they've chosen to uphold that law for almost a thousand years while everything around us died and the regent watched, uncaring for the hundreds of thousands of lives lost. That witch is my fate and if the Unseelie Court doesn't wish that fate to pass, then they'll need to give me the throne without our union. You shouldn't have come, Aura. You knew better than to try and now you're wasting my time with your theatrics. By coming here, you've risked the safety of the entire kingdom, and for nothing."

Her mouth opens and shuts, and then again as though she's a fish out of water, before she sputters in outrage. "I've done no such thing! I felt the curse break and I knew it had to be Airlie.

She was the only pregnant high fae in all the kingdom and I came straight here to be with her, as any mother should!"

Her words catch my attention, my curiosity itching without a way for me to scratch it. She felt the curse break as well. Tyton and Airlie feeling it could be explained, and the Goblin King didn't surprise me, but Aura? Does her magic writhe within her like an unruly beast, or do the high fae simply not recognize the power they hold within themselves? It's frustrating that I can't question them about this further and get a proper answer. Even if they trusted me, I doubt these people would know what I was asking them.

A cold smile stretches across Soren's lips. "And who did you tell about the curse breaking along the way? Who at Yris knows the reason you left? You might have loyalty, Aura, but you don't see the truth of how far our people have fallen under the reign of the regent. We're not untouchable—the witches have proved that time and time again, and my uncle has done nothing but look on as his people die."

She glances around the room as she murmurs, "You cannot speak of him like that, Soren, it's treason! I've proved my loyalties to you a thousand times over. There's nothing else I can do to sway the rest of the Unseelie Court to side with you. I've done everything in my power to preserve your reputation, even while you've worked against me. I live in Yris and adhere to the court's way of life, but there's nothing wrong with choosing comfort over this depressing and barren stone prison! I'm more use to you there."

Her gaze gets stuck on the scar across his face, and he shakes his head at her. "You fought for my reputation, and I fought for our lives."

She sputters out a protest, a denial of the severity of the war, but Prince Soren cuts her off. "Every last one of the royal families deserves to starve. I might be willing to risk the Unseelie Court by letting the regent traipse around the kingdom, but I won't have you risk Airlie or her son with your indifference to their safety simply to put on your act of a doting mother. The witch will care for her, you will stay in your guest rooms, and no one will leave this castle until I return. If I find out that you stepped so much as a single foot on the staircase to her room while I was gone, I'll kill you."

She gasps, taking a step back from him as she clutches at the lace paneling of her dress over her heart. Her gaze darts around the room, but there's no one else in here but us and the soldiers, a crowd of unsympathetic faces who would all lay down their lives at the prince's command.

He steps forward, his eyes devoid of emotion and his voice cold. "If you disobey my orders and risk her life, your own is forfeit. No amount of loyalty you've shown me will take priority over the two of them."

Turning away from her trembling form, he strides toward another exit on the far side of the Grand Hall from me. A cluster of soldiers there follow him without another word being spoken, all of them armed to the teeth.

There must have been another attack.

I wait with the maid for a moment, having my orders from the prince, but as the soldiers at the door finally move to let me leave, Aura lifts her head, her eyes meeting mine with cold loathing flashing through the endless blue depths. I can't sense any magic bubbling inside her, not like Tyton, but the fury she holds is like a vicious beast as it snaps its teeth at me.

"Whatever magic you've cast against him, whatever evil you are spreading here with my child, the Fates have said Prince Soren will win the war against your kind. It's only a matter of time before your scheming will be uncovered and he'll throw you aside."

The maid bows her head at the woman, as the household

servants do for all high-fae royals, before she leads me back out of the Grand Hall to the princess's rooms. Her feet are quick, the heeled shoes she wears clicking loudly on the marble floors.

The prince's soldiers' presence throughout the castle is more pronounced, out in the open and fully armed rather than casually milling around, and their gazes follow us the entire way. Men line the hallways and stand at every door with swords and shields at the ready.

I knew that the barracks here were full of soldiers, all of them loyal to their prince, but I'm surprised to see their numbers as they spread out around Yregar in its defense. The walls outside the windows are covered as well, the soldiers there readying themselves for an attack they're sure is coming.

I send one last prayer to the Fates as I speed up, an old habit I can't seem to break, though they've never been kind to me before.

Let this all be nothing more than a precaution, and keep any harm from coming to the prince. Send Roan home to his son.

TWENTY EiGHT

SOREN

Aura and the three guards with her had ridden through the gates of Yregar as though they were chased by monsters of the Fates all the way from Yris, and they have no idea how lucky they were to arrive here unscathed.

The reports of witches entering the icy plains of the Outlands arrived only minutes after they did, dozens of raving creatures moving on foot without flagging. I've often wondered if Kharl has the ability to sustain them through magic alone as they travel for weeks on end without stopping, but there's no way to be sure, and the knowledge wouldn't help us anyway. Roan has already moved his father's soldiers to strengthen their defenses, but there's something about this move from Kharl that doesn't sit right with me—a pattern appearing that grows only more ominous as the Fates tug at me.

No good comes from ignoring them.

I dismiss my aunt's arrival and sound the alarm for my soldiers to move into formation and for those I've chosen to ride out with me to be ready to leave imminently. Being forced to split my forces to ensure that Yregar is adequately protected while I ride out to meet Roan and the Outland soldiers isn't ideal, but that tug is growing more insistent as the minutes tick by, impatience raking at me until my temper ignites.

Aura forced me to meet with her, standing at the base of the stairs to Airlie and Roan's chambers as she screamed and wailed for her daughter. I was tempted to snap her neck right there and be done with it, only the thought of my uncle gaining the majority vote amongst the Unseelie Court staying my hand. That reason is beginning to wear thin, and as my fate looms, my aunt may soon find herself without its protection.

Defending the witch against my aunt wasn't a pleasant experience, but the long simmering rage in my gut for my aunt's apathetic and self-serving ways had only stoked higher at her words. She'd sat in the gilded halls of Yris and waited for her grandson to die. Worse still, she'd prepared to use his death to manipulate her daughter further. She'd treated this pregnancy the same as she had Airlie's first, never once offering help, just whining at her daughter to return home to her and be a pretty little puppet to wield for her own games. She's never done more than whisper behind the back of her hand, manipulating gossip and fabricating new stories in her efforts. Not a single time has she attempted to assist in the war efforts or even acknowledged we're fighting one in the first place.

She holds a seat on the Unseelie Court, but she also leads her own household, with several noble high fae under her command and many people over whom she holds responsibility. She may not have a castle of her own, but she has an entire wing of Yris that is hers to rule, just as the others on the Unseelie Court do. She has resources beyond just her vote and her influence, but no matter how dire the war has gotten, she's never offered her own soldiers or people in our aid.

She has no right to come to Yregar and question her daughter's decisions, and she's certainly in no position to demand we remove Airlie from a healer's care, no matter how loath we all are that the healer is a witch.

As I step out of the Grand Hall, Tyton and Tauron both meet

me, eyes sharp as they watch the sentries patrolling at the top of the walls. We're expecting retaliation for the witches' curse breaking, sure that Kharl will lead an attack on Yregar now that his most deadly defense against my people has been unraveled. Whether the witches have spies other than my uncle and my Fates-cursed mate living amongst the high fae I don't know for sure, but their newfound fixation on the Outlands is suspicious.

Kharl's armies haven't entered the icy plains of the Snowsongs' territory since Roan's mother died and laid a curse of her own with her dying breath, Seelie magic still strong in her veins and a mother's love at its most powerful when her son's life is in danger.

Now he's in danger again.

I turn to Tyton with a grim look. "Watch over Airlie in her rooms and have the soldiers report to you there. The witch is already tending to Airlie and the baby with Firna, all of them together so nothing can happen without your approval. Aura is not to leave the ground floor. She's been told it's her death if she does."

Tyton nods and claps his brother on the shoulder, then leaves to secure the castle. He's dressed in armor and dripping with weapons, ready should the witches attack Yregar. I'm not worried about leaving him behind; he's a competent and level-headed leader even with so many innocent lives in his care.

Tauron has his helmet tucked under his arm and a weary look on his face, his expression stark even with the determined set of his mouth.

"Have you slept at all?" I ask, and he shakes his head.

"How can I sleep while the witch runs riot through our castle, unchecked and plotting your demise? I feel as though the moment I shut my eyes, she's going to slit your throat and all hope for our future will be lost with you."

I huff under my breath as I walk, taking the steps two at a

time as he follows me toward the horses. "Have more faith in me than that, Cousin."

He shakes his head as Ingor brings out Nightspark, already saddled and armed for war. He hands the reins to me.

Tauron waits until we're both in our saddles and riding toward our waiting army, two hundred high-fae soldiers ready to defend this kingdom with their lives, before he speaks.

He murmurs to me in the old language, and softly enough that only high-fae ears can hear it, "The Fates wouldn't have given her to you unless she has the ability to change your mind and take a place in your heart. Are we so sure that the 'peace' you'll bring the kingdom isn't the demise of the high fae and the witches ruling the Southern Lands in our stead?"

He speaks my greatest fear, bringing it to life between us. The ambiguity of the Fates is a tricky thing. There are many ways to fulfill a destiny given to you, and sometimes what you think is a prosperous fate is nothing more than a nightmare of torture and blood-soaked death. My father's fate was to marry his mate and find happiness with her, to have a son and heir, and to rule over the Southern Lands.

Nowhere in his fate did it say he would be murdered, his household slaughtered alongside him, before his heir reached adulthood.

When my silence stretches on for too long, Tauron adds, "You cannot trust the witch, Cousin, no matter how many babies she saves."

I huff at the ridiculous suggestion. "I'm not so blinded by my desire for the throne that I've forgotten who our enemy is, Cousin. Besides, if the rumors are to be believed, there's no heart beating in my chest nor kindness to be found within me."

Tauron sends me a bold look, more aware than anyone else of my true nature and motives. "None of that matters right now. We can lose ourselves in the Fates' whims once we have Roan back at Yregar safely, naming his son and talking some sense back into his stubborn wife."

The villagers watch the army as we ride out, apprehensive as they stare up at us. Many of them make the mark of the Fates against their chests, though whether they hope for our safe return or simply for the fighting to not follow us home to Yregar, I don't know.

The moment we pass through the last set of gates, I kick Nightspark into a gallop and ride hard towards the Outlands. The entire army keeps up with the breakneck pace as we push toward our destination where witches lie in wait, a deadly barrier between us and Roan.

Hours pass as slowly as ever and the first gleaming rays of sunlight peek over the horizon before the ground changes to snow beneath Nightspark's hooves, our pace slowing as we hit the icy wastelands. The reason the trip is so treacherous isn't the distance but the conditions, the way the horses slip even as we slow our approach, and there's a very narrow path to follow to make it through the Outlands unscathed.

I would never lead an army this large through the Shard, though that's the more direct path, and we can go no faster than a trot over the ice that encases the earth beneath us. Without the lush forests of the more southern areas of the Outlands to break up the plains, nothing grows in this area.

When we finally reach the gully that lies at the eastern side of the Shard and follows the curve of the Lore River, we see the first signs of smoke ahead, and a ripple of impatience runs through me as we're forced to maintain our slow speed. The moment we step through the witches' magical sound barrier, I hear the vicious screaming. The pop and crackle of magic as it flies, and the singing of steel and iron cutting through the air as swords swing.

We reach the outcropping that overlooks the depths of the

gully, and I spot the colors of the Snowsong family ahead, Roan leading his father's soldiers into the battle, and the witches swarming like vultures over the dying. They're everywhere, hundreds of them, raving and mad, the black markings on their faces glowing. The battle sickness has taken them over, and they fight tooth and nail for Kharl's perverted aspirations of power, their lives meaning nothing to him.

I give the command, and my soldiers descend into the iced-over gully after the witches. The horses slowly pick up their pace as we ride into the fray, the first rounds of magic hitting and glancing off the iron we've covered ourselves in.

Horses to my left whinny and rear, bucking off their riders as the witches overrun us. Their numbers are hundreds more than the high fae. This is more than a simple attack or an ambush for supplies. They came here with every intention of killing us all.

I draw my sword and push Nightspark on, his huge body trampling witches underfoot. Their screams are cut short as their necks snap under his hooves, their bodies nothing more than uneven ground to my warhorse.

There are never enough horses for all of the witches, their true numbers unknown, but we've estimated it's at least six times that of the high fae, and their first wave soldiers always fight on foot. They're usually sacrifices, sent to tire us out before the more powerful witches arrive or to chip away at our defenses as a distraction for some other attack or tactical move of Kharl's. A shower of arrows rains down on us and I lift my shield to cover myself and Nightspark's head. I curse as more horses scream in pain around me, their riders caught unaware as their steeds pay the painful price.

I can't see where the archers are shooting from, but I can see the banner of Roan's house ahead and the shining silver of his helmet as the first rays of morning sunlight hit it.

I learned during the battles of our faeling years to stick close to my friends' sides, to not lose one another in the chaos and bloodlust, and I hack through the witches, pushing Nightspark forward as Tauron does the same at my side.

Together we pick off as many witches as we can, but they just keep coming, more and more bodies joining the melee. It's as though they found another fae door to stream through, countless numbers of deranged soldiers swarming us, no matter how many we kill.

I lift my shield in time to stop the piercing blow of a sword thrown through the air. It embeds itself in the heavy iron, and my arm goes numb on impact. There's no salvaging the shield with such damage, and I fling it to the ground, cursing as I do, then lift my sword to protect myself from another ball of power as it hurtles toward my head. The snow around us sizzles as it melts under the heat of the magic, black witch blood oozing into the ice and mixing to become a stinking slurry beneath us.

Tauron curses beside me, leaning down from his saddle to yank his sword from a witch's corpse and grabbing a shield from where it's fallen. A high-fae soldier stares sightlessly at the sky, his throat torn open as his blood soaks into the snow beneath us. My cousin hands me the iron shield, and I lift it just in time for the next wave of arrows to descend. Witches scream around us as they're killed by their own, eagerly sacrificed in the attempt to kill the high fae and those they rule.

I move the shield down to my side, swinging my sword at a raving witch as he attempts to climb onto Nightspark's back. As the body falls away from me, I look up and meet Roan's gaze across the icy, blood-soaked scene. There's blood pouring down his face and an arrow protruding from his shoulder, but his eyes burn as he pushes forward toward me, the sword in his hands blackened with witch blood.

I push on toward him just in time to see yet another arrow

land, this one alone as it hits its mark…dead center in Roan's chest.

I see fear in his eyes for the first time as blood spills from his lips and he slumps forward in his saddle.

The Outland soldier at Roan's side hooks an arm around his waist and keeps him in the saddle even as the others around us break formation, chaos spreading through the ranks. Tauron begins to scream orders, cursing and hacking at witches as he struggles to gain control.

I ignore it all.

I push Nightspark harder than ever before into the worst of the fighting ahead, my sword cutting down the witches that lie between Roan and I as though they are nothing but fresh snow against the early morning light.

As I reach him, another spray of arrows hurtles down on us, and I lift my shield just in time to cover my head and Roan's as the soldier holding him braces for impact. The moment he sees my protection, he reaches over to snap the arrows embedded in Roan, leaving the shafts in Roan's chest for the ride home.

I don't know the soldier's name, but he's efficient, moving his prince from his horse to mine and quickly wrapping a leather strap around his waist. He pauses only to kick at a rogue witch who makes it through the protective line of soldiers, putting the raving man to the ground and striking him with the base of his shield until blood pours from the wound.

I loop the leather strap around my own waist and tie it off once I'm sure Roan is secure.

There's another loud curse behind us, and Tauron barks out new orders, "Find the archers and kill them, for Fates-fucking-sake!"

The Outland soldier looks up until he finds the row of witches standing at the peak of the hill above us, bunkers dug out of the snow where they've lain in wait. He drops his shield and pulls his own bow from the back of his horse, then begins to fire arrow after arrow.

Other soldiers surrounding us do the same, trusting the rest of the army to protect them from the ground cover as they begin to pick off the archers above. Roan's breathing is haggard, his blood flowing steadily. I feel its warmth on my back in the few exposed areas not covered by the iron plates.

I meet Tauron's eyes, but he's already nodding, barking out more orders as he moves the soldiers around us. Kicking Nightspark forward, I spear through the mounds of the dead before us as I work toward the mountain and safety. The Outland soldier moves with me, putting down his bow and grabbing his shield as he follows.

When we break away from the melee, the soldier kicks his horse to take the lead. As he carves a new path through the snow, I glance over my shoulder and find the archers dead and the last real threat of the battle dealt with, nothing more to do but clean up the waves below.

I send a silent prayer to the Fates, and then I push Nightspark into a gallop, snow and ice be damned, as I trust the beast to keep his footing. The Outland soldier rides alongside me at the same speed, his own horse more practiced in the icy conditions. Even pushing the horses to their very limits, we're still hours away from Yregar, and the blood dripping down my back doesn't bode well.

As we ride closer to the edges of the Outlands, we find more signs of the witches, and the Outland soldier shoots a few strays running from the battle, picking them off even as his horse gallops beneath him with ease. Whoever this soldier is, I'd like to keep him amongst my own forces for such skill and loyalty to his prince.

I glance down and find the thigh of my riding leathers stained with blood, the silver of my chain mail now ruby red and, with a curse, I begin to pray to the Fates once more. I promise them endless submission if Roan survives this ride home, that I'll marry the witch and become the King of the Southern Lands.

I'll do it all if she's able to save Roan's life with no supplies, no tinctures, no herbs, nothing that the healers of old used, nothing but her bare hands. It's an impossible task; even someone as uneducated in such things as I am knows it, but I promise the Fates I'll follow through with their desires if they save Roan's life even with her at my side.

If the witch can break a kingdom-wide curse, surely she can fix a few simple arrows to the chest.

The soldiers at the outer wall of Yregar see us coming and shout to open the gates so we aren't forced to slow down. Word carries down the walls faster than our horses race, and the inner gates open before we reach them as well, the entire castle at attention and waiting for us as we clatter into the stables.

I pull Nightspark to a halt, the crowd waiting for us staring on in shock at Roan's slumped form as his blood drips to the cobblestones beneath us. The Outland soldier jumps down from his horse and loosens the strap securing Roan as he barks at the others to help.

"Where is the witch?" I yell as I flick the leather strap from around my chest and push myself up in my saddle to give them access to get a secure hold of Roan.

One of the soldiers on the stairs calls out to answer me. "The healer's chambers, Your Highness. She's been guarded down there while she fixes the princess's teas on Firna's orders."

The moment they lift Roan from my back, I look down to see the deathlike pallor of his skin, pale and lifeless as his lips begin to turn blue, his breath rattling in his chest. I take up his legs as I help the Outland soldier carry him, barking orders for doors to be opened and people to get out of the way as we move toward the healer's chambers. A maid scurries ahead of us to warn the witch of our arrival, her shoes echoing on the marble floors.

At the last moment I turn back and snap, "No one tells the princess about this, not a word or it's your death."

If anyone is to tell my cousin of her husband's death, it'll be me. Not a maid or soldier gossiping within her hearing—I'll be the one to look her in the eyes and explain that I failed her.

I feel my command travel through the castle, the entire staff dropping their gazes from Roan's prone form as we pass. When we arrive at the healer's chambers, the witch is waiting for us, tying an apron over her dress with her sleeves rolled up to her elbows and supplies already waiting. Two soldiers take up guard at the door to watch over her and a maid stands at her side, her head bowed but ready to take direction as the witch's mouth firms into a line.

"What in the Fates—how much blood has he lost? How far did you ride with him in this condition?"

The Outland soldier startles at the sight of her, looking over at me as though he hadn't heard me demand the witch. Even as he grimaces, he steps back and watches as she begins to strip away Roan's armor. Her fingers are practiced as the plates of leather-bound iron drop to the floor, and she pulls his shirt away from his chest and sucks in a breath at the sight of the snapped-off arrows still lodged in the flesh. Purpling veins extend from the skin surrounding the wounds, the area already inflamed and weeping.

"Poison," I say, and she nods, her hand hovering over his chest for a moment as she takes in the injuries.

She glances at me for the briefest of moments before gesturing a hand at his legs. "Hold him down. This is going to hurt."

Her eyes begin to glow, the silver coming alive with power, and every high fae in the room tenses as we ready for her attack. Her hand hovers by the arrows, and a purple-black liquid begins to bleed from around the punctures, the poison drawn out by the witch.

Her magic presses around his body as visible to me as the blood itself in its white glow, a sight that freezes the blood in my own veins as I fight my reaction to it. Though the tug of the Fates is still insistent in my chest at her presence, centuries of violence and war have primed my reflexes for my own survival and a cold drop of sweat rolls down my spine. Every muscle, nerve, and sinew is pulled taut to stop myself from shoving her away from Roan and drawing my sword, the pull between us both and my skepticism warring in my mind until my teeth groan under the immense pressure of my clenched jaw.

The witch moves back to the fire, unaware of the battle being fought within me, and picks out a small knife from the pot of boiled water. As she lays the blade on the cloths to cool, the magic around Roan never wavers as she holds his life in her competent care, his chest still rising and falling as his breath rattles out of his lungs.

The Outland soldier steps forward once more, murmuring to me low enough that she won't hear, "Your Highness, are we sure this is safe? Can we trust one of them to help him?"

I meet his eye. "Tell me your name, soldier."

"Reed Snowheart. I'm one of the elder Prince Roan's captains and I was helping Prince Roan return to his wife after the messenger arrived with the news. We were supposed to see him safely to the edge of the Outlands but made it only as far as the gully when we were snowed in, stuck there for a day and night. The weather wasn't normal, as if by magic the blizzard appeared and stopped us from traveling. As the skies cleared, the witches descended upon us."

His eyes flick toward Roan, and his mouth tightens. "I thought the prince would go mad, unable to move and waiting for them to strike. We could hear them coming."

I grimace, nodding at the haunted look in his eyes. Being trapped like that is something no one understands unless they've experienced it for themselves, the way your heart pounds and your skin crawls with anticipation, dread filling your body and slowly taking away your ability to find reason. It's a torture all on its own.

"We'd already killed the witches who attacked us at the base of Fates Mark. Prince Roan positioned more soldiers to secure the castle, and we couldn't call for help without risking the castle. When you arrived, we'd been there for two days, snowed in and then fighting through. The worst of the foot soldiers were dealt with already, hundreds of the disgusting things, but then they called in the archers and we got pinned down."

Three days in the snow, battling witches and hacking their way slowly toward us—it's a wonder any of them survived.

Reed's eyes widen, and he straightens as the witch lifts the blade over Roan's chest, tensing as though he's about to dive at her and rip it from her hands. I hold up a hand to stop him before I take hold of Roan's ankles once more.

I've seen healers remove witches' arrows before, and it's not as simple as pulling the specially carved wood from the flesh. The shafts are lined with rows of barbs, designed to do the most damage to the target, and the only way to remove them is to cut them out.

The work requires a steady hand, one that can't be distracted by the suspicions of those around her, and when the realization finally hits Reed, he cringes, his forehead breaking out in sweat.

"What pain herbs can we give him? Is there anything in the castle that can help?"

He doesn't address the witch, but there's no need—she's the only one in the room who can answer.

She doesn't look up at us as she murmurs, "I've already sent the maid to check the stores, but I doubt there's anything of use there. When you send your list of supplies to import from the Western Fyres, I suggest adding some plants to it. I can grow them here in the garden, and then I'll be able to heal without foraging around the Goblin Lands for scraps."

Her tone is flat and calm, but her words rake at my ego, already in shreds from Roan's ordeal. "You speak as though you're moving in."

With a sure hand, she begins to cut away the damaged skin at the entry point of the broken arrows. Roan's legs jerk beneath me, and a sigh of relief tears out of my chest. The color of his lips made me think he was dead, but even now his hue is better, closer to health. The pallor must've been a reaction to the poison, not the blood loss or organs hit by the two arrow shafts still embedded.

"I'll go insane if you lock me in this room without something to do, and I suppose you've had more than enough raving witches in your time. I'll play out in the garden, grow some herbs, brew some tinctures, and tend to the injured. What harm could it do?"

Her fingers are careful as she eases the wood from his chest—gentle but firm. She has experience with such things, and a determination to do it right.

"What's different? Only days ago you were pretending to be helpless and contained in the dungeon, and now you're dreaming up a future of digging around in a garden and healing people who would rather cut your hand off than be touched by it. Tell me what's changed."

She drops the arrow on to the countertop next to her with annoyance etched in her features as she moves to the second arrow, cutting and easing. The pain must be unbearable, and yet Roan hasn't reacted beyond the initial jerk.

Icy tendrils work their way down my spine as I check to be sure he's still breathing, but even as she works, his chest rises and falls steadily.

"I needed the time to adjust. I wasn't prepared for how bad things had gotten here in my absence, and I left one war only to travel home to another. I just needed to collect myself."

It doesn't feel like a real answer, but it's the only one she gives as she tends to Roan's wounds and slowly pieces him back together as competently as she'd walked into his wife's bedroom and broken a centuries-old curse.

TWENTY NINE

ROOKE

Digging the arrows out of Roan's chest is the easier part of healing him, even with the iron spines that jut out from the oak shafts. Cutting the wood from his flesh is a time-consuming process, and I use my magic to stop the bleeding and hold his life in safety as I pry out the jagged pieces of metal.

The hard part comes from the poison.

Being locked inside the dungeons for those long weeks has had its benefits, and even after the drain on my magic from breaking the curse, I still have more than enough to heal Roan as I need to. I'm able to coax the poison from his bloodstream, the purple hue ghoulish as the magic oozes out of the wounds and runs down Roan's chest. It sizzles as it hits the workbench, and I grab a handful of cloths to wipe it away, scrubbing until it's completely absorbed into the linens. When I cast them into the fire, the flames dance higher, burning iridescent for a moment as I send such evil back to the Fates on the smoke.

Soren and Reed both watch me, murmuring to each other low enough that I can't hear them, but I'm too focused to care about their opinions. Pulling the poison out of his body so it can no longer do any harm is one thing, but some damage has already been done.

The hours it took Soren to ride back to Yregar with Roan

strapped to his back gave the poison time to damage his body. Once it entered his bloodstream, his heart rate jumped as his body fought it off, moving it further through his veins and making the damage even worse.

I hold my hand over his chest again, my magic pouring out of me, and the horror emanating from all those around me is amusing, the telltale glow of my eyes clearly terrifying to those who have forgotten what power put to work looks like. High fae heal better than witches do, stronger and faster. I treated many injuries amongst the Seelie high fae in the Northern Lands that would've killed people of other races, but with enough rest and proper care hadn't left any lasting damage on them.

It's a coin toss, the gold still in the air as the Fates decide whether Roan will be left a shadow of the high-fae prince he once was or if I can get him through this in good enough condition to still wield his sword and hold his son. The life of a husband and father weighs heavy on me, especially after nights of caring for his family and hearing Airlie's excited anticipation for her husband's return.

I sigh and murmur to Prince Soren, "I need more supplies. Is there anywhere else you can go for healing herbs?"

He scowls at me. "Stop with your scheming. Just heal him with your magic and be done with it."

My magic pours over Roan's chest, ignoring the bite to his tone. "My options are limited, and even the strongest healers still need help."

Prince Soren shakes his head. "There are no other healers to help you. If there were, you'd be assisting *them.*"

Even after he's watched me dig poison barbs out of his best friend's chest, he still has the nerve to hurl around such words. "I'm not talking about another healer—I'm talking about the fact that those cupboards are bare and the shelves filled with rotting and decayed supplies. I have tinctures of milk thistle and nothing else, not even food or wine. My magic is strong, but no magic is limitless."

He moves toward the workbench, placing his hands against the wood as he leans over Roan's chest to peer at the wounds, still open there as my magic works through them. "He's healed from worse. It'll hurt like a Fates-cursed bitch, but he'll heal from this too."

I glance up to shoot him a sardonic look. "And how long have you been an expert in poisons? You got him here in time to save his life, but without assistance, he's going to be bed bound for the rest of his very long life. Is that the future you want for him?"

His mouth tightens into a line, looking down at his best friend for another moment before jerking his head at the soldier. "Go to the barracks and get cleaned up. See Firna for food and prepare yourself to ride back out. If Tauron and the rest of the soldiers aren't back here by noon, we're going back to the Outlands after them."

Reed nods and leaves, casting one last look at the prince before ducking out the door.

Soren walks to the small wooden chair by the bed and pulls it over to the workbench, stretching out his long legs as he takes the seat. There's the briefest hint of a wince on his face, a flash that he hides so quickly, I almost miss it.

"Are you injured too? I can take a look once I've finished what I can for Roan."

Soren's voice is a snarl. "It's bad enough you've gotten inside Airlie's head and now you'll work your way into Roan's with your magic. I'd rather bleed out."

I don't know whether to be insulted or flattered by his estimations of my abilities, but I watch him from the corner of my eye as I work. I can't help it; with the pull of the Fates between us I couldn't ignore him even if the entire kingdom depended on it, and though I'm thorough and careful in my work, I'm still far too aware of my Fates-cursed mate.

He looks exhausted.

In the long weeks since I arrived at Port Asmyr, I haven't ever seen him falter. He's been furious, enraged, cold, completely unreadable as he faced the Unseelie Court, in command and even weary as he's dealt with the games and gossip, but nothing like this. The high-fae males of Yregar all wear their hair shoulder length or a little shorter, no braids or leather ties to hold it back, and as he leans forward and rubs a hand over his face, his spills over his shoulders, ash and dirt stark in the silvery-blond strands.

The cold and cruel Savage Prince is now nothing more than a false rumor in my mind, the gossip of courts and the petty creatures within, and in his place is the very real and compelling Prince Soren. I see far too much of the soldiers I'd come to love and respect in the Northern Lands within him, an integrity and honor that cannot be faked, and it only makes his distaste for my people all the more cutting to me.

Blood covers him, too much of it, including a streak running across his cheek that I notice when he leans back once more. That one's not his own, but my heart clenches all the same. I've seen the worst of what war can do to a male, respected and loved many who fought on the front lines, but there's something about that red streak that makes my heart pound harder in my chest.

I hope he assumes the hard work of the healing is making it do that and not the Fates' cruel devices.

My magic spreads through Roan's veins, healing some of the smaller areas of damage, but the cluster around his heart is the most dangerous, and I have a difficult decision to make.

Would his own body's healing abilities do a better job of repairing the damage without scarring? Healing with magic is faster and can save lives, but it's not as perfect as the high fae's own healing ability. Any magic-aided recoveries always leave behind a scar, the white slash across Prince Soren's face a testament to that.

If I repair his heart myself, I could doom Prince Roan to a life of limitations, while his own body might be strong enough to renew the organ to complete health. An impossible decision but with only one correct answer.

Laying my hands on the workbench, I hunch over, sigh, and squeeze my eyes shut, my head throbbing as though it's going to burst.

"Tapped out?" Prince Soren says.

I shake my head. "It would take me an age to explain to you the nature of magic and how it works with fae bodies. There are other, more pressing things for me to do."

I look at one of the soldiers still guarding the door, though he doesn't meet my eye or acknowledge me even as I clearly motion to gain his attention. Prince Soren just watches me, not intervening, and my patience shortens even further.

I say, voice clear and commanding, "I must speak with Firna, urgently. Prince Roan's life depends on it."

The soldier still doesn't move until Soren jerks his head, dismissing him on the errand. I study the wall of vials, praying as though the Fates might've hidden some fae flowers there, or maybe a sealed vial of dragon's tears, but the same useless supplies stare back at me.

"You have to know that your behaviors are suspicious. Sitting in a dungeon for weeks on end when you could have fought back, only to run eagerly into a birthing room with a high-fae child's life at stake, and now suddenly you claim you want to help us? You saw the desperation the curse plunged us into and used your magic to exploit our weakness."

It's the first time any of his tirades have made perfect sense to me.

Centuries of watching their people wither and die—not just

the babies, but the soldiers out there dying by Kharl's orders, and the defenseless villagers at the mercy of these acts—it's warped his view of the entire race of witches.

By his age, I know that he's known nothing but conflict with my race, and I don't blame him for that, but I do blame him for assuming we're all the same.

There are no black markings on my face or my arms. There's no raving madness within me, no fire put there by Kharl Balzog and stoked until I'm nothing but a vessel of his hatred turned into a weapon against the high fae. Prince Soren knows that I left this kingdom. We spoke long ago, when I was barely more than a witchling, through our mind connection, and he knew my heart then to be pure and true.

How many other witches have been slain by him and his people without question, purely for the silver eyes in their head? Pemba didn't know my fate, but he was obsessed and furious at the rumors of what the Savage Prince was doing in the Southern Lands, hunting down every last witch and part-blood until there were none left but those under Kharl's control. There was never a fair trial for those people, or evidence of their supposed crimes. They never had a chance to prove themselves innocent.

If the rumors are to be believed, this man killed them all regardless.

I struggle but manage to keep my tone even. "I've never been good at sitting by and watching people suffer, even when they don't deserve my help. It's not how I was raised."

One of his eyebrows creeps up his forehead. "In the forest of madness? How did the Goblin King know you have family there—or was that a lie as well?"

A ripple of irritation works its way down my spine, the casual dismissal of my sacred home a greater insult than any other he's thrown at me. He watches me a little too keenly as I struggle with the indignant response I want to give him before I finally settle on a calmer option.

"All of the lower fae and part-bloods know of the Ravenswyrd Forest and what lies within. Many high fae as well. Just because it's outside your knowledge doesn't make it false."

Stepping over to the fire, I add more wood to stoke the flames. There's a small stack of logs that Firna dropped by earlier for brewing Airlie's teas, and as Roan begins to shiver and sweat with the first signs of a fever, I prepare myself to fight his illness right alongside him.

The healer's journey has always been to take the hand of someone in need and stand with them as they face the Fates' ruling, to heal them so they can go on with their lives, or to ease them from this world and into Elysium as gently as the Fates allow us to do.

Roan is strong and determined on the table, still breathing and fighting to return to his wife and family. I will fight with him for that too.

In the old language, I murmur a prayer to the Fates. It's an ancient incantation, carved within me from the moment I took my first breath, and one I keep murmuring for this man and his family.

When I finish, I glance up to find Prince Soren's eyes sharp as he meets my own. "You sound so devoted to the Fates, and yet you've sat by and waited for them to unfold for you. That's not the way the Fates work, and you know it."

My eyes narrow back at him, but he steps toward me, his tone cutting. "It's our job to reach out with everything inside of us and take our fate, even when every inch of your body rejects it, as does mine. No fate is simply given and plays out without work. We're told what we have to do, and then we walk that path until our legs give out. You speak of the high fae forgetting everything, and yet I know that better than you."

It's like a slap to the cheek, a reminder that I didn't just flee the conflict of the Southern Lands. I ran from *him*; I ran the moment the Seer spoke his name and the fate that tied us together.

I chose to run, and that choice led to two hundred more years of suffering for the people of this land, everything here withering away while I attempted to make a new life somewhere else. The Fates looked inside the little witch of the woods and knew that I would flee the moment I heard his name. I long for the hollowness I brought back from the Northern Lands that vanished along with the curse, because now guilt is twisting up inside of me once more. The Fates knew I wouldn't be able to face Kharl and help to fix the kingdom as I was, they knew I'd run to the Northern Lands and become the witch I am today.

Blinking away the tears that well in my eyes, I take up a fistful of the clean rags and press them against Roan's chest, easing my magic out of him as I let his body begin the natural healing process. The skin around the puncture wounds begins to knit together before my eyes as his body heals rapidly in the high-fae way.

"I didn't forget. I returned here and lost myself for a moment in the despair of the land, but I'm walking toward my fate now."

I speak with Firna, and she escorts me to the kitchens to look through the storage areas myself. I doubt I'll find something helpful within the meager supplies, but Prince Roan needs all the help he can get. Prince Soren stays behind to watch over the injured high-fae prince as he sleeps, his face grimacing and flinching as he heals.

I took his pain away and absorbed it into myself, burning my magic stores a little so I wouldn't have to feel it, but I can't keep up the connection while I'm elsewhere in the castle. Not without leaving behind a trail of light and glowing brighter than the full moon on a clear midwinter night, and I think I've pushed the high fae far enough for today.

The threat of the witches still hangs over my head like a monster of the Fates, my magic reserves strong enough to keep myself alive, but if they attack the castle, we're woefully unprepared. From the descriptions of the witch armies I've heard from the soldiers and villagers, the high fae are used to fighting the mindless rabble, and though their numbers give them an advantage, they're not a difficult enemy to outsmart and defeat.

If a powerful witch arrives, or a coven of them, the castle will fall.

The kitchen staff are prepared for my arrival, and none of them flinch or startle away from me as Firna leads me through into the large storage pantry. The cavernous size of it only makes the bare shelves more stark. There's nothing here, not enough food to get through the week let alone the coming winter, and I curse under my breath at how close they've come to ruin. Thank the Fates the Goblin King changed his mind about the trading route—whatever opportunity he saw in Prince Soren might just save Yregar.

There's nothing within the cupboards that can help.

The only herbs they have are for flavor, and they're in such bad condition that even if they once held medicinal properties, those would be long gone by now. Firna hovers behind me, and when I stand once more and shake my head, she frowns, deep lines between her brows as she presses a hand to her forehead once more. She's no longer afraid to show her true emotions around me, the prim façade gone. Maybe the bond that I felt in the birthing room wasn't just one sided; perhaps Firna and Airlie felt it as well.

"The princess heard that Soren has returned. She has a lot of questions about her husband, and I don't know how to answer them without causing her stress," Firna murmurs to me, her voice low and her eyes imploring as she looks to me for guidance.

I look around at the rows of flour sacks, an abundant winter store for a large family but not enough to get this castle and the villagers through the week. Even with the tight rationing and eagle-eye of Firna's command, we'd all starve if not for the Goblin King's grace.

I wonder how many of them will acknowledge that.

"You can tell her the truth, which is that he was injured during the fighting at Fates Mark as he rode home to her. I'm tending to his injuries, and I'll care for him as I've cared for her and her son. If Prince Soren allows, she's welcome to come see him, and I'll do everything I can to have him awake and meeting his son soon."

Firna glances at the small rows of dried leaves on the top shelf, where the warm air still circulates, and then around at the rest of the bare shelves, her face pinched.

"Is there more that you could do for Prince Roan if we had the proper supplies? Fae flowers and the like?"

I turn to face her more fully, crossing my arms and trying to ignore the pull of the fabric across my shoulders. I'm not going to soften my answer; the truth is always the best course of action. "There's a lot more I could be doing, not just for him but for everyone who lives within Yregar's walls."

Her eyebrows creep up her forehead as I continue, "I've seen the villagers. I know they need care as well. If I can fill the garden here with a proper healer's crop, I'll tend to them all, not just the high fae."

Firna shakes her head. "The prince will never allow it. We don't understand these things well enough to know that your intentions are true. The healers all left the Southern Lands when the war broke out, and we were left to fend for ourselves."

I scowl at her. "Why did the healers leave?"

She looks around carefully, but all of the maids are still working diligently in the kitchen, performing miracles with the ingredients to help the food stretch as far as it possibly can.

"Most healers in the Unseelie Court were witches, and the rest had witch blood. Millennia ago, the high fae had healers of their own, but they stopped teaching such things and their magic was lost. They didn't care about using it, they simply hired witches and provided good homes for them within their castles, living harmoniously, but then the war broke out. The high fae became suspicious of even the most loyal healers, even those who were part-bloods. Any attack on the royal bloodlines was blamed on the healers letting the witches in. Some were killed, some left to join the witches in their anger, and others just…disappeared."

My eyebrows tuck in tight as I curse under my breath.

She nods at my reaction. "The people here are afraid of you. The stories they've all been told are old, older than most of them are, especially the servants within the castle. They know that witches aren't a threat only to them, that being known to be friendly to one is to flirt with death. The high fae make no exceptions…even the Seers are gone now."

I have half a mind to walk back into that healer's quarters and throw these words in Prince Soren's face. How dare he sit there and lecture me about our fates with all the evil his people have wrought against my own?

I swallow around the lump in my throat, grief seizing me so hard that my chest aches with every breath. The covens are gone, all of them either killed or driven out. Thousands of innocent lives, witchlings and the elderly, those who served the kingdom and never caused harm. My fate has led me here to save a kingdom that has shown my people only the very worst of injustices. The desperation of the forest is an echo in my mind, and I can't help but fear that even ending the war won't be enough. The witches are gone, the survivors may never return, the land may continue to decline because the balance can never be restored.

My body fights against the chaos in my mind to keep working even as I want to lie down and die on the stone floor.

Firna wrings her hands as she watches this consume me, fretting silently until finally I get control of myself once more. My magic never once slipped, but the knowing look in her eyes is enough of a reminder of what fate will befall me if it ever does.

"Tell Princess Airlie that her husband will live. I dug the poison arrows out of his chest myself, my magic weaving around him as it wove around his son. A *filthy* witch helping another high-fae prince, even at great personal cost, because none of the high fae have ever given a blessed Fates-*fuck* about the innocent witches of this kingdom. Kharl Balzog's deceptions only swayed the weakest from our path—the rest wanted nothing to do with his madness. I know my role in honoring this land, do any of you?"

I turn and leave the pantry behind, ignoring the looks of the maids and soldiers as I walk back to the healer's quarters by myself. Unescorted, fuming, and uncaring of the consequences.

I ignore Prince Soren's presence in the corner, knowing well that if I open my mouth right now, a curse will fall from my lips and his life will be forfeit. The land would welcome his blood spilled in sacrifice, but the Fates would be swift in their own reply to my disobedience.

With a deep breath, I remember the terrifying sight of the tear in the sky and calm myself down. I don't think of the Ureen—I *never* think of them if I can help it—but the tear is enough to remind me of my purpose. It doesn't matter what the high fae have or haven't done. The Fates have spoken and I have no choice but to obey.

Seeing the ghastly pallor of Roan's skin helps to dampen the rage within me, reminding me of my purpose as a healer once more. Airlie doesn't deserve my scolding tongue, and I regret my temper unleashing in my reply to the waiting princess. With any luck Firna will soften some of the sharpness of my words, but I doubt it. None of these people have changed their opinions of me or my kind. I could save a thousand royal babies and still be loathed regardless.

Moving around the workbench, I start brewing the next cup of tea for Airlie, a ripple of irritation itching at my skin at the eyes still following me. No matter my feelings, I'll provide her and the baby with all the care in my power. With great determination, I force my mind away from Prince Soren's presence and slip back into a quiet contemplation once more, going through the motions and clearing my mind of the anger that spilled over. I left my grief and regrets behind in the Northern Lands and, though I don't want the icy casing around my heart once more, I don't want to live with such rage within me either, choking and consuming me until I'm nothing but vengeance and fury.

"I heard you speaking to Firna. Write a list of what you need to help Roan," Soren says from the corner, breaking the silence and my concentration.

There's censure in his voice, but a wave of satisfaction rolls over me. I'm *glad* he heard me, glad the words made their way to his high-fae ears, and I hope they haunt his every moment until he never knows peace again, just as my people have been haunted.

Unable to bring myself to look at him, I simply write out the list on the small scraps of parchment with the inkpot and quill Firna left behind for me. Those two simple items and the stove crackling with the fire behind me are the greatest gift the high fae have unwittingly given me, though I won't be able to make good use of them under such keen surveillance. The moment I'm able to prove myself to them, or if their scrutiny slackens, I'll do just that.

Not all fae folk need a horse and a long journey to send messages.

When I hold the list out to Prince Soren, he doesn't move to take it, so I place it carefully on the workbench and walk out of the quarters into the small walled garden, gulping in the fresh air to calm the storm within me.

Blind rage within someone as powerful as I am, the Mother of a coven as old as the Southern Lands itself, is a dangerous thing. I pull a small paring knife from the pocket of my dress, slipped in there earlier as a backup in case the one I selected proved too big for the work. I'd forgotten about it until now.

I walk to one of the overgrown planters, the stink of death in the air around me, and my magic swells in misery inside me.

Sitting down on one of the flagstones, I drag the blade across my inner arm and then press my hand against the dry and cracked remnants of soil. The earth reaches out toward me, greedily drinking in the magic I offer it in giant pulls that feel as though they're going to consume me whole. It soothes the hurt inside me, squeezing into the dark recesses of my mind as the exchange takes over everything, pressing me into its embrace as it fills me up. The small ache of hunger in my belly disappears as the earth sustains me, providing for me as I pour into it.

I feel Prince Soren step into the door frame to watch over my actions as I take a deep breath, my eyes glowing so bright I can see their reflection on the stone in front of me. My skin tingles as the magic passes through the planters around me, still filled with wilting and dead remnants of a once thriving garden. The dead plants begin to fall away to the ground as the earth within them churns, the soil reviving as my gift of life is multiplied tenfold around me. There's no saving the dead crops, but I've renewed the life within, giving the earth the ability to prosper once more. The milk thistle will grow now, and any other plants I find.

The problem, of course, is finding them.

When I stand back up, brushing the dirt from the horrible Unseelie high-fae dress I'm still wearing and then flicking the dirt away from my arm and admiring the perfectly healed skin there, I glance up to meet Prince Soren's eyes where he's still watching me from the open door, his shoulders spanning the frame. There's a scowl on his face, his eyes hard as he stares down at me, his arms crossed over his leather-bound iron chestplate, still spattered with blackened witches' blood. Even in the calm wake of my exchange, my temper simmers at his reaction. Any act of magic is distasteful to him, but I hold a palm out toward the gardens around me, silent as I gesture at the stark transformation I've wrought with a single act of giving and irreverent to his misplaced scorn.

Where dry and ashy dirt once lay, forgotten and sucked dry, now rich and abundant soil lies ready to nurture life. The first small buds of weeds have started to peek out, a nuisance for later but a positive sign for now. The very air in the garden has changed, the scent of life here once more, and even without my knowledge and skill, a garden can flourish here.

None of this needs to be said to Prince Soren. Not a single word could describe it better than what his own eyes are forced to see.

My mind still fills with them though, every word that would be wasted if given life, because he's already proven too stubborn to accept anything I say.

This is what the high fae have forgotten. This is why the land withers. Every innocent witch you killed, every one of my kind who chose to hold to our traditions and reject Kharl's war, all of them gave themselves to the land, over and over again. All of them lived in the cycle of life, and you murdered *them. Senseless killings because the high fae trust only their own, care only for themselves and those who they exploit.*

This is why your people are ruined. Not me.

THIRTY

SOREN

The witch spends the rest of the afternoon cleaning out the medicinal garden that she just revived, pulling out mounds of dead plants and piling them up by the wall in one corner of the grounds. I move my chair so I can watch her and Roan at the same time, but she ignores my presence. The resolute way that she can disregard me while I'm painfully aware of her is infuriating but there's nothing I can do about it, not without making my own obsession known.

She continues to duck back into the healer's quarters to check on him, but she never speaks, her eyes staying far away from me as she works around me. Firna's explanation of the witches' betrayal had caught her temper and set it alight. Working tirelessly to burn off that energy, she's a fury of limbs and brute force.

Watching her pour her magic into the earth was difficult, my hand hovering by the hilt of my sword the entire time as I waited for those silver eyes of hers to flick up to me and hurl that power in my direction.

My experience with witches is mostly limited to those on the battlefield and watching them run out of power within a few hours of casting small energy balls towards their enemy. She broke a curse a few nights ago, kept two high-fae soldiers unconscious for hours, broke out of her cell, held Roan's life in her hands as she dug poisoned arrows out of his chest, and still, her magic hasn't waned.

If anything, it's grown.

When she raged and opened another connection with the earth, the color in her cheeks came back, and as she stood up and flicked the dirt from her dress, she looked as though she'd just woken up from ten good hours of sleep and eaten a feast of only the finest foods.

If only she could give some of that health to Roan.

Just before the sun hits the center of the sky above us, Tauron and the soldiers who remained at the battle in the Outlands return, the slain soldiers slung over the backs of their horses as they bring them home to the funeral pyres here.

I hear this from Tauron himself when he bursts into the healer's quarters still streaked with blood, both Roan's and our enemies'.

"What news?" he asks, his gaze roaming over Roan desperately before he looks around the room for the witch. "Why isn't she here healing him?"

I turn toward the gardens and watch her work. "She's done everything she can for him. Without any supplies, he'll have to do the rest himself."

Tauron sneers and steps farther into the room, stopping to glance down at the state his own body is in. He doesn't care about appearances, but he watched as well as I did when the witch scrubbed everything that was to go near Airlie and the baby, the same way she scrubbed everything in the healer's quarters. She never once cared about the state of herself in the dungeon, so it points toward a care for her patients.

He gives the workbench a wide berth and steps toward me. When his gaze finally lands on the witch where she's working outside, he inhales, and his brow furrows.

"What in the Fates has she done?" he rasps, his voice ringing with wonder before he has a chance to hide it.

"She walked out there, gave a blood offering to the earth, and in return it gave her…life."

He takes another deep breath, and the long exhale quivers with unease. It mirrors the same uncertainty I feel in my own chest but, no matter our misgivings, there's no denying it. The fate of our lands, which I was so certain was to be destroyed by the witches, may yet find salvation.

"How many did we lose?"

Tauron scowls. "Twenty. It was those damn archers. They must have been waiting there for days, left over from the raiding parties Roan and the Outland soldiers had been dealing with since he arrived. It was an opportunistic fight, and far more deadly than it should've been."

I rub a hand over my brow and pull it away only to find I've spread the diseased blood of my enemy onto my palm.

Tauron grimaces at my hand and then me. "You're covered in blood. Go and get cleaned up so we can tell Airlie about Roan together."

I doubt that Airlie is unaware. Firna would have been forced to tell her something by now; our arrival wasn't a quiet affair, and my cousin has always been like a bloodhound when given a half-truth. I've been expecting the door to be kicked open and Airlie to stomp her way in, the baby tucked in her arms as she barks out orders for her husband's treatment.

"What's she *doing* out there?" Tauron mutters, scowling over his shoulder at the witch.

I lean forward in my seat. She's still just clearing out the planters, no shocking change to explain his ire. "I told her she's sleeping in here from now on, so I suppose she's decided to make the place her own. I doubt we're in any danger from her growing some herbs."

Tauron looks down at me, his face stern. "We just spoke about this, Soren, and this is *exactly* how she works her way under your skin. You allow her little freedoms and, before you know it, there's another curse laid on our people, only this one sees us truly over the edge to Elysium, the high fae never to walk the Southern Lands again!"

I look back at the witch, toiling away in the garden, grunting and heaving as she clears the last of an overgrown tree. It's long dead, but the roots are still deep in the ground.

That doesn't look like freedom to me, not as I know it.

"It's obvious she has knowledge of healing arts and magic that's been lost to our kind. Why not let her restock our stores and revive our lands while we watch for her treachery? The Fates demand I keep her, for now at least. This is more useful than having her sit in a cell and take up the time of my most trusted family. It's worth the risk."

Tauron stares at her for a moment longer, his eyes piercing like daggers thrown in her direction, before he claps me on the shoulder once more. "Go. You need to bathe, and while you're at it, figure out what we're telling Airlie. We need to have our story straight before we see her. I can watch the witch until you're clean."

I don't need any more encouragement.

When I get back to my chambers and into the bathroom, I remove my armor, the iron and steel dropping from my hands and crashing to the ground as pain makes me careless. Wincing, I raise my arm and find the dagger wound still marring my side. My movement opens it once more, and blood drips onto the marble floors, smearing all over my bathroom as I move. It would be far easier if I allowed an attendant to help me but my rooms have always been off-limits to the household, the one sanctuary I allow myself for now.

I'll have no choice but to accept their presence once I'm king.

Cleaning the cut with a rag and warm water, I'm careful to ensure none of the black witch's blood touches it and poisons me with its toxins. Once it's clean, I bandage the entire area tightly, mimicking the patterns that the witch made on Roan's chest. It's a much better technique than my own, which I learned on the battlefield out of necessity, and once I'm able to sleep, my high-fae healing will kick in to knit my skin back together, safe now that the wound is clean.

There was no sign of poison, no redness or purpling veins the way Roan's wounds had looked, and there's no reason for concern as I finish up in the bathroom. I dress myself slowly as I breathe through the stinging pain, the wounded area burning like the fires of the old fae if I'm too rough with my movements.

My mind can handle a lot more torture than my body can, my wits still strong and clear as my chest aches from the healing. I learned many centuries ago not to push too hard, not unless I was in my most desperate hour.

I leave my chambers and walk straight into Airlie's, knocking on the doors as I come through.

She calls out to me from her sitting area. Firna is hovering over Airlie as she sits and fusses with a baby's blanket in her hands, stitching away at a gift for her son as he sleeps in his crib in her room under the watchful eye of another trusted maid. She made dozens of them during her first pregnancy and none during this one, something I'm sure she now regrets, but I know guarding her heart from the devastation of that loss again was all she could do to get through it without losing herself.

"You better be here to tell me that my husband is awake and calling for me, Cousin. I will accept no other news."

Airlie's tone is saccharine sweet in her cutting defense as she worries about Roan. Firna casts me a long look over my cousin's bowed head, a soundless warning that I don't need.

"Your husband is alive and healing as we speak. I'll let you know as soon as there is any change."

She gives me a sidelong look. "I think you can do better than that for me, Soren. I'll be joining you in the healer's quarters just as soon as I finish tending to my son's needs."

"I don't want you moving through the castle, Airlie. The witches may be focusing on the Outlands for now, but I have no doubt Yregar is next. It's better if you stay in your chambers in the heart of the castle with Firna and my soldiers on guard. Roan is heavily guarded and taken care of; Tauron and I will both stay with him until he wakes. There's no need for you to leave the comfort of your chambers in this state."

Her spine snaps straight, her eyes flashing as she glares back at me. "And what state would that be, Cousin? My son is here, and we're both healthy and safe by all accounts. My husband is the one in grave condition, and I'll be at his side until he wakes."

My jaw clenches, and it takes me a moment to find an even temper to speak to her once more, imploringly. "It's not safe for the two of you down there. The witch is watching over Roan, and it's better for you to be up here."

Airlie scoops her son into her arms with practiced ease, no longer holding him as though he's nothing but a dream. She's come to terms with his safe arrival, enough to be sure he's not going to disappear the moment she closes her eyes, and pride shines in her every action.

"I trust that witch with my husband's life, just as I trusted her with my son. Roan said all along that the Fates have led you to her for a reason. She's not just your mate, Soren, she's the future queen of the Unseelie high fae and the Southern Lands. My loyalty is to you and your fate, and now with her. You and Tauron are suspicious enough for the rest of us. I'll spend my time tending to my family instead."

She takes another step toward me and the door, and then

her eyes light up. Turning back to Firna, she holds out her hand expectantly. "You brought the book I asked for, didn't you? I'd like to show it to Prince Soren before I go."

Firna cringes and shoots a glance at me before reaching into her pocket and pulling out a small leather-bound book. It's black and covered in gold lettering, swirling and looping so much it takes me a moment to see it's the old language. The library here at Yregar—and some of the tomes it holds—is as old as the castle itself, and though I spent much of my childhood in there with my tutors, I haven't given it much thought since my parents died and the war broke out.

I scowl, but Airlie waves it at me with a smile. "Rooke said to all of us that the high fae have forgotten. Maybe we should work on remembering some things, Cousin."

I scoff at her and the ridiculous idea from my Fates-cursed mate. A war is raging that doesn't care how many innocent lives are taken, and yet the witch wants us to spend our days reading and telling stories of a time long gone, a past filled with greatness that we can never hope to get back to? She's here to undermine us, to drive a wedge between me and my closest confidants, and I can see it happening right before my eyes.

Scrubbing a hand over my face, I wince as the movement pulls on my wound. I turn away a little so that Airlie doesn't see. "You're going to read old fairy tales at the witch's request? How novel."

Airlie looks at me with pity, and my skin tightens on my bones until I want to tear it all off with my bare hands. Her tone is soft, as though she's breaking bad news to a child, as she says, "No, Soren. I'm going to read our history and try to remember the purpose of the high fae—the one that led the First Fae to rule our kingdom in the first place. It might be too late for us all, I don't know, but maybe I can teach my son a different way."

The witch lets Airlie stay with Roan for an hour and no longer, answering her questions kindly and with patience. She explains to her the exact wounds he had, how her magic healed some of the damage but not all, what more she can do if necessary but the ways in which his body would be irreversibly changed in that case.

When Airlie questions her about other options, she explains the herbs she would require to make healing tinctures, even going as far as explaining how long it would take for her to prepare them and how long they would last.

Airlie soaks it all up, hanging on her every word, brow furrowed. I see the panic recede with every moment that passes until finally, she nods and accepts the witch's decision.

When the silence falls over the room once more, Airlie clears her throat and hands the witch the baby without hesitation. As she leans over Roan's sleeping form, her cheek pressed against his, she murmurs quietly into her husband's ear, low enough that the witch wouldn't be able to hear it, but I can.

Slow enough that I don't jar my wound, I step into the doorway overlooking the gutted garden to give her some privacy and take a deep breath to settle myself. It's the first real one I've taken since I returned to find Airlie in her labors and the baby arriving, but we're finally back in the safety of Yregar once more. There's nothing left for me to do now but keep watch as we wait. The witch's healing work has put some color back into Roan's cheeks, thank the Fates, and I'm glad Airlie didn't see him when I first got him back here.

I have no doubt she would still be sobbing.

Firna brought down a more comfortable cot, with extra padding and blankets, and before she sends Airlie on her way, the witch instructs the guards to assist me in moving Roan on to it from the stretcher-style bed she healed him on, watching with a shrewd eye to be sure we don't injure him further as we lift him down.

"Firna can bring another cot down here, and the crib for the baby. We'll stay here with him," Airlie says, tears in her voice as she presses her son's cheek gently into her own and inhales him as though his scent is her own form of pain relief.

At the sight of it, there's a pain in my chest that matches the one in my side, a longing for the life she's fought hard for and built around herself that the Fates keep holding just out of my own reach. Almost a thousand years of waiting only to have a witch for a mate, a queen no high fae will willingly bow to after Kharl's war, and the prospective mother to a part-blood heir she will no doubt twist against my own bloodlines. No matter how strong the pull between us is, I can't forget the future set out before me if I fail to keep my wits about me.

"There's absolutely no good in you wearing yourself out down here. I'm working hard to help your milk supply—we're not going to ruin it now by causing such stress. Roan will be under my constant care, and I'll send a maid if his condition changes, but I won't have you adding more work to the situation needlessly. In a few days we'll be able to move him up to your rooms but, for now, keeping him here is for the best."

She steps forward to clasp Airlie's shoulder with a gentle hand, ignoring Tauron and I as we react to the familiarity in the contact, but Airlie seems settled by it. A battle wages within me to tear them apart, but it takes only a glance down at Roan to keep myself in check. Until the witch proves my suspicions, it's better to sit back and watch her, to let her comfort Airlie and let her guard down.

When the witch speaks, her voice is low but strong, the confidence of a competent healer shining through. "Your task is your son, and mine is Roan. If we work together now, we'll see them both through this season and safely into each other's arms. We've already broken a curse between us—this injury is nothing to that."

Though tears fill her eyes, Airlie smiles and nods with a deep sigh. She ducks down to press a kiss to Roan's cheek, stroking his forehead as though checking for a temperature. When he doesn't wake at her touch, she straightens again and walks to Firna. The keeper clucks under her breath as she leads the princess out of the healer's quarters, a soothing noise and a motherly presence in all the ways my cousin needs her to be.

I've already banished Aura to the guest rooms and set a soldier on guard to ensure they don't cross paths in the hallway. It's everything I can do to respect Airlie's wishes that no one else meets their son before Roan does, but it doesn't feel like enough.

I had every intention of standing guard in the healer's quarters with the soldiers assigned there, but the pain from the wound in my side flares again, and I know it won't heal properly until I sleep. I have no choice but to make excuses and go back to my own rooms. I pass out cold the moment my head touches the pillow.

I wake before dawn, a cold sweat covering my body as the last of a deathly dream empties from my mind. I'm exhausted, my body seeming three times its usual weight as I drag myself from my sheets and into the bathroom. When I unwrap the bandages from around my stomach and wash away the cold sweat, I find my wound gone. The skin is healed over but still pink where the dagger was driven into my flesh, and it's tight as I move.

I dress in my battle clothes, everything but my armor, then head down to the healer's quarters with haste to check on Roan. The witch stands watch over him, tension in her stance and worry pinching at her brows that makes my stomach revolt.

Her eyes are grave as she meets my gaze. "There's no change. I'm not concerned about it…yet."

There's no arguing with the tone of her voice, no hesitation or wheedling, she's a healer giving her assessment, and though I might question everything else that spills out of those lips of hers, I have no doubt of her truth here.

I linger there for an hour, agitation at the wait crawling over me until I have no choice but to leave them, making my way to the barracks as a distraction. My presence might not be a distraction to the witch but if my impatience and irritation at my uselessness boils over, there's no doubt I'll become a problem to her.

I won't let my own failings risk Roan's life, not if I have control over them.

Commander Corym directs the soldiers through their daily tasks as the shifts go on around us. The castle and surrounding village are still on lockdown as we brace for an attack from the witches, especially as the raving masses had begun to swarm into the Outlands to draw us out.

Something inside of me warns that the witches' attacks aren't over yet, as though the Fates themselves are whispering in my ear that we've been too lucky. Roan's life being spared means there's still a price to pay for breaking the curse, a bounty on us all. It's the first real win the high fae have had in the war; even with the hundreds of small battles we've won, overall, the witches have still claimed more.

The tightness in my torso is a concern. The captain asks if I want to spar, a casual invitation to warm up and loosen my muscles in case we get the call, and I accept with a sharp nod. I change into my training armor and grab my dull sword, swinging it with ease even as my shoulder aches with an older injury.

I'm used to the pains of war.

I face the soldiers three at a time, each of them well trained and competent with a sword but no match for me. Every soldier who taps out has another jumping in, over and over and over again, until I finally make it down to the last three soldiers. As my chest heaves and my body drips with sweat, a flash of silver catches my eye, and I turn to find the witch staring at me as she walks past the training grounds. Her arms are full of dead branches, and a maid holding a crate of dead leaves stands at her side. The path they're on goes straight past the barracks and around the base of the castle to the royal gardens, once perfectly ornate and fruitful but now just another reminder of the barren state of the kingdom.

A soldier is with them, monitoring them and ensuring the witch can do no harm, but her eyes are trained on me, and I wonder how long she's been watching me put the soldiers through their paces. Whether she'll admit it or not, she looks impressed, a keen assessment of many long centuries of hard work.

One of my soldiers rushes towards me, sword raised and a war cry on his lips. I turn to block him and swipe his legs out from underneath him, waiting until his body crashes to the ground before I tap his shoulder with my sword to mark his death were we on the battlefield. Luckily for him, the enemies we face aren't high fae and most can barely lift a sword. Witches weren't made for fighting; they're weaker and mostly hide behind their magic.

I turn back to meet the witch's eye, but she's gone, her back quickly disappearing from my sight line as she strides back to the medicinal garden, her arms now empty as she's offloaded the branches for burning. The maid scurries closely by her side, her heeled shoes loud on the cobblestones as she struggles to keep up.

The soldiers don't comment about the witch anymore, something akin to respect in their eyes as they watch her pass. Saving Roan's life and caring for him through his healing might have been enough for her to creep beneath their defenses and go in for the kill.

No matter how many high-fae lives she saves, she will always be a witch first.

After I hang my training gear back up, I check in with the sentries at each of the main watchtowers along the inner wall of Yregar. Every soldier is on edge, preparing for the worst, but there's no news to report. No sign of the witches mobilizing to attack here or of any stray members of the Unseelie Court who might want a peek at the curse-breaking baby, not since Aura arrived.

When I step back into the castle, I find Firna waiting for me, a frown pasted on her lips as she shoots me a stern look. "Her Highness, Princess Aura, has requested an audience this morning. She impressed upon me the urgency of the matter about which she wishes to speak to you."

I raise an eyebrow back, and she scoffs. It's out of character for her, but Aura always did get on her very last nerve. "She's sick of staring at the same four walls and wants to know what she can do to convince you to let her see Airlie and the baby. She spent half the night telling one of the maids that it's her right as head of the family to see him, that their bloodline owes fealty to her, and no matter if you're the heir to the throne, she is still a Celestial princess and should not be ignored."

I huff and gesture at Firna to be on her way. "Tell Aura I'm too busy with the army of ravenous witches knocking at our walls to hear her woes, but I'll get to her just as soon as I can."

Firna smothers a smirk and bows at me, the long and plain skirts of her dress swishing as she leaves. She never did have much patience for the female. Long ago, when she was the handmaiden to my mother and forced to spend long hours with her sister as a result, she formed a deep dislike for my aunt purely due to her treatment of Airlie.

Aura would have more luck getting blood out of a stone than sympathy from Firna.

I walk down to the healer's quarters. Something about the perceptive look in the witch's watchful eyes earlier leads me through the maze of hallways into the bare and roughly hewn room tucked away under the castle, the quiet constant of the Fates pulling us together growing more insistent with every step.

It's colder down here than the rest of Yregar, the entire room carved from stone instead of the magnificently ornate marble, decorated with luxurious rugs, that covers the rest of the castle floor. It's a room built for function, not aesthetics, but the witch hums under her breath as she works. Her face is clear, the permanent scowl that once graced her brow gone as though it was never there.

She's wearing a different dress this time, one made of rough charcoal linen with sleeves that end at her elbows. It looks like something one of the maids would wear, far more functional than the dress Airlie gave her. She moves confidently as she brews another pot of tea and adds the drops of the tincture brewed from the milk thistle, still tending to my cousin's needs even though Firna and the maids could manage without her. Her fluid movements tighten up a little under my gaze, as though she's preparing to defend her actions against another round of my scrutiny, but I leave her to her work in silence as I shift my attention to her patient.

Roan's chest still moves steadily, no change in his condition, and my hand presses against the memory of the dagger wound at my side. I might have some lasting discomfort, but the wound is no longer bleeding through the bandages the way that Roan's wounds are.

The witch catches my frown in his direction and nods. "The poison did a lot of damage, and his body is struggling to heal because of it. My words to Airlie were the truth—it's a coin toss right now, and I fear the poison is winning."

My teeth gnash together, and my gaze drifts out the door to the soldiers standing along the wall. Yregar is the only safe place for us right now, everyone I care for is safe within these walls, and our priority is protecting everyone here if the witches attack. Leaving wouldn't just be a bad idea, it could be catastrophic.

"The herbs you need for him, do they grow in the Ravenswyrd Forest?"

She doesn't even try to mask her reaction to my words, her chin jerking up as her eyes clash with mine. "Of course. Everything grows in the Ravenswyrd."

I glance down at Roan and find no change in him even after hours of sleeping, the high-fae healing helping some but clearly not enough. It's a terrible time to leave the castle; every day that creeps by only brings more warning from the Fates murmuring within me, but I swore an oath to every one of my family and friends who chose to follow me. Leaving now will stretch us to the limit, pushing us so close to the edge that a breath of air would plunge us into despair.

When I look back up at the witch, the decision is already made. "Ready whatever you need to harvest it all. We leave within the hour."

THIRTY ONE

ROOKE

Prince Soren decides to leave Tauron behind in the castle and have Tyton and Reed—the scowling soldier who helped him carry Roan's lifeless body into the healer's quarters—escort us instead.

I'm surprised, knowing how concerned they all are that the trees speak to Tyton, but when I arrive at the stables, he's standing there, a determined look on his face as he waits for me. The calm and fierce mare Northern Star has been saddled for me once more, and the prince holds her reins out to me. I murmur a quiet thank you as I take them, because *my* manners are still intact.

Theirs are all strangely missing.

Tyton steps closer to me, his eyes not yet glowing or manic from the trees but the trip clearly playing with his mind already. "A Favored Child returned. Let's see what secrets you keep, witch."

Dozens of my secrets hide within the forest, many I would rather sit in the dungeon and die than face again. But the high-fae princes don't know where to look for medicinal herbs, and going back home is worth the risk to retrieve them. Spending my time cultivating a garden and restoring the healer's quarters as I count down the days until I fulfill my fate will be worth every second of Prince Soren's cold hatred. Going back to my ancestral lands and feeling my coven all around me once more, healing a long-since-accepted ache within me, will be worth it.

Loath as I am to admit it, Roan's life is too.

Prince Soren is dressed for the ride, back in armor and his leathers with weapons strapped to every inch of his long body, and there's a determined look on his face as he strides across the courtyard towards us, the midmorning sun catching on the silvery-blond of his hair and turning it into a white, blazing halo and making the cold depths of his eyes stand out even further. His gaze is sharp as he looks over the soldiers that surround the area, the courtyard and stables always full of them as they go about their duties. I hadn't expected him to change his mind easily about collecting the herbs for Roan, but I'm impressed with his determination to see the task out once the decision was made.

Tauron steps to his side with a sneer on his face as he argues with his cousin. "What if she uses that place to get into his head? She could be the reason the trees haunt him in the first place!"

Before I have the chance to worry that my trip home is going to be ripped away from me, Prince Soren shakes his head, taking his horse's reins from the stable master. "I need you here, watching over the castle, and you haven't gotten any sleep since we returned. Tyton is more than capable of this journey, and with the fae door, we won't be long. Watch over Roan, stop Airlie from killing someone to get to him, and keep the guard shifts watching the walls. They're going to strike back—this I know."

Whether a hunch or from his own connection to the Fates, Prince Soren truly does sound sure, but he mounts his snarling beast of a warhorse without another word, meeting Tauron's eyes one last time before we leave him behind.

Tyton takes up the rear, and the new soldier keeps pace

alongside me. He watches my every move, just the same as the rest of them, but his face is carefully blank as we follow Prince Soren through the village to the outer wall.

The village is quiet, subdued as the people all cower in fear, the military presence around them growing only more intense. My heart throbs painfully in my chest as we pass the temple. The doors are shut, and a long line of people are standing on the stones out the front as they wait for food to be brought down from the castle kitchens. I hope that the messenger Prince Soren sent to the Western Fyres has pockets full of gold ready to bring supplies home now, because if he went only to discuss terms, we're all going to suffer a long, painful death.

Reed reaches over to take my reins but nudges both of our horses through the fae door without dismounting, his control of the beast beneath him admirable. Several of the soldiers seem to have an affinity with the animals like that, while others aren't so confident.

The Augur Mountains stand out from the landscape, barren and dormant, a shadow of their once glorious visage.

My hands long to scrub over my face roughly enough to set my skin back onto my bones after the uncomfortable journey through the door, but the soldier is watching me a little too keenly, probably for signs of weakness, so I settle for a deep breath. Prince Soren pauses only long enough to see Tyton emerge from the door safely before he leads us down the path and toward the forest at the base of the mountain.

"We're like sitting ducks here, just waiting to catch an arrow to the chest to match Prince Roan. We'll be lucky to make it back alive," Reed mutters, and Tyton lets out a dry laugh behind us.

"Missing the snow already? I suppose we'll never convince you to join us at Yregar for the next battle."

Reed glances at Prince Soren as though questioning Tyton's words. My Fates-cursed mate doesn't look back at their conversation, his eyes constantly surveying the area as he watches for danger.

"I could be convinced, but only once we're sure Fates Mark is secure. There's no telling what fresh hell Kharl will send up there once he knows his latest attempt was unsuccessful, and my oaths are sworn to the Snowsong crest."

They're strong words, just as I expected from Reed. He's not one to play the high-fae games, I'm sure of it. I've met hundreds of soldiers just like him, and they're the type I prefer to spend my time with. No time for dissembling and ready with a brutal response if they find your own actions wanting.

I hope he does stay; his eyes would be useful to watch over Airlie and the baby.

The farther down the mountain we get, the softer the earth beneath our horses' hooves becomes. The ride becomes smoother as each step becomes more forgiving, the ground supple as we approach the life still thriving within my ancestral home.

The conversation breaks off when Tyton begins to fidget in his seat, growing more uncomfortable the closer we get, and I know the trees are taking hold of his mind.

I envy that he can hear them from this far away.

It's not until we reach the river, the path running alongside it as it cuts through the forest ahead, that I finally hear the song of the Ravenswyrd in my heart. A consuming calm takes over my body, my concerns easing away, because I'm home. This time, I'm not just passing by. I'll walk amongst the trees once more.

"Why does the witch look like she's going to burst out in song while Prince Tyton is fighting to not throw up?" Reed murmurs.

Prince Soren turns in his seat, his gaze dismissive as it moves over me and sticks on Tyton. "Just breathe, Cousin, we're only passing through."

Even as my heart sings wildly with the homecoming, the

forest a chorus of joyous welcome, I feel a small stab of pain as we get closer to the place I've longed for. Knowing that I'll finally walk amongst the trees once more only to be forced to leave them again is heartbreaking, the euphoria of the song within me dampening a little, and I have to force my mind away from that thought to focus on the good for now. I don't want to squander the reunion by thinking only of the goodbye ahead. It's still hours away, and the journey to my coven's village and the harvesting of the gardens is still to come. I can mourn my home on the return ride.

Tyton's eyes, already glowing brighter than before, widen, and his gaze snaps to Prince Soren. He frowns for a moment, likely to absorb the meaning of his cousin's words into his chaotic mind, before he finally nods. "They know we've brought her. They want the Favored Child. They want her to stay."

Soren glares at me before turning back to spur his horse on faster. "Tell the trees she's only stopping by. They'll have to find a different *child* to keep."

He says it sarcastically, as though he doesn't truly think the trees will listen, but they hear him. They're fluent in every language, both spoken and silent, and they don't like such disrespect. There's a rumble deep within the darkness as earth begins to groan.

Reed startles, his head snapping around as he tries to figure out what creature would make such a noise, and his horse lets out a whinny. Prince Soren is less easy to spook, and even as his beast of a horse paws at the ground, he remains still in his saddle, glaring ahead as he waits for an attack.

Tyton shakes his head, his horse still calm under a sure rider. "They don't like that. You shouldn't fight with them, Soren. They're older than we are."

He doesn't mean the trees that we can see before us. The Ravenswyrd Forest is older than the First Fae, older than the

Augur Mountains, but there's something *else* here. Something that came to live within these trees a long time ago and never left, something old and tired that chose to rest as the witches of my coven cared for it. For centuries unnumbered, as it slumbered, we tended to its every need.

It wants the Favored Children back.

As we reach the edge of the trees, Prince Tyton pulls his horse up short, jerking the reins with an unsteady hand. I've never seen him falter like this, exposed and vulnerable.

I edge Northern Star forward, her hooves hitting the moss, and when she jitters underneath me I stroke her neck, soothing her and assuring her she's safe with me.

I'm not so sure about the others.

Prince Soren turns to me. "How do we get in there without losing our minds?"

A smile flirts at the edge of my mouth and, misreading it, Reed cringes at my side. "We're going to trust the witch with our lives and sanity? Your Highness, please reconsider. This is a terrible idea."

The prince flicks a dismissive hand at his cousin. "That's why I brought a translator of our own, just in case. Tyton can speak to the trees, any deception by the witch won't get past him."

Reed and I both turn to Tyton, his eyes glowing and his lips moving. If he's forming words, they're for high-fae ears only, and he doesn't take notice of our interest. He stares unblinking into the darkness ahead, the way the trees cluster together so heavily that the daylight can't break through.

I hear the trees whisper in the depths of my heart, but it's as natural to me as the act of breathing. From the frenetic spill of his words from his lips I can tell the frenzy that runs riot through Tyton is different, and my guess is that his raw magic amplifies everything until he teeters on the edge of madness. Prince Soren obviously has a lot of faith in his cousin, because I'm not sure Tyton will make it out of here still sound of mind.

My gaze drifts back to the trees, unable to resist their call. "The Ravenswyrd protects the Favored Children. Walking amongst the trees unharmed is as simple as your intentions."

I speak to the soldier, because I already know Prince Soren's answer. "Do you wish me any harm, Reed?"

Reed swallows and frowns at me. "You're the healer who's going to save Prince Roan, the heir to the Snowsong family. I wish you no harm, if only to save his life."

A far more honest answer than I was expecting, and Tyton's face slackens as he turns toward the soldier. "The trees say you may enter. Leave behind a sacrifice, and they'll let you make your journey unharmed."

Prince Soren scowls as he stares into my forest, but he speaks confidently. "I'm not leaving the Favored Child behind. Her fate is tied to mine, but no harm will come to her unbidden."

The trees don't like that answer as much as Reed's, and it takes far longer for them to deliberate. A wind appears suddenly and rustles the leaves, the tall oaks groaning as they hold their conference with one another. They've been betrayed once before and will never be again, still paying the steepest price for the misstep.

I lean forward to stroke Northern Star's neck, soothing myself as much as settling her, and finally I hear the answer in my heart.

Tyton speaks, his voice quivering with the old power that lives within. "You can enter. They say you must give them a sacrifice, as well. They say it must be bigger for taking their Favored Child. It wants more. It needs the Favored Children returned."

Without waiting for Prince Soren's scathing reply, I nudge Northern Star forward and take the lead. "Don't stray from the path. You never know what you'll find here."

No one speaks as we walk our mounts on the path through the forest. The trepidation of the high fae riding with me is palpable, but my heart sings as I stare around at the untouched beauty of my home.

It thrives.

Even after two hundred years without my coven, the forest lives and breathes with the magic we once shared. Moss covers fallen logs along the path, and birds sing above us, the sound of the melodies exploding through my senses now after weeks of silence at Yregar.

Prince Soren stares around at it all as though he's waiting for an attack, poised and ready to fight.

The farther we ride, the more light filters through the tree canopy, and it's clear the trees themselves became a wall of defense around the outskirts of the forest. The small offshoot of the river follows our path, and I smile down at the water sprites playing there, the magic here still sustaining them even long after the rituals and practices of the Ravenswyrd Coven came to an end. The sacrifice of my family's and friends' lives, taken unwillingly and mournfully accepted by the trees, has kept the entire forest and the life within it preserved and protected from the drain of the war and the imbalance of the kingdom.

My throat closes as we pass a hollow tree, the echo of a memory within me. I realize now how slowly Pemba and I walked this path when we left, the way that my brother gently and patiently let me idle along. My heart was breaking inside my chest, not just at the loss of my coven but at the journey itself, and Pemba gave me all the extra time he could, a loving brother who always put me first. It was his gentle treatment, and the distraction and reassurance of Donn speaking to me each morning through our shared connection, that got me through that heartbreaking journey out of the forest for the first time. The last time.

The trees were terrified we wouldn't come home.

As a witchling, I didn't recognize that their song lives within me. It wasn't until I reached Sol City and found myself trapped in the silence within my heart that I realized something had lived within me and was gone, leaving behind a chasm of pain. The trees in the Northern Land speak, of course, the Seelie high fae even speak back to them, but it's a different language. Foreign to me in its difference to the song I grew up with, and a reminder of what I lost.

It became a comfort to me over the years, but never a replacement. I only wish Pemba were here with me, not back in the Northern Lands, but this journey was one for me alone.

I never told him my fate.

"What the hell is *that*?" the soldier hisses from behind me, and I glance up and see a small fawn foraging amongst the flowers ahead of us, content and unguarded.

There are predators within the forest, of course, other creatures and animals, but the deer is young and bolstered by an easy life so far. The Ravenswyrd Coven had hunted deer for meat, and I expect the herds have thrived here without us.

"Are there no deer left in the Southern Lands?" I ask as the creature spots us and startles away, running back into the thick line of trees and disappearing from sight.

There's no reply, and that's answer enough for me.

Whether they were over-hunted when the crops began to fail or simply perished when their own food supplies ran out, there's clearly no wildlife left elsewhere. The decay of the kingdom spreads like poison and takes all life with it.

"How much farther until we reach these plants you need?"

Soren asks, his tone utterly irreverent.

I look up at the canopy above us, searching for an answer there. "We have to follow the river into the heart of the forest. It won't take long with the horses."

"There are plants surrounding us now, everywhere we look, are none of these what you require?"

He doesn't trust me within the trees any more than he did before, whatever reverence he's found not extending that far, but it doesn't bother me. None of it does, because I'm finally home.

"It's better to wait until we reach the gardens than stopping every time I see something useful. They may be overgrown and unruly by now, but everything I need should be growing there, and it's a better place to start than running through the trees and moss without a clear path. Time is not on our side, nor Prince Roan's."

We fall into silence, each of us glancing back from time to time to check on Tyton, but he's silent, his eyes glowing and his mouth sealed shut as he takes it all in. The trees didn't try to stop him from entering or ask for a sacrifice from him, an endorsement all their own.

As we reach the thickest part of the river, the small lake-like swelling that had once been a fun destination for the children of the Ravenswyrd Coven to play in, with an abundance of fish and water sprites, I look across the riverbank and find ghoulish eyes staring back at me.

It can't be the same wraith that attacked my brother and I. The amount of energy it takes a witch to transform into the terrifying creature shortens its lifespan to no more than a hundred years, but it feels as though the past is replaying in front of me. Only this time, I'm not a naïve girl sheltered by her family within the protection of the trees. I've lived another life, wonderful and terrible, far away from the horrors here.

My heart hardening, I stare at the pitiful creature as its mouth opens and the screeching pours from the deepest recesses of its hollowed chest. The high fae pull up short behind me, and I hear one of them unsheathe his sword, but I raise my hand and send out a pulse of power in the wraith's direction. My control is ironclad now, even without my scepter, and when the ball hits it in the chest, it scrambles away, looking for an easier meal elsewhere.

"What the hell was that?" the soldier asks again, and this time I smile in return.

"That's a consequence of this war, and one with no one but the high fae to blame."

He turns to me, our eyes clashing violently as he fumbles for words. "Nothing else around here has been touched by the war. How can *that* have anything to do with our people?"

Firna's words still ring in my head, doing damage at every swipe, but I chose to lead the high fae into my ancestral home and so I must keep my temper. If the trees sense my anger, there's no telling what they might do to the high fae to protect me.

"A wraith is formed when a witch dies a wrongful death, a curse on their lips as they cast a terrible magic at their most desperate hour. The raving masses of Kharl's army don't have the power to perform such a thing. That wraith was once an innocent witch with a clear heart, following the teachings of our kind. That witch was *murdered*."

Hostile silence greets my words, but I find I prefer it that way. Better they keep their mouths shut than keep speaking their twisted truths and outright lies. I'm tired of teaching them things their kind should never have forgotten in the first place.

Nudging Northern Star until she continues down the path, I soak in the rays of the midday sun as we finally reach the clearing. The exposed and decayed poles that once held up the roofs of my coven's huts are visible through the thinning trees, and a lump forms in my throat as my hands tighten on the reins.

This is exactly what I wanted—to return here and see my home once more. But it takes everything within me not to pull Northern Star up short, turn, and run. My heart begins to thump in my chest, so hard I worry my bones will break around it, and I swallow down a lump as it threatens to choke me.

Prince Soren nudges his horse forward, squeezing onto the path next to me and glaring down at me. "You're leading us into a trap. I told the trees I wouldn't harm you as long as you didn't trick us, and you bring us to a coven? Can they save you from me now, witch?"

I shake my head at him, the decision made as I kick Northern Star into a trot. I ignore him as he hisses curses at my back only to stop abruptly when the remnants of the funeral pyre appear in front of us.

It's crudely made, nothing like the finely crafted and ornate pyres in the Northern Lands, but it was the best we could do at the time.

My brother and I had barely seen twenty summers each, but we'd piled up the bodies of our friends and family to send them on the smoke to the Fates, ensuring them a safe trip to Elysium. The arrows from Kharl's forces still lie embedded in the ground, with the telltale raven feathers of the fletching that are his calling card, and the horses weave around them as a grave silence falls over the group.

The forest has left the clearing untouched, an act of mourning and repentance for the single, detrimental misstep that cost the forest the Ravenswyrd witches it loved so dearly. Fae flowers grow everywhere, but in devastating patches, outlining each witch murdered there where their blood poured into the land. Though it was an offering the forest never wanted to take, it consumed every drop and has honored them with the blooms of the sacred flowers.

If I shut my eyes, I can still see my coven where they once lay in death. The memories are as sharp today as they were that terrible day. Pemba and I prayed to the Fates over each of the bodies before we moved them to the funeral pyre, slipping their eyes closed with shaking hands and fumbling our way through the rites. My chest ached as the sobs shook me so hard that my bones rattled within, but my brother had wept silently, his arms tight around my shoulders as he held me together.

The smallest patches of the fae flowers hurt the most, and when I slide down from Northern Star's back, I let the reins go and trust that she'll stay put. She does, well trained, but Reed steps forward to grab them anyway as he waits for orders, his mouth a tight line as he stares around us.

Prince Soren and Tyton both dismount as well, my Fates-cursed mate watching me while his cousin grows frantic. He walks between the fae flower blooms while the trees sing a mournful song, still grieving and sorrowful, but relieved that someone is here to listen to them finally.

"They're all gone," he whispers, his voice cracking as he kneels to press his hands amongst the blooms.

His eyes shine and despair colors his words as the trees sing our demise to him. "This was once a young girl. Sixteen. Still learning how to weave, her magic small but kind...she didn't fight back. She didn't want to hurt anyone, not even after she saw them kill her father."

Peony hadn't settled into her place within the coven yet. She was brash and bold but gentle in the way all Ravenswyrd witches were. Fiery red hair to match her wit, she was an only child, and so she spent most of her time with my siblings and I, never truly lonely in the coven bursting with witchlings. She was one of my closest friends, full of raucous humor, and she had a crush on my younger brother, Willow.

He was a summer younger than her and not interested in girls yet. He cared about building things, many things, anything he could dream up and for every purpose, it didn't matter. He just wanted his hands to be busy. My father had joked with my mother that the coven would be thrust forward three hundred years worth of advancement at his hand, if only he could sit still long enough to see his creations finished.

His fae flowers lie by my grandmother's hut.

From the cluster in the perfect outline of a growing boy on the cusp of adulthood, I can still see his sightless eyes staring up at the smoke-filled sky. When we built the funeral pyre and moved the bodies of our dead to it, Pemba told me he thought Willow must've run to her when the massacre began, thinking of her safety before his own. She was the Crone of the coven, our history and our lore living within her as she taught the younger generations what it meant to be a Witch of the Woods.

Willow loved her fiercely, we all did, with every fiber of our being from the moment she saw us into this world as a healer to our mother during all of her births. An entire coven full of traditions and stories and love, all of it destroyed in a single sweep of the war.

I murmur a prayer in the old language, futile because they're all already long since traveled to Elysium but it feels right to honor them. I've never forgotten them, not their faces or their pure hearts, and while I breathe, the Ravenswyrd way lives on.

As I walk farther into the clearing, ignoring Prince Soren as he follows close behind, I see that the huts are all still standing despite the damage and the long centuries passed. Each of them is partially burned, and the years of decay have rendered them hazardous.

A few on the outskirts have collapsed roofs, but the large healing hut in the center of the village looks safe enough, and the small garden, fenced off with reeds and woven vines, still flourishes even without care. The forest honors our work, the centuries passing the rest of the kingdom by but never touching this clearing, because the trees will never forget their Favored Children.

Walking out of the forest this time will hurt even more than the last.

I walk back to Northern Star to collect the leather satchels and harvesting supplies I brought with me, then I go back to the garden and begin my work, my sight blurred by the tears I fight to keep from flowing freely down my cheeks. I'm all too aware of my surveillance and the way Prince Soren's eyes never leave me, as cold now as the moment he first saw me and realized I was a witch.

THIRTY TWO⊙

SOREN

The witch works in silence as she harvests the small garden, but the forest is anything but silent around us. It's livelier here than the Goblin Lands have ever been. Lush and untouched, as though the war never came here, everything around us looks like a haven. That illusion is lifted only by the fire-damaged huts and the arrows that litter the ground, fletched with the same wax-tipped raven feathers we pulled from Roan's chest. A picture begins to form before my eyes, unsettling in its truths.

Tyton works his way around the fae flowers, but he doesn't pick any as he drops to his knees and presses his hands amongst the blooms, his eyes glowing as he mumbles nonsense under his breath. There's a manic energy within him, a crazed purpose pushing him onwards, and I watch him as closely as I do the witch.

When our horses first arrived in the clearing, those flowers sparked an ember of joy and hope within my chest, despite myself. It wasn't until I heard Tyton's words that I understood their creation, the outlines slowly taking shape until I could see the massacre that took place. The fallen members of the witch's coven, her family, nothing left of them but a field of the most sacred flowers.

This is the horror that drove her to the Seer and out of the

Southern Lands.

The force of her terror that morning had woken me and fueled my own fears for her safety, and though she wouldn't tell me what had frightened her so severely, the waves of grief had been a crushing echo of my own. I knew she had lost someone close to her, I knew that it put her own life in peril thanks to the fear that lingered and the small snippets of information I could ease out of her, but I didn't suspect something like this.

My suspicions of her true motives grow heavier within me, a weight I struggle to hold onto with the blooms of the dead surrounding us, but the survival of my kingdom and my people rely on my clear head. I cannot afford to accept this witch as my mate and put her on the throne beside me without thought of the consequences simply because of her past and the truth of the forest before me.

Reed stays with the horses at the edge of the huts, his eyes shrewd and careful as he watches the trees around us, but there's nothing else in the forest nearby. No danger lies within our hearing, just the peaceful sounds of a lively forest existing happily around the perfectly preserved clearing.

When the witch begins to hum under her breath, a content sound of busy work, I step back over to Tyton to distract myself. "Are you still in there, Cousin, or has the forest taken hold of your mind?"

He blinks up at me as though he forgot my existence and frowns as his hands push deeper into the earth, a long stream of madness falling from his lips.

"She was only eight. Eight summers in the forest, hearing its song in her heart. She hadn't yet learned how to light a fire with her magic, but she was close, and Mother was proud. She shared a bed with her sister each night, she read them both stories to chase away the bad dreams. She was scared of wraiths. They'd seen one while they were swimming in the river, she was sure of it, even when her brother said she was lying. The wraith has come to get them, should she have told her father, is that why the Favored Children are lost—"

The words stop short, the haze leaving him all at once, but his eyes glow brighter than ever. Maybe bringing him here wasn't the best idea—maybe I should've listened to Tauron's warnings about the madness within his brother.

I glance over and find the witch has stopped her work to look at us, her mouth pulled in tight at the corners as she holds in a grimace. Her eyes flick down to avoid mine only to land on the fae flowers, tears welling there before she looks away again quickly. Her movements are jerky as she gets back to her harvesting, her shoulders tight, and she lets out a long, shaking breath.

The dead walk amongst the trees of the Ravenswyrd, of that I'm sure.

Tense moments pass as I watch the tree line, but when the witch finally stands, looking satisfied with her bounty, Tyton and I meet her at the garden gate to collect the satchels and get them secured on our horses. She hands them over without a word and then stoops to a small pot by the gate to grab a handful of the smooth stones there, white and clinking a little as she slips them into her pocket.

I think nothing of it, walking to the horses and watching as the witch fusses with the satchels, careful to make sure that her precious supplies aren't crushed or damaged. When I make a move to mount Nightspark, she stops me. She takes a moment to collect herself, straightening and clearing away the grief that grips her, and when she finally meets my eyes, the tears are gone from her unerring silver gaze.

"Your fate is to marry me and mine is the same," she says, her voice sorrowful.

I scowl at her, ignoring the incredulous look on Reed's

face. No matter how persistent the gossip at Yregar is, he still somehow missed that small detail of the atrocity I'm trapped in.

The witch takes another deep breath. "My fate specifies that I need to marry you in your tradition and mine. Before you assume I'm doing something sinister, there's something I need to retrieve from my parents' house. My customs demand this, and I can't marry you without it."

There's absolutely no way I'll be sitting through a witch ritual during our marriage. I don't even know what their practices look like or what the expectations of my participation would be, but I do know that I want no part in it.

She takes one look at my face and clicks her tongue at me, shaking her head as though I'm disappointing her. "You can make this choice now, Prince Soren, but you won't get your throne without it. I'm happy to come back here when you realize your mistake."

I never want to step foot amongst these trees again, and at even the possibility, I'm quick to make up my mind. There's no harm in following the witch now, no way she can overpower me or outsmart me, and so seeing more of the place she once called home can only help me discover more of her motives and the past that had shaped her.

Turning with a nod at Tyton, I flick a dismissive hand at her. "Lead the way."

She grimaces but gets moving, snapping at me over her shoulder, "I'd rather you not step foot in my mother's house with that attitude."

I follow her to the largest of the huts, close by the garden and the communal space. Fae flowers surround the footings and the steps leading up to the roughly hewn door, and she murmurs a small prayer before pushing it open.

There are no lights within the hut, and the sunlight that crawls through the small window barely lights the room. It takes a moment before my eyes adjust, but when they do, I find it's not just a hut, but a *home*. Sitting untouched for two hundred years, but ready as though waiting for the family to return.

There's clutter everywhere for children, and lots of them. Toys, boots, and jackets in a dozen different sizes. There's bedding and pillows strewn everywhere, as though they all fell asleep where they landed at the end of each day. A long table has plates still laid out, ready for a meal that never came, dust covering everything. There are paintings on the walls, simple and crude but full of color and life. There's a scratching of ink in the corner by the door, barely legible, but scribed in the looping characters of the common tongue.

I murmur, "Pemba... What sort of a name is that?"

The look the witch gives me is enough to flay the skin from my back, another warning of the predator she hides beneath the calm demeanor of a healer. "A strong name given to a firstborn son as wise and as cunning as an owl. You would learn a lot if you were ever so lucky as to meet him."

She steps farther into the large room and ducks down for a moment to press her hands against the wooden slats that make up the flooring of the hut before striding into the adjoining bedroom. It's far too small for me to follow her, barely big enough to fit the downy mattress within it, and so I stay in the larger room to watch over her from here.

My gaze gets caught on the patch of floorboards she touched. The wood is stained, and it's only on closer inspection that I realize the dark mark is dried blood, and quite a lot of it spilled. Another witch was slain in here, a member of her family dying at my enemy's hand.

The walls of the hut begin to close in on me, the air heating up and squeezing from my lungs until I'm sure she's cursed me. The thumping of my heart in my chest breaks me out of the spiral, loud enough to stop my racing thoughts and center me in the tiny room once more.

This place is evil.

I snap at the witch, "We're leaving, grab your trinket, and let's go."

She ignores me, taking exactly as long as she would like as she moves around in there. A snarl slips out of my mouth when she finally steps out of the room, her face oddly blank and a large wooden box in her hands.

Fixing my attention on the box, prepared to defend myself if she's finally going to reveal her true intentions, I grasp the pommel of my sword, but she ignores me. Without fear of my aggressive stance, she walks straight past me out the front door, giving me no choice but to follow her.

Reed frowns when she approaches the horses, but she simply rearranges the satchels already tied on the back of Northern Star until she can secure the box there as well, checking the leather bindings three times before she's certain it's secure, then climbing back into the saddle without offering a word.

She's too practiced at all of this for my liking, too comfortable in the saddle and steady with Northern Star. Everything about her is too confident, as though she knows more about the world than we do and has superiority over us as a result.

Standing before her, I meet her eyes and snap, "You can't take that into Yregar without telling me what it is. You could be carrying in a death curse, for all I know."

I've seen one in action, and I'll never forget it.

Before Kharl had perfected his process to transform the witches into the raving masses we now face, we fought smaller groups with stronger magic. In the weeks after my gravest injuries, the scarring permanent thanks to the aid in my healing, we fought the witches at Yrmar, and they took control of the castle with a death curse.

The witch holding the cursed object rode into the walls,

her eyes glowing silver as the magic began to eat her alive. We stood by and watched, frozen in horror and confusion, because she never faltered in her path. Even when her skin began to melt from her bones and screams of agony tore from her lips, she pushed her horse harder until she entered the inner walls.

The moment the curse broke out, thousands died in the blink of an eye, their bodies ripped apart by a blast of power.

We survived only by chance, the outer wall encasing enough of that evil to aid our retreat. Prince Valorys, the Lord of Yrmar, and his forces were killed where they stood within the inner walls as they fought to defend their home.

It belongs to the witches now, at the heart of the Witch Ward they thrive within.

The witch's face stays blank, and she tightens the reins, guiding her horse back to the path. Reed jerks his hands on his own reins to trot after her, intent on dragging her back before me. "It's a dress, nothing more and nothing less. I'm bringing it in the box because I don't want it to be damaged on the ride home."

Tyton and I mount our horses and trot after them, riding quickly to catch up and then matching the witch's pace. The path is too narrow and too slippery with disuse to go much faster, but I find my skin itching to get away.

Reed mumbles under his breath for only high-fae ears, "Why would she need a dress? Why would that have anything to do with a witch's wedding? I thought they just dance naked under the moon—"

He cuts his jesting off, possibly realizing that if it's true, I'll be forced to do the same.

Tyton cuts through the dismayed silence, his voice echoing with power. "Robes. The Ravenswyrd witches are bound together by the Fates and wear ceremonial robes passed down from Mother to Maiden. The Fates have commanded the

Favored Child be returned to us, you *must* honor us."

I'll be happy when we're back at Yregar and no longer tiptoeing around the old gods that walk amongst the trees, something I no longer question now that I'm here to feel it for myself.

As we reach the river where the wraith hunted, chased away by the witch's magic, she pulls her horse up short. "You both still need to fulfill your sacrifice to the forest."

Reed scowls at her, but I lean down and pull a dagger out of my boot. A quick slice through my palm, and I'm holding out my hand to let the blood drip down on the mossy path, watching as it soaks into the green and disappears. The forest drinks it greedily, the sound of the trees louder for a moment before the witch nods. The forest accepts the sacrifice.

Reed does the same, surly and almost pouting, but when the forest is satisfied, the witch nudges at her horse and directs us back on the path out of this cursed place. How Tyton has fought off the claws of the trees and whatever old gods live here to keep his mind is beyond me. I'd rather face a hundred raving witches with nothing but my sword.

When we make it out of the trees and back to the deadened lands at the base of the Augur Mountains, the peace and calm have left the witch, leaving behind a scowl as she stares into the darkness of the night, the moon lighting our way up the side of the mountain.

"When I arrived at the Seelie Court, I found out the truth of what happened to my parents and our coven. My brother and I were unaware there was a war happening outside of the forest. It protected us well, but Kharl and his forces had centuries trying to figure out a way in...and that day, they did."

She turns to me, eyes clear and honesty ringing through her voice, as though she's passing judgment on us and finding us truly wanting. "The high fae forget that the first victims of

Kharl's war were the witches themselves."

Reed stares at her, his mouth tight as he holds in a grimace, but her words just keep tumbling out. "Do you think the mindless raving masses want to be that way? Do you think they knew what he would do to them? When he first came to the Southern Lands, he gave them two options—join him, or die. Any witch who escaped him, fleeing their covens and ancestral lands, found themselves at the mercy of the high fae. Painted as enemies and hunted for nothing more than the blood in their veins and their silver eyes. All of the witches in the Northern Lands were there because they had no better option. I heard countless stories from them of the hunt for our people that drove us all from our homes and the trees that love us. *That's* the truth of the kingdom you're fighting so hard for. That is the truth of your war."

We cross through the fae door and back onto Yregar land after the moon has reached its peak in the sky, shining down on us and casting an ethereal light over the starkness of the castle and its surroundings.

As I wait for the others to cross through, I can't help but look over my shoulder at the pastures that lie beyond the stone wall. Through the large iron gate manned by the soldiers, my home is in ruins.

We've been desensitized by years of slow decay, but seeing the Ravenswyrd Forest, and even the Goblin Lands, has made the desperation within me grow. It doesn't have to be this way. We can find our way back to a flourishing kingdom, stronger than ever before, I know it.

Tyton rides alongside me, his eyes now back to the same simple blue of the Celestial bloodline. His expression is clearer than it has been in many months, and when he feels my eyes on him, he turns.

"I can't hear it anymore," he says to me, shooting me a long look and keeping his gaze pointedly away from the witch. "I've always heard the ramblings of madness for days after the forest took my mind, but there's nothing there now."

The witch's voice is uncharacteristically soft in the cool night air. "We left the forest a sacrifice, a gift for seeing you safely through. You listened to what it had to say, and so now it will let you be until you meet again. That's the Ravenswyrd way. That's the old way, of the trees."

Tyton's brow furrows. The horses still move briskly along the cobblestones, delayed only by the inky blackness of the night as it blankets the road to the village. Even simple things like torches and firewood are now in great demand and not to be wasted lighting paths that are sparingly used.

"Who was the girl? The one who saw the wraith, who died thinking the massacre was her fault. What was her name?"

Reed glances over, apprehensive, but he looks to the witch for her answer. She stays silent for a long part of the walk, her hands tight on her reins and the horse fussing underneath. Northern Star calms and snorts happily when the witch runs an absent hand down her neck.

We make it through the village, past the homeless sleeping on the streets and into the inner walls before the witch finally speaks. "Tawnie. Her name was Tawnie."

Tyton nods, happy enough with just this information, but the name niggles at the back of my mind.

At the stables, we dismount and hand the reins off to Ingor and his stable boys before we unpack the supplies from the saddles. The witch insists on carrying the leather satchels herself, and I insist on carrying the wooden box she recovered from her parents' room, jerking my head for her to follow as I lead the way to the healer's quarters.

When we arrive there, Tauron is standing in the doorway, a scowl on his face, but he bows to me and says, "There's been no change. He still mutters in his sleep and jerks like he's fighting off banshees in his mind."

The witch moves around him and begins unpacking her bounty, lining up freshly scrubbed jars and placing cuttings within them as she waits for water to boil on the woodburning stove. She takes no notice of any of the eyes on her, blocking us all out as she gets to work.

I dismiss Tauron and send Reed and Tyton off to get cleaned up and rest, aware there's a long night ahead of standing watch over the castle for us all.

The witch moves about the kitchen area confidently, pausing only long enough to press a palm against Roan's forehead. Frowning, she presses her fingers to his throat and she shuts her eyes for a moment, then continues checking and testing him in all the little ways of a seasoned healer confident in her craft.

I watch on as she crushes flowers and chops up stalks, grinding leaves into paste and rolling seeds between her palms, slowly adding all these things to the bubbling pot of water on the woodfire.

A fragrant smell begins to waft through the room, honeysuckle and the intoxicating scent of the fae flowers dancing together in a promise of life. The witch didn't take any of the flowers blooming from the fallen witches, instead harvesting them from a small patch in the garden where they were once cultivated in abundance by her coven's diligent hands.

She removes the pot from the direct heat, letting the water simmer as she stirs, but doesn't make any further moves to add to it. The mixture slowly thickens as she toils above it, her watchful eye calculating every step of the process until finally she pulls out a smaller spoon. Dipping it in the pot and then slowly dripping liquid from it, she checks the consistency. It's the exacting sort of work that means the difference between life and death, the sleeping high-fae prince on the floor reliant on this concoction.

When she finally deems it finished, she dips the spoon in once more, taking a few drops of the emerald liquid. After letting it cool for a moment, she ducks down to carefully siphon it between Roan's lips, watching him like a hawk. It's such a small amount that he doesn't need to swallow, thankfully. Instead, it melts onto his tongue, and we both watch as his skin begins to glow, golden and vital, as the fae flowers infuse him.

The rattle in his chest eases away until it disappears entirely, and a great sigh heaves from his chest. He finally stops muttering and falls into a deep sleep. The witch watches it all, shrewd eyes narrowed, and at his relaxation, she nods to herself, satisfied it's a job well done.

"Tawnie is a type of owl, as well. Is it customary for witches to name their children after creatures in the forest, or just a practice within your family?"

She doesn't answer with words, but her shoulders push back as she straightens. My guess is correct—the eight-year-old was her sister.

Ignoring my presence, she gets to work as though the Fates themselves command her. Pulling out the vials she carefully emptied and scrubbed out days earlier and then placed in boiled water, she lines them up on the bench for filling. All of the work she did over the past few days in preparation suggests she knew that, at some point, we'd have to procure these ingredients for her, one way or another.

She spoons the elixir into the vials slowly, her hands steadfast and sure, until five of them sit sealed with a cork on the bench before her. The journey into the forest, her hard work, and the ingredients boiled down to five tiny vials, an illusion of a small yield from her work, but I know better.

If two drops can save a high-fae prince's life, then a great bounty lies before her.

Shifting on her feet, she begins to scrub all the tools that she used, diligent and steadfast. She doesn't seem to care that there are maids and servants within this castle that she could demand service from. For the work she's done, no one would deny her, even being a witch. She treats every person she comes across the same, addressing my family by our royal titles but never attempting to bow. She's humbled herself to no one but the Goblin King.

I place the wooden box on the workbench, and she turns to look at me, her eyes guarded as a seething anger simmers behind them.

I motion toward her prize. "You're going to open it and show me, or I'll destroy it for the safety of the castle. Maybe Tauron's right and I've let my stupidity over the Fates and your acts of healing fool me into letting you bring it in here in the first place. I know better than to believe in your lies."

She steps forward and pulls the lid off the wooden box as simply as she'd stirred the pot, no reverence in her hands. It's as though it holds no memories or connection to her, a very convincing act.

"Fabric. You're all fretting about a bundle of silks and linens. The high fae have a lot to be worried about if this is terrifying to your kind."

She turns away from me, once more plunging her arms back into the soapy water, and I let my own gaze drop to the dress. Tyton was right, they're clearly ceremonial robes. White silk with embroidery down the edges of the lapels, fae flowers and oak leaves dance and play until they form into the pattern of the old oak trees of the Ravenswyrd. The colors are vibrant and lush, a true image of the forest.

I can't feel anything around the box, just the same as Tyton.

There's nothing to say that the witch hasn't concealed it from us both, but I place the lid back on and pick it up once more, the wood warm in my hands as the weight of it surprises me.

"I'll lock it in my chambers until you manage to convince me that going ahead with our marriage is the best thing for the kingdom," I say with a smirk.

She shakes her head at me, clicking her tongue disapprovingly. "You've got it all wrong, Prince Soren—you're the one who's going to have to convince me of such a thing, because right now, I'd set you on fire just to watch the flames consume you."

As I turn away from her, a smirk stretching across my lips at getting under her skin, she calls out to me again over her shoulder, "If my sister's name ever crosses your lips again, or my brother's for that matter, I'll end your bloodline. I'll do it and laugh as the Fates open to destroy us all, I swear on my coven's name."

She says it with the same sincerity that she explained to my cousin her husband's condition and the way she told us about the wishes of the trees. She says it like there's no question of her capability, like every word is as indubitable as the Fates' commands of us.

For the first time, I believe the words falling from her lips are true.

THIRTY THREE

ROOKE

In the last moments before dawn, Prince Roan wakes from his healing sleep.

He blinks rapidly and a low groan vibrates from his chest, his body tensing as he jerks his limbs. A cold sweat breaks out over his forehead, and before he truly regains consciousness, he speaks.

"Airlie. Where is my wife?"

A lump forms at the back of my throat, his devotion to her as beautiful as hers to him, and I step forward through the darkness of the room, lit only by the woodburning stove still burning to ward off the healing chills. "She's alive and she's safe. I'll bring her down to you if you'd like?"

His eyes don't turn in my direction, the sweat beading on his forehead until it drips down his temples. He grits his teeth together and nods, a simple jerk of his head. I quickly dart to the door to ask the soldiers to call for the princess, their presence a constant that I've learned to put out of my mind already as I work.

Tauron arrived at the healer's quarters moments after Prince Soren left, the box with my mother's robes in them tucked under his arm. I should regret my brash words to him, and I'm sure he'll make me do so soon enough, but my sister's sweet name falling from those cruel lips was untenable, worse even than the sarcastic drawl of my brother's name in the hut.

Pemba would have *so* much to say about this Fates-cursed mate of mine.

Prince Tauron slumbers as Roan's groans get louder, the pain of the poison's effect on his body rolling through him in waves, and I retrieve the tincture to measure out two more drops. If only he could down an entire bottle of it and walk away a new man…but it's too strong for that. Any more than a few drops a day would kill him as his body burned bright and short.

Tauron wakes with a start moments before I feel a tug in my chest and hear the rush of footsteps coming down the hall toward us, jumping to his feet as he rubs a hand down his face with a sheepish look. Our eyes meet, and I raise a brow at him, smug at his lapse. These princes are running themselves ragged protecting the castle and running around the kingdom collecting supplies for their beloved family, but I'll make no excuses for any of them, no matter the consequences. I'm done giving kindnesses to those who spit in my face in return.

The doors to the healer's quarters open as I ease the spoon with two drops between Roan's lips, murmuring quiet instructions and reassurances that it's going to help him. He takes it without any trouble, his chest heaving as he pants through the last of the pains. The elixir soaks into him, and his skin begins to glow once more, brighter and brighter until he lights up the entire room.

"Roan," Airlie says, the word breaking on a sob that wrenches deep from her soul.

Her arms are full of their sleeping son as she stumbles into the room, distraught from her worry and exhaustion. Prince Soren catches her elbow, keeping her feet underneath her, but she turns to hand me the baby as sobs begin to rack her body. I take him easily, folding his tiny form into my own chest as I soothe him back into a content slumber.

The princes look away from the little bundle, but I'm not worried about their actions. Airlie made it clear she wanted no one else to hold the baby until her husband could see him and, besides Firna and I, no one has even attempted to look at the infant. There is a lot of talk about him throughout the castle, maids and soldiers whispering joyfully at the curse finally being broken and the arrival of a new Snowsong heir, but they've kept their eyes averted.

Prince Soren made his command perfectly clear.

Airlie hovers over Roan's still form, dropping to her knees by the pallet as tears roll down her cheeks. Her hands frame his face, and she whispers to him, "My love, you've returned to me safely."

He swallows as he frowns, his mind still clouded, but he raises a hand to thread through the golden curls that fall over his chest. "You're alive. I thought the curse would take you, Bluebell, I thought it would take everything from me this time."

She smiles through her tears and leans forward to press a gentle kiss against his lips, pulling away to scowl at the sweat on his forehead. She tucks a hand into her sleeve and wipes the moisture away.

Her voice attempts a teasing tone, but the tears are still too thick to pull it off well. "I would never leave you, Snow-boy, the Fates themselves couldn't part us. Something happened while you were healing. The Fates have granted us a miracle."

His eyebrows bunch together as his eyes start to focus, the elixir continuing to work its magic in aiding his body to heal and the clarity in his face growing as each moment passes by.

Airlie looks up at me and reaches out for her son, and I step around the pallet to gently place him back in his mother's arms.

When his gaze falls on his infant son, Roan's eyes don't just widen in disbelief, they grow until they seem to take over his entire face. He stares at the small bundle, the same awed disbelief radiating from him in waves just like Airlie when she'd stared at her newborn son on the birthing bed. The desperate hope he was too afraid to put into words shines through his eyes too, even as the young baby wakes and begins to mewl, eager for his next meal.

Airlie whispers, tears heavy in her voice, "He's alive, Roan, we did it. We broke the curse, and our son is here, just as the Fates promised us."

Stepping away from them both, I turn my back to give them some privacy, and I look out the window for a moment. As the sun breaks over the horizon and the first rays of morning filter into the healer's quarters, I feel the Fates begin to sing under my scars.

It's a magical moment, filled with the simple wonders of the kingdom around us, and I never grow tired of such a thing. There were many mornings when I worked surrounded by the injured and dying in the Northern Lands that I thought it might be the last time I saw a sunrise. For many of those I tended to, it was.

Prince Soren dismisses Tauron to get some rest, the two of them careful not to disturb the reunion of their closest kin. Tauron never breathes a word about his failure to stay awake on his guard shift, an offense punishable by death in the Sol Army—he just walks out of the healer's quarters and disappears to his own rooms.

I get back to my preparations, moving the cuttings I gathered from the healer's garden at Ravenswyrd and setting them out on the large window sills for cultivation. My magic seeps into the water and fuses with them, strengthening and giving them life as I eagerly plan out the garden to ensure a plentiful crop.

I couldn't take cuttings of everything; there weren't enough leather satchels for that, and some plants are far too delicate to travel in the satchels, but I chose the plants I thought would be most useful to the people of Yregar and the victims of this war that find refuge here.

Wounds from the battlefield, pain management, and everything a newborn baby could possibly require to thrive through his first year, the months ahead ticking through my mind. Babies grow so quickly, moving through many different stages, and I want to be sure to see him through them as gently as I can. The ordeal of the curse that haunted him as he grew in his mother's belly has opened up a soft spot within me for the baby, not just that he survived it all, but some sort of penance for the evil acts of my kind.

"When can Roan come back to our rooms? I want to tend to him there—our bed is far more comfortable than this cot," Airlie says a short while later.

When I look over, she's cradling her squirming son to her chest as he begins to fuss for his food in earnest. There's no good option to host her down here, but I can't have them moving Roan quite yet either.

Glancing at the maid standing at the door, I ask her, "Can you bring the princess a more comfortable seat, please?"

The maid ducks her head and scurries off, clearly eager to leave my presence, and I walk around Prince Soren to gently guide Airlie to a roughly carved wooden seat for now. My gaze drops to Roan's prone body, finding him asleep once more, the loving reunion and joyful news having wiped him out of his small reserve of energy.

"He's going to need one more dose of the elixir, and then I'll reassess his condition. You're welcome to stay in here with him for a few more hours this morning, and we'll move him up to his own bed once he wakes. The walk will be good for him."

Airlie sighs in relief, her body deflating as all the tension that she held inside rushes out of her at once. "Thank you for the elixir, Rooke."

It's the first time she's used my name, at least to me, and the melodic sound of it is different to the way the Seelie high fae had spoken it, different even than the Goblin King, with his very particular accent. It sounds the way my brother says it, the way my family once said it, and I nod my head to acknowledge her courtesy as I turn away, a lump growing in my throat again that makes it impossible to speak.

The maid brings down a more comfortable chair, as I requested, plush and with plump pillows spilling from it as the maid struggles to carry it. As she gets it placed close to the cot, Airlie murmurs a thank you before she sits to finish feeding her son, singing a quiet melody under her breath as she watches me work.

Prince Soren squeezes her shoulder before leaving as well, barking orders to the soldiers as he goes, and I sigh and busy myself with preparing more tinctures as I shove the thoughts of him out of my mind once more. My efforts this time will be focused on pain relief and shortening fevers, the two most likely ailments to be brought to me.

I don't attempt to make conversation with the princess, but she doesn't seem bothered by my silence, minding herself and her son as she leaves me to my work. I smile at the pretty tones of the song she sings to her son and husband, the old language falling from her lips in the sweetest of melodies, a beautiful sound on its own.

The song is ancient, a lullaby about the way that the Southern Lands look in the winter and the provisions it's required to bring forth during the equinox. It's a timely reminder of the rites we should be preparing for and, as I hum along quietly under my breath, I find myself puzzling over Airlie and her folk.

If the high fae have forgotten such things, why does the princess know the words to this ancient rhyme?

Stumbling and supported by two of his closest friends, Roan walks to his own chambers later that afternoon to finish healing under the watchful eye of his wife and in the presence of the miracle that is his son. The next morning, I wake before dawn and begin moving the jars of plant cuttings outside with me, placing them in the planter to map out my garden.

It's an important task to ensure there's enough space for each of them to thrive. There's no way I will be able to convince Prince Soren to escort me back into the Ravenswyrd forest anytime soon, so I have one opportunity to get this healer's garden growing as it needs to.

I can't let something as simple and avoidable as root binding or conflicting growth patterns ruin this.

One of the maids comes looking for me midmorning with a tray ready for Princess Airlie's morning cup of tea, and I prepare it for her as well as another for Prince Roan.

The maid scowls at it as though presenting the Snowsong prince with a remedy is a difficult task, and I warn her, my voice stern, "He must drink it if he wants to continue his quick healing, otherwise he will be stuck in that bed for weeks to come and will be a burden on the castle should we be attacked."

She dips her head and carries the tray carefully from the room, and I curse under my breath as I watch her go. I chose my words with care, knowing exactly which ones would itch at a high-fae male's ego, and when she returns hours later with an empty tray, I note he's consumed it all.

The days pass in the same pattern. I wake and tend to the garden and then spend my days preparing teas for the high-fae royals and tinctures for good health and various ailments in the afternoon. I use all the supplies that I collected from the forest, ensuring none of them go to waste. All of them except the small cluster of moonstones that I tucked into one of the leather bags. I'd found them in the small pot by the garden gate where my coven had placed them to charge with power, and now they're infused with centuries-worth.

No matter how many times I tell myself that I'm a healer and nothing more, that this war is not my own and my fate is to marry Prince Soren and aid him to take his throne, not to protect these people, I can't deny that I grabbed them without thinking of a tincture or elixir.

I thought of war.

How far do I offer such knowledge and protections? How far am I willing to go for these people?

Even the part-bloods and lower fae look at me with fear and wariness. Though Firna explained why the Unseelie fae folk recoil from me, I know the people of this kingdom are never going to thank me or even think kindly of me, no matter my words or actions here. I knew this before I stepped foot in the Ravenswyrd Forest once more, and I knew the Fates were not commanding me to take the moonstones from the garden, yet I did it, and the die was cast. No matter how busy I keep myself, they whisper at the back of my mind until I have no choice but to make a plan.

The Ravenswyrd Coven does whatever needs to be done with no payment required, but I never expected preparations for war to be included in this creed.

When the maid comes down the next morning, bright and early, for the tray of teas, I hold up a hand to her to stop her from taking them. "This is Prince Roan's, and you may take it to him, however Princess Airlie will need to come down here to see me with the baby."

The maid looks taken aback at the instruction, but I don't give her time to make protests as I continue, "I need to check the baby and discuss with Airlie her condition before I continue making tea, otherwise it could bring her harm. I must discuss this with her and no one else. Her medical decisions are hers alone to make."

I almost feel sorry for the maid when she blanches, but she takes the freshly brewed cup and places it on the tray, then steps out of the room.

I brace myself for Prince Soren to appear in the doorway, slinging insults and curses faster than he can draw his sword, but I'm pleasantly surprised when only minutes later, there's a sharp knock and Airlie steps through.

The baby is sleeping in a simple sling across her chest, stretchy fabric in the royal blue hue bound through a silver ring. The princess is wearing a far more simple gown than her usual attire, still in the royal blue and trimmed with silver but without the lush skirts or intricate embroidery. With buttons down the front to assist her in feeding her son and sleeves that are looser on her arms for her comfort, it's exactly the type of gown she should be wearing.

She smiles at me as she steps in, no signs of worry on her face, and when she steps up to the workbench I gesture at the small wooden chair there. "Sorry it's not more comfortable. I would have come up to see you instead, but I have something I need to discuss with you as well."

There's no point dancing around the topic, and though Airlie's brows pinch together at my revelation, she nods, rubbing a hand over the fabric of the sling and resettling her son as he squirms against her.

"Whatever it is, I'll be happy to help. Is Soren giving you trouble about your garden? Because I've already told him there's nothing to fear about plants."

There's plenty to fear about plants.

Her husband was almost killed by a poison derived from

one of the flowers growing a few paces away from us in the freshly tilled soil, but I keep that small observation to myself for now. It won't help my case, and I need her help for this.

"If nothing else, I hope I've proved to you that I mean you and your son no harm. I'd do just about anything in my power to stop harm from befalling him."

She cocks her head and nods. "Roan and I have agreed on that much, though my cousins are still skeptical."

I think skeptical is far too soft a word for their feelings, but I'm not about to muddy the conversation by pointing that out. I finish brewing her tea and push the china cup across the table to her, meeting her clear gaze as she thanks me for it.

"I have a lot of knowledge of magic outside of healing. When I was a young girl, I was trained to take over as the Mother of the coven someday, and I learned the skills to create talismans for many uses. I brought back enough ingredients from the forest to create a ward around the castle. Do you know what a ward is?"

Her frown deepens, and she takes the tea cup, sipping at the bitter flavor without wincing, accustomed to it now after days of my care. "I've never seen one myself, but you're talking about a boundary around the castle."

I nod slowly, reaching out to take the baby from her and laying him on a small bundle of cloths on the workbench. I check him over, carefully looking at his reflexes and feeling the hefty weight of him now that he's flourishing with her milk and hard work.

"It would be undetectable to the high fae and the witches, but it has many uses that could help if they attack."

She purses her lips and turns to look out the window at the guards that walk the walls. The extra protections haven't eased up, and while reports of more attacks throughout the kingdom arrive every day, there's been no sign of the witches advancing here yet.

My greatest concern now are the wagons that should be traveling here from the Western Fyres, carrying a month's supply of food for the people of Yregar. There's no doubt of where the witches will attack Prince Soren next. It's outside of my abilities to protect them—I'm limited by the prince's distrust of me—but the wards aren't. Better they all know as little about them as possible; it will help me to convince them to allow it.

I keep my eyes on the prince in front of me as I fuss with him, keeping my voice light as I say, "Think of it as an early detection system. I'll know the moment they arrive at the wall, and I'll be able to help you guard the baby until the soldiers have fought them off."

Airlie sighs and looks down at her son, sleeping once more on the table, undisturbed as I button his small suit back up. I'm happy with the flush of his skin and the plumpness of his limbs, all great signs of a healthy baby.

"I was taught how to swing a sword from the same age as Soren—all Celestial children are. I was apt at the skill, but I'd rather not fight with my son in my care, not unless I have to."

Leaning forward, I clasp her hand with mine. "You're heavily guarded here and are the priority of the entire castle, not just your husband and cousins. From what I've seen of the people here so far, I doubt you'll be taking up a sword anytime soon, Princess."

I wrap the baby back up in the blankets, and she finishes off the last of her tea. "Did you fight while you were in the Sol Army, or were you only a healer in your time?"

A sad smile stretches across my lips. "Every healer in the Sol Army fought at one point or another. We didn't have the luxury of healing camps or the safety of castle walls. If you didn't know how to use a sword, you'd die alongside those you were trying to help. If an enemy makes it all the way to your chambers, you won't have to pick up a sword, Princess. I'll make sure of that."

She smiles and takes her son from me, easing him back into the sling and nodding to me once more. "What do you need for the ward? I'll help you to lay your talismans wherever they need to be."

With a sigh of relief, I explain the process to her. She listens intently and asks questions where she needs to, an intelligent ally to have. When she leaves me once more, humming under her breath at her son as she goes about the tasks, I begin assembling the pouches. Moonstone and unopened sundrop buds, leaves from the fae flowers and drops of my blood, I seal them together with the words of power my mother taught me. Using a small spool of thread and a sharp needle Firna brought me, I sew together pouches from torn scraps of linen until they're assembled and ready. I'm not sure I have enough to cover the inner walls of Yregar but there's no going back for more moonstones, so I'll have to make it work.

The guards watch it all but whether it looks like a banal task or they've been instructed to merely observe and report, I don't know but they leave me to my task in peace.

A maid comes down with a simple slice of bread and the smallest wedge of cheese for my lunch, hours of work passing the day quickly. I take the food with a nod of thanks and, as she leaves, Airlie steps back into the room. She's changed out of her comfortable dress and into one more suited to walking, but the sling is still securely wrapped around her, her precious cargo sleeping steadily.

She smiles at me in greeting, delivering her news without preamble. "I've spoken with my husband, and we both went to Soren. I told him that it's nothing more than an old tale, that couldn't possibly do anything, but my cousin still wants to escort us as we work. I'm ready now, if you are?"

Curse the man, I want nothing to do with him even as my stomach clenches in anticipation.

My spirit is still sore from the last time I was forced to endure him, but I nod to her, grabbing the leather satchel holding the talismans as I shove the bread and cheese into my mouth. There's not much there, and in two hearty bites, my lunch is done.

I follow the princess out of the healer's quarters and through to the courtyard, taking a deep breath before I face my Fates-cursed mate once more, shutting off the soft healer's heart within me so he can't do any further damage to my fraught temper.

THIRTY FOUR

SOREN

The witch stands with a leather satchel bound around her arm and a frosty look on her face as she descends the last of the castle steps into the courtyard beside Airlie. Her eyes never turn toward me, whatever attempt she was making to find common ground now abandoned, and a cold smirk of satisfaction stretches across my lips.

"Soren, you promised me a peaceful walk," Airlie snaps.

I glance back to find her scowling at me, disapproval dripping from her. The baby is sleeping in the sling across her chest, and she's wearing a comfortable dress. Her beloved heels have been switched out for a pair of flat boots for the walk.

Worry still tugs at my chest, the small bundle in the sling too precious to be out on errands like this. "Is it safe for him to join us?"

The witch raises an eyebrow, but her gaze stays glued to the soldiers lining Yregar's inner wall that encases the castle. "I'm certain that *you're* the one joining *us* for the walk, but it's good for the baby and the princess to get fresh air and a bit of light exercise. We won't go too far—this doesn't all have to be done today."

Airlie tilts up her chin in victory, gloating as she waves an arm at the witch to lead the way, and we walk through the courtyard and up one of the staircases on the inner wall. Two soldiers—Reed and Alwyn— flank us, just to be sure that none of the villagers attempt to approach my cousin, and I called ahead orders for the soldiers already patrolling the village to prepare for our arrival.

The northern expanse of the inner wall is the only barrier between the village and the castle. Though we keep the gates open and guarded throughout the day, the deep unrest within the village isn't something I take lightly. What snippets of truth I can discover here with this fruitless task is worth the risk and though three of the talismans the witch wants to bury will put us in contact with the village, the guards will stay with Airlie and the witch to ensure nothing goes awry. No matter how sure I am that I won't need it, my sword hangs ready at my side as I guard my cousin and her baby.

"Do witches have naming days?" Airlie asks, and I roll my eyes, tipping my head back to stare up at the sky and the Fates above for a moment.

The baby's life is worth a lot of things, even the witch becoming Airlie's new favorite obsession to dissect, but that doesn't mean I'm going to enjoy being forced to listen to all of this, no matter how soothing her tones are to me when she's speaking calmly to my cousin and not the harsh ones she gives to me.

"We do. The next new moon after a baby is born, we hold the naming rites. It's usually a quiet affair, calm and supportive for the mother's health, but we do call the baby's name out to the Fates before the sun rises again. Witches believe that we're all given to this earth by the Fates to serve its needs, of course, but claiming the baby as one of our own and bringing them into the fold of the coven is a vital part of our beliefs."

Airlie nods, casting a long look toward the haggard line of villagers at the temple below us. "The high fae do the same, I suppose, but with a larger party and more wine. I finally let my mother come to see the baby, and she's insisting on inviting the entire Unseelie Court to meet him."

I shake my head, my voice cold, but only about her mother's involvement, "It's too risky for such an event. She's going to have to get over her desires for pageantry and gloating."

Airlie chuckles under her breath, adjusting the sling a little as the baby wriggles within. "Oh, she would love nothing more than to parade us both around under the regent's nose and fawn over my son publicly so that everybody could congratulate her for such a wondrous gift. Roan and I discussed it, and we'd like something much smaller. We're hoping you will name him for us, Soren."

A lump forms in my throat but she meets my eye with a small smile before she turns away, happy to leave my own reaction to such an honor private and not display it to the witch. Amongst the high fae, naming a child doesn't mean choosing the name for them, of course, Airlie and Roan will do that themselves. Naming refers to the ceremony that our people once took part in before the curse. It's an honor they're giving to me, and I would give my blessing to the baby first out of those in attendance.

Even now that Roan is home and well, I've barely laid eyes on the child. Airlie is far too protective to hand him around, fearful of the baby catching an illness or somehow having harm befall him, but I have seen that he looks just like his father, with perfectly Seelie-gold eyes shining back up at us.

Firna told Airlie that the color might still change, some babies' eyes do during the first year, but my cousin only smiled and nodded, happy to have as much of her husband shining back up at her as the Fates choose.

The witch pauses, looking over the side of the inner wall as she assesses the spot below, and Airlie clears her throat delicately and says to her, "Roan and I would like you to join us for the naming ceremony as well. Please, Rooke, it would be a great honor for us to have you in attendance."

The glare I send my cousin is clearly expected, because the moment I turn to her, she's already glaring back at me defiantly, one eyebrow raised and her head cocked as she baits me to argue with her.

The witch studies Airlie carefully as we pass the sentries, and when my cousin gives her a questioning look, she nods. "You're moving well, it's good to see, and I thank you for the honor of the invitation. I wouldn't miss it."

Airlie smiles, and her expression is like the first rays of sunlight after a great storm, her shoulders rolled back and her posture perfect as she radiates joy. It's an emotion I haven't seen from her since her first pregnancy, a joy I wasn't sure she would ever be capable of again. I know that the memory of her first son still lies heavy in her heart, but with her second son sleeping safely on her chest, she once again has hope of a future she always dreamed of. Children she shares with her husband and a long lineage for their house.

A future the Fates are also dangling before me, only a twisted and distorted version of that joy.

I step away from the two of them to speak to one of the soldiers, checking that the village has been peaceful all morning and there's no sign of danger down there. If anyone attacks, the staircases can be sealed to keep Airlie safe up here, but I'd rather not leave her side.

I have more experience with the rituals and talismans of our enemy than Airlie does, thanks to the war, so when she sought me out to ask about the ward, I was well aware of what the witch was doing. Casting a boundary around the castle and claiming it for herself, so that any witches who come here will know she resides here and will look for her.

It's nothing more than a declaration of inhabitation, and

harmless to the castle. We've crossed a hundred ward lines in battle and never lost a single high-fae life because of them. I don't know why the witch is bothering, but if she wants to wave her flag over this castle, then I'll play along, let her weave her deceptions…and drown her in them the moment I can.

She's watched so closely that we'll know the moment she prepares to strike.

My first reaction was to say no, of course, but I need to draw her out, let her think she's slowly worked her way into our good graces so when she eventually moves to betray us, I'll be three steps ahead. I'll step into the game alongside her and entrap her with her own confidence. She'll have to get over her seething fury at me if she wants to get back to digging her way under my skin. Too bad for her there are no cracks in this armor.

Airlie and Roan will be devastated when her acts of salvation to them are proved nothing more than calculated moves, but that will spur them on for retribution. I waited a thousand years for this Fates-cursed mate; my patience is now ironclad and ready for the tumultuous future ahead.

The witch presses her hands against the stone, staring over the small turret and the village to the barren farming plains beyond the outer wall. Her gaze follows the Lore River as it runs past the castle, and I'm certain she's planning out the positions of her little pouches of deception.

She ignores the murmuring of the high-fae soldiers around her as she closes her eyes and takes a deep breath. The air up here is clearer than in the castle or down in the village, the desperation and stink of a crowded population beneath us waiting for our return.

Her eyes open, and she looks at Airlie.

Her voice is firm, that of a healer who expects nothing but full compliance from her patients. "You and the baby need to stay up here where it's safe. It'll be too strenuous for you to walk up and down all of these stairs needlessly."

As meek as a springtime lamb, my cousin nods and leans against the stone wall. She, too, looks out at the destroyed plains that were once a thriving farmland and are now a dust bowl. "I'm quite happy up here. Although, I have so much energy after all those days being cooped up in my bedroom that I'm quite looking forward to the walk around the perimeter."

I frown—there's no way I'm going to let her walk the entire distance with us—but the witch simply nods. "I'm not sure Prince Soren has time to make the entire journey, but I'm happy to take it easy. With some breaks to sit down, the walk will be good for you."

Airlie smiles again and watches happily as the witch follows me down the second set of stairs that lead to the outer side of the wall. The small door at the base of the wall, tucked closely to the gate, is made of solid iron and with steel bars locked into place, one each at the top, middle and bottom. It's impenetrable and always has been, and the witch takes no notice of the offending metal as she drops to her knees and murmurs a prayer to the Fates in the old language, the words rolling off her tongue like a melody.

Even with the trowel, it's hard work for her to bury the satchel in the hardened clay, but once she deems the hole deep enough, she drops it in without ceremony and then scoops the clay back over it. As she presses on the mound to flatten it out, her magic seeps into the earth around it, her eyes flashing silver as she murmurs words of anchoring and concealment.

I'm expecting her to cut her hand open and press her blood into it as well, but she doesn't, simply sending the tendrils of her power down to secure the talisman in place. I watch as her hands glow, the shine from her eyes lighting up the clay, and the magic soaks into the earth. It's subtle and peaceful, but my stomach clenches as I feel the magic, a foreign sensation to me.

It's a lesser but similar sensation to the fae door, something *else* around me that I can't see or hear fully but there's no doubt it's there. I don't usually sense magic like this, at least, not anything more than the Fates tugging and pulling at me, and yet…as she pushes power into the talisman, something stirs deep in my chest.

When the witch straightens and brushes at her skirts, she doesn't show any concern at my scowling fury or the suspicion written all over me, just follows me without a word as I lead her back up the staircase. I lock the door securely behind us, my hands steady despite the overwhelm in my mind, her calm demeanor irritating me further.

I want to poke at her, to claw at her mind the way she does mine, but her promise of death still lies between us. The threat was treasonous enough to have her hanged even if she wasn't a witch, but I keep all the cutting words trapped inside my chest as I observe her instead.

Walking with them both for a third of the castle wall, I listen as Airlie leads the conversation, asking question after question about the work of the witches and their former role within our kingdom. The witch answers her patiently, setting a snail's pace and watching as Airlie comes to life the more she moves. This outing *is* good for her, if nothing else.

When we reach the watchtower to the north, I see horses riding toward the castle walls—messengers arriving—and I leave Airlie and the witch there under the protection of Reed and Alwyn and make my way back to the castle in haste. Far too much of my day has already been taken up with this fruitless task.

I stop outside my reception room only to find my aunt waiting there, forcing me to take a calming breath as I try to remember all the reasons I can't kill her. Aura's arms are crossed, a haughty look across her face, and one of her guards stands at her shoulder, cringing away from the ire she's emanating.

Too bad for her, I'm not so easily cowed.

I give her a smirk as I say, "I have messengers to see first, Aura, you'll have to wait."

Though I was hoping my irreverent treatment and the long wait would scare her away, Aura stomps into my reception room two hours later, more irate than I've ever seen her before. I have no sympathy for her, the sound of her silver and diamond bracelets clinking together grating on my last nerve.

"I'm not leaving this room until you assure me that you're going to pry this witch out of Airlie's heart and push her into the flames of the Fates where she belongs," Aura snaps as I shut the door behind me, no greeting or respect given as she rages.

I raise an eyebrow at her until, grudgingly, she stands and bows, every part of the action clearly grating on her as shown by her jerky movements. I walk around the desk and take my seat before I nod for her to do the same, accommodating even as I bite my tongue against the hard truths I want to hit this female with.

Shoving her out of the castle gates is the only course of action I want to take but, without offering her an escort, it isn't safe for her to return to the Unseelie Court, and if anything were to happen to her, the vote she holds doesn't pass on to her daughter.

Unfortunately, Aura has a cousin who, by the twisted and fickle laws of the Unseelie high fae, would take her seat on the court before Airlie. Ayron is obsessed with the regent, all of my uncle's syrupy lies and philandering ways singing to the indulgent corners of the male's heart, and with a single rash action the regent would gain the majority.

Someday I'll change the laws and wipe the simpering, useless heads of families from the court I will cultivate, but for now, Aura's loyalty to the direct bloodline of the Celestial family works in her favor.

"I can't kill the witch, Aura, you've already been told why. I wouldn't be so concerned about your daughter's heart, it's far stronger than you will ever know."

She scoffs and pushes back in her seat, her hands flapping in front of her dramatically. I wonder how she ever learned to navigate the Unseelie Court if it's this easy to rile her, or whether this is just a show, a carefully cultivated relationship between us that she's now trying to exploit to get her way. The birth of Airlie's son didn't go the way she expected, and now she's lost ground in her efforts to bring her heir and new grandson home.

Her distaste for Roan is the reason I'll never trust this female, no matter what pretty stories she weaves, and she knows it too.

The day the two of them married, many centuries ago now, was the first time I told Aura exactly what I thought of her, brash in my youth and uncaring of the consequences. I hadn't yet watched hundreds of thousands die, hadn't experienced the true depravity of the war, and there was still an arrogance within me that thought I could convince the Fates to give me my mate sooner. It was a hard lesson to learn, the Seer's words were immovable, but an effective one; I've never again forgotten the power they hold over me.

She tries again, her tone wheedling and edged with the fury she won't ever truly show. "The days after a baby is born are very delicate, Soren. You wouldn't know this because of the curse, but this is the perfect time for the witch to enchant Airlie and twist her mind away from reason. Roan has never been strong enough to call his wife into line. If you don't do it, no one will."

I count my breaths.

It's a slow act to give myself time to find my patience, reminding myself of all the reasons this woman should stay alive. Granted, the list is small and growing shorter by the minute. Every lashing insult strikes another line from it, until I'm left with the balance of the Unseelie Court and that alone.

Eventually I'm able to speak with a level voice once more. "What happens between Roan and Airlie has never been and will never be any of your business. Your daughter is married to her Fates-blessed mate. They're a family now, and what they choose to do with their lives is none of your concern. Before you start up your tirade against Roan, Aunt, I should remind you that he's upstairs healing from the injuries he took while defending our kingdom from our enemy, all while your own husband didn't bother to leave the wining and dining of the Unseelie Court to wish his daughter well and meet his new grandson."

The insults and critiques fly straight past her, glancing off the armor of arrogance she wraps around herself, her mind focusing on one thing alone. "Injuries Roan took while fighting *witches,* and yet while he was traipsing around the Outlands, abandoning his pregnant wife at her greatest hour of need, there was a witch here in this castle, granted freedoms by all of you, simply because she knows the names of some plants and can brew a pot of tea! These are not the decisions of a king, Soren! Not one strong enough to lead this kingdom and restore our way of life."

It's a peculiar feeling to defend the witch so vehemently, but for Airlie's sake I will. "I think you forget that your grandson is alive because the witch broke the curse. He is the first full-blooded high-fae baby born in centuries, a whole generation of life to come, because that curse is gone. Accept that this castle is under my rule and my word is law, or leave. Make the journey back to Yris and the Unseelie Court with nothing but the guards you brought with you, but know that it's a long way home, Aura, and a miracle of the Fates that you made it here unscathed in the first place."

I smear a hand over the parchment in front of me, her gaze following my fingers as I run them over the numbers from the messengers. "The attacks are doubling every day now that the witches know the curse is broken, and they're scrambling to keep the high fae too busy to recover from the evil they held over us all this time. Who knows if they'll be able to cast the curse once more, or if my Fates-blessed mate will be able to break it again if they do. For now, the kingdom is a bloodbath, and your choices are very limited."

Aura's face sours like old milk, the lines deepening around her mouth as she grimaces. It detracts from her natural beauty, the same she passed on to her daughter, and I struggle to see that beauty now that her sharp tongue and meddling ways mar it.

"Your Fates-*blessed* mate? What are you going to do, Soren, marry her? You'll marry a witch and place her on your mother's throne? I'm glad she's not here to see how far her son has fallen. You're supposed to protect your people, not shove a crown on your enemy's filthy head!"

I shuffle the papers once more, carefully looking for the exact parchment and plucking it out of the pile where I'd hidden it. Her eyes flick down, an eyebrow rising as I've caught her attention.

"I sent messengers across the seas to speak with the Sol King about trading routes and a treaty between us once I am king. One of the messengers brought this back, a warning of what's to come if I turn my back on the path the Seer laid out before me."

I slide the image across the table at her, the carefully rendered likeness that the Sol King himself had brought to life with his magic in the most horrifying way. Hamyr told me that the regent was being sent one as well, a thorough warning to any and all who may rule to understand our responsibilities to the Fates and wholly surrender ourselves to their commands.

It's a warning and a promise—the Seelie Court won't take any defiance of the Fates lightly.

I watch Aura's face crack, her grimace turning into gaping terror as she shoves it away again and cringes against her chair. There's no color left in her cheeks, a fine tremor rippling over her. My own reaction was similar, the creature unlike any I've seen before and more horrifying the longer I stared at it, and one thought has plagued me since Hamyr held the parchment out to me, his own hand trembling as well.

The witch has seen one up close.

There's none of my own reaction in my voice as I say firmly, "That's a Ureen, Aura. Do you know what they are? The nightmares that haunted the Northern Lands for centuries, falling from the sky and consuming *everything*. I think only of my kingdom, as I have from the moment my parents were murdered. I can't share your sentiment, though—my mother's death lies heavy on my shoulders."

Her breaths heave out of her chest, her hand clutching at the lace panel on the front, delicately tatted and sewn on by skilled hands. There are jewels decorating her pointed ears and her hair, diamonds around her wrists interspersed with sapphires, and a large ring sits on her finger, a symbol of the vows she spoke with that spineless husband of hers. All of her finery is on display, and in the dire situation we're in, it's nothing but gaudy and tasteless.

I motion toward the door, dismissive and done with her games. "You need to leave, Aunt. I have too much business to see to and not enough hours in the day to argue like this with you."

She trembles in her seat, still horrified by the image, and I move a stack of parchments over it once more to help her regain her wits.

When she finally leans forward in the seat, gulping dramatically, the color is still absent from her face as she croaks to me, "I'll help you arrange the wedding. Airlie is of no mind for such things while caring for the baby, and this isn't a simple ball to leave to the castle staff. The Unseelie Court will be in attendance, all of them, and it must be strictly planned and executed if you're to take your throne. The regent himself cannot deny you the crown, so long as we do it right."

I might just slip Airlie that image to use against her mother, if this is the result.

There's a new meekness to her form as she reaches out with a shaking hand once more, taking a blank piece of parchment and one of the ink pens I have sitting on my desk. "I'll write the list of the families you must invite along with all of the Unseelie Court. We could arrange it for the autumn equinox, but winter solstice is better, more apt for such an occasion."

She glances toward where the monster hides under a stack of other papers now, gulping as she rasps, "If we have time to wait, that is. If the Fates demand it happen sooner, then I'll make the necessary changes."

I shake my head, looking at the list of attacks before me. The messengers arrive daily, stepping through the fae door and riding their horses as though chased by the monsters of the Fates as they battle their way back to me through the enemy-infested lands.

There are hundreds of villages between here and the Witches Ward, hundreds of thousands of lower fae and part-bloods within. All of them have long been abandoned by the regent, but now I'm forced to pull my forces back to Yregar, leaving them defenseless and without hope of aid. While we don't have room for more refugees, I sent out word through my scouting riders regardless.

Come to Yregar. We will not turn you away, we'll find space for you, and food.

No one has arrived at the castle gates yet, but whether that's a hesitancy to travel this far south with a long winter ahead or simply the fact that there are no survivors, I won't know until more scouts arrive. Each of them has been tasked with the most dangerous work, and many won't return, more casualties in this fruitless conflict. Despair takes hold in my gut as I fear the worst, the spiral into oblivion for our people only spinning faster as the days drag on.

Aura glances around my sparse reception room, her eyes disapproving, but she chooses her words with far more care now that she's been forced to face the reality of our situation. "The Unseelie Court demands a traditional high-fae wedding. The Celestial family's Fates temple here in the castle will have to be prepared, decorated, and cleaned thoroughly. The witch will need a dress for the ceremony, and another for her introduction to the court. Celestial family jewels to adorn her, but only after the cleansing preparations have been done to her body. The feast after the ceremony must be enough to sustain an entire day and night of festivities. Then there's the marriage bed. Someone will have to stand guard and herald the consummation—that will be a very *delicate* position to fill."

She looks at me again and clears her throat, the prospect of anyone bedding a witch enough to rattle her, but she continues, "I'll send out the invitations to the Unseelie Court, but is Yregar prepared to host such an event? The kitchens have only sent up bread and a few paltry apples for my meals. Will there be enough food to feed a thousand high fae for the wedding and however long they choose to stay afterwards in celebration of your nuptials?"

I flick a hand in her direction, my eyes again on the correspondence in front of me so she can't see my reaction to

---

the list of rites I'll be forced to undertake.

The noose tightens around my neck with every breath as my fate begins to edge toward me.

"You worry about who's coming and where you're going to sit them in the Fates temple. Leave the provisions of Yregar to me."

As she stands and takes the parchment with her, ready to work on it up in the guest chambers, I grimace and drive home the last of the bad news. "Ensure the Goblin King is on the list. He's already confirmed his attendance."

THE CROWN OF OATHS AND CURSES

THIRTY FiVE

ROOKE

The ward sits perfectly around the castle walls, undetectable and strong thanks to the moonstones, ready to assist when the witches finally come to call. They'll come to Yregar, there's no doubt in my mind, and the Fates sing beneath the skin of my scars as they direct the dance we're all forced to endure.

Reed has been assigned to watch over me for now, or maybe he volunteered for the duty, and he shadows me closely as I go about my days in the healer's quarters once more. As the days turn into one week and then two, it becomes clear his only duty is to watch my every move.

When I'm sure I have as many tinctures and elixirs brewed as I can until the next crop flourishes in my gardens, I stop to take stock of what needs to be saved. Some of these vials hold liquid far too precious to use except in times of dire need, and I push those to the back of the shelves and pull forward those I'll be able to replace readily. Some plants take an entire year to establish roots and flourish enough to withstand a harvest, while others, such as the milk thistle, spread in a matter of days, making for only a few short weeks until an abundant crop is established.

A vitality elixir is quick and easy to make, vials lined up on the shelves waiting for me to find a use for them. One drop diluted in clean water is enough to fortify a child, but only once they've cycled through their first year, and it's no longer effective once they reach adulthood. I set aside a bottle of it for Airlie and her son, ready for him next summer, and my mind wanders back to the children I saw in the village, their eyes following me in despair each time I rode past.

When I turn to Reed, I find him sitting on the wooden chair, balancing his chin on his fist as he watches me work. There's a keen sort of interest in his gaze as he soaks in the daily tasks of a healer, as though he's learning everything there is to know about my life's work just by sitting here with me in the quiet.

"I know that look," he says, sighing as he rubs a hand over his face.

This feels like the beginnings of banter between soldiers, entirely too familiar for the stilted interactions we've had until now, but whether I'm softening thanks to Airlie's quiet friendship or just bored, I fall into it.

"How could you possibly know what this look is? You've only been at Yregar for five and a half minutes, ten at most."

He lets out a chuckle, the tips of his ears poking through the long blond hair seen everywhere in the castle thanks to the strong Unseelie bloodlines. He wears it down, with braids on either side of his head—uncommon for a high-fae soldier—but he carries himself with the same confidence as the soldiers of Yregar do, sure in his own abilities.

I haven't seen him fight, but if he's been trained like the rest of them, I'm sure he's a force to be reckoned with. I've watched the soldiers here spar, the barracks visible from the garden over the low-lying stone fence that runs the perimeter, and, though I loathe admitting any positives about Prince Soren, his men are nothing short of impressive.

With vastly honed skills—both unarmed and with swords— they show sharp reflexes and have been well-trained in all forms of combat. The commander puts them through their paces on a daily schedule to ensure they're primed and ready to defend this castle to the end.

Watching Prince Soren step into the sparring ring and demolish fifteen of them as though they were nothing but children had been a sight to see. Hearing rumors of the abilities of the mate the Fates have chosen for me and seeing his prowess in the flesh had left me with a new, if uncomfortable, appreciation for the male.

It was a valuable lesson for me. Prince Soren didn't get the moniker the Savage Prince simply for the scar that runs across his face, despite the snobbery of the Unseelie Court and their unquenchable thirst for perfection. The high-fae male is a beast, and every inch as good with a sword as the rumors declared. A better swordsman than any I've seen myself. If he ever learned to harness the magic within him, slumbering but present as it is in every Unseelie high fae I've come across so far, he'd be unstoppable even against a powerful witch such as Kharl.

It's exactly what he needs to win the war ahead of us.

Whether the Fates put us together for me to teach him to use his magic is beside the point—any teachings I might give him will fall on deaf ears if the man can't get his hatred of my kind out of his mind.

"That's the exact look that you gave Prince Soren right before you tore into him about the morals of our race. I'm just trying to figure out what I did to piss you off and start that lecture back up. I'm not one to take such treatment willingly, and certainly not from a witch."

His tone is lighthearted, but his eyes are serious. It's the first time anyone has acknowledged what I said, but the fact that he's not denying the truth of my words or attempting to minimize them softens his response now. I'm now hoping that Reed will stay at Yregar, for more reasons than just the safety of Airlie and the baby. A voice of reason amongst the high fae is a rare occurrence, one I'm not eager to lose.

I hold up one of the vials. "There's enough elixir in this to improve the health of three hundred children. Do you know how many there are in the village of Yregar?"

His brows pinch together as his eyes stay trained on the ruby-colored liquid within the vial, calculating but not suspicious.

"No, but I can ask. Prince Tyton is sparring in the barracks today to put the soldiers through their paces and ensure no one is slacking off. He should know the answer," he drawls, as though he finds it hilarious to even suggest that the soldiers might lose their edge.

I simply nod back and slip the small glass vial into the pocket of my dress, fussing with the front of it and trying not to wince at the awful cut of the fabric. Reed sees all of this, his eyes far too sharp, and he follows me into the garden to take the shortcut to the barracks. It was only after we cleared the dead tree and debris away that I found the small gate there. I haven't used it until now, but I was quick to tell Firna of its existence, in case any soldiers or returning messengers should need immediate assistance.

My shelves are now stocked with mounds of clean bandages and pain relief in dozens of forms, and I even convinced Firna to bring me a sewing kit. The messengers are all part-bloods, many with high fae in the mix, but there's every chance they won't have heightened healing ability. Blood loss is not something to take lightly, and a few clean stitches will help to aid where the body might struggle under catastrophic damage.

Tyton's eyes narrow as we approach him, his casual smiles and joyful heart having disappeared somewhere in the Ravenswyrd Forest. I'm not sure if his happy nature will ever return after what he experienced there, but I meet his suspicious glare with my chin tilted up, determined never to cower from any of their ire.

"The witch has brewed tinctures and healing remedies. She has one that could help heal the children of the village," Reed says, and I shake my head at him, shifting between the two males to make sure they understand me perfectly.

"Not heal them, but it will help them grow. The children out there are starving and not getting the proper variety of foods and nutrients that they need to develop well. Even once the trading wagons arrive, they'll probably still bring simple foods that can stretch to feed as many as possible. Correct?"

Tyton scowls deeper. "We'll do what we can for everyone, but we only have three trades before midwinter. Our options are limited."

I nod, my face carefully blank. "Keeping them fed is all we truly need to do until the war is over to ensure they survive, but with this elixir, they'll have a better chance of *thriving*. All of the important properties of the foods they're missing out on won't matter so much anymore. Rebuilding a kingdom takes a lot of work—the next generations can't be lacking."

I pull out the vial and hold it in my hand, and I feel the raw bounds of his magic touch it. He might not have full control over his power, but he trusts it, and when his eyes flash bright white for a moment before he nods, I know the biggest hurdle is over with.

He knows the elixir won't hurt the villagers.

I glance between the two males once more and push on. "I've set some aside for Princess Airlie and the baby, but he can't have it until he's passed his first birthday, a full cycle of the seasons complete. There's enough here for three hundred children to get a dose, and I can make more once the garden has settled in. One dose will see them through until next summer and, if Prince Soren deals with the food shortage, things should be better for them all by then. Is this enough, or should I grab another vial?"

Tyton stops to pull off his training armor and place it on the small crate outside of the barracks doors, with a wary look at us both as I stare back at him unflinchingly.

This the most lively area of Yregar I've seen so far, hundreds of high fae going about their duties under the rule of their prince. The soldiers who stream in and out of the building bow their heads to Tyton respectfully even as they murmur quietly amongst themselves about my presence here, not at all worried about me seeing the malice in their eyes as they pass. There are even a few whispers about Reed and his assignment to watch over me, but I ignore those just as easily. Idle gossip is at the base of every community, and to entertain it is to invite it to take root and flourish—better to let it die on bored lips looking for weaker prey.

Tyton lets out a breath finally and shakes his head. "There are only a hundred or so children outside of the orphanage, and fifty who live there, so that's plenty, but you'll have a hard time convincing the parents to take this elixir from you. They won't trust you, and interacting with a witch is to invite death—they all know it well. If you go down there, they'll turn their backs on you or refuse you at their doors."

I look down at the red liquid once more before I take a deep breath and hold it out to him. "One drop in a glass of water, one glass to each child. It's only effective until they reach adulthood, whatever age that is for their race, so there's no use giving it to the adults or the elderly of the village."

Tyton looks at the vial before he takes it, gently squeezing his palm around the glass as though holding an act of magic he's not eager to lose. Whatever else has transpired between us and the song the forest sings in his heart, he trusts my abilities as a healer enough to take up this quiet task.

As he moves to duck back into the barracks and bark out

orders to the soldiers to assist him, I call out to him once more, "I'll go to the orphanage. With Reed at my side, they should let me in, right? I want to go there myself."

Tyton shrugs and agrees, then moves off while I get to work fortifying the castle in every way I possibly can while high-fae soldiers do the same. I can't undo the damage the witches have done to these children and their families, but I can strengthen them and give them the best chance at life. No matter what else happens here at Yregar, I won't forget the fae folk who live beyond the castle walls.

———

Reed stares at the small iron fence around the orphanage as though he's afraid that diseases and a rabid pack of wraiths live within, and I stop myself from pushing the small gate open and turn to him with censure.

"You can't walk in there and be around orphaned children looking like that. They're already set apart from this community, and you'll only make things worse."

I gesture at the fence to prove my point. It's there to keep the children safely within the grounds of the orphanage, but the fact that it's made out of iron is abhorrent, in my opinion. My magic protects me from feeling the true pain of the ghastly metal, but the part-bloods and lower fae within won't be so lucky. They can't open the gate without feeling excruciating pain, and so they're trapped inside.

The high fae have their gloves and leathers to protect them from the iron they wear and wield. They've been smart to use the metal in the first place, to find ways to overcome their own aversion to it to protect themselves from the weaker magic of the raving armies, but to see it here, circling a house built for orphaned children, makes my stomach churn with unease.

I have no reason to believe that anything untoward happens here, but these iron gates have eaten away at the back of my mind until I had to figure out a way in to do a welfare check of my own. There's every chance Tyton is right and the people in charge will deny me access, but I'll use my magic if I need to, send a pulse of power through the building to check the health and well-being of those vulnerable children within.

I don't need the high fae to support me. If I find something I don't like, I'll deal with it myself.

Reed glances at me and runs a hand over his face, unable to shift the scowl there. "I hate these places."

It's hard to stop myself from reacting to the typical high-fae sensibilities, and I *tsk* and shake my head at him, the easy familiarity between us loosening my tongue as I slip back into soldier banter easier than breathing. "You don't want to be around small helpless children? Or is it the part-bloods and lower fae that worry you? You know they're not that different from the high fae, not really. It's a shame you lot never mix with those below your station."

The scowl between his brows deepens. "I don't care about their heritage. As long as they're not witches."

He tacks his disclaimer onto the end as though being sure to clear up any confusion our conversation might expand within me, and I roll my eyes at him as he continues, "Every one of these children has either been dumped here out of desperation by parents who once loved them but couldn't feed them, or they've lost their families to the war."

He stops for a moment, cringing before giving me a sidelong look. "Well, there's a third option, and you should be prepared for it, because I don't need you stomping off back to Prince Soren and blowing up at him."

Nothing will shock me at this point, but I just gesture at him to continue.

"Some of the part-bloods within are probably the bastard children of the high fae, dumped here because they didn't want to suffer the embarrassment of the Unseelie Court gossiping about their trysts with the 'lower folk.'"

I take a deep breath to hold down my anger, but this isn't surprising to me.

These things happened in the Seelie Court as well, though during the war, a great change happened within the heart of the Sol King. As he watched every race of his land come together and fight the Ureen, tooth and nail, to the death, he came to treat every soldier, no matter their race, the same, with respect for their service. They all fought for their kingdom.

After the war, the Sol King made it clear that, while the princes, princesses, lords and ladies of the high fae would still hold their titles and their lands, they were no longer allowed to rule over the lower fae and part-bloods to the fae folks' detriment.

He couldn't change everyone's minds, and there were still many within the Seelie Court who resented such changes, old prejudices and arrogance running deep, but it was the first step toward change and before I left I saw the way the Sol King and his queen were raising their son. The young prince was surrounded by all the people who lived within the Northern Lands, as his father taught him not only to be their king but to lead them all as equals.

Perhaps that's why I judge Prince Soren and this kingdom so harshly. I've seen a far better path laid out, lived within that culture, and offered healing to them all, only to have the Fates lead me back to the Unseelie Court and their destructive ways. I miss the unity of the Northern Lands.

Giving Reed a sidelong look, I shrug and push open the gate, then step into the courtyard of the orphanage and stride confidently to the front door. It's nearing midmorning, and yet the children are still inside, no one playing or enjoying the clear autumn air around us. I don't like the implications, but I raise my hand and knock against the old oak door before I let myself jump to conclusions.

The building is made of stone, three stories that jump and twist into the air above us in a fantastic sort of way, with rows of windows far too small to let in good light but enough of them that perhaps it isn't so gloomy within. The front door is old enough—there are signs of wear and decay around the frame—but the front steps have been swept clean and the garden beds have been stripped bare, as though perhaps long ago, before the land died, flowers were cultivated there. Maybe someone within truly cares about this place and its lost souls.

The door swings open, and a part-blood female squints at me, her face apprehensive and slipping into fear when she gets a good look. Reed steps forward and slides in front of me as though hiding me now will help the situation.

"We're here at the prince's request to offer medicine to the children."

He carefully doesn't say which prince, I notice, but after giving him a good once-over, the part-blood woman nods her head sharply and steps aside. Whatever challenges she's faced at Yregar, she trusts the soldiers here and the high-fae prince who leads them.

Reed glances over his shoulder to give me a nod before stepping into the building, carefully ensuring I'm following him and this hasn't been one big ruse to slip away from his guard. Stifling my eye roll, I step into a small reception area and blink against the small orbs of magic that light it.

I wasn't expecting to see magic like this here. The castle has the same lighting, old magic placed there by high fae of generations ago who still used their magic, but someone here is tending to these orbs and keeping them lit. The part-blood woman has pointed ears and blue eyes, some Unseelie high-fae blood within her, but the long curly tresses of red hair that fall over her shoulders and the golden hue to her skin belies other heritage.

"I was just watching the soldiers in the village speaking to the families with children. I did wonder if someone would come to us, but I wasn't expecting the witch."

There's an accent to her voice as well, and it takes me a moment to place it. She grew up speaking the goblin tongue first and the common tongue as an afterthought, the words forming in her mouth a little strangely as she works hard at forming the extra syllables and stringing them together fluently.

A part-blood raised within the Goblin Lands, finding herself at Yregar during the worst decades of desperation—she's a puzzle indeed.

I reach into my pocket and pull out the small vial there, showing it to her on the palm of my hand as Reed looks around the reception room. His eyes widen, and I suspect he finds himself impressed. It's not only clean, but well lived in like only a loving home can be. A rug on the floor that's seen better days after so many small pairs of feet traipsing over it and a door frame with etchings of heights and names scrawled all over it, the marking of time a triumph in this war. There are small piles of toys in baskets here and there and a large painting hanging over a small, unused fireplace, many little hands having touched the canvas and leaving behind impressions in a vibrant wash of colors.

It's a testament to a woman trying desperately to create a loving home, and I like her already.

"Foxfire elixir? That's not so easy to get right," she murmurs, her eyes flicking up to meet mine as she nods to me. "When I first arrived at Yregar, I had such supplies, but they're long gone now. I'd be very grateful to offer it to my children."

Hope balloons in my chest—a victory for the most helpless, finally!—and when I hold the vial out to her, she takes it confidently.

"One drop in a glass of water—" I begin, but she waves me off.

"Yes, I know the dosage. One drop in one glass for every cycle of the seasons. There's enough in here to see us through the next few years, at least for the small ones. I have ten older children who'll get only a year or two."

The smile on my face grows bigger. "You have knowledge of such things? I'm glad to hear it."

There's a thumping noise upstairs, and her gaze creeps upwards. She sighs as only a mother can at whatever mischief is afoot. "I had once hoped to be trained in such arts, but my heart led me to a different calling. Now I only remember the things that are useful to the children—all else is lost in my mind as I try to remember bedtime routines and how to braid hair."

Reed looks up with her, smiling at whatever noises his fae ears are picking up, but I take the moment of honesty and push it a little further.

"Why are the children inside on such a nice day? There's plenty of space out there to run out their energy and save your furniture." I gesture toward the ceiling, and her face shutters as her defenses kick back in.

I fear I've misstepped and insulted her, but she meets my eye confidently. "It's too dangerous out there for them at the moment. The extra soldiers and the waves of new folk in the village aren't kind to them, not like they once were. The place is large enough to keep them inside, and the hall upstairs might be bearing the brunt of their play, but I'd rather lose every piece of furniture within these walls than hear the disgusting things some people say to my children."

Reed's expression slowly loses its joy and wipes clean,

becoming nothing but a mask, and I find myself struggling to hold back my own temper. The woman meets my eye and nods at whatever she sees on my face, a knowing look shared between us. Her eyes flick to Reed as she hesitates, carefully choosing her words in front of him, but whatever prejudice lies within the high fae about my kind, it's not taken root within her.

I'm beginning to suspect I have the Goblin King to thank for that.

"My name is Whynn, and I thank you for offering the foxfire elixir to my children. If there's anything I can do in repayment, please let me know. I'm the only keeper here—the other women who used to live and work here left as things got worse in the kingdom, but the older children have stuck close as they've grown up, and I have enough help to keep everyone safe. I might not be able to spend time away from here, as some of my children are too small to be left unattended, but anything within my abilities is yours."

The way she structures the sentences is an echo of dozens of goblin soldiers I spent time with in the Seelie Lands, and I bow to her respectfully, the goblin way.

She smothers a grin as she bows in return, the two of us interacting in a manner foreign to Reed, who scowls at us both.

The thumping upstairs grows louder, and a sigh ekes from Whynn's lips.

I smile once more. "We'll be on our way. If you or the children ever have need of a healer, please come and see me at the healer's quarters at the castle. There's a gate and a side entrance, and both are always open to you."

THIRTY SIX

SOREN

With no word from any of my scouts about the supplies from the Western Fyres, I take stock of just how little we have left and what I'm going to do if the Goblin King has betrayed us.

My scouts who act as my eyes within the kingdom have been waiting at the edge of the Goblin Lands for days, knowing that Darick should be coming through with the first fleet of wagons at any moment, and yet there's nothing, no sign of the supplies we'll soon perish without. The two weeks that have passed isn't enough time for the wagons to get to Yregar, but they should have left the Goblin Lands by now.

The morning that Firna comes to tell me they've cooked the last batch of bread and halved everyone's rations to see us through the following day, I refuse to eat anything myself, sending the food back with her to put on Airlie's plate instead.

The Keeper of Yregar looks apprehensive, but she nods. "Prince Tauron and Prince Tyton did the same. None of us have told Prince Roan that it's the last of the food, because the witch said he needs to eat to regain his strength, but he has his suspicions. He's been giving the princess more of his share anyway. She's hungry with the feeding of the baby, and we've all been slipping her more from our own plates."

She's not saying it for praise. She's saying it because that's the truth of the matter and how concerned the entire castle is. If the wagons don't arrive soon I'll have no choice but to ride out myself in search of them and travel through the fae door, leaving the castle in a fraught state once more, but there's no use protecting us all from a witch army attack if the people within the castle have already starved to death.

I go to the barracks to discuss such a plan with Corym there only to find Roan in the sparring ring, moving through his paces as he fights away the aches and stiffness from weeks healing in a bed.

He looks haggard, but when he sees me, he grimaces and shakes his head. "I'm fine, I just have a very hungry son calling for his mother at all hours of the night."

Despite the heavy feeling pressing over me, I smile, watching as Roan turns and blocks a sword from a soldier to his left. Spinning and turning together like a dance, they move around each other in the ring. Corym watches them both just as closely as I do, nodding in approval when he likes what he sees, and I do too. The soldier holds his own against Roan, but the Snowsong heir moves smoothly, taking each blow easily as he puts them both through their paces.

He's less brutal with his movements than I am, more graceful on his feet, and his technique has always been flawless. We were trained together by the same swordmaster as faelings, but over the years I've dropped the precise actions we were once so eager to get right. Now my own technique can only be described as a brutal and damning display of the depths of my rage for what has become of my kingdom and the fae folk within.

As Roan taps his training sword on the soldier's chest, marking his victory, he jerks his head for another to enter the sparring ring. There's a fine sheen of sweat over his forehead, but his color is good.

He sees my assessing gaze and calls out, "Stop standing over there and fretting about me. I was given the all-clear by the healer, and I'm not likely to drop dead from a bit of light sparring."

I frown at his choice of words, but he stares back at me in defiance, the golden hue of his eyes unwavering as he very artfully calls me out. None of the soldiers would guess that's what he's doing, but there's no question in my mind. By pointing out the witch's good work he's pointing out all the ways he expects me to accept my fate to her.

Good thing I already have an answer for him. "Have you spoken to Aura lately? She's having quite the fun, planning our winter events."

His eyebrows rise, but his eyes remain trained on the soldier moving toward him, no war cry on the male's lips as he hacks away at Roan. He's far less technical but a mirror of my own footwork, effective and more of a challenge for Prince Roan.

"I heard rumors that she's planning the nuptials, but I thought it was nothing more than idle gossip," Roan says as they break apart again, effortlessly keeping up with the conversation and the fight before him.

Many eyes bore into my back, but there's no easier way to break such news to my household than to discuss it openly like this, sending the correct information out amongst those most loyal to me so there's no obscuring the truth of the matter.

"The Fates demand I marry her. It doesn't mean I have to like it or treat her as anything other than the witch she is, but I'm sick of being stuck under the whims of others, and by marrying her I fulfill the requirements of the Unseelie Court and take the throne. This is the only way to end the war, and I'll choose my kingdom over my own wishes, always. I'm a Celestial Prince— that doesn't come without sacrifice."

I look across the barracks and find Corym watching the

fight, a stern look on his face. He nods along to my words as if agreeing with the path I'm choosing. Every last one of my soldiers knows their meal this morning was smaller and that tomorrow's will be their last. They all know that fighting off the witches and reclaiming our kingdom has been made impossible by the regent splitting up our forces and refusing to take the offensive, protecting Yris and his lifestyle over the good of the land. That will change only under my rule, and after centuries of living this way, there's no denying the truth of it.

There's murmuring along the wall, soldiers slowly sharpening their gaze and standing at attention. Roan and the soldier in the sparring ring both pause as well. All the eyes of Yregar turn toward the commotion, and we hold our collective breath as we wait for confirmation of the witches' attack.

Just as I'm about to snap, one of the sentries steps back over to lean down and call out, "The wagons are here, Your Highness! Darick has returned with the supplies!"

I scowl, disbelief rippling in my stomach as I meet Roan's eyes.

The castle doors open again, and Tauron jogs down the stairs, a sneer on his face. "How could he have returned and not passed by the scouts?"

I move with them both to the stables, Ingor holding out Nightspark's reins as the stable boys quickly saddle horses for Roan and Tauron as well. The only explanation is the scouts' deaths—that the witches found them waiting at the edge of the Goblin Lands and killed them—but that doesn't explain how the wagons have arrived here safely.

The answer to that becomes clear as we begin to ride out, one of the soldiers calling along the walls, "Soldiers! There's an army of goblin soldiers waiting out there!"

An army of goblin soldiers.

My own soldiers open the gate of the inner wall of Yregar,

and we ride out hard and fast to meet the wagons as the villagers all look on. Hundreds of gaunt and dirty faces line the streets, all of them depending on me and those wagons to be full and undamaged.

As we approach the outer wall, I slow Nightspark to a walk, the murmuring of the soldiers keeping watch on the wall drifting down to me as they worry amongst themselves.

"—at least a hundred of them. If we're under attack, they're going to win. Look at the size of that one! Since when did goblins get that big? They can't be out of food—"

"Open the gates," I call out, and the soldiers startle to attention, too distracted to have taken notice of our approach but moving to do as I command without question. Their preoccupation is a lapse, but one I won't punish too harshly as they were focused on the approaching army, as they should be.

Tauron sends me a sidelong look. "Should we really let them in? If there are a hundred of them, and three of us waiting to welcome them, should we not have more soldiers down here? This is the perfect time to kill you and take Yregar for their king."

The Fates sing under my skin, whispering to me in a language long forgotten but the meaning clear. "If the Goblin King wanted to take Yregar Castle, he would simply cross the fae door and take it. He knows exactly how dire things are here."

Roan's mouth firms into a disapproving line, but loyally he doesn't contradict my word as the gates open.

We're humbled by the sight of the goblin troops, lined up perfectly as they surround the fleet of wagons carrying the supplies in a protective wall of heavily armed and fierce-faced soldiers. Darick rides at the head of the group with one of the goblin soldiers alongside him, and as they approach the gates, the lead soldier calls out an order in the harsh goblin tongue. The rest of the soldiers stop outside the walls, pulling their horses up short in perfect rows. It's a powerful display of an obedient army, ruthlessly bred and trained to do their king's bidding.

Darick and the goblin leader walk through the gates of Yregar together, the wagons following them by magic as though a horse pulls them all. They approach us without preamble, Darick bowing his head deeply and, after a moment of tense silence and a steely gaze, the goblin soldier does the same, paying his respects, if somewhat grudgingly.

"Your Highness, I've returned with the supplies from the Western Fyres. The goblin army escorted me through their lands just as the Goblin King promised, but when we arrived at the border, there were witches waiting for us there. They knew of our movements and were prepared to take the supplies and keep them as their own. The goblin soldiers killed them all and escorted the supplies the rest of the way through the kingdom to Yregar."

The soldier doesn't move or speak, and I assume he doesn't know the common tongue. The Goblin King himself doesn't speak it, and it's obviously not the language used in his lands, so there's no reason to assume otherwise. I incline my head slightly, a thank you given just as grudgingly as he had bowed to me.

I speak, even knowing he probably can't understand me. "We thank you for your gracious assistance and the Goblin King for his honorable aid to Yregar and my household. I offer you and your people the hospitalities of Yregar Castle to rest before your long journey home."

I see Tauron's hand twitching on his reins at my words, but the goblin soldier's face remains unmoved, his eyes deep pools of darkness as he takes his measure of us all. There's no recognition there, nothing but a shrewdly assessing gaze as the silence grows between us.

Darick glances between us before he settles his gaze on the

soldier, shifting in his seat as he murmurs, "I know a few words now in the goblin tongue, just enough to make it through the journey. I can try, Your Highness?"

It's a question, and an apprehensive one, but before I can answer, the soldier finally moves, rolling his shoulders back and sharpening his already perfect posture to the exacting edge of a sword. He's fluid and graceful in a way we don't think of goblins as being, and my own hand moves toward my sword on instinct alone. After almost a thousand years of war and politics, I've become adept at reading people, and that movement from him tells me a lot.

This soldier is far more dangerous than he looks.

He gestures to one of the wagons, small and covered, and says slowly in the common tongue, "For the witch. A gift from the Goblin King."

No matter how we question the goblin soldier, he doesn't speak another word to us, as though he was instructed by the translator to relay the Goblin King's message and only the phrase he would need when he came before me.

They didn't choose to stay with the wagons on a whim.

"This wagon was picked up from the Western Fyres along with our supplies. The goblins are trading with them as well. The soldier added some packages to it, but I don't know what's in them," Darick says under his breath, soft enough for only high-fae hearing.

I give the soldier a once over before I nod my head again, turning our horses to lead the way into Yregar. The soldier follows, leaving the army waiting outside the castle walls without concern. It's an act of good faith on his part, doing everything he can to appear nonthreatening, and it doesn't raise only my suspicions. Roan's shoulders are tight as he rides at my side, and Tauron practically vibrates in his saddle.

As we make the slow ascent to the castle with the wagons behind us, the villagers all stand and stare as the rations go past. There's no relief in their faces, just a stony silence as we move through. It looks just as desperate here as the situation truly is.

The soldier is careful not to show too much interest, his eyes fixed on the castle ahead as we reach the courtyard. Coming to a halt at the main steps, I find Firna and Tyton waiting for us there. Both of them look apprehensive as they stare at the soldier.

"Bring me the witch," I say to Tyton, and though his eyebrows rise he turns without question.

I send Darick off to rest while Firna instructs the staff to begin to unload the wagons, her eyes steely as she takes note of the stock and watches it all like a hawk as the maids take it in. Food is far more precious than gold; if that wasn't abundantly clear to us before, it is now. No matter how well we treat them, the servants could be driven to steal. There's every chance that, in their desperation, someone might pocket some rations. I might not excuse it, harsh punishments already prepared for any who might try, but that doesn't mean I don't understand why it would happen.

Footsteps sound around the side of the castle, and the goblin soldier swings down from his saddle, acute interest lighting his eyes as the witch steps into the courtyard in front of him, Tyton leading the way and Reed following closely behind her.

I have to clamp down on my temper when she greets him in the goblin tongue, bowing before a simple soldier with such respect. Rage just keeps boiling inside my chest at them both as he bows back, a smile tugging at his lips as he answers her.

She seems taken aback by his words, and when she glances at me, the softening she showed in his direction vanishes as though it had never been. "He says he has a gift from the Goblin

King for me. An early midwinter gift."

She doesn't say that it's a wedding gift, but then she's probably unaware that the preparations have gone ahead, something I'll have to tell her at some point. The Fates require her consent to seal our souls together, whatever torture I'll have to exact to get it.

I look at Reed, still shadowing the witch as he has for days, having taken on the task, at Roan's request, to learn everything he can about her.

He steps forward, nodding his head slightly at the soldier as the witch did, before he reaches for the straps on the smallest of the wagons, which came to a halt directly behind the goblin soldier.

Reed lifts the covering. His eyebrows rise, and he glances back at me. "It's plants. Dozens of plants in pots, all looking in full bloom and in perfect health."

The witch's eyes light up as she scurries over to him, murmuring quietly in the goblin tongue. The soldier smiles at her, his face transforming as they converse in that harsh foreign tongue like old friends. After a long stream of this, the witch finally remembers she has an audience of high fae, poised and ready to slit both of their throats for the scheming and conniving the two of them are clearly doing.

She turns back to me and says, with a carefully sedate face, "The Goblin King has gifted Yregar with a full crop of medicinal plants and herbs. He's even preserved a fae flower in full bloom for us—the plant is in spectacular condition. Most of these will flower straight away, I won't have to wait for them to take root, like the cuttings I brought from the forest."

There's a carefully controlled joy in her voice, but she's very careful about the way she's choosing her words, as diplomatic as even the most seasoned Unseelie Court member.

It doesn't fool me. The soldier was clear. This is not a gift for Yregar—this is for the witch alone, and he was sent here with an army to deliver it to her.

The Goblin King had every intention of denying us the trading route and leaving my people to starve. A single conversation with her was enough to change the male's mind and win his favor, if the witch is to be believed. It was the mention of her name alone that caused the change.

Roan stares at the wagon with his arms crossed tightly, calculating and making his own guesses of what's happening, but Tauron is barely containing his ire, his temper coming to life. He murmurs to me, low enough that only the high fae can hear and in the old language to hide it further, "It's not just plants! Don't be blinded by his aid, Cousin—he's offering her allegiance over you. He's siding with the witches."

Roan makes a dismissive noise. "Only if the witch is truly our enemy. Otherwise, he's offering his loyalty to your mate and the queen who will sit at your side. Your father fought for *centuries* to gain that man's respect and failed. She's gotten it with one meeting. I wouldn't dismiss that easily, Soren."

We had discussed the interaction at length, all of my family picking over the smallest of details, but without knowing what was said between the witch and the Goblin King, we didn't have much to go on. This *gift* only raises more suspicions within me.

Firna steps back out of the castle, her eyes shrewd as they trace over the small wagon still burdened with greenery gifts for my witch mate, but she bows as she addresses me. "All of the supplies are there, Your Highness, everything we sent for. This should see us through an entire moon of feeding all of Yregar, with extra in case more refugees arrive in the village."

The soldier murmurs with the witch, taking her through each of the plants as though he has some knowledge of these things, and when he pauses at Firna's words, he turns to the witch with a question. It's hard to tell the inflection with the goblin language. To the casual observer, they look as though they're fighting with the harsh tones, but the witch hesitates before she turns back to me.

"The Goblin King has offered his forces to see the wagons across the kingdom and to Yregar for the next two trips as well. He has another gift he would like to send to me. He didn't bring it this time, because it's far more precious than the plants, and he didn't want us to turn them away at the wall."

Her tone is apprehensive, aware of the suspicious nature of such an offer, and I look over the soldier once more.

He's taller than the others. His skin is the same color, but he doesn't have the tusks or horns of most goblins, though his tail whips around. Whether he's simply younger and hasn't yet grown into such features or is maybe a part-blood, his station within the forces and his being trusted with such negotiations speaks to a higher position. The way he holds himself and moves is that of a seasoned warrior, a confidence that can't be taught or faked. The Goblin King chooses his ranks by skill alone, and there's every chance that, though he lacks the fearsome features of the goblin army outside the wall, he's the most dangerous of them all.

"The wagons wouldn't have made it here without them," Roan says softly, and I look at Tyton for a moment, trusting his magic and the way the Fates speak to him more clearly than they've ever spoken to me.

He scowls at the empty wagons, already picked clean by the staff as they rushed to store the provisions. His gaze runs over the wagons and lingers on the goblin soldier for a long while before he turns to me.

With a grimace in his brother's direction, predicting Tauron's reaction to his words, he says, "They're just plants."

Nothing else matters—the offer is impossible to refuse. There's no telling what the next gift could be, but unless we're willing to form our own army to wait at the Goblin Lands' edge for the next shipment, our hands are tied. We would have to leave Yregar with half its forces to do that.

Darick was clear that the witches killed the scouts and were waiting at the border of the Goblin Lands for the supplies. Whatever spies the witches have, they know our movements. They got so close to dealing us a devastating blow, one we couldn't recover from.

My eyes turn toward my Fates-cursed mate as she bows and smiles at the goblin soldier, and my suspicions of her grow stronger.

Was our meeting truly the first time she'd spoken to the Goblin King, or did they know one another before? How is she getting information back to Kharl and his forces, and how did she transform from the little witch in the Ravenswyrd Forest who lost everyone into a supporter of his regime? She plays her part well, fabricating her stories of loss and grief to pull at our heartstrings, the venom in her voice as she snarls at any degradation of their memory, and yet there's no doubt she's hiding her true nature from me.

"Tell him we accept the offer and thank the Goblin King most humbly for it."

The witch stares at me, suspicion dripping in her gaze, but she nods and murmurs to the soldier at my command. She smiles at something he says in return, then leans forward to pick up a potted plant as they get back to their jovial interaction once more. She turns to Reed and asks for help moving the bounty to the healer's quarters and, with a distrustful stare from Reed at the goblin soldier, they leave without another glance in my direction. All the soldiers of Yregar watch them as they pass, the castle filled with tension at the goblin soldier's presence.

Tauron shoots the male a ferocious look before he follows them, muttering viciously under his breath.

I stand and wait until the last of the wagon is emptied of the Goblin King's gift, the smell of dirt and life still clinging to the wooden slats. Nothing about this gift bodes well for me, but with the lives of hundreds hanging in the balance, I have no choice but to accept it for now as I prepare myself for whatever deception is to come.

THIRTY SEVEN

ROOKE

In the Seelie Court it's known as a curse of the Fates to be born a second son.

I've met dozens of such males in royal families and, amongst the lords, even for the lower fae and part-bloods, it's considered a difficult burden to bear. And yet...speaking with Prince Gage, the second-born son of the Goblin King, I don't think he's felt his position to be much of a burden.

His mother is a full-blooded goblin, a healer in her own right and fated to marry the Goblin King, by all accounts a happy partnership that has brought forth a burgeoning plenty of royal children. Her skill with crafting tinctures and elixirs is renowned in all the lands, whispers of her particular remedies reaching across the many kingdoms of the high fae and beyond, and I've always wanted to meet the skilled and dutiful female. No matter her station, elevated with her marriage to the highest position within her land, she's toiled and worked in service of her people.

My respect for her, based on the whispers alone, knows no bounds.

When I walked down the steps of the castle and my eyes met those of the prince, I recognized who he was straight away. The high-fae bloodline is difficult to miss, and the insignias over his chest proudly declare him the son of a king, a warrior in his own right, and not someone to take lightly.

The high fae around us have no idea.

Prince Gage helps to ferry the gift from his father to the healer's quarters. He's careful about how obvious he makes his assessments known, but he's making them all the same, murmuring quietly to me as he goes.

"My father wanted to be sure you were safe, Mother Ravenswyrd. He was very concerned at your meeting and regretted not sending soldiers with you that day. Fates are undeniable, but how we reach them is not. There are many horrors that could befall you before you complete the requirements."

Ignoring the name he used for me, I smile at the prince as I carefully lay out the armful of plants on the workbench and then help him place his. Reed watches us both, scowling all the while as we converse, but nothing about our tones seems to alert him to any danger.

"I am more than capable of taking care of myself, Prince Gage, but it honors me to know that your father has concerns for a witch such as myself."

Prince Gage sends me a knowing look, one that's a little too astute for my liking. He glances around the healer's quarters, not bothering to hide the curl of his lip at the bare state of them.

"You're to be married to the prince, and this is where he houses you? My father would kill any male who tried to lock my mother in such a miserable place."

I look around and struggle to see what is offending him so badly. "It's a welcome relief to me, and everything I need. It's not the Ravenswyrd way to live in opulence, though it warms my heart to know that your mother is treasured. Such a wealth of knowledge and hard work must be respected and protected."

He likes the approval in my voice, his tail whipping around and sneaking toward me even as he smacks it into submission with a rough hand. The look of shock on Reed's face is comical, and I find myself choking on the laughter attempting to burst out of me.

Prince Gage only shoots me an apologetic look. "It has a mind of its own. I mean no offense, Mother Ravenswyrd."

It's the official title that I hold in my coven, but even after centuries, hearing myself referred to that way is still jarring. "Rooke is more than fine, Your Highness. I prefer it."

He grins at me, a row of white sharp teeth shining back, and he ducks his head in respect. "Gage is good for you to address me as well. I look forward to staying here at midwinter for the solstice and speaking with you at length. I think we'll be fast friends, Rooke."

After the Fate Wars ended, I didn't think I'd ever make friends again, and yet I've found myself with a high-fae princess inspecting every inch of my life, Airlie vehemently determined to befriend me, and now a goblin prince with a wagon full of gifts and kind words.

He hesitates before he speaks again, his brow drawing in a little as he tries not to show too much of his concern. "My father's next gift is for you alone, but the high fae will question it."

I shrug. "They've questioned everything about me and my life so far. I'm not concerned."

He cringes a little, his tail wrapping around his body, and he shifts it out of the way once more as though by habit. "We've sent aid to the Western Fyres in the past and helped with some of the conflicts on the borders, just to keep peace with King Salem and his dragonriders. The last time we were there, two moons passed, and we found some fae folk fleeing our kingdom. They were part-bloods, a mix of high fae and lower fae, and we had no intention of keeping any of them or halting their escape. None amongst them were witches known to be taking part in the war, but when we questioned them and searched the cart they traveled with, we discovered they were holding a high fae captive."

I stop my work and scowl at him, stepping around the bench as I cross my arms and wait for more information. Reed looks alarmed at the change in my demeanor, but I wave him off, too busy to placate him.

"A high fae *captive*? Not simply traveling with them and fleeing something themself?"

Gage blows out a breath and rubs a hand over the back of his neck, his hair cropped short with only a few curls falling over his forehead in the traditional goblin fashion. "It was a female, young and terrified, and the condition she was in…there's no doubt she was being held against her will. She won't speak, even after my mother tended to her wounds. We've offered her sanctuary, but she sits in terror, trapped in her mind with whatever memories plague her there."

A missing high-fae female.

While the part-bloods and lower fae live within the kingdom at the whims of the war and those with more power, the high fae are different. Even those without a title are usually accounted for, soldiers or citizens within the castles, and any harm that befalls them has consequences. They're protected more than any others in this kingdom, and a female wouldn't simply disappear without someone knowing about it.

There's every chance that Prince Soren knows of her, even with the hundreds of high fae without royal titles who grace the castles spread throughout the kingdom. This isn't something he'll brush off or ignore—I've learned enough of my Fates-cursed mate to be confident of that—but still I hesitate to make my own assumptions of what may have led to this female's plight.

Gage says, his voice careful but steady, "We've always

intended to send her back into the other Unseelie lands once we learned where she was taken from, but without knowing who she is, it makes it difficult to get her home. A goblin army transporting a damaged and terrified high-fae female would not reflect well on my father or the way he conducts his kingdom."

I nod slowly, frowning at the possibilities, and finally Reed loses grasp of the patience he's long held. "What has he said to upset you? Tell me, witch."

Gage's eyes flick to the soldier, and he raises an eyebrow at me. "Do none of them know your name, or is it simply the high-fae way to address people so abhorrently?"

I shake my head. "They know my name, but trust is hard won amongst their ranks. I'm still finding my way there. Your grasp of the common tongue is quite good if you caught that with his brusque tone."

The goblin prince steps back toward me, putting down the plants he is holding as he smirks at me, ignoring Reed's intense surveillance of us both. "I'm fluent in the common tongue, but why should I make their lives easier by speaking it to them when it's never occurred to any Celestial King of the Southern Lands to learn our language?"

Biting back my own smirk at his defiance of the high fae, I nod and turn back to Reed. "There's nothing wrong. He was just explaining a conflict at the borders, and I was concerned for the lives lost there."

Every word is the truth, just turned slightly so I reveal nothing of the gift that's to come. I have one cycle of the moon to figure out how to convince Prince Soren and his family that the Goblin King means them no harm, even as a terrified high-fae female is transported back here.

How hard could that possibly be?

Gage bows to me again, clasping a hand over his heart in a great show of respect, and I do the same back. It's a great honor to me to know I've been able to form a relationship with the goblin royal family, based only on our mutual respect for the kingdom and the ways of old.

"Well met, Rooke. I look forward to seeing you again, and I will send your gracious thanks and well wishes to my father."

I nod and step to the doorway to watch him go. He walks back to the front of the castle unescorted but with the eyes of every high-fae soldier on him. They watch him with nothing short of distrust, and I shake my head at their stupidity, the way they all shun anyone who isn't a mirror of their Unseelie high-fae image because they're obsessed with themselves. I might be harsh in my assessment of these people, but I think after my treatment here, I'm allowed some sharp edges, if only in the privacy of my own mind.

Reed leaves me to my silent seething until we see Prince Soren climb back on his horse and ride out to see Gage back to the outer wall of Yregar and the army sent on their way. The hard lines of his shoulders and his form in the saddle are impossible for me to ignore, and I silently curse to myself for the Fates' whims I'm pulled into.

"That conversation was too long to just be about the fight at the border. Prince Snowsong asked me to stay with you and be sure that you're no harm to the princess. I can't offer him that reassurance if you don't tell me what you discussed with the goblin soldier."

I turn back to him and smile. It's guarded and not the genuine one I gave Gage, but it's more than I offer most of the high fae.

"He told me about his mother and her healing practices. He has a lot of knowledge about these plants and wanted to be sure that the entire crop flourishes here. The Goblin King wanted to be sure that the gift arrived safely and unharmed. He wouldn't want to have his gift twisted into an insult against his people."

Reed watches me carefully, his own eyes guarded, but I

continue without waiting for a reply, "The soldier said he'd come and check on me when he brings the next gift, and I'm sure the Goblin King is still concerned for my safety. He certainly was when I met him, and I told Prince Soren then that he offered me sanctuary. I declined it, but the soldier offered it again just now."

I look around at the stone walls of the healer's quarters and smile as I shake my head. "He seems to think that Prince Soren is insulting me by housing me here, and it took some time to convince him that I'm more than comfortable and happy." I raise an eyebrow and shoot Reed a sardonic look. "I was kind enough to leave out the details of my first few weeks in the castle and how much of a step up this truly is to the dungeon and the cell down there. I offer Prince Soren far more kindnesses than he extends to me, and yet you all still treat me so poorly."

Face slackening for a moment, it takes Reed a second to recover before he picks up some of the potted plants and follows me outside to the garden. Despite the bleak conversation and his ignorant questions, joy expands in my chest. I'm eager to get to work and see this area thrive, thrilled to have a small space to care for once more. It's been a long time since I've been responsible for cultivating life in this way, and my heart could burst as I move the lush pots around the area.

The Goblin King is a very astute gift-giver.

"Why was he suspicious of your treatment here? You're not in chains, you're dressed in clean clothing, well fed, given your own rooms to work in…what else could Prince Soren do for you?"

None of that is a kindness; surely he must know that.

Digging my hands into the now-rich soil, I begin my work. "It was pretty obvious to the soldier that none of you use my name. You must have heard me offer it to him, didn't you? Well, I offered you all the same, and it has yet to cross your lips, or the lips of any other male here. Only the princess has chosen to use it. Perhaps if you're trying to hide your contempt for me to the goblin soldiers and their king, you should start there."

He doesn't answer me, but I'm not expecting him to, the amicable silence we cultivated now gone and a fraught tension left in its wake.

After I've spent two full days planning out the gardens and caring for the plants to be sure they take root there, Firna sends one of the maids to the healer's quarters to summon me at Princess Airlie's request. I'm expecting her to require a task regarding her son or perhaps Roan's healing progress, and so I pack a small leather satchel of useful tinctures and herbs just in case.

Reed watches me, brow furrowed, and I slowly talk through each of the items that I place into the satchel as though he were an apprentice learning the fine and delicate art of medicinal properties and not a soldier expecting me to carry their death right to their door.

"This one is vyrane and can help should the princess be feeling any pains. It's not safe for the baby, of course, not many of these are, but it's safe for her to ingest even while she's feeding him."

I hold up another. "This is Seelie Sun, and I couldn't give this to her while she's feeding the baby. However, if Roan is in pain from lasting side effects of his wounds or perhaps from pushing himself in the sparring ring too early, then it's a suitable remedy for him."

Reed doesn't make comments, but his eyes are sharp on each of the vials as I pack them, taking note of what I'm saying just as well as the young trainee healers did back in the Seelie Court. It took me a long time to take on apprentices, and I did so only once the war had ended. Only once I knew I would return home for my fate did I do it in earnest, but I know the look of concentration of a student, and Reed wears it well.

If he gets stuck on this guard duty for the long term, it'll be useful to me for him to know what lies within the vials on my shelves, especially if the witches finally come to call.

With the leather satchel filled with my remedies, we make haste to the princess's rooms, through the winding halls lined with soldiers, passing maids as they go about their daily chores. I know now that this entire wing of Yregar is known to the staff as the Snowsong lodgings, and it bustles with life.

As I approach the first set of doors, the soldiers open them without a word, clearly expecting my arrival. The reception room is unchanged, but Reed leads me through to a small dining area. I find signs of busy family life everywhere. A blanket thrown over a chair here and a teeny tiny grow suit and knitted bonnet splayed over the table. There's a woven rug and small knitted toys laid out on the floor where the princess might lie with her son in the morning, doing his exercises and strengthening his muscles at my advice.

Firna steps in after us, a tray in hand laden with fresh food and a steaming pot of tea. There's a calm about her that I'm sure has everything to do with the stable food supply the wagons brought in.

She meets my eyes with a smile as she says, "The princess will just be a moment. The young prince decided that now is a good time for a diaper change, guests or no guests."

She makes herself busy as she collects the baby items and puts them away, carefully restoring the area to its perfection. I have to bite my tongue not to stop her. There's nothing wrong with the signs of a growing family, nothing to hide about the messy and joyous evidence of the hard work that comes with tending to a baby's needs, but it's the high-fae way and none of my concern.

I move to place the tray's contents on the table and gesture for Reed to take a seat, but he shakes his head and takes up watch by the wall, a good vantage point for the entire room.

I scoff at him. "You can't honestly think I'm going to hurt the princess or the baby! You people are ridiculous."

He shrugs and crosses his arms, choosing to stay silent. Before I can push him further, the princess walks in, her arms filled with a squirming baby and a smile on her face.

"I'm supposed to be hosting you, and as my guest, you're not supposed to be setting the table. We're doing everything wrong," she says, but she laughs and joins me, holding out her son for me to hold.

I take him and admire all the growing the young boy has done, the alertness in his eyes as he stares up at me and makes faces. With a grunt and a big yawn, he settles himself in my arms. I check his color and his reflexes subtly, careful not to alarm the princess into thinking anything is wrong, but when I look back up, she's watching with a knowing eye. "He looks good, doesn't he? Firna and the maids keep saying he's growing well, even with his early arrival."

I nod and idly stroke a hand over the crown of his head, watching as he yawns and snuggles into me, content in the warmth and safety of my arms. "He looks perfect. It's an old habit—I can't help it. It's been a long time since I've held a baby for any reason other than to offer care."

Airlie smiles and nods, slowly pouring out a cup of tea for each of us, and when she spots her son taking a nap, she gently takes him from me and eases him onto the small blanket where he'll be in our view at all times. I wonder if the small boy will ever draw a sword or learn to ride a horse—by the looks of things, his mother will never allow such things to happen.

When I murmur this to Airlie, a smile on my lips as I sip the tea, she laughs, a bright and joyful sound. "I've already told

Roan, no swords. He's never allowed to ride off to war with his father. If anything should happen to him, I will simply die. I'll lie down on the ground and expire instantly, racing after him to the clutches of Elysium."

I look back down at him and find myself thinking the same thing, an affection for this baby that I haven't felt in years pulling at me.

In the Seelie Courts, I knew my duties as a healer—to give the utmost care and support to those who needed it, but to hand the responsibility of loving those infants to the mothers and the families and continue down the path before me. Growing attached to babies is dangerous, even in the most peaceful of kingdoms. The work of a healer is hard and requires a soft heart, but one that can also let go and move on to where it's needed most, never straying from our calling.

"I've been reading a lot since the baby's birth."

I smile back at the princess, prepared for an idle conversation shared between friends, nothing too serious, over a simple lunch. A breath of fresh air for the princess as she adjusts to her new life as a mother.

I should've known better.

"There's an old tome that Firna brought to me that was hidden quite well in the library upstairs. It discusses the cycle of the earth in the Southern Lands and who's responsible for each of the rites."

I put down the cup of tea and sit back in my chair, watching as she picks at her food and nibbles away at everything, trying to be delicate and polite as she was taught but with the rabid hunger of a breastfeeding mother. The girl who picked idly at apples, leaving much of them behind, is long gone.

She glances out the window at the clouds lingering above Yregar. The days are growing colder around us, the warmth of summer long gone. The next shipment from the Western Fyres will need to include firewood, or we're going to freeze before hunger sets in.

"The tome says that the autumn equinox is an important time to replenish the earth and replace the magic so it may recover during the long sleep of winter."

I nod at her slowly as she picks up another slice of apple and crunches away at it. I slide the plate closer to her, encouraging her to eat more.

Explaining the traditions of our lands isn't a labor to me; it's a joy to share them with her. "There are rites to be performed at each of the seasons' peaks. The autumn equinox is vital, but so is the winter solstice, spring, summer—all of them come together. The magic weaves through the land and holds it safe so it will prosper."

Airlie nods, looking back down at her son. "If we were to perform these rites at the autumn equinox, it would be enough to start the earth *weaving* once more, wouldn't it? We have to start somewhere."

I'm desperate to look over my shoulder at Reed's face to gauge his opinion of such things, but instead I nod. "It would be a good place to start, Princess, but there's no hiding an equinox rite. The sacrifice that a witch makes isn't going to go unnoticed, and Prince Soren will never agree to it. Burying the wards was one thing, harmless talismans he doesn't understand the power behind, but watching as I call on the depths of my magic to pour it into the land will definitely alarm him. The magic moving through me and into the land will be felt by all the people of Yregar, regardless of their own magical abilities, and the males of your family will see it as a threat."

Her eyebrows pinch together, her mouth setting into a line. I take a deep breath to prepare myself for the temper tantrum at my reluctance. She doesn't immediately snap back at me though, and it's clear she's different from Princess Sari. Airlie is a calculating sort of wit who doesn't accept no for an answer—she'll work endlessly for what she believes are the right results.

"Your wedding to Soren will be held on the winter solstice, and very little would need to change to incorporate those rites. There's already going to be a feast and a ceremony, rituals, and sacrifices—I'll tweak everything with my mother. I'll hate every second of working with her, but it's easy enough. The real challenge here is the equinox. Our best chance at a good spring and the land waking up renewed once more is to start the rites *now*."

I tilt my head, considering, and then shrug. "The best time to start anything is right now, but I have no desire to find myself locked in the dungeon again or to suffer the demise that Prince Soren describes to me every time he loses his temper. The people won't starve before midwinter now that the provisions have come in…but the first crop of grains will be meager at best without the rites."

Airlie scowls and pushes her seat back. She stands and disappears for a moment into her bedroom, then walks back to the table with a large tome in her hand. The old language is written on the spine in gold ink, flaking away with age, the leather cracked. Airlie drops it onto the wood with a thump and flicks through it until she finds the page she's looking for. The artwork in it is stunning, ink paintings of golden leaves falling to the ground, red and yellow flowers decorating the pages. It's a beautiful representation of the equinox that quickly approaches.

Her hands run over the black ink on the page, her mouth moving slowly as she reads through the old language with narrowed eyes as though looking for something that could convince her cousin. "Pouring your magic into the land on the eve of the equinox as the moon hits the sky, giving abundantly and without demand, will send it into the long sleep of winter with stores."

I nod my head. "If I were to do it, and a high fae as well, it would be a strong start. The earth hungers so ravenously, it'll take everything we give without question."

She looks up at me, her bottom lip pinched by a row of perfectly white teeth, and her eyes flick to Reed for a second before coming back to me. "Tyton has magic. He doesn't know how to use it, but he has it."

I smile at her. "You *all* have magic—his is just unrestrained and eager to come out to play. But you all have magic within you."

She nods as she presses a hand against the page, a determined set to her mouth, and I begin to fear what retribution I'm about to face from Prince Soren when she begins her own campaign of war against him.

THIRTY EiGHT

SOREN

A messenger from the regent arrives, escorted by six of the regent's guards in an obvious display of how serious this message of his must be. Tauron meets them at the stables and splits them up to lessen their show of force, sending four of the guards into the barracks to rest there while the remaining two are escorted with the messenger into the castle.

I see them in the Grand Hall, sitting on an ornate chair a few paces in front of my parents' thrones in what I'm sure my uncle would see as a sign of submission to him, but the members of my family and the families of Yregar that surround me look on that deference to my parents' legacy and my current position with respect.

Only a king should sit on the Celestial thrones spread throughout the castles in the Southern Lands. It's the Unseelie way, and yet, my uncle has sat on them all. A ploy to manipulate the court, to twist their opinions and make them bend to his will, he pushes the boundaries of the law to the very limit in his desperate plan to claim the crown. For some, this tactic has worked, convincing half the Unseelie Court that he's a just ruler and will be a good king. Others see through it.

He's never gone as far as wearing any of the Celestial crowns, dozens crafted over many generations to mark occasions and some gifted from other rulers as signs of the bonds that once existed between the kingdoms, but the regent has employed a fleet of silversmiths and jewelers to create hundreds of tiaras for his daughter. He walks a fine line between what's acceptable and what's considered a treasonous act, but he plays his manipulation games well, ensuring the Unseelie Court looks at Sari as the Heir Regent and wishes for that softened and proper beauty as the future of the throne, a stark contrast to myself.

My rule will not be kind to any of them.

Airlie leaves her son in her rooms with Firna and a fleet of maids to watch over him as he sleeps, the babe wanting for nothing in her absence. Standing with Roan at my left side in a clear sign of loyalty and power, they both stare defiantly at the guards, who glare back at them. Both of the males' gazes drop down pointedly to her now flat stomach. It feels like a threat, and one I won't take lightly. Airlie is dressed in her old finery, dripping with jewels and exquisite laces as she puts on a show for them, her chin tilting up as she dares them to approach her or ask questions.

Roan's sword is sharp where it hangs at his hip.

This is the first time I've held an audience in the Grand Hall since before the wagons of food arrived, and though we're being careful about wastage, I've ordered a good lunch for those who attend, the royal families, servants, and villagers alike.

Two dozen of the lords and ladies living at Yregar make up a portion of the crowd, but they keep mostly to themselves, as always. Standing huddled together, they're here to listen to the messenger and my reply as a show of support, but they're clearly still nervous of everything going on. They're loyal to me, but without a seat on the Unseelie Court, there's nothing they can do with that loyalty except attend these events and attempt to sway those with more power than they hold.

"His Majesty, the Regent, has heard a tale of woe whispered

throughout the kingdom," the messenger says, his voice loud and booming off the opulent walls of the Grand Hall.

The crowd is quiet, far more subdued than my uncle's traveling troop, and the messenger smiles at what he must think is a respectful sort of silence. He doesn't understand that they're shocked and appalled, contempt for him and the regent rife.

He lifts his chin further into the air and speaks again, a declaration he rode a long way to give. "Goblin soldiers were seen by passing scouts making haste to Yregar with supplies of war. He sent soldiers to aid you in such a brazen attack, but as they arrived, they witnessed you opening the gates and welcoming these soldiers into Yregar in an unwarranted act of defiance."

There were no soldiers sent to Yregar at my uncle's command.

Not for our aid nor any reason other than to spy on my movements and loyalties. I was expecting this confrontation, and I'm prepared with my answer, my household moving around me easily after so many years of dancing like this with the regent. Roan and Airlie step closer to my side, Roan carefully moving his wife ever so slightly behind him. When other high-fae males do this, it's often a show of power, dismissive of their wives' own agency, but only an idiot would miss that Roan is ensuring Airlie's safety while they show me their support, a united front as always.

I cock my head at the messenger and place an elbow on the ornate armrest of my chair, the plush cushioning there catching the weight of my limb and holding it fast as I drape myself over the seat in a leisurely fashion. This pose is a common one for the regent, a sign of his comfort in his rule, but I wield it like a warning.

My household knows it too.

The crowd stares as I raise an eyebrow at the messenger,

replying, "I have to admit, I'm confused by such an accusation. The Goblin King is not our enemy. He signed the accords centuries ago and has lived well within them from the moment the ink hit the parchment. Is my uncle suggesting that we're at war with the goblins? Because I have no knowledge of such a thing and, from when we last spoke, neither does the Goblin King. He simply offered aid and loyalty to the Celestial Heir, as is his right."

The messenger slowly fills with tension, his posture straightening like the edge of a knife as his face betrays his anger. My uncle clearly made a guess at my true motives for going to the Goblin King rather than begging at his feet at Yris to keep my household fed, but he didn't pass on those assumptions to this male. Perhaps the regent's spies aren't as rampant as I've assumed.

"The Goblin King has offered no such loyalties to the kingdom. There have been dozens of attempts to speak with him and discuss his responsibility to the accords, and he has spurned them all. He has shown great contempt to the regent, and yet he meets with you and sends you aid? This does not sit right with the Unseelie Court."

The messenger looks around only to meet Aura's eyes, his head ducking into a bow and a grimace curling the corner of his lip.

There's no denying her position within the kingdom, and though my aunt takes very particular handling, after our recent confrontation in my chambers, I've made peace with her. I smile and gesture to Aura, a cold expression on my face, and her answering look is just as frosty, playing along with the game of war waged amongst the high fae at such gatherings.

My tone is carefully neutral as I speak loud enough for the lower fae and part-bloods attending to hear my every word. "I simply reached out to a member of the Unseelie Court and invited him to our midwinter ball. We've been very careful to follow the exacting laws of the Unseelie Court while planning my upcoming wedding, ensuring that nothing impedes it or my coronation. The Goblin King is eager to form lasting bonds once more within the kingdom, and his gesture in escorting our supplies to Yregar was a welcome congratulations gift for finding my mate."

The messenger blanches, his gaze darting around, but the witch is in the healer's quarters, guarded heavily by an extra band of soldiers I placed there the moment I heard of his arrival. She toils away in the garden unimpeded, and moving her there was the best idea I've had yet. She's able to be useful to the castle while freeing up my cousins while we wait out her end goal of betrayal.

The guards standing over the messenger are trained, but neither of them is as disciplined as my own men. Their faces show nothing but contempt toward me as they watch the spectacle.

I know the messenger, if only by the gossip and assumptions of the court. Syrus, a fifth son of the lord of Yrell. With no hopes of inheriting his own lands or any titles and a resentment for his bloodlines, he signed on under the regent, even though the rest of Yrell sides with me. It's a gamble he's going to lose, despite the regent crest that's pinned to his chest giving him a feeling of power over others. The two soldiers I don't recognize, but their loathing of me runs just as deep, etched into the sneers that twist their lips.

"You've invited the Goblin King to the winter solstice at Yregar, even knowing he holds the regent in contempt. The Unseelie Court won't be able to attend—not if the safety of the regent and his beloved heir Princess Sari cannot be promised, and with the goblin hordes here, it can never be assured."

I look at Aura, but she's staring at the messenger, her eyes only flicking away from him to send me a sidelong glance, waiting for my nod before she answers. "The laws of the Unseelie Court are clear. If Prince Soren sends out invitations in good faith to the head of every family who holds a seat, it doesn't matter if they come or choose to shun his Fates-filled day—he's fulfilled his duties. This law was put in place generations ago. Should we not all remember the long and arduous battles of King Soral and Queen Merynn, the regent's great-grandparents, may Elysium hold them safely? They were forced to endure centuries of turmoil before the Unseelie Court found peace once more, time that chipped away at the integrity of our kingdom. Their reign was short and full of heartache because of the court's indecisions and squabbles."

Aura steps forward and glares at the messenger, disapproval coloring her tone as she swipes a hand dismissively at him, theatrical in the exact way I need her to be. "I should remind you that the Goblin King holds a seat on the Unseelie Court, whether we welcome him openly or not, and without that amendment to the Unseelie laws, His Majesty, the Regent, would never have been able to take the throne into his care during the wait for Soren's fate. The Goblin King has not sat in any of these halls for many long centuries, and Prince Soren's long and arduous toil to reach the Goblin King and negotiate a meeting with him is the act of a good ruler and nothing short of heroic. A sign of the lengths the Celestial Heir will go to for his kingdom."

No doubt those exact words will ring in the regent's ears for weeks to come. My aunt wields her power skillfully and, when she's not trying to control every moment of her daughter's waking life, she does so very effectively. Keeping my temper for long enough to subdue her ambition to hold more influence within the court may prove to be a great victory in my campaign.

One of the messenger's guards inches forward as though asserting himself, and Tauron and Tyton both stalk toward him from the outskirts of the crowd. They halt a few feet from us, Tauron's arms crossing his chest and death in his eyes as he stares Syrus down, waiting for the moment the messenger is stupid enough to interrupt the silent interaction. Feeling the danger approaching, the guard touches Syrus, and he shuffles back, effectively neutered as he's outmatched.

From across the room, one of the ladies smiles invitingly at my cousin, no doubt enjoying such a display, but Tauron is filled with rage and retribution, a readiness bubbling up within him to tear every last one of these people apart.

I look back to the messenger. "Return to my uncle and extend to him my reassurance that no harm will come to him or any of his bloodline at Yregar under my rule. We look forward to seeing them all at the winter solstice."

I have long dreamt of seeing my uncle's face in the crowd as I take my seat on the Celestial throne, taking the power from him and ending this war once and for all.

Tucked between the looming stone structure of the inner wall and the castle, the old castle garden is the last area of Yregar with any sign of greenery left, but even with the tireless efforts of the gardeners, it's nothing but a small patch of dead grass and an orchard full of dormant trees. The shrubs, once a lush and carefully cultivated display, are nothing but groups of sticks jutting from the ground. The flower beds are bare, nothing but cracked earth fills the stone planters, and the entire area looks long abandoned.

Roan stands at my side, his sleeping son bundled up in my arms and tucked into the blankets his mother has been dutifully and obsessively sewing for him. His face is plump and healthy-looking, dark eyelashes fanning his warm cheeks as he dozes, the weight of him a shock to me. He feels as though he's doubled in size since I first held him only a week ago, growing well under the care of his mother, Firna, and the entire castle as we all flock to fulfill their every need.

I send a dry look to his father. "Maybe Aura was right and you truly can't control your wife, if she has convinced you of the merits of *this*."

The look Roan sends me could kill a man and would subdue most, but not me. "I think we both know I'm the first to tell Airlie when she's wrong. What you and her mother are forgetting is that she's smarter than most of the Southern Lands combined, and there's no good to come from ignoring such a female."

I do know this but, as we stare at the spectacle before us, I feel unease churn in my gut until I want to throw up, the potential consequences of taking this risk pressing down on me. There's a confidence in the witch's movements, a fluidity that sparks flashes of the goblin soldier's image in my mind, and the churning only gets worse, doubled by the fury I felt at their instant connection. She's hiding something beneath the calm mask of the healer and this dutiful caretaker to the land, of that I'm sure.

With Reed standing guard at her side, Airlie stands only a few paces away, ignoring us as she watches the witch and Tyton begin their work together, a book clutched in her hands as she memorizes their every move and murmur.

Tauron refused to join us, furious that we're going through with the rite in the first place, but when he'd snapped at us all, Tyton had turned to him with haunted eyes. "The trees need it. The trees will not be ignored forever, Brother, and it's not the madness taking me over, but a change of heart."

Tauron couldn't argue with that. He didn't even try, simply walking away to join the watch for the witches somewhere else. The events within the witch's forest had eased a long-held pain within Tyton, but whenever any of us had questioned him about it, his reply was always the same.

I sleep better now. I know what the trees want, and I made my own sacrifice in the forest, a promise to make things right.

Airlie went to him before approaching me or even letting her husband know of her plans, a calculating and manipulative move as she knew Tyton would agree wholeheartedly. The forest changed something within him a long time ago.

It took Roan and I more convincing, and only after I read the passages of the book she brandished before me did I even consider allowing the rites.

After hearing his wife out, Roan placed the final log on the funeral pyre of my apprehensions, no mercy in his brutal honesty. "You're beholden to the Goblin King. Until we're able to restore the kingdom's prosperity, anything he asks of you must be considered and, ultimately, you have no room to say no. Expanding the borders of his kingdom, giving up another Celestial castle, letting more goblins live within the kingdom, more rights given to him than any other royal family—he could ask for any of it, and while he controls the trading route and our survival with it, you'd be forced to say yes. There are many bad options laid before us, Soren, and you have to choose the ones that lead us out of this devastation with the least amount of sacrifice to our kingdom and your people."

Before us, the witch murmurs quietly to Tyton as she directs him with seemingly endless patience, her instructions clear on how to reach the magic within him and bring it forth for the rite. She presses a hand over his chest as she speaks, pushing at him, a physical direction to aid him in finding the power locked within him.

My temper at her touching him simmers away within my gut, a *need* that borders on obsessive to put a stop to it almost breaking the steely grips of my control. I fight the urge to walk over and tear them apart, to stop her from ever laying hands on my family and protecting them from her poison as she fools them, one by one, into believing in her innocence. I pointedly refuse to think about the other reasons I want the witch away from my cousin, my possessive nature I cannot abandon and can barely control.

The baby stretches and yawns in my arms, and I send Roan a long look. "Traitor. You gave him to me as a distraction, and I won't forget it."

He doesn't look away from Airlie's tense back as he grins. "I handed him to you as a reminder of what we're really fighting for, but keeping your hands full and away from your sword is an added bonus. Tell me, oh mighty Prince Soren, how many times have you envisioned killing the witch since we dragged her here to Yregar?"

Airlie shoots us both a reproving look, making it clear she's been listening all along, but I answer him regardless. "Countless times. Right now I would very much like to cut off that hand of hers."

Roan clicks his tongue and arches an eyebrow at me. "That sounds very 'Unseelie fae mate' like to me. Maybe Airlie can stop fretting about the sad state of your upcoming union and your heir requirements after all."

He ignores the ire sent his way, but before I can hand Airlie her son and beat the life out of her husband, there's a small popping sound and a flash of light. Airlie's gasp rings out in the courtyard as Tyton's skin begins to glow.

His magic springs forth and floods the area with power, his eyes glowing from the magic within as it rushes to the surface, and the witch quickly grabs his hands and presses them into the earth below. Her mouth moves quickly with more instructions, the sound of her soothing tones like a salve over us all that rankles me, her own magic glowing alongside his as she performs the rite by memory alone.

The feeling around us is like nothing I've ever felt before, the hunger of the land now not just words the witch used to describe it, or even Tyton's ramblings of their demands, but an *ache* within me that expands until I feel as though I might never take a full breath again. All I know now is pain, desperation, and longing, a cavernous void that can never be filled, the damage permanent and devastating. *We did this. We ruined it all, we took until there was nothing left to give, we forgot it all...* The words ring through my mind until they weave their way into my very being.

The earth feeds from Tyton and the witch, guzzling down their magic and power with such a ravenous hunger that terror fills my veins with ice. It's going to take too much. It's going to kill Tyton, it'll kill the witch, I'll never save my kingdom...but the force of their power creates a barrier between us. I can't get to them even if I try.

My arms curve protectively around the infant as I shield him from the waves of power, cursing the Fates for allowing him to be here in the first place. Airlie's hand reaches out to cover my arm reflexively as she steps into the protection of Roan's body, her gaze glued obsessively to Tyton and the witch.

Frantic footsteps sound behind us, and Tauron arrives, his voice sharp as he bellows, "What in the Fates is happening?"

The soldiers lining the wall come running to see for themselves, but even with the mounting fear within them at the formidable display of power, they stand ready to fight. As we all stare, the glowing chasm before us grows brighter and brighter, searing our eyes until we have no choice but to look away from the heat of it. The ground shakes beneath us, the power building to a crescendo that might tear us all apart.

Then, as quickly as the rite began, the connection snaps into nothingness, leaving behind only the witch and Tyton. They're both panting as though they've fought ten rounds in the sparring ring with no break, alive and whole while their skin still glows with the last vestiges of power.

Tyton stares at the witch, dazed but unharmed, and when Tauron makes a move toward him, Airlie's hand snaps out to stop him, her nails digging into his arm when he tries to shake her off.

"They have to finish the rite. If you interrupt now, the power exchange will have been for nothing. The instructions are *very* clear, Cousin, and Tyton agreed to them."

Tauron turns to her, a snarl on his lips savage enough that Roan steps between them, but it doesn't stop the onslaught of his words. "You all sent him to that cursed forest with her, and whatever madness has haunted him has now taken root in his mind. This is all her! The witch is controlling him, and you've all just sat back and let it happen for the sake of a fate!"

He doesn't say my fate or even the kingdom's fate, respectful even in his ire, but only as far as that. His temper burns as hot as the Seelie midsummer sun, and with the smallest push we could send him into a manic rage the likes of which Yregar has never seen before.

Airlie has endured centuries of her cousins' outbursts, along with those of all the many male-folk she surrounds herself with, men she trusts more than any others in this kingdom, and she simply stares at him before turning back to the rites at hand.

Her tone is dismissive. "Either you trust Tyton to be strong enough to know his own mind or we all wither and die, Tauron. Perhaps that fate of yours, so terrible it turned your heart, has truly taken all hope from you, but *my* hope is not gone. There's nothing bad about choosing to give back to the earth once more, and we all agreed performing the rite was worth the risk."

He snarls back savagely, "I agreed to *nothing,* and you have no right to speak of my fate when yours is a happy life ahead!

A husband and a son, a future laid out before you, when ash and blood and heartache are all I'll ever know."

It's the closest he's come to actually telling us what future the Seer once revealed to him, but the moment the words leave his lips, he turns and stalks away from us, keeping a perimeter around the witch and Tyton but staying close to his brother all the same.

Airlie glances at her son, but he's still sleeping peacefully in my arms, undisturbed by the magic and the cacophony that surrounds us all. It's a handy ability to have, particularly being born amongst this family of ours with barely a peaceful day within our grasps.

Roan wraps an arm around her waist, and she nestles against him, muttering furiously under her breath, "Stubborn, idiot men! I'm going to have to drag the lot of you into the future we all deserve to have, kicking and screaming against your own best interests. How am I going to raise a son with such a heavy burden on my shoulders?"

I turn my attention back to the witch as she murmurs to Tyton low and patient explanations of what is still to come for them both, and no matter how hard I try, I can't find any obvious danger within her actions…none except for the looming sense of foreboding hanging over us all, a carefully laid trap waiting to consume us whole.

THIRTY NINE

ROOKE

The autumn rite is nothing like those I took part in for the Ravenswyrd Forest or even in the Seelie Court. There are no celebrations nor involvement of anyone at Yregar but Tyton and myself as we contend with the voracious hunger of the land.

The power it takes from us is more than I've ever experienced before, and the moment the connection finally ends, my vision is spotty. I choke down the bile that creeps up my throat as waves of nausea overtake me, carefully taking control of my body and not looking up to meet Tyton's eyes until I'm sure I'm not going to vomit. He looks just as stunned as I feel, his face green and his mouth turned down as he swallows a few times, but his eyes are clearer than they have been in many days.

"Is it supposed to feel like this?" he murmurs, and I sigh as I shake my head.

"It's been too long since the last rite here at Yregar. Each rite will probably feel like this for decades to come until the balance is restored and the stores within the earth are replenished."

He frowns, rubbing a hand over his chest as he contemplates the emptiness within him. The deep recesses of his powers are now spent, and there's a long road of restoration ahead for him as well. It's as simple as resting and eating well, the same as recovering from any injury or exhaustion, but the ache within is different. A mournful loss at the depletion of power.

As I pull myself to my feet and look around at all the high fae standing and staring at me, poised and ready to strike, my situation becomes startlingly clear. My own power hasn't been emptied quite as much as Tyton's has, but I'm more vulnerable now than ever before. Even the close proximity to the leather-bound iron plate of armor strapped over Tyton's chest is far more unpleasant than it usually is, pinpricks of pain rippling over my exposed skin. I have to fight not to cringe away from it, not to expose my weakness for all to see, and I'm careful to look nothing but composed as Princess Airlie steps toward us.

Her voice is low but firm as she says, "It's complete? There's nothing left to do now but wait?"

A statement posed as a question, her eyebrows inching up as a hopeful air emanates around her. I nod with a sage smile, careful not to look at the scowling faces of the princes behind her. Tauron in particular looks as though he's envisioning a blood-soaked death designed just for me.

I'm too drained to put up much of a fight, and it's the most precarious position I've been in since I stepped foot back in the Southern Lands.

"The earth is preparing to sleep over the winter to repair itself and bring forth a fruitful spring. Prince Tyton did well. It's a difficult task, and not one to take lightly."

Airlie's eyes flick toward her cousin, but he's still scowling at the ground as he rubs a hand over his chest. Her eyes are calculating as they shift back to me, noting my own lack of reaction. I hold my blank expression and motionless body carefully.

I never played cards amongst the Sol Army the way that other soldiers did to pass the time, but I watched my friend Hanede hundreds of times, and I know he'd call my own act a perfect deception. I can hear the pride in his voice now, and my chest aches with such a sharp clawing sensation that my breath catches. Grief and longing choke me as I yearn to hear that voice once more, far off in the Seelie Court and out of my reach now, the wheels of my fate having finally begun turning.

Reed steps toward me, and I bow my head to the princess once more, then walk back to the healer's quarters slowly so none of them can see the wobble in my legs. Though I'm careful with every step about the placement of my feet against the cobblestones, my legs are like jelly, even the awful pinching of my toes forgotten from the numbness that's flooded me.

When I reach the healer's quarters, I take a seat on the small wooden chair there and blow out a breath as I rub a hand over my face. No amount of scrubbing will wipe away the aftermath of the rite, but I try anyway.

Reed huffs. "So it did affect you, then? Tyton looked like he just faced the full brunt of a death curse while you were unaffected. I thought for a moment maybe you'd directed all of his power into the rite to spare your own."

Stupid high-fae male...but he has a point, if not the one he intended to make. This is a fine dance I've found myself in, a ruse I'm enacting to ensure they don't suspect me of foul play while hiding my vulnerability.

I lean down and pull off my shoes, an action I usually take only at the end of the day when I'm spent, and he knows it after all his shifts guarding me. His eyebrows creep up his forehead as he watches me sigh in relief, my toes blistered and throbbing. Keeping up the pretense of a complaisant prisoner has never been less appealing to me, and every last pair of high-fae shoes should be sent to the very depths of Elysium on the fires, never to grace my feet again.

"The rite has weakened Tyton so severely because it's his first time channeling his power, and he has no idea how to control the raw magic within him. He'd feel the same way after any magic act, not just a sacrifice. Think of magic like fire, useful and vital to our survival but damaging if handled incorrectly. He doesn't yet have the resilience within him to withstand that fearsome power yet without being burned."

I look at my hand, the calluses there proof of my own work within the Sol Army to find resilience within myself. I have no doubt Prince Tyton could be trained in magic—any soldier could—because perseverance is the hardest skill to learn, and he's already honed it well.

Reed's eyes fill with recognition as his gaze traces over the same roughened skin of my palms. He nods as he steps toward the small fireplace and places a few logs on the dying embers for me. He's never attempted to help me with any of my work, and I send him a speculative look.

He clears his throat, tone grave as he murmurs, "I felt the earth's magic for the first time while you both fed your power into it. I felt the hunger, and the way it's been abandoned by us all. When Prince Roan and Princess Airlie spoke to me about the rites, I wasn't convinced by your stories or the passages of those old books. I thought there was a good reason it had all been long forgotten."

His eyebrows pinch together, and he stares out the window at the small garden there, thriving beautifully due to my magic and tender care. "Fates Mark has changed a lot since I was born there. The War of the Witches had only just begun when I was a faeling, but the land has grown colder and dug deeper into its dormancy as the years have gone by. I never understood how they could be affecting our land so much if none of them ever stepped foot in the Outlands, not since the last healer was driven out by the elder Prince Roan after the curse took effect."

Something about his tone stops my temper from flaring. Maybe it's the extra days I've had to process the motives behind the high fae's stupidity and malicious ways, but I'm able to sit and listen as the words spill out of him, a sad story of the fall of the high fae.

His pose is relaxed, but his eyes are just as sharp as the sword at his side. "I had no idea that life was flourishing elsewhere in the kingdom. The winters are colder in the Outlands now. The trees in the Stellar Forest are mostly dormant too, never truly waking up in the spring, and the deer that once lived there in abundance are gone. I almost forgot what they looked like until we saw that one in the Ravenswyrd, and I remembered the winters when we hunted them for food...all of this came to be because we stopped using our magic and giving it to the land?"

Sitting back in the chair, I ignore the uncomfortable support of the wood and wiggle my toes as I finally gain some sensation in them once more. Fatigue and exhaustion eat away at my bones as I tilt my head at him, considering my answer and just how honest I can be with a high-fae male like him.

Without the passing of knowledge and an open and willing heart to accept it, nothing will change.

"When the First Fae came to the Southern Lands, all the land flourished with magic and life. The witches were already here."

His eyes narrow as he listens, but he doesn't refute my words or interrupt, and that's enough encouragement for me to continue. These are important lessons that need to be passed on, but only to those willing to learn.

"Every forest in the Southern Lands had a coven living within it, and some more than one. There are too many different accounts of how they came to be there to ever truly be sure, but the Ravenswyrd lore says we came from the trees themselves. They had need of caretakers and loyal servants to cultivate and tend to them as they rested, so through an act of the Fates and the trees' own devotion, the Ravenswyrd Coven came to be, the first Crone, Mother, and Maiden of many generations to come."

I press a hand against my mouth for a moment, taking a deep breath and letting my body calm. The emptiness within me is an echo of the ache within the ground, mourning together at the despair that cloaks us.

"The high fae came to the Southern Lands and left us to our forests. They formed the kingdom and ruled over the lower fae who followed their journey, promising a good life and a peaceful kingdom in this land that flourished. When they came to the forests for supplies and aid, they made an agreement with the trees. A sacred oath of sacrifice, and that gift, given freely, would always be honored with abundance from the land. The sacrifice was always given as blood, magic, or life itself, but when the high fae forgot their promise, it became a cycle of taking, each harvest slowly eating away at all resources, until the land had nothing left to give."

I glance at Reed, and he's listening intently, his gaze shrewd.

I continue, happy the lore of my people isn't falling on ignorant ears for once. "The Ravenswyrd stays lush and green because the coven died there, all but two of them, and that was enough of a sacrifice to sustain it all this time."

The magic still dances there amongst the trees, in the river as it rushes past and the fae flowers that grew as a memorial. The spirits that spoke to Tyton were echoes of the witches who died there, remnants of their magic that the earth had soaked in as a sacrifice accepted. I'd wager that there are many centuries left for the Ravenswyrd before that sacrifice wanes.

I smile sadly at Reed's expectant look, collecting myself to continue. "Everyone but my brother and I died there. We were on our way to see the Seer to find out my fate, to learn Prince Soren's name and of our unlikely union. You're right, though, the Ravenswyrd has thrived thanks to all that power our coven once held returning to it."

He swallows and glances away, looking out the window

again so he doesn't have to see the raw grief in my gaze. "Doesn't that make you angry? That the forest let them die and then used their power for itself?"

I shake my head at such an arrogant way of thinking, and so unlike my own mind. "The power was the forest's to begin with—it simply returned home. My family lived and died exactly where they wanted to be, at home in the trees."

I take a deep breath, the truth tumbling out of me so quickly that I couldn't stop it even if I tried. "The forest *didn't* let us die—it was betrayed. Kharl used that story to turn the hearts of many witches, to convince them this war is about returning the lands to the glory of the time before the First Fae and taking back the forests. He's lied to thousands of them, and now, after so many years of distorting our traditions and building his army of madness, he no longer needs to spin his web of lies. He already has what he needs from the covens—all that's left is the high fae, waiting the Unseelie Court out while you fight and squabble amongst yourselves. He's proved himself a patient male. The time of the high fae is drawing to an end, and there's no one but yourselves to blame."

Reed blows out a breath and scratches the back of his neck, his eyebrows pinching together once more. "How were you not convinced then? Why are you immune to this promise of a return to the old times and restoration of the land? You care for it deeply—Tyton said you sat in a cell and bled onto the stones there just to give it crumbs of your power. Why don't you want the forests filled with witches once more?"

The smile I give him in return is a cold promise of death, and I watch as he gulps at it, a shock to his system after the quiet and peaceful tales I wove throughout the room. The promise of retribution I wear so boldly is a stark reminder that even the most docile of prisoners is guarded for a reason.

"The Ravenswyrd witches were living peacefully in the

forest for millennia. Kharl deceived the trees with his intentions. He could have left us alone, and yet he hunted for centuries to find a way into the trees, desperate to kill us all.

"Even if he were the last witch left in the Southern Lands and our only hope for survival, I would hunt him down. No matter what the high fae choose to do in this war, Kharl the Betrayer's death is mine alone."

That man owes me lives, dozens of them, and the Fates have promised him to me. Heartache and ruin may follow in the wake of my ill-Fated marriage, but I will see my coven avenged.

I only hope that, from where she rests in Elysium, my mother will forgive me for how far I've fallen from the Ravenswyrd way.

I sleep like the dead, but I'm woken in the early hours of the morning by frenetic energy under my skin, the Fates singing an executioner's toll underneath my scars. The weight of the death to come presses heavy on my heart, pushing at the muscle until I'm sure it's going to burst.

I lie there, my eyes squeezed tightly shut, as I pray to the Fates that I'm just worried about my magic and the days ahead as it replenishes, but I've sensed this feeling too many times in the past to fool myself. Even before my scarring, I felt the call of the Fates and woke too many times on the edge of a battlefield, knowing the devastation to come.

By the time Reed takes over from the night watch, I'm awake and preparing supplies, cutting linens into strips and boiling hot water to ensure they're clean and ready for wounds, moving the tinctures around obsessively on the shelves to ensure the healing and pain management vials are within easy reach, keeping myself busy in the only productive way I can as doom grows thicker around us all.

He steps up to the workbench and presses his hands against the wood as he leans his weight onto them, a stern look on his face as he says, "You feel it as well. The whole castle woke up as if marching toward a funeral pyre. Tyton has been pacing for hours, and everyone is avoiding Tauron like the dragonpox."

A grimace tugs at my lips, but I stoke the fire and keep to my work. "Prince Tyton needs to rest and ensure he's eating well to recover. If there's an attack coming, he needs to be ready."

He nods as the usual maid steps in for Princess Airlie's morning tea, her eyes on the stones beneath our feet. I set the cups out while he relays this to the maid, and she bows to him before scurrying away, eager to be out of my presence and off with her morning work.

I send Reed a dry look, the grimace still lingering on my lips. "I wish Firna would come down instead. That female's no-nonsense way is far preferable to the meek and terrified maids in her employ. Honestly, they're all ridiculous."

"She's busy with the princess—they're supposed to name the baby tonight. The entire castle has been preparing for the naming ceremony for days, and now this war is going to take that from the prince and princess," he says, and despite the dread forming a lump in my throat, the corners of my lips tug up into a smile.

"I have to admit, when I returned from the Northern Lands I wasn't expecting to find such loyalty in the Unseelie high fae, especially from a soldier without blood ties, but the way you speak of them both is a relief. I know they're safer with you around."

Reed pulls up a chair and sits at the workbench, then grabs one of the piles of linens and begins to tear them into strips. They're the perfect size, thanks to his ever-watchful gaze calculating and weighing my every move, and I don't have to direct his actions at all.

His reply is low but firm, a declaration if I've ever heard one. "My family has always served the Snowsong royal bloodline, but I have a great respect for Roan and the princess. When all the other families closed their doors to their people and hid amongst their riches, they both heeded the calls for aid. Both of them have fought for their kingdom. They stayed true to Prince Soren's claim to the throne, even when offered great riches to abandon him for the regent's claim. Prince Roan didn't learn how to swing a sword merely to prove himself as a high-fae male, he did it to lead armies and protect the Outlands. When the witches came for his father's lands and the people he'd sworn to protect there, he returned home. Even as the princess battled against the curse to bring their son into the world, he trusted his family here to keep his wife safe while he did what was right…even though it nearly cost him his life. Prince Soren isn't the only future leader of this kingdom. Prince Snowsong is the heir to Fates Mark and will lead the entire army of the Outlands. I'm proud to follow him, regardless of the Unseelie Court's opinions."

We fall into silence once more, the workload halved thanks to his help, and when I finally run out of supplies to prepare, I thank him quietly before moving back to the stove.

The truce between us makes things more comfortable for me, but I can't let myself slip, not even for a second. The easy air exists between us in the first place only because I'm not acting in a suspicious way. The moment I do anything outside of our agreed upon tasks, I'll find myself shackled in iron, the pleasant and easy patterns of my days ripped from my grasp once more. This wasn't such a terrible prospect before, but the ache in my chest at the loss of my magic reserves is a grave warning and could bring my torture and death should I ignore it.

I begin to write out instructions and tasks on small pieces

of parchment, careful to wait until Reed's interest in my actions wanes before I quickly write out a message. I click under my tongue as though I've made a mistake, a familiar action of mine, and cast the parchment into the fire. I stand in front of the stove as I stoke the flames to hide the flicker of magic lighting blue as my message is sent on its way.

Reed follows me out to the gardens and watches as I kneel to weed the planters, inspecting each and every leaf and picking off any insects that dare to snack on my hard work. I'm not usually so fussy about them, but I can't afford to lose any of my precious supplies. Once the garden is yielding an abundant harvest, I'll relax about the pests, aware of the cycles of nature that we're desperate to cultivate once more. All food chains start with these minuscule creatures and will lead to the wildlife returning to the lands.

"Why don't you make a sacrifice to the earth and let it replenish you? I can see how tired you are from yesterday. Why not let the earth give back to you if it's always so eager to help a Ravenswyrd witch?"

I press my hand against the stones that separate the planters, warm under my touch even in the weakened light of the autumn sun as the hot springs below Yregar work year-round. Some of the tightness in my fingers eases, and I sigh as I soak it in, turning his words over in my mind. He listened well to me before, and while I'm not going to expose my vulnerable state to him, I can answer him this.

"I'm perfectly well, just a little fatigued. A good night's sleep is all I need to ease away the last clutches of the rite. I could give to the land right now, but it has little left to give me in return—it's replenishing and storing nutrients for the long winter ahead. Besides, a sacrifice is about what you can give, not what you can get. The forest didn't need to demand such things from me when we entered, or from Tyton. It knew our hearts and knew what we would do without ever being asked. It was your heart and Prince Soren's that were in question."

Reed scowls, but as he opens his mouth to reply, he jolts, his teeth snapping together as he glances up at the soldiers on the walls. My gaze follows his, and we watch as they begin to move about, a warning sign of something arriving at the gates. The sentries don't shout for aid, so I doubt it's a witch army ready to enact retribution for the curse, but I stop my work and watch regardless.

Reed's eyebrows begin to rise, his own hearing picking up details of whatever's being said up there, and I curse my own limitations, not for the first time and I'm sure not the last. High-fae hearing would've come in handy a hundred times before today.

When it's clear he's not going to tell me anything about the ruckus taking place, I shift my focus back to my work and I leave him to eavesdrop without my scrutiny. I have the last of my preparations finished with and the workbench cleared once more when a tension finally fills Reed, his shoulders growing rigid as the familiarity we've grown together melts away and the immovable Outland soldier materializes before me once more.

When his eyes flick back to me, a small seed of dread takes root in my gut, my lack of power never so concerning as it is right now. More noise and movement on the wall is drowned out by sounds within the castle, doors opening and soldiers' footsteps rushing down the hall toward the healer's quarters. I don't need to see Reed's reactions to know this isn't a good sign for me, but it plays out for me regardless.

Apprehension colors his eyes before he wipes his expression clear, his shoulders rolling back and a command in his voice as he says, "Get up. I'm taking you before the prince to answer for your crimes."

FORTY

SOREN

When the messengers begin to stream into Yregar, riding through the gates as though chased by the monsters of the Fates while the sun sets on the horizon before us, I call for a full attendance of my household in the Grand Hall.

Airlie brings her son with her this time, knowing that only our most loyal supporters live within these walls, and though the ladies flock to see the baby, she doesn't remove him from the sling for their curious eyes. She stands, rubbing his back gently through the fabric as she chats quietly with them all. She's careful to ensure there's always a healthy distance between her infant and the crowding females cooing after the miracle of her curse-breaker child.

Roan stands at my side and watches their every interaction carefully, his eyes narrowing when Aura arrives and immediately rushes to her daughter's side, but the female has been subdued by the consequences of our potential failure and is no longer eager to convince her daughter to leave Yregar. If anything, she's now desperate for them both to stay.

Her loyalty to me may have started out as a desire to keep the throne passing directly down the bloodline of the Celestial family, as it has since the time of the First Fae, but there's a newfound respect in her as she comes to terms with the reality of the war around us. With her arrival at the castle so close to when the rations ran out, I put her in the guest wing that looks over the dying farmlands, just to be sure her mind can't be swayed by the regent's honeyed lies. There's no twisted, gilded perception of Yris Castle here, no denying the truth of our situation and writing my words off as some ploy to scare the Unseelie Court into siding with me in the war.

The death that surrounds us is inescapable.

Tauron and Tyton both mingle in the crowd, smiling and laughing with the soldiers and grimacing as they're questioned about the castle's protections by the lords in attendance. Many of them have sons who serve me as soldiers, and they hear much of the war efforts directly from them, giving them the very misguided impression they know the extent of the battle we're bracing for. None of them are truly prepared for what will happen if the castle comes under attack, but their loyalty is enough for now.

Firna hovers by the banquet tables, which are laden with just enough food for those in attendance and not a single scrap more. She fusses as she makes Airlie a plate, her eyes narrowed on my aunt as Firna monitors Airlie's every move. Firna's temper paces like a dragon before its most treasured possessions, ready to pry the woman away. In her latest stay at Yregar, Aura has learned the hard way that no matter her royal title, the Keeper of Yregar has my ear and my full support, especially when it comes to Airlie. If Firna suspects even the slightest wisp of tension from Aura toward her daughter, she'll find herself banished to the least comfortable and most reclusive rooms in the castle.

My gaze moves away from Airlie only when Fyr steps up to me, bowing deeply as the chatter of the room dissipates. His eyes are solemn as he takes a deep breath, his news marking the beginning of the fight for the throne.

"The regent has locked down Yris Castle and is refusing to

let any of the families there leave. Prince Doryn met with him and discussed his urgent desire to be with his wife and daughter during such trying times, but the regent refused to let him go. Princess Tylla did the same, asking to travel here to be with her sons, only she approached him during a banquet in front of the entire Unseelie Court, and instead of dismissing her from his presence, the regent has detained her in her rooms. She's now heavily guarded and not allowed to repeal his decision or go in exile to her family's lands."

Tauron's face doesn't change at the news of his mother's treatment, but Tyton scowls as the eyes of the lords and ladies slowly turn toward them both. He still looks exhausted from the rite that drained his magic at the witch's direction, his scowl deepening as he meets my eyes across the room.

I motion for Fyr to continue, his voice carrying through the murmurs with ease. "Any of the Unseelie Court families who have sided with you have also been put under house arrest within the castle. Those who were neutral to him and happy that the laws are being followed have been told that it's a safety precaution as the witches prepare to attack. Doryn, Tylla, and a handful of other more vehement supporters of changing the succession laws to give you the throne before your Fates-blessed marriage have been told that the arrest is to stop them from undermining his rule. The regent claims to know of a plot to kill him and place you on the throne, regardless of the laws."

More gasps ring out, but I was expecting this from him. The news of my nuptials to the witch have rattled him, but my uncle has been planning for this for a very long time, assessing every last move he'll need to make to keep the throne until he's sure of his success.

Anything he can do to degrade my reputation, to weaken my position within the Unseelie Court's minds...nothing is off-limits to the male.

I incline my head at Fyr and say, loud enough that the part-bloods and lower fae in attendance can hear me clearly as well, "I thank you for your good work. How many families have been imprisoned?"

There are forty-two seats on the Unseelie Court, held by the royal families that descended from the First Fae, thirty-six of which live within the perimeter of the regent. Even several who are loyal to me are content to live within the protection of Yris. It's the Unseelie way to live near the court, but it rankles me all the same.

Of the six seats missing, Aura is safe here at Yregar, and the Goblin King in his own lands. Roan's father stays at Fates Mark, ruling the Outlands and scorning the Unseelie Court's venomous gossip. Mercer, the Prince of Yrell, still holds his castle and defends it against the witches, his borders inching smaller every day as the Witch Ward grows in power. The Seer holds an honorary position, but she holds it all the same.

I hold the last seat, passed to me from my father upon his death.

The regent has the support of twenty households, and I have the same, with only the Seer and the Goblin King choosing not to cast a vote.

The Seer has never voiced a preference—it's not the Seers' way. They were given a spot in the Unseelie Court as a mark of respect to the Fates, and never in all the millennia that we've lived in the Southern Lands has a Seer cast a vote.

Even with his statement of intent to join us at midwinter, until he declares loyalty to one of us the Goblin King is neutral ground, a wasted vote during the long centuries past. No king in the goblin lands has cast a vote for generations, not since the first of the high-fae princes were banished to live there and told to control the rabble as punishment. That one action led to the eventual uprising and civil war, the same that my grandfather fought in to bring peace to the kingdom once more. The accords were drawn up and signed, but only after much bloodshed and loss on both sides of the conflict. The Briarfrost family had agreed to continue to serve the Celestial King but only if they held sovereignty over their own lands, thus the line of the Goblin Kings began.

The divide within the kingdom has remained ever since.

"All eighteen of your supporters at Yris have been put under house arrest."

Fyr pauses to glance at Prince Roan and Princess Airlie before he speaks again. "Princess Sari has also been moved to her chambers and denied the right to leave."

It's hard to keep the surprise from my face, but it ripples through the crowd regardless as unease begins to pool in my gut, swelling with every passing moment.

The regent has always treated his daughter like a pretty trinket, something he owned and could show off to his people. My efforts to get her to acknowledge the war around us may very well have put her life in danger. If anything happens to her, I'll have no one but myself to blame.

"He says there are spies within the castle and she's safer that way, but there have been many rumors that the princess was spending much time in the libraries before that, asking questions that aren't befitting of the Heir Regent Apparent." There's a sardonic lilt to his voice, the first sign of his own opinion of the message.

It's a slip, and one Fyr never makes, always faultless at his job, but his own opinions of the regent and his daughter are nothing short of vicious.

He and Firna have a good life here at Yregar, but my keeper was the eldest of three part-blood sisters. The youngest died in the war long ago, having run a successful tavern in one of the villages along the eastern edge of the Mistwyrd Forest that was gutted by the witch army in one of the first waves of violence across the kingdom. Firna's middle sister, Fyrla, worked at Yris alongside Firna, but when Firna and I chose to leave the castle behind after my parents' deaths, Fyrla stayed on.

There were many accounts of what happened to Fyrla, but the only thing anyone can agree on is that she bore a child of high-fae blood and died during the birth, unaided and with no family to build her funeral pyre.

That child now works in Princess Sari's employ, a confession all of its own. Sari collects the bastard children of her father, his ego enjoying watching them work and toil for his full-blood daughter. Though my cousin might be naïve in many ways, she's calculating and careful in this one aspect of her life, doing what she can to protect her sisters from her father's egocentric power plays.

Fyr hasn't met this cousin of his in any meaningful way, only passing by her in the castle of Yris whenever he delivers messages, but he never stops thinking of her. He and Firna both implored me to remove the girl from Yris, but no matter what tactics I tried, my requests were denied. The only solace I could give them was the promise of Sari's devotion to the girls and the way that she offered them whatever protections she could. It's not enough, it never could be with the regent's twisted games, but it's all I can do for now. I've promised Firna many times to hold my uncle accountable someday, and I won't fail her.

That day is swiftly approaching.

With nothing left of his news and another deep bow to me, Fyr steps back and melts into the crowd, his message passed on and his job well done. He makes a beeline to his mother, and she puts together another plate from the banquet, this one far smaller than Princess Airlie's, but still she fusses with the food for her beloved child.

As I look around the room, I find that all of the plates are far smaller than my cousin's, proof of the awareness within my household of the tenuous agreement I've brokered with the Goblin King to keep the castle fed and the mutual unspoken agreement to prioritize Airlie and her infant son's needs. Their respects for my cousin and the baby are exactly why each and every one of the fae folk in attendance have been allowed to stay at Yregar under my protection and with my solemn oath to provide for them, even as my resources dwindled away to nothing.

Another of my messengers, Rome, steps forward. He's smaller than most high fae, with eyes as black as coal and hair shorn close to his scalp. There's banshee blood somewhere in his heritage, which isn't often seen within the high-fae castles. His skin is darker than Roan's, and it's only the pointed tip of his nose and the tilt to his ears that show his pixie and high-fae descent. He meets my eyes with a deep bow, shifting on his feet in discomfort as he straightens.

He never did like to give news in front of my entire household, but he speaks without preamble, voice loud and clear as it echoes through the Grand Hall. "The witch armies march to Yregar in the largest assembly I've seen in many decades. There are reports from the scouts stationed farther north that they began the journey south when the curse was broken, and they now ride at speed, as though following a beacon of light. They know there's a witch within the castle walls, and they come for her. They ride to Yregar to take her back into the fold."

Reed escorts the witch into the Grand Hall with a blank face and a firm hand around the top of her arm as he marches her at his side, keeping her close as though he's sure she'll disappear in a cloud of magic and leave us all with questions he won't have answers to if he allows even an inch of space between them. They'd waited outside the closed doors while the messengers spoke, the witch's ears too weak to hear their words, but Reed would have heard it all.

He avoids looking at Airlie, who stares daggers into the side of his head, her mouth a thin line as she fumes. Although furious that this is taking place, she knows her place and stays silent in the crowd. She stands surrounded by the ladies of my household with her mother's hand resting on her shoulder, a silent reminder to hold her tongue.

I'm never going to hear the end of this from her, but at least she'll be alive to rage at me. If the witch had succeeded, she'd be the sort of silent only the dead can achieve.

Reed brought the witch straight here from the healer's quarters with dirt on her skirts and her sleeves rolled up to her elbows. Wisps of her dark hair have fallen from the hasty braid she always wears. Her expression is serious and her silver eyes guarded as she stares directly at me. There's no sign of fear of the consequences she's here to face, nor any sort of deference to the throne she stands before as she holds my gaze with the defiance of an angry god long since gone from this earth. She's as sure of herself as if she were the Seer handing down my fate, every inch of her certain of the path ahead.

It's not my fate to be with this female, no matter what the Fates may say.

Reed stops in front of me and bows deeply, his hand tightening around her arm and jerking her into the same motion when it's clear she has no intention of bowing with him. Arrogance rolls off her like an incoming thunderstorm, her expression darkening with fury as she jerks her arm out of his grasp and straightens once more.

A ripple of shock works through the crowd and turns into a murmur of anger, my household deriding the witch's disrespect, and when Reed straightens, a scowl of his own shot in her direction, I dismiss him without another word. Her actions speak louder than her words ever could. Reed takes two steps back but stays at the front of the crowd, watching the witch with the intensity of a loyal soldier. His hands hang loosely at his sides, a façade of relaxation when I know exactly how quickly he can draw that sword of his, swing it and cleave her head from her body at the first sign of an attack.

He wouldn't hesitate either, which is the reason he's been assigned to her in Tyton's stead.

I look at her with every inch of the disdain I feel for her. "You've been brought before my household to answer for your crimes."

The witch doesn't look to Airlie for any help nor do her eyes ever flick toward Roan, who stands at my side, alive and whole thanks to her care. Her healing acts are just a piece of her plan that hasn't come to fruition.

Instead she stares directly at me, the high-fae heir she's fated to be with, and her chin tilts even higher as she holds my eye unwaveringly. "And what crimes would those be? I wasn't aware the high fae had outlawed planting a garden or offering aid to new mothers and soldiers returning from the war."

Murmurs spread through the crowd, gazes darting between the Snowsong couple and the bundle still sleeping on Airlie's chest, but that was always the witch's plan. An act of good faith so strong, helping my closest family so I wouldn't notice her true intentions here.

"The scouts have come back and said the witches ride to Yregar for you."

Her brows inch up her forehead, and she tilts her head consideringly. "My crime is breaking the curse and thwarting your enemy? Are you planning on winning this war entirely by yourself, Prince Soren, without aid from any other? I'll be sure to ignore any further acts of destructive magic and leave them to the *capable* hands of the high fae. You still remember how to use your power, don't you? A powerful high-fae prince must be adept at such a basic skill."

Gasps of shock ring around the room from the high-fae lords and ladies in attendance, but the lower fae and part-bloods aren't quite so offended by her cutting observation of Yregar and the desperate state we have all fallen into. They avert their eyes, staring at their feet rather than letting their own opinions show.

A cold smile settles on my lips and her eyes focus on it, her jaw flexing as she clenches her teeth.

"You were close, I'll admit. Our little trip to the Ravenswyrd Forest had you close to convincing us all that you wanted nothing to do with Kharl. Do the witches of the Ravenswyrd still walk there, are they the ones who taunt us if we dare to enter? Do they know that you repaid their deaths with loyalty to Kharl and his armies, or did you find out your fate and take it straight to him to be crafted into a weapon against us?"

She shakes her head at me, her body rigid and her words lit up with clear disbelief. "You're ignorant to any true sign of reason. If you want to watch as your people die around you, then throw me back in that cell and leave me there. I'll return to my connection to the land and leave you all up here to wither, riding your pride and baseless thoughts of grandeur all the way to the oblivion of Elysium. I hope your bloodline judges you harshly there."

I jerk my head at Reed and motion toward the doors. "Take her to the dungeon and keep her from casting her magic, with whatever force is necessary. There's no point listening to her rambling any more than we have to. The witch seeks to sow terror amongst the high fae, to weaken our ranks and ensure we fall victim to the stinking, worthless hordes of her people as they advance on Yregar."

When Reed reaches for her arm once more, the witch pulls it away from him and steps toward the door without fighting, and it's only when she reaches the soldiers standing guard in front of them that she comes to an abrupt stop. Reed, following closely behind, almost walks into her as he halts as well, rocking on his feet to keep them steady under him.

She murmurs for my ears, though all the high fae in the room are privy to it, "Your people will wither and die, all while you're busy pouting about your fate. When you realize your mistake, you'll have to *beg* me for my help, and still, I'll refuse to give it, because you're nothing but a useless, arrogant male. The regent might be drinking and dancing his way to ruin, but you're right alongside him, riding a horse with a sword into the very depths of darkness and taking your whole kingdom with you."

Reed finally captures her arm and drags her out, hissing under his breath to censure her for her disrespect, but she walks peacefully enough alongside him. As the large doors shut behind them both, quiet overtakes the Grand Hall, and I nod at Tauron to join Roan and I as we figure out what our next tasks are, the simmering, indignant fury still heating my blood almost impossible to put aside but for my people I must.

Tauron stalks across the marble floor, flicking an angry look around the room as he dismisses the lords and ladies to go back to their conversations. The few hours of this paltry party are the only time any of them will spend outside of their rooms while the castle is on high alert.

"You and Tyton can swap out with Reed for guard duty. Someone needs to be down there at all times with her, and it has to be one of us."

Tauron glances over his shoulder at his brother, who is smiling even with tight lines around his mouth and talking to one of the ladies, reassuring her that nothing untoward is going to happen this evening now that the witch is locked down in the dungeon. "He's still recovering from his ordeal with the witch stealing his magic. After everyone goes back to their rooms, I'll take over from Reed for the night shift and make sure she's not powering herself up again."

Roan glances between the two of us before he says, "I can take guard shifts as well."

His tone is baiting, waiting for me to deny him and claim he's under the witch's spell, but I just shake my head dismissively. "You need all the energy you have to stop Airlie from slitting my throat for dealing with the witch, and I need help convincing Aura that the wedding must still take place, only now we need further accommodations to force the witch into submission."

Tauron's jaw flexes but he nods. "There's nothing in the old laws that say she can't be chained to the temple or that we can't torture her consent out of her. It'll be a wedding for the history books, for sure."

Roan's eyes flick between the two of us and he shakes his head slowly. "I know your reasoning, and the accusations are damning, but the witch must be the best actress I've ever seen, far better than even Aura. It's hard to fake such indignant reactions, or the care she has for my son."

The silver of her eyes flashes in my mind once more, raking against me until my head pounds, and I grit my teeth as I shrug. "She was trained for this, I have no doubt, and that's why she came so close to convincing us all. The Fates have tested us all; the kingdom came close to ruin."

Tauron shakes his head. "She never got close to convincing me. No acts of healing or good faith can cover the stink of a witch amongst our ranks."

I nod slowly, and Roan groans quietly, rubbing a hand over his eyes before he murmurs, "And the Goblin King? How are you going to explain your witch mate standing in a temple draped in chains with Tauron looming over her, his plans of torture finally unleashed? It might just be enough to make him choose a side and finally support someone, and it likely won't be you. He could break the Unseelie Court's stalemate and crown your uncle as revenge on her behalf, especially if your suspicions of his own plans for unchecked sovereignty are correct."

I've long since recognized the meager possibility for that to happen because, no matter how hard the Goblin King spurned me and my messengers, his loathing of the regent was always threefold. My uncle's messengers were sent back to Yris in pieces whereas mine were simply turned away at the border.

It's a real possibility that the witch who charmed him in a single conversation might turn his loyalties to my uncle just as quickly.

I shake my head at them both. "We still have weeks before the winter solstice, and the witches to deal with before then. We'll see Yregar through it all before we worry about the Goblin King."

Roan nods slightly. "I'll send word to my father for Outland soldiers, but there's every chance the witches will arrive first. We'll have to defend Yregar on our own."

Airlie leaves the Grand Hall shortly after Reed and the witch do, Firna hurrying after her with another plate of food as the keeper sees her up to her rooms safely. A frown settles on my face. I worry not only about harm coming to my cousin on the trip back to her chambers with her son secured in the sling, but about the very real possibility that she might attempt to sneak down to the dungeon and offer aid to the witch.

Either prospect is a very real concern.

Roan watches the path of my gaze and then turns back to

me. "I'll take care of Airlie. She's not going to commit treason and go against your commands."

When I shoot him a droll look, he grimaces back. "I'm not saying she'll obey without an argument, but she knows your word is final."

I nod, confident that I'm going to hear every defense possible for my Fates-cursed mate from Airlie, every second of her ire a lesson in patience, but it's a virtue I'm now well-versed in, thanks to the Fates and their cruelly twisted games.

Tyton leaves the gathering early, rubbing a hand over his temple and making excuses, fatigue etching deep lines into his otherwise eternally youthful face. Tauron stares after him and makes his own excuses, then follows his brother.

I stay in the Grand Hall until the last of the lords and ladies retire. Long gone are the days of wanton drinking and partying, but everyone is reluctant to return to the solitary confines of their own rooms. The witches will arrive whether they go to bed or not, and yet they drag their feet.

The Fates murmur to me, their warnings growing louder and louder in my mind as the hours pass us by. I don't even think to attempt to get some sleep, the frenetic power that bubbles in my veins promising that the time of reckoning for the curse being broken by the birth of the high-fae prince is close.

When the first of the sentries begin to call out sightings of lit torches on the horizon, I go down to the stables and find Tauron waiting there for me, our horses already saddled and another prepared for Roan.

I raise an eyebrow at him, but he only shrugs back. "He'll be here any minute. We both know he's delayed only by Airlie and her opinions."

Before I can answer, the door above us swings open and Roan takes the castle steps down to us three at a time, dressed once more for war with a steely set to his golden eyes as he takes stock of the preparations around us.

"Have you sent out the archers? Better for them to pick off as many witches as possible before the masses hit the wall. We don't need a second wave coming through while we're trying to make repairs."

I nod, then lift my eyes to the lines of soldiers waiting on the inner wall, looking out over the village as we move our forces steadily into position. "Make sure the iron cages are fitted between each section of the wall. I haven't forgotten the climbers, and neither should you."

Tauron shudders at the very mention of the witches that scaled Yrmar's walls, killing the soldiers there before opening the gates and letting through the death-curse witch and her box of destruction.

The climbers then were barefoot, using their fingers and toes like hooks digging into every tiny hole and crevice as they scaled the stone structure in seconds. Black spittle dripped from their mouths and their eyes rolled wildly in their heads, their screams and screeches as destructive as banshees, seeming as though they'd been overtaken by the madness within the Ravenswyrd Forest, only worse. Murderous and unforgiving, they didn't flinch or falter as we picked off their comrades, ignoring the arrows that pierced their backs and limbs and stopping only when their hearts refused to pump. They were death incarnate and enough to make anyone's skin crawl at a single glance.

The soldiers open the gates of the inner wall for us to ride through, and at my instruction they leave them open for now. I direct soldiers to move the villagers into the Grand Hall as a safety precaution. With the extra defenses I've put in place, there's no reason to believe the witches will breach the outer wall, but I offered these people my protection and protect them I will.

Bands of soldiers stream into the village and begin rounding people up, throwing children from the street over their shoulders as they bark out orders. They move quickly, quiet and determined in their work as they take no excuses for delay. The Grand Hall is big enough for a thousand high fae reveling and dancing, and it'll shelter all the villagers, as emaciated and damaged as they are.

The horses jog steadily beneath us, traveling farther and farther until we close the distance to the outer wall and the fae door that lies beyond. The soldiers there are watching the black, writhing mass roll over the desolate plains ahead, no coverage for the witches as they descend.

I stay on Nightspark's back as Corym stands on top of the wall, calling down to me as the horde grows closer, "There're at least a thousand of them, all but the commanders on foot. They're not holding formation, it's definitely a rabid pack. They're wearing black, no insignias or defining marks, and they're yelling amongst themselves. There are no wagons or any sign of a curse box, no protected riders amongst them. We'll keep watch for one."

I nod and think of those cursed trinkets the witch buried, biting back my anger at my own stupidity for allowing her to plant the talismans in the first place. I pray to the Fates now that it won't be our undoing.

Roan doesn't look as concerned about the witch's involvement, his eyes narrowed as he stares up at Corym. A frown slowly grows between his brows.

"What is it?" I murmur in the old tongue, years of fighting alongside each other kicking in as I obscure our conversation from the other keen ears around us.

The old language is long dead to the majority of the high fae and those we rule over. Only a handful of princes and princesses still speak it, most of them trapped at Yris.

Well, and the witch.

Roan answers me, his frown growing deeper, "There are too many soldiers down here. If they take the wall, they take them as well. You need to move more archers to the inner wall."

Tauron scowls and shakes his head. "They're not going to take the outer wall. A thousand soldiers from the festering pits of the Witch Ward aren't going to make it inside of Yregar. They only got Yrmar in the first place because we were caught unaware."

Roan hisses at me, furious, "They caught us aware because of our arrogance. Do you really want a replay of that? I took two arrows to the chest because I was sure I could read the snow of the Outlands better than they ever could. Listen to me, Soren—you can't underestimate them."

Even as the soldiers on the wall above us call down their descriptions of what's coming, I feel for the tug of the Fates within my chest. No matter the twisting and winding path they've put me on, they've still promised that my kingdom will flourish under my rule, the crown rightfully mine but also better off in my hands than in my uncle's callous clutches. I listen to them now as they sing their somber songs.

They call for the witches' deaths, I know it.

I call out to Corym to split up the archers, and Tauron, Roan, and I ride with them back through the village. As the evacuation continues at a frantic pace, several of the archers grab children or duck under the shoulders of the elderly and ailing to support them, leaving them at the castle steps before Roan begins to give the archers their orders. He has a good head for strategy and dispensing resources, thanks to training under his father and his time in the Outlands, a valuable skill.

Tyton watches us from the battlement over the gate at the inner wall, keeping command at the castle in my stead, bowing to me as he meets my eye with his own sure gaze. My confidence in Yregar and our defenses hasn't wavered, but only a fool would keep skilled battle advisors at their side only to ignore their advice out of nothing but arrogance.

While there are a lot of witches coming here, we've faced worse odds in battle and won through grit and might alone. It's not ideal to be so outnumbered, but we'll hold off this siege and kill as many of the stinking witches as we can before they retreat.

After the last of the lower fae are through the inner wall and the villagers are secure in the Grand Hall, the sentries from the outer wall call out their warnings, their voices carrying easily in the early morning air. The witches have made it across the dead plains and stopped before the wall, held back only by the iron gate in a raving, writhing wave, the screeches and screams of their war cries bellowing through the clear and cold night.

From our own position on the incline at the base of the inner wall, I can see the army that awaits us.

A roiling sea of soldiers, ready to die at Kharl's command for a cause that was never theirs to begin with. Whatever else his magic is capable of, the mercilessness of the power he holds over these witches is second only to the cruelty of the now-broken curse.

We hold our position as the inner gates start to close behind us, our gazes steady on the waiting masses. The witches stand within the archers' range, but Corym holds his command, staring at the horde with a critical eye as he waits for them to make the first move and show their hand. He's a good commander with the patience to draw them out, form the best plan, and protect our home and our people from the evil that's come calling.

The screams get louder and more intense, and the soldiers on the outer wall hold a perfect line with their bows in hands, arrows nocked and at the ready as they wait for the command.

The first flash of light takes us by surprise, because it comes from the wrong direction, off to the western side of the outer wall and barely within our sight line. The fae door begins to glow, the old oaken branches winding together to slowly form an empty doorway. Burning brighter and brighter, with searing white light, until those branches catch fire, flames climbing into the air as the gate behind us finally seals shut. A low pulse of a sound surrounds us, one so deep and powerful that even at this distance it rattles our chests and presses against our hearts, the organs struggling to beat in their cavities at such a sound. To our mounting horror, the fae door opens, and Kharl himself steps through.

Though centuries have passed since I last saw him, he hasn't changed at all, aging unnaturally slowly for a witch. He looks no older than the cusp of adulthood, only the deep and motionless voids of his silver eyes speaking of an ageless cruelty that has wrought much evil. He's taller than most of his people, dark hair cut short and skin tanned and decorated with white lines as his power shines through them. Every inch of his stance is confident and assured, the battle already won in his mind.

He's more than just a powerful witch, strong not only amongst his own kind but in the entire population of the Southern Lands. Whether born with such power or gaining it in some grotesque way, he seems to radiate with the strength of the Fates themselves. He tilts his head back to stare at the walls of Yregar, and I see the cold calculation of a warlord, none of the raving madness that his army is prey to. The witches under his command may stand in a writhing crowd, but they hold their position as though fixed in place by magic, their yelling and screaming quietened by his presence alone.

Kharl's hold over them is absolute.

His eyes don't even flick to the high fae soldiers who are gaping at him from the battlements of the outer wall, and as he widens his stance, a clear sign of him readying his attack, Corym calls for our archers to fire. They take aim at the High

Witch himself, but no arrow hits its target, all landing uselessly in a perfect circle in the deadened grass around him. They aim for the troops instead, and the first waves of the witch army begin to fall, magic popping and sparking light around them as some still wield just enough power to shield themselves.

Kharl looks on, unmoved and uncaring as lives are lost around him. He lifts a hand, and a pulse of power arcs through the air. Before we can see the damage the witch is inflicting, Roan throws his arm across my chest to grasp my arm and shake me.

"We need to get behind the inner wall. Call a retreat *now*, Soren. It's no good riding out to meet this madman at the outer wall," Roan says, his words breaking through to me, but I don't want to act on them.

My hands tighten on Nightspark's reins, the weight of my sword heavy at my hip as I prepare to draw it, but Tauron snaps out a hand to grab my other forearm. "Listen to Roan! We can't ride out there. If he kills you, the Fates will break and the castle will fall. Come, Soren, you're no use to your people dead. For once, just listen!"

I don't listen.

I can't, the obliviating rage at the destruction this man has wrought consuming me and, finally about to face him, I can think of nothing but his death at my hand. I kick Nightspark to urge him on, but as he takes his first step, the air in my lungs suddenly evaporates, choking me and the others as Kharl's magic reaches over the entirety of Yregar's land and the castle within.

The wave of magic swells and fills everything until it finally snaps, a blast of power hitting the outer wall and the gate in a deafening *boom*, my ears ringing and my senses momentarily dazed. As Nightspark startles and rears, I'm barely able to keep myself in the saddle as the soldiers above us yell out, Tyton screaming at us all, but it takes me a moment to get my horse under control and my wits about me.

When I finally glance over my shoulder I find an entire section of the outer wall missing, blown apart, and dozens of soldiers dead in a single, devastating blow from our enemy. It's a crushing display of the power he wields and illustrates just how little we know of his true abilities. The gate lies twisted and distorted on the ground as the witch army advances around the iron remnants, the witches screaming their victory to the Fates.

We could ride to them now and fight them, even outnumbered as we are. We're stronger than the raving soldiers we've faced countless times before, stronger than them all...except Kharl, untouchable in his power. If he has any magic stores left to use on the inner wall after that burst, we're doomed.

Yregar will fall.

As my mouth opens to give the command to send out a battalion of our own to ride out and meet their advance, there's another rumble of power within the earth, and our gazes are dragged as if by command to the fae door. The air shimmers within the burning branches, and the door opens again, only this time a stream of countless witches travel through, screaming and running as they descend like a plague of raving death into the village.

The true might of Kharl's armies have arrived.

FORTY ONE

ROOKE

I take up my position by the wall in the cell once more, refusing to meet Reed's eyes as he cringes at the guard post, leaving me to wallow in the heavy air around us.

It's different down here, thanks to my power exchange with the earth, my magic weakened at the worst possible time, and the barrier of the iron presses around me as the cell doors are locked once more. They've been repaired and fitted with extra locks, all of them clicking into place behind me as I fume in the corner. There'll be no easy escape this time, not until I'm back in good health, and the castle above me could be gutted by the approaching army by then.

Prince Soren deserves to be burned to nothing but ash.

I should never have helped any of them, should've left them all to the consequences of their actions. The results of generations of high-fae arrogance and stupidity, their obsession with themselves and their own kind leading them here.

"You might want to rein in your temper before Prince Soren and his cousins come down to check on you. Your anger is only going to prove them right."

I ignore Reed, pushing my back against the stone and letting my eyes slip shut as I check in with the earth. It's quiet beneath us, deceptively so after so many weeks of listening to its ravenous hunger, but it reaches out to greet me kindly. It's glad to feel my loving presence here, joy radiating from it until the storm in my heart calms a little.

"Prince Tauron told me not to let you bleed yourself down here, so don't try any of your magic, witch."

My eyes snap open, and I finally meet Reed's gaze with a glare. A secret part of me, dark and malicious and every inch the monster they believe me to be, is overjoyed when he flinches back from the heat of my ire directed right at him.

My words drip with every bit of the venom I feel within me, "A messenger comes to say that Kharl and his army are arriving at Yregar, and that's enough for you all to be convinced I'm evil. I'm nothing more than a witch to any of you, and yet when the trees in the orchard bloom in spring, the crops finally take hold in that dust bowl outside the castle walls, I suppose you'll come crawling back to me to beg for more of my magic."

I shake my head, an incredulous laugh falling from my lips as I look away from him and back up to the stones hanging overhead. "What am I saying? The high-fae male arrogance couldn't possibly admit to any fault. You'll probably take responsibility for the harvest."

Reed doesn't answer, and silence falls between us once more. My skin begins to itch, and it takes me a moment to realize it's not due to the iron that surrounds me, but the Fates singing as the doom of Yregar rides here, the consequences of breaking the curse finally come for their ounce of flesh. There's no changing the facts, the die is already cast for the battle. The high fae soldiers are strong, but Kharl is stronger. If he joins the battle, then Yregar will fall.

Princess Airlie and the baby will die.

The evening crawls by in silence. Reed grows more agitated as the hours creep by, his hands constantly picking at his clothing and scratching the back of his neck, pulling on his skin as though he's trying to fit it back over his bones, only this time the correct way so the itch will settle.

There is no settling the itch, no way to stop the Fates when they come for you, and we're forced to sit in excruciating anticipation and wait.

In the early hours of the morning, we hear the first sounds of the attack.

Reed's head snaps up.

I shut my eyes and try to reach out with my magic to get a read on what's happening, but I have only enough to cover the castle, now locked down and protected. All of the high fae that Soren kept far away from me are holed up in their rooms while the soldiers monitor all of the hallways and open spaces of the castle. The maids and servants are in the kitchens, still toiling away but secured there for their own safety should the castle be taken.

Airlie and the baby are in her chambers with Firna, and a half dozen soldiers watch over them. They're alive and well for now, but there's no sign of Prince Soren or the other high fae princes.

A rattling sounds deep within the earth, and Reed curses viciously, turning on the spot as he runs a hand through his hair and tugs at it. Frustration leaks out of his pores, but I ignore him, pulling my magic back into myself and trying not to sweat or shake at the effort that took. I'm practically useless now, my act of good faith rendering me nothing more than a burden. It will take another three days of good sleep and a full belly for my stores to be replenished.

Reed begins to pace, his footsteps quiet against the stone, but he doesn't mutter or curse under his breath at being trapped here, guarding me. His head tilts as he listens, his pacing an attempt to burn off some of the frenetic energy within him. When he does finally curse, vicious and long, the door above us opens and careful but speedy footsteps run down the stairs, the clink of heels against the stone an announcement of their own.

I open my eyes in time to see Princess Airlie walking toward the cell. There's a harried look on her face, and she's unkempt, dressed in a way that looks so deeply foreign to her usual appearance that I can't help but stare. The baby is in his sling across her chest, and pain blooms in my chest at the reminder of all the innocent lives within the castle walls. If the Savage Prince fails to stop the siege tonight, they'll all die.

Reed starts toward her, alarm in his voice as he says, "Princess, you can't—"

"Do not *think* to tell me what I can and cannot do, Reed Snowheart. I will *end your bloodline*."

Reed's mouth snaps shut, his head bowing in deference to the princess as she hitches the sling across her chest a little higher, approaching the iron bars without missing a step.

"Are you okay, Rooke? Don't worry, I'm here to get you out."

I raise an eyebrow at her and gesture around the room. "There is no getting me out, Princess, not without facing your cousins for treason, and I'm not about to let you do that."

She scoffs at me, pulling a key from the many folds of her dress, and Reed finally steps forward to clasp her arm gently and grudgingly, as though he is cursing the Fates themselves for forcing this upon him, but he does it nonetheless. "The witch is right. It's treason to go against Prince Soren's command. This isn't a game."

She stares him down with a look that could set fire to stone. "I'm well aware of what I'm doing, and there isn't going to *be* a Prince Soren to take the throne at this rate. The witches have taken the outer wall already, blown a giant hole in it, and hundreds of them have spilled into the village. The people have been moved inside the inner wall, thanks to Soren's forethought, but it's only a matter of time before they get through that, too."

Reed curses viciously again, and Airlie steps up to the iron bars. She flinches as her fingers take the key without the protective gloves, and there's a sizzling sound as the metal burns her skin, but she fits it into place with nothing more than a wince. She unlocks the door and pushes at the bars until they give, sliding open with ease.

I don't move from my seat on the ground, and she stands in the doorframe with her hands on her hips, the baby squirming on her chest in discomfort at being so close to the iron. For a moment, she ignores his protests and simply stares down at me. "You promised you'd protect us if the witches came to Yregar. You *promised* I wouldn't have to lift a sword to defend my son, and I'm here to call in that oath."

I scoff and glance away, staring at the etchings on the stone around me as I avoid looking at the fierce mother who broke the curse through her determination and belief.

"Even if I wanted to help you, I can't. I gave my power to the earth for the chance of a spring harvest. I'm as useless as any other," I say, my tone dismissive, but the princess is not one to accept the answer *no.*

Airlie reaches into her pocket and pulls out a small dagger, shooting a glare at Reed when he mutters furious protests at her. "I guessed as much. Tyton has been lagging, and you both gave your power to the earth, but what you gave can be returned. You said so yourself—it's a never-ending renewal of sacrifice."

She steps into the cell with me, confident and without hesitation over the uneven stones, and holds out the dagger. I have my own stored away, but whether she knows about it or not, I can't tell. It doesn't matter—a sacrifice isn't an option right now.

The corner of her lips quirk upwards, a shadow of a smile there, but her face is set with a furious determination. "If nothing else, imagine how pissed off Soren is going to be when he's forced to admit he was wrong. That's the only thing that stopped me from tearing a new hole in my cousin's throat to breathe through as he whined and simpered in that *stupid* meeting."

Reed looks not only horrified but shocked by her words, gaping as though he's never seen the princess before, but none of this shocks me. Loyalty does not mean following blindly, not to all, and Princess Airlie has always been fiercer than most. She knows her mind—no one will change it.

Another vibration shudders through the earth, and both high fae cringe. The baby begins to cry in earnest from the safety of the sling. I take the dagger from Airlie, and she shifts him into her arms, soothing him through the sound of the attacks and the war that rages above us.

Reed finally comes to terms with his unwitting role as an accomplice in this mess of treasonous actions. "The girl in the forest, the one that Prince Tyton connected with while he was there…the little one who was scared of the wraiths and was killed by Kharl's forces. She was your sister, wasn't she?"

Airlie glances at me, looking surprised by this information, and I turn away from them both, furious that the high fae continue to speak of my dead so flippantly, but he continues, "You said that's why you'd never join the witches, no matter what else happened. Prince Soren might not have believed you, but I did, and I still do. Whatever help you can give us now, it'll spurn Kharl directly. He's out there, *right now*, trying to take Yregar from us. He's taken the fae door, and hundreds of his troops arrive by the minute. If they breach the inner wall, we all die, and Kharl gets away with our deaths and your sister's too."

My gaze snaps to meet his, my fingers tightening around the handle of the dagger, and a deadly calm settles over my bones. "Kharl Balzog is here now? He came with the army?"

Airlie nods. "That's how they got through the gates. His

magic is stronger than that of any of the raving masses they've faced before. We were prepared to face a thousand of the witches alone, but with him at the forefront and the fae door acting like a bridge to the Witch Ward, Prince Soren is outmatched. He can't get close enough to kill the witch."

I drag the dagger up the length of my arm, my skin splitting open as the steel bites deep into my flesh, far more than a simple opening of a vein.

I offer a sacrifice the earth hasn't seen in generations.

Airlie scrambles toward me, a protest on her lips, until the white light from the earth below begins to surround me and fill me, the earth giving and pouring into my very soul as it thanks me for my sacrifice. I spill enough blood to kill a less powerful witch, but I let it run down my fingers and into the earth without hesitation. My heart pumps faster with the pain, and the crimson stream pours out of me, flowing until my vision begins to white out, too much too soon for my body to sustain, but still I give and *give* to the earth, and it accepts it all gladly.

It takes until there is nothing left of me, nothing left as I'm transformed into an empty vessel, everything pouring out of me and into it and so, when the earth returns my power to me, there's a cavernous void within me to accept it, the earth's magic filling me until I'm burning with the true power it wields. I take as ravenously as it has taken from me until every inch of my body and mind is nothing but vengeance and raw power.

The high fae cowering within the castle walls feel it. The witches, raving and streaming into the empty streets of Yregar's village, feel it. The trees of the Ravenswyrd feel it, singing their mournful song to call me home.

The Goblin King, sitting in his own kingdom four days' ride from the battle beginning here at Yregar, feels it too.

When I open my eyes and find Airlie and Reed both staring back at me, their eyes mirror images of shock. I ignore them both, no time to explain the power of the earth or the magnitude of the sacrifice I gave for the power burning within me now.

"Reed, take Princess Airlie up to her rooms and bar the doors. Don't let anyone in until the siege is over."

He blinks rapidly, coming back to himself, and his mouth snaps shut. He steps in front of the princess as he gently nudges her back out of the cell. "You can't just go up there—Prince Soren will assume you're escaping to be with the witches, and he'll kill you without stopping to hear you out. That's why they put you in the cell in the first place."

I stare at him for a moment before I move back to Princess Airlie, repeating my instructions, "Go to your rooms and stay there. Barricade the door, and don't open it unless it's to a member of your family."

My words fall around us uselessly as she shakes her head as well. "Reed isn't being dramatic, that's exactly what they're going to do. We need to get you out of the dungeon and onto the inner wall without bumping into any of them. I don't want you wasting any of that power knocking our own people out. Are you going to be able to use the power against Kharl? How strong are you right now?"

Stronger than any of them have any ability to conceive of, but Reed sputters and waves a hand in my face. "She's glowing like a fucking star right now—I'm pretty sure she can handle this fight! She doesn't have to go out there and face Kharl all on her own anyway, she just needs to let him know we have magic on our side as well. If the armies stop coming through the fae door, then we might have a chance."

If only these two knew my fate and what carnage is still to come.

I walk out of the cell and glance down at the uncomfortable

dress I'm still wearing, impossible to fight in. Airlie cringes as she follows my gaze, finally realizing just what her meddling has done to hinder me.

She's brusque as she says, "Do you need fighting leathers to cast magic like this? I need you to tell me what I can do to help you, Rooke, and time is not on our side!"

I raise an eyebrow at her and flick a hand down the front of my body, enjoying the awe and disbelief radiating back at me from them both as the high fae dress melts away and shifts into the traditional fighting robes I arrived in when I returned to the Southern Lands, the same ones she threw away after the disastrous bathing incident.

The firm strips of black linen, held in place by pins made of silver, ornate only in their casting as simple oak leaves. The traditional symbol of the Ravenswyrd Coven, I insisted on wearing it even when I lived in the Northern Lands and turned away from the Ravenswyrd's teachings. Peace and neutrality to the point of destruction, but not mine, and not Pemba's. We formed a different way, together, to survive, and Kharl has no idea what vengeance comes calling for him today.

My feet wriggle in my new boots, and I turn on the thick heel to march up the stairs, ignoring the two high fae as they scramble after me.

Airlie mutters, "Why are you wasting power on getting changed? We could've found you something upstairs. You need every drop of power you can get to go out there to face that male. Kharl blew the front gate to pieces and took out half the outer wall with it without so much as a flick of his wrist! The male is insane, Rooke, and a healer—even with the power of the earth's gift to you—is going to be at a great disadvantage."

I ignore her as I make my way up the stairs, my mind already planning miles ahead of the two of them. "Do any of the high fae here today have the ability to test a lie?"

They're both quiet for a moment, and then Airlie answers me, ignoring Reed's indignant huff. "Tyton. Not in the traditional way, but his magic will flag any dangerous untruths."

I nod, and when we open the door at the top of the stairs, I peek my head out for a moment to be sure there are no waiting soldiers. The hallways are clear, every man available outside and fighting. I can hear the skirmish and taste the power in the air, the way it sings to me a mournful song of corruption and evil.

"Airlie, this is the final time I'll say this, and you need to listen to me, or I'll force you to follow my instruction. Go now to your rooms and barricade the doors. I cannot be thinking about whether you and the young prince are safe and having that distract me while I'm out there."

Her mouth firms into a line, but she nods, then hesitates before she says, "Reed, you'll come with me."

I glanced at the soldier and shake my head. "No, Princess, I need him here. He's going to watch the front entrance of the castle and ensure the villagers have been moved into the Grand Hall for safety. If anyone asks you, Reed, you don't remember being assigned to watch over me. Your mind has been scrambled by the evil witch downstairs, and you have no true knowledge of any orders from the prince. You'll act as though it's reckless of anyone to ask you such a thing while the witches attack."

He doesn't like this at all, his loyalty and sense of honor far too strong for such deceptions, but Airlie turns back to face him, juggling her son in her arms as she keeps the baby quiet.

Her tone offers no space for argument. "This is a direct order, Reed, as your Princess Heir Apparent of Fates Mark and wife of the Commander of the Outland Forces. You must do as Rooke instructs. Once all is said and done with the battle, I need your support, and if you're beheaded on the spot for treason, you're no good to me or my son. We're all moving along our own paths to put Soren on the throne and save his kingdom. Someday he'll thank us for this. We just have to survive to see that day."

Reed mutters something unintelligible to my ears before stomping off in the direction of the front doors, his sword in his hand and his posture the perfect rigid form of a soldier prepared to fight to the death, all for the chance of peace for his kingdom.

Airlie groans and mutters one last truth. "Reed said all people committing treason would say such a thing, but he already knows the sacrifices I've made for my cousin and he for me. I would *never* endanger him or his claim to the throne. Never, and I'll fight for it even when he missteps." With that, she turns to the stairs and goes.

It's not a warning to me, I'm sure, but I take it as one, a reminder that she's backing me and formed a friendship with me not only because I saved her son, but for the fate that still aches in my heart, a calling to step outside and face the army crafted of my people's demise.

The witches there were born and bred in madness, twisted and deformed until they no longer crave the feeling of the forests around them, the loving embrace of a coven, or the magic in their own veins. They're nothing more than grunts to be directed and sacrificed in the name of Kharl's perversions, their magic stolen to fuel him. The fae doors aren't strong enough to transport armies of witches like this, the land has been depleted for too long, and I'd wager that Kharl is the one holding them open for this attack.

I follow Reed toward the front door but pause as we pass the Grand Hall to check in on the villagers there. I've cast a simple glamor around myself so the soldiers standing guard can't detect me, and I find the room burgeoning with bodies, huddled together and terrified.

I throw a blanket of my power over the crowd, but no

matter how many times I check, there's no sign of Whynn or her children. The orphanage didn't make it to Yregar before the witches took the village.

They could all already be dead by now, or worse. Far, far worse.

I keep the glamor over myself as I step through the front doors. Reed is there by himself, sword in hand and eyes squinted as he listens to the battle beyond the inner wall.

Hundreds of soldiers line the top of the wall, standing with bows in their hands as they fire stream after stream of arrows, the screeching of the witches following as some hit their mark. Magic lights the air above, shadows flickering as the fighting rages around us. The witches are still coming through the outer gates, as though an endless supply of them streams through from nowhere.

Though he can't see me thanks to the glamor, I speak once more to Reed. "The orphanage wasn't cleared. Whynn and the children are out there. If the witches aren't focused on the orphanage, we can still get them to safety."

He glances over his shoulder, his eyes unfocused as he looks straight through me and mutters quietly, "You're supposed to be saving your power for Kharl and whatever trick you're going to use to scare him off. We can't think about the orphans right now, or we're all going to be traveling to Elysium together, no funeral pyres to see us safely on our trip."

I click my tongue at him. "You should know by now I'm not just going to leave them out there defenseless. Will you help me, or will you prove yourself to be as useless as the rest of the high fae?"

His jaw flexes as he grinds his teeth. "I *really* wish you'd stop saying that, because it might be your impression of us all, but should I remind you that the Grand Hall is filled to the brim, bursting with lower fae and part-bloods. Prince Soren didn't just leave his kingdom to wither to care only for his own kind. He's been feeding them, protecting them, offering sanctuary to whomever he could, all while his uncle worked against him. His soldiers, all of whom are high fae, are out there ready to die to protect this castle and the fae folk within. The prince is wrong about you, I'm sure of it, but that doesn't mean he's useless."

Now isn't the time to examine the intentions of my Fates-cursed mate. I look around at the soldiers near us, and then I press a hand against Reed's chest, the glamor rolling over me to cover us both as it seals him into the magic.

"Go to the orphanage and bring Whynn and the children back. Speak to her and tell her this is an act of the Ravenswyrd, tell her that I'm the Mother of the coven, and I sent you to get them to the castle."

I pause, thinking better of it for a moment, but I need to convince the female that Reed is telling the truth and it's not a trick of the witches. An act of faith to both of them, another sacrifice I'm giving in the times of war.

"Tell her that I have the support of the Goblin King as the Mother of the Ravenswyrd Coven, and I'm using that power to get the children to safety. Place your hand on each of them, and the glamor will shift. Tell her the Goblin King trusted my power and my coven's reputation so much, he sent his son to Yregar with gifts for me, an offer of a powerful friendship."

Reed's eyes widen at the admission, but I ignore him. "Whynn grew up in the goblin lands—she'll understand exactly what an honor that is, and it should be enough to get her to follow you with her children. Be sure you touch each and every one of them, your palm on their skin, to pass the magic along. Go now, and hurry—I won't face Kharl until you're all safe."

He scowls at me again before taking off without another word, but when he gets to the steps that climb up and over the wall, none of the other soldiers see him. Some glance around at the sound of his feet against the stones, but when they see nothing there, they focus back on the fighting in front of them, no time to waste on a trick of the ear.

How he's going to get past the ravenous hordes of witches clamoring at the inner wall, I have no idea, but I've interacted with the male enough to trust that he'll figure it out. I need him and the children safely within the inner wall before I can deal with Kharl—I just need Prince Soren and his soldiers to hold the line until then.

I move to another set of stairs that climb the inner wall farther along and behind the iron partitions that have been locked into place as extra protection. This section has been shut off in case the witches make it over, dozens of the metal cages put in place so if one section is breached, the others can still be contained. The soldiers here are protected as they fire round after round of arrows into the crowd. It's smart, a solid defense tactic, but it's not enough to stop the madness below.

When I reach the top of the wall, the sight I find waiting below me is sickening. Bodies of high fae soldiers already torn apart lie scattered at the base of the wall, and the village is overrun. There are far more witches here than the scouts had warned, a plague of them spilling out over the streets as they tear down any buildings that aren't made of solid stone. Fires burn and spread through the thatched roofs, the small bakery that was out of business burned to the ground. Horses whinny and scream below, commands are barked as the soldiers move into position to defend the castle. It's clearly a last stand, as the witches dig into the siege, endless resources at their disposal as more witches stream through the outer wall as if conjured.

I can't see Prince Soren or any of his cousins in the bedlam surrounding me, but I watch as the orphanage door opens, my sight line perfect from this vantage point. Sending out a small pulse of light, nothing more than a glow bug dancing through the wind, I light a safe path through the village for the children's escape.

Reed is smart enough to follow it, the long stream of children holding hands trailing behind him. The little ones are paired with the older partlings, the infants and toddlers carried as they firmly press their hands over their mouths with Whynn taking up the rear to ensure none of the children stray from the path. Reed must've been sure to warn them to stay silent to avoid detection, and they're all obedient as they follow him through the village to the far side of the wall, my light guiding the way. I won't make my move until they're safe behind the inner wall.

I won't leave them behind.

FORTY TWO ✦

SOREN

Thanks to our preparations and cautiousness, the villagers are safe within Yregar as the never-ending wave of witches streams through the outer wall and the decimated fae door. I dismount from Nightspark to climb up the inner wall and watch as raving madness decimates the village.

The archers pick off as many as they can, but the witches begin to brace themselves against the gate, pooling there at an alarming rate until there's no way to guess at their numbers. We stand on the wall and listen to the sound of sizzling flesh below, the masses pressing against the iron and getting burned horrifically, their screams rending the air. Still they push on, throwing themselves to a torturous death for the sake of their war, , their pain and suffering meaningless in the face of their leader's aspirations for victory over the high fae.

Kharl's blank eyes filled me with nothing but rage, that fire still burning as I stare down at the destruction of Yregar. My home and my charge, these people relying on me to see them safely through this carnage.

Tauron moves to a section of the wall to my left and secures the dividing cages in case the witches take the outposts. The iron structures separate the battlements from one another, a setup resulting from a lesson learned in the most catastrophic of ways.

Roan begins barking orders, still atop his horse as he rides around the inner wall and ensures the soldiers there are positioned and ready, moving them to better vantage points and securing the surrounding courtyard to protect the door and those most precious to us, who wait within.

Tyton takes up the far end of the wall that overlooks the river, his face no longer clouded but lines cut deeply around his mouth as he calls for the archers to fire, again and again. There's a bow in his own hands as well, ready should he need to step in and take up arms.

We might not have anticipated Kharl's arrival at the castle, but we were prepared for one of his generals, a stronger witch than any we'd faced before, and even in our planning we prepared for the loss of the outer wall. The witches aren't the only ones with something up their sleeve.

Our information on the generals themselves may be limited, as is our information about the true happenings within the Witch Ward, but we've fought some before, and though they're stronger than the other witches, we came out the victors. They're not consumed by the madness of the masses—their witch markings are white, and their eyes are still clear—but they fight as though the Fates themselves command them, and they're far more competent with swords than any other witches we've faced. None of them showed signs of the level of magic Kharl just wielded, though they certainly have more power than the small balls of stinging light that fizzle out against our iron armor.

I turn to Darick and nod to him, and the messenger runs with my instruction, his feet moving so fast he practically flies to move into our next defense.

Streams of soldiers work their way up each of the sections of the castle walls, dozens of pots between them filled to the brim with witcheswane. The poison has been stored and guarded within the barracks for centuries, in preparation for just such an attack on my home. I readied myself for this moment and took every lesson learned in the war into account, never needing to be taught twice.

We wait until the first of the climbers begin their ascent before we give the command, all three of us speaking as one. "Ready, take aim, hold…fire!"

Half the pots of witcheswane now have arrows sticking out of them, the wood soaking in the liquid, and the archers use the pots as quivers, pulling the arrows out and shooting rapid-fire. Our stores of weapons are enough to see us through continuous fire for a month, thanks to the hard work of my household, my obsession with the war and our protection holding us in good stead.

The other pots of liquid are shoved forward and hatches in the battlements opened. The liquid is poured down the stones, coating them, and as it splashes onto the witches pressed against the walls, their screams of agony fill the air, the smoke from their burning flesh an acrid scent that fills our nostrils and coats the backs of our throats. The sound of their agony is deafening, so loud I can't think of anything but my grim satisfaction, hundreds of our enemy dying in a single sweep.

"Archers ready," I call out once more, and the two soldiers that flank me both pull an arrow from the witcheswane pot and hold it up to the torches burning above us. The oil catches light faster than ever before.

I give the fire command, and they shoot at the writhing mass of witches at the bottom of the wall, their bodies lighting up like wildfire beneath us. Flames crawl up the side of the wall as the oil burns, and the hatches around me slam shut, the soldiers preventing that fire from reaching us.

The witcheswane is mixed with dragon oil, a substance that

burns endlessly unless smothered, and water only spreads its devastation. Though there's every chance that Kharl will be able to perform such magic, he stays where he's standing in the far corner of Yregar Village and watches as his streams of witches continue to pour in through the fae door. He's unmoved by the screams of his burning soldiers, remaining unflinching as the witches sacrifice themselves for his ambitions.

The mass below continues to destroy the village, picking apart the buildings as though that's their true intention here instead of getting through the inner wall.

Fraught minutes tick by as the arrows continue to rain down on their forces, but for every fifty witches we kill, a hundred more arrive, their population tenfold to our own. The arriving forces melt into the masses and press against the burning mounds of flesh, now silent in their death but still adding to the fight with their weight, and the gate below us—the single point of weakness of the inner wall—buckles beneath them all.

The acrid smoke fills the air and pollutes our line of sight, so it's only after another wave of witches arrives that Tauron calls out from the left side of the wall, "The stone is breaking around the iron! There are too many of them, too much force and magic pressing against it. The wall cannot hold!"

Roan hears his warning and calls the ground soldiers to attention once more, lining them up and commanding them to draw their swords and lift their shields, preparing for the wave to hit them next. That crushing wave that has destroyed everything in its path, unstoppable as the witches keep streaming through.

Spikes have been erected around the castle, giant structures of iron jutting out to impale as many of the raving creatures as they can. Every wall and door inside Yregar and out has been soaked with witcheswane by now, Firna and the maids having been ordered to shower the castle with it as a final act of protection before they take up guard over Airlie and the baby and barricade themselves in the Snowsong wing.

If the gate breaks and the witches make it through, Yregar is lost. The witcheswane will only slow them down.

Tauron curses, and I glance at him, but his eyes are on the courtyard and not the raving battle below. The archers are still firing streams of arrows into the air as they try to stem the flow bracing against the iron, moving at our orders and never faltering.

Following Tauron's gaze, I see Reed standing on the steps in front of the courtyard with his sword drawn as he prepares to defend the castle, no shield but his steel held confidently in hand.

I look around him, but the witch is nowhere in sight. If the Fates are kind to me, she's still locked downstairs in the cell, fuming and leaving us to the fight, but I fear the Fates took a look at me long ago and found me wanting.

A thud sounds on the wall to my right, standing out against the melee around me, and I turn back to find Tyton unconscious on the stone, the witch now standing on the wall and looking out from the battlement. Her eyes glow silver and her skin shines with power, her magic pulsating out of her as she glows like the beacon her people followed here. The soldiers around her are still firing their arrows obediently, unaware that their death stands with them now as the witch returns to her people.

Tauron takes up one of the bows and nocks an arrow, then shoots without thought of the Fates' punishment, but the witch sidesteps it without so much as a glance in his direction, magic falling from her in waves that beckon and call out for all who surround her to take notice of the power she holds.

I glance down at Tyton. His chest is still moving; he's alive but unconscious at her whim once more. I draw my sword and work my way across the wall, screaming orders at the soldiers to continue firing and ignoring Tauron's screams of retribution, his fury at her appearance, as I prepare to stop the witch before she strikes. The tug of the Fates in my chest is like a fist, so much pressure I have to fight against it too, but my people are depending on me, and I can't forget that.

The witch turns to stare at me as I reach the iron partition, erected for our protection but now holding me back from stopping her.

The old power that whispered to Tyton shines through her face, settling once and for all who was speaking to him. The evils of her magic are boundless, but she barely gives me more than a once over before turning back to the battle before us, watching as the archers continue to pick off dozens and dozens of witches. Stream after stream of the arrows fall, and the fires still burn as the masses press against the door, the rumbling beneath our feet growing louder as the sheer mass of the witch army begins to move the iron structure as though it hasn't been anchored within the stone and standing safe for millennia.

The witch raises a dagger, and the stones in the handle of it glint at me. Sapphires set in silver—a Celestial dagger that she's found somewhere or pulled from someone. Fates above, if she's killed Airlie on her way out here, it's all been for nothing. Every sacrifice will be worthless if my cousin is lost.

The witch draws the blade across her hand, the blood pooling there for a moment before she reaches out to let the drops fall in a long and tumultuous journey down the wall until they hit the land below.

Yregar is hit with a second wave of power, this one so strong it blows us all off our feet, chaos consuming the ranks, and I'm consumed by white light.

The world is far too bright. I blink rapidly to clear my vision only to realize that my senses weren't knocked out of me by the burst of power from the witch's spell—we're surrounded by that white light. A shimmering shield now follows along the inner wall of Yregar, a magic blanket covering us as far as the eye can see.

I lean over the battlement to find it reaches the grass below, and when I stare up into the sky, it domes over the castle to protect us from aerial attacks, a complete blanketing of power that pulses with life.

There's a small gap between the shield and the stone wall. A handful of witches are still alive within that space, and they stare up at it, aghast, awe and terror wiping away some of their madness for a moment. One of them reaches out to the shield, but the moment it touches the magic there, it screams and clutches its head before falling dead on the ground, black liquid oozing from its open mouth.

One of the archers, thinking fast on his feet, pulls arrows from the oil barrels and picks off the rest of the live witches on our side of the magical barrier, their bodies falling to the ground as the writhing mass presses into the shield now instead of the failing gate. The shield doesn't move; it stands firm as the enemy pushes themselves to their deaths.

Pillars of light that line the shield shine brighter where they dig into the earth, their spacing perfectly aligned to where the witch buried the talismans with Airlie. Her magic is anchored to the small pouches, digging the shield into the earth below as it holds us all safely within.

My Fates-cursed mate stares into the distance, her eyes still shining bright with power, and a hush falls over the raving crowd below. The screams quieten down, and the long stream of troops finally eases as they all stare in wonder at the display, fear creeping into their eyes at the scale of such magic.

I'm stepping forward to lean against the stone of the

battlement, a plan to breach the shield myself to face the witches and fend them off already starting to form in my mind, when Kharl's voice reverberates around the village, booming with power.

"We have come to free you, good sister! We heard a rumor of one of our own held captive by the Savage Prince, and we've returned to bring you into the fold. Such power does not belong with the high fae, chained at their feet as we have been for too long. Join us now so we may take you home."

There's cheering below from the mindless masses who agree with his every word, but the witch looks at Kharl without flinching, her chin never dropping and her shoulders perfectly straight. A breath catches in my throat as I stare at her, humbled at the power she wields.

She answers him, her own voice strengthened by the magic within her, no need to raise her pitch to be heard over masses. "I'm no sister to you, no sister to any of these creatures. You should never have come here, Kharl Balzog. You should never have come to the Southern Lands to begin with. Your fate was sealed the moment you stepped into our kingdom and met the Seer."

The cheering continues underneath us, and Kharl chuckles lowly under his breath, a farce of humor in a joyless man.

"The high fae and their stories. They've twisted the truth to you. They locked our kind in their castles, away from the forests, and forced us to work in servitude. They forgot how to give to the land. They do nothing but take and destroy. Why should we give to them what should be given only to each other and ourselves?"

A ripple of unease works its way down my shoulders, my sword gripped tightly in my hand as I inch toward the witch. It's an echo of the words she said to us, only twisted and vicious.

In her tales, she didn't want any of the power for herself.

They continue to speak as though thousands aren't listening and waiting with bated breath, the coin still in the air as the entire castle waits for the outcome of the toss.

"I've heard your tales of grandeur, the propaganda you fed the covens to take their Maidens and twist them into these creatures, the witchlings you took from our forests and never returned. I know it all and more. I'm here, Kharl Balzog, to deliver your fate."

My eyes narrow, and footsteps sound behind me as Tauron finally reaches my section of the wall, standing beside me with the bow in his hands as he watches the interaction. His gaze lands on the witch and gets stuck there as he witnesses the fearsome power that emanates from her, the shield holding strong around us all and pulsing with that same power.

"My fate? Good sister, I don't have one. The Seer delivered it to me, and I killed her for it, then I rewrote my fate to my own liking. Even the Fates themselves bow before me. If you think yourself strong enough to stand against me for the sake of the high fae, then come down here to face me as hundreds have before, all of them now nothing but ash."

She lifts her arms, the sleeves of her robe parting at the slits that run up to her elbows. She holds her hands out before her as a small pinprick of light shines from each of her elbows for a fraction of a moment, fast enough that it could be confused for a trick of the early morning light, except for the *pops* of power that pierce the ear and make way for a sword to appear in one hand and a long scepter in the other, a ribbon tied through the twisted wood and a raw emerald glowing at the top within the clutches of the oak staff.

She holds each of them with the calm confidence of not just a soldier but a warrior, trained to fight with magic and blade. Finally, something close to apprehension worries at Kharl's brow, his lips curling up as he stares at that scepter.

The witch nods, grim death in her eyes. "I know your fate, Kharl Balzog. To die at the hand of a Ravenswyrd witch, generations of neutrality and tradition broken for your demise. Your fate is a death toll calling."

My heart stops dead in my chest, the Fates screaming underneath my skin as though they speak through her, my mate nothing but a vessel for their commands.

Kharl sneers, curses falling from his lips before he snaps, "The Ravenswyrd are dead, I killed them all! That is not my fate anymore."

With one hand, steady and sure, she lifts the scepter and points the raw jewel directly at him, only the shield between them, and his eyes fill with horror at the sight of the relic.

"You missed me."

A pulse of power bursts out of the emerald and through the shield as though it isn't there, a beam of light that cuts through the masses below and tears them apart in a single blow like a bolt of lightning. The earth opens up around the light as it absorbs the power, but the enemy screams as they're decimated.

The earth sings in triumph.

With every high-fae eye on her ignored, my Fates-cursed mate climbs onto the battlement with the sword hefted in one hand and her scepter held firmly in the other before she steps off the stone to plummet to her death on the other side of the wall. My heart stops dead in my chest, a strangled command to stop her trapped in my throat as I throw myself against the wall of the battlement, too late to do anything myself but watch her fall. The soldiers around us shout as they all scramble to look, all of us expecting her blood-soaked death at the bottom, only to find her standing tall on the grass.

She steps through the shield, unharmed and determined, and moving faster than I ever thought possible, she launches into battle. Her sword cuts through the witches there, the light of her magic bursting forth and cleaving them apart—it's a massacre the likes of which I've never seen before.

Alone and with no regard for her own safety, the witch fights for Yregar.

FORTY THREE

ROOKE

The shield holds true.

Even without the moonstone talismans as anchors, shields have always been my strongest gift, an affinity for protection I've carried since birth, and the shimmering dome of magic that encases Yregar Castle is impossible to breach. The witches learn that the hard way, my magic killing them violently, but the high fae are more cautious in their explorations. There's no need for their hesitation; the shield is held in place by my magic, and it won't harm them, but they can't cross it either.

I don't need any distractions down here.

The power of the earth races through my veins, burning me with the glory and vitality of the land. It's like holding fire, a devastating force that's vital to our survival but could kill me if I hold on too tightly. The trick to not burning out is to channel the power and use it, to wield it freely until there's none of that heat left within my veins.

I lift my scepter and cleave entire swaths of the raving mass of witches as somber screams fill the air, and I widen my stance as the first wave of them hits me, Kharl's voice still ringing in my ears. It's a sound I imagined for many decades after I learned who he was and why he came to the Ravenswyrd Forest. A fate to be killed by a witch born of neutrality, and I've already raged and mourned the fickle ways of the Fates we follow.

If he hadn't come to kill my coven, I would have never left the forest.

I would have never become the witch I am now, the only version of myself who can fight Kharl and kill him. I would have never learned to hold a sword, the calluses still rough on my hands from decades of fighting in the Northern Lands.

These skills are so intrinsic to me now that I slip back into my soldier form, swinging and cleaving the witches apart, the magic in my scepter magnifying every blow as I fight them off two-handed and leave devastation in my wake. Two centuries in the Sol Army training every day, fueled by my desperation to somehow convince the Fates to change my fate through my acts of selfless service, these weakened creatures don't stand a chance against me. I've learned to fight against all fae folk, the high fae and part-bloods and myriad fae in between, and though I mostly wielded my sword and magic against the Ureen on the battlefields, I'm more than adept to face the enemy before me now.

The raving army of witches pouring in from the fae door finally stops as Kharl realizes his fatal error, the victory he wrapped tightly around himself as a comfort now quickly unraveling as the lie is brought for all to see. He doesn't call for a retreat—every last one of these witches is expendable to him—but as I fight my way through the masses, I hear the cries of his own retreat as he leaves them behind.

He shoves one of his protectors off their horse and climbs onto the saddle then rides back to the fae door as he runs from his fate and my wrath. He's wearing the traditional robes of the Unseelie witches with ornate embroidery on them, the symbols a twisted cacophony of the covens he's destroyed to create this new one of his own, and the long cloak of black and red trails in the wind as he flees.

I don't chase him down.

This isn't the marker of our fate, the moment his death becomes mine. The Fates were clear of my path and my union to the prince, in his tradition and mine. My sacrifice is still to come, after I join my soul to his in the old way.

Instead, I focus on releasing these witches from the torment he has them locked within, black spittle oozing from their mouths and their eyes as they swarm to me. As the steel length of my sword bites into them and tears their flesh apart, arcs of the earth's true power radiate down the blade to magnify the damage and send them on their way back to the Fates. They may return to Elysium, but their souls can never be cleared of the evil Kharl sowed there, and I can't help but wonder if the Fates will look kindly on the witches who willingly turned from their way.

I don't have the heart for such a question; their death is all I crave as penance for their crimes, but it'll never be enough. No amount of bloodshed and torture could ever atone for the Ravenswyrd Coven and the hundreds of others lost here.

The witches who were born within the Witch Ward know nothing but this chaos, and they snarl at me in their final moments, but I see other witches amongst the crowd, a glimmer of fear tempering the madness before their deaths, and "Mother" on their lips as the power arcs from my scepter. My robes spin and twirl as I become nothing more than the force of retribution, my sword swinging elegantly as I perform an old dance. One I can never unlearn, and I thank the Fates for that.

I feel the moment Kharl crosses the fae door once more, the smoke curling into the air but the scent of it obscured now by the burning flesh of the witches. They've been destroyed by the witcheswane and the dragon oil, the stink of it all consuming as it coats the back of my throat until bile threatens to choke me, but the magic the earth gave me holds off the effects of it for now.

The blood of the witches begins to poison the land underneath us, stinking and rotting and doing more damage to Yregar. Another devastating blow against the healing I've so desperately tried to offer it, and some of the calm I'd slipped into during the power exchange wavers. My temper flares as the magic of the land protests within me at such treatment.

They've taken *everything* from us—taken away the rites, taken away those who cared for us, until there was nothing left of our great legacy. My mind fills with the song of the trees as they mourn the damage to the kingdom. I hear their pain through the power given to me, the deep-rooted oaks spread throughout the Southern Lands older than the kingdom itself burning in misery as Kharl leaves nothing but destruction in his wake.

His death will be mine, and the trees will sing their glory once more.

The cobblestones of the village are slick beneath my feet, every inch of my body covered in blackened and poisoned blood, and the stink of it is streaked across my cheeks. My stomach protests the moment I take notice of it, roiling dangerously. The piles of dead are everywhere as I cast my magic out to be sure none are left behind, none are left to take root here and spread Kharl's poison further.

The village is destroyed.

My own temper, unaided by the land, flares, and the next witch I find still mumbling under his breath takes the brunt of it. He stares up at the sky pleadingly, the pain across his face ending at the vicious swing of my sword as I put every ounce of my fury behind it.

The inequity of it all sinks its teeth into me, biting down until I'm holding on to my clear head by a thread. The high fae castle stands untouched, while the villagers and the refugees are left with nothing, always losing out in this vicious war with no one to defend them or the lands. It will take months just to repair the buildings and replace the belongings that were lost today, and the cold grip of winter fast approaches.

High fae soldiers stream down the stairs on the inner wall, but the shield stays true, keeping them securely held within the protection of my power.

There's a loud *pop* ahead, and through the wreckage of the wall I see the fae door open once more, magic sustaining it even as it burns. I look over to find riders coming through, no longer the raving masses but witches who sit securely in their saddles with a calm that none of the other witches have held.

Kharl has sent his generals for me, witches with magic strong enough to face me and change his fate once and for all. I count as six of them cross on horseback, wearing the same black cloaks as he did, their power rippling through the battlefield of Yregar. They cross one by one, not waiting for each other as they each ride toward me at a breakneck pace.

Shouts sound along in a wall as soldiers attempt to cross the shield, swords drawn to join me in the fight. Dozens more stand waiting, arrows drawn and desperate to fire, but the shield doesn't just keep the enemy out, but them within. I don't want help, I don't need the distraction, and I turn my back on them all as my magic holds the shield in place.

It will not fall.

I don't look back as I focus on those six riders, their horses snorting and snarling beneath them as they push them harder. The beasts are bred for war, riding hard enough to kill themselves, and the calls of the high fae grow louder. Reed's voice is in the mix as he desperately tries to get my attention, but I ignore him as I move. I step into the path to the fae door to meet my enemy upon their arrival, lifting my scepter toward the sky and letting out a burst of power. The once raving masses of the dead jerk and twitch before falling still once more, one final check to be sure the army is dealt with as the generals approach.

A single twisted witch with a dagger could be the end of me if I'm taken by surprise in the middle of a fight.

Power isn't something to be taken lightly, and I know no arrogance in this fight. My eyes slip shut for just a moment as I murmur a prayer to the Fates. This isn't my time; many battles lie ahead, Kharl's death at my hands to restore the lands just one part of the greater whole, my fate too intricate to end it all now.

I faced the Ureen and the possible end of all time in the Northern Lands. I survived the very worst that war can bring with my friends at my side and under my brother's watchful presence. I'm not going to die here and now by these generals. I won't cross to Elysium until I've seen my brother again, not until I bring him home to the forest with the land renewed and the war here over. I'm not going to die today and let the Fates tear the sky open once more.

I open my eyes just in time for the first of the generals to reach me, steel arcing through the air vibrating and glowing red with power, but I lift my own sword to block the blow, pushing my magic into the strike and watching as he tumbles from his saddle. He catches himself to land on his feet in a telling action.

These are not the raving hordes lying dead around me, these are soldiers and powerful witches in their own right. This witch doesn't wear a hood, and the markings on his face proclaim him a member of the Nightsyde Coven. He's long since betrayed them to their demise, but they once lived in the Mistwyrd Forest nestled within the Blood Valley, an ancient forest of great sacrifice that stands tall and proud.

That power is distorted in this man whose eyes flash silver, framed by dark marks and a cruel twist of his lip.

"Mother," he taunts, the word a curse on his lips.

There's no relic in his hand as he lifts his sword and strikes at me, stronger and taller than me, but I was trained by the Seelie high fae, who are far stronger and taller than any witch could ever be. I take the blow without fault, letting his momentum pull him forward to shift his balance. I widen my stance as I spin around him, watching as he barely blocks my own blow. Our robes fan out as we spin and hack at one another, power running down the length of our swords as we use every skill at our disposal. Any misstep now will be my last. I block out the screams of the high fae on the wall until I know nothing but my sword and scepter.

When he finally loses his temper and swings at me recklessly, I duck and slash at his ribs, the bite of my Seelie blade slicing through the robes, and blood, still red, pours from his side in a confession of his compliance.

Kharl didn't have to twist this male's mind—he followed willingly.

The blood soaks into the land, an unwilling sacrifice, but still not enough. I turn, and the two of us are side by side as I lift my sword and spin. My arms are numbed by the magic pumping through me, so I barely feel the strain as the sword hits home this time, slicing through his neck and cleaving his head from his body in a single powerful stroke.

There's no time for me to rest, no time to take stock of the situation, as the sound of hooves on cobblestone echoes louder, more of their kind coming for me. I don't need to think; I learned that long ago. My body acts on instinct alone, honed for centuries, and the sound of my sword clashing with another rings through the decimated streets of Yregar Village, echoing through the burning buildings and bouncing off the cobblestones.

My boots move smoothly underneath me, my footwork so ingrained in me I don't have to think about it as I spin and turn, facing the witch as she flings herself from her horse. The beast gallops away, terrified and frantic as it weaves through the piles of bodies. Long tresses of red hair spill out from the witch's dark hood, and the witch markings on her hands glow black with her power.

Her hand runs down the length of her blade, ornate and ceremonial but sharpened for this purpose, the embedded stones of citrine and smoky quartz lighting up in the hilt as her magic takes hold of the weapon.

She's stronger than the last witch, and when she turns to face me, the hood drops and the silver of her eyes flashes at me, showing her rage. The witch markings over her face are etched deeply into her skin and the unnatural black lines glow, a distortion of our traditions and an insult to every Crone, Mother, and Maiden before her.

More horses ride toward us, a promise of outnumbered sword play, but as she looks at the wall, her lips curl into a sneer and she speaks to me. "A pet of the high fae—you're disgusting! They're the reason we were stuck in the forests for so long, forced to do their bidding to keep the balance while they laughed at our stupidity and thought themselves better."

I study the markings around her eyes, placed there long before she joined Kharl's ranks. Each stroke of the ink is a legacy she's betrayed, and her shame will be known amongst the forests until the last tree dies.

I shake my head at her, the oak of my mother's scepter warm in my hand as I feel the endless generations of Ravenswyrd witches who clasped it tight before her, only to end with me. The last Mother.

"You think yourself better than the high fae when you've forgotten the language of the trees? Or do you still hear them screaming and simply ignore them, far worse? I'm not here for the high fae. I'm here for the Ravenswyrd Forest and the coven within."

She flinches, her eyes tracing over me for witch markings, but my mother never had the chance to give me any, murdered at Kharl's command before I was old enough to receive them. I've never let another witch mark me. If I couldn't have my mother's mark on me and the ink of my coven on my skin, then no other would do.

"The Ravenswyrd are dead, all of them," she hisses, and the corner of my mouth tugs up into a cold and cruel smile.

I watch her comrades ride toward us, death on swift horses. Each of them bolted through the fae door as fast as the old magic would push them, and now they race straight to me to kill me at Kharl's command.

"Did your leader not tell you he failed? Ah, I see. He told you he defied the Fates themselves and scorned them without retribution, somehow better than the Sol King, more powerful than the old magic."

She gapes at me but the cold smile on my lips grows wider. "He lied. So filled with his own arrogance and importance that he can tell a good story, but he lied to you all. The Fates are not bowing to him and his whims. The Fates bow to no one, not even a king, or a witch who traveled far from his own forest to burn ours to the ground. You followed a false god, and it led you here."

I lift my scepter, and her eyes widen with dread as the magic arcs from it, white light flowing through me and into the wood. Magnifying my power, the emerald groans as the white light rains down on the four horses and their witch riders. Their screams fill the air around us as my magic tears them apart, limb from limb, and the screaming stops as their body parts hit the ground.

The witches were strong enough to be sent to fight me, but their magic was no match for what burns within me, a neutral witch called to war with the power of the forest in her veins. The old gods that walk amongst the oaks, resting there for a time unknown, nurtured me and protected me so that I may protect it now.

Kharl might have killed my coven, but their legacy lives on in me. The heart of a healer beats within my chest, but I've long since made peace with the war that lives in my mind. A soldier who no longer fears the sword I must take up and the death that must be given by my hand.

The witch backs away from me slowly, tripping over the burned body of one of the raving masses, falling and then scrambling on her hands and knees as she cowers away from me. Every lie Kharl ever told her has unraveled before her eyes, and though she's a pathetic creature, no empathy tugs at my heart.

The witches who murdered my coven at Kharl's orders shot my sister in the back as she ran, terrified and sobbing, the tears still wet on her cheeks when I found her.

They slit my mother's throat and killed the baby nursing at her breast where she sat in our family hut. Her blood poured over the son she was sure would grow up safe and strong in the forest, dead but still clutched within her arms.

My father had twelve arrows embedded in his chest, so deep that the fletching of raven feathers was buried in his flesh. In his dying moments, he crawled through the dirt, desperate to reach my mother to protect her and the children they had brought into this world together. He died alone, face down, the screams of his coven the last thing he knew before Elysium.

My brother died before my grandmother's hut, arrows in his back and a dagger slashed across his throat as they finished him off, his hands digging into the dirt just the same as my father's as he desperately held on through pain and blood and fear to reach our beloved Crone.

I know my siblings' deaths, every one of them still an open wound within me that time can never heal. A single command from Kharl, and they wiped out an entire legacy of peaceful healers, protectors of the trees, those who never asked for anything in return of their services, who poured into the land selflessly and never ask for more than simple shelter and safety, the forest's song singing deep within our hearts.

None of those witches showed mercy to my coven.

No matter how deep in my healer's heart I look, I can't find any for this witch either.

Terror shines from her eyes as she looks up at me, prayers to the Fates falling from her lips, but I hope they don't look kindly on her and the depths of Elysium reject her soul and leave her to wither into nothingness, an eternal torture for the devastation she's wrought.

I lift my scepter once more, the emerald singing within the clutches of the oak, and the burst of power hits her full force, a hole opening in her chest and her blood pouring into the land. Red and vital, still a willing accomplice to Kharl and his ambitions.

I murmur my own apologies to the land for giving them such a violent sacrifice, but it guzzles it down all the same. Power is power, and though a willing sacrifice is always preferred, an unwilling one is just as strong.

The village is silent around me.

For hours the battle raged, but it's over now, no more riders crossing the fae door to face me. I wait, not one to be caught unaware, but there is nothing to greet me but the piles of stinking dead.

I send out another pulse of magic through the village just to be sure they're all dead, and when I sense nothing but corpses, I take aim with the scepter once more and put out the fire ravaging the fae door. When there's nothing left there but the charred structure, I seal the door shut, pushing the magic back into the land to ensure Kharl can never come through it again.

The earth groans and shudders beneath us as it accepts the old magic of the First Fae, a powerful morsel to consume, and then I turn to the bodies of the witches. Their blackened blood is burning as it seeps through the cobblestones, scorching everything with its poison.

Without proper care, the land here at Yregar will never recover.

Still ignoring the shouts and protests from the high-fae soldiers on the walls above me, I hold out my sword, and light flashes from the point at my elbow as I put it away. Grasping my mother's scepter in both hands, I direct the last of the land's magic through the wood to set fire to everything around me, containing the flames to only the poison as I burn it all away. There'll be no funeral pyres for these dead, no comfort to see them to Elysium safely, and I hope they don't find peace wherever they end up. I don't have any kindness left within me for them; that version of me died in the forest with my family. Smoke funnels into the air and arches around the dome shield I still hold, curling at the top as it gathers there.

I don't put my mother's scepter away until the last of the bodies and the blackened blood are ash. I untie the ribbon, a creation of centuries of my own handiwork, and slip it into the inner pocket of my dress, then the light of my magic pops as the scepter returns to where I store it, the small pin point on my other inner elbow glowing for a moment with power before it disappears. There's no other sign of the magic there, nothing but a light freckle easily missed in every search of my body so far.

I turn to face the inner wall of Yregar, the lines and lines of soldiers staring down at me with their weapons still in hand but no longer pointed. Their eyes are too far away for me to see them, but we all watch as the enemy we faced drifts toward the sky as nothing more than ash and smoke.

I take a deep breath, and I let the shield for the Battle of Yregar go once more, its job well done.

FORTY FOUR

SOREN

As the arcs of light burst out of the witch's scepter, the soldiers around the wall take cover, bows still in hand as they duck under their shields and the large stone battlements, but her power isn't aimed toward us. No matter how far the dying hordes of witches are flung by that power, none of them cross the shield.

I stand in the safety of that shield and watch as my Fates-cursed mate decimates the army that was so close to victory. With a sword in one hand and her scepter in the other, she spins and swipes as she fights with the skill and grace of a seasoned warrior. She swings the blade with ease, cutting through the witches who approach her as the steel sings through the air in a song I know well.

Though my heart clenches in my chest at first, the mate I waited centuries for fighting alone down there, as she moves confidently cleaving through our enemies, my throat closes over at the sight. Something close to awe begins to bloom in my gut, warmth spreading through my limbs with every passing moment of the display before me. She is a sight to behold.

I was expecting a fumbling technique from her at best, the skill level of a healer forced to pick up a sword only by the devastation of the war she faced in the Northern Lands. That motivation to learn is all wrong and usually cultivates a poor swordsman, but even as she uses her magic to kill dozens of the raving witches in a single blow, her technique with the sword is nothing short of perfect.

The witches quickly become nothing more than piles of dead, their poison leaching into the ground as their screams slowly peter out. The witch glows with the power of the earth, a glorious dance of death as she defends the castle. I've fought two-handed and it's tiring, your body using twice the energy and burning out faster, but she doesn't falter once as she decimates them.

The wall is silent as we stare, the shock at her skill and defense palpable amongst the ranks. Even Tauron has nothing to say as he gapes at the scene before us, and when the anticipation becomes too much for Roan, still in the saddle keeping command over the soldiers in the courtyard, he sends Reed up to see what's happening.

The Outland soldier is quiet as he approaches me, but his apprehension melts away as he sees the flare of her robes and watches her turning to slash and hack with each pulse of magic she sends out. Roan's agitation only worsens at our silence, but Reed can't find any words to describe the witch as she cleaves through the battlefield and leaves piles of her dead kinsman as she goes.

I turn back to him. "Come and see for yourself, there's no enemy left for you to defend against down there."

Roan's eyebrows shoot up his forehead, but he dismounts from his horse and hands the reins to another of the soldiers, then takes the steps up the inner wall to my section three at a time, the only sound on our side of the shield the clink of his armor. When he comes to a halt at my side, standing between Reed and I, all the confusion melts from his face, leaving behind awe. The same emotion is in the expressions of all the soldiers as they stare down, a reprieve taking over the ranks as we forget that the battle could change at a moment's notice.

"Why didn't the witch just tell you her fate," Roan mutters.

Reed doesn't say anything in reply to his prince, but his jaw tightens and his chin lifts just a fraction, a reaction that speaks loudly enough.

There's no point in lying, the truth undeniable as the witch fights before us. "We wouldn't have believed her. We barely believed that she was fated to me."

Roan's eyes widen at my honesty, but the scene before us can't be argued with. If I tried, I'd be no better than the Unseelie Court, basking in my uncle's presence and hanging on to his every honeyed word as the castles around me wither, clinging to his lies for the sake of nothing but comfort.

The witch will kill Kharl and restore the land. If nothing else, I'm sure of that.

Reed's eyes narrow as he watches the witch walk through the village, ensuring none of the enemy have been missed in her efforts, and when he speaks, it's with a carefully neutral tone. "Maybe you should start making your peace with her by calling her by her name. Perhaps then she won't keep her word and force you to beg her to marry you."

Roan turns to look at him, censure in his eyes at his soldier's impertinence, but the lull in the battle is broken before he can form words.

"Riders approach!"

The sentries from Tauron's section of the wall cluster as they call out to us, their position having a better viewpoint of the fae door and, after a moment, they begin to call out to the witch too, warning her of the danger approaching. Tauron leans forward on the battlement stones, cursing under his breath at the scene.

"The fae fucking door, they're still crossing over from the

Witch Ward. Kharl's fled, but he's sending more of his kind to kill the witch."

Her words to Kharl ring in my mind once more—her fate is to kill Kharl and hold him to justice for the hundreds of thousands of lives lost in the Southern Lands at his command. Her coven was just a drop in the ocean of his evil, but it's the drop that spilled the bucket of his death. The witch fated to me will kill our greatest enemy and free Southern Lands from his reign of terror.

I'm only furious that she'll take his death from me.

Reed steps away from us, ducking down to open one of the hatches the soldiers used to pour the witcheswane over the stones and then dropping down to the outer staircase there. It's encased in iron, but he doesn't let its effect hinder him as he calls out to the witch, "Let us through the shield! We're ready to help you, Rooke, you can't fight them off alone forever!"

She ignores us all, her steps even as she walks toward the advancing horses. We hear the hooves as they bolt toward her, witches of power on their backs sending small balls of magic sparking through the air only to stop at the shield, testing its strength. One, two, three...we count until six of them have ridden out, and the witch walks out to meet them, sword in one hand and scepter in the other.

She holds them both comfortably, the ribbon tied to the end of the scepter dancing in the breeze and the raw emerald held within the clutches of the wood glowing bright across the smoky battlefield-turned-massacre. Her posture is still perfect, no signs of injury or fatigue, and yet my skin crawls with the uselessness of standing here and watching her.

The soldiers try calling out to her again, but as she faces her enemy, Roan puts a stop to that potential distraction.

My Fates-cursed mate lifts her sword and knocks the first witch out of the saddle with ease, his horse whinnying as it bolts away from them both, snorting and panting in terror as it flees.

One on one, we see the true power of the witch's sword technique, the perfect dance as their swords clash and part and clash again. The male she faces is desperate as he hacks at her while her sword moves almost lazily through the air; she's comfortable in the way only a true master of the art can be.

She doesn't waste time drawing out the duel, cleaving her enemy's head from his shoulders as she turns on her heel and her robes flare around her once more. The blood that drips onto the cobblestones is still red, the powerful witch a willing accomplice and still of sound mind.

I watch as the blood disappears between the cracks, the words of the Ravenswyrd Forest a lesson of what magic is taking place there. A sacrifice unwillingly made but accepted all the same, and hopefully one that sends the witch more power.

There are footsteps behind me, and Tauron and Tyton both fall into place at my side as they watch the witch fight. Tyton is rubbing his temples, but he's awake and watching closely as the next rider approaches. The female jumps from her saddle willingly, holding up a sword confidently but with none of the technique of the warrior she faces.

Tyton turns to Tauron with narrowed eyes and snaps at his brother, "You heard what she said to Kharl. There's no denying her loyalties now. I told you the forest said she would save us all—the forest promised me she was honest and true and like nothing else in the Southern Lands. The last Ravenswyrd Mother cannot be overlooked or disrespected."

Tauron grimaces, but for once he has nothing to say, his writhing anger dormant within him as the wrath of a witch the trees love scorches the enemies before us.

She speaks to this new witch, fury rolling off her once more. She lifts the scepter, and light arcs from the top and kills the approaching riders instantly in their saddles. She tears them apart with her power as though theirs is nothing. Kharl's assumptions of what it will take to defeat her are so far from the truth.

My own assumptions are also being blown apart right now, though at least I'm not running away in terror from her wrath like the self-proclaimed High Witch did.

As the defeated female crawls away desperately, the witch finishes her off, her anger merciless in all the ways I thought she would be with the high fae, but here we stand, protected by her magic. She stands and waits, not letting the shield down, and when she's sure that the riders have stopped coming, she turns to survey the village, careful in her assessment. When she confirms them all dead, the emerald of the scepter glows, and she burns the rotting witch-flesh and destroys the poison they leach. I'm sure this isn't about helping us with the cleanup but rather protecting the land from taking in too much of that toxic blood.

The smoke and the stink become unbearable as she turns back to the fae door, the flames still burning high as the magic fuels them. She lifts her scepter again, only this time, we all feel the magic in our bones as she closes the door and pushes the magic back into the earth, the flames snuffing out as though they were never there in the first place. The earth accepts the old magic back into its depths, swallowing it down until there's no trace of it left.

Our shortcut through the kingdom is gone, but the witches' attacks are halted once more.

With small pops of light, her weapons disappear back into the ether where she hides them, the question of the missing dagger answered. Her hands flare out at her sides, and she tilts her head back and lets the early morning sun shine down on her face, her skin still glowing and a calm falling over her once more. The tense lines of fury melt away from her expression, and the serene female appears—her most dangerous form, because seeing her standing there that way turns the unspent fury within me into something I don't want to admit to.

It's impossible to see on her black linen robes, but spatters of witch blood cover her face and hands in a gory display of her ruthless battles. There's a tear in the skirts at her side, and the black leather boots she's now wearing look nothing like the Unseelie high fae ones Airlie gave her. She's dressed for war on her own terms, a female to be reckoned with.

Her hair is secured back in the same braid she wears as she tends to the injured and ill with gentle healer's hands and a thorough eye, the same braid she wore while pouring magic into her garden and cultivating the plants that grow under her careful eyes, the same braid she wore as she eased my cousin's baby into the world, breaking curses and holding the infant with care.

All of these females are one and the same, each a facet of the same witch, driven out of the Southern Lands long ago by a war and a fate that terrified a child of the forest who'd known only peace and neutrality.

My Fates-blessed mate.

The witch doesn't move from the village. She continues to soak in the gentle rays of the sun, as the soldiers on the wall begin to dig our way out of the smoldering piles of ashes left behind.

The mounds block the gate, and we're unable to get it open. Teams of soldiers are sent down the outer staircases to get to work, but they don't approach her. Instead, they choke back their reactions to the already rotting corpses as they clear the gate and then start to work on a path out.

When the iron door, creaking and damaged but still secure, swings open, there's a collective sigh of relief. Sentries still cover the battlements and hold watch; the battle is over now, but our guard must never come down.

Kharl's fate must be ringing in his ears, tormenting him now that he's learned it still stalks him, and his armies are still plentiful. This battle might have been a defeat, but I'm sure he won't even notice the loss of his soldiers back in the Witch Ward. Every count we've made of his forces, every rumor we've heard and every tale of the writhing masses of his armies tells of far greater numbers than what we've seen today, a sobering thought for all.

I take grim satisfaction that his numbers may recover, but his mind certainly won't. I've lived through centuries of torture over my own fate, a promise of good things just outside my grasp, but there's nothing good coming his way. Nothing to keep him from falling further into his insanity.

When a path is finally cleared, I look back toward the witch only to find her gone, vanished as though she was never there in the first place. My heart clenches in revolt, but Tyton steps forward ahead of me, his eyes narrowed as he stares toward the outer wall. He glances at me before nodding in that direction, and I follow his gaze.

The witch moves to each high-fae soldier who was lost in the first wave of the witches' attack, their bodies strewn over the cobblestones by the force of the wall coming down. There's no sign of discomfort in her posture, not at the battle she just fought on her own or from the witcheswane that surrounds her, and I wonder if the magic of the land strengthens her against it.

I don't need the tug of the Fates in my chest to lead me to her. I might have been wrong about her allegiances and her motives, but she's definitely a beacon, only I'm the one drawn to her and unable to resist the pull.

I call for Ingor to bring me Nightspark as Tyton lets out a breath, raw and full of pain. "She's praying for our dead, to see them safely to Elysium. The same soldiers who've whispered their hopes for her suffering and death at your hands, and she's out there reading them their last rites to see them on their journey safely."

I have nothing to say back to that, no way to describe the twisted mess that only grows more intricate inside my chest.

Ingor finally brings Nightspark to me, his head bowed and his skin still pale from shock but his eyes clear after our victory. He didn't see the worst of it from the stables, but no one missed the shield of the witch's power as it protected us, pushing Kharl's forces back and saving the wall just as the gate had begun to break. We all know how close it came.

One of the sentries from the wall calls out, "Riders from the Outlands approach! Dozens arrive to Yregar. The Snowsong colors fly strong; Prince Roan is here."

My stomach drops.

The Outland soldiers won't stop to ask questions, they'll kill any witch they find…but the only witch still left at Yregar is my fated mate, in their direct path, whispering prayers to the dead. After seeing her wield that sword of hers, I'm not so certain the Outland soldiers would come away from an attack against her the victors.

Roan's father or his most loyal soldiers will fall.

I swing onto Nightspark without a word, Roan cursing behind me as he calls for his own horse where it's still saddled and ready in the stables. I kick Nightspark straight into a gallop and jump and weave through the debris of bodies. His hooves are loud on the cobblestones as we race to beat the Outland soldiers to the outer wall. The witch has eyes only for our dead, ignorant to the danger approaching as her kindness in seeing to their passing.

The village is all but destroyed as I ride through, buildings torn apart and burned. The bodies of our enemy cover the doorsteps, and some even fell within the houses they were ransacking until their demise, hundreds of my people now needing shelter within Yregar Castle until we can restore their homes. This village has stood here for thousands of years, and it's now barely more than rubble.

I kick Nightspark again, pushing him as hard as his legs will go. The banners of Snowsong approach, the calls of the soldiers ringing through the air, and the witch finally looks up and sees them. She rises to her feet, but even as they descend upon her, she doesn't draw a weapon. She just stands there and watches them swarm.

As calls for her death ring through the air, Roan calls out from behind me his own orders to stand down, and the Outland soldiers slow a fraction in their approach. It's just enough for me to reach her first, Nightspark brought to an abrupt halt and the momentum almost throwing me out of the saddle as I place his body between the witch and the high fae soldiers.

The group of them circle us as though ready to watch me kill her, their eyes bright and cold beneath their helmets, their faces shielded as they stare down at her with contempt. Even as her own eyes glow back at them with magic, she doesn't cower and no harsh words cross her lips as her righteous fury emanates.

She's not going to accept our apologies or admissions of wrongdoing easily.

"A witch? Prince Soren, what is the meaning of this?" The words ring out, and the hooves approaching finally come to a halt.

Roan answers his father. "This is Prince Soren's mate, Rooke, determined by the Fates themselves, and the battle of Yregar was won at her hand. The siege was held off by the high fae, but the enemy was destroyed by her."

The soldiers glance first at each other and then at the mounds of dead that surround us, disbelief cutting deep lines around their mouths. When they finally look back at her, they size up the

Ravenswyrd witch and decide for themselves that she's nothing to be concerned about. Her slight stature in comparison to their horses is a cunning ruse of the Fates.

If only they knew the power that lies within her, or the mastery in the swing of her sword. They missed out on the humbling spectacle that my own soldiers witnessed. It was an important lesson learned by us all, one I won't soon forget.

"Thank you for heeding our call for aid, Father. Please ride with me back to Yregar to help with the cleanup. The gate and inner wall need to be repaired with haste—they're our only protection against the witches' return."

His words are formal, full of respect, and the soldiers finally shift away from the witch. Their horses step away from her as they reluctantly leave her alive, a murmur of disgruntlement working through them all.

The older Prince Roan guides his horse over to Roan and clasps his shoulder, pride shining in his blue eyes as he stares at his beloved son. "I'm desperate for news of Airlie, but I won't ask in front of the witch. Let's leave it behind so you can tell me of my daughter's health."

A ripple of irritation breaks through the protective haze clouding my mind at his dismissive words towards my mate, the witch who has saved us all today and proved just how obedient to the Fates she's been all of this time. She chose to stay in the dungeons and endure our treatment, she chose to leave the iron cage behind to break the curse and save the baby, and then again she chose to come out here and fight for Yregar. She didn't deserve the mistreatment or scorn then and she certainly doesn't deserve it now.

With a deep breath, I remind myself that Prince Roan has just arrived and has no idea of what the witch has done for us here.

None of the contempt that Aura feels for Roan is reflected

in the older man's regard for his son's mate, accepting her into his heart and family with nothing but joy. There's no deception or manipulation in his words—he's desperate to know if the female he treasures as a daughter survived the birthing bed.

The messengers haven't dispersed any information of the baby throughout the kingdom. Aura's own messengers were stopped before they made it out of the gates; there's been not a word breathed about Roan's miracle, a healthy wife and son.

His own golden eyes flick toward the witch, and he holds out a hand, gesturing at her as his father scowls. "Prince Soren's Fates-blessed mate is a gifted healer and saw Airlie through the birth. The rumors that run rife through the kingdom are true, Father, the curse is broken. My wife is alive and well, waiting for us in the safety of the castle with our son. Your grandson, the Snowsong heir."

Ripples of disbelief and whoops of joy work through Roan's most loyal males as his father jerks him forward in his saddle for a raucous embrace, all of the celebration he deserves but was robbed of by the witches' attack. The soldiers are staring at the witch with far too much interest for my liking, and I guide Nightspark to step around her, blocking her from the sight line of the high fae. The soldiers look away as I move between them, their gazes dropping in respect for me, but they murmur speculations of her to each other regardless.

I want her out of here and away from this scrutiny.

I hold out a hand to her with the intention of carrying her behind me on Nightspark for the trip back to Yregar, but she stares at my hand like it's a death curse.

When her eyes flick up to meet mine, she grimaces. "That doesn't look like begging to me. I'd rather walk until my feet bleed."

She speaks in the old language, obscuring our words from the soldiers around us, but the elder Prince Roan hears them and understands, his brow furrowing. His son slaps him on the shoulder to distract him, and they begin to walk their horses back toward the village.

The Outland soldiers all follow and leave me to my witch mate, the cold fury radiating from her, and the calm before the storm.

FORTY FiVE

ROOKE

The effects of the earth's power still thrum through my veins as I stare up at Prince Soren, sitting rigidly in the saddle on his beast of a warhorse's back, the creature snorting and pawing at the cobblestones in his impatience to follow the others back to the castle.

After an intense moment of glaring between us, Prince Soren swings down to stand in front of me, deft and confident as he holds out the reins to me. He clicks his tongue at the horse's protest, quieting it with nothing more than that little sound.

I'd almost forgotten how tall this high-fae prince is, how broad his shoulders are, as he looms over me, the breathtaking beauty of the high fae shining in his face. His charisma is only magnified by the scar running through it, no matter what the Unseelie Court may think.

My fury at him deepens the longer I stare back.

His armor is covered in dust and debris, dirt and witch blood coating him to the knees, and as he steps closer to me, a deep unease pools in my gut. My skin is itching, and at first I think it's a physical reaction to every last one of the missteps and malicious acts this male has orchestrated against me, but then I smell it. The witcheswane. His people used the vile substance against Kharl's armies effectively and brutally to protect the castle from the siege. My stomach's roiling reaction now that the power of the earth has left me makes sense.

If he touches me, I'll burst into hives, welts that cannot be soothed covering every inch of my skin. I would have to wait them out as my body healed from the damage. Either he doesn't care about that, or he's forgotten about the poison he's coated with, because his mouth turns down at my response.

"Take my horse and ride back. I'll wait here for the soldiers to arrive to take back our dead for the funeral pyres. We can't delay in sending them into the fires to Elysium. The witches could strike again at any moment."

My body begins to weaken, the power of the magic burning bright within my veins almost burning me right along with it. I drop my gaze and finally step around him. We move as though we're dancing around each other, an intricate pattern of steps as we circle and refuse to make the first move. Whether we're making amends or killing each other makes no difference; the dance is the same.

I call on my last vestiges of magic, and my eyes glow so bright that even I can see the whiting out of the landscape around me as the earth below us begins to groan.

The horses of the Outland soldiers, Prince Roan, and his father stop a few hundred paces away. They're making the journey back to the castle at a snail's pace, giving the horses time to cool down from the hard ride here. Even my witch ears pick up on the concerned murmurs between them, the alarm as the last of my magic begins to fall away from me and spread around the wreckage we stand within.

The stones of the wall strewn around us began to tremble, shuddering and rattling until slowly they rise into the air, lifted by my magic and the power of the earth.

Curses and shouts ring from the inner wall, calling for reassurance, but Prince Soren doesn't speak or move as he watches me slowly piece back together the castle's first line of protection. The white light sears and burns, sealing the stones and melding the wall back together perfectly once more.

The buckled iron gate groans as it lifts into the air, the crunching and snapping sound of it straightening out so loud that the high fae around me cover their ears, groaning themselves as their sensitive hearing is assaulted. I slot the gate back into place, my power patching the holes that Kharl tore through it. I reinforce the hinges and locks until it's even better than before, everything repaired as I strengthen every part of the wall that my magic touches. The power flows through the wall and binds it into a formidable structure once more.

With my very last drops of magic, I turn to the inner wall and lift my hands, directing the power to wash over the gate there too. It held strong until the last possible second, but the damage of that struggle shows, and my magic fills the cracks and fuses the iron back together, reinforcing it the same way I did the outer wall. When the protections of Yregar are secured once more by my final act of magic, the white glow finally dissipates, and the last of the power leaves me.

The magic simmers away to nothing, gone as quickly as the earth had poured into me in the first place, the sacrifice given and honored as Yregar was saved in our most dire hour of need.

I can't wait here for Prince Soren's final decision about my intentions and the dangers of my power. Exhaustion hits me as hard as a horde of witches, and my feet move reluctantly as I walk back toward the castle.

I focus on my steps, counting them as I use every last one of my tricks to stay conscious. Stubborn pride is spurring me to walk on my own and ignore the high fae on their horses around me, making the journey alongside me in silence as their eyes burn into my rigid back. My breathing quickly becomes ragged, but I ignore it. Prince Soren doesn't get back in his saddle, instead leading his ebony beast beside me as we wind through the streets of the ruined village.

I murmur a curse to myself for not fixing it while I was shoring up the walls. But my magic wouldn't have spread that far, not right now, and our safety trumps the houses while the Grand Hall is able to offer shelter to villagers and refugees alike.

My vision begins to waver, black spots appearing wherever I look as I reach the inner wall. The soldiers there are cleaning up the piles of rotting witch flesh, but they all stop and bow respectfully to their prince as we pass.

Their eyes all linger on me.

I can't see or focus well enough to read what they're thinking. They should be happy I've taken care of the witches, but they're probably sticking to their prejudices and are terrified of me now.

I have to make it into the castle and down the stairs into the dungeon. In there, with the iron bars in place, I can sleep for as many hours as my body wishes, get every minute of rest I need to recover from wielding that much power.

It's not such a terrible trial to walk—I've been forced to endure worse—but my feet falter once more as I reach the castle steps, the smell of the witcheswane coating everything around me turning my stomach anew. The last of my energy leaves me in an unstoppable rush.

My last coherent memory is of hands catching me before I hit the stone, lifting me into strong arms that smell like the same poison, leaching the life out of me, and then I know no more.

SIGN UP FOR MY NEWSLETTER TO
HEAR ABOUT UPCOMING RELEASES

ALSO BY J BREE

The Bonds That Tie Series

Broken Bonds
Savage Bonds
Blood Bonds
Forced Bonds
Tragic Bonds
Unbroken Bonds

The Mortal Fates Series

Novellas
The Scepter
The Sword
The Helm

The Trilogy
The Crown of Oaths and Curses
The Throne of Blood and Honor

The Mounts Bay Saga

The Butcher Duet
The Butcher of the Bay: Part I
The Butcher of the Bay: Part II

Hannaford Prep
Just Drop Out: Hannaford Prep Year One
Make Your Move: Hannaford Prep Year Two
Play the Game: Hannaford Prep Year Three
To the End: Hannaford Prep Year Four

The Queen Crow Trilogy
All Hail
The Ruthless
Queen Crow

The Unseen MC
Angel Unseen

ABOUT J BREE

J Bree is a dreamer, writer, mother, and cat-wrangler. The order of priorities changes daily.

She lives on the coast of Western Australia in a city where it rains too much. She spends her days dreaming about all of her book boyfriends, listening to her partner moan about how the lawns are looking, and being a snack bitch to her three kids.

Visit her website at http://www.jbreeauthor.com to sign up for the newsletter or find her on social media through the links below.